Joanna Hines was born in _____ _____ _____
and the LSE. For over _____ _____ _____
worked on the Lizard, _____ _____ _____
husband. She has a step-d_____ _____ and a son.
This is Joanna Hines's sixth novel. Her earlier books are the
contemporary novels *Dora's Room*, *The Fifth Secret* and
Autumn of Strangers, and two earlier novels of seventeenth-
century Cornwall, *The Cornish Girl* and *The Puritan's Wife*.
All are available in Coronet paperback.

Praise for Joanna Hines:

The Cornish Girl
'A fine novel of Cornwall, beautifully written' A L Rowse
'A long, escapist wallow in the seventeenth century'
Daily Mail
'A fantastic tale of trust, honour, courage and fate'
Company

The Puritan's Wife
'An enjoyable historical novel . . . the love story is engaging,
with a pair of very credible protagonists, and the background of the period well felt besides being well researched
. . . but perhaps the greatest merit of this very readable
novel is its underlying sense of the horrors of civil and
religious war'
The Tablet

Autumn of Strangers
'A well written novel with a large cast of characters, a
pleasing, gentle wit and a strong awareness of the countryside's historical continuity'
Sunday Telegraph
'I greatly enjoyed this well-written analysis of contemporary
life in a picture-perfect English village, its various inhabitants and their interaction all portrayed with sensitive,
intelligent precision'
Jessica Mann

Also by Joanna Hines

Dora's Room
The Fifth Secret
Autumn of Strangers
The Cornish Girl
The Puritan's Wife

The Lost Daughter

Joanna Hines

CORONET BOOKS
Hodder & Stoughton

Copyright © 1999 by Joanna Hines

The right of Joanna Hines to be identified as the Author
of the Work has been asserted by her in accordance
with the Copyright, Designs and Patents Act 1988.

First published in Great Britain in 1999
by Hodder and Stoughton
First published in paperback in 1999
by Hodder and Stoughton
A division of Hodder Headline PLC

A Coronet Paperback

10 9 8 7 6 5 4 3 2 1

A CIP catalogue record for this title
is available from the British Library

ISBN 0 340 65371 X

Typeset by Hewer Text Ltd, Edinburgh
Printed and bound in Great Britain by
Caledonian International Book Manufacturing Ltd, Glasgow

Hodder and Stoughton
A division of Hodder Headline PLC
338 Euston Road
London NW1 3BH

For Allison
completing the trilogy

PART ONE

Perdita
March 1661

Chapter One

A raw wind was gusting up the Thames from the marshes beyond Rotherhithe, ruffling the surface of the incoming tide. Perdita pushed open the high window and, leaning her forearms on the sill, drew in deep breaths of air: smells of salt and fish and decay from the river, noise of carts and voices rising from the street below. If she leaned out further Perdita could see the masts sticking up like bean-poles above the roofs on London bridge. Most of the ships had only pennants flying, all but one which was coming up-river, its buff sail spread to catch the wind like a pale homecoming bird gliding upstream with wings out-stretched.

She tilted her face, enjoying the stinging wind against her skin. From the depths of the room behind her, Kitty broke off her instructions to the dressmaker and said plaintively, 'Perdita, close the window before we catch our death of cold.'

'In a moment, Mother.'

Perdita could imagine the shouts from deck to shore as the ship came into the quay. Her heart flew to join them. She longed to leave this stuffy upstairs room and the endless talk of cloth and fit and trimmings. The rough wind was biting against her cheeks. There had been rain earlier in the day and the rooftops and alleys of the city were streaked with wet. Storm-clouds were still massed above the horizon. And then, as she leaned out to see the final settling of the ship, the sun broke through and the wide sails of the returning vessel dazzled copper bright against the solid dark of the sky. Perdita felt a lift of excitement, the lure and adventure of the sea.

'Careful, Mistress Treveryan,' said the dressmaker, crossing the room to her side. 'A child fell out of a window only last week in the next street. Broke her head in three places and was dead the next day. There now.' As Perdita drew back, the woman shut the window firmly and the noise from the street was muted. What the dressmaker had meant to say was, 'My daughter and I are the ones who must stay up all night long finishing these clothes for your journey. We can't afford to let the heat go to waste. Not that you'd know anything about working all night or making do with only a small scoop of coal, a fine lady like you with nothing to worry about but watered tabby underskirts and embroidered gloves.' But all she said out loud was, 'What a fine young lady Mistress Perdita is now, Lady Treveryan. She'll turn all the men's heads in Cornwall, no doubt about it.'

Perdita could no longer see the ship. Her shoulders drooped and she scuffed her bare toes on the edge of the rug. She felt as if she'd been trying on clothes all afternoon. She was bored and impatient to be gone.

Kitty said, 'Make sure those two gowns are ready by tomorrow evening. My velvet can wait a day or so more.'

'Are you not going to Cornwall then, Lady Treveryan?'

'No. Perdita is travelling alone with her father.' Kitty's mouth set in a narrow line of disapproval.

On the way home, while Kitty rattled on about silks and underskirts and cambric with lace trim, Perdita's thoughts drifted to the homecoming ship. She never tired of seeing them, the effortless flow of their movement over the water, the mysterious beauty of their destinations, far-off places with names like poetry: Virginia and Cathay, Hispaniola and Oporto and the Indies. Her father's wealth had been built on ships laden with fat cargoes that braved the floating ice of the northern seas and the boiling miasmas of the tropics . . .

'Really, Perdita, you never listen to a word I say,' said Lady Treveryan crossly, as they battled through the busy street. 'I do declare these crowds are worse than ever. Where do they all come from? We must remember to call in at Master Ashe's and see if those new powders are in yet. Ah, there's the reason.'

As they turned into Thames Street the crowd was flowing

more thickly, away from the gibbet which had been set up at the crossroads by the Anchor. Evidently the spectacle had only recently ended. A small child, hoisted on his father's shoulders and being carried away, was whimpering that they had arrived too late and he'd missed the treat of seeing them die.

Two bodies, very much dead now, were dangling from the crossbar. From this distance their feet looked as though they were grazing the spectators' heads. Two women, one white-haired, the other somewhat younger. Their heads lolled, like chickens waiting to be plucked, but gradually one turned towards the other, giving the eerie impression they were continuing a conversation begun in the cart that had brought them from Bridewell. A misting rain was furring their heavy skirts with moisture. Two small boys lobbed stones at the corpses, aiming at the feet.

Kitty, Lady Treveryan, tutted her annoyance as she bustled past. 'I knew we should have brought the coach,' she said, barely glancing towards the two women. 'There is always some inconvenience to delay us. Here we are at Master Ashe's. I've heard his new cream is excellent for the hands.'

'I'll wait for you outside.'

Perdita felt that if she had to endure another of Kitty's endless encounters with tradespeople she would surely scream. Besides, there was always a freakish fascination in any execution, even that of two poor women past their youth. She wondered what their stories were. Not rebels, surely, or they'd have met a worse end than this. Witchcraft, probably, or theft.

As she waited on the corner outside the shop, she became aware that she was being watched. Always sensitive to the reactions of others, Perdita sensed it in the same way one feels a light breeze, or the warmth of a fire. Instinctively, she adjusted the angle of her head a fraction so that her features showed to advantage while she caught a glimpse of her observer.

He was a young man with yellow hair and a country-fresh face who was selling pastries from a tray. Perdita stood quite still for a few moments, enjoying his admiration. She was growing accustomed to the attention of young men but had not yet had time to grow bored with it. Their gaze was drawn not just by the obvious wealth of her costume. With her dark hair and eyes, her sallow skin and her thin face she was far from the fashionable ideal of chubby blonde prettiness, but Perdita knew that her features, even in repose, had an animation and character that were immediately attractive. What she did not know, but what the pastry-seller had recognised at once, was that there was something restless and unsatisfied in her appearance, an urgent hunger to be noticed and admired that set her apart from other genteel young ladies.

She picked her way through the slime of the street to join him. A warm smell of butter and baking rose from the tray. Tempting.

'Only a penny, mistress,' he told her. 'Four for threepence.'

He looked at her boldly. His jacket was open at the neck, in spite of the chilly March wind, and there was a glimpse of muscled shoulders and pale hair.

Perdita's eyes gentled slightly as she asked, 'What was their crime?'

'Murder,' he said cheerfully, 'if you can call it that.'

'Is murder ever in doubt?'

'Plenty of people would call it a service, though of course no one is going to stand up and say so in their defence. Midwives, both of them,' and here he paused, watching her carefully before he finished, 'but given to disposing of unwanted burdens, if you know what I mean.'

'Unwanted burdens?'

'Of the bastard kind.' He grinned. He had wondered, when he began, how quickly this elegant young gentlewoman would catch his meaning. He imagined that she had always been sheltered from the harsh necessities of those who lived close to the street, the kind of unfortunates who'd made use of the midwives' skills. But she had known right away, though she had recoiled daintily enough at the word bastard. He went on cheerfully, 'Smothered most of them, so they say, though a few were strangled with their own cord. Not that I agree with it myself, of course, but many believe they did everyone a favour. No shortage of bastards in this world already. Try one of these pastries, I'll do you a special price if you like. Fresh baked by my mother this morning. She knew there'd be a good crowd here today.'

Perdita's eyes held his but her expression was hard and unflinching. She said, 'Thank you, no. The rain has already spoiled them.'

She turned abruptly and hurried back across the street, just as Kitty emerged from the shop.

'There you are,' said Kitty. 'I thought you had wandered off again. I can't seem to keep track of you for more than a moment.'

'Are we going home now?'

'Indeed we are. We can see how Cullen's managed with your new hat. She is good with a needle so long as she's not allowed to rush the job. You must remember that when she's your responsibility in Cornwall.'

'Yes, Mother.'

As she walked past the gibbet, Perdita was careful to avert her eyes. Somewhere in the throng a lonely infant was crying. Kitty talked of Master Ashe's new lotion and the art of trimming hats. Perdita no longer felt like screaming with boredom at Kitty's preoccupation with hand cream and silver gilt ribbons: the young man's words had kindled the terror that lay always just below the surface of her life. Bastard infants were fit only to be murdered, cast out like unwanted kittens and drowned in a sack. No one cared what happened to them.

The magic of the ships was set aside. It was safer to play the part of the young lady of quality, with nothing to occupy her mind beyond proper accomplishments and adornment, rather than remember the dark trade that had brought those two women to the gallows.

'Unwanted burdens' . . . The phrase haunted her. Was that what she herself had once been to her own mother? To her natural mother, that is, not Kitty, Lady Treveryan, her father's lawful wife, but that other woman, the one who had given her birth, then handed her over to be reared by a stranger. She knew almost nothing about her. There had been stories, tales of magical practice told by the servants when they thought no one was listening or had forgotten that the small child with the dark hair and the watchful, eager eyes had crept into the kitchen quarters for company and warmth.

Kitty had been prepared to take her husband's bastard into

her own home; more than that, she had reared her with as much love as she was capable of, just like her own two boys. Clearly there was something unnatural about Lady Treveryan's devotion to her husband's ill-begotten, cuckoo child.

Rumours had been strange godparents gathered about Perdita's cradle . . . Whispered secrets and innuendo had clung to her, closer than shadows, ever since. Would she never be able to shake them off?

She had been reared a gentleman's daughter, in spite of her birth, and she was too proud ever to settle for second best. She was determined to direct all her intelligence and energy to attaining the position her dubious origins might have denied her. The beautiful ship glimpsed over the rooftops of the city was forgotten. Better by far to pick out the exact shade of grey for her doeskin gloves, to feel the grip of the fine leather pulled taut between her fingers. Impeccable behaviour and all the trappings of legitimate status, every artifice known to womankind, all these she must rally to her aid. One day, she vowed to herself in a silent prayer, one day she'd be raised so high in wealth and power that no hint of slander would ever touch her again.

That evening Kitty brought her jewel case down to the main chamber of their rented London lodgings and took out a pair of earrings.

'Try these, Perdita,' she said. 'My first husband gave them to me when I was not much older than you are now. Take them with you to Cornwall. Nothing looks better on young skin than pearls. I was always much admired when I wore them.'

In her excitement when she tried on the earrings, Perdita forgot her usual caution. 'How do I look, Father? Are they not truly elegant?'

Sir Richard Treveryan, who happened to be passing through the room on his way out of the house, paused to regard his daughter. She felt her confidence waver. Something deep inside her always shrivelled up and became hard and angry when she felt his dark gaze on her face, as though he was comparing her with some other image that she always failed to live up to.

'They'll do well enough.' But he spoke with a singular lack of enthusiasm.

Kitty leaped to Perdita's defence. 'Is that all you have to say, sir?' she demanded shrilly. 'Do you want to undo all my hard work with the girl? Just what you think you'll gain by rushing off to Cornwall with her at this time of year I cannot imagine. And on horseback too, when every woman of quality takes a coach these days, at least as far as Exeter. Her face will be exposed to wind and rain, and her hair will be quite undone. I do believe you must be the most vexing and contrary man that ever was born. You never hear a word I say!'

Her most vexing and contrary husband interrupted the flow of words with a curt, 'I cannot help but hear you, Kitty, though it's true I try hard not to listen.'

She tilted her cross little face to look up at him. 'You, sir, might find it amusing to despise the proper clothes of a gentleman, but Perdita has been brought up a lady. I will not let her be reduced to a mere vagabond.'

Richard glanced towards the foot of the stairs and the pile of trunks and portmanteaux in which Perdita's wardrobe had been packed and repacked many times during the past few days. He said drily, 'Your fears, madam, may prove to be somewhat exaggerated. Besides, I too wish our daughter to be a lady.'

Kitty was not to be pacified. Her face was pinched with misery. It was an anxiety that went far deeper than gloves and creams and proper clothes, but its true cause could not be spoken of. This young girl on the verge of womanhood, this child who should have brought her nothing but shame but whose existence had given her a joy as great as any she had known, was being wrenched from her protection and there was nothing she could do to prevent it.

Worse, Richard was taking her to Cornwall. She had no idea of the purpose of this journey. All she knew – and the knowledge clawed at her heart – was that long years ago she had lost her husband's love in the bleak moors and misty headlands of Cornwall, and now she feared she was going to lose her daughter too.

Sir Richard Treveryan strode from the house, and the front door fell shut behind him with a bang. Deprived of the real object of their anger, Kitty and Perdita fell to squabbling with each other, until Perdita flounced out of the room saying she could not wait to leave for Cornwall and Kitty said good riddance, she'd been nothing but trouble ever since her father had come back to England six months before.

During her childhood Perdita had seen little of her father. A late convert to the royalist cause, Richard Treveryan had placed his ships in the King's service in 1644. After Charles I's defeat, imprisonment and execution, he remained in exile with the martyr's son and visited his family only a couple of times when royal business sent him to England as a spy. For Perdita then, his firstborn child, he was an almost superhuman absence, much talked of but hardly ever seen.

The previous year, 1660, Charles Stuart, son of the murdered king, had returned to London and a hero's welcome. In September Richard himself returned and was reunited with his family. To Perdita's disappointment he was cold and distant, a dismal contrast to the wise and loving father her imagination had created. The sense of hurt increased when he attended to her two younger half-brothers, but continued to ignore her cruelly.

Until the day of his audience with the King. While his family waited with him in the crowd that habitually gathered in the anterooms of the King's palace at Whitehall, Richard had been accosted by a scoundrelly-looking man who claimed to have helped him at the time of his escape from England after the King's defeat at Worcester. Perdita had seen this argument, but never heard or knew what was said. All she knew for certain was that her father had been much moved when the summons came to see the King; he had called for her specially and told her they would talk together alone. For the first time, he had looked at her with affection.

Later that same day he invited her into his study and spoke to her of her mother – her natural mother, Margaret Hollar, who had lived and died in Cornwall. He told her that though she had not been born in wedlock, she had been a child of great love, and so had no reason for shame. 'Your mother,' he said, 'was the finest, stubbornest, truest and bravest woman it was ever my pleasure to know. Loving her was the one good thing in my life, the only thing I have ever had cause to be proud of. As I am proud of you now.'

Perdita could hardly believe what she was hearing. She had

come to think he must have hated her natural mother, and that that was why he always looked on her with disfavour. 'Then why did you part from her?' she asked. 'Why did she give me over to your wife?'

'Because . . .' On that October evening of his audience with the King, Richard had risen from his chair and moved slowly to the window. 'Because it was a muddle and we did not see our way straight, not then. She thought she might save her son if she gave up what mankind calls wickedness. And I was too proud and disbelieving, and a pitiful blind fool. And have been well punished since for my folly.'

'But why did you—?'

'Enough.' He had turned his face away, but Perdita could tell by the break in his voice that he was still much moved. 'Enough for now. We'll talk more of it another day. Now leave me.'

She did not insist. She had slipped away and left him alone with his old man's memories. Her curiosity was far from satisfied, but she had his brief words to gloat over and she was sure that before long they would speak of it again.

That night, however, he was gripped with a fever, one of the recurrent fevers that had plagued him since the days when he had sailed the tropics on his own ship. For several weeks only Viney, his elderly manservant, was allowed to tend him.

Perdita found other distractions to occupy her. That first winter of the restored monarchy, London was a city given over to light-hearted pleasures, a fine place for a young lady from a wealthy family to enjoy herself. Mean-spirited gossips might refer to her behind her back as Lady Treveryan's cuckoo child and exclaim over the woman's tolerance in rearing her husband's bastard with her own two sons, but to Perdita's face most people were civil enough. She discovered a natural talent for flirting, and soon had a couple of suitors to amuse her through the winter. The young men, however, tended towards caution, since it was by no means certain that the Treveryans' indulgence towards the girl would be reflected in the size of her dowry.

As soon as his health improved, Richard dispatched his two sons, now sixteen and fifteen, to Oxford with a tutor and strict instructions not to waste their time in gaming or cock-fighting. He was occupied with business affairs, and though there was no return to his former coldness towards Perdita, his manner did not invite confidences either. She sensed it would be pointless to press him.

Conscious from her earliest years of her precarious position in the Treveryan household, Perdita had always known it was vital for her survival to find favour with those close to her. Other daughters could be wayward and disobedient, but never Perdita. At any moment the cuckoo child could be thrown from the nest.

When Richard noticed the two young men who were paying court to his daughter, he told her she might divert herself as she wished but to give neither any encouragement. He had other, and better, plans for her.

Perdita was curious, but she sensed that he was more likely to tell her if she did not pester him with questions. Now that she was nearly eighteen and reaching the age when these matters must be decided, her own views on marriage tended to see-saw between two extremes. Occasionally she found herself thinking it would be a fine thing to love and be loved, and she imagined a handsome suitor who declared his undying passion for her. At other times, especially if she had been snubbed, or had overheard a piece of malicious gossip, she persuaded herself she must be guided by her head alone: a respectable marriage to a wealthy man, a good name and a position in society, these were all that mattered. Marrying for love was a luxury that only well-born women could hope for. For the time being though, she was content to flirt with any man who attracted her attention, but wait and see what her father had planned for her.

She guessed she'd not have to wait for long. This journey to Cornwall with her father must have some clear purpose.

Two days later, in the grey chill of a March dawn, they were at last ready to set off. Perdita had a new chestnut mare, a fur-trimmed riding cloak and warm gloves. Richard Treveryan was mounted on a tall bay. His manservant, Viney, was sunk in gloom at the prospect of the long ride ahead; Adam the groom was full of excitement and Perdita's maid, Cullen, who had never set foot outside London in her life before was terrified of the wild countryside and strange people they were likely to meet. Kitty fussed and fretted, the two packhorses waited with drooping heads as the luggage was balanced and tied down, Richard controlled his impatience with difficulty.

And then, at last, they were clattering down the street towards the green fields beyond St James's. Soon the noises and smells and bustle of the capital were behind them. After less than an hour the city of London, with its teeming alleys and festering gutters, its airy mansions and its poisonous cellars, all the raucous, filthy, glorious wonder of it, was reduced to no more than a smudge of smoke on the far horizon, then dipped from sight entirely.

A melody threaded its way through Perdita's mind: a song about travelling west, towards the setting sun and the prospect of adventure.

The following morning, as they left the comfort of their inn for the stableyard where their horses were waiting, all thoughts of adventure had vanished. Perdita was so stiff that she could barely walk, and remounting Nimble was a form of torture. But she was nothing if not determined, and she managed a stoic smile when her father came up beside her. 'Are you sore, daughter?'

'By no means.' Perdita found it hard to speak for the chattering of her teeth and the pains in every part of her body. 'I am looking forward to this day's journey.'

He laughed. 'Lying suits you,' he said, and patted her gloved hand.

Cullen had no such reason for fortitude and she was snivelling loudly as she rode out of the inn yard, a captive pillion seated behind Adam the groom.

As they journeyed west the sky grew darker and the air colder, and Cullen's grizzling settled into a rhythmic moaning that kept time with the stride of the horse. Once or twice Richard dropped back to see how his daughter did and she protested her cheerfulness, since stoicism was clearly to be the fashion on this particular journey.

About eight miles short of Reading it began to sleet and the raw cold invaded Perdita's bones. In a dazed way she remembered tales of mariners found dead and frozen to the rigging of their ships. Every ounce of her strength was now required to keep her upright in the saddle; the cold had become a greater pain, overlaying the soreness of her limbs. Though she had wrapped a muffler about her face the sleet filled her eyes and stung her skin. She no longer had any idea of where she was, and it was some time before she recognised that her father had once more dropped back to ask after her well-being. She tried to assure him she was well, but her arm was too cold to lift and she could not move the muffler from across her mouth, so he did not hear her.

She saw Richard frown and catch hold of her reins before halting both their horses. He seemed to be telling her to dismount, but she was so rigid with the effort of staying upright in the saddle that she was quite unable to move. He shouted to the other riders, then slid from his horse and came to her side. He reached up his arms, but still Perdita did not move.

His hands were about her waist and he pulled her down. A new pain shot through her legs as her feet touched the ground and in sudden darkness she continued her downward descent. Richard caught hold of her and held her pressed against his side. She heard his voice. 'The child is half dead with the cold.' He was speaking to Viney. 'Why didn't she tell me?' And then to her, 'Here, drink this.'

Cold metal pressed against her lips, then strange liquid in her mouth, burning her throat. Perdita coughed and opened her eyes very wide. Her father's grim face was watching her.

'Thank you,' she gasped.

'Can you move around? Here, stamp your feet. Like this. Now move your arms.'

She did as she was told. After a few moments she felt warm enough to say, 'That's better. I'll do well enough now,' though the words sounded strange through the rattling of her teeth. She went to mount Nimble once again, but Richard stopped her.

'You're stubborn enough, I grant you,' he said, 'but I think I'll keep you with me for the rest of today.' He lifted her on to his horse and swung up behind her, then wrapped his arms and his cloak around her, and the little cavalcade set off once more.

Perdita had never known such joy.

'Are you warmer?' The question came from just above her head.

'Much warmer. But I wouldn't mind some more of that delicious tonic.'

He laughed. 'We'll cheer you with spiced wine when we reach the inn. You cannot start getting a taste for brandy on the second day of our journey. Your mother would never forgive me. Tonic, indeed.'

Perdita leaned her cheek against the textured surface of his buff coat and breathed in the warm smells of leather and cloth, of horse and man. With her father's cloak pulled half across her face her vision was obscured. From time to time the speckled nose of Viney's cob came alongside, then fell behind once more. She could see her father's thickly gauntleted hands holding the reins. She could see sleet falling from a pewter sky and a dreary landscape, ruts and puddles and pot-holes along the road. She could sense the growing happiness of the man who sat behind her, and after a while she began to understand the reason.

As they reached the outskirts of Reading, Richard said to his manservant, 'We'll have to travel by shorter stages if this bad weather continues, more's the pity. It's good to be travelling west again, eh, Viney?'

'It's been a long time,' was the laconic reply. A major speech for the taciturn Viney.

As it happened, Richard did not have to curb his impatience so very much. That second day, of sleet and mud, was by far the worst. On the third morning the sun shone down on a frosty landscape and by the fourth day, when they set out from Newbury, even Cullen had become reconciled to the endless travelling and looked about her with hesitant curiosity. For her part, Perdita began to have some sympathy for her father's loathing of carriage travel. As her limbs became accustomed to the long hours of side-saddle she found this journey more enjoyable than the one from Plymouth with her mother the previous summer. Rattling around in the stuffy interior of the hired coach she had endured agonies of motion sickness and boredom. Now, mounted on her amiable mare, she was content to follow the man mounted on the tall bay who rode always a little way in front.

The man she hardly knew at all, but who happened to be her father.

Chapter Two

Their journey was taking them across the Somerset levels, a mournful area of huge skies and solitary birds. Such dwellings as there were hardly rose above the level of the reeds and there was no protection anywhere from the scything wind. Perdita glanced up to watch a skein of geese winging their way towards the far horizon.

Her first thought was that Nimble must have stumbled. She tried to gather up the reins, but a man's head was level with her knee and a man's hand was clutching the bridle. Two eyes glared up at her from a face as bristly as a hog's.

'Down you get, mistress,' he said, breathing hard and fast. 'We'll have the horse and let you on your way.'

Perdita heard Cullen's terrified scream, her father's roar of anger. Half a dozen men must have been concealed in the ditch and all leaped up at the same moment. At least two were tackling Treveryan.

'Get away from me!' she shouted.

The man caught hold of her skirts to pull her down. Instinctively she lashed out with her booted foot and caught him a blow on the shoulder. He swore viciously and grabbed her by the ankle. Nimble pranced and plunged, and Perdita leaned over, clung to her mane and kicked as hard as she could, but the man had tight hold. She began to slither towards the ground while all around her were the sounds of fighting.

A pistol shot exploded close to her ear. A horseman loomed up beside her, his arm raised to strike. Holding his pistol by the barrel, Richard brought the stock down on the man's skull with such force that he released his grip on her at once and staggered backwards, blood pouring from a deep gash just above the ear. Perdita, who had been more off than on, scrambled back into the saddle as best she could, gathered up the reins and wheeled around to see what was happening.

Viney had been unseated at once; he was staggering down the road after an old fellow who was leading his horse away as fast as he could. Richard thundered past him, caught the thief a blow to the side of the head and recovered the horse. By now the footpads, who had never expected such resistance from a small group of travellers – two men past their youth, two women and a lad hampered by the presence of a pillion rider – were now in disordered retreat.

Suddenly Perdita let out a wail of dismay. While they had been distracted by the fighting, two of the footpads had detached the packhorses and now they were racing across the flat moorland, the two laden ponies trotting behind them with necks outstretched. Perdita was appalled to see all the bags and portmanteaux in which her precious hats and skirts and petticoats were packed being borne away. Her father, who was still busy with the ruffian who had stolen Viney's horse, had not noticed. But then Adam the groom clapped his heels to his horse's flanks and set off after the vanishing luggage. Cullen, still seated behind him on the pillion saddle, squealed with fright at their sudden acceleration, flung her arms tightly around his waist and pressed her face against his back. All at once high drama was transformed to comedy and Perdita, once she was sure her possessions were safely recovered, burst out laughing.

Leading the packhorses, Adam trotted back towards the road. Cullen was still moaning with fear and hugging him close as ivy round a tree trunk. His hat was askew and he was panting, but his broad face was lit by a grin of triumph.

Richard rode up to his daughter. She regarded him with shining eyes.

'You like adventures?' he asked. 'I did not know you were so brave.'

Perdita wished she were not shaking with shock. 'I was not frightened in the least,' she said, before adding truthfully, 'I thought I would be.'

18

Richard nodded. 'Now we must decide how best to deal with our captives.' He regarded the two men with distaste. The ruffian who had first attacked Perdita was still on his knees and holding his head between his hands. Blood seeped between his fingers. The other, an older man with white hair and a grizzled beard, looked up at Richard with empty eyes.

Richard leaned forward. 'Are you their leader?'

'We have no leader,' the old man replied steadily, 'but I'm the oldest by many years. Punish me, but leave the others be.'

'I'll do as I see fit,' said Richard thoughtfully. 'Are you a local man?'

'Born and raised in Lancashire, sir. A labourer's son, but no one will give me work now, not after twenty years a soldier.'

'In Cromwell's army?'

'For King Charles until Marston Moor. Then the Parliament side. I was in Ireland many years.'

Richard turned to Perdita. 'Well, daughter, what shall we do with these rogues? Shall we hand them over to the justices?'

'Of course, Father. Whipping is too good for them. They deserve to hang for their crimes.'

He regarded her thoughtfully. 'You're mighty free with men's lives,' he told her. 'Your mother would probably have rewarded them for their impudence. Isn't that right, Viney?'

Viney caught his master's eye, and smoothed his hand across his mouth, but as usual he said nothing.

Perdita was incredulous. Only last month Kitty had herself thrashed a servant for stealing a pat of butter. But then she realised he had been speaking of that other woman, her natural mother, and she said nothing. She thought, however, that she must have been a very peculiar woman if she did not believe in the proper punishment of criminals.

Richard was suddenly impatient. He wheeled his horse round and motioned the others to follow, while to the two felons he said, 'Go on, then, be off with you. I should have you up before the justices in Taunton, but that would only slow me down. I intend making a full report, so go find honest work. And far away from here.'

The two men stared at him stupidly, not yet able to believe they were being set at liberty. Adam gave the younger one a nudge with his toe. Cullen was peering at them over his shoulder.

Suddenly the older man came to his senses. He picked up his hat, which had fallen to the ground during the battle, took his wounded comrade by the elbow, and walked slowly away from the road. In a short time they had vanished in a dip in the land. The group of riders moved on.

Perdita kicked her mare to a trot so as to catch up with her father. 'Why did you let them go?'

He shrugged.

'You were thinking of her, weren't you?'

'Maybe so.'

'Why did you say she would have rewarded them? That's not right, surely.'

'Ask Viney.'

'He'll not tell me. He never speaks.'

'His greatest merit.'

'Please tell me, Father.' The upset of the attack had put a temporary stop to Perdita's self-restraint.

'You're very persistent.'

'Because otherwise I learn nothing.'

'True enough. Very well, then. Viney came to me from your mother's household. Her manner of hiring him was somewhat unorthodox.' As he spoke, Richard glanced back at his man-servant, who was staring straight ahead of him as though oblivious to this discussion of his past.

'How so?' asked Perdita.

'They first met when he was trying to rob her home. I believe he may have been hungry at the time. She fed him, clothed him and kept him on.'

'Why did she not have him punished?'

'As I remember, it was something to do with the fact that he reminded her of a black-faced sheep.'

'But that's nonsense!'

'So people said at the time. Especially me.'

'I mean, Father, surely . . .' Perdita was so scandalised she had grown quite breathless. 'If everyone acted that way, where would it end?'

'Where indeed? Don't fret, Perdita. Luckily Kitty has

brought you up to have proper ideas on all topics. You're my wife's child to the core.'

But from the way he said it, Perdita knew he was disappointed in her. She could tell that he had preferred this other, crazy woman who made a guest of robbers but then gave up her own child to be reared by strangers. She felt more frightened by her father's nonsensical reaction to the robbers than she had felt during the attack.

And then a spark of rage flared inside her. She intended to have no rivals for his affection, that affection she had glimpsed when he thought her brave and stubborn but which was fading now, and all because of some contrary woman who'd had no sense of what was proper and right.

On the Somerset levels, the dusk seemed to start in the form of a darkness, growing upwards from the earth. As the exhilaration of their encounter with the footpads dwindled, Perdita rode on towards the denser darkness ahead that was Taunton. She was frowning, and deep in thought.

By the time they rode into Taunton it was almost dark. Perdita loved entering a strange town beside her father. Sir Richard Treveryan might despise fashionable clothes but he was so obviously a man of wealth and importance that people stopped what they were doing and stared as his party rode by. No matter how weary she was, Perdita always sat very straight in the saddle at these times, turning back the fur trim on her hood to show off the pearl-drop earrings Kitty had given her, and adjusting the folds of her cloak so that her skirts and petticoats and fine leather boots were revealed for all to admire.

On the evening following their encounter with the footpads, as they turned down the cobbled side road that led to the Mitre Inn, she noticed they had rivals for the crowd's attention. Just beside the entrance to the inn, lit by a tall flare, two men were standing on a rough wooden box. One wore a wide-brimmed hat and a loose shabby coat. He was playing a sprightly tune on a violin. The other, who was perhaps Perdita's age, was beating a small drum and announcing in a strange sing-song voice the entertainment that was to take place in the Mitre's yard that very evening. 'Music, juggling and dramatic interludes . . . come see, come see . . .'

And then Perdita saw something she did not understand at all. As Richard rode up to the covered gateway that led into the inn yard, she saw the fiddler glance up at him with a frown, then turn away quickly so that his face was hidden beneath the wide brim of his hat. As though he was afraid of being recognised.

A chill ran down Perdita's spine. Was he perhaps in league with the footpads who had attacked them earlier in the day? The next moment Richard had passed under the arch, the fiddler turned his head once more and looked straight up at her.

Perdita caught her breath. It was the oddest sensation. She was quite certain she had not seen the man before in her life – she could never have forgotten such a face, with its dark, tilting eyes and its wide, sensuous mouth – yet he looked at her as if he knew her. His eyes seemed to be penetrating deep into the heart of her, though he did not smile or make any sign of greeting. Impossible to wrench her gaze away from those all-seeing, all-knowing eyes.

Then she was past him, Nimble's hoofs ringing out on the cobbles of the yard, grooms and potboys running to attend them. Perdita slid from her mount and followed her father into the taproom of the inn, which was already crowded with townspeople awaiting the evening's performance.

A couple of hours later, when Cullen had washed Perdita's hands and feet in a tub of hot water, and she and her father had eaten a good meal in front of a cheerful fire, Perdita had almost forgotten the incident by the entrance to the Mitre. If she thought of it at all she put her reaction down to the excitements and fatigues of that day's journey. By now the courtyard was full of a boisterous crowd, flares had been lit against the dark night and the performance was already under way.

Perdita tilted her head, the better to see through the small-paned window.

'You wish to see the play?' Richard was observing her.

'Very much. Can we watch it, Father?'

'I must find the justice and report on the men who attacked us.' He glanced over at Cullen, who was nodding with exhaustion, and then at Viney, who was staring mournfully into his empty pint pot. He said, 'You may see it if you wish, but keep Viney with you at all times. These country places can be as rough as any Cheapside tavern when there's a crowd.'

Cullen awoke and insisted that she was not at all tired and wished to watch the entertainment with the others. Richard departed. Viney escorted Perdita to the front of the crowd and cleared a space for her on a rickety bench.

The performance was taking place on a stage, which extended from an ancient cart. The audience was already laughing and shouting loudly at the players. A fat man with a shining bald head was waving a club and chasing the youth around the stage, while the youth, who was dressed in women's clothes, was pretending to be much afraid, shrieking and tripping over his skirts and leaping wildly. The crowd loved it and soon Perdita was laughing as loudly as anyone.

Abruptly her laughter stopped. Standing in the shadows to one side of the stage was the long-legged man who had stared at her as she rode into the Mitre yard that afternoon. His face, in the dancing light of the flares, was strange and other-worldly. He held his fiddle in one hand and appeared to be watching the antics of the two actors on the stage, yet Perdita would have sworn on her life that he was aware of her presence in the front row, that he knew without looking at her when she laughed or was solemn. She knew it by the way the skin on her shoulders tingled, by the dryness in her throat.

While she had been observing the tall fiddler, the youth with the skirts had somehow wrested the club from the shiny-headed giant and was pretending to beat him senseless, much to the delight of the crowd who cheered him on wildly. Then they both made a speedy exit and the fiddler stepped into the brighter lights at the centre of the stage.

He tucked the fiddle against his shoulder and began to play a lilting tune, which the audience quickly recognised as one of the marching songs of the Cavaliers in the late wars. They began to sing raggedly, some in a rowdy drunken roar, but others, perhaps those who had lost friends or kin in the fight, with tears springing to their eyes. Perdita glanced at Cullen. Like most Londoners, the maid's family had been loyal to Parliament throughout the conflict, and it was a little while before she could bring herself to

23

join in the songs her enemies had marched to. Then Perdita glanced the other way, towards Viney. He was not singing either: he was staring at the fiddler and for once the manservant's lugubrious features were troubled with a frown.

Two more songs followed. At the start of the third the two actors returned to the stage. The youth was dressed in the exaggerated style of a great lady. He minced and smirked at the giant, who was now wearing the long coat of a fashionable gentleman – though both their costumes were so greasy and rumpled that the effect was grotesque. They began to execute an elaborate dance, a parody of courtly fashions; their satire delighted the audience.

More dances followed. The girlish youth grew more flirtatious, the foppish giant ever more lewd in his advances. Only the tall fiddler remained detached from the mayhem around him; he appeared wholly absorbed in his music. Finally the giant lunged forwards and grabbed his partner's skirts between her legs and hung on gleefully while the 'maiden' pretended to swoon with shocked delight.

And then, quite suddenly, the fiddler turned towards the audience and fixed his eyes on Perdita. He did not scan the other spectators to seek her out: as she had guessed, he had known from the first where she was sitting and had been waiting only for this moment. Once again, Perdita felt his gaze press down into the very heart of her. She gasped, the colour flooded her face. And then he smiled, the merest trace of a smile, the slightest movement of the lips. Almost a secret smile, to be observed by her and her alone. Yet it did not feel like a smile of friendship, far from it. Nor yet of enmity either. More a smile of certain knowing.

Perdita felt a sense of imminent danger, greater by far than that of the footpads who had attacked them earlier, because this was a danger that was almost welcome.

The entertainment ended. A strange agitation took hold of her and she felt herself to be on the verge of swooning away like the mock-maiden on the stage, yet she knew herself to be very much awake and alert to every detail of the scene.

The stage was empty, the applause died down and the audience began to disperse. Perdita stood up, aware suddenly that the air was clear and cold and smelt of frost. The chill restored her to her senses. Foolish to imagine there was danger: Cullen walked behind her, Viney in front. At this very minute her father was probably returning from his meeting with the justices, and here she was, surrounded by a noisy, friendly crowd of townspeople. No fear of any harm in the courtyard of the Mitre Inn.

As they entered the steamy warmth of the taproom, Cullen yawned and groaned and said, 'I'm so weary I could sleep a month.'

And a man's voice said quite clearly, 'Viney, old friend, a moment of your time.'

Perdita looked about her rapidly, but the crowd was packed so tight she could not make out the speaker. Viney said, in a low voice, 'You go on to bed now, Mistress Perdita. Cullen will see to you. I'll wait here for the master.'

It was only when she had begun to climb the main stairs and turned back to survey the crowded room below that Perdita was able to pick out the man who had spoken just now. Viney was standing near the fire, a pint pot in his hand. The fiddler was beside him. She saw the fiddler put what looked like several coins into Viney's hands, then the old man embraced him. Perdita, baffled, remained motionless, and watched.

Cullen stumped on ahead. 'I'll go and make sure your bed is aired, mistress. I'll be asleep on my feet else.'

'Go on, then, Cullen. I'll follow soon,' said Perdita distractedly.

The maid disappeared along the corridor that led to her room, leaving Perdita alone overlooking the bar. As she observed them, the two men below embraced once more. Then Viney, draining his pint pot at the speed for which he was famous, was heading towards the landlord for more while the fiddler had slipped out by a side door.

How strange, she thought, strange and yet vexing too. Everyone knew that Viney must never be given cash, for it was immediately converted to liquor. Liquor that transformed the loyal, taciturn old man into a senseless drunkard. Her father would be furious when he discovered, and Viney would be sore-headed and sick in the morning. The next day's journey was sure to be miserable for everyone.

Suddenly decisive, Perdita picked up her skirts and turned to go back down to the bar to put a stop to Viney's drinking. Although she had always been a little in awe of her father's manservant, this was clearly the moment to assert her authority.

A man's voice, speaking from the shadows of the landing above, stopped her in her tracks.

'Mistress Perdita, do you want to know your story?'

Chapter Three

Perdita spun round so quickly that she came close to toppling back down the stairs.

He was standing in the shadows on the landing. A tall, slim-built man whose features were half lit by the guttering tallow against the wall. She must walk past him to reach her own room. Close to, she could see that his clothes were shabby and his hands and face not entirely clean, but he spoke with the gentle Cornish intonation that she remembered from Dorcas, the woman who had cared for her in her early years. She saw, too, that he was older than she had first thought, perhaps thirty or more. Not good-looking at all, but those uptilted eyes and that generous mouth might well exert a powerful fascination.

'Well, then, Mistress Perdita,' he said, when she did not at first reply, 'are you not curious?'

'You're mighty bold with my name, fellow. If you wish to speak with me you must call me Mistress Treveryan.'

'Why? That was never your true name, Perdita Hollar.'

She gripped the stair rail tightly. 'How dare you call me that?'

'Why not? Are you ashamed of your own mother's name?'

'Who are you?'

He shrugged. 'A mere go-between, Miss Call-yourself-what-you-will. But I know a woman here who is sometimes visited by unquiet spirits. She has been contacted today by one who wants to talk with you. It was this same talker with spirits who told me your true name. She will see you now, if you wish.'

Perdita felt a thrill of fear. This man was just the sort of devious fellow to have dealings with those shadowy areas where the living and the dead intermingle. She glanced nervously behind her. Viney was nowhere to be seen, her father had not yet returned. Despite her curiosity, she did not wish to dabble alone in the dark arts. She assumed a haughtiness she was far from feeling.

'I don't believe a word you say. Let me pass or I shall call the landlord and have you thrown out.'

His face relaxed into a smile. It changed him completely. Suddenly he appeared no more threatening than a child, and Perdita began to think perhaps she might trust him, after all. He said, 'Why? Are you afraid to know the truth about yourself? To hear the words of the woman who might even be your own mother? Are you such a coward?'

Perdita stared at him. She could feel her heart thumping under her bodice. She hated to be called a coward and she did not doubt that what he said was possible. All her life Perdita had heard tales of discourse with the dead, of ghosts and goblins and the impish tricks played by babies who had died before they could be baptised and so were forced to roam the earth in torment through all eternity. Kitty and most of her acquaintances paid frequent visits to astrologers and cunning men for advice with their problems. But she guessed her father would not want her to listen to this man. She remembered the way the stranger had turned his face away, so that Richard would not see him. Yet, still, her curiosity was overpowering.

While she wavered, the fiddler had somehow moved closer. He reached forward and caught hold of her left hand, slipping the doeskin glove from her fingers.

She tried to pull away. 'What are you doing?'

He did not release her, but flipped her hand over and examined the palm closely. 'You can learn much from reading men's palms.' He spoke always in that lilting, Cornish voice. 'Women's too.'

'What can you see in mine?'

'I am not so skilled as others . . . But I can see you will encounter many obstacles on the way to the happiness you seek. And – yes, look – it says here that you will learn much to your advantage this very evening.'

'You made the last part up.'

He raised his eyes from her palm and looked at her with that uncanny directness she found so unsettling, but once again he was smiling. A gentle smile, which told her she had no reason to fear him. 'Maybe I did not read it in your palm, but it is true all the same. Will you visit Goody Carbin?'

'Who is that?'

'The woman visited by spirits.'

'Where is she?'

Apparently taking her question to signify agreement, he said, 'I will show you.' Still gripping her hand in his, he led her down the passageway, past the door to her bedchamber, where Cullen was now waiting for her, past her father's room and past all the meaner chambers that lay at the back. Holding a candle aloft in his free hand, he led her down a winding stairway in what must have been the oldest part of the building, then came to an abrupt halt in front of a low doorway. He released her hand. 'Wait here,' he commanded.

'Where are you going?'

'To tell Goody Carbin you attend her.' And before she could protest further, he had whisked away around a corner, leaving Perdita alone in the icy darkness.

'Wait!'

He was gone. Not a glimmer of light anywhere. Through the thickness of several walls came the ebb and flow of far-off voices and laughter, like waves from a distant sea, but all around her was only this eerie silence and the numbing cold. Perdita was angry, not because the stranger had brought her on a fool's errand but because he had abandoned her so abruptly. She must find him at once and give him a piece of her mind. He was just a common musician and needed to be taught the proper respect due to a lady of quality.

She groped about her in the pitchy black, recoiling swiftly as her bare hand plunged into a net of cobwebs. Her left glove was missing. Her heart skipped with fear: it was well known that those who practise magic will take a lock of hair or an item of personal clothing if they intend to injure someone. So long as the man kept her glove, he had the power to do her harm, no matter how far away he was. She must retrieve it at once.

Reaching out with her other hand she felt the outline of a door, then a metal latch. The moment she touched it, the latch began to lift against her fingers, as if by magic. The door swung open. Light filled her eyes.

A woman stood before her. Tall, and strongly built, she was dressed with extravagant finery, richly coloured velvets and lace that once, many years ago, must have belonged to a fine lady. It was clear from a single glance that this woman was anything but fine. She had a short nose and bulbous eyes, like some snuffling breeds of dog. Her thick features were smeared with paint and she gave off a sickly perfume. 'I've been expecting you, my lady. Come in quickly and close the door behind you.'

Perdita did not move. The room was lit only by a single candle, but there was enough light spilling through the open door for her to make out the means of her escape, the narrow stairway down which she had come.

'There, there, little lady. Don't be afraid. The poor soul who wants to speak to you is a friend. Maybe more than a friend.'

'I'm never afraid,' said Perdita crossly. 'Is it true you can tell fortunes?'

'No, little lady.' Goody Carbin spoke in a guttural, mannish voice and with an accent Perdita had never heard before. 'Fortune-telling is a common gypsy's trick. I'd not stoop so low. My gift is a rare one. Sometimes troubled spirits use my unworthy body to speak to loved ones who remain on this earth. And there's one poor soul has been begging to be heard ever since you came here this afternoon with your father.'

'Who are you?'

'I told you, little lady, I am Goody Carbin.'

'Why should I believe you? How do I know you're not making this up?'

Goody Carbin had seated herself in a low chair on the far side of the room, which seemed to be some kind of store. She looked at Perdita. There was a challenge in her gaze. White powder clung like frost to the hairs above her lip. 'Put some money on the table, Mistress Perdita. You'll soon discover if I'm speaking the truth or not.'

'I'll not give you a penny until you've proved your worth,' said Perdita. But without being aware of what she was doing, she had entered the room and come to stand in front of the woman. A small table stood between them. There was a scuffling and a squeaking behind the walls. The Mitre must be overrun with vermin. She hoped desperately that it was nothing worse.

The woman was smiling at her. It was not a pleasant smile, but it was infinitely better than what followed. Slowly, gradually, even as Perdita stood and watched her, a change came over the woman's face. Her calm expression gave way to a look of great anguish. Her eyes grew very large and round, and her pupils rolled up under her lids. A strangled noise escaped from her throat. She clutched at her hair and shook and quivered like someone possessed by demons. Then it seemed as if all the room was full of invisible whispering. Just as Perdita was looking about her in terror, a thin high voice emerged from the woman's mouth.

'Perdita, oh, my Perdita,' the unearthly voice entreated, 'will you not listen to me even for a little while? I have waited so long, so very long to talk to you. Oh, my sweet Perdita, do as this good woman commands. Let me unburden my heart to you. Is that so much for a mother to ask? Oh–oh!'

The pleading ended on a heartrending cry, and Goody Carbin collapsed against the back of her chair. Hardly knowing what she was about, Perdita scrabbled frantically in the purse at her waist, extracted a couple of coins and flung them down on the table.

Reviving, Goody Carbin opened her eyes, shot a disdainful glance at the coins and demanded, in her own voice, 'More.'

Perdita emptied her purse.

With a sigh Goody Carbin settled back in her chair. She closed her eyes and then flinched, as though prodded by an invisible presence. Once again Perdita could hear a faint scratching sound and that mysterious, hidden whispering, which changed every now and then into a low murmur. She looked around the room in bewilderment, half expecting to feel the draught from angels' wings fanning through the shadows.

Goody Carbin had begun to speak again, low and guttural and with that foreign-sounding accent. 'Yes, I can hear you now. The little lady is here. Perdita is listening now. We can begin, yes . . .' And then to Perdita she said, 'She tells me her name is Margaret. She wants you to know she has waited a long time to talk to you. There are things you must know so she can find her eternal rest. Pay attention. You must listen carefully.'

'Who is she?'

'I told you, she said her name was Margaret.'

'Yes, but—'

'Don't interrupt, girl. I am trying to hear.' Goody Carbin was frowning, straining to make out a whispering voice that Perdita could barely hear. Like smoke flowing into an apothecary's jar, the room was filling with an unseen presence. Perdita pulled her shawl more tightly round her shoulders and looked behind her: the door was still open, but the stairs down which she had come were all swallowed up by darkness. The distant noise from the taproom mingled with the strange, unearthly whispering. Goody Carbin let out a long breath, and continued, 'She tells me you must know she was born near a place called Porthew.'

'Where is that?'

Goody Carbin waited. 'In Cornwall, she says. Far from here. Near the sea. She says her mother was a foreigner . . .'

'A foreigner? Where from?'

'Don't interrupt me, girl. Listen.'

Perdita was not used to be spoken to in such a manner. She was about to berate the woman, but already Goody Carbin was continuing, 'She wants you to know her story. She wants you to know that when she was still a girl, younger even than you are now, she was got with child.'

'By my father?'

'No. Not he. Pay attention. It was the priest, the village priest. He was a good man, she says. He had always been a father to her and also her teacher, but he could not marry her. So she married Master Hollar.'

'Who?'

'Quiet. I'm trying to hear what she says. Master Hollar dealt in cloth, she tells me. He was a kind father to her son, but she did not find happiness with him. For many years she knew only sorrow. Then she had the misfortune to meet a scoundrel called Richard Treveryan.'

'A scoundrel? My father? How dare you!'

A weird noise filled the room, like a winter wind blowing

through the cracks in the plaster. Goody Carbin opened her eyes very wide and glared directly at Perdita. 'I only repeat what the lost soul tells me. Do you want to hear her out? Have you any idea what the spirits risk when they try to break through the barriers between their world and this? What I myself am risking now? Can't you imagine what this woman is to you?'

'Tell me, then. I'm listening.'

The woman settled back once more in her chair. Her chest was heaving under the soiled velvet of her bodice. She closed her eyes and frowned, straining to hear across the divide between life and death. 'She wants you to know Treveryan was wicked from the beginning. He had married for money and he came back to Porthew a rich man. Everyone hated him. He was cruel and did injury to those who stood in his way. She says, she says . . . Her voice is growing faint. I cannot make it out.'

'How did he injure people? You must tell me how.'

Goody Carbin opened her eyes and regarded Perdita coldly. 'You will have to pay more if you wish to hear the rest.'

'I have given you all the money in my purse. I have no more.'

'Your earrings, then. They'll do.'

Perdita gasped. 'These?' She reached up a hand and touched the pearl drops hanging from her ears. 'You cannot have these, they're not even mine to give. They belong to my mother.'

There was a silence while Goody Carbin looked at her with veiled and snake-like eyes. Then suddenly there was a violent scratching noise behind the wainscot, and the woman asked her, 'Your mother? How so? Surely it is your mother who speaks to you now?'

'No, not her. My other mother. I mean, Lady Treveryan.'

Goody Carbin let out an anguished groan and clutched at her throat, rolling her eyes towards the ceiling and falling sideways in her chair as though buffeted by a great wind. 'No!' she shrieked, and once again it was the thin, high, other-worldly voice that cried out. 'How dare you call that woman mother? She stole my child, she took my baby from me. Oh, Perdita, I have waited in torment these many years to speak with you and now you will not hear me and all because of that vile woman's trinkets. Shame on you, unnatural daughter!'

Perdita's fingers were slippery with sweat as she unfastened the precious pearls from her ears and set them down on the table. Although Goody Carbin was still heaving and shaking with the passion of the tormented presence who spoke through her, some part of her remained alert for she reached out a long arm, snatched the pearls and tucked them in the folds of her dress.

'Well?' asked Perdita. 'What more? How did my fa – how did Richard Treveryan injure those close to her?'

'She says . . . Her voice is growing faint now, but I think she says he did an injury to some people in the town, something to do with a farm that was disputed. Yes, yes, I am sure she says it was a conflict over property. Treveryan fought with her sister's husband and maimed him, and he put a cripple and his family out of their home. She says it grieves her to say it, she sees the folly of her ways now, but then she was blinded by love and could not see his many faults. She turned her back on her own people and went with him. She lived with him in his house at Trecarne for many months. But he left her when the war began, as such men always will, though she was expecting his child.'

Perdita opened her mouth to ask the next question, the obvious one, but her throat was dry and no sound emerged.

'That child was you.' Goody Carbin answered it anyway. She sighed. 'She says she wants you to know that she never meant to give you up, but that William Hollar, her husband, said he would put you in a foundling home. She fell sick and did not expect to live. That was when she sent you to Treveryan's house. It was her servant Viney who took you there. She wants you to know . . .'

But Goody Carbin had stopped talking. The strange whispering and scratching noises had ceased and the room was invaded by a chilling silence. Goody Carbin seemed to be straining to hear.

'Yes?' Perdita could hardly breathe for impatience. 'Tell me more. What else does she want me to know?'

'I cannot make it out. Her voice is fading.'

'Listen harder! There is so much I want to ask her. Surely you can bring her back.'

'I am trying . . . Oh, no, I fear she is prevented . . . I fear – oh!'

34

And with a final cry, Goody Carbin fell sideways in her chair in a faint.

For a few moments Perdita stood quite still. Gradually her impatience turned to anger. 'Wake up!' she commanded. 'Wake up, you have not finished. There must be more.'

When there was still no response, Perdita stepped round the table and tapped Goody Carbin on her broad, velvet-clad shoulder. 'Tell me more, woman. I've not had my money's worth yet and—' But when Perdita touched her again, the woman shuddered violently and fell forward, her thick hair covering her face.

It occurred to Perdita then that if she was to hear no more she might as well have the pearl earrings back: she had never meant to let Goody Carbin keep them. She glanced around her, half fearing that the tortured spirit might still be observing what she did, and the candle flame flickered and burned sideways in a rush of cold air. Perdita shivered, then resolutely began to search through the folds of Goody Carbin's skirts.

There was a sound in the corridor outside the room. The fiddler was standing in the open doorway, the candle dripping on to his hand. 'What are you doing?' he asked sharply.

'I am looking for my pearls. I gave her money, but she wanted my pearl earrings too and they were not mine to give. If my father learns she has them, she'll be arrested for theft.' Perdita's search for the pearls had grown more insistent, but in spite of Goody Carbin's faint her arms were clamped immovably at her sides and her fists were clenched tight. 'Help me, please. I must find the pearls.'

The fiddler crossed the room to join her. He regarded the slumped figure for a moment or two before drawing Perdita away none too gently. 'Enough, leave her. I'll get your pearls back for you later. Surely you can see Goody Carbin has been deeply affected by her ordeal. She needs rest and quiet. To disturb her now might well prove fatal.'

'But my pearls—'

'I told you, I'll have them for you in the morning. You'd not want her death on your conscience.'

'No, but—'

'Then cease fussing. Tell me, did you learn anything of interest?'

'It was most strange . . . I do not know what to make of it at all. Sometimes she spoke in her own voice, and sometimes the spirit woman spoke through her.'

Goody Carbin made a muffled choking noise and slid forward on the table, her face hidden behind a thick curtain of hair. Her large torso was shuddering. The man looked at her. His face was disfigured by loathing.

'We must leave her in peace,' he said, steering Perdita firmly away from the unconscious woman. 'She needs a period of rest to recover from these seizures.'

'Do you promise you'll get my earrings back before my father finds they're missing?'

'Didn't I tell you I would? Trust me.' There was a dangerous edge to his voice that had not been there before. Perdita was acutely aware of the pressure of his hand against her arm. Even as they passed through the doorway she allowed her body to incline slightly towards his, so that she brushed against him as though by accident.

'I'll take you back to your room now,' he told her. 'Let us hope you have not been missed.'

Holding the candle aloft he went up the stairway and along the corridor that led back to the main part of the inn. A roar of voices and the smell of sweat and tobacco rose up from the taproom below. Perdita had a sense of returning from a foreign place. This was where the stranger had spoken to her first, it seemed like hours before. Remembering, she glanced over the banisters into the crowded bar. Viney was sprawled across a bench, a tankard in his hand. A few minutes more and he would be insensible.

She turned back to the fiddler. 'My father's manservant recognised you, but said nothing to my father,' she said. 'How was that?'

'Viney and I were friends, but that was in another life,' was all the reply.

'What do you mean?'

He frowned. 'I will leave you. But first you must promise, on your honour as a gentlewoman, not to breathe a word of this to anyone before morning. It is vital no one disturbs Goody Carbin until she has recovered from her fit. Do you understand?'

'I think so.'

'Then you promise?'

'Yes.'

'Good.'

'And you will return the pearls?'

'Of course. I gave you my word.' He smiled. 'Good night, Perdita.'

'Good night . . .' This time she did not challenge his right to call her by name. It seemed an altogether natural thing. 'But how can I bid you good night when I still do not know who you are?'

'I'm sure you will find out. Soon enough.' He was no longer smiling. He pressed the naked lobe of her ear between finger and thumb and she felt a tremor pass through her body. His fingertips slid down and circled her neck. She was not afraid in the least. She knew he did not mean to harm her. Even stranger, she was not angry either. It was as though she half expected him to kiss her.

The moment passed. He released her throat. 'Remember this,' he said, 'when we meet next.'

And then he was gone.

Chapter Four

———◆◇◆———

'Why did you stop so soon? We could've had that ring off her finger easy as wink. I swear it was a ruby.'

'You're getting greedy, Maria. You have the earrings, isn't that enough?'

'How do I look?' The woman had clipped the pearl drops to her ear-lobes and bobbed her head provocatively. She looked grotesque: the delicate jewellery only accentuated her coarse features and leathery, painted skin. Despite the fiddler's concern for her health, Goody Carbin's recovery had been dramatic. By the time he returned to the little storeroom at the back of the Mitre she had drunk a good deal of Canary sack and was in uproarious good spirits.

'Like a queen,' he told her, but his voice was edged with contempt.

'Liar. More like an old nag with a ribbon in her mane. Still, these will fetch good money in Bristol. We can split it two ways if we don't tell the others.'

'It is all yours.'

'What?'

'You've earned it.'

'Ha, easiest hour's work of my life. Goody Carbin indeed. My only worry was I'd laugh and give the game away.' She chuckled, a deep, satisfied chuckle, then adopted a high-pitched, mincing voice. ' "Listen harder, Goody Carbin, surely you can bring her back. There is so much I want to ask her." Sweet heavens above, however do rich people rear their daughters to be so stupid? She deserved to lose the clothes off her back. And she would have done if you hadn't stopped me.'

'You have the earrings. Their loss will cause upset enough.'

The man threw himself down in a chair and took a measure of wine. His earlier good-humour had evaporated and he was frowning.

Maria gazed at him thoughtfully. 'Why so considerate all of a sudden? First you stop our game just when we're moving in for the kill, now you tell me you don't want a share of the money. You're not getting a conscience, are you?'

'The sport grew tedious. As you do, Maria.'

'Tedious, is it?' She reached down and slid her hand around his neck, but he flinched away from her touch. She withdrew her hand. 'Suit yourself,' she said.

He stood up. 'Tell the others to pack up at once and be gone by morning. The sooner the better. I told our fine lady not to speak of this to anyone till daybreak, but she will probably break her promise. And you, Maria, want to be a hundred miles away from here when her father discovers she's been duped.'

'Treveryan? That same villain you told her about?'

He nodded.

'And is he such a terrible man?'

'Most people believe so.'

'How do you know him so well?'

He smiled slowly. 'Oh, I hardly know the fellow at all.'

'But you hate him all the same, it's written all over your face. Is that why you tricked his daughter?'

'Perhaps. Reasons aren't important, Maria, you know that. Besides, the girl should be grateful to me. I only told her the truth. It appears no one had bothered to tell her that before. There's no need to profit from it as well.'

Maria was not convinced. She did not know the fiddler well – he had only been travelling with them since Christmas – but she knew he was a complicated and secretive man, easy-going and cheerful for most of the time but a prey to dark moods and impulses. It had been entirely in character when he came rushing to find her that evening and persuaded her to take the role of Goody Carbin while he hid behind a flimsy partition and whispered the information necessary to deprive the rich young lady of her surplus finery. It had all been a piece of fun. But now his mood was altered completely. She was shrewd enough to know that his earlier appreciation of her efforts had changed to disgust.

'Don't linger here,' he told her. 'If you hurry, you'll be gone by midnight.'

'And you?'

'I'm leaving. But not with you.'

Maria let out a long sigh. She had always known he was only with them for a short while, but that would not prevent her from missing him. She asked, 'Where are you going?'

'It's better I don't tell you, Maria.' He stood up and patted her shoulder. 'Those earrings are my parting gift to you. Don't let anyone give you less than fifty pounds for them.'

'So much?'

'At least.' He was at the doorway.

'Luke, wait.' She came to stand beside him. They were the same height. 'How did you know so much about the girl's family? About her mother and the parson and the people Treveryan injured? Do you come from that village you talked to her about? That place in Cornwall by the sea.'

He smiled, a strange and secretive smile. 'Maybe I do,' he said, 'but perhaps it goes deeper even than that.'

'Deeper?'

'Supposing I told you I was that spoilt girl's kin.'

Maria stared at him hard then burst out in a roar of laughter. 'Dear God, Luke, you almost had me fooled. You must think I'm as gullible as her ladyship if you expect me to believe you're kin to the likes of her.' She chuckled once again before kissing him firmly on the lips. 'Oh, but I hate to see you go. I'll miss your teasing as much as your fiddle-playing. Are you sure you don't want any of the money we had off her?'

'Keep it. Only make sure you share it with the others.' He was grinning broadly now, confirming her belief that he had been jesting earlier. 'Or I'll tell them you've swindled them.'

'God keep you, Luke.'

His smile faded at once, and he quickly went to the inn yard to gather his few belongings from the back of the cart. The bald-headed giant and the pretty youth were curled together under a

41

heap of dirty cloaks and curtains. A thin-faced mongrel growled a warning, then thumped his tail when he recognised Luke. Hurriedly he stuffed his few belongings into a canvas bag and swung a thick cape over his shoulders. He had already settled his bill.

The night-watchman was snoring in his booth as Luke strode through the empty streets of the town. Beneath his feet the road was slippery with rubbish, but above him the sky was spangled with stars.

He left by the western gate, but almost at once he took a road to the north. He, too, was travelling to Cornwall, but he did not want to cross Treveryan's path again. Not yet. He would follow the side roads he knew so well. There was no hurry. When dawn came he would find a place to sleep. He preferred to travel by night. He preferred the sheltering cover of darkness to the glare of day.

God keep you, Luke . . . Maria's parting words echoed in his ears. A mockery and a cruel reproach.

Long ago God had shown his opinion of Luke. It was not God who kept him, not any more. Not for a long time.

His father had been a dedicated Puritan, convinced that a precious few men and women had been chosen by God to fulfil His preordained purpose. There was never any doubt in his mind that Luke, his only child, was one of God's elect and therefore different from the common race of men. The boy had grown up with a sense of his favoured place in the scheme of things.

Until, when he was still little more than a child, he was torn from his home and left to find his own way in the world. His disillusion had been swift and complete. Such calamities did not happen to the chosen few, therefore he must be one of those cast out from God's grace.

There was no chance, for the growing boy, of finding a place in the middle ground. Like Lucifer, the fallen angel, if he was not one of God's elect, he must be damned utterly and for ever. He ran away and found a home of sorts among the soldiers of the Parliament army where he saw and did many things that confirmed him in this view.

Since then, it had been easy to believe that he was a wretched sinner, beyond all hope of redemption. He did not like himself much, and saw no reason why God should either. From time to time his dissatisfaction with himself and his life grew to such a pitch that he left his respectable life behind him for a month or so and took to the roads with a band of players or travelling rogues.

He had been shocked to see Treveryan again the previous evening, but he realised now that it had been inevitable, given the few resting places on the roads between Cornwall and London, that he would encounter Treveryan one day. It was nearly twenty years since they had last met, but he would have recognised him anywhere: that craggy, uncompromising face, the brooding dark eyes.

And he had known at once who the young girl travelling with him was, though he had never set eyes on her in his life before. It was something to do with a familiarity in the wide mouth, her eager intelligence.

At first he had thought merely that he might have some fun from the coincidence. He had long believed in seizing any crumbs of opportunity that fate threw in his path. He was surprised to discover that tricking Treveryan's daughter was a perverse and bitter-sweet satisfaction.

Perdita, her mother had called her.

The lost one.

But now he had found her, and he knew where they were headed.

He told Maria that he had tired of the game, but that was not strictly true. He had not really expected her to be taken in by his deception. The whole escapade had disturbed him almost as much as he was sure it had disturbed her. He had found himself remembering people and events he had always struggled hard to forget.

When he heard her questions and sensed her great hunger for any crumbs of information about her mother, he was so struck by the horror of their separation that he had felt physically sick. He had always known that it had broken Margaret Hollar's heart to give up her infant daughter; he had never imagined that the child, though reared in luxury, had suffered nearly as much.

He reckoned she must be about seventeen. Under the fine clothes and the ladylike manner, she was not much more than a child – and a vulnerable, lonely child, at that. When he felt her brush against him as they left the storeroom, he had sensed the force of her yearning, had wanted to put his arms around her and comfort her himself. He had wanted to warn her of the dangers ahead.

But he knew he was powerless to help her.

Besides, since when could one of those cast out by God bring anything but misery to those around him? Hadn't he known all along that he was a black-hearted monster, whose only gifts were cruelty and deceit? As that evening's work had demonstrated once more to his own perverse satisfaction.

Daybreak at the Mitre Inn that March morning of Perdita's visit revealed an even more shambolic scene than usual. The potboys and scullions who had fallen asleep near the fire were roused from their brief rest by a roar of rage: Sir Richard Treveryan was berating his manservant, who had been sprawled unconscious on the bench since his collapse the previous evening. A bucket of cold water completed the awakening process, whereupon Viney gurgled and began to vomit long and noisily. So occupied was the old fellow in parting with the contents of his stomach that he barely registered the loss of his livelihood as well.

'Drunkards are two a penny,' Richard told him. 'If anyone else wants a tosspot for a servant, they can have you and welcome. I want never to see you again as long as I live.'

Viney only rolled his eyes and groaned, before staggering out to the privies at the back. Richard, grim-faced, returned to his bedchamber for some bread and boiled meat before the journey. He did not notice Perdita's hollow-eyed and suspicious gaze when she joined him a little later.

She had lain awake all night thinking over what she had been told during the evening. Increasingly, as dawn approached, her anxiety shifted to the fate of Kitty's pearl earrings. She had believed the fiddler when he said he would get them for her: there was something about him that she trusted instinctively, but still, she could not rest easy until she had them in her hand again. She did not doubt that the spirit woman had been real, but she had increasing doubts about Goody Carbin. It seemed to Perdita to be sadly in keeping with what she was learning of her natural mother that Margaret Hollar had chosen such an unsuitable conduit for her communication with the living.

Perdita was in a hopeless tangle over what she had heard. A shadowy picture was growing in her mind, a picture of a woman unhappy with her husband who had formed an unsuitable liaison. It meant a lot to her to know that her mother had given her up only because she believed she was dying, and that her husband had threatened to place the baby in a foundling home. The spirit woman's – Perdita could not think of her as a mother – bitterness towards Richard Treveryan must have been caused by his abandonment of her. But, then, her father had spoken of her with such tenderness, as though he had truly loved her and regretted that ever they had had to part, even after so many years. She wished now that she had thought to mention this to the troubled spirit: the knowledge might have helped to set her heart at rest.

Watching Richard now as he drank his morning ale and gave orders to Adam to saddle Viney's horse with the rest but that Viney himself was on no account to join them, it was easy to believe him the scoundrel of Goody Carbin's description. His irregular, gaunt features were more suited to his present fury than to gentleness. She could not quite bring herself to believe that he would maim a man, or make a cripple and his family homeless, but it was easy to imagine he might have enemies.

He glanced up, noticed her eyes on his face. 'Eat up, girl. We leave right away.'

Perdita had hardly touched her food and at the mention of leaving, her appetite vanished altogether.

'We cannot leave yet,' she told him.

'Cannot?' The single word was dangerous.

'I mean . . . poor Viney is not well . . . We ought to wait for him, surely.'

'He is dismissed.'

'You weren't serious when you told him to quit your employment?'

'Indeed I was.'

'But it wasn't his fault, not entirely. That man gave him the money deliberately.'

'What man?'

'Oh . . . no one.'

Richard stood up, impatient. 'I'll not be delayed by drunkards. Nor by anyone else. Meet me downstairs in five minutes.'

Perdita reached the taproom before her father. She looked through the half-open door into the inn yard. It seemed larger than it had the previous evening. The space where the covered cart had stood was empty. Heart pounding with alarm, she found the landlord, who was writing out her father's bill.

'Where are the players staying?' she asked him.

'Under a tree, for all I know. They were on their way by midnight. A change in plan, so they said.'

'What about Goody Carbin?'

'Who?'

'The tall woman who was with them, the one with the strange voice and the velvet coat.'

'Oh, you mean Maria Carabini. She left with her menfolk, of course.'

'And the fiddler?'

'He was the first to go. Paid his bill and left straight away.'

Perdita's squeal of rage was loud enough to be heard by her father as he crossed the taproom to pay his bill.

'What ails you, girl?' he asked irritably.

'How dare they?' Perdita stamped her foot in her fury. 'Father, do something quickly! I've been robbed!'

'Robbed?'

'Goody Carbin has stolen my pearl earrings!'

'Maria Carabini,' said the landlord helpfully, confusing Richard still more.

'She has stolen your mother's earrings?' asked Richard.

'I gave them to her last night. Only the man promised I would have them back again this morning. And now they've gone. Oh, Father, you must catch them. They must be punished, hurry, I'm sure you may still catch up with them!'

Richard caught his daughter by the shoulders. 'What in God's name are you babbling about?'

Perdita realised quickly that the events of the previous evening did not reflect to her credit, but she saw no reason why her father should be angry with her. She wondered whether to resort to a few maidenly tears, but calculated rapidly that this would only inflame his anger. However, her eyes were filling with tears without any effort on her part – although they were tears of impotent fury. 'Oh, to think of such wickedness! Just wait till I get my hands on them both!'

Richard took a deep breath. 'Perdita, I'd like to get my hands on them too, but until you tell me who they are and how they have wronged you, there's precious little I can do.'

And so she told him. Not the whole story, but the salient facts, leaving out only the unflattering things she had heard concerning his character, and that the spirit had claimed to be her natural mother.

Richard, however, noticed the omission. 'Perdita, without doubt you are an addle-brained imbecile, but even you would not part with your mother's earrings just to speak with a ghost.'

'She told me things. I do not see how she could have known them unless . . .'

'What sort of things?'

'About Porthew. The ghost came from a place called Porthew.'

'Sweet Jesus, I cannot believe you are such a simpleton. To fall prey to a couple of common fraudsters the moment I let you out of my sight. I've a good mind to send you back to your mother and wash my hands of you.'

That stung Perdita to protest. 'How was I to know? Besides, I thought it was all right to trust the fiddler. Viney greeted him like an old friend.'

Richard's eyes narrowed. 'Viney?'

'Yes.' Perdita saw a way to shift some of the blame, which seemed, most unfairly, to be attaching itself to her. 'The fiddler said they had been friends in another life. They even embraced each other. Then he gave Viney the money for his drink.'

'Thus leaving you unprotected. What did this fiddler look like? No, wait—' Richard broke off as Viney himself staggered back into the room. He collapsed beside a table and raised a pot of ale to his lips. Richard was beside him in an instant and knocked the tankard to the ground.

'Who was it?'

'What, sir?' Viney looked up, his eyes bleary with drink and sickness. 'Who was who, sir?'

'Who gave you the money last night?'

Viney's cheek convulsed in a mighty twitch. He began, 'I don't exactly remem—' but Richard seized him by the throat and lifted him clean off the bench.

'Was it the boy?' he demanded.

As best he could in that dangling posture, Viney nodded.

'Luke?'

Another nod and a strangled, 'Yes, sir.'

With a furious oath Richard threw Viney sprawling in the sawdust on the floor. 'Why in the name of all that's holy did he have to cross my path now?'

The question was addressed to no one in particular, but Perdita stepped over the body of the old servant and asked her father, 'Do you know the villain too?'

He did not appear to have heard her question. He was breathing heavily and staring at a patch of damp plaster on the far wall.

She asked again, 'Who was he, Father?'

He turned to her then with a look of such contempt that she felt shrivelled and small. 'An idle rogue from Porthew,' he said. 'God knows what tired local gossip he revived to part you from your pearls.'

'It'll be easier to catch him, won't it, Father, if you know him? I shall be glad to see him punished.'

The landlord did not want the Mitre's reputation sullied by tales of robbery. He had been attending carefully, and now he said, 'I shall alert the justice right away, Sir Richard. They cannot have gone far, not with that lumbering slow cart. And the fiddler too.'

'You'll not hurt the boy, though,' said Viney quietly, picking himself up from the floor.

Richard flinched. 'Damn you, Viney,' he said. He turned and crossed the room slowly. He was staring at the empty space beyond the window where the cart had been. 'Why must it always be this way?' Nobody answered him. Suddenly he came to. 'Let's be off,' he said, and to the landlord, 'No need to trouble the justice. I'll deal with this myself.'

Perdita ran after him. 'Shall we hunt them down, Father?'

'No. You must learn to do without your pearls. Most likely they've already been sold on. Besides, I've wasted time enough already.'

Perdita was incredulous. 'You cannot mean to let them get away with their crime? I *must* have my pearls back!'

'Then chase after them yourself. Maybe next time you hear a pile of lies about unquiet spirits you'll stop to think before parting company with your intelligence. If the pearls are lost, you have only yourself to blame.'

'Aren't you going to do anything at all?' Perdita wailed, following him into the yard where their horses were saddled and waiting.

'Yes indeed. I mean to continue my journey to Cornwall. Nothing will hold me up. Not you, not your wretched jewels, not any number of petty felons. Now, on your horse, Perdita, unless you wish to remain here with Viney. It's all the same to me.'

Red-faced with helpless anger, Perdita allowed Adam to help her mount and rode out of the inn yard after her father. She could scarcely believe that he could be so unjust: to blame her when she had been the innocent victim of a malicious trick!

During that day's journey she had plenty of time to contemplate just how completely she had been hoodwinked by the fiddler and his accomplice. All night she had lain in bed and pondered the story of Margaret, her unhappy marriage and her alliance with Richard Treveryan despite his reputation. For the first time in her life she had felt she had some idea of her origins, however muddled. Now she did not know what to believe. Goody Carbin and the fiddler were clearly liars and impostors, and yet they must have known something. Even unreliable local gossip was better than nothing at all.

But then she remembered how she had believed their story about unquiet souls. That Carabini woman had even pretended to speak in her mother's voice! Her outrage was intensified by the curious attraction she had felt to the low-life fellow, an attraction she had no way of explaining and which now troubled her deeply. She was furious that they were to get away with their crime, but her father rebuffed all her efforts to talk to him on the subject, and told her angrily to hold her tongue.

She spent the rest of the day hating her father and convincing herself that all she had learned of him from the spirit woman was surely true. He was cruel and heartless and unfair, and both Kitty and Margaret had undoubtedly been fools to have ever cared for him at all.

Towards evening on the second day after their disastrous stay at the Mitre, Richard's horse went lame and they had to remain two nights at Okehampton while a replacement was found. This delay enabled Viney to catch up with them. He slid off the back of a haulier's wagon and shuffled into the Bull, where Perdita and her father were just sitting down to their dinner. Without a word Viney took the platter of meat from Adam's hands and served his master as if nothing had happened. Richard merely glanced up at him and grunted. No more was said about dismissal.

But it was only when they had crossed the Tamar and were in Cornwall itself that Richard's humour improved sufficiently for Perdita to feel it was safe to pester him again. They were crossing some open, moorland countryside and he was singing, loud and tunelessly, as he looked about him at the high-flying hawks and the gusting clouds. A fresh wind was blowing and there was a new scent in the air.

When her father had told her they were to travel to Cornwall, Perdita assumed he meant to go to her mother's old house in Saltash. Now she realised they had passed Saltash to the south some time before. She was travelling further west than she had ever been in her life, into those mysterious regions of which she had heard talk since infancy, but had never really expected to see. It was a remote and harsh county, famous for fish and tin, and a dogged loyalty to the martyr King that had cost them dear during Cromwell's years.

She dug her heels into Nimble's flanks and trotted to catch up.

'Is it far now, Father?' she asked him. 'Where exactly are we going?'

He turned to her and smiled for the first time in several days.

'I am taking you home, Perdita,' he told her. 'Or as near to home as we can get. I am taking you to Rossmere.'

Chapter Five

A flock of white doves rose up, like a flurry of snowflakes in a wind, wheeled about in a leisurely arc, then sailed downwards, wings uplifted, to land on the slate roof above the stables.

Sir Francis Sutton glanced up from the contemplation of his ledger to watch them. He sighed. Twenty times a day he looked through his window at the small movements of the doves, and each time he saw them he sighed. Though beautiful, the doves ate the corn that should properly go to the farm poultry, corn he could ill afford to squander. But the doves were descended from two white birds given to his great-grandfather in the reign of Queen Elizabeth by Mr Godolphin of Godolphin. They were a link with another time, a time before the late wars, when there had been a sufficiency of good things at Rossmere, and that link must remain unbroken, in a thousand ways more costly than the feeding of the doves, though the burden of it put all their futures in jeopardy.

He frowned, rubbed his eyes, and forced himself to look once more at the columns of figures in his ledger. 'Item: 2 barrels of bay salt.' For some reason he had drawn a line through that item the previous day. The page, though only half used, was already covered by an untidy scrawl of alterations. Francis hated the lines of figures because they told an unending tale of declining income and increasing debt; because he hated to do the job he did it badly and the job had to be done again and took the whole day. And now, for the life of him he could not remember why he had put a line through those two barrels of bay salt he had entered in the book only the week before and which must be paid for somehow, crossed out or no.

With another sigh he dipped his pen in the ink and laboriously began writing again: 'Item: 2 barrels—'

The door of his office burst open. His pen skittered across the page. A spray of ink spoiled the clean paper. 'Mother, please . . .'

Alice Sutton swept into the room on a tide of her own breathless words and did not notice her son's gentle protest. 'Arriving tomorrow. Or maybe even today. He says yesterday but then again he says he may be held up. Something must have detained him, pray God until tomorrow at least, though I would not wish him an accident. Lord, I hope he has not met with an accident – why did he not come yesterday? But tomorrow is better. Now we have time to prepare the rooms . . . So much to do I cannot think where to begin.'

Sir Francis Sutton leaned back in his chair, placed the pen down in exact alignment with the ledger and asked, 'What has happened, Mother?'

'If only he had sent word sooner!' Alice's flowery perfume filled the room as she buzzed back and forth, a sheet of paper dangling from her plump fingers.

'Who had?'

'Richard, of course.'

'Richard?'

'Richard Treveryan. *Sir* Richard Treveryan, as he is now, though why he should be specially honoured by the King when it was your poor dear father who gave up his life . . . Well, there you are, nothing is ever how it ought to be, we've learned that much if nothing else.'

Francis was still struggling to grasp the essential facts. 'Sir Richard has sent you word?'

'His letter came just now. He is on his way to Rossmere.'

'Ah.'

'Maybe this very day.'

'I see.'

'We must make haste and prepare.'

'Yes.'

As so often during the course of his life, Francis was aware that decisive action was required of him. The realisation produced only a kind of paralysis. His large frame drooped visibly, and he gazed at the ink-spattered page of his ledger. At times of crisis, Francis's mind had a tendency to latch on to small problems: now, unable to deal with his mother's present urgency, he wondered only what was the meaning of those two barrels of bay salt.

Alice rattled on regardless. 'We must get in some decent wines, for he's sure to expect the best of everything. And the table has to be properly filled. There must be five kinds of meat at least or he will consider us paupers. And I simply cannot delay any longer getting fresh lace and linen. We must send to Porthew at once, or the Lord alone knows what he will think of us all.'

'But, Mother—'

'Now, Francis, pray do not start being tiresome and saying we cannot afford it. We *must* afford it, and there's no more to be said.'

'But how?' Francis made a great show of peering through a pile of bills that covered a good third of his work table. 'We cannot have goods in Porthew on credit – the tradesmen there will not allow us any more.'

'Then we must go elsewhere. Oh dear, no, there is not time. Surely you have some money put by, Francis, for just such an emergency as this?'

Francis sighed heavily and lifted himself from his seat. He was not yet thirty, but all his movements were ponderous, like those of a man twice his age. He lumbered across the room, took a key from a string about his neck, opened a small chest and took out a handful of coins.

'There,' said Alice in triumph. 'I knew you must have something.'

'Mother, these bills on the table, all of them, should have been settled a year ago at least. The ones that are twelve months overdue alone come to one hundred and forty-three pounds. And on Lady Day we must pay the eight pounds due to Sir Michael Roper on the mortgage for the Barton Farm. And on the very same day the interest is due on the loan from Solomon Daniels. That is seventeen pounds. And there is another seven pounds must be paid to the money-lender at Penryn on the same date. All I have here is less than ten pounds. And then there's the repairs that are needed on the house – but, of course, they must wait. We must find an extra twenty-five pounds to service these two debts in the next ten days as well as the eight pounds and—'

These figures had been haunting Francis day and night for weeks, and it eased his mind to confide his worries to his mother, but she dismissed him quickly. 'Clearly that is quite impossible,' she said firmly. 'Sir Michael Roper will be tolerant, I know, he is a friend of ours and would not demean himself to come hounding the family of his dear dead friend. And as for those thieving money-lenders, well, they will have to do without for once. Lord above, I don't see why they have to thrive at our expense. Everyone knows Solomon Daniels is as rich as can be. Yet my children live like paupers and they are a gentleman's family. It is not right, Francis, surely you can see that. Tell them they must learn some patience.'

'I told them so at Michaelmas, Mother. And Lady Day last year. What happens to us when their patience runs out?'

'How am I to know? Oh, don't be such a worrier, you'll give me a headache, and there is far too much to do. I'll make them see reason, leave it to me. In the meantime, there are a hundred and one things to be done before Richard gets here. Lord above, I don't know where to begin. There's no sense in arguing, Francis, my mind is quite made up.'

Francis stood no chance in debate with his mother. Her strength was due to a refusal to see any point of view but her own. She had honed her skills in litigation with the County Committee during the difficult years when the Suttons had been branded delinquents by the Parliament men ruling Cornwall and it had seemed that Rossmere would be taken from them. Nor was Francis altogether sorry to be overruled, since it relieved him of the burden of responsibility which had lain heavy on him since his father's death.

He had been only twelve when his father Nicolas Sutton was killed. A serious and conscientious lad, he had struggled from that day onwards to fill his father's extravagant shoes. Small wonder that he had grown to manhood crushed by impossible expectations. Nowadays he avoided decisions of any kind, avoided almost any activity save a restless rearranging of the papers on his desk that spelled out the family's approaching ruin.

'If you insist, Mother.'

'You must get more rents in,' said Alice. 'That will provide money to service the debt.'

'There are only two farms left, Mother. Their rents are in already.'

'Then we must sell livestock.'

'Uncle Stephen says we have sold too much already.'

'Uncle Stephen, Uncle Stephen! That man is always so doomish. Lord above, what does he know about anything anyway?'

Francis was unable to answer this question. 'Ah,' he said, thoughtfully.

Alice fidgeted. 'Well, there you are, it can't be helped. We must just get on and make the best of things. There is no question of not receiving Richard Treveryan here properly. Your dear father would have wanted us to make this sacrifice, Francis. Richard has not been to Rossmere since the day when Nicolas's poor broken body was laid out in the main hall and . . .' Her eyes were filling with tears, but she recovered herself quickly. 'Well, there you are, it can't be helped.' But then she burst out in a passion, 'Oh, Francis, if only you had seen how we entertained at Rossmere when your dear father was still alive. It was nothing for us to have eight meats on the table just for the family, not to mention fish and pies. And Rossmere was famous for its marchpanes, though of course the cook left us when the hard times came. And we had open house, and everyone visited and was made welcome, and never any talk of mortgages and debts and scrounging and pinching just to have a decent meal and—'

'Yes, Mother, I know.' Francis was desperate to interrupt her reminiscences, not simply because he had heard them a thousand times before but because they upset her, and he always felt guiltily responsible for her unhappiness. As though, had he been a better manager, she could have been spared their present humiliating poverty. A glance at the estate ledgers, however, would have shown anyone that the land had been heavily in debt even before Nicolas's death and the crippling effects of the

Royalist defeat, but Francis was too blinded by day-to-day worries to see this for himself. 'Come,' he said, 'we'll draw up a list of what we need.'

'A list, yes, that's the way to start.' She brightened at once. 'Now, then, I must have fresh lace. And there must be at least five different meats at table and—'

In her agitation, Alice had let the letter fall to the ground. Francis stooped to pick it up and grunted. 'You did not tell me he was bringing his daughter with him,' he said, glancing at the large untidy handwriting.

'His daughter? What daughter?'

'See here. It says so quite plainly.'

'I was so surprised by his news that I did not read to the end.'

'He writes that he is bringing his daughter.'

'There must be a mistake. Richard has two sons, I never heard tell of any daughter.'

'He says her name is Perdita – Mother, what's the matter now?'

The colour was draining from her face. 'Surely not!'

'What is it?'

'He would not! That woman's child!'

'What woman?' Fragments of an old local scandal assembled themselves in Francis's mind. 'Ah, yes. The Hollar woman. I remember now.' And then, as the enormity of what his mother was saying sank into his brain, he said, 'Ah. I see. You mean . . . Surely he would never bring his bastard child into our home.'

Alice had plumped herself down on a chair. 'It must be her. I heard tell his wife had taken the child in, but I never imagined he would attempt to bring her here.'

Shock had at last galvanised Francis into an appearance of activity. 'The fellow must be stopped. It is preposterous. God knows, we may not be so wealthy as we used to be, but we still have our dignity to consider. I will not permit my wife to be humiliated by sitting down at table with a bastard. I will give word to the servants to refuse her entry and—'

'There, there, Francis,' said his mother, standing up so that she could pat her scandalised son on his arm. 'Save your indignation.' To his great surprise she turned on him a smile of almost girlish charm. He was not to know that Richard

Treveryan had been her first suitor when she was still young and untroubled by talk of mortgages, rents and the interest on debt. Long ago Richard and Nicolas had even come to blows over her, and the memory of that skirmish had cheered her often when her handsome young husband began to seek his pleasures elsewhere. The memory of their rivalry, and much else besides, was cheering her now.

Francis looked at her in amazement. 'I cannot believe you intend to allow some trollop's love-child to be a guest in our home.'

'I understand your sentiments entirely, Francis. But I know Richard of old, and you do not. Save yourself the trouble of protesting, it will get you nowhere. No buts, Francis, you will find out soon enough that once Richard Treveryan has made up his mind to do a thing, neither you nor I nor anyone else stands a chance of thwarting him. You'll see.'

'Yes, Mother.'

Well satisfied with the money she had managed to extract from her son, Alice paused before leaving the room to glance at his ledger. 'What a mess you have made of the page, Francis. I've never known anyone so untidy in their book-keeping as you are. Why are you writing in the bay salt again? I told you yesterday we had sent it back. I told the merchant it was tainted, but in fact we did not need so much and I ordered it returned. So you see, Francis, no one can say I don't know how to make economies.'

And with that she swept from the room, leaving her son even more anxious and perplexed than before.

They had passed the night just south of Truro and set out on the last leg of their journey soon after dawn. About midday it began to rain, a soft but penetrating drizzle. They were crossing an area of desolate moorland, empty of habitation or any signs of life. Perdita, peering out from the shelter of her fur-trimmed hood, thought they must be nearing the end of the world. Cullen was clearly of the same opinion: she was moaning pitifully from behind Adam's broad back, something she had not done since the early days of their journey. Adam turned and spoke to her encouragingly. During their long enforced proximity on the dun-coloured gelding an understanding had been growing between the groom and the city-born maid.

Richard reined his horse to a halt for Perdita to catch up with him. The rain did not seem to trouble him in the least and he was in a high good-humour. He laughed when he saw how she had retreated tortoise-fashion beneath her cloak.

'Not far now,' he told her. 'Rossmere is just beyond that far line of trees.'

Perdita looked where he pointed; she saw a patch of scrub-land, nothing she would have deigned to call a tree.

She did not, however, let her father see her misgivings, merely asking brightly, 'Why are we going there, Father?'

'It used to belong to my friend Nicolas Sutton.' Richard kept his horse to a slow pace so they could ride together side by side. 'He was injured at Lansdown Hill in the second year of the war and died from his wounds before he reached home. He loved Rossmere above all else. You'll see why soon enough.'

'Who lives there now?'

'His widow, Alice, and their children. I dare say the older ones are off and married by now. It's nearly twenty years since I was there. It's bound to have changed a good deal.'

Perdita had never known her father mention friends before: there were men who had fought alongside him and men with whom he did business, but no friends. She wanted to learn more, but did not know how to ask.

Remarkably, Richard provided the information without prompting. 'Nicolas Sutton was a more loyal friend than I ever deserved. A Cornishman through and through. He often dis-agreed with what I did, but he stood by me all the same. He never understood why I stayed neutral when war first broke out and it grieved him deeply. It was a long time before he could accept the care I had for your mother. But the last time we saw him, he gave us both his blessing.'

The cold and damp were all forgotten. Riding along beside her father while he talked to her in this comfortable manner about his early life, Perdita was glowing with happiness enough to melt ice.

Suddenly she remembered the name of the place the

imposter Carabini had mentioned. She asked, 'Are we near Porthew?'

'About four miles to the south-east. You could see the sea from here if it wasn't so misty.'

The track led them downhill, and the land was changing. The bleak moorland gave way to small fields enclosed by tall hedges, farmsteads, streams and densely planted oaks. They were riding through a deep lane, hawthorn and holly forming a tunnel above their heads. The sheltered valley was enfolded in silence. Then, at last, they turned in between stone gateposts and rode down an avenue of bare-limbed trees.

Richard was looking about him with every appearance of satisfaction. 'The last time I saw these limes they were young saplings. How Nicolas would have loved to see them like this.'

Perdita looked ahead eagerly as they passed between the dripping trees. And then, a turn in the driveway, and Rossmere was before them. At the same moment the sun emerged from behind a cloud and the scattered roofs of the house, still wet from the day's rain, shone golden in the dying sunlight. A flock of doves rose up, white and gleaming against the grey sky. It was a picture that was to remain with Perdita for a long time.

Protected from the western gales by a gentle hill, Rossmere had grown over several hundred years to its present spacious accumulation of buildings. There was no single part of it that was outstanding, no symmetry or elegant façade. From time to time, as need arose, an enterprising or ambitious Sutton had constructed a wing here, a stable block there; an arch joining the two had been added at a later date. Then a few more rooms were placed at an angle and a courtyard appeared in its midst, until now the whole place possessed a rightness, a harmony with its surroundings as natural and satisfying as an outcrop of moorland granite.

Their horses sensed journey's end and tossed their heads eagerly. Perdita adjusted her clothes and prepared herself to make a good impression. But on whom? A strange silence enfolded Rossmere as they came to a jingling, stamping halt. Richard was looking around him uneasily. Where were the stableboys and servants who should have come running at their approach?

A door at the side of the house opened and a young woman emerged. She was a few years older than Perdita, but her status was not immediately apparent. She was clad in the kind of old-fashioned hand-me-downs usually worn by a serving-maid or poor relation, but her manner of greeting them was all familiarity. And then again, she had picked up her skirts and run across the forecourt with no more thought for her appearance than a child.

'Sir Richard,' she exclaimed, catching hold of his horse's bridle and caressing the tall bay's velvety nose, 'welcome to Rossmere.'

'You must be Nick's daughter. Is it Sophie?'

Her hazel eyes were shining up at him. 'How clever of you to remember my name.'

'You've not changed at all. Except maybe to grow more beautiful.'

'Doubly welcome, Sir Richard,' she said, with an easy laugh. 'Compliments are in short supply in this part of the world.'

'Then your local gallants must be blind fools, every one of them.'

Perdita listened with growing astonishment to their bantering exchange. Never had she heard her father play the courtier before, and certainly not to a woman whose clothes were darned and whose nails were cracked and broken, even if she did have a pleasant, laughing manner. She noted also that the fingers caressing the horse's nose were bare of any ring. Poor Sophie was well on the way to being an old maid, Perdita thought, with just a touch of contempt.

Richard was dismounting. 'Where are your servants?'

'Uncle Stephen has just now gone to rouse them.'

As she spoke a tall man strode under the arch that led to the stableyard at the rear of the house. He had an honest, serious face. Like Sophie he was dressed in a yeoman's coarse clothes, yet he had the air of a gentleman. Behind him came two servants, though one was so old and the other so lame it seemed unlikely they could manage a day's work between them.

'Richard,' said the tall man, 'it's good to see you.'

'Stephen?'

He nodded. 'Come inside. You must be weary after your journey. Alice is all eagerness to see you again. Amos and Sithney will see to your horses and make your servants comfortable.'

Richard looked sceptical at this last remark. Amos and Sithney did not look capable of the simplest task. But then a small cough somewhere above and behind him indicated that Perdita, still seated on Nimble, had been ignored for quite long enough.

'I almost forgot,' said Richard, placing his hands around her waist and lifting her to the ground. 'This is my daughter, Perdita.'

Sophie stepped forward at once and put her arms around Perdita, damp cloak and all. 'Perdita,' she said warmly. 'What a pretty name. You are most welcome at Rossmere. I hope your visit will be a very happy one.'

Perdita extricated herself as quickly as she could.

Stephen said, 'It's a pleasure to see you, Perdita. I'll help Amos with the horses. Sophie will take you both through to Alice. You'll find her in the winter parlour.' He himself took Richard's horse and led it towards the stables. The two servants hobbled after him with the other horses. Viney trailed behind with Cullen and Adam.

Perdita followed Sophie and her father into the house. They entered the great hall, the oldest part of Rossmere. The high-vaulted ceiling was richly decorated in the old style and the stone walls were hung with ancient weaponry and banners. All this splendour, however, was barely visible because of black smoke billowing from a vast fireplace.

Sophie beat vaguely at the smoke and turned to Richard with an embarrassed smile. 'I apologise for the unpleasantness, Sir Richard. We do not usually trouble to light the fire in here. This room is seldom used and the chimney has not been swept in an age, but my mother insisted—' She broke off awkwardly, as though fearing she had already given away too much. 'Here, let me take your outdoor clothes.' She fussed round them performing the tasks that should properly have been done by a servant. 'My mother and brother attend you, Sir Richard. And Perdita.' She turned to Perdita and gave her a smile of encouragement as she pushed open the door into the winter parlour. 'Mother, Francis, they are here.'

The winter parlour, a pretty panelled room, was in shadowy darkness. It was that dusky time of evening, when the light from outside has faded but the candles have not yet been lit. Between the two lights, as the country people called it.

A fire was burning in this room too, and here there was no problem with smoke. There was, however, an unmistakable chill in the atmosphere, which no amount of blazing fires could quite disguise: the frostiness of respectable folk who fear they are being compromised. Perdita smothered a burst of panic. She should have expected no less: God knows, it was a hazard she had encountered many times before. Now she understood the reason for the exaggerated generosity of Sophie and her uncle: clearly they had anticipated that the rest of the family would be less welcoming.

Two figures, apparently deep in conversation, moved apart guiltily as she and her father were announced. Alice and her eldest son had been engaged in a heated debate about how best to deal with this base-born intruder, and were anxious as to just how much had been overheard.

Adjusting the spotless new lace at her throat and wrists, Alice took a hesitant step towards the door. 'Richard . . . after all this time . . .'

'My dearest Alice.'

Richard began to cross the room towards her, but after only a couple of paces he halted. He, too, had noted the frozen expression on the face of the portly young man, who must surely be Nicolas's eldest son. He stood quite still. No one else moved. Richard pushed his unruly hair back from his forehead and looked about him thoughtfully. He had caused upset enough in his youth to detect the musty smell of outraged morality when it was all around him.

Very deliberately, he smiled, then turned and motioned Perdita to join him. Slipping his arm over his daughter's shoulders he said, 'Alice, it gives me great pleasure to introduce my daughter, Perdita.' He spoke with deceptive gentleness, but there was steel behind his words as he went on, 'I know you will wish to make her feel at home at Rossmere.'

Alice wavered only for an instant. Her brown eyes fluttered upwards to Richard's face, as implacable and ruthless as ever she remembered it. She flushed slightly, made some conversational but indistinct noises, then extended her small plump hand and said, 'Of course. Of course. Perdita, yes, yes. How like your father you are. And your . . . yes, well. Delighted to meet you. Richard, this is my eldest son, Francis. Francis, come and meet Perdita.'

When the newcomers were announced, Francis had been in the middle of telling his mother that she might do as she pleased but that he was not about to compromise his family's standing in the county by offering hospitality to other men's bastards.

Richard gripped his hand firmly. It was warm and flabby. He said, 'Francis, it is a pleasure to see you again.'

Francis smiled weakly at the newcomer. Then he found himself crossing the room and greeting his most unwelcome guest. It was hard to be certain in this dim light, but the girl was clearly dressed with greater elegance and richness than anyone who had previously visited his home: more importantly, she held herself like a lady.

'Sir Richard,' he said, all the time speaking and acting as though directed by Treveryan's fierce gaze, 'you are most welcome at Rossmere. You . . . and your daughter. I am sure my father would have wanted . . .' His voice faded. He coughed.

Perdita dipped her head in the smallest of curtsies. She had steeled herself to show no trace of her dismay: in fact, her imperious manner implied that she had been expecting only courtesy.

The social niceties having been completed under Richard's hawk-like vigilance, everybody unbent. There was obviously no question of turning back; they must all get on and make the best of the situation.

'Thank you, Francis. And Alice,' said Richard. 'It's good to be here at last. I sometimes wondered if I would ever see this place again.'

Alice's hands fluttered constantly. She had nothing to do, but was unable to be still. Her voice fluttered also, as she bustled to create a semblance of past normality. 'Sophie, see to the candles. We'll eat by and by. We were expecting you and so delayed our meal. Oh, what a time it's been, Richard. You've waited long enough.'

'I was living abroad until last year.'

'Cornwall never held you long, did it?' asked Alice, then, as she felt herself begin to blush, she wished she had not asked Sophie to light the candles so soon. She glanced nervously at Perdita.

'Mistress Sutton,' said Perdita, forcing herself to speak out, though she would much rather have remained silent at her father's side, 'it is such a pleasure to see Rossmere after all these years of hearing it praised. My mother always assured me that there wasn't a house in the whole of Cornwall that could match it for elegance and comfort. And now I find it is even lovelier than I was told. You and your family are most fortunate to have such a home.'

Richard observed with some interest the opening shots of his daughter's campaign to win over the mistress of Rossmere. He had not witnessed her social determination before and he was intrigued to see it now. Obviously veracity was no part of her armoury, since Kitty had always loathed anything associated with this western part of Cornwall and would have spoken of Rossmere and its occupants only to criticise them. Truth aside, he had to admit it was an artful performance, combining just the right mix of deference and composure. Even so, it irritated him. Like a practised mountebank she had gauged her audience and was tailoring her performance to their response.

He was about to cut short her masquerade, but then he hesitated. He had not, after all, undertaken this long journey west for the sake of his health. There was a purpose to it, and the purpose concerned his daughter's marriage prospects, as she had guessed.

Well done, Perdita, he thought, as he observed the skill with which she drew the pallid and reluctant Sir Francis into her orbit. Only carry on like that and my plans will be much easier to achieve.

Chapter Six

A crystal bright morning. Perdita awoke to distant cockcrow and the nearer scratch and murmur of doves. For a moment she thought this was yet another inn on their journey west, but then she remembered. Rossmere. They had arrived at Rossmere the previous evening.

She cast her mind back over the events following their arrival. The confusion of unfamiliar faces, the strain and forced jollity of their hosts. The two who had greeted them first, Sophie and her uncle Stephen, had gone out of their way to be hospitable, but their warm welcome had only emphasised the resentment of the others. Mistress Alice Sutton had fussed over Richard and ignored Perdita. Francis followed his mother's example. So, too, did his wife Honor, a dismal-seeming woman, Perdita thought.

The younger sister, Louisa, was hardly any better. She was about twenty, as pretty as her elder sister, Sophie, but with none of her easy-going charm and generosity. She was surly with Perdita to the point of rudeness but, then, she was the same with everyone. Perdita maintained a pose of regal serenity. She had learned that in situations like this it was advisable to act as though she was doing this rustic family an enormous favour by condescending to honour them with her presence and to ignore any hints of discourtesy as beneath her notice. In time these tactics were usually effective.

But undoubtedly it was hard work and she had been exhausted when the evening drew to a close. There had been some unpleasantness over the arrangement of bedrooms. Sophie had volunteered to give up her own room to Perdita, which Perdita thought was a fine idea but to which Louisa, who shared a bed with her elder sister, objected strenuously. Perdita was puzzled that such a large house seemed to possess so few bedchambers, but the smell of damp plaster upstairs indicated that only a few of the rooms were habitable during the winter. She settled the matter by sending Cullen to help Sophie make the necessary alterations. Louisa fell into a sulk and did not speak again for the rest of the evening.

Perdita stretched in the large bed. She was glad she had brought her own linens with her: everything in this bedroom, as in the rest of the house, was old and shabby. She lay for a while and pondered which clothes to wear on this her first day at Rossmere, then got up and went across the room to look out of the window. The weathered beauty of Rossmere that had so impressed her the previous evening was enhanced by the spring sunshine. Suddenly she was eager to be outside and to explore.

Just as she was about to turn away from the window she noticed a man emerge from the house by the side door beneath her room. It was her father. He was speaking to Stephen.

Perdita was curious. Last night she had noticed her father asking various apparently unrelated questions of Mistress Sutton and Stephen. She was determined to find out what lay behind his enquiries. She pushed the window open quietly.

Her father's voice rose up in the clear morning air. 'Stephen, I must talk with you in private.'

'As you wish. I'm on my way to prepare a saw for the men. We can talk together while I continue with my work.'

The two men strode off in the direction of the farmyard, which lay at a short distance from the main house.

An important discussion. With Stephen Sutton. In private? Was it possible that her father had brought her all this way to see her wed to a man more than twice her age? He must have been a handsome man in his youth, but now . . .

'Cullen, come quickly!' she shouted. 'Come and help me dress. I am going out.'

★   ★   ★

Sir Richard Treveryan was moved neither by the freshness of the spring morning nor by the time-weathered beauty of the buildings at Rossmere. Where Perdita saw lichen-yellowed granite and mossy thatch, he saw only dilapidation and decay. He had been out and about since dawn, and the more he saw the angrier he became: roofs and windows in need of repair, hedges overgrown, weeds tearing at the masonry of the house, ditches and gutters clogged and smelling. Worse still, livestock was in poor condition, the grain stores and hay barns were practically empty and there was hardly an able-bodied serving man to be found anywhere.

He kept his anger reined back until he and Stephen had reached the privacy of the near barn, but then he burst out, 'What, in God's name, has been going on?'

Stephen had settled down on a small stool and did not answer until he was working on the saw blade. He had a lean, serious face with clear grey eyes and an economy of movement and gesture that gave weight to his words. He asked calmly, 'Is something troubling you, Richard?'

'Of course there is. This whole place has gone to ruin. What the devil have you been playing at?'

'You're very swift in your opinions, Richard. You've been here only a night.' Stephen's voice was quieter, but had a resonance that carried well.

'I've seen enough to know that Rossmere is crumbling around your ears. Everywhere I look I see signs of incompetence and neglect. It's downright criminal.'

Stephen frowned. 'Why not find out the facts before you jump to conclusions?'

'That's what I'm trying to do now.'

'Francis is the master here. I suggest you talk with him.'

'Don't hide behind your nephew, Stephen. It's plain to see he is ruled by his mother. And Alice has never had a head for business.'

'Is that so? Before you see fit to criticise my sister-in-law, maybe you should bear in mind that she fought long and hard to keep this place for her son. Many Cornish landowners lost everything under Cromwell.'

'I know that better than anyone. My own home was forfeit

long since. But, still, keeping Rossmere in the family was one thing. Making it prosper was your responsibility. Francis is a dullard. He doesn't look capable of the simplest decision.'

'My nephew does the best he can. Everyone knows a colt broken too early to the shafts will never gain his full strength.'

'Meaning?'

'Francis was twelve when his father died. When I returned to Rossmere in the autumn of forty-five he had been carrying a man's burdens for two years.'

'All the more reason for you to take those burdens from him.' Stephen began to speak, but Richard went on angrily, 'And what of his sister? What of Sophie? She's a beautiful girl and she should have been wed long ago. Yet you keep her on here doing the work of a serving wench. Have you no shame, man?'

'Be careful, Richard.' Stephen's voice remained calm, but it had grown ominous. 'Sophie stays at Rossmere of her own free will and for the same reason I do. Because she loves this place, and her family too.'

'Yes, and you have let her sacrifice her own chance of happiness to suit the family. Have you never thought of that?'

Richard's furious question hung in the silence, while Stephen continued steadily moving the file over the jagged edge of the saw blade.

Richard took a step towards him. 'How can you sit back and let these wrongs continue? You've eaten at your brother's table for nearly twenty years but you've not even begun to make up for his loss.'

'Spare me your indignation, Richard.' Suddenly Stephen's voice no longer sounded angry but infinitely weary. 'You've not been near Rossmere since the wars and now you turn up on a whim and are angry because you find things not to your liking. You know nothing of what has been happening.'

'That is precisely why I'm asking you.'

'Why? What's it to do with you after so long? Why have you returned here now?'

'Does there have to be a particular reason? Isn't it enough that I should want to see the family of my oldest friend after all this time?'

'If that is all your purpose.'

'What are you suggesting, Stephen?'

'It is common knowledge that my brother Nicolas had borrowed heavily from you before his death.'

'And?'

'There are fears you have come to collect your debt.'

'Who thinks so? Francis?'

Silence. Only the rasp of the file on the saw's teeth.

Richard burst out, in a passion, 'Sweet Jesus, what do you take me for? I may have the reputation of a blackguard in these parts, but even I would not dun the family of my oldest friend for money when it is plain to see they cannot afford to put decent clothes on their backs. God damn it, man, I loved Nick. He was a brother to me, more than a brother, and it grieves me now to see his children reduced to beggary. Can't you see I only want to help?'

Another silence. This time even Stephen's labour had ceased. He set down the file slowly and placed his hands on his knees. At length he looked up at Richard and his austere expression softened. 'Well, Richard, you have an odd way of showing it, but I do believe you are sincere, though your reputation never led me to expect a benefactor.'

'I have no patience with gossip.'

'Nor I, neither.'

'Well, then, we are agreed on that much at least. Now, tell me what's been happening here. You know I'll not get a straight answer from Francis. Both he and his mother are determined to have me think nothing has changed.'

'It is worse for Alice now.'

'Why?'

'When Parliament ruled, she understood our problems. She endured hardship and humiliation from the County Committee, but she never let them beat her down. No matter how bad things were, she was convinced that as soon as the King was restored all her troubles would be over. She simply cannot understand how it is that King Charles is safe in London yet our situation is unchanged. If anything, it has grown worse.'

'Worse?'

Stephen sighed. 'Alice does not want me to tell you but, God knows, it is common knowledge hereabouts. Better you should hear the truth from me than a garbled version from someone else. Rossmere is weighed down with more debts than can ever be paid off, short of a miracle.'

'Go on.'

Stephen said, 'The estate was already encumbered at the time of Nick's death. When Alice was forced to compound for delinquency, she raised a loan with the money-lenders, chiefly Solomon Daniels at Penryn. From time to time she and Francis have borrowed further sums just to pay the interest on the debt. There seems to be no prospect of ever paying off the principal. Honor brought some money with her when she married Francis, not much – I believe it was a love match primarily – but that was soon used up.'

'What about the income from rents?'

'All but two of the farms were sold years ago. Alice had no choice. And the two that are left are the ones that no one bothered to make an offer on. The Barton Farm is mortgaged to the hilt and Widow Firth has Polcreath – the land there is so poor that she and her son can barely scratch a living. There have been other losses besides. If you wish to know the details, you will have to ask Francis.'

'I am content to hear it from you.'

'I have told you all I know.'

'Why this ignorance? How can you pretend to help them when you withhold your advice in the one area it is most needed?'

Stephen stood up and walked across the little shed. He turned slowly. In general, he was a self-contained man, generous and gentle with those he loved but giving away little of his true feelings.

The expression in his grey eyes was sombre as he said, 'When I came back to Rossmere, Richard, I wanted nothing more than to be useful to my brother's family. I was weary of slaughter and destruction. I wanted to make things grow and prosper, not for my own sake but for Alice and the children. I knew they were likely to be all the family I would ever have.' Richard raised his eyebrows in surprise at this, but Stephen ignored the implied question and continued, 'My father was still living at that time, and he had some hare-brained notion of making me the children's guardian in place of Alice. It came to nothing, I saw to that. The only consequence was that Alice came to see me as a rival. For a while she thought I wanted to seize Rossmere for myself. Nothing could have been further from the truth, but I have had to tread carefully ever since. Any suggestion known to come from me is certain to be disregarded. And I have never been admitted to their discussions.'

'Surely Francis has more sense than to be prejudiced against you.'

'My nephew, as you have already observed, is ruled by his mother.'

Richard threw up his hands in a gesture of exasperation and swore vigorously. There was a clattering sound from outside the barn, as if an iron pot had been kicked over. Richard glanced suspiciously through the half-open door, then turned back to Stephen.

'What a confounded tangle,' he said.

For the first time the ghost of a smile lit up Stephen's eyes. 'My thoughts precisely, Richard. I never thought I would wish myself a soldier again, but there have been times when I'd rather face a battery of Roundhead cannon than carry on struggling in this swamp of debt and suspicion.'

'I heard you were a fine soldier. Nicolas always said you had all the courage in the family.'

'My brother was an excellent soldier, and he died bravely. I have often wished . . .' Stephen did not finish his sentence, but Richard had anticipated him.

'That it was you who died? I've thought the same myself, in an idle moment. No one would have mourned my passing.'

'Surely your wife—'

'Kitty must have wished me dead a hundred times.'

'And Perdita's mother?' Stephen had been observing him closely.

'Yes, long ago. Only I did not know until it was too late.'

'We have both been unfortunate, then,' said Stephen.

Silence filled the barn once more, but this time it was a different kind of silence, that of thoughts shared with no need to speak them plain.

At length Stephen said, 'Now it is your turn, Richard. You still have not told me your real reason for coming to Rossmere. I do not believe you have undertaken this long journey, and brought your daughter with you, all for memory's sake.'

'You're right. And I am concerned for the girl's future. Her origins are dubious enough. I want to see her well settled, and, if possible, in the country her mother knew.'

'Is that wise?' Stephen asked. 'People round here have long memories. It might be easier for her to bury the stigma of her birth where her story is not so widely known.'

'And risk being found out? I have always been of the opinion—'

Here Richard broke off suddenly. Unmistakable sounds of commotion came to them from outside the barn. He strode out into the morning sunshine and almost tripped over a small white puppy, followed by his daughter. He caught her roughly by the arm.

'A peeping Tom?' he demanded angrily.

It was one of the accomplishments that Perdita valued but saw no reason to boast of. She had little patience with the old adage that eavesdroppers never hear good of themselves, since she had always found the practice useful. As a child she had learned in this manner of Kitty's father's revulsion at the idea of receiving Richard Treveryan's bastard child into his home. She had also overheard Kitty's efforts on her behalf. She had immediately set about gaining a place in the old man's affections and a year later she had overheard a conversation that proved her success: not simply tolerated, she had become his particular favourite.

She had discovered that a small animal often made a useful pretext on these occasions and so, when she set out to follow her father, she had gathered up a milky-coloured puppy who was harassing one of the maids. Following her father down to the farmyard, she had seen him step inside the low-roofed barn with Stephen and had hidden herself behind it to listen. Luckily the building was built of stone and cob and, like most other things at Rossmere, had fallen into disrepair. She had found a useful spy-hole and was able to see as well as overhear the conversation between the two men. Unfortunately she was so absorbed in hearing her father's plans for her that she forgot all about the puppy. He quickly grew bored and, in an effort to persuade her to play with him, sank his needle-sharp teeth into the heel of her soft leather shoe. Gasping with pain and surprise, Perdita had spun round, slipped, seen the puppy race round the corner and run after it.

Straight into her furious father.

'Oh, Father, whatever are you doing here?' she exclaimed breathlessly. 'I was just looking for the little puppy. One of the house cats had frightened him and he ran off, so I followed him and—' Shaking off Richard's hand, she dived forward and scooped up the puppy, who licked her cheek with enthusiasm.

Her father did not look as if he believed a word of it. However, he turned to Stephen, who had emerged from the byre and said smoothly, 'Perdita has strayed too far from the house after some foolish puppy. I'll walk back with her. We must continue our conversation later, Stephen. I dare say I've kept you long enough from your work.'

Stephen bade them both good day and set off towards the saw pits with the newly sharpened blade over his shoulder. Perdita doubted if he was convinced by her story, but she had an idea that Stephen Sutton at least could be relied on not to mention it. 'I'll take the puppy back now,' she said hurriedly. 'I never knew I'd followed him so far.'

'Come, Perdita.' Gripping her arm firmly, Richard led her not towards the house, as she had expected, but down a grassy track that led away from the farmyard. She began to be frightened.

They arrived in a small meadow containing three white geese and a slime-covered horse pond. Richard wheeled about and faced her. 'How much did you hear?'

'Hear, Father? Why, I heard nothing. I did not even know you were there. I—'

Swiftly he clamped her elbows to her sides and lifted her clean off the ground. 'I trust you're a strong swimmer. Lie to me once more and you go head first into the water.'

'Set me down this instant!'

'How much did you hear?'

'Just about everything, I should hope.'

He released his grip. 'That's better. Don't ever presume to lie to me again.'

Perdita picked up the puppy, who had fallen to the ground, and hugged him tightly. Richard still looked inclined to pitch her into the green depths of the pond. He said coldly, 'Just as I always suspected. My wife has brought you up with the appearance of a fine lady and the scruples of a kitchen cat.'

'That's not fair!'

'You deserve to be thrashed. That might teach you to mend your ways.'

'Beat me as much as you like, but I'll not change.'

He advanced towards her. She took a hasty step back.

'Are you not afraid of me?'

'Of course I am! I know you can hurt me in all sorts of ways worse than beating.'

'Yet you still persist?'

'Yes, I have to! I *have* to know what concerns me most, no matter what the cost.' And still she gripped the puppy. Her heart was beating very fast, in spite of her brave words. The look on her father's face was murderous, but for once her sense of outrage was stronger than her fear and she forced herself to return his stare.

All at once his expression changed. He burst out in a laugh and exclaimed, 'Bravo, Perdita. Maybe you're not the ninny I took you for.'

She let out a long breath. 'Then you will tell me your plan?'

'No. For one thing, you have discovered more than enough already, and for another, I have no fixed plan, not yet.'

'But you wish to see me settled.'

'That is every father's wish.'

'And you would like me to make my home near here.'

'Perhaps.'

'My guess is that you have a mind to see me married to someone here. Am I right?'

He was regarding her thoughtfully. 'And how does such a plan appeal to you?'

'I cannot say until you tell me who you have in mind. I thought at first you might be thinking of one of your friend

Nicolas's sons. Francis is, as you so rightly said, a dullard –'
Richard hissed with vexation at hearing his unflattering words
thrown back at him, but Perdita continued unabashed – 'but he
is married already, so I presume you mean one of the younger
sons. I gather there are four.'

'And?'

She smiled. 'May I take my pick?'

His expression remained stern. 'In theory, I have no objection at all, but in practice it might prove difficult.'

'How so?'

'Charles, who is next to Francis in age, lives in Camborne
and married a maltster's widow a year ago. The two middle
boys, Nicolas and John, were sent to work for Alice's cousin
who has interests in Barbados and Newfoundland. I believe they
are both overseas, and likely to remain so for some time.'

'And that leaves?'

'Young Richard, my namesake.'

'He is also abroad? Or married perhaps?'

'On the contrary, he has been visiting friends at Launceston
and is expected to return home at any time.'

'Then I look forward to meeting him. I thought at first that
Stephen was the man you had in mind.'

'Stephen? I had not thought of that, but now you mention it
. . . How would you like it?'

'Does my liking count for anything?'

'A little. Marriages are more likely to be successful when
there is neither strong dislike nor strong passion.'

'I understand the need to avoid dislike, but why passion?'

'Because when it fades there is nothing to take its place. The
best marriages are those which are based on a similarity of
background and a reasonable degree of liking. The rest can
follow from that.'

'Yes, Father.'

He turned and began walking back towards the house. She
hurried after him. Similarity of background and a reasonable
degree of liking . . . He was right, of course, all the world was
agreed on that. So why did she feel disappointed?

A sudden image came into her mind of the man who had
tricked her of her earrings at the inn. She forced herself to dismiss

75

the thought. She told herself firmly that she had every reason to be thoroughly satisfied by this conversation with her father.

Since he had returned to England the previous autumn, she had struggled to win him over with the sweetness of her disposition and feminine wiles. She had wanted his love because he was her father, she needed his affection because otherwise her future was worse than uncertain, but the harder she tried, the more he seemed to disdain her.

And now she had discovered that all the time she needed only to stand up to him to win his respect. It was a lesson she would not forget in a hurry, though she had an idea she would not have been so brave were she still in Kitty's household. Something inside her had altered during the long ride down to Cornwall. Or maybe it was all to do with this bright West Country air.

But when they reached the forecourt and were about to enter the house, Richard paused and said in a low voice, 'Perdita, this afternoon I have private business in Porthew. It does not concern you at all. And I warn you, if you make any attempt to follow me I will tie you to the gatepost and leave you there until my return. Do I make myself plain?'

There was no question but that he meant what he said, so 'Yes, Father,' was all her reply, with a demure lowering of the eyes as she spoke, which was for the benefit of anyone who might be watching but which did not deceive Richard for an instant.

Stephen Sutton delivered the newly sharpened blade to Sithney at the saw pit and then went to help with the spring ploughing. He worked hard, as always, but his conversation with Richard Treveryan had troubled him. It gave him no satisfaction to see the place through a stranger's eyes, nor to be reminded of the impossibility of running the farm when there was neither money nor men to do the job properly. Had it been a question of hard work alone, then providing food for the household at Rossmere and a surplus to sell for cash would have been a simple matter. But fate had a way of undermining all his efforts.

In October the harvest had been safely gathered in, one of

the best for years, and then a month later a gale blew the barn roof away and a mountain of grain was ruined by the wet. A healthy calf was born only to sicken and die within the week for no reason anyone could see. The plough horse went lame just as the ploughing was about to begin. Small wonder that country folk's lives were riddled with superstition, since amulets and incantations gave at least an illusion of defence against calamity.

It did not help, of course, that money that should have been put back into the farm was invariably taken to pay the interest on their crippling debts. The more hopeless the situation became, the harder Stephen worked. It was the only thing he could do.

When Stephen had returned from the wars in 1645 he had had his own reasons for wishing to plunge himself into work. The events of that fateful summer, when the Royalist army had suffered its crushing defeat at Naseby, had been overshadowed for him by his own, more personal catastrophe. That year, when he was garrison commander in a small Midlands town, he had fallen in love, wholeheartedly and impossibly, the way a man does who has come late to the experience. As that summer ended and the old King's cause was lost, his own chance of happiness vanished also, seemingly for ever.

Hard work and the care of his brother's fatherless children were the panaceas he embraced with gratitude. He had come close to destroying his health in the process and it was difficult now to have to recognise that, in spite of all he had done, his efforts were likely to be in vain.

Following West Country practice, the main meal of the day was still taken at noon at Rossmere. Now that Perdita had a clue as to her father's intentions, she was more than ever eager to study this new family in which she found herself. No general, surveying his own troops and those of his enemy before a battle, made a more exact reckoning than Perdita when she took her place at table on that first full day at Rossmere. At the same time she remained careful, as ever, to make a favourable impression on all those present.

Since Mistress Sutton was almost entirely taken up in talking over old times with Richard Treveryan, Perdita kept her best efforts for the eldest son. She recognised Francis's antipathy towards her, and set to work to thaw him out, praising the beauty of his home, its situation, the landscape, the Cornish climate and anything else she thought might gratify his countryman's pride.

Nor did she neglect his young wife, Honor, who took her seat now next to her husband. Privately Perdita considered her a pitiful, sickly-looking creature, with watery blue eyes and mealy skin, but it was clear that Francis doted on her. No doubt, Perdita thought, he was delighted to have found a bride who was even less animated than he was himself . . . but no one watching her charming chatter that dinner time would have guessed she felt anything but admiration for them both.

Meanwhile, she was busily reassessing her opinion of both Stephen and Sophie. Perdita had been brought up by Kitty to judge people according to their appearance and their social standing, and neither Stephen nor Sophie rated very high by either measure. But Rossmere, she was beginning to understand, was not Kitty's world. She had learned from that interesting conversation in the barn that her father regarded both uncle and niece at least as highly as he did Alice and Francis, if not more so. Perdita had always been swift to learn. She was afraid her manner towards them both the previous evening might have seemed a little offhand, and she was scrupulously attentive now.

She observed, however, that Stephen was impatient to get back to his work on the farm and that Sophie had to be restrained by a sharp word from her mother from helping the serving-maid clear away the dishes. This elegant and leisurely meal was clearly a deviation from the normal state of things at Rossmere, whatever Mistress Sutton might pretend.

That left only Louisa. The younger of Alice Sutton's two daughters did not appear to have Sophie's generous charm. She might have been just as pretty, Perdita thought, since she had the same rich brown hair and well-shaped features, and her dress was neatly cared for, though shabby. But the effect was marred by her air of reckless boredom. She had stumped into the room as though she had lead weights in her shoes. When Perdita tried to draw her into the conversation, Louisa glanced up, her eyes clouded with gloom. Not even Perdita's highly dramatic account of their battle with the footpads on the Somerset levels, which made Alice Sutton pause for a moment in her reminiscences with Richard and attend to her with interest, was able to engage the dismal girl.

Just as Perdita was despairing of ever finding a way of winning a smile from Louisa, a diversion burst upon them. Hard on the heels of the serving-maid bearing a tray of sweetmeats scampered the white puppy she had commandeered that morning. Much to her vexation he made straight for her place and began jumping eagerly against her skirts. She tried to thrust him away surreptitiously, aware all the time of her father's mocking gaze.

'How did that puppy escape?' asked Francis. 'I ordered the whole litter drowned a week ago. God knows, there is no shortage of dogs to be fed at Rossmere.'

'This one seems to have taken a liking for my daughter,' said Richard. 'I cannot imagine why.'

Perdita was on the point of denying any association with the nuisance when Louisa, showing animation for the very first time, exclaimed, 'You cannot drown it, Francis. It's Kip's favourite. He begged Amos to spare him.'

'Kip?' asked Perdita.

'My youngest brother,' explained Sophie. 'Richard, but he's always known as Kip.'

'Ah.' Perdita swept the puppy into her arms and fed him a choice morsel from her plate. 'What a dear little fellow he is, and he does seem to favour me,' she exclaimed. 'Does he have a name?'

'Kip just called him Puppy,' said Louisa.

'How about Peeping Tom?' suggested Richard.

Perdita darted him a furious glance. 'Tom,' she said firmly, 'Tom is a fine name for such an adorable creature.'

She ignored her father's snort of derision, noting only that her friendship with the puppy seemed to have endeared her to Louisa. With luck it would have the same effect on young Richard – or Kip, as she must learn to call him – when he eventually returned to Rossmere.

*   *   *

That afternoon, a lone horseman set off from Rossmere and rode slowly along the lane that led towards Porthew.

The little town was no more than a cluster of houses and a couple of streets in a rocky bay, a place smelling of sea and tar and, above all, the rank stench of pilchards being salted in barrels ready to be sent overseas.

Those residents who recognised the stranger gave him a wide berth. They remembered the stories that had gathered around him when he had made his home nearby, more than twenty years before.

He rode slowly past the forge and into the little town, following the road along beside the harbour and the alehouse, only stopping when he came to the church. Here he dismounted and, leaving his horse by the lych-gate, he went into the graveyard where an old man, the sexton, was smoothing the soil on a fresh grave.

The two men spoke together for a short while, then the sexton laid down his rake and hobbled over to a narrow plot, marked only by a rotting wooden cross, on the seaward side of the cemetery. The stranger indicated that he wished to be alone, and the old fellow returned to his task.

Clouds were beginning to obscure the sun, a white haze drifting up from the sea. The air grew chilly and damp. The sexton felt the tell-tale twinges of rheumatism in hands and knees and retreated to the vestry.

Some while later, when the sexton emerged from the church, having packed up after his day's work, the sea mist had obscured the scene almost entirely. As he crossed the graveyard to return to his home, he noticed that the stranger had not moved from his place by the lonely grave. He was standing quite still, head bowed as if in thought or prayer, while the rooks squabbled around the church tower and the muffled boom of the waves broke against the rocks beyond the harbour wall.

At length, as dusk was falling, Sir Richard Treveryan placed his hat once more on his head, returned to his waiting horse and rode back the way he had come.

Chapter Seven

The fog that had gathered around Richard in the graveyard persisted through the following days. Swathed in white, Rossmere shrank to a mere huddle of stone floating in a sea of mist; distances were blotted out and the sounds of cockcrow and footsteps on cobbles echoed muffled and strange.

Perdita had known fog before in Saltash and in London, but this was different, and oppressive. Here there was no clatter from city streets, no bustle from taverns or shops, no pedlars shouting their wares, no racket of porters and dray horses, but only a dripping stillness and the veiled routine of the household and the farm.

Two days after her conversation with her father by the horse pond, she was gazing idly from her bedroom window at the white-shrouded roofs and chimney-stacks of Rossmere and wondering how in the world the Suttons and other country folk condemned to a rustic life avoided going mad with boredom on days such as this. She had already done a circuit of the house to see what was happening on this damp morning.

Mistress Alice Sutton was closeted once again with her eldest son in his office. As far as Perdita could make out they spent a good deal of each morning in these private conversations, sessions from which both emerged grey-faced with anxiety. Perdita had loitered in the passageway outside Francis's office long enough to learn that their talk was all about loans that must be serviced by Lady Day, a topic of no interest to her at all.

Her father, she learned, had ridden out at first light, no one knew where. Sophie and Stephen, predictably enough, were hard at work, Stephen helping the men with the spring plough-ing and Sophie busy in the kitchen with the maids. Perdita was not yet so starved of occupation that she was prepared to contemplate housework, so she went in search of Honor and Louisa.

Honor, as she discovered when she met her on the stairs, had awoken that morning with a sick headache and was already on her way to lie down on her bed.

'You may come and read to me, if you wish,' said Honor, with a supplicating smile. 'It sometimes distracts me from the pain if I have company.' And her pale eyes watered with tears as she spoke the word 'pain'.

'Later. Maybe,' said Perdita, who was feeling far too fidgety to sit by a sickbed all morning, though it occurred to her that if nothing more interesting materialised she might take the op-portunity to pump Honor for information about the family. She added, as an afterthought, 'Did you say you were feeling sick, Honor? Maybe you are with child at last.' For Honor and Francis had been married for nearly three years and there was still no sign of an heir to Rossmere.

Pale though she already was, Honor turned even paler at this casual remark and put trembling fingertips to her brow. 'I do not think so . . .' she said, in a low voice, but she looked so dejected that Perdita assumed she had said the wrong thing.

'I'm sorry, Honor, that was tactless of me.'

'Not at all.' Honor's hand was trembling on the stair rail. 'It's just that I feel so faint.'

'Here,' said Perdita briskly, 'I'll help you to your room.'

When she had escorted Honor to lie down in the large tester bed, Perdita was heartily relieved that she had not consented to read to the invalid. The bedroom had a queasy smell of patent medicines. Despite the mildness of the morning, the windows were tight closed and the air was stale and musty as a closet. When she went to throw open a window, Honor cried out in alarm, 'Don't, it's so cold! I shall perish, I know I will.'

Perdita was going to contradict her, but when she came back to the bedside she found that Honor was indeed shivering.

'There now.' Perdita found a loose wrap and put it across her shoulders. 'The fire has gone out. I'll send one of the maids to attend you.'

Honor's eyes were brimming with tears. 'They will not come,' she whispered. 'Sophie will not let them.'

'Why ever not?'

'She always says they have work to do in the kitchen and cannot be spared and I must fend for myself.'

'What nonsense,' said Perdita. 'I'll send one of the girls up with a hot posset to drink and a warm brick for your feet. You'll soon be feeling much better.'

Honor blinked up at her hopefully.

But when Perdita entered the massive kitchen across the courtyard at the rear of the house, she found that Sophie was determined to keep all the Rossmere servants hard at work. Worse, she intended to recruit more. She was filling the neck of a large capon with a mixture of chopped giblets, herbs and oatmeal; her sleeves were rolled up and her hands and wrists were flecked with the glistening mixture. Perdita kept her distance.

'Poor Honor, she's always unwell with something or other,' was all the sympathy Sophie conceded when Perdita had described the girl's plight. 'I'll go to her myself when I have a moment, but we're all run off our feet just at present. And, Perdita, now that you're here, can you have a word with your woman Cullen and tell her that at Rossmere even a London-born lady's maid has to pitch in and help from time to time?'

'Cullen? But I need her myself this morning.'

'Oh, no. Why?'

'I want to alter the trimming on my Genoa bonnet.'

'Is that all? Unless your bonnet is on the menu for today's dinner it will have to wait till later. Have a word with Cullen for me, Perdita, there's a dear.'

Perdita opened her mouth to argue, caught sight of the exasperation on Sophie's handsome face, thought better of it and smiled sweetly. 'Of course, Sophie. I'll speak to her at once.'

Cullen was moving a wooden spoon around in a pot of cold custard. Her distaste for the work was evident in the extreme slowness with which she worked. Perdita told her to listen to what Mistress Sophie told her.

'I'm a lady's maid, not a serving-wench,' grumbled Cullen. 'It's not right.'

'Don't fuss, Cullen.'

'Your mother wouldn't approve neither. It reflects badly on you, Mistress Perdita, me being used as a maid-of-all-work.'

'It won't be for long.' Perdita could see a fierce-looking woman with a scarred forehead advancing towards them. 'Just do as they tell you.'

'Adam says it's the same in the stables,' Cullen sniffed. 'He's only supposed to look after your father's horses, but he has to fetch and carry for all of them and—'

She was interrupted by the arrival of the fearsome cook. 'Do you mean to ruin the sauce?' she demanded angrily, seizing the pot and spoon from Cullen. 'Beat it properly, girl. Like this!' And she stirred it with such vigour that both Cullen and Perdita instinctively stepped backwards in alarm. Her hands and arms bulged with strength enough to wring the necks of chickens and geese – and, no doubt, slovenly maids as well.

The cook thrust the pot back at Cullen with such force that she almost fell over. Perdita decided to retreat. She ran up the wide stairs and poked her head around the door of Honor's room just long enough to tell her that Sophie would be up to see her shortly.

'She won't come,' moaned Honor. 'No one ever pays me any attention. They don't realise how I suffer. Do stay, Perdita. You promised you would read to me.'

'Oh, I will,' said Perdita, 'but later.' And she began to walk away swiftly down the passageway. 'Only now I must . . .' Her voice faded, the excuse unfinished.

She found Louisa, hemming a pillow-case in the winter parlour. On one side of her on the settle was a pile she had already completed, on the other were those waiting to be sewn. Perdita dutifully admired the neat little stitches, so tiny they were scarcely visible.

'I do all the sewing,' Louisa said sullenly. 'That way Sophie can't drag me into doing things for her all the time.'

'She's very busy,' Perdita conceded. 'And poor Honor has a headache and is lying down.'

'Honor is always lying down with some sort of ache.

Especially when there is work to be done.' Louisa's pretty face drooped into the familiar pout of discontent. 'Not that she'd have to do much anyway.'

'Why not?'

'Why not? Because she is *Lady* Sutton and she is *married*.' She said the last word with especial venom.

Perdita pulled a stool near the fire and sat down. 'Isn't there anyone you would like to marry, Louisa?'

'Oh, I never even think about marriage!'

'But you're nearly twenty-one. Surely you must have thought about it sometimes.'

'Why? What's the point of thinking and dreaming when nothing will ever come of it and I'm cooped up here with no chance of anything ever being any different? Just look at Sophie. She'll be twenty-eight this year and she's no nearer to being married than she was at my age. It's hopeless. I'll still be here, in this very same spot, and still hemming sheets when I'm an old woman, and all my life will just have been for nothing. Nothing!' Her bottom lip trembled.

Perdita said brightly, 'Don't fret, Louisa. I'm sure you'll meet the right man soon.'

'And what if I do?' The fury behind the question was startling. 'What good is that going to do me?'

'Well, surely—'

'Oh, it's all very well for you, Perdita. You're only seventeen but you're bound to be married soon. Your father will make proper provision for you. I dare say he'll be especially generous, seeing as how you're—' She broke off with a sneering smile and concentrated fiercely on her sewing.

'As how I'm what?'

Louisa said nothing. Perdita rose to her feet. 'What were you going to say?'

'Oh, nothing,' said Louisa, but then she muttered into her stitches, 'but it's only the truth. Everyone knows. And I'm a gentleman's proper daughter, but where does that get me, I'd like to know? It's just not fair.'

'I suggest,' said Perdita icily, 'you learn to watch your tongue if you hope to find a husband.'

'As if that would make any difference,' grumbled Louisa, and then, as Perdita stalked out of the room, she wailed, 'Oh, I wish Kip were home again. It's so dull here without him!'

For once, Perdita agreed with her.

She was left to her own devices. But not quite alone. As she emerged from the winter parlour she almost tripped over an energetic white bundle: Tom, who had been hunting for her in hope of some attention.

She scooped him up. 'Come along, then, Tom. No one else can be spared. You will have to help me trim my hat.'

But when she was once more in her bedroom she found she no longer had any enthusiasm for hats. Louisa's spite had unsettled her; besides, what was the point of dressing in the latest fashion when she was surrounded by people wearing clothes that looked as if they dated from the days of Queen Elizabeth?

Irritated, she threw the hat on the floor. Tom pounced on it and attacked a ribbon. She rescued it and placed it on the oak chest. She thought of teaching the puppy some clever trick that would impress Kip when he returned, but she quickly discovered that training puppies was more arduous than she had imagined. Then he piddled on the hem of her petticoat so she banished him altogether. For a while he fussed and scratched at the door. Then there was silence.

Perdita put her elbows on the sill and gazed morosely out where the view should have been.

Fog. Everywhere fog.

He'll be especially generous, seeing as how you're . . . Everyone knows.

Knows what?

Illegitimate. Misbegotten. Bastard.

The disfiguring stain of birth that would never be washed away. The rotten heart of her that no amount of fine clothes could ever quite disguise.

It's not fair, Louisa had said. But what did she know about the unfairness of things? Louisa was just a spoilt miss and Perdita hoped she never found a husband to put up with her sulks and spite. Let her die an old maid.

'Good riddance,' said Perdita, out loud. 'I'll show her. Just wait. She'll be sorry.'

Her voice sounded strange in the white silence.

And then, through the stillness, she heard the muffled thud of horse's hoofs on damp ground, the chink of a bridle. Peering into the mist, Perdita made out the shape of a man mounted on a thin, pale horse. Not her father. Not anyone she had seen here before. This man was riding with slack reins and one knee crooked over the pommel of the saddle, ready to slide to the ground as soon as he reached home. He wore a tall hat and a coat that was far too small. Strain her eyes though she did, Perdita was unable to make out the newcomer's features.

'Hallo-oo! I'm home! Where is everyone?'

Perdita's bitter mood vanished at once. Even before she heard Louisa's excited cries as she raced through the house to greet her brother, Perdita knew exactly who this was: the young man her father had brought her here to meet. Richard Sutton, known to his family and friends as Kip.

Perdita whirled around, peered in the mirror to make sure that all was well, and sped downstairs.

Chapter Eight

The family resemblance was striking.

Like Sophie and Louisa, even like the pale and ponderous Sir Francis, young Richard had the attractive Sutton features, the brown hair and full mouth, the well-shaped eyes and trim nose that were giving Perdita a good picture of what their father Nicolas must have looked like as a young man. Not yet twenty, Richard Sutton had a fresh-faced vigour and health that made him immediately appealing. Perdita, observing him with interest when he arrived and then in more detail during his first meal at home, could imagine that he was a popular addition to any social group. She noticed how Mistress Sutton's eyes softened when she gazed at him, the youngest of her brood. Louisa had become almost merry and Sophie treated her youngest brother with smiling indulgence.

He had greeted Perdita cheerfully enough, but showed no great interest in her presence in the house. If he had heard of the scandal associated with her name then he was either too courteous or too unheeding to show that he remembered it. His greatest enthusiasm was reserved for little Tom, who was frantic with excitement at seeing him again and wagged his white tail into a blur.

'Hello, little chap. Been missing me, eh?' Kip crouched down and tumbled the puppy on to his back.

'Sophie has already banned him from the kitchen,' said Louisa. 'Cary nearly tripped over him when she was carrying a pan of scalding water.'

'You little rascal,' Kip grinned.

The main meal of the day had just ended when the puppy had made one of his surprise entries into the room where they had been eating. Perdita had kept back a choice morsel of food to make sure Tom demonstrated his affection for her, but to her intense annoyance the puppy ignored her completely, lavishing all his devotion on Kip. Ungrateful wretch, she thought crossly, while smiling sweetly and telling all and sundry how utterly she adored all young creatures.

'Don't spoil him, Kip,' said Alice, as she left the room. Francis had already quitted the dining table to go and see to his wife, who had been too unwell to attend the meal. Stephen had returned to his work in the fields, but Sophie for once remained behind to enjoy Kip's company.

'Piers has a fine young dog,' he told his sisters. 'Part deer-hound, but smaller. And fast. You've never seen a dog take off at such a rate. I thought we'd lost him for a while. Gave the hare a good run, though.'

'Piers?' asked Louisa. 'When did you see him?'

'He was staying at Boswinnow when I visited two days ago.' Kip had flung himself back in his chair, placed the puppy on his stomach and tickled his one white and one black ear fondly.

Perdita observed Louisa throw a sly look towards Sophie as she asked, 'And was his cousin at Boswinnow too?'

Sophie frowned and pushed crumbs into a little pile on the table with the edge of her hand.

Kip grinned. 'The handsome Edmund? Yes, he stopped by for an hour or so the day I arrived.' He slid a teasing glance towards his elder sister. 'It could have been coincidence, of course. He was most courteous in his enquiries after my family. *All* my family.'

Two spots of colour had appeared on Sophie's cheeks. She allowed her hair to fall forward, covering her face.

Kip continued, 'He was especially interested to hear news of my elder sister, the lovely Mistress Sophie. He stammered somewhat as he spoke your name, Soph – can you imagine that? The faultless Edmund actually reduced to stammering. "H-h-h-how is your l-l-l-lovely s-s-s-sister?" '

'Oh, Kip! Hold your peace, I never heard such nonsense.'

Laughing, Kip rocked in his chair. ' "The b–b–b–beautiful S–S–Sophie" '

'Enough!' Half angry, but laughing in spite of herself, Sophie swept across the room and cuffed her brother. Tilting back in his chair he ducked to avoid the blow and had to grip the edge of the table to save himself from ending up on the floor. Both he and Louisa were almost helpless with laughter.

'It must be love!' squealed Louisa in delight. 'Look how angry she is, Kip. Sophie's in love with the noble Edmund – oh!'

Sophie whipped about and cuffed her sister too, and Louisa was not quick enough to duck. 'Really, the pair of you! Have you nothing better to do than waste the afternoon with nonsense? For goodness' sake, make yourselves useful for once!'

Kip and Louisa were still laughing as she swept out of the room.

'Poor old Sophie,' said Kip, while Louisa rubbed her head and said ruefully, 'All the same, she didn't have to hit me.'

They became aware of Perdita, silent throughout this scene, but watching it all intently.

'Who is Edmund?' she asked.

'Edmund Menheire,' said Kip, pulling a pair of dice from his pocket and rolling them idly across the table. 'His family have Trecarne.'

'Trecarne?'

The question was out before she had a chance to consider. She knew at once it had been a mistake to ask.

The name had a familiar ring to it, reviving fragments of conversations overheard when she was still too young to understand their significance. Echoes of servants chatting in low voices around the kitchen fire on a winter's evening when they thought she was safely dozing in her corner seat. As a child she had always tended to dismiss any talk of her Cornish origins, preferring to imagine that her early life had always been identical to that of her legitimate younger brothers.

Trecarne. A name that was somehow linked with her mother. Had the imposter who pretended to go by the name of Goody Carbin spoken of Trecarne? That whole conversation in the back room of the inn had grown so strange and dreamlike in her memory that Perdita had difficulty distinguishing what was real and what imagined.

Kip and Louisa had both stopped laughing. They were staring at her. Staring as if everyone in the world knew where and what Trecarne was, everyone but her. And staring at her as if she, of all people, should know the significance of Trecarne.

'I mean—' She broke off, not knowing what she meant.

It was Kip who answered. 'The house your father built.' Again the rattle and roll of the dice.

'Oh, yes. Of course.'

Nobody was fooled. Kip shrugged and continued rolling the dice aimlessly across the table, but Louisa was gazing at her triumphantly. 'Surely you've heard of Trecarne, Perdita. It's famous in these parts. Your father built it as a love-nest.'

'Lou—' Kip's protest was half-hearted. If anything, Louisa had gained confidence from his presence.

'It was quite the scandal round here for years. That great huge house, the grandest for miles around – very new and vulgar, of course, but still – and his lawful wife never even set foot in it. He kept the whole place just for a common strumpet.'

'Oh, Lou—'

'Mother always said she was a wicked woman. Some folk believe she used witchcraft to trap him. No wonder she came to a bad end. Such people always do, thank the Lord. Just a common shop-keeper's wife and a loose-living fool. Mother said it was a lesson to other women to know their place in the world and stick to it. But some people don't seem able to learn, do they, Perdita?'

Perdita's cheeks were burning with shame and rage. She forced herself to hold Louisa's contemptuous stare, but for once in her life she could think of nothing to say.

Louisa pressed on, 'It is well known that a lack of morals is inherited through the female line. Cat will after kind, isn't that how the saying goes? I'm astonished that anyone with such a parent would risk going back to the very place where the scandal took place. But there you are, some people are born with no pride at all.'

'Oh, Lou, leave it be.'

'No pride – and no name either!'

'How – how dare you?' Perdita had leaped to her feet and raised her hands, as though she meant to box Louisa's ears. 'You don't know what you're talking about!'

'I know more than you do, little Miss Ignoramus.'

'Oh!'

'Do stop arguing, you two,' said Kip lazily. 'It's such a stupid waste of time.'

Louisa shrugged and went to get her work-basket. 'I was only saying what everyone else thinks. Much better to have it all out in the open, don't you think, Perdita?'

Kip grinned and shook the dice in his hand as he said to Perdita, 'Do you ever play at tables?'

'What? Tables?' She was still almost panting with fury and had found it hard to take in his question. 'Oh, well, yes. I play draughts sometimes with my brothers. And chess occasionally.'

'How about tick-tack? Irish? Backgammon?'

'I have played backgammon once or twice.'

'Tick-tack is better.'

Still smarting from Louisa's attack, Perdita agreed without thinking. She had difficulty concentrating while Kip explained the differences from the game she knew, as she was still busily plotting painful revenge on the girl, and she lost several games in a row. Since it turned out that Kip only played for money, no matter how small the amount, she soon found she had lost three shillings.

Meanwhile Louisa sat in her usual spot near the fire and hummed to herself as she worked at her sewing. It was an irritating little tune, but it took Perdita a while before she realised just why it was so annoying. The words, which she did not doubt Louisa knew quite well, concerned a foolish girl who was seduced and ruined by a wealthy but hard-hearted lover.

Kip grinned across the board towards her. 'Ready for another game, Perdita? Shilling stakes, this time?'

Louisa stopped humming. 'Do you know this song, Kip? The words are really most amusing.'

Perdita had recovered her outward poise by this time and she placed her hand against her mouth as though stifling a yawn. The gesture also served to show off her delicate wrists and the sapphire in her ring. 'I know the song well,' she replied. 'It was popular in London a couple of years ago. No one who cares about fashion would bother with it now. Only serving-maids and common people.'

Louisa snapped a thread with her teeth and her mouth drooped back into its habitual pout.

'Shilling stakes?'

'Oh, Kip, you're too good at this game for sure. I'll have to stop before I am ruined altogether.'

'Tell you what, then, we can double or nothing. If you win the next game you get your three shillings back.'

'And if I lose?'

'You're sure to win next time. You're getting much better.'

'It helps to know the rules,' said Perdita tartly. She suspected Kip of having withheld certain vital aspects of the game until they cropped up to his advantage. But then she directed her smile at him and said, 'We'll have to play again some other time. Just now I think I'll take a turn around the garden. It's so stuffy in here, don't you think? And too much close confinement indoors just makes people disagreeable, and that is so ill-bred.'

Louisa accidentally dug her needle into her thumb and yelped with annoyance.

Kip was reluctant to let his partner go so easily. 'I'll give you a game of hazard, if you like. Penny stakes. Or merels. Surely you play merels?'

'Nine men's morris, you mean? Now there's a game I'm expert in.'

'Then you'll play?'

'Later, certainly. Just as soon as I've recovered from my defeat with some of your lovely Cornish air.'

Kip sighed. 'I suppose we could always play skittles,' he said.

'We'd never see them in this mist. I intend to walk down as far as the main gate. My father is likely to return at any time.'

'Oh, very well, then. I may as well come with you,' said Kip grudgingly. 'There's nothing else to do.'

'Watch out for Uncle Stephen,' warned Louisa. 'He was muttering at lunch that he needed extra help with the plough-ing.'

'He can count me out. I don't mind giving him a hand

sometimes, but I draw the line at field work. Are you coming, Louisa?'

Perdita's heart sank as Louisa put away her work and accompanied them from the room. At the foot of the main staircase, they met Francis who was coming down, his pale face more anxious-looking than ever.

'Oh, Perdita,' he said, 'just the person I wanted to see. Honor said you promised to read to her and she is desperate for company.'

'I'd love to, but I'm afraid I cannot just now. I am going to walk down to the gate to meet my father.'

'Oh dear.' His anxious gaze settled on Louisa, who had been studiously avoiding his eye. 'Then you will have to go to her. Don't argue with me, Louisa. It's not so much to ask. You only need stay with her until she sleeps, the poor creature is quite worn out with the pain.'

Louisa showed her fury by stumping up the stairs as loudly as she could. Her footsteps could be heard banging down the passageway. Perdita listened to them with some satisfaction.

Perdita went to put on her cloak with the fur-trimmed hood, her outdoor shoes and a clean pair of gloves. She was still seething with rage over Louisa's spite and her own shameful ignorance. Little Miss Ignoramus . . . Why had her father never told her about Trecarne? She remembered now what he had said as they were crossing the wild moorland country on their journey west. 'I am taking you home, Perdita. Or as near to home as we can get. I am taking you to Rossmere.'

As near to home as we can get . . . So 'home', her father's home, the place he regarded as her home also, was near to here. Home was Trecarne.

Two bright spots of colour were the only symptom of her inner turmoil as she joined Kip on the forecourt, and these, which she had noted in the mirror before she came down the stairs, were not altogether unflattering. Ever sensitive to the reactions of those around her, Perdita knew she had yet to make any real impression on the youngest of the Sutton brood. She guessed he was not an easily impressionable young man.

The mist was thinning in patches as they set off down the avenue towards the road; there were glimpses of blue sky above bare branches and an occasional shaft of sunlight. A few pale primroses were flowering between the stones at the side of the driveway. The puppy ran back and forth, occasionally tripping over his own front paws in his haste.

'My father named him Tom,' said Perdita. 'Do you think it suits him?'

'Tom will do well enough. There are no others here with that name. Here, Tom! Tom! So long as he answers when called.'

He stooped to reward the puppy with a piece of biscuit from his pocket, and they walked for a little while in silence.

At length Perdita said casually, 'I did not know Sophie had a suitor.'

'Edmund Menheire? I would hardly call him a suitor.'

'What, then?'

'Lou and I think he's had a soft spot for her since the first time they met,' he said, and then added with a younger brother's scepticism, 'Lord alone knows why.'

'Sophie is very agreeable.'

Kip shrugged. 'Nothing will come of it anyway.'

'Why not?'

'Mother and Francis would be horrified just to think of it. They can't abide the Menheires. And by the way, Perdita, I'd be grateful if you didn't mention to them that I said anything about seeing him. Or his cousin.'

'Is there such bad feeling between the families?'

'Of course.'

'Why?'

'Well, for one thing Colonel Menheire was a Parliament man, and one of the worst of the County Committee in Cromwell's time. He got the house at Trecarne and he would have had Rossmere as well if he could. Mother spent years battling to keep this place from his clutches. She says he is an evil, grasping man who would gladly see us all ruined.'

'Then you can understand her feelings.'

'Oh, of course. But one cannot live for ever in the past, you know. Edmund and Piers can't help it if the Colonel is a rogue. People ought not to be held to blame for their family's faults.'

'Louisa thinks they should.'

'Oh, don't mind her. She never thinks of what she says.'

Perdita disagreed, but did not choose to say so. She asked, 'Does Sophie return his feelings?'

'She hardly knows him, but Sophie is inclined to like everyone. If she was going to marry, Edmund Menheire would be a fine catch, but she never will.'

'Because of his father?'

'Partly that. And she's not really the marrying type. I mean, she'd never dream of leaving Rossmere.'

'Surely she does not want to die an old maid.'

'I don't suppose she thinks of it like that. She knows Mother could not manage here without her. No one could. She's needed at home, and so she'll stay. We tease her about Edmund, but it's just teasing, nothing serious.'

Perdita remembered her father's indignation on Sophie's behalf. 'That doesn't sound very fair to me,' she said.

Kip just shrugged. 'She's happy enough the way things are,' he said.

Perdita was about to protest, but then she saw a rider coming down the road towards them and quickened her pace. 'Oh, look, I do believe it is my father.'

The horseman came closer. Treveryan swung down from the saddle.

'Father, this is Richard Sutton.'

'Ah yes, my namesake.' He was examining the young man carefully. 'I'm pleased to make your acquaintance, Richard.'

'His family all call him Kip.'

'Glad to meet you, Sir Richard.'

Kip greeted her father with his usual indiscriminate good-humour. His main interest, however, seemed to be with Richard's mount. He ran a practised hand across the horse's rippling shoulder, then down the length of his fine leg. 'What a handsome animal, Sir Richard. There must be Arab in his blood.'

'Apollo's grand-dam was one of the late King's Barbs. He gets his speed and delicacy from her.'

'Are you going to walk to the house from here?' Kip asked eagerly. 'I can ride him back to the stables if you like, save you the trouble.'

Richard smiled at the youth's enthusiasm. 'By all means. But make sure my own man Adam sees to him. Your brother's groom means well, but he's apt to be careless.'

'He's only ever had plough horses and ponies to tend before.' Kip had sprung up in the saddle before Richard had a chance to change his mind. 'My, what a beauty. I don't think even the Menheires' stallion Charger has such a stride. May I take him once around the near field before he settles?'

'Don't let him work up a sweat. You may try his speed another day, when he is fresher.'

Kip was grinning broadly as he nudged the tall bay to a trot and rode off towards the field at the side of the house.

Perdita and her father began walking slowly after him.

'When did young Richard arrive?'

'This morning.'

'Hm. And already he is escorting you on your afternoon stroll. No one could accuse you of wasting time, Perdita.'

'I should certainly hope not, Father. But I think it would be easier to impress him if I had four legs instead of two.'

'How do you find him?'

'He is amiable enough. Which is more than can be said for his sister.'

'Sophie has been troubling you?'

'Oh, no, not Sophie. The younger one. Louisa is a spiteful vixen and ought to be thrashed.'

Richard frowned. 'You are a guest, Perdita. You must try to be agreeable to your hosts.'

'Yes, but—'

'But what?'

Perdita did not reply. She hoped that most of the time her father forgot that she was not his legitimate daughter, and she did not see how she could tell him of her recent humiliation without reminding him of what caused her the greatest shame. Hoping rather to please him she said, 'You were anxious to know why Sophie has never married. I believe I can tell you the answer to that one.'

'I had forgotten your habit of listening at doors. What have you learned this time?'

'I heard it in open conversation. In fact, Kip was telling me when you arrived. He said his mother would never allow Sophie to marry because she was needed here.'

'Just as I thought.'

'But there is a man who has her affections. And who cares for her as well. Or so Kip thinks.'

'Go on.'

'His name is Edmund and he lives at . . . His father has the house at . . . Mistress Sutton cannot abide the family because they were strong for Parliament and now they have the house . . . your house . . . Oh, Father,' she blurted out, through sudden tears, 'why did you never tell me about Trecarne?'

'Trecarne?' He stopped and looked down at her while she tried to block her useless tears with her hands.

'I hear everything from other people . . . My ignorance is held against me . . . It makes me a butt for every kind of spiteful talk . . . It is not fair!'

'Louisa?'

She nodded. 'I hate her. She deserves to be whipped.'

'A fine way to endear ourselves to the Suttons.'

'Then you must speak to her! Tell her to mind her manners.'

'And if I do? There will never be any shortage of righteous citizens ready to slander you, Perdita. Your only real defence is to be proud of who you are and who your mother was, and to treat such gossip with contempt.'

'But how can I be proud when I do not even know? She called me an ignoramus, and all because of that place.'

'Trecarne. Yes, I should have told you. I meant to tell you in good time. It seems I leave everything too late. Don't cry, Perdita, don't ever let them see you cry. Here.' He handed her a kerchief, since her own had been forgotten. 'Listen to me. Are you listening? Good. Tomorrow is Sunday. Look out your finest costume. We will ride to church in Porthew. That is where your mother lived and where the memory of scandal is strongest. Together we can face down any number of petty gossips, just you see.'

Perdita liked the sound of 'together', though the rest of his plan filled her with foreboding. 'Must we go?'

'Certainly we must. But after, I will show you something that touches you.'

'Will we ride to Trecarne?'

He shook his head. 'Colonel Menheire is hardly going to welcome us with open arms. He is already in a sweat of panic because he assumes I have come back to reclaim my property.'

'And will you, Father?'

'No. I have looked into it this past two days, and his title is strong enough. If I took him to law then the case could drag on for years. I have no wish to play into the hands of a bunch of corrupt lawyers. Besides, I vowed years ago never to set foot there again.'

'Because?' She looked up at him. His eyes were warning her not to ask him. There was no need. She felt a sharp despair. 'So I will never see the house where you lived with my mother?'

'Do you want to so very much?'

'More than anything in the world.' It was the truth.

'I suppose that is natural. We could perhaps ride as far as Crousa Beacon. Part of the property is visible from there. But first we must show ourselves at Porthew church. After that we will see about a visit to Trecarne.'

Chapter Nine

Perdita left nothing to chance.

Cullen had been busy from daybreak to make sure that when her mistress made her first appearance in Porthew she was every inch the grand lady. Dressed in bodice and skirts of raised blue velvet, her finest tabby petticoats showed beneath, while her hair was a tribute to Cullen's skill with curling tongs and paper. Her face and hands had been liberally smoothed with Imperial water and creams, her gloves scented with lavender; her exquisite flounces of linen and lace were spotless. She wore boots of softest Cordoba leather. Strict instructions had been sent down to the stables the previous evening, and Nimble was groomed until her chestnut coat shone in the March sunshine, her hoofs oiled, saddle and bridle polished to a glow. The good folk of Porthew could not fail to be impressed.

Having devoted so much attention to her first regal entry into the town, Perdita was disappointed to discover the smallness of the stage on which she was appearing: hardly more than a main street curving around by the harbour wall and a few dozen low grey houses. It was not much of a town at all, more an overgrown village. They had passed the forge and the corn mill as they approached; in the town itself there was only the church, a couple of alehouses and a few mean-looking shops. Perdita realised she would have caused a stir had she taken half the trouble; merely to be riding a horse that was of decent size, neither lame nor sway-backed, would have been cause enough for comment.

Perdita had only a hazy impression of the service. They took their seats in the Suttons' box pew at the front, the congregation's responses ringing out forthright behind them. The minister seemed to her a person of no account, the church was chill and smelt of damp plaster and drains. She paid no attention to the sermon and nor, from the shuffling and whispering that drifted from the back, did anyone else. When the time came for them to leave, she walked out proudly beside her father ahead of the rest, and almost persuaded herself that the low murmurs that pursued them like the buzz of insects were nothing whatsoever to do with her.

As Perdita stepped out into the spring sunshine, Richard took her by the elbow and said, 'This way.'

He led her down a grassy path between the gravestones to the farthest end of the churchyard, which was bounded by a low wall overlooking the sea. Pale clouds floated above them in a clear March sky and the wide sea shimmered all the colours of amethyst and opal beyond the wall. Thinking she had been brought here to admire the view, Perdita said dutifully, 'This is indeed a fine prospect, Father.'

'Prospect be damned,' he told her. 'See this.'

She saw that they were standing in front of a newly cut gravestone, a good deal more ostentatious than the simple ones all around. And when she read the words that had been carved in the granite, a chill ran down her spine:

MARGARET HOLLAR DIED 1653

'My true mother,' she whispered.

'Yes,' was all his reply.

'But the gravestone is new.'

'I had it placed there yesterday.'

'Oh.'

She felt more was expected of her. An insistent voice inside her head was saying: why now? Why leave it for so long? But she dared not show her anger to her father, since he held the key to so much that she wanted. At length she said, 'What do those other words say?'

'They are Latin.'

'Yes, but . . .'

He read out slowly, '*Nullus amor talis coniunxit foedere amantes.*'

Perdita remained silent. She wished she had paid more attention when her brothers were set their lessons.

'It is from Catullus,' said Richard.

'Who?'

'Have you no knowledge of Latin at all?'

'Well . . . my mother . . .' She stumbled at the awkwardness of it all, then continued, 'Your wife, Lady Treveryan, always says an educated woman is an abomination and will never make a good wife.'

'And I suppose it never occurred to you to question such a ludicrous belief?'

'It is what everybody says.'

'That does not make it right. Your true mother grew up among poor farmers, but she fought tooth and nail to keep her precious books. But I can see that Kitty has reared you to be as empty-headed and frivolous as she is. Dear God, I am wasting my time.' He turned on his heel and strode away across the churchyard.

Perdita remained where she was, too bruised and angry to think what to do next. How had she displeased her father so abruptly? She had always studied to be a good daughter to Kitty and now she was being punished for her diligence. If he had ever once bothered to tell her that learning was what he valued in a woman then she would have become the most scholarly of daughters. It was hardly her fault if Kitty and he had never seen eye to eye on such matters, nor her fault either if the recent wars had kept him from home and so prevented him from supervising her education himself. It was not fair. Here she had been up since dawn making herself look the fine lady because she had thought that was what was required, and now he told her the time would have been better spent with her nose in some Roman book.

Gradually her feelings of hurt gave way to an angry determination to make her father see how unjust his contempt had been. She stood up very straight, smoothed a couple of bitter tears from her cheeks and began to walk back towards the church.

And then she saw him.

Leaning against the wide base of a yew tree, one knee bent in an attitude of casual repose, he must have been there for some time. She realised he could have watched and listened to all that had taken place. How had her father not seen him?

A gust of wind blew off the sea and Perdita felt an irrational thrill of fear. She remembered the spirit voices in the inn; she remembered all that she had heard from Maria Carabini about Porthew; she remembered how she had thought herself deceived – but perhaps the voice from beyond the grave had been real after all.

The man was better dressed than he had been at the Mitre Inn: no longer the tattered clothes of a travelling player, but the plain and respectable coat and breeches of a townsman. The wide-brimmed hat, though, was just as she remembered it. And that penetrating, all-knowing regard.

Perdita glanced rapidly towards the church. Her father was there, standing in the spring sunshine and talking with Stephen Sutton and another man. She could call out, her father would come at once, the felon would be arrested and punished just as he deserved: still smarting from the humiliation delivered by her father, Perdita decided there was nothing she would like more than to see that thieving rogue suffer.

She was on the point of calling out when the stranger raised his finger to his lips, signalling silence. And then he smiled. An intimate smile, linking them together in secrecy. Suddenly she was reminded of the feel of his hand against the skin of her neck. Her fear and anger were overlaid by a disturbing attraction. Perdita hesitated, waiting to see what would happen next. He indicated, with a slight movement of his head, that she was to join him. Without hesitating she did so.

'Where are my mother's earrings?' she demanded breathlessly. 'You promised you would return them to me.'

'So. I broke my promise.'

'Do you have them now? Can you get them for me?'

'No. They will have been sold long ago, or exchanged for a keg of wine.'

'You stole them!'

'On the contrary, I distinctly remember that you gave them to Goody Carbin of your own free will.'

'She was an imposter.'

'But you learned much that you wanted to hear.'

'Did you tell her?'

'Of course. I was hiding behind the partition.'

'Oh!'

But Perdita had long since guessed as much. He was smiling at her but she could not tell if it was a cruel or friendly smile, nor what she thought of him at all. His face was not handsome exactly but interesting, with long eyes that tilted slightly, high cheekbones and a wide mouth. She knew she should be angry with him, but that seemed impossible now. She noticed the small lines fanning out from the side of his eyes. At length she said, 'You ought not have tricked me out of those earrings. They were valuable.'

'They were trinkets only. Besides, you learned a useful lesson at the Mitre. Someone less scrupulous than I am might have exposed you to real danger. You'll never be so gullible again.'

Perdita fidgeted. Of course it was outrageous of him to dress up his trickery as a kindness and yet, to her amazement, he sounded as though he was genuinely concerned for her. Or was this, perhaps, yet further evidence of his trickery? She asked, 'What are you doing here?'

'Porthew is my home.'

Somehow Perdita felt she had known this all along. She wondered if all her care that morning over her appearance had been because, deep down, she had been half expecting to see the mysterious fiddler who had tricked her into her first knowledge of the place.

'If this is your home, then what were you doing with the travelling players?'

'Travelling, of course. And playing the fiddle, as you know.'

'Why?'

'Porthew is a small place. From time to time I get restless and take to the road for a while.'

'So I see.'

'And what do you think of your mother's headstone?'

'It is very elegant.' More than ever Perdita wished she knew the meaning of those Latin words inscribed beneath her mother's name. She assumed – and hoped – they were something suitably pious and appropriate. She said, 'It demonstrates my father's great devotion to her memory.'

'Your father's devotion, my dear Perdita, is not worth a rush.'

'He had it made specially.'

'Goaded by his guilty conscience, nothing more.'

'You're a fine one to talk of consciences. I should have him arrest you here and now.'

'Treveryan will not harm me. Not here, not now. Call him over if you like and see for yourself.'

Perdita remained silent.

He said, 'You had better go to them now. You don't want people to see you talking with me. I'll come and visit you one day at Rossmere.'

'There? You'd be thrown out.'

'On the contrary, my father and I have always been made welcome at Rossmere. I may decide then to renew my acquaintance with your odious father.'

'Where do you live?'

'I told you, here in Porthew.'

'Yes, but—'

'Off you go. We'll talk again by and by.'

That seemed more a promise than a threat.

On the way back to Rossmere Perdita was so quiet that Richard, believing her distressed by his harsh words in the churchyard, attempted briefly to cheer her up. She hardly noticed. All her thoughts were with the stranger in the wide-brimmed hat whom she knew and yet did not know at all. He had answered all her questions, so why had she not asked him the one thing she most wanted to know? His identity. And how did he know so much about her background? Was it all just common gossip in Porthew, or was there a more particular reason?

She had not asked him because she knew he would never tell her until he was ready. Nor did she intend to ask anyone else, though presumably if he lived in Porthew and was welcome at Rossmere he was well known to everyone.

Everyone except her.

But she would not ask. There was a curl of pleasure at the

base of her stomach and all because he had said they'd meet again. Besides, she was tired of betraying her ignorance to all and sundry. She was learning to be patient. And she had no doubt that she would find out soon enough.

The following morning four riders left the stableyard at Ross-mere. Sir Richard Treveryan was mounted on his strong bay, Apollo, and beside him Kip struggled to keep up on his pale gelding. Perdita followed behind on Nimble and Sophie, on a plodding cob, brought up the rear.

Perdita had been surprised when Sophie declared her intention to join their excursion, since she associated her entirely with household tasks. Sophie, however, had been adamant. 'If Kip is to ride with you, then I shall come too. This is just the morning for a ride.'

And, indeed, it was. A soft wind was blowing from the south and cloud-shadows were racing over fields and moorland while all the birds in creation seemed to be singing in the spring sunshine.

They rode down muddy lanes and across small, stone-bound fields until they reached a stretch of open country. Kip, who had been urging his horse to a trot to keep pace with Richard's, was eager to discuss horseflesh with the older man. As Richard was endeavouring to question Kip about his education and future prospects, neither of which were subjects of any interest to Kip, their conversation was decidedly lopsided.

Perdita, following at a dainty pace on Nimble, heard their disjointed phrases floating back to her on the breeze.

'– useful for one member of the family to have an understanding of the law in these contentious times—'

'– a Camborne lawyer I heard of had a charging horse with such courage it burst its lungs in a race last year—'

Beside her, Sophie lifted her face to the sun and closed her eyes, revelling in the mild air. Perdita sat very upright on her horse as she had been taught. Even though there was no one to see her but an occasional labourer toiling in the fields, she was too well schooled to forget her appearance for long.

They came to an expanse of moorland, with pale sedge

grasses and heather, and a skylark singing overhead. Here, at length, Richard relented. Dismounting, he said to Kip, 'You may try his speed now, if you wish. Apollo is as eager as you are and the ground is soft and will do his feet no harm.'

Kip needed no second invitation and within a moment he was in the saddle, adjusting the stirrups. Apollo, with an unaccustomed weight on his back, capered sideways and threw up his head.

'Keep him steady to begin with,' Richard told the young man. 'Take him slowly to that far hawthorn, then you can let him have his head on the return.'

'Yes, Sir Richard.'

It might have been that Kip intended to do as he was bid, but was not strong enough to control the powerful horse. But the eagerness with which he crouched down in the saddle and urged the animal forward indicated that the temptation to feel Apollo at full stretch was simply too much. Kip galloped as far as the hawthorn and beyond, only wheeling about when he had dwindled to a tiny figure on the horizon. Richard frowned and signalled that he was to return. Kip appeared to wave back at them, but then, instead of returning along the route he had just followed, he came around in a wide arc. They could hear the thunder of Apollo's hoofs as Kip, making no attempt to stop the horse until he was almost upon them, raced down the hill towards them, finally bringing Apollo to a chaotic, prancing halt.

Furious, Richard caught hold of the reins, but Kip's face was aglow with excitement and he did not even notice. 'What an animal! That was magnificent.'

Richard was endeavouring to soothe Apollo whose shoulders were flecked with sweat as he blew and stamped and shook his head in agitation. 'Get down at once,' he commanded.

Grinning, Kip did as he was told and exclaimed, 'You should try him now, Sophie. You've never seen a horse with such mettle.'

Richard said, 'Apollo is hardly a lady's horse.'

But Sophie, to Perdita's amazement, was already sliding off her weary nag and going across to where the tall bay was still plunging and puffing.

'Oh, Sir Richard, do let me try him.'

'Wait until he's calmer, and then I'll lead you.'

Kip laughed at this notion. 'No need to worry about Sophie. She's a better rider than anyone. Always has been.'

'But the saddle—' Richard began.

'I'll manage,' said Sophie firmly. She had taken hold of Apollo's bridle and was stroking and soothing him with her large, strong hands. His ears came forward and he whickered a gentle greeting. 'May I, Sir Richard? Please.'

He was smiling at her. 'Are you sure you know what you're doing?'

'Oh, Sophie always knows that,' Kip answered for his sister. 'Here, I'll give you a leg-up.'

And without further ceremony he made a stirrup of his hands and hoisted Sophie into the saddle. Perdita gasped. Never in her life before had she seen a woman sit astride a horse. It was clear, however, that Sophie had done so many times, judging by the practised way she gathered her petticoats between her legs and sat on them in the saddle, a little tail of pale cambric feathering out behind her. She let her overskirts fall down on either side, but bunched about her legs so they were not too much in the way. Her pale calves showed above her boots.

'There,' she said, smiling as she caught sight of Perdita's horrified expression, 'not very elegant, I'm afraid, but it will have to do.'

Richard had still not let go of Apollo's reins. 'If I tell you to ride slowly as far as the hawthorn and then return at a canter, is there any chance of being obeyed this time?'

'I'll do my best,' she promised.

They watched in silence as she rode off down the grassy track. Apollo's stature seemed exaggerated by the smallness of the figure seated on him, but he walked steadily, his tail swishing contentedly from side to side. When she reached the hawthorn she turned around at once, allowed him first to trot, then his stride stretched to a slow canter, which she curbed in plenty of time to bring him calmly back to his owner.

'Well?' asked Treveryan. 'How does he suit you?'

Sophie's eyes were shining. 'He's perfect,' she said. 'More

than perfect. Is that possible? But now I've ridden him like a lady's horse, may I try something more?'

'What did you have in mind?'

'To test his speed as Kip did. And to see how he does over a low wall.'

'A low wall?'

'Well, not a very high one.'

Richard was appraising her carefully. Perdita was amazed. She hardly recognised the dutiful daughter and industrious housewife in this woman who was burning with energy and adventure.

'Your horse is in good hands with Sophie,' said Kip.

'So I'm beginning to realise. Very well, then, Sophie. I ask only that you treat Apollo with the care you would have if he were your own. Don't keep us waiting here too long. And, please, no broken bones.'

They watched as Sophie set off down the grassy track once more, but this time at a leisurely canter. They were still watching as she turned off to the right before reaching the hawthorn and gave Apollo his head. They watched with growing excitement as horse and rider streamed across the open moorland fast and light as a bird and they were still watching as she collected him once more, set him at a low broad stone wall and cleared it with a yard to spare.

'Where in God's name did your sister learn to ride like that?' asked Richard.

'Oh,' said Kip carelessly, 'she's always been good.'

'Good? I've never seen a woman ride like that anywhere.'

Perdita, still seated on Nimble, felt a pang of vexation. Here she was, elegant enough to turn heads in St James's, and all the attention was being taken by a country girl in patched clothes who rode like a stableboy.

But when Sophie finally returned, the enthusiasm shining from her face was so infectious it was impossible not to share her happiness. She swung her leg over Apollo's neck and sprang down to the ground as Richard once more took his horse by the bridle.

'Oh, Sir Richard, thank you, thank you!' she burst out. 'I've never been so happy!' And she flung her arms around his neck and hugged him.

Richard was startled, but by no means displeased. He placed his hands on both her shoulders and held her at arms' length, regarding her intently. 'You are a woman of many surprises,' he told her.

She laughed easily at the compliment. 'Oh, no,' she said, 'I love to ride, that's all.'

'I wonder,' said Richard, half to himself. 'Anyone who rides as well as you do should have a better mount than that pitiful creature.'

Sophie went over and patted her pony's neck affectionately. 'Billy's just a bit old. He can't be blamed for that.'

'Indeed not,' said Richard, still thoughtful as he mounted Apollo. 'Shall we continue our ride?'

Perdita was about to fall in beside her father when Sophie said casually, 'By the way, Sir Richard, it might be a good idea not to mention this to Mother or Francis. They tend to fret, and there's no point worrying folk for no reason.'

He nodded his agreement and they rode for a while in silence. Perdita was still struggling to reconcile her earlier impression of Sophie, the tireless labourer in the kitchen and this wild, radiant-looking woman.

At length she said to her, 'I never knew you liked to ride.'

'More than anything. I often take one of the horses out in the afternoon or evening when most of the work is done.' And, after a while, she added, 'If we've all been at sixes and sevens in the kitchen, it clears my head and puts me to rights with the world again.'

She spoke with such a depth of feeling that Perdita wondered what it must be like to ride in that way, to be fearless and full of energy and happiness. Just thinking about it was alarming. Kitty would have been scandalised, but just now Kitty's world seemed a long way away. Suddenly Perdita felt stiff and foolish in her dainty riding clothes, her carefully prepared gloves and boots and hat, like a little doll. Very decorative, to be sure, but right now that did not seem so very important.

They had been riding for nearly half an hour when the open, high country fell away. They were returning to an area of farmland and woods. As they approached the crest of a small rise,

Richard reined Apollo back so that Perdita could catch up with him. 'Look,' he said. 'There it is.'

A dense canopy of oaks was spread below them, their branches still bare of leaves but shimmering grey and softest green with lichen and moss and the first swelling buds of spring. Beyond the falling expanse of woodland lay the sea, green and blue and silver in the March sunshine. It was a wide bay, bounded on either side by headlands that went down to a rocky foreshore. And not a house in sight.

'What a beautiful situation,' said Perdita, disappointed.

Richard did not answer, did not even seem to have heard her.

A thin plume of smoke was rising at the far edge of the trees. Smoke that came from a chimney. A chimney, she saw it now quite clearly, that rose from the side of a house, which was almost entirely hidden by the oaks. A thin high tower and a brief stretch of slate roof. Trecarne.

She must have said the word out loud because her father turned to her and said, 'Yes, that is Trecarne.'

Sophie and Kip had ridden up behind them but Sophie, with instinctive tact, found some pretext to draw her brother to one side.

Glancing back at them to make sure she could not be overheard, Perdita asked cautiously, 'The place you built as a love-nest for my mother?'

'Is that what they say? Well, they're not so far wrong. I was building it anyway, but I only really cared for the place when she came to join me. So, a love-nest, if you wish.'

Perdita's heart was beating fiercely. 'Can we see it properly?'

'This is as far as we go. Beyond here it's all Menheire land.'

'But I must see it!'

Richard laughed at her eagerness. 'Then you'll have to disguise yourself as a wandering tinker and hope for the best. We cannot go on as we are. This is all you'll ever see.'

He wheeled his horse about and started back the way they had come. Perdita followed reluctantly. But she knew that, for once, her father was wrong. She would see the house again and next time she would see it all. She did not know how this would come about. But she had already learned that if you fix your mind on a thing and are prepared to wait and scheme, sooner or later the opportunity will present itself.

She was sure she could find a better way than to disguise herself as a wandering tinker and hope for the best, but if that was what it took, then so be it.

Evening had fallen the next day, and the winter parlour was deserted.

As 25 March – Lady Day – was approaching, Sir Francis and his mother were once more closeted in his office and Honor had retired early for the night, not a headache this time but she feared that the change in the weather had brought on an ague. Sir Richard Treveryan had set out early that morning and had not yet returned.

For a while Perdita sat in lonely state in the parlour, then, growing bored, she set off in search of company.

She found it in the kitchen.

It was a large, high-vaulted room, far too big for the present needs of the household but a legacy of an age when the Suttons' home had been a byword for hospitality throughout Cornwall. The fire had been damped down for the night, all but the vast log at the back which would burn slowly for weeks, making it easier to start the fire again in the morning. The people ranged about the hearth shared a comfortable informality, which spoke of countless evenings passed in a similar manner.

Stephen and Sophie had the favoured positions on either side of the fireplace. Stephen was puffing at a long-stemmed pipe. His eyes were half closed and his clean-drawn face showed the weary contentment of a man who has been toiling in the fields since before daybreak. Sophie sat opposite him on a high-backed settle. She was spinning, but using the old-fashioned distaff she preferred to the modern wheel. Next to her sat Louisa, a piece of rough sewing in her lap. She had set it down when the light began to fade. Kip, on a low stool, was attempting to teach Sithney the game of doublets. He appeared frustrated by the man's inability to understand why three die should be needed instead of the more usual two, and also by the fact that the fellow had nothing in the whole world to lose.

The servants, Viney, Cullen and Adam among them, were seated at a slightly greater distance from the fire. In pride of place on a sturdy wooden chair was the cook with the fearsomely scarred face who had scolded Cullen a few days before. A child of about ten was sitting by her on the floor, her head leaning against the woman's knee. A couple of large dogs had flopped down by Stephen's feet and little Tom, curled up and snuffling in his sleep, lay between them. The air smelt of woodsmoke and tobacco, fresh baking and the residue of roasting meat, sweet herbs on the floor and the men's damp workclothes steaming gently in the evening warmth.

Perdita observed the scene for a few moments before her presence was noticed and she felt a strange conflict of emotions. Part of her was shocked: in Kitty's household formal relations were maintained between masters and servants. Kitty would never have compromised her dignity by associating with them in this casual manner. But then she remembered when she herself had been a small child and had crept downstairs on dark winter evenings in search of warmth and comfort. She remembered the affection she had found as a little girl in the company of servants.

It was Sophie who spotted her first. 'Perdita, come and join us. We've just been trying to persuade Cary to tell us a story.'

Louisa picked up her sewing and made room for Perdita on the settle. 'There you are, Cary, here's a new audience for you. Perdita has probably never even heard of the Grey Lady.'

'Never heard of the Grey Lady?' The child on the floor gazed across at Perdita, awestruck at such woeful lack of knowledge.

Perdita flushed with annoyance at this fresh exposure of her ignorance, but the cook admonished the girl, 'Nonsense, Het, how can Mistress Perdita know the story of the Grey Lady? She's London-bred, nothing to do with Tilsbury at all.'

Sophie said, 'Go on, Cary. You haven't told us a story in ages.'

'I told you one two nights ago.'

Perdita had gathered by now that the fierce-looking cook was Cary, the storyteller.

'Yes,' said Louisa scornfully, 'but that was just "Hop o' my Thumb", and your own stories are much the best.'

'That's because they are all true, every word.'

Stephen slid Cary a glance and smiled. '*Every* word, Cary?'

The child Het wriggled with excitement. 'Do, Mother. Tell the story of how you blew up all the Parliament's ammunition and saved Father from a terrible death and nearly won the war for the King. Do, Mother, please.'

Perdita was examining the cook with a new interest. Clearly, in her time, she had done a good deal more than baking pies and plucking chickens.

'No, Het.' Suddenly Cary's face was sad. 'Not that one, love. Not tonight.'

Kip had given up his attempt to teach the serving-man doublets. He said to Perdita, 'Would you like a game? It's really very simple, though Sithney here can't seem to make head nor tail of it. Halfpenny stakes?'

'I was hoping Cary would tell us a story,' said Perdita swiftly.

Cary looked towards Stephen. 'Captain Sutton?' she enquired.

He smiled across at her easily, a smile that indicated long friendship and trust. 'If you're not tired, Cary. It's always good to hear the Tilsbury stories.'

'Have you been there?' Perdita asked him.

'Oh, yes. Long ago.' His grey eyes softened at the memory.

'Well, then,' said Cary, 'I'll need a drop of ale for the voice . . . Thank you, Mistress Sophie, that'll do nicely. The Grey Lady, Mistress Perdita, was a famous tale in the town of Tilsbury, which is the place where I was born. Are you sure you all want to hear the story again? Very well.'

There was a general shuffling sound, like chickens settling on their perches at evening; the gentle movements of people making themselves comfortable to hear a good tale. Kip had finally resigned himself to not finding a partner for his game; he flopped down on a bench. Cary took a long drink of ale and shifted her ample buttocks on the chair. She could have been a sturdy queen surrounded by her courtiers. Her accent was not Cornish, Perdita had noticed that already, and certainly not London, like Cullen. A Tilsbury accent, obviously. But where was that?

As if reading her thoughts Cary began, 'In the county of Gloucestershire, that is to say, somewhere to the north of Bristol, there is a town by the name of Tilsbury. It's a fine place. Wool merchants built their grand houses there, and it has a market for sheep and cattle and horses, which was famous for miles around. In the old times it was famous also for its priory. Once upon a time the good Catholic folk sent their sons and daughters to be educated by the nuns in Tilsbury Priory. The nuns wore grey clothes, all grey from head to toe, and they never even spoke to a man, not even their own brothers and fathers.

'But then, in the time of King Henry word was sent all round the country that there were to be no more monks and nuns, nor priories nor abbeys nor convents at all. Now, the monks were a feeble bunch, most of them, and they gave way with hardly a murmur, but the nuns were not so easily shifted. The abbess of Tilsbury was a fine, strong woman. "Who will care for the sick and the poor and the children if we are sent off into the world?" she wanted to know. And six of her women stayed with her and refused to leave the priory, no matter what terrible threats King Henry sent down to them.

'So the King sent a troop of wicked soldiers to drive the women from their home. They were terrible men who liked nothing better than to ravish helpless women and then tear them limb from limb . . .'

Here Cary paused for another generous measure of ale. Perdita was somewhat startled at the direction this story was taking and she glanced at Cary's daughter, still seated on the floor and listening intently. But Het's eyes had the dreamy expression of someone hearing a well-loved tale for the hundredth time.

'Well, they broke down the door of the priory, no problem there. Then they seized all the nuns, all screaming and praying to the Lord and terrified . . . as well they might be. But the abbess was too fast for them. She ran through the whole length of the old church and began to climb the tower. The men ran after her, but she climbed up swiftly, swiftly, as though the Good Lord was giving her the strength and speed of an angel, but the soldiers followed close behind. There was blood dripping from their hands from the evil things they had done to her sisters and a terrible bloodlust in their eyes, but when they reached the top they stopped.

'There she stood on the very highest parapet of the tower with all the whole county of Gloucestershire spread out below her, hills and valleys and woods and streams, so small and far away, and the birds flying underneath her. "Come one step closer and I shall jump!" she told them. But they just laughed, black-hearted villains that they were. And so, "The Lord have mercy on my soul!" she cried out, and stepped off in the air.'

'Dear heavens,' exclaimed Perdita, 'what a terrible way to die.'

'Ah, but she did not die, not straight away. Some say her skirts slowed her fall, some say it was a miracle and they saw an angel appear in the sky beside her and guide her gently to the ground.'

'So she was saved?'

Cary gave her an odd look.

Kip guffawed. 'No one ever escapes a gruesome end in Cary's stories,' he told her.

'That's right,' said Cary firmly. 'The angel only broke her fall and prevented her from dying outright which, considering what happened next, would certainly have been a merciful release. The angel could not save her. No one could. While she was lying there on the ground, her body twisted and broken, the soldiers came and taunted her. And then they ravished her, just as she was, all bleeding and mangled from her fall. Then, last thing before she died, she asked God to forgive them. But Our Lord had more sense than that. Each one of those men died in great agony. One of them—'

Stephen was looking at Het. 'I think, Cary,' he said, 'we should end your story for now, or poor Het will have nightmares.'

'I'm all right,' the child protested. 'Tell how the Grey Lady came back to haunt the tower for ever more. And how she helped the Irish soldiers when they were all going to die and how you helped her and how—'

Kip caught Perdita's eye and smiled. 'Go on, Cary. That's a good story too.'

'She did haunt the priory,' said Cary firmly. 'No one would ever go there. Even foxes and badgers never went there after dark. Once, a stranger came to Tilsbury and did not know the story. He tried to drive his horse up to the walls of the priory but the horse would not budge so he beat it and beat it but still the horse would not move. And finally the man drove the poor animal forward two steps, its skin all hanging from the beating, and it fell down on the spot. Dead. Of fright.'

She looked at her audience with satisfaction and finished her pot of ale at a single draught.

Chapter Ten

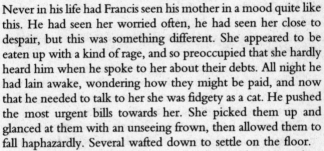

Never in his life had Francis seen his mother in a mood quite like this. He had seen her worried often, he had seen her close to despair, but this was something different. She appeared to be eaten up with a kind of rage, and so preoccupied that she hardly heard him when he spoke to her about their debts. All night he had lain awake, wondering how they might be paid, and now that he needed to talk to her she was fidgety as a cat. He pushed the most urgent bills towards her. She picked them up and glanced at them with an unseeing frown, then allowed them to fall haphazardly. Several wafted down to settle on the floor.

Francis grunted as he stooped to recover them. 'Mother, please, give this some thought. We have less than three days before the money is due.'

Alice wandered towards the fireplace. Some half-charred papers, the remnants of Francis's most recent effort to organise his affairs, were all that remained of the winter fires.

'When I first came here as a young bride,' she said, 'your father's family welcomed me like a queen. There was open house for weeks. I do believe the whole county must have visited.'

'I know, Mother. But what are we going to do about these debts?'

'No one ever talked of debts in those days. We were so young and light-hearted. Not like you and Sophie. No one had any troubles then. Your generation doesn't know what pleasure there was, you're always worrying about something or other.'

'I know, Mother, but—'

'It's the war that changed everything. That's what turned me into an old woman. And all for what? We have a king again. All those lives, all that money, all gone for nothing!'

'They say Sir Richard has done well from it.'

'Richard always knew how to look after himself. When we were young, everyone thought he'd go to the bad, but I knew he was different. He made all his money for himself. Of course, his marriage helped. And everything was so much easier in those days. People still knew how to enjoy themselves.'

'I thought we might ask him to lend us the money.'

'What?'

'Just for a month or two. Just enough to pay the interest on the loans. By the summer I'm sure something else will turn up and we can pay it back and—'

'I will not scrape and beg to Richard. You'll have to think of another way.'

'But I do not see that we have any choice.'

'Dear heavens above —' Alice's eyes were brimming with tears — 'don't I have humiliation enough without that too? How can you even think of such a thing?'

And with that she swept out. She was intending to retreat to the privacy of her room, but she saw Honor and Louisa on the stairs and, unable to face anyone, she bolted into the garden.

In all the years of her battles with the County Committee she had never felt the indignity of her position as keenly as she did now. It was not just the lack of money that was so painful: now there was the knowledge that she had become an object of pity, ageing, plump and dowdy. No longer the tragic young widow, battling bravely for her fatherless children, but the pathetic dowager, clinging to memories of vanished happiness.

And how had these bitter insights been revealed to her? She had seen the lesson in Richard's eyes, that was how. She had seen the way they still glowed with warmth and admiration and respect — but only when he looked at her elder daughter. On the rare occasions when he was obliged, for courtesy's sake, to turn his attention to her, his expression was dulled by boredom.

Oh, the bitter agony of being jealous all over again, and at her age too! Had she not suffered enough when her husband was alive? Why must the seething torment begin all over again, and this time because of her daughter? It was not fair, it was not just, it was too much.

Sometimes, though she knew it was wrong, she was eaten up by bitterness towards her late husband. It was all very well for him to die the young hero in the futile glory of battle, but she was the one left to grow old grappling with the chaos and fighting off the creditors and the County Committee. This was a battle of a different kind, a battle with no end and no glory and, increasingly, no prospect of victory.

Alice was so agitated, this mild March day when Richard had ruined everything by his blatant admiration for Sophie, that for some time she was incapable of doing anything but pace up and down the remnants of the formal garden. It was here, a little later, that he found her.

'Alice, I must talk with you privately.'

'Why? What can we possibly have to discuss that cannot be said in front of my family?'

'Patience, Alice. I know why you are upset. Shall we walk a little way?'

It was not really a question, Richard's never were. Alice might have been able to do battle with grasping Parliamentarians, but she had never been a match for this man. She glanced up at him briefly as he took her arm and set off down the gravel path that led away from the house. As a youth he had always appeared too strange and irregular to be handsome. Now that his unruly shock of dark hair was streaked with grey and his youthful anger had been replaced by the confidence of maturity, he had grown imposing. Still not handsome, never handsome, but a man to be noticed. Alice could well imagine how her gentle Sophie might be attracted by such a man.

But what was she thinking of? He had a wife already. Yes, and had shown his opinion of her in the past by setting up house with his mistress. Well, her Sophie might have no money and therefore no chance of a suitable marriage, but Alice would never contemplate anything less. The girl must remain a spinster at Rossmere and care for her family.

Richard was speaking.

'Alice, we have known each other since we were children. I think all the hardships we've been through since the wars began have made us older than our years. I find I have reached that time of life when a man wants to put his affairs in order. That is why I came back to Rossmere and why I brought my daughter with me.'

Alice bristled at the notion that she looked even older than her age.

He went on, 'There are, of course, certain irregularities to consider, but they need not stand in our way. I believe Nicolas would have wanted an alliance between our two families.'

'That is for me to decide,' she said swiftly.

'What concerns me most at this time is the boy's complete lack of any real education.'

'The boy? What boy?'

'Your son Kip.'

'Kip?'

'I thought you knew what I was talking about. I have been considering him as a prospective son-in-law, but at present he is so ignorant and boorish I'd not foist him on a dairymaid.'

'Kip?' Alice repeated, but this time she laughed out loud. Partly from relief that they were not, after all, to talk of Sophie and partly because the very idea of her precious boy united with a bastard, even if that bastard was the daughter of Sir Richard Treveryan, was utterly laughable.

Richard said, 'The lad has been badly spoiled but I trust it is not too late to make something of him.'

'I'll not hear a word against him.'

'That, dear Alice, has been his downfall.'

'Whatever do you mean? Everyone sings his praises.'

'In your hearing, perhaps. Are you aware that he has not a single word of Latin? He is barely able to write in a legible hand. Nor does he make himself useful. I heard him yesterday telling Stephen he'd not help with the farm work. He is so idle and ignorant I'd not even hire him as a serving-man.'

'What nonsense, Richard. Kip could never be a serving-man. He is a gentleman's son.'

'Nicolas was no scholar but at least he knew enough not to make a complete fool of himself. My first thought was to send Kip to the university with my own boys, but I've seen enough of his character to know that he would fritter away his time in idleness and, no doubt, corrupt them too.'

'How dare you slander him so? He is always busy.'

'Yes, gambling and rabbiting and visiting his friends. He needs to learn discipline. I only hope it is not too late. I intend sending him on one of my ships. I expect he will make a confounded nuisance of himself to begin with, but Captain Boulter has turned idle boys into useful seamen before now. With any luck he can do the same again.'

'I won't hear of it.'

'How so?'

'Well, for one thing, Kip is too young to be sent from home.'

'At twenty? Alice, he is a grown man.'

'Not Kip. He has a delicate constitution.'

Richard snorted. 'The boy is as strong as an ox.'

Alice felt a rising panic. She said, 'There is no point arguing with me, Richard. I'll never allow Kip to endure life on one of your ships. His place is at home with his family. He is too sensitive for the rough and tumble of shipboard life. I'll not let him go.'

'Consider his needs, Alice. You've done your utmost to ruin him. Now he must learn to make his way in the world.'

'Never. I need him here.'

'Then you'll have to learn to manage without him. It gives me no pleasure to grieve you, but my mind is made up. I want to talk to Kip immediately and take him back to Saltash with me when I leave. I know it is what Nick would have wanted for him.'

'Nick? Nick? That is not fair.' Suddenly Alice was weeping. 'Three of my sons have left home already. Surely I can keep my baby with me just a little longer.'

Richard was silent. They had stopped walking while Alice cried for a while and then composed herself. Then she said, 'I will talk to Kip. He will never agree to your plans.'

'Then you must persuade him.'

She wiped her eyes on a kerchief.

Richard said, 'My aim is to help you. You and your family. It is almost Lady Day and—'

'And what of that?'

'You know well enough. The interest must be paid on several loans that you and Francis have raised.'

'Who told you our private business?'

He laughed. 'It's hardly private, but don't fret. No one at Rossmere has answered my questions. Your financial problems are no secret in Porthew. I had forgotten what a confounded gossipy place this is. There's not a tradesman or money-lender for miles around to whom you don't owe money, and some of the debts go back more than ten years. Don't think I'm blaming you, I can imagine how difficult it has been and I only wish I had been here to help you sort it out sooner. I've never come across such a tangle.'

'You have been misinformed.'

'Have I? There is over seventeen pounds due on the loan to Solomon Daniels at Penryn and nearly nine pounds owing to Sir Michael Roper, as well as the nine pounds you failed to give him at Michaelmas last year. Do you want me to go on? Since you have been lavish in your spending of ready cash over the past week, no doubt because of my own presence here, it is thought unlikely you will have the wherewithal even to pay off the interest. Is that not right?'

'I'll get the money.'

'In three days? How?'

Alice had forgotten what it was like to be cross-examined by Richard, to feel the full force of those piercing black eyes. All at once, she buckled. 'I did wonder if you might perhaps consider lending us what is necessary. Only till the summer, or the harvest at the latest . . .' She had been planning to broach the subject more subtly but now she had come to the point there seemed to be no easy way of doing it. Nor, after her recent fit of weeping was it possible to resort to feminine wiles to sweeten her case. Richard was their last hope, their only hope. She had sold everything that could be sold, borrowed from everyone she could think of, even the servants and most of them had received no pay for years. It was hopeless.

'Alice. I'll not lend you a penny.'

'Oh—'

'Here, sit down. Here, on this bench. Listen to me carefully. I'll not lend you the money, Alice, because that would just add more muddle to the whole impossible tangle. I intend to give you all that is necessary to pay the interest on the major loans and to pay off the petty ones entirely.'

'Oh, Richard—' Alice was gripping his hand fiercely.

'In return I require merely that you hand Kip over to me. I do not believe he is a bad character, only that he has been indulged by you since his infancy and allowed to run wild. You will thank me in time, Alice, I am sure of it. And if he makes good progress then in a year or two it may be possible to consider a union between him and my daughter. In the mean-time I intend to take over the loan repayments on all the debts at Rossmere.'

Alice felt the blackness that comes before a faint, but the hard wood of the bench was pressing into her spine and she did not lose consciousness. After nearly twenty years of ceaseless anxiety, it was too much to take in all at once. To have her precious Kip wrenched from her was a torment she could not imagine. But there was no question of turning down Richard's offer – only a mad woman could do that. As Richard had known from the beginning. She wondered why she had ever bothered trying to stand up to him. Hadn't she herself told Francis only the previous week that opposing Sir Richard Treveryan was a waste of time? And in so many ways it was a relief to be told what to do, to lean on someone stronger than herself. Stronger, and with apparently limitless wealth.

She opened her eyes, saw the gravel path, its lavish crop of weeds and the unkempt border beyond. 'I can't quite take it in. And I thought you wanted to talk about Sophie!'

'Sophie, yes. I almost forgot.'

'No more surprises, Richard. I don't think I could bear it.'

'Your eldest daughter is not only beautiful she is one of the finest women I have ever come across. It is an outrage to keep her cooped up here as a skivvy. She should have a husband, a family of her own. It has come to my attention that there is someone who might wish to pay court to her, but you have prevented it.'

'No one will marry Sophie. Or Louisa, for that matter. There is no money for dowries.'

'That can be remedied. Besides, the man I have heard about

is wealthy enough to marry for love if he so chooses. But nothing can possibly come of it so long as you prevent them from meeting.'

'What man?'

'I understand your dislike of his father. I have even less reason to care for him than you do. But the wars are over and we cannot expect our children to continue the old hatreds. If Edmund does wish to marry Sophie then—'

'Edmund?'

'Edmund Menheire, of course. Wouldn't you like to see your own daughter settled at Trecarne?'

'Are you telling me there is some kind of understanding between them and I have been kept in ignorance?'

'Calm yourself. There is no understanding that I know of, not yet. But I believe he has expressed admiration for her.'

'That is ridiculous.'

'Alice, I insist. I promise I will do nothing to forward any such association, but neither will I let you stand in their way. From now on they will be allowed the kind of familiarity natural between neighbouring houses. I shall tell them about it myself.'

As they walked back down the gravel path Alice was surprised only that the afternoon continued pleasant and mild, that the house remained just where she had left it and the season was still spring. Her world had been so thoroughly rearranged during the previous hour that she half expected to see a corresponding change in her surroundings.

Edmund Menheire and Sophie . . . Her beloved Kip to be torn away from her and thrown to the wolves. She would never forgive Richard for his high-handed ordering of her family's fortunes and would thwart him if she possibly could.

But, oh! To have their debts removed! Not just the half-yearly interest but the monstrous hateful burden of it.

Now that a solution was within her grasp she saw how close they had all come to disaster. Perhaps even the unthinkable calamity, losing their home, had been closer than she had allowed herself to know. Her hidden fears of destitution, her children friendless and alone, she herself dying in miserable poverty, all these terrible images surfaced now.

Richard had not exactly agreed that he would pay off everything, but she was determined that he would before she was finished. Perhaps his tenderness towards Sophie could be put to the family's use. Like him, Alice knew how to drive hard bargains when she had to.

Sir Francis Sutton climbed the stairs to his bedchamber and for once his footsteps rang out purposefully.

Honor heard the weight of his tread. Suddenly apprehensive, she was feigning sleep when he entered the room.

With uncharacteristic determination, he disregarded her need for rest. 'Honor, my dear, wake up. I must talk with you.'

Honor simulated a yawn and said, 'What's the matter? Is it bad news?'

'I hardly know what to make of it. One might suppose it to be thoroughly good news, yet I am afraid there may be something I have overlooked.' He set the candlestick on a side table and lowered himself ponderously on to the bed.

Honor sat up and reached for a shawl to put over her shoulders. 'You had best tell me what it is,' she said, gazing at her husband with timid affection. His kindly, tender, handsome, pallid and always anxious face was rumpled like that of a child who suspects some devious trick.

'Mother is so certain about it, and I must endeavour to trust that she knows what she is doing, but all the same I'd be easier in my mind if I understood more.'

'Dearest, you are talking in riddles.'

'Yes, of course.' He took her hand and kissed it. She smiled, then removed her hand from his grasp and placed it under the counterpane as he continued, 'I did not like to worry you with all this before, but I must confess that for the last few weeks I have been half out of my wits with anxiety.'

'My poor Francis, why?'

'In a couple of days the interest falls due on those loans I may have mentioned to you once or twice before. We had set a small store of money to one side, though not nearly enough, but when Sir Richard arrived Mother insisted we use it to entertain him properly. Of course, I understand how important that was, but then again I did not see how we might survive without some means of paying our creditors.'

'My dearest heart, why didn't you tell me about this sooner? I can't bear to think of you anxious and not confiding in me.'

'You are so good.' He put his arm around her shoulders. After a little hesitation she leaned forward so that she was pressed lightly against him. He went on, 'But you have not been well recently and I did not want to add to your burdens. Besides, there was nothing you could have done.'

'Oh, Francis, what are you going to do now?'

'That's what I can't understand. Sir Richard has offered to meet all the interest payments himself.'

'Good Lord above, why has he done that?'

'I only wish I knew. A man like him is hardly going to play the benefactor unless he expects something in return.'

'You'll surely not refuse his money.'

'I couldn't, even if I wanted to. He has arranged it all with my mother.'

'Did she tell you why he was doing it?'

'Because of the old affection that he had for my father. And she hinted, though it was only a hint, that there had been an understanding between them in the past.'

Snug inside the circle of her husband's arms, Honor smiled, and her doleful face was almost pretty. 'Your mother and Sir Richard? Surely not!'

'It must have been a long time ago.' Francis was as puzzled by the thought of his mother ever having been a young woman as he was by the idea that a near-stranger was coming to their rescue.

'So long as he pays up now, it hardly matters, does it?' asked Honor. 'You don't think she'll marry again, do you?'

'Lord, no. Besides, he has a wife.'

'But, still, you suspect him of something.'

'It gives him power over us. From now on we are all in his debt. Mother said he wants Kip to go away for his education. Also that Edmund and Piers should be allowed to visit here sometimes.'

'As for Kip, I thoroughly agree with him. The boy has been mollycoddled far too long. But why on earth would Sir Richard want to encourage closer ties with the very family who turned him out of his own home?'

'That's what is troubling me. I cannot fathom his motives at all.'

Honor twisted round to face him and, at the sight of his baffled expression, she said, 'Oh, Francis, dearest one, just look at you. All your worries wiped out at a single stroke and still you find reasons to fret. Maybe Sir Richard simply wanted to be kind? From what I've seen of him so far he does not merit his reputation.'

He gazed down at her uncertainly. 'Are you sure?'

'I believe he is a hard man, but not deceitful.'

'Oh dear –' he looked more anxious than ever – 'it would be so terrible if we were mistaken.'

'Poor Francis, try to stop worrying. The money will be paid. Surely that is enough for now.' And then, when he continued to look wretched, she touched the edge of his cheek with her pale fingertips.

Still frowning Francis reached down and kissed her gently on the lips. Then he drew back and said, 'Maybe you're right.'

'Let us hope so. You should have told me your worries sooner.'

'I only wanted to protect you.'

'I know.'

The knowledge of his kindness, a kindness that she had never known from anyone in childhood, filled Honor with an answering tenderness for her husband. She reached up and kissed him once again.

'Oh, Honor,' he murmured.

She wasn't quite sure how it happened. She had only meant to kiss him lightly, as she had, and he had responded with his usual restraint. But then she found herself curling her fingers around his head and pressing her lips against his with greater purpose. Startled, he drew back briefly. Her eyes were misty with affection, and something else besides. 'Oh, Honor,' he murmured once more. She arched her body towards his, seeking out his mouth. Clumsily he wrapped his arms around her thin shoulders, crushed her body close to his own. Her heart was racing. She wanted to offer herself to him completely. His hands were on her breasts, and the surface of her skin felt dry and hot. He pulled back the counterpane a little way, stretched himself beside her. Even though he was still fully dressed, she could feel his urgency pressing against her and her body was coming alive with an answering need. He pressed her back against the pillows. There was a sound of screaming inside her head, a woman screaming and coming closer. Terror flooded through her, banishing desire.

'Francis, please, not now. I am not ready. Not yet.'

'But surely . . . if we just . . .'

'No.'

He let out an agonised breath, his head dropped against her shoulder. His hands were limp. Then he pulled back. 'I'm sorry,' he said. 'I don't know what . . .' And then he groaned and said in anguish, 'Are you sure, Honor? Don't you think we might just try? I promise I won't hurt you.'

'It's not that.' Her eyes were filling with tears. The screaming inside her head was fainter now, but had not vanished entirely. 'You know it's not that.'

He hung his head.

'Oh Francis, I wish . . .'

'It doesn't matter,' he said. He was turning away. 'Please don't cry. I'm sorry, Honor. It was my fault.' He stood up and blew out the candle before undressing and getting into bed beside her. Beside her, but not touching.

After a while she said, in a small voice, 'Maybe in the summer, dearest. When my strength is greater.'

He did not reply, but she knew he wasn't asleep. Neither of them would sleep for a long time. Never before had she wanted him so badly, and that made it harder for both of them. But stronger even than the desire was the fear. Not of the sexual act itself, but of its consequences.

Her earliest memory was of weeping in lonely terror as she listened to her mother in the room where she was closeted with the midwives when her little brother was born. At first she had merely cried out in pain, and they had told the waiting child that it would soon be over. But as the day turned into night, so her mother's cries changed, shrieks that seemed to last a lifetime, terrible sounds that endured all through the night and the next day as well until Honor was almost demented with fear and could not eat or sleep or do anything but listen and wait. Not that anyone noticed: by then the whole household was so taken up with the drama in her mother's bedroom. Her mother survived. It had been a difficult birth, they said, but there had been worse. The next time, when her sister was born, the worse came. That time she saw the midwife go into her mother's room with strange-looking implements and knives, and the murderous sounds went on for days. Again, they said, she had been lucky. Her mother survived. The baby did too. After that her mother said she must not worry any more, there would be no more babies. But her mother was wrong. When Honor saw her mother's shape begin to change for the third time she clung to her fiercer than drowning, but it did no good. The third time the shrieking did not last so long, but it was different, fainter, yet more terrible. The howling of a wounded beast, no longer human at all. The banshee wailing stopped abruptly; no swaddled infant this time, no mother building up her strength slowly. Only the mourning bell and the winding sheet and the two coffins laid in the earth.

Each time her husband touched her Honor could hear her mother's dying agony shrieking in her head. She had thought that when she married her kindly, anxious, ponderous husband, her fears would be soothed by his tenderness, but it was not to be. Honor loved Francis, and wanted only to make him happy. But to suffer in torment then die an agonising death, and all for a few moments of carnal pleasure, surely that was too much for anyone to risk.

Chapter Eleven

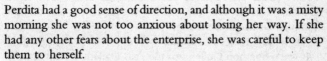

Perdita had a good sense of direction, and although it was a misty morning she was not too anxious about losing her way. If she had any other fears about the enterprise, she was careful to keep them to herself.

Cullen, however, had no such inhibitions. 'I'm a lady's maid,' she grumbled. 'I do your hair, I care for your clothes and I never complain. But no one ever told me I had to dress up as a beggarwoman and I won't do it.'

Perdita had ignored her protests. Over the previous days she had considered the problem long and hard, and she could see no other solution to her dilemma. She wanted to see Trecarne. No guest of the Suttons would ever be welcome there, especially not if that guest was the daughter of the man whose house it had once been. And every time she puzzled over it, her father's words floated into her mind: 'You'll have to disguise yourself as a wandering tinker and hope for the best.'

Well, then, if that was the only way she'd ever get to see Trecarne, then so be it. A travelling tinker – or, at least, a pauper woman – was what she'd have to be, for one morning of her life at least. One of its main attractions was that he would never believe her capable of such an escapade.

They rode past the stretch of open ground where Sophie had galloped on Apollo, and in less than an hour they reached the place overlooking the oak woods and the bay where they had been obliged to halt. There, once again, was that tantalising glimpse of roof and tower and the gentle smoke curling about the chimney-stack in the damp air. The landscape was deserted.

Perdita dismounted quickly and looped Nimble's reins over a low branch before untying the small bundle that was strapped to her saddle. 'Hurry up, Cullen. Help me with these.'

'Dear heavens above, you're surely not going through with this!'

'Indeed I am. And you will help me.'

Shivering in the morning chill, Perdita removed her outer garments and put on the shabby old gown that Cullen had borrowed from the woman who came to Rossmere to help with the dairy work.

'Ugh.' Perdita wrinkled her nose in disgust. The dress had neither shape nor colour, but a pungent smell. The fabric scratched her skin, even through her fine linen shift. She thought anxiously of lice and vermin.

'How do I look?' she asked.

It was a question Cullen was used to, as a lady's maid, though never in quite such a context as this. She replied truthfully, 'You look like a grand lady who's borrowed a poor woman's dress.'

'What must I do?'

'Muss up your hair . . . like this. And your face and hands are far too clean and white.' Gaining courage, Cullen was almost enjoying herself as she tousled Perdita's dark hair and rubbed patches of mud into those pink and white cheeks and hands.

'Is that better?' Perdita was scowling.

Cullen stood back to examine her once more. 'Your shoes are much too dainty.'

'They are my oldest boots and almost worn through.'

'Yes, and the finest Spanish leather and made by a fashionable London cobbler too. You'll have to go barefoot.'

'Barefoot! I can't do that!'

Cullen made no attempt to hide her smile. 'That's what poor folk often do.'

'Very well, then.' Perdita sat down on the damp grass and tugged off her shoes, revealing small, unblemished white feet. 'Now you must do the same,' she said.

'There's no need for that. My shoes are very old – just the sort of thing a tinker woman might wear.'

Perdita took a deep breath and looked around. No one had seen them. Along the edge of the wood the birds were singing and far off a rooster crowed. The ponies were grazing contentedly.

They began to walk through the oak woods that led down to Trecarne. Perdita had never imagined a path to be so varied and rough. Dried sticks of bramble stuck in her flesh, sharp stones cut her. Soon her feet were throbbing and painful. But she discovered that dead leaves and grass were soft as a caress. She hitched up her skirts and picked her way carefully.

Cullen said smugly, 'You are walking like a lady. That will give you away faster than anything. You must stride out like you've tramped for miles and are used to carrying heavy loads.'

'It's all very well for you to talk, you've still got shoes on. Oh! Watch out!'

It was too late. The man had seen them and was approaching up the woodland track.

'You'll have to talk for both of us,' whispered Perdita. 'My voice would betray us at once.'

'What shall I say, mistress?'

'Stop calling me mistress, you simpleton. Just tell him we've lost our way and—'

The man drew close. He was young, not much older than she was herself, with an honest face and the clothes and manner of a labourer. Perdita had the unpleasant sense of being somehow exposed in the coarse dress. She was used to wearing clothes that held her firmly, that formed a barrier and a defence as well as being ornamental. She was reminded of the two women she had seen hanging from the gibbet. They, too, had been shapeless and vulnerable in their rough skirts.

She was about to whisper to Cullen what she must say but, to her amazement, the man paid them hardly any attention. He glanced briefly in their direction, dismissing them with a contemptuous glance, and his eyes had a hard, closed-off look. They might have been invisible. He walked on briskly.

Perdita's heart was pounding. She, who was accustomed to respectfully lowered eyes or expressions of envy and admiration, felt herself shrinking almost to nothing in the young workman's eyes. Then it dawned on her that his reaction at least proved her disguise was effective. The light was dim in the wood, and that undoubtedly helped, but even so the transformation was disconcerting. She had planned the disguise in order to see Trecarne: she had not thought what else it might mean.

'Come on, Cullen,' she said briskly. 'Let us hope no one else sees us. We'll stay close to the woods.'

'I don't like it. Suppose they set their dogs on us?'

'Dogs?' said Perdita. 'What dogs? Why should they do that?'

'They won't want two poor women skulking close to their big house. What will we do?'

'I don't know. I can't think of everything. Stay here, then, if you want, but I'm going on.'

The thought of being left behind all alone in the woods was even more terrifying than marauding dogs, so Cullen hurried after her.

They were at the edge of the trees and looking towards the back of the house. Always before, Perdita realised, when visiting grand houses with Kitty, she had seen them first from the front: the imposing façade and the public face. It was strange to approach a house from the rear, to see its underbelly of stables and servants' quarters, privies and workshops, bakehouse, dairy and mews and . . . Gradually, as Perdita peered out from the edge of the woods into the misty morning, the hugeness of the house built by her father before her birth was revealed.

'Blessed heavens above!' said Cullen. 'It's a palace.'

'We must see it properly. Come on.' Perdita stepped out from the shelter of the woods.

'But you said we'd stay hidden. You promised!'

'Don't be such a weasel.' The rough grass behind the house was cool and damp underfoot. She felt a rising excitement. She was so close to the house she could smell it, hear the clang and bustle of servants going about their morning tasks and the energy and life of a well-ordered household.

Cullen scurried after her. Keeping always at a safe distance, they went round in a wide arc until they had reached the driveway. There Perdita turned and examined it properly.

Trecarne, she thought. The house my father built, but where he was only happy when my mother was with him.

A happy house, perhaps. Certainly a beautiful one. Louisa had said it was vulgar but, then, she had never really seen it.

Two towers at either end, similar in appearance but not

identical, were linked by a long and elegant façade with tall windows and a wide flight of steps leading to the main door. Unlike Rossmere, which had grown over the centuries from a simple semi-fortified structure to its present haphazard arrangement of buildings, Trecarne had been created from the beginning to a single unified plan.

Perdita longed to go closer and enter the rooms her mysterious mother had once inhabited, but men were weeding the gravel paths near the house and she knew they would only be turned away. Or worse.

'There, now.' Cullen was panting with fear. 'Now we've seen it. That was what you wanted. Let's go back to the horses.'

'Don't be so impatient. I want to look at this so I never forget. Lord above, what's the matter now?'

Cullen had grabbed hold of Perdita's arm and was whimpering in fear. Shaking her off crossly, Perdita saw two brindled hounds racing towards them through the mist, baying. Cullen hid her face in Perdita's back. Perdita stood quite still. A man was running behind the animals, shouting. The hounds had long heads and bodies built for speed. There was no point in trying to run away, though at the sight of those savage teeth Perdita was sorely tempted. She pulled her shawl over her head and wished she had thought to bring a stout stick.

The lead hound, a male, was still baying when he reached her, but he did no more than leap about and wag his tail. The other did likewise. The man caught hold of their leather collars and ordered them to lie down. Only when they did so, and Perdita let out a long sigh of relief, did she realise she had been holding her breath. A chill of sweat trickled down between her shoulderblades. She reached back and pinched Cullen. 'You do the talking,' she whispered. 'I'll tell you what to say.'

'Don't be alarmed,' the man told them. 'They won't hurt you.'

Cullen emerged slowly.

'What are you doing here?' he asked. 'Don't you know this is private land?'

Perdita examined him. A youngish man, medium height and slender built. He had hair that was almost black, its darkness accentuated by his pale skin and the bluest eyes Perdita had ever seen. They were regarding her now with a quick intelligence. His clothes, though neither fashionable nor grand, showed him to be a person of modest wealth, perhaps even a gentleman. His hair reached his shoulders, too short for fashion, too long for a Puritan. Pulling her ragged shawl half across her face Perdita whispered to Cullen.

'Please, sir,' said Cullen, in a suitably contrite voice, 'we mean no harm, but we have been walking since daybreak and must have lost our way.'

'Where are you headed?'

More whispering, then, 'Porthew, sir.'

'That's nearly six miles from here. Where did you start from?'

Perdita glared at him. She had no idea what answer to give and could not see that it was any of his business anyway.

When no whispers were forthcoming to help her, Cullen ventured, 'I don't rightly remember, sir. Maybe it was Truro.'

'Not very likely,' said the man, 'not unless you have seven league boots.' Here he looked down at Perdita's bare feet; following his glance, she noticed that most of the dirt had been washed away by the wet grass and her feet were pink and white and tender-looking. When he raised his startling blue eyes to her face once more, he was frowning.

Perdita was growing uncomfortable. The coarse fabric of her dress was prickling her skin and she longed to scratch her arms and chest. Worse, she was not used to being stared at so directly, and had no idea how to respond, especially as she could neither snub him nor flirt with him.

'What about your friend?' he asked. 'Can she not speak?'

Perdita whispered fiercely that Cullen should tell him to mind his own business and not be impertinent, but the maid, more accustomed to the ways of diplomacy, replied, 'My la – my friend, I mean, my companion, has an affliction of the throat and cannot be easily understood by strangers.'

'How most unfortunate,' he said, and shot another piercing glance at Perdita. 'Clearly you have travelled a great distance. You look weary and half famished.' Here Perdita opened her mouth to protest this fresh insult, then closed it again. 'Come with me and I'll arrange some food for you before you resume your journey.'

Perdita's heart leaped with excitement. To see inside Trecarne, to see it properly, this was more than she had dared to hope for.

Cullen began nervously, 'We should be on our way, sir,' but Perdita was already moving towards the house.

'No need to be anxious,' he said. 'Come along.' He turned on his heel, whistling his hounds to follow. Perdita accompanied him, but kept always a good distance between them. Something in his manner disturbed her.

She grasped Cullen tightly by the arm and hissed, 'Say as little as possible. He suspects us, I'm sure of it.'

Cullen, however, was beginning to enjoy herself, and the young man chatted with her easily enough, drawing her out. By the time they reached the broad gravel path in front of the house he had learned that they were from London, a place they had left on the death of their father (they were sisters, apparently, which Perdita considered an audacious liberty on Cullen's part) and were trying to find relatives who might give them work and a home. As they passed the centre of the enormous building, Perdita automatically began to climb the wide steps to the main door. Cullen caught her by the arm.

'That's for grand folk, not us,' she scolded.

The young man's dark eyebrows lifted in surprise. Furious at her mistake, Perdita pulled her foul-smelling shawl a little further over her face. Most of the windows were draped in heavy curtaining, so she could see nothing inside, but one was open and, looking through, she caught a glimpse of an elegantly panelled room, a plaster ceiling decorated with leaves and flowers, an elaborate fireplace and magnificent paintings. A clean smell of polish and sweet herbs wafted out on the spring air. She was consumed with a desire to go inside and explore.

They went around the side and into the back kitchen, where the young man set them in a corner out of the way. The whole area was full of noisy activity and they attracted little attention. A maid fetched them a wooden platter with bread and cheese and a mug of small beer and set it down before them without ceremony. Perdita went to sip the beer but it was of poor quality and she was too fastidious to drink it. The young man was watching her. She met his curious gaze and forced herself to swallow several gulps in what she hoped was a suitably famished manner. As soon as his attention was distracted by a serving-man with a query about a lame colt she quietly emptied it into a pail of dirty water and fed the crusts of bread and the cheese to a couple of waiting dogs.

'Fraser will see you safely on to the Porthew road,' he said, coming back to their corner. 'I'd show you myself but I have been called away unexpectedly.'

Cullen began thanking him profusely, but he interrupted her with a brisk, 'Not everyone has forgotten the old custom of hospitality. Good day, and may your journey be successful.'

With a nod of encouragement and a final puzzled glance at Perdita's bare feet, he strode from the kitchen. It became immediately apparent, from the altered attitude of the servants, that the old custom of hospitality had departed with him.

Perdita was trying hard to think of some excuse to see the main part of the house, but she could think of none and the man called Fraser told them roughly to make haste as he didn't have all day. He was gangling and dishevelled, with a rolling eye and a sagging mouth and he scratched unceasingly at every part of his anatomy with red hands.

When they had walked in silence a little way down the drive, he stopped. 'What's the hurry?' he asked.

Perdita did not want to walk too close to him, so she stopped as well, and turned around. She was glad of this final chance to look at the magnificent house her father had built and which she was unlikely ever to see again. She wanted to fix every detail of it in her mind before it was once more swallowed up by the mist. The windows were still heavily curtained.

Then, as she watched, there was a movement at one of the top-floor windows. A hand drew back a curtain, a woman's face looked out. A servant, it must have been, but for a moment it was as if the unknown woman had been looking out just to see the lonely figure standing barefoot on the driveway in the mist. She felt a shiver of recognition. And then she was seized by an ache of longing so fierce it was a kind of pain – homesickness, perhaps, but for a home she had never known.

To her annoyance, the fellow Fraser came to stand in front of her, blocking the view. He had the most extraordinary expression on his face. She stepped to one side. He did likewise, then placed his hands on her waist and grinned. 'How about a kiss then? A thank-you for the guide. I'll give you threepence if you come into the woods and give me something more.'

Perdita was astonished. The fellow was obviously quite mad, and she had no experience of madmen. She couldn't think what to say to him.

He leered at her. It was a repulsive sight. He said, 'You're not bad-looking under all that muck. And, anyway, I'm not fussy, can't afford to be. How about it, eh?' He tugged her towards him.

Perdita twisted free. 'How dare you, you impudent rogue? I'll see you whipped for your impertinence!' She delivered a stinging slap. The lecherous grin was replaced with fury and he punched her hard in the stomach. Perdita gasped with pain. 'Don't go acting the fine lady with me.' He had thrust his face up against hers. 'You're nothing but a common drab!'

'Get away!'

He caught hold of her arm, but Cullen sprang forward, tore at his hair and scratched his face. Still gasping from the blow to her stomach, Perdita beat him with her fists and soon the man was in full retreat, covering his face with his arms and protesting that he meant no harm.

Panting, they watched him run back towards the house.

'That showed him,' said Cullen. 'Are you all right?'

'Yes. No. Of course not. I don't know. Let's get away from here. The fellow must have been a lunatic to act so.'

'Why? Because he thought a poor woman with no man to protect her would be glad of the chance to earn a few pennies?'

'Ugh. He thought we were common trollops. Hurry up, Cullen, for goodness' sake. We're finished here.'

Perdita picked up her skirts and ran through the wood as fast as she could, no longer worrying where she put her feet or noticing the stony ground. She was not running from the man, or from the risk of discovery: she was running back to her own clothes and the protection of wealth and status that she had so unthinkingly cast aside. Never again would she take such a foolish risk. Not if it meant that every lewd scrounger thought he could insult her with impunity.

She was still shaking with fright and anger when they reached the ponies. Nimble had broken free of the blackthorn but had not strayed far and was easily caught. Perdita ripped off her ragged clothes and looked down in horror at the hem of her petticoats, torn and muddy. Kitty would have had fifty fits if she could see her now, and quite right too.

Puffing from the steep hill, Cullen joined her.

'Here, help me with my boots.'

A lady's maid once again, Cullen knelt down and eased the leather boots over Perdita's bruised and swollen feet. Perdita winced, but said nothing.

She did not speak all the way back to Rossmere, though Cullen was so relieved that nothing worse had befallen them that she chatted away anyhow. Perdita was distracted by all that had happened and this time she missed the way. They had to retrace their steps. They were both exhausted and hungry when at last they rode into the stableyard at Rossmere. Adam came out of the groom's loft to take the horses, but otherwise the place was deserted as the servants were all at their dinner. Perdita pulled her fur-trimmed hood right over her forehead and hoped that no one noticed her dishevelled appearance.

She slipped into the house by a side entrance and Cullen disappeared towards the kitchen to fetch hot water. From the parlour came the noise of masculine voices and laughter. The midday meal must be nearly over and it sounded as if the family had been joined by guests, a rare occurrence. Suddenly conscious of her filthy hands and face, her rumpled hair and the muddy feet inside her leather shoes, Perdita ran up the stairs and disappeared into her room.

She could not wait for Cullen to come and help her. She pulled off her clothes, all but the fine linen shift she wore next to her skin. She threw her soft leather boots across the room. She did not want ever to wear them again.

There was a knock at the door, which opened at once.

'Set the water down and send for more,' she said, without bothering to turn around.

'Where the devil have you been all morning?'

Her father's voice.

She spun round. 'Father! I thought you were at table.'

'Where have you been? And don't waste my time with any of your paltry lies. I want the truth.'

'Trecarne,' she said, with just a hint of pride.

'Trecarne?'

'That's right. I wanted to see Trecarne again, but properly this time, not just a chimney and a bit of roof. When we went there before, you said I'd never see it again unless I disguised myself as a travelling tinker and hoped for the best. And so I did.'

'A travelling tinker?'

'Well, a poor woman anyway.' She remembered the feel of Fraser's hands around her waist, his disgusting face so horribly close to her own, and she shuddered. Cullen came in carrying two pails of hot water. At the sight of Sir Richard, she almost dropped them both.

'Did you see what you wanted?'

'Better than before, but still not enough. I saw it all from the outside, and a little bit within.'

'How did you like it?'

She hesitated, then sighed and said, 'It's more beautiful than any house I've ever seen in my life before.'

'Did anyone see you there?'

Perdita glared at Cullen. 'No one much,' she said.

Her father was grinning. 'You should have told me your idiotic plan, I might have saved you the trouble. If I ever hear of you traipsing around the countryside like a vagabond again I'll pack you straight back to your mother. Is that understood?'

'I have no wish to do so again anyway.'

'I'm not the slightest bit interested in your wishes.'

'Yes, Father.' He was no longer angry: on the contrary, he seemed to find it all highly entertaining.

'Come down as soon as you are ready. I want you to meet our guests.'

'Yes, Father.'

Cullen was still standing by with pails, soap and towels. Treveryan nodded towards her as he went once more to the door. 'And be quick about it,' he said.

'Yes, Father.'

* * *

143

Despite his instructions, it took several more pails of water and a great quantity of soap before Perdita felt clean enough to be dressed. Cullen rubbed salves on her bruised feet, liberal quantities of tansy cream on her hands and face, and flower waters on her hair. She put on a clean shift and her embroidered velvet slippers, her blue taffeta skirt and bodice and her opal necklace. Clothes fit for a grander occasion than this, it was true, but Perdita was determined to bury all trace of the ill-kempt vagabond she had been that morning. She wanted Cullen to take away the ragged dress and shawl and burn them, but Cullen refused, saying that the dairy woman who had lent them would wear them for a good many years yet. Cullen even insisted that Perdita give her sixpence for her trouble.

At last Perdita felt sufficiently restored to her normal self to face company again. Half-way down the stairs she stopped abruptly. The meal had finished and the diners were streaming out of the parlour and into the great hall. Richard Treveryan, Mistress Alice Sutton and Stephen went to stand beneath the display of ancient Sutton armour that hung from the walls. Francis and Honor stood a little apart. Sophie, Kip and Louisa were still joking with their guests by the door.

Their guests.

Perdita stared down at them in horror.

'Ah, there you are, Perdita.' Her father detached himself from the others and came to the foot of the stairs. 'I was beginning to despair of you.' There was an odd look in his eyes.

Somehow Perdita reached the bottom of the stairs. Richard took her arm and led her to meet a man she had never seen before. He was perhaps thirty-five years old. His clothes were expensive but he wore them awkwardly. His features were regular, and might have been attractive, except that there was something bleak and unyielding in his appearance. A man altogether without softness or grace.

'Perdita, this is Edmund Menheire,' Richard told her. 'His father lives at Trecarne. I believe you were interested in the house.'

Edmund Menheire greeted her briskly, with a minimum of courtesy. At once Perdita realised that he knew all about her irregular parentage. After her experiences that morning she was more than usually sensitive to any suggestion of contempt. She touched the opal at her throat and allowed him a brief, haughty smile, but she was too distracted to gauge his response. All her attention was taken by the young man who stood behind him and who broke off an animated conversation with Kip to come forward and be introduced. Though obviously related, he was more slightly built than the older man. He had hair that just touched his shoulders, eyes of an intense blue fringed with dark lashes and an expression of amusement and surprise.

Amusement and surprise that were all directed towards her.

Her father's voice continued, but it had gained an oddly echoey quality, as if he were a great distance away. 'And this is Piers Menheire,' he was saying. 'He is fortunate enough to live with his cousin at Trecarne.'

Piers's mouth twitched with the beginnings of a smile. He glanced down at her feet, now safely shod in their dainty velvet slippers, then he raised his eyes to meet hers. 'I am delighted to make your acquaintance, Mistress Treveryan,' he said as he stepped forward and took her hand.

And then, for her ears only, he murmured softly, 'Again.'

Chapter Twelve

While they had all been inside the house, the mist had burned away and the green landscape was steaming in the sunshine. Kip was determined to organise some kind of entertainment and he suggested a game of skittles.

They spilled out through the front door, dogs crowding at their feet, and made their way along the wide walk that led to the area set aside for skittles and bowls. Edmund Menheire walked beside Sophie. He made no effort to converse with her; in fact, his general air of assurance made Perdita wonder if some kind of understanding had already been reached between them. Mistress Sutton, however, was always nearby; once or twice she attempted to draw Sophie away, but Edmund followed close behind, as if joined to her by an invisible thread.

Perdita was equally determined not to let Piers Menheire out of her sight until she had extracted a promise of discretion from him. This left her no time to find outdoor shoes; her embroidered slippers must be sacrificed to the present need. To her surprise her father seemed intent on sharing her company. As she hurried to catch up with Piers and Kip, Richard strode along beside her.

She said, in a low voice, 'I thought there was enmity between that family and the Suttons. When did this change come about?'

'Yesterday. I spoke to Kip in the morning. After what you told me concerning Sophie's affections, I decided to act without delay. Kip must have taken the invitation over to Trecarne at once.'

'But what about Mistress Sutton? How did you persuade her to receive them?'

'My methods are my own business.'

'Will Colonel Menheire be equally friendly?'

'I expect so. Now that England is a monarchy once again, he can only benefit from cordial relations with his former enemies. He has achieved his material gains and desires to be accepted on equal terms by the old Cornish families. And the Suttons are a very old family indeed. Where they lead, others will follow.'

'I wish you had told me,' said Perdita crossly.

'It would have saved you the trouble of disguise,' agreed Richard. 'By the way, who did you say you saw at Trecarne this morning?'

Perdita did not answer.

They were nearing the area of smooth ground where the skittles were set up. She asked, 'Will you also visit your old home?'

'Certainly not.' Richard's reply was swift and certain.

The first game was between Kip, Stephen, Louisa and Piers Menheire. Perdita was obliged to watch and wait. Edmund had once again manoeuvred himself next to Sophie. Mistress Sutton was watching them and fidgeting, but nothing in Sophie's manner betrayed any special partiality for their handsome neighbour. She was attentive when he spoke, smiled warmly when he said anything of interest and replied with energy – but, then, she did as much with whoever she spoke to, even the old man who cleaned out the drains, so there was nothing special in that. It was obvious, however, that Edmund Menheire was well on the way to being badly smitten.

Ever sensitive to the undercurrents that others missed, Perdita quickly decided that Mistress Sutton was squandering her anxiety on the wrong daughter. It was Louisa who was making a bid for Piers. Probably no one but Perdita had noticed this, since Louisa's symptoms were mainly a kind of tongue-tied surliness – and Perdita was in favour of anything that caused Louisa to be tongue-tied. A desire to impress their visitors made Louisa more anxious than ever to win, especially to beat Kip. Perdita observed Louisa's sullen competitiveness and Sophie's easy-going good-humour and thought that if this was how country girls behaved in the company of eligible young gentlemen then they both deserved to die old maids.

Soon Perdita had an opportunity to demonstrate how such situations should properly be handled. Louisa withdrew from the game in a fit of temper after accusing Kip of cheating and Perdita took her place. As it happened, she was good at skittles, having beaten her two brothers many times, but she had no intention of betraying this fact and, within a short time, Kip, Piers and even Edmund were gathered round to help her master the basic techniques. When Perdita sent the skittles flying, she was full of amazement and assured them that it was all due to their excellent tuition. Louisa was grumpier than ever.

This was a small triumph, and satisfying in its way, but Perdita was beginning to despair of an opportunity to talk with Piers privately. Until he gave her a promise to say nothing about her unorthodox visit to Trecarne, she felt she was teetering on the brink of a precipice. Meanwhile, she was trying to assess what methods would best work with him. She had thought at first that he and Kip were two of a kind: they both threw themselves into the game as if skittles were the most important business in the world. From one or two casual remarks, she gathered that, despite the feud between their two families, they passed a good deal of time in each other's company.

In the end, unintentionally, it was Louisa who provided Perdita with her chance. Seeing how her rival was gaining all the attention, Louisa had returned to the game as soon as she could when Stephen retired to smoke his pipe and watch. But whereas Perdita had to struggle to hide her skill, Louisa was just the opposite: the harder she tried, the more she fumbled and the crosser she became.

'Lord above, Lou,' said Kip finally, 'what's the matter with you today? Perdita's only a novice and already she's much better than you are.'

It was the last straw. Her pretty face flushed and furious, Louisa spun round and hurled the ball, not at the skittles, but at her brother. Even now her aim was appalling. The ball sailed wide of Kip, but whacked her mother on the side of the head.

Alice's hand flew to her face. She groaned, then swayed. Louisa shrieked and burst into tears. Sophie, Edmund, Kip and

Stephen all hurried to the injured woman's aid while Richard scolded Louisa for her ill-temper. The game was over, with everyone talking at once – except Mistress Sutton, who cradled her upper jaw in her hands and moaned pitifully. The party moved in an untidy gaggle towards the house, and Perdita was about to follow when she noticed that Piers had remained to gather up the skittles. She picked up one ball from under a bush, retrieved another from the mouth of an amiable dog, then went over to join him. 'Master Menheire,' she said at once, 'I hope I can rely on your discretion.'

He picked up the last of the skittles, tucked them all under one arm and turned to her. 'How are your feet?' he asked.

'My feet?'

'There is blood on your shoes.'

She glanced down. Her velvet slippers were ruined and, now that she was reminded of it, her feet were throbbing and painful. 'No matter. They will mend.'

'A stoic attitude.'

'You still have not answered my question.'

'Was it a question? I assume that your visit to Trecarne this morning was undertaken in secret.'

Perdita said haughtily, 'Not entirely. My father knows all about it.'

'Now you do surprise me. Sir Richard does not strike me as the kind of man who encourages his daughter to roam around the countryside dressed in rags. But I'm curious to know which is the truth and which the charade. Are you a gentlewoman who likes to play the vagabond, or are you a vagabond posturing as a gentlewoman?'

'Your question is an insult.'

'Just as I feared. A pity – the other explanation had a definite romance.'

Perdita had had enough of his teasing. She smothered her annoyance and gazed up at him through her lashes, smiling demurely. 'Master Menheire,' she cooed, 'I can see that you are a man of sound judgement, but there are others who might not be so judicious.'

'Sound judgement, eh? I am flattered. Most of my acquaintance are not so generous.'

'I would not like people to gain a false impression. Obviously, I have done nothing I need be ashamed of—'

'Then there is no cause to worry.'

'—but all the same, I would be grateful if you would promise never to mention this morning's visit to anyone else. Please.'

'Are we to be bound by promises already?'

Perdita responded with her most engaging smile, the one she had perfected in London the previous winter, before asking softly, 'Why not? This can be our secret. Yours and mine.'

He was watching her very closely. He asked, 'First you must tell me why you did it.'

'Are you trying to bargain with me, Master Menheire?'

'Maybe I am. I must be curious. After all, it is a little unusual – a vagabond one moment, a fine lady the next. Like some character from a children's story. What was your reason for the subterfuge?'

'I wanted . . . I wanted to see the house my father built. Where he lived with my mother and was happy.' Perdita had intended to keep her voice sweet and low, but all at once the intensity of her longing to see Trecarne came back to her in a wave and her eyes filled with unwelcome tears. 'For he did love her, you know, whatever lies people spread about them. And my father said I would never see it, not properly, because of the enmity with your uncle, not unless I dressed as a tinker who had lost their way. He meant it in jest but I did it all the same. Please don't tell anyone, they would never understand.'

'No, I don't suppose they would.' Piers paused, considering. Then, 'Very well then. I will take your secret with me to my grave.'

'Do you promise?'

'I was under the impression I just had. Yes, I promise. On my honour – such as it is.'

'Thank heavens for that.'

In her relief, Perdita forgot that she was supposed to be hopeless at ball games and shied a ball at a post. It made contact with a satisfying thwack. She was glad her tears had done the trick, but annoyed that Piers Menheire had observed her weakness. Now she wanted only to be rid of him. She said, 'I will go indoors and see how Mistress Sutton does.'

'I dare say her jaw is smashed, poor lady, but she has plenty of people to fuss over her. Don't go just yet. Edmund is going to invite Kip and his sisters to visit Trecarne three days from now. Why don't you come with them? If you like, I can show you the whole house – a proper grand tour.'

'I would like that very much indeed.'

'Excellent. I look forward to it.'

Perdita decided to make use of what might be only a temporary advantage. She said, 'You should get rid of that servant, though. The one who escorted us from your home.'

'Fraser? Why?'

'I've never met such a rogue. His behaviour towards women is deplorable. He was perfectly civil to me –' Perdita had her pride, after all – 'but he was abominably rude to my maid Cullen.'

'I am sorry to hear it. I will certainly talk to the fellow myself, but that is all I can do. Edmund and my uncle pay no attention to my opinions.'

This information was given as a statement of fact. They had been strolling down the grassy path that led back to the house. Now that the front door had come into view they both slowed their pace, reluctant to rejoin the others just yet.

Perdita asked, 'How did you come to live with them?'

Piers stopped to break off a hazel wand that was bending over the path. 'That is simple,' he said. 'Edmund's mother and mine were sisters. I believe they married at about the same time, but there the similarities ended. One husband prospered and the other declined. My aunt tried many times to help her sister and family, but the Colonel believed my parents' problems were of their own making. Nine years ago my mother and father both died of typhus in the same month. Colonel Menheire relented and gave in to my aunt's request that I go and live with them. He insisted, however, that I take his name, which I have done. My unfortunate aunt died a year later, but by that time I believe the Colonel had grown used to having me in his house, and so that is where I have remained.'

'How very sad.'

'In parts, I agree. But in general I have no cause to complain.'

There was no bitterness in his account, which surprised Perdita, for in her experience dependent relatives usually became resentful and crabbed by the petty indignities of their position. Even though Piers Menheire was clearly a poor relation, and therefore of no consequence, Perdita found that she enjoyed his frankness, and she was encouraged to ask him something that had been bothering her.

She said, 'When I came to Trecarne this morning, did you guess that I was not what I seemed?'

'I did not suspect. I knew.'

'Was it because of my feet?'

He grinned, his blue eyes shining. 'Why so curious? Are you thinking of trying your experiment again?'

'Certainly not! I'd rather die than wear such clothes again!'

After some thought, Piers said, 'You're right. It was the feet. It was obvious you'd never walked barefoot in your life before. Nor worn ill-fitting boots like a working woman's.'

'Pray God I never do so again,' said Perdita, with feeling, as they walked towards the house.

Piers was smiling. He did not tell her, as he might have done, that it had not been the soft flesh of her feet alone that had betrayed her that morning at Trecarne. More revealing still had been the expression in her dark eyes. He had been struck by the intensity in her gaze when she looked towards the house. He had invited them into the kitchen quarters to see if he could discover the reason for her crude disguise. Edmund's announcement that they were both to leave at once to dine with the Suttons had compelled him to cut his investigations short.

He had been delighted to discover that the answer to the mystery was waiting for him after his meal at Rossmere. Piers decided that a gentlewoman of dubious birth who was prepared to masquerade as a vagabond to achieve her ends was likely to be a welcome addition to the ranks of respectable families hereabouts.

Perdita had devoted the best part of two weeks to winning a place in Kip's affections. She had discovered early on that the feminine wiles which worked so well on the young men in London were wasted on Kip. The way to his heart was more straightforward but, from Perdita's point of view, often tedious. She spent long hours playing every kind of backgammon, nine men's morris, card games and even dice, though she was afraid that dice was not a game that someone with her precarious hold on respectability could afford to be seen playing in company. When the weather permitted she played skittles, bowls and shuttlecock. She listened to him while he talked about horses and dogs, racing and hunting until she was ready to scream with boredom.

She was still undecided about the idea of marriage, though she tried to calculate the prospect carefully. On the one hand he was amiable enough and, though his family were poor, their standing in the county remained equal to anyone's. A marriage between them would be a simple trade: money for respectability. Sometimes she thought wistfully that Kip, with his rosy cheeks and his boyish delight in games, was someone she could neither respect nor love, but then she told herself sternly that such considerations were a luxury she could ill afford.

But there were more serious drawbacks to an alliance with Kip. She suspected that it might be better for her to make a home somewhere where her mother's story was not so well known. Added to that was the danger that Kip would squander any money he laid his hands on, and as his wife she'd be hard put to prevent him doing as he wanted.

He was three years older than her, but often Perdita felt as if she were the elder by far. He had no interests apart from horseflesh and petty gambling, and knew of no world beyond Rossmere and the homes of his friends, all similar. All his life he had been the indulged youngest of the family, free to spend his days as he chose. He had never known what it was like to be lonely or afraid. By temperament he was easy-going and believed himself content.

Perdita was surprised, therefore, to find him gloomily lobbing walnut shells into an empty grate on the afternoon before they were due to visit Trecarne. She suggested a game of draughts, and he agreed, but was then too distracted to go in search of the board. Kip not inspired by a game of draughts? This was a sign of serious malaise.

'Do you not feel well, Kip?'

'What? Oh, yes, I'm fine. It's not that . . .' He let the sentence hang unfinished and gazed moodily at his fingernails.

'What, then?'

He sighed heavily. 'It's no secret, I suppose. A couple of days ago your father called me in to talk with him. He had some notion I ought to go to sea. I didn't think much of it at the time. I've never wanted to go to sea – or anywhere else, for that matter. I thought it was just some whim of his that would blow over and nothing would come of it. But I spoke to Mother this morning and she says everything is arranged. I am to leave Rossmere when he does and put to sea under some fellow called Master Boulter. Yet I know she would rather I stay here. I cannot understand it.'

Perdita smothered a smile. 'What a terrible shock for you!'

'The trouble is, I don't see the point of it all. Your father started up with some nonsense about making a man of me and all the rest of it. Of course, I agreed with him at the time but I wasn't really listening to any of it. Thought it best to let him ramble on and then everyone could forget all about it.'

'I wish you'd told me sooner. I could have warned you that once my father has decided on a thing it usually happens.'

'It might be easier if I could see what it has to do with him,' Kip continued, in an aggrieved tone. 'I even told Mother I'd help Uncle Stephen on the farm if she thought that would help, but she says that wouldn't make any difference. It's all so damned unfair. I mean, what about little Tom? I ought to start training him in a month or so. No one seems to think about that.'

'I hope you did not mention that to Father.' She could imagine Richard's likely response to the notion of putting off a career at sea for the needs of one small puppy. She said, 'I'd forgotten about poor Tom. Do you want me to look after him for you?'

'Would you? I'd trust him with you.' Kip sighed again. 'I suppose I won't mind being at sea. So long as the food is all right and there are some decent fellows to have a bit of sport with. I don't suppose I'll have to work much. You never know, it might even be quite jolly. And, if it doesn't suit me, I can always come home again.'

Perdita was silent. Her knowledge of life at sea was limited, but clearly Kip's optimism was unbearably misplaced.

She said at length, 'That's right. I think it's wonderful how you've adapted to the idea so quickly. My father is sure to be impressed.'

'Do you think so? I'd like that. He can be quite – quite fierce, sometimes, can't he? I've never met anyone like him before. But I dare say his bark is worse than his bite.'

'Don't be fooled, Kip. With my father, it is always the bite you must watch out for.'

Kip looked depressed at this. Perdita did not consider it necessary to tell him that Captain Boulter had a reputation as an unflinching disciplinarian. She thought it most unfair of her father not to mention his plans for Kip sooner. It would have saved her a deal of bother. Now he would probably be at sea for a year or even two, and who knows what might have happened before he returned? It was infuriating to think that so many hours of tedium had been wasted at backgammon and doublets. Still, she had grown quite fond of him and didn't like to see him looking so downcast.

'Come along then, Kip. How about a hand of piquet? Sixpenny stakes.'

'Sixpenny stakes?' He brightened at once.

They were just beginning their third game when they heard sounds of commotion at the front of the house.

'Whatever is going on?' asked Perdita.

They went to the window and, kneeling side by side on the low seat, they looked out. There on the forecourt was her father, mounted on Apollo. Next to him, being walked in wide circles by Adam, was a Barbary stallion. Dappled grey, with pewter-coloured rump and paler mane and tale, he was all fine-boned delicacy and prancing strength. Francis and Honor, Alice and Sophie had already tumbled out of the front door to view the new arrivals.

'My God,' breathed Kip. 'I've never seen such an animal!'

He was across the room and out through the door before Perdita had a chance to reply. She hurried after him.

As she emerged from the house she saw Sophie clap her hands to her mouth in amazement. All the others had turned to look at her. Kip's face was bleak with disappointment.

'Oh, Sir Richard,' Sophie gasped, 'it can't be!'

Richard's face wore the gentle expression it often had when he was talking to Sophie. He said, 'I wanted to give you a present before I left. I thought Falcon would be more to your taste than jewels.'

'Falcon! Oh, Sir Richard!' Sophie was laughing in disbelief.

Alice had barely spoken since the ball struck her jawbone, since any movement was painful, but in her agitation the discomfort was forgotten. 'Whatever are you thinking of, Richard? That horse is quite unsuitable for a woman.' The words emerged cloudy and indistinct.

Kip agreed eagerly. 'You're right, Mother, but I could manage him well enough.'

'This is Sophie's horse or no one's,' said Richard. 'The girl is far more likely to crack her bones on one of your broken-winded nags. Falcon will take good care of her, I promise. Well, Sophie, don't you want to try him out?'

'Oh, Sir Richard!'

'Stop repeating yourself, girl. Just ride him.'

She shook her head, still incredulous, then walked over to the dappled stallion. He arched his neck and greeted her cautiously as she ran her hand across his shoulder. His muscles rippled like grey silk. Adam crouched down, made a stirrup of his hands and Sophie sprang up into the saddle – a lady's saddle this time.

'Sophie, for mercy's sake, be careful,' mouthed Alice.

Sophie did not reply. It was clear that she had not heard, that she was oblivious to the crowd of onlookers, oblivious to everything except the grace and beauty of the stallion. She touched his mane and neck with her hands, shifted slightly in the saddle and then, with an invisible nudge of the reins, urged him gently forward.

Stephen had come round to the front of the house. 'Whose is that?' he asked.

Kip said bitterly, 'Sir Richard has given it to Sophie.'

Stephen glanced at Richard, who was dismounting stiffly. 'That's a remarkable animal,' he said.

'You'll not find a better horse this side of the Tamar,' said Richard. 'Your niece deserves only the best.'

'I know,' said Stephen quietly. 'But I thought I was the only person who did. Well done, Richard.'

Sophie had entered the near field and was cantering in a slow circle. When she returned to the silent group of onlookers, her cheeks were glowing. 'Oh, Sir Richard!'

'Please, Sophie, not again.'

'I never thanked you.'

'There's no need. Just take good care of him and enjoy yourself.'

'Falcon. I will. You know I will.'

Kip caught hold of the bridle and looked up at his sister. 'Let me try him now.'

'Of course.'

Sophie was about to slide down when Richard held up his hand. 'No, Sophie, that's not allowed. Falcon is your horse and yours alone. No one else is to ride him, not the grooms, not even Kip. He would easily be ruined with rough handling.'

'Oh, but—'

'That's not fair!' Kip burst out.

'Fairness be damned. Your sister has more than earned her reward while you've thought of nothing but your own pleasures. When I hear good reports of you from Captain Boulter, then I might reconsider.'

'What use will that be when I'm cooped up on some stinking ship?'

'Be careful how you talk about the *Fearless*. That stinking ship is the jewel in my fleet. No need for you to argue with me either, Sophie. It's a waste of time. You are the only one allowed to ride Falcon, do I have your word? Good. Now, take him for a proper airing and the two of you can get better acquainted.'

Sophie smiled her thanks and set off down the drive. As he watched her departing back, Kip's face was a picture of discontent and envy. Louisa's expression was exactly similar. For once, the two youngest Suttons were united in outrage at their sister's preferential treatment.

Perdita had some sympathy with them – or with Kip, at least. She was delighted to see Louisa's spiteful nose put out of joint. But, like them, she was piqued that her father had made such a show of singling out Sophie for praise and attention, when she so desperately wanted all the admiration for herself. She began to hope that the dancing, dappled stallion might prove too much for his rider and that Sophie would return muddy and humiliated. But then she checked herself. It was not true: she did not want that at all. Anyone else, and she would have been more than ready to hate them for their good fortune, but for some reason it was impossible to resent Sophie. To her surprise she found she was glad that her father had given Falcon to Sophie, even though they were sure to eclipse her and Nimble if they ever rode out together.

Feeling suddenly light-hearted, Perdita crossed to where her father was standing with Stephen and Alice.

Mistress Sutton was still grumbling painfully. 'Another stallion, Richard. It will cause nothing but trouble in the stables. It is sure to be vicious and unmanageable. And Sophie will be distracted from her work. It'll be a seven-day wonder and then we'll just be left with the feed bills and the farrier. As if we didn't have enough to consider already.'

Richard did not bother to answer. He watched with satisfaction as the pale shape that was Sophie and Falcon disappeared between the long lines of trees.

Stephen said, 'That's the best sight I've seen in a long time.' There was pride and affection in his voice.

And Perdita silently agreed.

Chapter Thirteen

Two visits to Trecarne in less than a week, and they could not have been more different. The first occasion had been in mist and drizzle; the second was sunny with a clean wind blowing from the south-east. Primroses and celandines, the paler yellow scattered among the bright, grew thickly along their way.

Three days before, Perdita had had only Cullen for company. Now she was part of a lively group, with servants to attend them. At their head Sophie rode the speckled Falcon; the stallion stepped out as graceful as a shadow and Sophie's happiness was so intense that all were affected by it. Kip's easy-going nature had reasserted itself: he had forgotten his approaching exile, forgiven Sophie her good fortune and was attempting to lay bets with Adam the groom on Falcon's chances in an open race with the Menheires' best horse, Charger.

Perdita was resplendent in her favourite gown of tawny red paragon and her velvet cloak with the fur trim. Her hair had been dressed with more than usual attention, her gloves perfumed and her leather shoes carefully oiled. There was no chance that anyone would notice the slightest resemblance between the unfortunate creature trudging barefoot to Trecarne three days before and the grand young lady mounted on her elegant chestnut mare.

Only Francis was impervious to the general air of good-humour. He did not like to leave his delicate wife, nor his even more delicate account books, but Alice had insisted. 'I am not at all happy about this visit,' she told him that morning. 'God knows, we suffered enough from Colonel Menheire when he sat on the County Committee. I do not see why we must now regard him as our friend. Keep an eye on matters for me. Make sure he does not find out some new way to do us harm.'

Francis felt bowed down by a familiar weight of responsibility: once again it was up to him to keep disaster at bay – but precisely what disaster, or how he was to hold out against it, he had not been told, so as usual he had no idea how to act for the best.

Perdita, with her instinct for the anxieties of others, was aware of his discomfort, though she could only guess at the reason for it. She had ridden beside him from time to time on the journey from Rossmere and had done what she could to raise his spirits. Although it was obvious that Francis did not wield much power in his own home, he was still the titular head of his household and therefore an ally worth cultivating. As they rode along a wide, stony track, Nimble missed her footing and stumbled. Instinctively Perdita reached for the nearest fixed point to catch hold of, which happened to be Francis's plump knee. Nimble recovered, Perdita righted herself and turned to apologise to Francis. He was regarding her as if he was just waking up, and covered his confusion by demanding to know if she was unhurt. She pretended not to notice his exaggerated reaction, and assured him that she was quite recovered, but she stored away this incident for future reference.

As they passed the point where she had looked down on Trecarne with her father, and where she and Cullen had left the horses, Perdita felt a quickening of excitement. There was to be no barefoot skulking through the woods today. They followed the wide road that swept round in an arc with the shimmering sea on one side and the broad façade of Trecarne, more beautiful than ever in the spring sunshine, on the other. Her father's house.

Elated, she turned to Francis. He, in contrast, was a study in foreboding. Beads of sweat glistened on his broad forehead and he looked as if he were riding towards the gallows, not on a social visit to a neighbour.

She said, 'You are so brave to be visiting the Menheires today, Sir Francis. There is nothing I admire half so much as a man who can offer forgiveness to an old enemy. It demonstrates true greatness of spirit and generosity. Such rare gifts.'

'Oh, really, you are too kind . . . but all the same . . .' Briefly Francis allowed himself to bask in her praise. His face cleared, like sunshine after rain.

When they came to a halt at the front of the house, he hastened to dismount so that he could assist Perdita from her horse before the grooms reached them. He grasped her hand firmly as she jumped down from the saddle and looked at her with obvious admiration. She congratulated herself that whatever misgivings he might have had about receiving a child of scandal into his respectable home had now been all forgotten.

The next moment she had forgotten all about him. Kip bounded up the broad steps to the front door, which was opened by a liveried servant, and Perdita followed eagerly. As soon as she entered the building, she felt as though she was entering another world. Despite the gloom of the massive hallway, there was a sense of space and height and great beauty. Her eyes quickly became accustomed to the dimness and she made out a wide staircase sweeping upward in a smooth curve, and high above their heads a domed ceiling tricked out with intricate plaster decorations. But the tightness in her chest, the flutterings of excitement beneath her ribs, had nothing to do with the magnificence of the building. She drew in deep breaths of air and wondered what the cause might be.

The servants took their outdoor clothes and withdrew silently. The Rossmere party were left alone. Uncertain what to do next, they moved randomly around the shadowed hall.

'Are they expecting us, do you think?' asked Francis, perspiring freely once again.

'I feel as if I'm being watched,' said Sophie.

'And so you are,' Kip told her. He went to stand beneath the enormous portrait that dominated the space: a man who bore a definite resemblance to Edmund Menheire had been painted in full Parliamentary armour, a painting of sombre black and brown, with only the pale face and the uncompromising glare of the eyes shining clear through the gloom. Kip struck a pose similar to that in the portrait, but exaggerated and pompous. Then he squinted and twisted his features into a mocking gargoyle.

'Oh, Kip, stop it!' exclaimed Sophie, but she was laughing.

'Death to King Charles!' said the gargoyle Kip, just as a side door opened and Edmund Menheire came in.

They smothered their smiles and hid their embarrassment as best they could, but Edmund did not appear to notice. With a brief nod in the direction of the others, he said at once to Sophie, 'Mistress Sutton, I'm sure you must be tired after your long ride. I have ordered refreshments. Unfortunately my father is suffering with a headache. He hopes to be well enough to receive you later.'

He led them into a large, high chamber. Like the hall, this room was as murky as a tomb: the windows were covered by dark hangings, which blocked out all the light.

'My father, Colonel Menheire, is much afflicted with headaches,' he explained. 'This spring sunshine is torment for him.'

Edmund made these statements as though they were matters of public interest, without any trace of emotion. His voice seemed tuned to address subordinates or large outdoor gatherings. At this first mention of Colonel Menheire, Francis and Kip exchanged uneasy glances. For as long as they could remember, his name had been spoken with dread and their mother had frequently wished him into an early grave. There was an awkward silence. It was impossible for any of the Suttons to express their true feelings, nor were they skilled in the art of hypocrisy.

Perdita, however, had no such inhibitions. She said smoothly, 'An ailing parent is such a worry. I do hope your father is soon returned to full health.'

For the first time Edmund looked at her. It was not a comfortable experience. Never before had she had such a sense of being weighed up – almost literally. She would have sworn that at the end of his appraisal of her Edmund must have a shrewd idea as to her weight, size, age and the value of her costume, but nothing else. He then turned to Sophie and said, 'My father wishes particularly to make your acquaintance, Mistress Sutton.'

For once in her life, Sophie was at a loss for words and another awkward silence fell on the group. In the stillness they could hear Falcon whinnying to the Trecarne mares as he was led round to the back of the house.

164

Kip looked about him. 'Where is Piers?' he asked.

'He is detained,' said Edmund curtly. 'He will join us by and by.' He gestured to a servant to ladle wine into glasses for his guests, then watched with satisfaction, and no further attempt at conversation, while this was done.

Still smarting from her host's rudeness, Perdita took her glass and went to stand beside one of the tall windows. She drew back the curtain slightly and a shaft of light sliced the gloom. Outside she could see formal gardens with geometric beds edged in low box hedging, and beyond that the wide sweep of the valley leading down to the rocky shoreline and the sea. All at once Edmund's slight was forgotten and the strange sensation that had possessed her when she entered the house returned: she would be content to remain in that same place all day.

Francis had interpreted his mother's instructions as meaning that he must remain as guard dog near his sister. Kip, though, had no such mission, and he wandered over to join Perdita. He soon grew bored with looking at the view and said, 'Sixpence says the old man will not be well enough to see us.'

'You advised me never to bet unless I knew the odds.'

'Threepence, then.'

She smiled. 'No.'

'A penny? Ah, heaven be praised, here's Piers.' Kip turned with relief to his friend. At once the atmosphere was transformed. Piers performed the simple actions necessary to make his guests feel welcome that his cousin had either not bothered with or not known were necessary, and all the while Kip was talking excitedly about Falcon and his hopes for a race. 'You've never seen such an animal, Piers. I lay odds he can beat Charger over any length you choose.'

'A race, eh?' Piers looked delighted at the idea. 'I'm warning you, Kip, there's not a horse in Cornwall has beaten Charger yet.'

'Half a guinea says you're wrong. How about it?'

Piers laughed. 'Wait, wait. How can I bet when I've not even seen him? The way you talk he must have wings at least.'

'Falcon doesn't need wings. He goes like the wind anyway. Why don't I show him to you right away?'

'All in good time. I have certain promises to keep first.'

'Promises?'

Kip's face was a picture of incomprehension as Piers turned to Perdita. 'Mistress Treveryan,' he began solemnly, 'I believe I owe you a tour of the house.'

'A tour?' blurted Kip. 'Whatever for?'

But already Piers was crossing the room and pulling back the heavy curtains.

Edmund, who had been conversing with Sophie, called out angrily, 'What are you up to, Piers? You know my father cannot bear strong light.'

'The knowledge, dear cousin, is etched on my heart. But unless you have concealed the Colonel under a footstool I assure you the light will do him no harm. Not while he remains in another room. And I am unable to display the beauties of your home in pitch darkness. There, Mistress Treveryan. How do you like it?'

'The room is very fine.'

'Indeed it is. I am told this house was built by a gentleman of excellent good taste. Would you like to see more?'

'I'd like nothing better.'

'Perhaps we can persuade Sir Francis to join us. Edmund appears determined to keep Mistress Sutton all to himself. And, Kip, I know you have no interest in architecture or paintings whatsoever but it's high time you learned to distinguish a linenfold panel from a linen chest.' Piers spoke always in a light-hearted, bantering tone, as though he had not a care in the world.

Kip scuffed his boots and said, 'I wish you'd come to see Falcon.'

'All in good time, Kip.'

Gloomily, Kip followed them.

As far as Perdita was concerned, the tour of the house could not be long enough. Each room seemed to her more beautiful than the one before it, and she was proud to think her father had created a building of such magnificence. She considered it a shame that the Menheires had not furnished it with such sensitivity, and as they passed from one chamber to another, she mentally supplied the defects, adding a Bruges tapestry or half a dozen Turkey rugs to fill the gaps.

They were in a charming, circular room at the foot of the old tower, with windows looking out at the sea in front and the woods behind, when a servant came and told Piers that the Colonel was now ready to see his guests.

Kip's gloom increased, Piers pulled a rueful face, Francis looked more wretched than ever. Perdita alone was undaunted. Having wormed her way into the reluctant affections of Kitty's father when she was a child, she expected Colonel Menheire to be a comparatively easy challenge. Besides, it meant they would be able to see the long gallery, which she understood to be the crowning glory of the house.

It stretched the whole length of the building between the two towers and, like the rooms on the lower floor, it was heavily curtained. As they entered they could make out a seated figure visible in the light from a turf fire at the far end. A manservant stood sentry behind the chair and Edmund and Sophie were already ranged before him. No one spoke as they walked over polished wood, their footsteps ringing out in the stillness.

It was hard at first to recognise the soldier figure from the portrait in this elderly man sitting huddled beneath furs. This Colonel Menheire wore a velvet cap, his skin was translucent and stretched tight over the contours of his skull. But there was a light in his eyes, yellow and rheumy though they were, that was undimmed. The light of a born fighter.

Piers said briskly, 'Here are our guests, Uncle. I see you've already met Mistress Sophie. This is her brother, Sir Francis –' at this, Francis made a bow, so stiff and unyielding he might have been made of stone – 'and his brother, Kip.'

'Kip? Kip? What sort of name is Kip?'

'His name is Richard, Uncle, but everyone always calls him Kip.'

'Why? Why fool around with a good name? I've no time for that nonsense. If you were christened Richard then Richard is what you're called. Isn't that right, boy?'

Kip looked puzzled. 'I suppose so, Colonel Menheire.'

'Suppose so? What's the good of supposing? Either a thing is true or it is not true. No supposing about it. Am I right, eh? Of course I am. Richard is a worthy Christian name. Kip is a name fit only for a dog. And you're not a dog, are you, boy?'

'Well, of course not, Colonel Menheire.'

'And how about you, Sir Francis? Are you managing that place at Rossmere any better than that idle father of yours, eh?'

Francis was perspiring freely, but Perdita was no longer watching, nor did she hear his stammered response. As her eyes became accustomed to the dim light in the long gallery, she noticed some words carved in the mantel over the fireplace. A massive length of oak, its only decoration was two lines of lettering cut deep in the wood. She read the words with a shock of recognition. She moved closer, to be sure, and read them over again.

Nullus domus tales umquam contexit amores
Nullus amor talis coniunxit foedere amantes

Words carved on a new headstone in the far corner of a churchyard by the sea. The epitaph for a woman she had never known.

'What is it?' Piers had come to stand beside her, close enough to speak without being overheard.

Perdita glanced at the Colonel, but he was wholly absorbed in grilling the unfortunate Francis about farming techniques and the numbers employed on the demesne farm at Rossmere. She said, 'Why is there an epitaph carved on the mantelpiece?'

'I believe it was always there. And, besides, it is not an epitaph. They are lines from a poem by Catullus.'

'My Latin is not so good. Can you tell me what they say?'

'Translating loosely, let me see . . . "No other house was ever home to lovers such as these," ' he spoke quietly, so as not to be overheard, and his voice softened as he continued, ' "No other lovers were ever joined in such a bond." Fine sentiments, don't you think? Whoever put them there must have been a person of great feeling.'

'But that is beautiful. I never imagined . . .' She blinked back unexpected tears. 'You said the inscription has always been there?'

'So I believe.'

She said, 'My father had those words inscribed on my mother's headstone. I didn't know what they meant, but . . .'

Piers nodded. 'He must have had it put there when the house was built. I remember hearing the older servants talk of your mother when I first came here. They described her with great affection – but, then, I am sure you know all about that.'

She shook her head, then reached out and touched the words with her fingertips. She imagined her mother, a woman who, in her mind, had no particular face, sitting in front of this very fire on a winter evening, Richard Treveryan at her side. *No other house* . . . She felt as if she was close to something, but she had no idea what that something might be. It could not possibly be her mother, since the woman known as Margaret Hollar had died when she herself was little more than a baby. And after her humiliation in the back room of the Mitre Inn, she no longer believed in ghosts.

At length she said, 'I had no idea . . . It is beautiful.'

'Catullus was a fine poet,' said Piers. He was scanning her face intently, but for once Perdita did not notice.

'Whispering? What's this?' It was the Colonel's voice, raised and rasping. 'Haven't I taught you better manners than that, Piers?'

Piers turned to the old man. 'I did not want to disturb your conversation, sir.'

'Don't do it again. I'll have no whispering in corners. If you have anything to say then speak it out loud and plain. Like a man, eh?'

'Yes, Uncle.'

Slowly the Colonel's gaze fastened on Perdita. He looked at her closely. Perdita knew she should drop her eyes respectfully, but for some reason she found she could not. She held his look steadily.

'And who is this overdressed miss you've been tittle-tattling with?'

'This is Mistress Perdita Treveryan, Uncle.'

Perdita dropped him an elegant curtsy.

An expression of cold relish crept over his face. 'Mistress Perdita Treveryan, eh? Would that be the daughter of Sir Richard Treveryan?'

'That's right, Uncle.'

Colonel Menheire glanced briefly at Piers. 'Go and fetch my

green drops, Piers. Barnes forgot to bring them earlier. Go on, then, hurry up. I should have had them at noon.' When Piers, with only a brief hesitation, had strode from the room, Colonel Menheire turned once again to Perdita and said, 'But you are not the child of his lawful wife, are you, madam? Sir Richard's pretty bastard, that's who you are, isn't that right?' There was an astonished silence. The Colonel continued, 'Call a thing by its proper name, that's always been my belief. And the child of a whore is a bastard, isn't that right?'

Now Perdita understood why Piers had been sent from the room. The Colonel must have known that he alone would have defended her. Kip did not seem even to have heard what was said: at the first opportunity he had moved away from the group by the fireside and was attempting to make one of the young deerhounds sit to command. Francis was incapable of speech.

At length Sophie said calmly, 'Perdita is our guest at Rossmere, Colonel Menheire.'

'More fools you, in that case,' said the Colonel. 'Your father would never have stood for it, you can be sure of that.'

Perdita was so startled by the suddenness of Colonel Menheire's attack that she was briefly winded and could not think what to say.

'Well, then,' he continued, still with relish, 'you haven't much to say for yourself, have you, for all that you're dressed up like some Bartholomew's Fair trollop? Did you know that in New England they manage these matters better than we do here? They cut the noses off adulteresses, and an excellent thing too, in my opinion. At least they still know right from wrong. What do you think of that, then, eh?'

There was a horrified silence. The viciousness of Colonel Menheire's attack seemed to have deprived everyone of speech. Francis cleared his throat and shifted his weight from one foot to the other. Sophie took a step towards Perdita, as though to protect her. Kip pretended to be wholly absorbed in the dog.

Perdita felt utterly alone. She realised there was no one who could defend her, not even Sophie. Instinctively she glanced at the words carved over the fireplace. She had the sensation of floating. She said coldly, 'I am grateful to you for the information, sir. Tell me, what punishment is meted out in that enlightened country to foul-mouthed old men who break all the rules of hospitality and courtesy?'

Another, longer silence.

Colonel Menheire's smile faded as he stared back at her. 'What did you say, girl?'

'I am sure you heard me perfectly well. You are not deaf, though it would be better were you mute.' Perdita was aware of all eyes watching her now. Watching her, and waiting. The manservant, Barnes, was leering at her with glee. No doubt he had witnessed his employer's viciousness many times before and was enjoying the contest.

'How – how dare you speak to me like that in my own home, you brazen female?'

'Oh, so it is permissible for you to be as rude as you please, but no one is supposed to answer in kind, is that it?'

The Colonel was gasping. 'I've never heard such impudence, never!'

'The more's the pity.' Now it was Perdita's turn to observe him with contempt. 'It's a shame it has to be the daughter of a whore, as you so elegantly call my natural mother, who has to be your teacher.'

This time the silence seemed unending. All eyes were fixed on Perdita, so only she observed that Colonel Menheire was fighting for the breath to speak. His thin fingers scratched at his chest. She said coolly, 'I believe the Colonel wishes to say something. Let us hope he is trying to apologise. I dare say it is his own guilty conscience has caused this fit.'

'My drops,' he wheezed. 'Where's the boy got to with my drops?'

Running footsteps echoed down the long gallery. Since everyone else still seemed deprived of speech, Perdita said calmly to Piers, 'Master Menheire, your uncle is in urgent need of his medicine. I believe he must be suffering an excess of bile and choler. He would do well to control his temper in future.'

Piers looked at her in surprise, then stooped over the old man to administer the precious drops. Perdita had a sudden urge to knock them from his hand and let the Colonel perish for want of them. Instead, she reached out and touched the lettering above the mantelpiece briefly with her fingertips. She was aware that

Piers, having tended Colonel Menheire, was about to ask her what she meant, but she avoided him altogether and swept haughtily away, glad of the long gallery's protective gloom.

Their retreat from Trecarne was swift and confused. Amos and Adam had been just settling down to a jar of ale and a gossip with the Menheires' servants when they were roused unceremoniously and told they must get the horses ready to leave at once.

Francis flapped and fussed and blamed himself for the catastrophe. 'But what could I have done?' he kept asking anyone who would listen.

Sophie was concerned only for Perdita, who brushed her sympathy away angrily. Perdita was too proud to let anyone see how bruised she had been by the old man's attack.

They had ridden almost to the boundary of the Trecarne land when they heard horses' hoofs on the turf behind them. Piers was galloping to catch up with them.

'I'd almost given you up,' said Kip. 'Look, Piers, look at Falcon. Isn't he even better than I told you?'

Piers ignored his young friend and drew alongside Perdita. 'Mistress Treveryan,' he said at once, 'I wish to apologise to you for my uncle's outspoken behaviour. It was most unfortunate.'

'That is not the word I would have used to describe it,' said Perdita.

'My only consolation was that it gave you an opportunity to demonstrate your skills in debate.'

'Believe me, sir, it was an opportunity I could have done without.'

'I trust it has not soured your opinion of Trecarne.'

There was genuine sympathy in his voice. Perdita felt herself close to tears. She fought them back. She was not going to give any of the Menheires the satisfaction of seeing she had been hurt. She said coldly, 'I do not hold the house responsible for the bad manners of its inhabitants.'

'Then I hope that you will visit it again.'

'Oh, yes, I shall visit this place again.'

She did not elaborate. She could not have said just then why she was so sure that this was not to be her last visit to the house her father had built, and despite her bravado, she felt flayed to the bone by the Colonel's vicious attack, hurt, angry and confused.

But when Piers had bade them farewell and ridden back down the hill, she could not resist turning for one last look at Trecarne. She vowed to herself that one day she would return, one day she would be received there with all the honour due to a lady of rank and fortune, one day she would bury the memory of this present humiliation and see the Menheires grovelling at her feet. At that moment, this was the best and only consolation she could imagine.

Chapter Fourteen

The soft smell of spring was in the air.

It was her last evening at Rossmere and Perdita had strolled with Sophie to the near field where Falcon was grazing with a couple of the Rossmere geldings. Despite the differences between them, Sophie and Perdita enjoyed each other's company, and it was Sophie whom Perdita was going to miss most when she left. They lingered a while by the gate, admiring the beautiful stallion as the sun sank below the western hill.

'Poor Kip,' said Sophie. 'He's going to miss all this.'

'You never know,' said Perdita, 'he might take to life on ship like a duck to water and never come home again.'

'Not Kip. He'll be back as soon as he can. He'd be miserable anywhere but here.'

'Could you ever be happy away from Rossmere?'

Sophie smiled. 'Your father surely doesn't have any plans to send me off to sea as well.'

'None that he's told me yet.'

'Then where would I go?'

To Perdita's amazement Sophie's question was innocent of artifice. 'To Trecarne, of course. If Edmund Menheire was to ask you . . .'

'He never would.'

'But just suppose he did.'

Sophie considered the question carefully. She looked around her, at the horses contentedly grazing in the meadow, at the buildings that had always been her home, bronzed by the dying light.

At length she said, 'When my father was injured at Lansdown Hill, his first thought was to come home. He died on the journey. Some plants thrive only in their native soil.'

Perdita was wondering what it must be like to be as deeply rooted in a place as Sophie and her family were at Rossmere. She asked, 'Then do you mean never to marry?'

'I don't think about it. I'm needed here and I'm content, and that is enough.'

'Aren't you afraid of dying an old maid?'

Sophie burst out laughing. 'How desperate you make it sound!'

'Then you don't care for Edmund Menheire?'

'He's an admirable man, I'm sure . . .' Her sentence trailed into silence, more eloquent for what it omitted.

Perdita said firmly, 'I think he is a man any woman could be proud to care for.'

'Really?' Sophie looked at her curiously. 'I would have said it was his cousin who had caught your eye.'

'Piers? He is of no consequence.'

'Because he has no fortune?'

Perdita smiled. 'I never admire a man unless he has at least the prospect of wealth.'

'Cary says the servants at Trecarne all speak highly of him.'

'How is Cary so well informed about the Menheires?'

'You know how servants gossip. She is friendly with the Menheires' dairymaid and they get together in Porthew whenever they can. I'm sure the dairymaid knows every detail of our lives here.'

Perdita had long been puzzled by the Suttons' fearsome cook, who held a place in the family unlike that of any servant Kitty had ever employed.

'How did Cary come to work here?' she asked, as they turned and began strolling back to the house.

'Have you not heard the story? Her husband was an Irishman who fought with Uncle Stephen during the late wars. The Irish were all captured by the Parliament soldiers after Naseby. They were imprisoned and dying without food or water. Cary claims that she was responsible for helping them escape – aided, of course, by the Grey Lady.'

'That ghost she was talking about the other night?'

'That's right.'

'And do you believe her?' asked Perdita.

'I don't know. When it's dark outside and the wind is blowing down the chimney and she tells us the story, then I do. On an afternoon like this it's not so easy to believe in ghosts. Sometimes I think Uncle Stephen knows more about it than he lets on. Kip and I believe he had a sweetheart in Tilsbury – it's the look in his eyes when Cary tells her stories. But he never talks about it himself.'

Perdita tried to imagine the serious, self-contained Stephen Sutton as the hero of a romance: to her surprise it was not difficult at all. She said, 'What about Cary's husband? Did he go back to Ireland?'

'No. It's so sad, you mustn't say anything about it in front of her. He was one of those brave men who joined with Captain Penruddock when he tried to raise a rebellion in Cornwall against Protector Cromwell. He left her one night – he wouldn't say where he was going – and he never came back. It was weeks before she heard any news. First she heard he had been killed, then that he was injured, not killed at all. Then, just as her hopes were raised, she got word he'd been sentenced to go in chains to Barbados – and that's near as good as dying. She set off at once to Plymouth to try to see him – Uncle Stephen went with her – but they were too late. The ship had already sailed. She's heard nothing since. So many men die on the journey out, and life is so harsh on the plantations that no one ever returns. But she always says it is the not knowing that is hardest to bear.'

'My father has ships that sometimes go to Barbados. Maybe he could find out for her.' Perdita had only a vague idea of the size of Barbados, but Sophie shook her head.

'It's cruel to raise her hopes for nothing. Uncle Stephen has tried many times, but he's never heard anything. Apparently it is so terrible there that even supposing he managed the crossing he's unlikely to have survived more than a few months. We are all the family Cary and Het have now.'

They had reached the house. Perdita and Sophie paused to look back at the trees and meadows that surrounded Rossmere. Surveying that tranquil scene of fresh greens and sun-flushed sky, it was hard to imagine a tropic hell where men were starved and worked to death in a matter of months.

'I hope Kip will be all right,' said Sophie suddenly.

The same thought had been in Perdita's mind.

In pensive silence, they went into the shadowy coolness of the house.

It was still too early for the candles to be lit. Sophie threw a couple of logs on the kitchen fire and the flames leaped up. Cary's daughter, Het, sat on a little joint stool near the hearth and watched the sparks dance upwards in the blackness. 'The hounds are chasing the hare,' she said. It was an age-old belief: the first spark – and there was always one that led the rest – was the hare, and all the rest were the hounds.

Sophie said, 'But they'll never catch her.'

'Why is the hare always a her?' asked Perdita.

'I don't know,' said Sophie, and then she smiled. 'Maybe because she always gets away. Would you like a hot posset, Het, before you go to bed?'

Het nodded vigorously, but Cary, coming in from the dairy and wiping her hands on an old clout, said fiercely, 'You'll spoil that child, Mistress Sophie. She's already had her supper.'

'Children are meant for spoiling,' said Sophie, as she fetched the milk to be warmed. 'Will you tell us a story, Cary? It's Perdita's last evening. And Kip's,' she added, more sadly.

'That depends on Master Kip. Where's he got to anyway?'

The general opinion was that he had been out rabbiting with a couple of friends and was now in the stables, spending a few last precious minutes with horses and dogs.

There was a strange atmosphere in the large kitchen on that final evening of Perdita's visit. Alice and Francis had left Rossmere at midday to see a Helston lawyer. Sir Richard had accompanied them and had insisted that Stephen go as well. With all the older members of the household absent, there was an unusual air of informality that might, under different circumstances, have led to singing and merry-making. But the knowledge of Kip's approaching exile cast a shadow that had affected everyone, family and servants alike, and no one was in the mood to be merry. His three older brothers had all left home, one by one, when they were younger than Kip, but their departure had never caused this sombre mood. Kip was the spoiled darling of the household and the void he left behind him would be impossible to fill.

Louisa wandered in, her arms full of shifts to be mended. 'Will you tell us a story, Cary?' she asked. 'Kip's leaving tomorrow.'

Even Honor had come to join the sombre group by the kitchen fire. 'Do tell us a story,' she coaxed. 'No one tells them quite like you, Cary.'

'You've heard them all a hundred times before,' scoffed Cary, but it was evident that she loved the ritual of persuasion.

'Perdita hasn't,' said Honor. For once she was almost animated. 'And just think of poor Kip. He won't hear a proper Cary story for months and months. Maybe even years.'

'Just as well. He'll have better ways to fill his time,' said Cary, settling herself in the large chair in front of the fire and filling a pipe with tobacco. When she smiled, as she did now, the damaged skin above her eyebrows puckered alarmingly.

'Tell us how you took the secret message past the enemy soldiers and then blew up their ammunition wagon,' said Sophie, handing Het a mug of warmed milk.

'And lost all my looks into the bargain.'

'But gained a father for me,' said Het.

'Well . . . yes . . .' Cary was thoughtful, then she said, 'We'll leave it to Master Kip. It's his decision.' She was growing annoyed that Kip was choosing to spend these last moments at Rossmere away from her little fiefdom in the kitchen.

'Where *is* Kip?'

Just as the question was being repeated, Kip himself appeared at the back door. His clothes were muddy, his hair was tousled and half a dozen rabbits were strung over his shoulder. At once a clamour of female voices were raised insisting that he persuade Cary to tell a particular story. 'All in good time,' he said, with a grin, dropping one shoulder to let the rabbits fall in a pile on the bench. He crossed the room to where Perdita was seated beside the fire. 'Perdita,' he told her, 'there's someone outside who wishes to have a word with you.'

'Who is it?'

He shrugged. 'See for yourself.' But as Perdita rose and began to cross the room to the back door she heard Sophie repeat the question. Kip stooped, whispered a few words in his sister's ear and she threw Perdita a troubled glance, but Perdita was already going out into the stableyard, and never saw the other girl's expression.

It was as she had expected. He was standing, loose-limbed and waiting, in the shadows by the horse trough. Some instinct had told her she would see the fiddle-playing stranger again before she left Rossmere.

'Good evening, Mistress Perdita,' he said, as she approached. 'I trust you are in good health.'

'Excellent, thank you.'

'I'm glad to hear it. Shall we walk a little way? Somewhere we'll not be overheard.'

'I'll fetch a lantern.'

'There's no need for that.' He caught her lightly by the arm. 'The moon will be rising shortly and it's only two days off the full.'

'A moonlit stroll, sir? When I do not even know your name?'

'Surely someone has told you by now.'

'I have not asked. I wanted to hear it from you.'

'That is one of the reasons for this visit.'

'Only one of them?'

He nodded, and Perdita felt a quickening of excitement. There was a bantering familiarity in his manner that had been absent at their first two meetings. As if he were an old friend . . . but no. Never with an old friend had she felt this thrill of apprehension.

'How do I know I can trust you?' she asked lightly.

He touched his hand to the wide brim of his hat and said, with a small bow, 'Mistress Perdita, you should know by now you cannot trust me at all. Shall we walk?'

He linked his arm through hers, and they went slowly away from the stables and down the grassy path that led towards the mews – or towards the sheds that had been the mews in the days when hawks were still kept at Rossmere, but which was now a store for animal food and farm tools. There was a flutter of wings above their heads as the doves returned to their roosts.

'Well, then,' asked Perdita, 'will you tell me now?'

'When I am ready.'

'You are very secretive. You're not Rumpelstiltskin, are you?'

She saw his shadowy smile in the dusk. 'I'm taller than that angry little fellow by a yard at least. Or had you not noticed?'

'Oh, I've noticed everything about you. Now, stick to your promise and tell me who you are.'

'First there is something I want from you.'

'From me? But that is scandalous! You've already had my money and my earrings and—'

'Hush, hush. Don't be angry with me, little Perdita. That was a fair exchange. How else would you have ever heard the truth about your mother?'

'If it *was* the truth. And you were certainly wrong to speak so badly of my father.'

'That was just my way of telling the tale. A story is always more vivid when it is coloured by strong opinions.'

'Anyone hereabouts could have told me as much.'

'But they did not. Besides, no one knew your mother as well as I did.'

'How can that be?'

'I'm coming to that.' They had reached the farthest extent of the grassy path; from here the way grew brambly and uneven and they halted. Perdita was not quite sure how it had happened, but as he turned to face her he put his hands on her waist. Yet it seemed an altogether natural thing to be so close to him, as though there was a bond between them that she could not have explained to anyone but that he understood too, perhaps even better than she. As her eyes grew accustomed to the fading light she let her body lean slightly towards his and looked up at him. His face was strange, but she no longer detected any cruelty in it.

'Tell me,' he said, and the pressure of his hands about her waist increased slightly, 'why is your father helping the Suttons with their debts?'

It was not at all what she had been expecting. She drew back, but he did not release her. Nor, in truth, did she want him to. 'Is he?' she asked. 'I did not know.'

'Can you think why he might do such a thing?'

'Perhaps because he wants to help them,' she said, not really thinking about it much. She was wondering what it would feel like if he were to adjust his position so that they were touching. 'Nicolas Sutton was his greatest friend.'

'If that was all . . .'

'Why this interest in the Suttons' affairs?'

'Everyone around here takes an interest in their affairs, and there are many who wish to see their ruin.'

'Ruin?'

He nodded. 'When an important family falters it creates a void. Some will certainly be ruined with them, others may profit. No one can remain unaffected.'

'I never knew their problems were so great.'

'Their debts are too large ever to be paid off. Your father's interference only delays the inevitable. The time is coming when they are sure to lose Rossmere.'

Perdita shuddered at the certainty behind his words. She tried to tell herself to be on her guard, that this was probably just another of his tricks, but for once she was finding it difficult to think clearly. Her breathing had become rapid and shallow. She said, 'Then that must be the answer to your question. He has acted from friendship.'

'Treveryan does not know what friendship is,' he said swiftly. 'He must expect to gain something for himself.'

'That only goes to show how little you know him. He *does* want to help. That is why he has found Kip a place on one of his ships.'

'So that the young fool will be transformed miraculously into a worthy husband for you?'

'How do you know so much?'

'It is my business to know these things.' His tone was still teasing, but Perdita felt an edge of danger. His hands, circling her waist almost touched each other, fingertips to fingertips. He asked lightly, 'How would you like to be married to a boy like Kip?'

'I will do as my father chooses. But I would rather—'

'Yes?'

'It does not matter.'

'You would rather be married to Edmund Menheire and be mistress of Trecarne. Is that it?'

Perdita sprang back, freeing herself in an instant. 'I've never told a living soul! I've hardly even thought it! You must have—'

'Magic powers? There's no need. It was merely a guess and, by the look of you, it was an accurate one. Don't be angry, there's no shame in your ambition. If I had been humiliated as you were when you visited Trecarne, then I dare say I'd want to return in triumph. You and I are much alike.'

'Who told you about the Colonel?'

'As I said, I make it my business to be informed.'

'He is a vicious old man. Did your spies also tell you that I was more than a match for the old fool?'

'They say you were a tigress. Nearly drove the rogue to a seizure. But don't waste your anger on him. His sickness is terminal and he'll not be in this world much longer to trouble us.'

Perdita absorbed this, then looked up at him slyly. 'If you know so much, have you also heard about my first visit to Trecarne?'

'You were taken there as a baby. Viney and Dorcas took you, if that is what you mean.'

Perdita was relieved. 'So there are some things you do not know.' She had begun to think this mysterious man must really have the gift of second sight.

'What other first visit do you mean?'

'I might tell you one day. If I choose.'

He smiled. Perdita could see his expression quite clearly now because the moon had risen behind her: his face almost handsome, after all. He raised his hand and gently brushed a strand of hair off her forehead. A tremor ran from the back of her neck right down to her feet.

From the region of the house and the stableyard came the sound of horses whinnying to each other in greeting, dogs barking with excitement.

'Sir Francis must have returned,' he said. 'I did not expect them back so soon. Time for me to be off before I overstay my welcome.'

'Wait . . . you promised . . .'

'Of course I did. Here.' He put his arms around her shoulders and drew her towards him, almost as if he meant to kiss her. Instead he turned his face slightly and whispered into her ear, so that it tickled, 'My name is Luke. Luke Hollar.'

'But Hollar was my mother's name. Are you a cousin, then?'

'I'm closer kin than that.' And this time he did kiss her, very lightly, his lips grazing the surface of her cheek.

'How can you be closer than a cousin?' Perdita was shivering so much her teeth were chattering. 'I do not understand.'

He drew her to him and held her tightly. 'Don't be frightened, I will explain it all—'

Then there was a rush of movement and a roar of sound. Luke released her and stepped backwards with a cry of pain. Perdita screamed as a dark figure half fell from his horse and knocked Luke to the ground. Horses' hoofs and running footsteps and a clamour of voices – at once the little space beside the mews was full of people and horses and dogs and the two men fighting in their midst.

'Adam! Viney! Hold him down!' It was her father, struggling to free his arm so he could strike Luke with the stock of his whip.

Someone had brought a lantern, and in its yellow light Perdita watched in horror as her father's servants ran forward to prevent Luke from defending himself. The older man had had the initial advantage of surprise, but Luke's youth and vigour would soon have gained the upper hand had not Adam and Viney – but mostly Adam – fallen upon him and stopped him from retaliating. Richard Treveryan brought the whip down with all his strength. Luke's arms were pinned beside him, so he could not even protect his face; his knees buckled and he fell to the ground.

'Sir Richard, no! You're killing him!' Sophie had flung herself against him and seized his right arm with both her hands. He thrust her off in a fury and kicked his victim in the ribs and shoulder.

'Let that be a lesson to you to leave my daughter alone!' His voice was thick with rage and he raised the whip once more.

This time it was Stephen who restrained him. 'That's enough, Richard. That's punishment enough.'

Taking their cue from the warning in his voice, Viney and

Adam released their hold of Luke. He rolled over, drew his knees up towards his chest, coughed and spat out blood. Sophie dropped to her knees beside him. She reached out and touched the blood that was pouring from a gash on his forehead.

'Why?' Perdita was shaking so much it was difficult to speak. 'Why?' It was all she could say.

Luke raised himself on one elbow. His other hand covered his ribs. Seeing that he was about to speak, Richard tried to get to him but Stephen, his muscles hardened by long days spent working in the fields, was stronger by far and held him back.

'Your father doesn't want you to know your own flesh and blood,' gasped Luke. 'Isn't that right, Sir Richard?'

'Quiet, or I'll kill you!'

'Why?' Luke looked up at him with pure hatred. 'Can I not speak with my own sister?'

'*What?*'

'It's true, Perdita.' Luke's lips were bruised and swollen, but still his words were distinct enough. 'Everyone here knows, everyone but you. Margaret Hollar was my mother too. You and I are . . .' The effort of speaking was too much for him. As he spoke the words, '. . . brother and sister,' his strength gave way. His supporting arm crumpled beneath him, but just then Sophie reached out and caught hold of him tenderly.

The last thing Perdita remembered seeing was Sophie, her hair golden in the pool of lamplight and her expression wondering, as she cradled Luke's battered and bloody head in her arms.

PART TWO

———•———

Sophie
September 1661

Chapter Fifteen

There was going to be a fine apple harvest at Rossmere this autumn. Sophie tilted her head to gaze up through the branches to the blue sky beyond. Two small birds were hopping nervily from one twig to the next and the air hummed with the drone of greedy wasps. She cupped one of the large, sap green fruits in her palm and twisted it gently, but it did not come away. A couple of weeks yet before this tree, a favourite for cider-making, was ready to be harvested.

She picked up a withy basket full of small yellow apples and walked back through the lush weeds of the orchard. She could feel the sun's warmth through her shift and the sharp prickles of sweat under her arms. As she crossed the stableyard the doves who had been strutting and pecking among the cobbles lumbered into the air and floated round in a wide curve before breaking like a crest of foam on the stable roof, their white feathers brilliant in the September sunshine. From the front of the house came the noise of hammering. After years of neglect, the roof was at last being replaced.

She went up the back steps into the kitchen and set the basket down on a trestle table near the door. She took out one of the apples, smoothing its soft film of powdery grey with the ball of her thumb. These early apples, small and yellow and smelling of a frosty morning, were best stored and eaten around Christmas time. Yellow Jacks, they were called at Rossmere.

But it was not thoughts of apples that preoccupied her.

'Sophie, wake up. Here's a letter for you.'

Lost in thought she had not noticed Francis, who was making

one of his rare appearances in the kitchen wing of the house. There was ink on the middle finger of his right hand and a familiar pucker of anxiety on his forehead.

'For me?'

Sophie smoothed her hands on her apron before taking the folded sheet of paper. A letter for anyone at Rossmere was a rare event, and to be enjoyed with due reverence. She pulled out a bench and sat down at the table, pushing the basket to one side. 'Maybe it is from Kip.'

'Or a gallant suitor.' Francis smiled tentatively as he sat down opposite her. Only with the elder of his two sisters did he occasionally hazard a clumsy humour.

Sophie broke the seal and unfolded the letter. 'Neither,' she said. 'It is from Perdita.'

'What does she say?'

'She is still in Plymouth with her mother and she hopes we are in good health,' said Sophie, reading slowly and with great concentration. 'She sends her best wishes to you and our mother, she has not seen Kip since he came back from Bordeaux but she expects a visit from him when the *Fearless* is next in port . . . la-di-da . . . The gist of it is that she hopes to accompany her father when he visits here later in the month.' She looked up. 'I did not know Sir Richard was coming back so soon.'

Francis glanced behind him to make sure they could not be overheard, but for once the kitchen was empty. 'He will need to be here when the interest is due at Michaelmas.'

'Can he not send a bill of exchange?'

'He said in the spring that he wanted to handle it himself.'

'And? What is it, Francis?' Sophie reached across the table and placed her hand on his. 'You look so anxious. Sir Richard has promised he will come and deal with the money. Why are you still worried?'

'He may change his mind.'

'Surely not.'

Francis shifted his ample thighs on the bench and glanced behind once more. 'I fear he will lose patience with us altogether.'

'But why?'

'Well, for one thing, I don't believe he knows anything about this new loan Mother has secured to pay for the roof. I know the work was necessary, but it is going to end up costing nearly two hundred pounds and she refuses to tell anyone who she has borrowed the money from. She is so sure of Sir Richard's help that our debts have grown yet larger, just when we might have begun to pay them off. In many ways our situation is now more precarious than ever. If some accident befalls Sir Richard, or he changes his mind for any reason, then . . .'

'Then?'

'Well, I do not like to think . . .'

'Francis, tell me, truthfully, how bad would our position be?'

'Well . . .'

'So bad that we might lose Rossmere?'

He dropped his eyes but did not answer.

'As bad as that,' said Sophie thoughtfully, and then she burst out, 'Poor Francis, it's not fair. You worry about it night and day, and then Mother takes out a fresh loan without consulting you at all. But just think of all the times when our situation has been desperate in the past and we've managed somehow. I'm sure it will work out again.'

He gazed at her. On his face she could see hope battling against certainty. She felt a surge of compassion for him, her kindly, cautious, struggling older brother.

'Try not to worry so much,' she told him gently.

For a moment neither spoke. From the yard came the cooing of the doves, the splash of water as a bucket was dipped in the horse trough, Amos grumbling at the dogs. They were both remembering the first few months after their father's death, when their mother had been so distracted by the horror of her position that all the care of the household, the younger children and the demesne farm had fallen to Sophie and Francis, then eleven and twelve.

He squeezed her hand and said, 'When I talk to you, Sophie, I almost believe we'll be all right. I couldn't manage at all without you.'

She smiled.

'I know,' she said.

★　　★　　★

Honor had been searching for Francis everywhere. She had been resting on her bed after lunch when she heard the lad from Porthew clatter up to the house on his little pony and call out that there was a letter. It might be for her, she thought eagerly, though in truth no one wrote her letters any more, not since her old aunt in St Ives had died the previous winter – and she had only ever written once.

She pulled a shawl around her shoulders and nestled her feet into soft slippers. Despite the warm September sunshine she had been feeling shivery since mid-morning and she feared she might be coming down with a chill. Or maybe something worse still. It was vital to take precautions against such perils. No one else understood what a terrible battle she fought against every kind of ailment. Even now, as she struggled to rise, she felt as though her bones had turned to gruel. Instinctively she hugged her arms: they felt so thin, so pitifully thin. Why did no one take better care of her?

By the time she had searched for Francis in his office, in all the rooms at the front of the house where he was usually to be found and had crossed the kitchen courtyard, she had a stabbing pain in her upper chest that was causing her serious alarm.

She stepped into the silent kitchen and there he was. Lord be praised, she had found him. He was seated at a rough table at the far side of the room, near the back door. The room was filled with the mellow scent of apples. Speckled shafts of sunlight slanted in through the high windows, touching his hair – and Sophie's too – with gold. Brother and sister were wrapped in a web of intimacy so profound it had no need for words.

Honor experienced the first tremors of fever as her initial relief gave way to something altogether more sinister. In a jumbled way she remembered the rumours she had overheard in the spring: people had whispered that Sir Richard Treveryan's great rage against Master Hollar had been because he had discovered the scoundrel paying court to his own sister. And now here was her own husband . . . Oh, vile, unnatural thought! She was finding it hard to draw breath.

Sophie smiled as she caught sight of her sister-in-law. 'Honor, what brings you here?'

The distance across the slate floor seemed huge as Honor waded through the sunlight and laid her trembling hand on Francis's shoulder. 'Oh, my dear, I could not find you.'

'I was just here.'

'Yes.'

He did not let his eyes meet hers. He was patient and he was kind, but Honor sensed at once the way he withdrew into himself as she approached. There had been a time when his whole face lit up at the sight of her. No more.

The pain in her upper chest intensified.

By now, she and Francis should have been united by ties closer than ever brother and sister could enjoy. In their marriage bed, that crewel-work-shrouded four-poster where she spent long, lonely hours of sickness, they should have found their deepest union. It was her own cowardice that prevented it. But maybe Francis no longer regarded her as a wife; maybe he no longer found her desirable.

Too terrible to contemplate.

Timidly her fingers stole across the shoulder of his worsted jacket and touched the pale flesh at the back of his neck. She raised her hand to smooth his brown hair. Francis leaned forward, evading her, and reached for an apple.

'Yellow Jacks,' he said. 'My favourites.'

Sophie noticed his evasion. She saw, too, the way Honor flinched and drew back her hand and the hurt that showed in her pale eyes. She was often exasperated by her sister-in-law but, still, she was dismayed by Francis's coldness. All the girl needed, in Sophie's opinion, was some tenderness, and then a baby or two to care for, and her health was sure to be marvellously improved. But it was beginning to look as if poor Honor was unable to conceive: more than three years married and still no sign of pregnancy. Plenty of men cooled towards their wives at the first hint of barrenness. Sophie hated to think her brother might be one of them.

She stood up. 'Perdita has sent me a letter, Honor. You may read it if you wish.' And to Francis she said, 'These apples need wrapping before I put them in store. Do you have any old papers I can use?'

'I'll find some for you. And I'll tell Uncle Stephen about your letter. It shows Sir Richard will be here at the end of the month. Do you know where Uncle Stephen is?'

Sophie was picking bits of leaf and twig off the apples. She said vaguely, 'I think perhaps he had to go to Porthew.'

'Porthew?' Cary had just trudged in through the back door. She was carrying two pails of water which she set down noisily. 'Captain Sutton's gone to Polcreath, I reckon. He had that look in his eye all morning.'

'Polcreath Farm?' asked Honor. 'What business does he have there?'

'Oh . . . well . . . Something for the farm, I expect.' Francis and Sophie glanced at each other over the basket of apples and each smothered a smile. Both were shy of telling Honor the real purpose of their uncle's occasional visits to Widow Firth at Polcreath.

'Farm business?' asked Cary derisively, and then she said, 'Oats, more likely!' and she burst out with a roar of laughter.

A couple of scruffy chickens had wandered in through the door, but Biddy Firth was so absorbed in her litany of woes that she did not notice.

'Tod's a good lad, really,' she told her visitor. 'He means well, but sometimes he forgets and he must have left the lower gate open. Or, at least, not fastened it securely. Lord knows how long the cows had been in there. It can't have been more than an hour or two but they'd tramped it down good and proper. Not that it wasn't a pitiful crop beforehand – the far side hardly grew at all and the rest was all spoiled with thistle and charlock. But, still, it's enough to break your heart to see so much barley all trampled into the ground.'

'I looked at it on the way over,' said Stephen. 'Most of it can be saved.'

'I wish I thought so.' Biddy Firth was not given to optimism. 'Maybe if it's not left too long. Can you spare me a couple of men to give us a hand? If the rain holds off and it isn't all ruined by the wet.'

'I'll help you myself,' said Stephen. 'A small field like that won't take so long.'

'Tod's not very good with a scythe and the pain in my shoulders is so bad, these days, I have to stop all the time.'

'You work like a Trojan.'

Biddy was not sure what a Trojan was but she smiled anyway, pleased with the promise of help. Her face was so lined by work and weather that when she smiled, which was not often, her mouth and eyes vanished in deep creases. Sometimes she reminded Stephen of a little monkey he had seen on a sailor's shoulder in Porthew, but he was careful never to mention this. She might have liked the comparison less than Trojans.

'Well, then, Captain Sutton, if you've finished your ale we can go upstairs. The boy won't be back for a while yet.'

Stephen nodded and rose from his chair.

She led the way up the narrow stairs, so steep and roughly put together they were little more than a ladder. One end of the loft room over the kitchen was used as a store: coils of rope, a neat pile of sacks and a couple of unwashed fleeces. At the other end a bed had been built into the span of the roof.

Biddy straightened the counterpane with a housewifely gesture. She loosened her skirts and let them fall to the ground, shrugged off her bodice and pulled her shift over her head before turning back, quite naked, to Stephen. 'Lord, what a time you take,' she said.

He placed his hands on her bare hips and drew her towards him. Her skin was white and soft, all but her face and neck and hands. He stooped slightly and kissed the pale flesh just above her breasts, but she turned deftly aside.

'None of that foolishness,' she told him.

'Just a kiss?'

'All right, then. Just one.'

She stood perfectly still while he kissed her on the mouth, then she moved away and climbed on to the bed and sat there, large and white and brown-tipped like an exotic starfish, waiting for him.

In the beginning he had been puzzled by her manner. She was so comfortable with their nakedness, but so dismissive of any signs of tenderness or caress. Now he was used to it.

When he, too, stood naked before her – and he was as pale and brown-tipped as she was, though he did not know it, having no mirror – she lay back and wriggled a little lower on the bed to receive him.

'That's better, Captain Sutton,' she said, as he entered her, 'oh, yes, that's much better.'

Her pleasure flared up at once, as if all the time she had been busy with her work on the farm she had been waiting only for when he came to her. She gripped his shoulder-blades and moved under him with fierce joy. Her eyes were shut tight, then all of a sudden she cried out and released him at once. His climax followed hers. He let out a groan and rested his cheek against hers.

Biddy raised her head to peer at him, then, when she was sure that he was still, she moved briskly away.

'That's that, then, Captain Sutton,' she said, as she swung her legs off the bed and wiped herself with her shift. 'Would you like a bite to eat before you go? I don't need to fetch the cows yet a while. We could walk down to Parc Grous together, take a look at that swelling on Maidy's leg. I can't seem to put it right no how.'

Stephen clasped his hands behind his head and watched her as she padded around the little loft room, chattering and expecting no reply. However intense her pleasure, she seemed always to have forgotten it the instant their coupling ceased. There were obvious advantages for him in this arrangement, and it was simpler to ignore the residue of disappointment he was always left with.

He followed her down the stairs, refused the hard lumps of bread and cheese she was offering and then, just before he left, placed a couple of coins on the cup shelf. She swept them off at once and put them in a small jug where her son was not likely to find them.

'You're welcome any time, Captain Sutton,' she said. 'You know that.'

He nodded. Seven years ago, when Biddy's husband died from a mysterious sickness, Stephen had visited Polcreath to offer the family's condolences. Old Tod Firth had been a tenant, and his father before him, but as well as the legal niceties Stephen was willing to help the widow if he could. He learned that she meant to keep the farm on and work it with her son Tod, who was somewhat feeble-minded but able to do a good day's work if given clear instructions. He discovered also that her husband had not contributed much to the running of the farm in recent years and she was well able to manage without him. There were, however, some aspects of husbandly activity that she was missing intensely and those, having misjudged the real reason for Stephen's visit, she invited Stephen to supply. Which he had done from time to time ever since. He listened to her woes, which were unending, and helped occasionally with the farm work and the animals. And she was always pleased to see him.

When they had examined Maidy's leg, Biddy said, 'I saw those men again last week. Down by the spring, they were. It must have been well past midnight.'

'Smugglers, do you think?'

'What would smugglers be doing in a place like this?'

'Poachers, then?'

'Maybe so.'

'If you recognise any of them, let me know.'

'I thought perhaps they had buried something, the ground was all dug over. But Tod and I dug through all of it the next day.'

'And?'

'Nothing, more's the pity. I wouldn't mind turning up a few hogsheads of wine. Or even some decent tobacco.'

Stephen pondered the mystery of Biddy's nocturnal visitors as he walked back towards Rossmere, then forgot about it. The moment he crossed the stream and saw the clustered roofs of his home ahead, all the familiar preoccupations crowded back into his mind.

Just before Richard left in the spring he had insisted that Stephen be included in family discussions. Francis had silently welcomed his uncle's help, but Alice had accepted with bad grace and Stephen himself sometimes wished he were back in his previous state of comparative ignorance. For years he had toiled unceasingly on the farm to provide a livelihood for his brother's family. This past few months he had worked just as hard, but now he had to drive himself to do so: he knew that, no matter how hard he worked, the situation was doomed to worsen with each year that passed. The stark truth was that too many farms had been sold off; the rents from the few that remained – smallholdings like Biddy Firth's, for instance – were too small to support an establishment like Rossmere.

Richard's help with the interest on the loans had offered a chink of hope, which Alice had extinguished by borrowing yet more money to repair the roof. When Stephen and Francis had protested, she told them she was not prepared to lose her home to weather and decay, not yet. Besides, the slates had already been purchased, the money spent. Francis was unable to stand up to her, and Stephen had no right to.

The only consequence of their protest was that she refused to tell them how much she had borrowed, the rate of interest, or who the lender was. She was convinced that not only would Richard continue helping them indefinitely, but that he would use his influence with the King to ensure a favourable response to her new petition for recompense for all her family's losses during the late wars. She had spent much of the summer drafting and redrafting her loyal petitions. She was sure the royal heart would be moved to action, but Stephen feared that her petition was just one among thousands. He knew he must consider how best to help his nephews and nieces if the unthinkable happened and they lost Rossmere.

As he walked down the grassy track that led from the old mews to the stableyard, he saw Sophie going towards Falcon's field. He changed course, and followed her.

Though Stephen had always tried to treat all his brother's children the same, it was Sophie who had his heart. When he considered the catastrophe waiting to befall the entire family, it was her he worried for most.

She had fed Falcon two small apples and was leaning against the gate, her chin resting on her forearms as she contemplated the stallion. Her eyes were filled with the dreamy, faraway expression which had, during the summer months, become increasingly familiar.

'Sophie?'

She turned to him with a sleepy smile. 'Uncle Stephen, I did not hear you coming.'

'What were you thinking of?'

'Oh, this and that . . . nothing, really.'

'You're as poor a liar as I am.' Stephen smiled.

'Look at Falcon. Isn't he beautiful?'

'Are you going to ride him now?'

'Later. When the flies are less troublesome.'

'Perhaps I should have asked you *who* you were thinking about.'

Sophie rubbed her chin thoughtfully against her knuckles. 'What makes you say that?'

'You've changed.'

'I'll never change.'

'I think I began to notice it around the time Treveryan was here.'

'You never used to be so inquisitive, Uncle Stephen.'

He accepted the rebuke. 'There was never any need before now. When Edmund Menheire visited last week I had the distinct impression he was sounding me out. I thought it best to encourage him.'

Her reaction was not at all what he had been expecting. 'Edmund?' Her nose wrinkled with obvious displeasure.

'You must have realised the reason for his visits.'

'Surely it is natural for neighbouring families to be on friendly terms.'

'Either you are blind or too modest for your own good. My guess is that Edmund will ask you to marry him. He let me know his father has no objection.'

She said, 'I could never marry Edmund.'

'Try to think of yourself for once, Sophie,' said Stephen gently. 'I know you've always been content to stay here and help your family, but the present situation . . . may change.'

'How?'

'I will be honest with you, but please don't repeat this to Louisa or any of the servants. It might be that in spite of all our efforts we have to leave Rossmere.'

'So . . .' She let out a long sigh. 'It is true, then. I thought it was just Francis being Francis and worrying, but if you say so too . . . Do you really think it will happen?'

'I hope to God it does not, but it is certainly a possibility. Yes.'

She was frowning. 'If that happens, then Francis and Mother and everyone will need me more than ever. How can I abandon them just when their need is greatest?'

'You would not be abandoning them. Just imagine, if you were mistress of a fine house like Trecarne, you'd be in a better position to help them. Louisa and your mother might be able to live there with you. At the very least it would be one less person to worry about.'

'I had not thought of it like that.'

'I only mentioned it now because I thought you maybe cared for Edmund. I did not want you to turn him down simply from a misplaced loyalty to your family.'

'No. I would not turn him down because of that.' She was still frowning, all the same.

'You could be very happy with him.'

She hesitated, then said, 'Maybe our situation is not so desperate. Maybe our fortunes will improve next year.'

'Maybe.'

There was silence for a while. Then Sophie asked, 'What about you, Uncle Stephen?'

'Oh, I shall manage somehow. There are plenty of places I could go.'

'No, I meant, have you ever been in love?'

Instinctively he stiffened. 'Why do you ask?'

'I *am* asking,' she said, with a smile. 'Never mind the why. Tell me, then, have you?'

'It was a long time ago.'

'During the wars?'

'Yes.'

'So you were far from here?'

'Yes.'

'Why did you not stay with her?'

'It was not possible.'

'Because?'

'Sophie, you must not ask.'

'Is that why you have never married?'

'I suppose so.'

'Did Cary know the woman?'

'No more questions. Why this sudden interest?'

'Because you never talk about yourself at all.'

'I'm not very interesting.'

'That's where you're wrong. And now, the very last question and the hardest one of all: do you love her still?'

All unaware of what he was doing, Stephen began to smile, a smile of pleasure that sprang from a hidden source. In his mind's eye he could see a woman's face, darkly beautiful and suffused with pain and strength and a desperate, hopeful love. The image blurred, grew faint, yet despite the aching void deep inside him, he still smiled, with happiness at what had once been.

'I don't know how to answer that one, Sophie,' he told her quietly.

She placed light fingers on his sleeve and smiled. 'There's no need to, Uncle Stephen. You already did.'

Chapter Sixteen

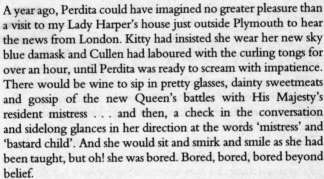

A year ago, Perdita could have imagined no greater pleasure than a visit to my Lady Harper's house just outside Plymouth to hear the news from London. Kitty had insisted she wear her new sky blue damask and Cullen had laboured with the curling tongs for over an hour, until Perdita was ready to scream with impatience. There would be wine to sip in pretty glasses, dainty sweetmeats and gossip of the new Queen's battles with His Majesty's resident mistress . . . and then, a check in the conversation and sidelong glances in her direction at the words 'mistress' and 'bastard child'. And she would sit and smirk and smile as she had been taught, but oh! she was bored. Bored, bored, bored beyond belief.

Kitty, Lady Treveryan, sat opposite her in the coach as they rattled over the cobbled streets past St Andrew's church towards the Old Town Gate. Every inch of her costume was encrusted with embroidery and semi-precious stones, like a rock all covered in barnacles and molluscs. Perdita wondered only that she could remain upright under such a weight of ornamentation.

'Well, miss,' said Kitty tartly, 'are you going to give me a civil reply?'

Perdita was startled out of her reverie. 'Of course, Mother.'

'And?' Kitty's little face was as unyielding as the whalebone busk in her bodice.

Perdita looked out of the window. There had been a question, obviously, but she had not noticed it. A couple of labourers sprang out of their way as the coach bowled along the narrow street.

'If you would only pay attention for once!' shrilled Kitty.

'I will try, Mother.'

But there was no need. Kitty had forgotten her question too, swept away on a strong tide of complaint that was likely to keep her fully occupied until they were disgorged on the gravel forecourt of Lady Harper's elegant mansion.

Through a gap between an alehouse and a chandler's shop, Perdita caught sight of buff sails and a gallant three-masted ship. She twisted her head to keep it in view. Yes, it was the *Fearless*, Master Boulter's ship, leaving Catwater to sail out past St Nicolas Island on a brisk south-westerly to Oporto and beyond. Gulls swarmed around the masthead. Perdita felt a tug of something that might well have been envy. The *Fearless* was her father's ship, and Kip was sailing with her.

She sank back against the hard leather seat and thought of the young man who had dined with them only two nights before. Veteran already of two voyages to La Rochelle and Bordeaux, Kip had changed since he had travelled with her and her father to Plymouth in April. Gone was the soft roundness of jaw and cheek, gone too the bland contentment in his brown eyes. This Kip was grown leaner and harder, as was to be expected after six months as a sailor.

More disturbing, Perdita thought, was his shifting vigilance: she saw how he slid a glance at her father when he thought no one was watching, his eyes never settling for long but flickering swiftly away. He was unable to look at Treveryan directly when they spoke and avoided talking to Perdita altogether. He seemed to find refuge in Kitty's piercing torrent of words, since with her nothing was required of him. As Perdita watched his abject discomfort she had a sense that the easy-going hunter of Rossmere, the youth with whom she had played endless games of backgammon, slam and merels in the spring, had become one of the hunted, watchful and uncertain.

During the meal he evaded all Richard's questions.

'How was the crossing to La Rochelle?'

'I believe it was rough, they called it a swell.'

'Did you take your turn on watch?'

'It was not . . . required.'

Kip stared at his plate and pushed the venison from side to side with his knife.

Kitty, with unintentional tact, launched herself into the gap in the conversation with a detailed account of why the flesh of roe deer was preferable to that of fallow at this season. Richard was observing the youth with obvious exasperation.

At last the truth came out. Perdita, intending to offer Kip the chance of some more neutral topic, asked mildly, 'And is the food on ship as bad as everyone says?'

'I . . . I suppose so.'

'You must have an opinion,' her father pointed out.

'Well . . . yes.'

There was a silence. Suddenly Kip looked up from his plate and threw a furious look at Richard before saying, 'I cannot eat on board.'

'Why ever not?'

'I am sick all the time. I can take no food or drink at all.'

Richard laughed, but not unkindly. 'Everyone is queasy to begin with. It's nothing to be ashamed of. You'll get used to it soon enough.'

Kip pushed his food away, barely touched. 'Yes, sir.'

Afterwards Perdita suggested a game of crib and allowed him to win three times in a row, but the stench of misery clung to him like a miasma, which not even winning could shift. Once or twice she thought she detected him cheating, a thing he had never done before.

When he had left and was on his way back to the *Fearless*, Perdita said to her father, 'Maybe Kip is not suited to life at sea. What then?'

'Kip does not yet believe he is suited to any existence save that of a gentleman's idle son. Master Boulter is a fair captain. He'll make a sailor of the lad.'

Perdita hoped he was right. Seeing Kip had reminded her of how much she too was missing Rossmere, more than she had ever expected. When she and her father had left Cornwall in the beginning of April she had never expected to go back, still less that she would want to. During her visit she had been exposed to the disapproval of Alice and Francis, though both had softened towards her by the end. Louisa had never missed a chance to put her down, and on the few occasions when Perdita went to Porthew she had been alert to the echoes of old scandal on people's faces when they saw her pass. Still, she could have overcome all of that, she could even have hardened herself against Colonel Menheire's attack, for then at least she had the satisfaction of knowing she had made a spirited defence.

It was the final evening, the discovery that the mysterious fiddler was Luke Hollar, that he was her own brother and that everyone had known this but her – that was what had made her glad to leave and want never to return. She had left Luke being cared for by Sophie – though as she had been careful to keep him out of Sir Richard's sight it had been easy for Perdita to avoid him also.

Perdita's feelings of horror and revulsion had clung to her all through the journey back to Plymouth.

She could not accept that Luke was her brother. She had two brothers already, Kitty's sons Nicolas and Ralph, now both at university with their books and their tutor and their father's warnings ringing in their ears. Those boys she had known always. She remembered standing on tiptoe and gripping the sides of the crib so she might peep in and examine their pearly pink baby faces. She remembered holding out her hands when each made his first wobbling steps, her envy and pride as first one, then the other, was breeched. She remembered squabbles and rivalry and teasing and the times when they drove her to distraction and she wished one or both of them dead, and other times when she watched out eagerly for their return because she longed for company again. Brothers were a nuisance and familiar. Luke Hollar was altogether different.

And yet, as her anger and shock subsided, she gradually acknowledged that there had been something different about him from the beginning. He must have known, of course, when he first set eyes on her as she rode under the covered way that led to the Mitre Inn. He had known, and he had used that knowledge to swindle her out of money and jewellery and make a fool of her. Yet even then her anger had not lasted long, almost as if she had known that this first encounter had been just an opening skirmish between them.

What disturbed her most was not Luke's actions, despicable though these were, but her own unguarded response. Even now, she could feel the press of his hands around her waist, the teasing trace of his lips against her cheek.

At the time she had hardly been aware of it, but on that last evening with him all the lessons she had learned from Kitty about the dignity and proper behaviour of young ladies had begun to unravel. She sensed that he was inviting her to flirt with danger, to take a risk – and her body had accepted that challenge. She knew not just that he had kissed her, but that she had been inviting that kiss.

For the first time in her life she had allowed herself to follow her instincts and be ruled by her heart – and the consequence had come close to disaster. It was a lesson she was not likely to forget.

She was not sorry that her father had beaten Luke like a common scoundrel: it was only what he had deserved. Next time they met, she would find it easy to maintain a proper distance.

She did not doubt they would meet again: it must be so. It was one of the reasons why she was so determined to return to that remote, south-western tip of Cornwall.

That, and the urge to see Trecarne again.

She thought nearly every day of the fine house her father had built at Trecarne. Its beauty and the pain of her humiliation there had become entangled in her mind: no other place she had ever seen had affected her so profoundly.

Had she been a young woman of more fanciful nature, she might have thought she had gained the strength to counter the Colonel's attack from the lingering spirit of her natural mother in that gloomy, velvet-shrouded house. As it was, she consoled herself by imagining her triumphant return to the house where she had been treated so rudely.

There was a faint possibility that Edmund Menheire, heir to Trecarne, might be persuaded to shift his devotion from Sophie to herself. Perdita was too much of a realist to think this a likely outcome and she had no intention of pinning all her ambitions of one fragile possibility, but there was no harm in having a goal. If her heart had led her to Luke and disaster, then from now on she would be ruled solely by her head. And her head might well lead her to Trecarne.

How she itched to take command of that magnificent house, to pull back the dark swathes of fabric shadowing every room and let in the light and air . . . and if the loathsome old Colonel suffered headaches as a result, then so much the better.

'I cannot imagine what is so amusing, Perdita.' Kitty's voice pierced her thoughts. 'I would have hoped for more respect from you, but since you came back from Cornwall you think you know best about everything.'

'I'm sorry, Mother.'

'Oh, don't bother about me,' said Kitty, adopting a martyred air. 'Here we are at Lady Harper's. Just make sure you don't inflict that supercilious smile on her or I don't know what she'll think.'

'Yes, Mother. I mean, no, Mother.'

'Be a lady, Perdita. Remember all I've taught you.'

'Yes, Mother.'

And she did try. She showed interest in the London tittle-tattle, though it varied hardly at all from the gossip she had heard in town during the previous winter. She feigned laughter at Lady Harper's pitiful jokes and made a fuss of her two disgusting lap-dogs. She marvelled at the little black boy whom Lady Harper had recently been given by her husband and who looked enchanting in his silver waistcoat and lace and elaborate turban, apart from something lost and empty in his eyes – even when he laughed – which reminded her, surprisingly, of Kip.

At last Kitty announced it was time to leave and Perdita's performance was nearly over. A message was sent to the coach-man, the carriage duly creaked and rattled over the gravel, they were handed in and Kitty's dissection of the afternoon com-menced, a breathless monologue that, with any luck, would keep her occupied until they reached home once more.

Perdita was surprised at how impatient she was with Kitty these days. She blamed her weeks at Rossmere. When she had heard the vacuous gossip with Lady Harper, she found herself yearning to be settled instead in the comfortable informality of the kitchen at Rossmere while Stephen and Cary filled their pipes with tobacco and everyone clamoured for a tale of the Grey Lady. And when Kitty worked herself into a frenzy of indecision over two different varieties of Brussels lace, Perdita's thoughts flew to Sophie – Sophie in her old gown of threadbare worsted. She remembered how she had gathered her skirts between her legs and stuck her petticoats out behind her like a tail on Apollo's rump, so she could gallop over the yellow moorland and be free . . .

As they rattled down the hill and came within sight of Sutton Pool, with Catwater and the Sound beyond, Perdita pushed up the blind on the window and searched the wide expanse of blue, but among all the traffic of ferries and barges and fishing boats, and the fine big ships that plied back and forth to the Americas, there was no sign of the *Fearless*. Out of sight of land. She imagined Kip vomiting and miserable, and she fervently hoped that he found his sea legs soon. Maybe that hazy point of darkness near the horizon was–

Perdita was so startled that her head jerked upwards and she struck her cheek against the window's edge. 'Mother, stop the coach!'

'What's the matter?'

'I must get out. Quick, tell the coachman – Oh, never mind, I'll do it myself.' And she poked her head through the window and banged against the side and shouted to the coachman.

Pandemonium. The man roared at his horses, the carriage creaked and swayed more than ever, harness jingled while all the time Kitty was squawking like a ship's parrot and demanding to know why and what, and telling Perdita to stay where she was or—

'I cannot, Mother. I must get out.' Perdita laid her hand briefly on Kitty's jewel-studded fingers in a pointless gesture of reassurance. 'I – I feel sick. I have to walk. I'll be home before you know it. Please don't worry.'

She pushed open the carriage door and jumped down.

'Your shoes!' shrieked Kitty.

Too late.

'They'll be ruined – oh! Watch where you're going!'

Her mother's protests were drowned in the hubbub of voices all around, coopers hammering, mariners and beggars and poorly dressed women, and two shepherds driving half a dozen sheep down towards the harbour.

Perdita hitched up her sky blue skirts, dodged these obstacles as best she could and ran back to where she had glimpsed a familiar face that ought by now to have been far away to sea.

Yes, there he was, hurrying down a side street that led to the huddled homes and taverns where the sailors congregated.

And she had been right. It was Kip.

Perdita was so intent on keeping him in view that she barely noticed where she was going. Some instinct warned her to watch Kip, and not to make herself known right away. He looked like a man who was walking with a purpose and she was curious to know what that was. Only when she saw him enter a low doorway under a sign with a crudely painted animal on it did she slow down enough to notice that she, too, was being followed.

At the same time she realised she had strayed far from the sort of streets usually frequented by persons of quality. She was at the entrance to an alley so narrow that if she stretched out her arms she could almost touch both walls with her fingertips, and the upper storeys crowded out the sky. Sunshine never penetrated this dank corner, the walls were slippery with damp and the ground underfoot was filthy. The stench was overpowering. Two gaunt children sat in an open doorway and watched her with hungry eyes.

She shivered. The footsteps that had been following her while she walked had stopped as hers had. She forced herself to look behind her.

Relief turned to annoyance. Kitty's footboy, a lad not much older than she was, stood some little distance away, observing her. 'What are you doing here?' she demanded.

He moved forward and assumed a pose of false humility. 'The mistress told me to see you came to no harm.'

'Did she, indeed? Then I am ordering you to go away and leave me in peace.'

'I cannot do that.'

'Cannot?'

'Orders is orders.'

'Would threepence be sufficient to change your mind?'

'Maybe.'

'Very well. Go and wait for me at the end of the street where we stopped. Next to the stocks. If I am not there by sunset you may raise the alarm and I'll see you do not get into any trouble. I need to be left in peace for a short while.'

'I think I understand you,' he said, with an ill-concealed leer. He must have seen she was following Kip, and assumed it was an assignation.

'You don't understand at all, but never mind that now. Off you go.'

When he had touched his cap and slouched away down the long street, Perdita realised that their conversation had drawn an audience. Several faces peered down at her from open windows. A woman's rough voice called down, 'Lost your sweetheart, my lady?'

Laughter reverberated between the steep sides of the alley. The two children leaned forward, eager to touch her dress.

Perdita picked her way carefully over the foul-smelling muck of the street and walked firmly up to the entrance where she had seen Kip go in. She pushed open the door.

There had been little enough light in the street outside, but here it was as dark as an underground burrow. And silent too: as she stepped inside all the hubbub of talk and laughter had ceased. Blinking, she looked around her. Through the fug of pipe tobacco she could make out many eyes, gazing back at her intently. About a dozen men were ranged about the walls on rough benches, some with tankards in their hands, and all staring at her in amazement.

She looked around once more, just to be sure. Over a dozen men, but not one was Kip.

She said, 'I'm looking for Master Richard Sutton. Kip. I saw him come in here.'

No one spoke. They continued to stare at her.

She said again, 'I know he came in here,' though even as she spoke she began to wonder if she had mistaken the door.

A lean-faced man said, 'Kip? I'll be your Kip if you like.'

Her eyes were smarting from the smoke and she was on the verge of leaving. But then she heard a cheer, followed by the piercing screech of a rooster. It was coming from the other side of a door at the back, a door so smoke-blackened that she had not noticed it before.

She moved towards the far door, bumping against the corner of a low table as she did so, but the lean-faced fellow intercepted her. 'You don't want to go through there,' he told her.

'Out of my way!' she snapped. She lifted the latch and pushed the door open.

There must have been about thirty people, men and boys and a handful of eager-looking women. They were crowded into the tiny space behind the alehouse, an area small and dark as the bottom of a well. It was a moment or two before Perdita could make out what they were doing, but then there was a screech and two fighting cocks rose up in the air in a flurry of feathers and blood, spurs thrust forward for the kill. There was a roar of encouragement from the onlookers, which grew louder as the battle intensified. Everyone was jostling to see the birds as they tore at each other with increasing frenzy, their savage talons drawing blood at every blow.

Suddenly it was over. A mangled carcass was swung high in the air, its neck broken and the wings covered in blood though the body continued to twitch convulsively. The victor was seized by its triumphant owner. That was when Perdita caught sight of Kip among the throng. He was laughing, red-faced and excited, just as she remembered him from countless games of chance at Rossmere. She could tell at once that his money had been on the winning bird.

But then his eyes met hers, and all the merriment drained out of his face. He looked horrified, and afraid.

'Kip!' she called out. 'What are you doing?' She started to push her way through the jostling crowd of spectators but a man's hand caught her by the arm. She assumed it was the lean-faced fellow who had tried to hinder her in the alehouse. 'Let go of me,' she exclaimed, angrily shaking him off.

'Mistress Treveryan,' said a voice that was oddly familiar. 'Wait a moment.'

She spun round and found herself confronting the intensely blue eyes of Piers Menheire. She gasped. 'What are you doing here?'

'I was about to ask you the same question. And with more reason, I think. You have ruined another pair of shoes. It seems to be becoming a habit.'

She glanced down at her feet. It was true. The blue satin slippers Cullen had picked out for her visit to Lady Harper's were dirtied and torn beyond repair.

'No matter,' she said briskly, 'I must speak with Kip.'

But when she looked around for him once more, he had vanished.

Walking back towards the broad street that led down to the wharf at Sutton Pool, Perdita was glad of Piers Menheire's presence beside her. A small crowd, mostly children, had gathered in the alley to observe her when she emerged from the alehouse. She was conscious of the wealth betrayed by her sky blue damask costume, its hems now weighed down with filth. And of her poor ruined shoes. Conscious too of the way Piers negotiated all hazards with cheerful ease.

Only when they reached a clean-paved street where the salt tang of the sea was stronger than the stench of the crowded tenements did Perdita draw a deep breath.

She paused. Piers also stopped, and waited.

She said, 'What were you and Kip doing in that place?'

'Kip?'

'Please don't waste time pretending he wasn't there. I know I saw him. And you deliberately distracted me so he could make his escape. But why?'

'Kip has always loved a cockfight, even a botched affair like that one.'

'But he was supposed to be on the *Fearless*!'

'I believe he changed his mind.'

'He must be mad. He was as good as ordered to go. My father will be furious when he finds out.'

'And when will that be?'

'What do you mean?'

He hesitated. Despite his affable manner, Perdita sensed he was weighing her up. He said, 'Mistress Treveryan, in the spring you asked me to keep a secret for you and I did, gladly. Now I am asking you to keep this to yourself, to help Kip out. Just for a few days at least.'

Perdita's eyes narrowed. 'Are you threatening to betray my confidence, if I do not do as you ask?'

'Of course not.' He looked genuinely surprised at the idea, and Perdita was ashamed even to have thought such a thing. 'How very suspicious you are. I told you then that your secret was safe with me and I meant it. No conditions. I am merely asking you, for friendship's sake, to do the same for Kip.'

For friendship's sake. It was a novel idea, and not at all unappealing, though she wondered if he meant Kip or himself as her friend. She looked out across the crowded harbour. A pilot boat, its dozen rowers exhausted, was coming alongside the quay. It occurred to her then, as Piers Menheire waited for her answer, that this friendship could be useful to her in her campaign to win over Edmund, and so Trecarne.

She raised her eyes to look at him directly. 'Are we to be friends, then, Master Menheire?'

He held her gaze. Laughter, and something else besides, glittered in his eyes. Then, with an extravagant gesture, he plucked off his broad hat and swept her a bow. 'Madam, if you would honour me . . .'

She burst out laughing, a sudden release of tension. 'I promise I'll say nothing to my father. Though he's bound to find out soon enough, and then heaven help poor Kip.'

'Your father is a tyrant?'

It was on the tip of Perdita's tongue to make an unfavourable comparison with Colonel Menheire, but all she said was, 'He hates to be disobeyed. I cannot imagine why Kip was so rash.'

'To tell you the truth, nor can I.' They were strolling slowly back to the street where Perdita had escaped from the coach. 'I can think of nothing I'd like more than to be aboard the *Fearless* right now. But it was different for Kip. He suffered horribly from sea-sickness.'

'My father told him he'd get used to it in time.'

'I don't think Kip was prepared to wait. Watch out.' Piers drew her to one side of the street as a cart, weighed down with bales of fleeces for loading, careered out of control down the hill.

Half a dozen carters were struggling to slow it down before the draught horses were overwhelmed.

As the commotion died away, Perdita asked, 'Would you really like to sail on the *Fearless*?'

'A ship like that, yes.'

They had reached the top of the rise. Perdita said, 'There is my mother's servant.' The fellow was lounging by the stocks and sharing a piece of pie with the prisoner, a well-known local drunkard who was frequently to be found there, chatting with his friends and complaining of his lot. She turned to Piers. 'You do not have to accompany me further.'

'It is no hardship.' He smiled.

'What brought you to Plymouth?'

'Some business for my uncle. I am due to return to Trecarne in a day or so. Seeing Kip has delayed me.'

'I am hoping to go back to Rossmere at the end of the month.'

'Why wait till then? It is St Ewan's Day in Porthew next week. You should see it if you can.'

Perdita did not think her father would consider the Porthew saint's day sufficient reason for a change of plans. She asked, 'Will your cousin also be at Trecarne?'

'Yes. Why do you ask?'

'Oh . . . no reason.' The footboy had noticed her approach. He spoke a few words to the man in the stocks then walked towards her. She said, 'Goodbye, Master Menheire. Tell Kip I will keep his secret for him, but he'll live to regret his rashness all the same.'

'I'll warn him. And thank you, on his behalf.'

She echoed his earlier words. 'It is no hardship, sir.'

His eyes held hers. For a moment she was sorry their encounter was ending so soon, but then she reminded herself that from now on she was to be guided in all matters by her head alone: the attractions of a pair of remarkably blue eyes in a lively and intelligent face were of no interest to her whatsoever. She bid him a brisk farewell.

When she joined the servant, she could tell by his smirking expression that, having first observed her following Kip then returning with an altogether different young gentleman, he had drawn all the wrong conclusions about her desire for privacy. In the end it cost her sixpence to buy his silence, and even then she was not sure she could trust him. She set her mind to devise some story that would explain her absence. She must not allow any suspicion that Kip had been involved.

In the event her precautions were superfluous. By nightfall Sir Richard Treveryan knew all about Kip's desertion: he had been alerted by the pilot who had guided the *Fearless* through the treacherous waters near the mouth of the Sound and who had been sent back with a message for the ship's owner from Master Boulter.

Richard flew into a rage. Assuming that Kip was already on his way back to Rossmere, he was all for setting off in pursuit at once and catching up with him near the outskirts of Plymouth. Perdita thought it best not to mention that he might have more luck looking for him in the taverns down by the harbour. It was Viney who pointed out to his master, in an uncharacteristic burst of eloquence, that they'd do better to go by boat to Porthew. That way they might reach Rossmere before him.

As Richard calmed down he saw the wisdom of this advice and sent Viney off to make enquiries about boats sailing west. Viney, who found long days in the saddle more than his old bones could manage, set off willingly to the harbour. When his manservant had departed, Richard was surprised to receive a visit from his daughter. 'What do you want?' He barely looked up from the pile of papers that must be sorted before he left.

'Father, I want to sail with you to Porthew.'

'Out of the question.'

'You said you'd take me when you went back to Rossmere.'

'This is different.'

'But Sophie will be expecting me. I wrote telling her I hoped to visit them soon.'

He glanced up briefly, then returned to his work, saying merely, 'I did not know you were in correspondence with Sophie.'

'She will be so disappointed if I let her down.'

'Don't pretend to me that you care two farthings for Sophie Sutton. Why this sudden eagerness?'

'I want to see Rossmere again. Please, Father.'

He surveyed her carefully. 'You're up to something, Perdita. You've a scheming look about you.'

She tried hard to make her expression blameless. 'I want to see Sophie and her family. I want to go to Porthew.' Still he looked suspicious. 'Very well, then, I want to go on the ship with you. I've heard about it so much and I've never been on one. Please, Father. Please don't say no this time.'

There was no doubting her sincerity this time. Richard's eyes softened briefly. 'Very well, then. If you can be ready in time. I'll not wait for you.'

Perdita was so excited she could have hugged him. 'Don't worry about me, Father. I'm ready now.'

Dusk was falling, and the last touches of sunset glow were fading from the surface of the water when the ferrymen began their long haul across the Tamar. Their only passengers were a couple of young men and the small ponies they had purchased for the journey west. The ferrymen were reluctant to set out so late in the day, but the travellers were impatient and offered good money.

With every stroke of the oars, Kip felt his spirits lift. He knew he'd not feel right again until his feet touched the damp soil of Rossmere and he heard the doves murmuring on the rooftops, but this, at least, was a beginning. The motion of the ferry dragged at his stomach but he hardly noticed it. Sea-sickness had been a misery. From the moment he set foot on the *Fearless* his guts had revolted against the unnaturalness of the enterprise. For days he had wanted only to die.

But even that was mild compared to the agony of home-sickness, which he knew would never ease. His longing for the sights and sounds of Rossmere and the company of his family was an iron fist around his heart, a pain so acute that the misery of sea-sickness was almost a relief by comparison. Even now he felt it. To be home again was a physical necessity: there was no sense of making a choice.

Still, if he hadn't bumped into Piers that morning he'd probably be on the *Fearless* now, though he was convinced this third voyage would have killed him. Seeing Piers had reminded him more fully than ever of all he was leaving behind. More to the point, Piers had been prepared to lend him the money for the journey west. And this evening he had assured Kip that his secret was safe with Perdita.

Still, seeing her at the cockfight had jolted him into making a move right away. He'd not be content until the whole length of Cornwall lay between him and Sir Richard Treveryan. He was terrified now lest Sir Richard send men to apprehend him and force him back to sea. But all the ogres of hell would not get him back on board. He'd sooner jump into the sea and drown.

Gradually, as the glimmering lights of Plymouth were swallowed up by darkness, and the shadowy form of the Cornish land mass appeared before him, he felt a growing certainty that he had escaped. Now his fear gave way to truculence. He didn't care about Sir Richard: he had given the sailor's life a fair try and it had turned out not to suit him. No shame in that. Alice and Francis would understand – surely that was all that mattered. It was really no business of Sir Richard's.

Then, as the ferry's bow bumped against the wooden jetty and he jumped ashore, all his morbid thoughts gave way to a great and growing joy at the prospect of home.

Chapter Seventeen

Perdita had been on deck since first light. Dawn had brought a slack wind and a damp, numbing cold, but she hardly noticed. She was determined not to miss a moment of these last precious hours at sea. The crew of the small coaster they had boarded the day before were alternately amused and exasperated by her ceaseless questions and interference. When Sir Richard came on deck in the morning the master jerked his head in her direction and said, 'If your two lads take to the sea like she has, Sir Richard, I reckon they'll do you proud.'

Richard observed the small figure standing near the prow. Her head was tilted back slightly so that the breeze buffeted her face, and there was something about her, a quality in the way she stood with her feet braced against the rolling of the ship, that he had never noticed before. He went and stood beside her. 'We'll reach Porthew before noon,' he said. 'It's just around that headland.'

'So soon?'

'I thought it was your dearest wish.'

'Well . . . yes. But I don't want this journey to end yet.'

'You like it?'

Perdita nodded. She had a feeling that if she tried to put her pleasure into words something would be lost. Last evening she had seen cormorants skimming low over the water and the curved backs of three porpoises as they played beside the boat. She had seen the evening star and the crescent moon and the way the surface of the water changed from one moment to the next. She had listened to the sailors as they joked among themselves and told their tall tales. One said he had been captured in his youth by Sallee pirates and had been a galley slave for three years before being rescued by a Dutch privateer. He had offered to show her his scars and the others had laughed. They talked of shoals of cod off the coast of Newfoundland that were so thick a man could walk over them from one ship to the next and only get wet to his ankles. And when she had stood on deck in the starlight she felt a sense of the hugeness of creation and what the Bible meant when it spoke of the mighty heavens and the waters of the deep.

At length she said only, 'I begin to see how it is for Sophie when she rides on Falcon.'

'You are growing poetical, Perdita. How is the Latin progressing?'

'I brought the grammar with me,' she said, before adding dutifully, 'I hope I'll be reading Catullus soon.'

Richard smiled. He was struck by the contrast between his daughter when sincere and when she said what was expected of her. He said, 'Your mother always longed to go to sea.'

'Did she?'

'Yes, she liked nothing more than to hear me talk about the places I had been. Maybe you take after her more than you think. Certainly the sailors don't mind having you on board. Usually they complain bitterly about women – they're supposed to be bad luck.'

'To hear them talk you'd think everything was bad luck.'

'It's dangerous enough. And a hard life.'

But Perdita, he could tell, was not convinced. Besides, the knowledge that her mother had wanted to go to sea, that perhaps they had something in common after all, had made her glow with happiness.

A little later they rounded the headland and saw the squat tower of Porthew church rising from a huddle of grey houses near the harbour. The early mist was thinning into wisps and trails as the sun broke through.

They drew closer still and Perdita exclaimed, 'Porthew looks different from the sea. More colourful, somehow.'

Her father looked over the glittering water. 'Ah,' he said thoughtfully, 'I had forgotten about that.'

'What is it?'

'St Ewan's Day.'

For that one day in the year, Porthew was transformed. Country families with baskets of produce and their silent, wide-eyed children; pedlars with packs of ribbons, pins, buttons and penny books; Brittany sailors and travelling rogues; a man with a parrot that blasphemed in five languages and an Irish apothecary selling St Bridget's charms guaranteed to protect the wearer against plague and the evil eye. There were pickpockets and charlatans, horse-dealers and runaways; sturdy beggars looking for work and packs of young boys looking for trouble. There was ale and music, Cornish wrestling that was organised and local fights that just broke out anyhow, canoodling and quarrels, bargains and betrayal, gossip, laughter and song.

Cary was gathering stories to be embellished for later enjoyment at Rossmere. Kip, who had reached home the previous evening, was in his element, all the miseries of shipboard life obliterated in the riot of sport and gambling which was his to enjoy just so long as his credit held good. He forgot his recent debt to Piers and dropped broad hints about the fortune he'd amassed during six months as a sailor.

Honor was listening spellbound while a distinguished-looking gentleman in a tall hat explained that a few grains of the powders he was selling, at a very reasonable price, were guaranteed to cure all but the most acute disorders. Even Louisa seemed to have left her sulks behind at Rossmere and was enjoying the novelty and the noise. Of course, it was heartbreaking to see so many tantalising delights and have no money to spend on them, but today even this deprivation could not damp her spirits. Besides, she had begun to think she might be making a good impression on Piers Menheire, who had returned from Plymouth at the same time as Kip. Since Edmund and Sophie seemed well on the way to making a match, what was more natural than for his younger cousin and her sister to be paired off likewise?

The old women who sat in their doorways with their spinning and their ale and watched the crowds go by were in no doubt at all that a wedding was on the way. You could see it in Edmund Menheire's satisfied air as he guided Sophie through the crush; you could see it in his eager purchase of some trimming that had caught her eye and the way he insisted on fastening the ornament to her jacket himself and the way his hands lingered when he touched her.

The general opinion was that the match was as near made in heaven as could be. Sophie Sutton was liked and respected locally and she was a lovely-looking girl, but that did not alter the fact that she was nearly thirty and, with her family's debts threatening to become a local scandal, she would be lucky to find a suitor with a quarter of Edmund Menheire's advantages. The Suttons were an old family, and proud, but Edmund was a respectable man and obviously thought well of her. If there had been enmity between the two families in the past then the union would be a symbol of the new mood of reconciliation in the country since King Charles's return.

Everyone hoped the whole business would be settled by Christmas, and everyone was delighted.

Everyone, that is, except Sophie Sutton.

It wasn't that she didn't try. After her talk with Stephen, she had deliberated long and hard – for the first time in her life – about her own future. It felt a strange thing to be doing.

When Perdita had asked her in the spring if she wasn't afraid of dying an old maid, Sophie had been honest in saying she never gave the subject any thought. She had always imagined her future in terms of Rossmere, the work that was needed, supplies to be laid up for the winter, the progress of her brothers. The yearly rhythms of farm and orchard and kitchen were so central to her life that she could imagine no other. But she trusted her uncle, and if he told her to prepare for catastrophe, then so she must.

It was obvious that if she were settled at Trecarne then the rest of the family was sure to benefit. And Edmund Menheire had much to recommend him: he had regular, agreeable features; he had no known vices; he was due to inherit a large amount of money on his father's death. More to the point, he seemed devoted enough to ignore the absence of a dowry, and not many men would do that. After all, she had hardly been overwhelmed by the press of suitors beating a path to Rossmere to ask for her hand.

She was fortunate, and she knew it.

So why was she so dejected? Usually no one enjoyed St Ewan's Day more than she did. She loved the laughter, the crowds and the music. Of course, there had been plenty to worry about since her conversation with Uncle Stephen, and since Kip's return she had been anxious about him too. Added to that was her unease concerning Francis and Honor – altogether plenty of reasons for feeling out of sorts.

Still, she could have put her troubles to one side for the day. Since her father's death she had learned to savour to the full even the briefest of pleasures. A naturally contented person, she inclined towards happiness as plants turn towards the sun.

But for once in her life she dared not follow her instincts. During the summer she had seen a good deal of Edmund, and though she had no reason to dislike him, she did not particularly relish his company. She did not want to spend all of St Ewan's Day with him, and the prospect of a lifetime as his wife was even less appealing. She felt oppressed by his nearness. None of this was worth mentioning to anyone else: she could not even explain it to herself. Maybe it was just that she had enjoyed her spinster state for too long and was afraid of change, even a change so obviously for the better.

Louisa, who was walking a little way ahead with Piers, let out a squeal of delight. 'Oh, look, Cary has found a fortune-teller! I must have mine told. It's only a penny – oh, Sophie, do give me a penny, please!'

Sophie frowned; Louisa knew full well she had no money with her, but Piers promised he would oblige when Cary had finished. Louisa dimpled her thanks. Sophie was watching Cary closely.

No one else would detect the tension on that strong, scarred face but Sophie noted her exaggerated calm, the way she seemed almost to have stopped breathing, so desperate was her hope, against all reasonable expectation, that the fortune-teller had some news, hidden to others, of her missing husband. A slight hardening of the eyes, resolute in her disappointment, showed that the fortune-teller's skills did not stretch as far as the steaming shores of Barbados.

'Nothing?' asked Sophie, when Cary stood up, shook out her skirts and joined them once again. Louisa had plumped herself down on the upturned barrel and thrust out her hand. The gypsy examined it fastidiously, as though Louisa were not quite clean.

Cary said cheerfully, 'The usual stuff about not starving and never being rich neither. I could have told her that myself. And some vague words about fearing what I don't fear and not fearing what I do.'

'What is that supposed to mean?'

'I asked her the same myself, but she wouldn't say. She must have made it up.'

Honor had joined them and listened anxiously to Cary's doubts. 'Don't you think it's true, then, Cary?' she asked.

Sophie smiled at her wide-eyed sister-in-law. 'Why so curious, or are you thinking of having your fortune told too?'

'I have already,' said Honor.

'Really?' Sophie was astonished. 'What did she say?'

'Well . . .' Honor glanced anxiously at Edmund and Piers, then whispered in Sophie's ear, 'She said I'd have a child within a twelvemonth.'

'Honor, that's wonderful news.'

It was the look Honor gave her when she had uttered this commonplace remark that so surprised Sophie. One would almost have thought the girl had seen one of Cary's ghosts.

On the other hand, quite clearly, Louisa had had only good news. When she stood up her pretty face was flushed with excitement. 'Your turn now, Sophie,' she exclaimed, 'I really do believe she has the gift. It was quite amazing.'

Piers held out a second coin and Sophie laughed and said, 'What nonsense, Louisa.'

But Edmund stepped forward to place himself between Sophie and the gypsy woman. 'I advise you not to meddle with such foolishness, Mistress Sutton.'

'Why ever not?' Sophie asked, unthinking.

'Is the reason important?' he asked stiffly. 'I would have thought the mere fact that I have cautioned against it would be enough to make you reconsider.'

Sophie was so surprised that she couldn't think what to say.

Piers said, 'Don't be so pompous, Edmund. It's only some harmless fun.'

Edmund's mouth curved into a smile, the humourless smile of a man who is certain of his position and expects to be deferred to. He said, speaking to Sophie, not his cousin, 'On the contrary, I consider this dabbling with the dark arts to be highly dangerous, not just some trivial amusement. I am confident Mistress Sutton wishes to be guided by me.'

Sophie avoided looking at him directly, but she forced herself to say, 'I am sure we can find some better entertainment. Why don't we have a look at the play?'

'Maybe my cousin objects to that too,' said Piers.

Edmund considered this possibility at some length before delivering his judgement, 'I believe the life of St Ewan is harmless enough. In its way it may even be edifying. If my companion wishes to see the play, then I see no reason to object.'

Sophie turned away abruptly and began to walk away from the harbour. Edmund had to lengthen his stride to catch up with her.

He was satisfied that Sophie had demonstrated her meekness over the fortune-teller. Her placid nature was one of the things he most valued in her – but it was always best to be sure of these matters.

When he had caught up with her, he said, 'Please do not think, Mistress Sutton, that I thought you were in danger of being taken in by that gypsy woman's foolish lies. You have far too much sense for that. I am sure you understand how important it is to set a good example for our families and servants.'

'Let's watch the play,' said Sophie.

'By all means,' said Edmund.

The ritual of the saint's life was enacted each year on a raised piece of ground behind the alehouse and soon they could hear the booming voices of the actors – on this occasion a seine fisherman and the Porthew blacksmith. When Piers, Honor and Louisa joined them, Sophie dropped back. 'Heavens, I almost forgot,' she said, flushing slightly. 'I'll come back in a little while. I promised my mother I'd do an errand for her.'

'In that case I will accompany you,' said Edmund. 'The crowds can be troublesome and it is not seemly—'

'Please don't bother,' Sophie interrupted him. 'I shall be much quicker on my own.'

And before he had a chance to ask her where she was going, she turned and almost ran away from them and back down towards the harbour.

Kip had been on a winning streak all morning. Intoxicated as much by his good luck as by large quantities of ale, he decided to stake all his gains on a single throw. His opponent, a scrivener's son from Penryn, held his breath while the dice rattled – and then his face cracked into a grin of relief. Kip conceded defeat with a good grace – it was something he'd had plenty of practice in – and the victor bought a flagon of ale for them both.

While he drank, Kip tried to persuade one or two of his cronies to continue the game on credit, but he already owed all of them so much money that he had no further takers. In time he grew bored, and looked about him for fresh diversions.

A small coaster had dropped anchor just beyond the harbour wall and a few passengers were being rowed ashore. From this distance Kip could not see them clearly. He wondered what Piers was up to and whether he might be good for a few shillings more. At least they could lay some plans for the horse race between Falcon and Charger that Kip had first thought of in the spring.

He ambled down towards the harbour. The crowds that had been dense around the stalls were thinning as people drifted towards the open space where the Life of St Ewan was being enacted. Kip cadged a piece of pie from the miller's son who sometimes went coursing with him and wandered in the direction of the play. He was thoroughly content. Only a fool would be any place but Porthew on St Ewan's Day: the crowds, the friends, the entertainments and the drinking . . . Suddenly he became uncomfortably aware of the large quantity of ale he had consumed already: he turned off into a narrow passageway near the shambles and was just about to relieve himself on a steaming dung pile when a man's voice roared out, not ten feet away, 'Well, then, boy! What do you have to say for yourself now?'

Horrified, Kip spun round.

Sir Richard Treveryan, his face dark with fury, stood at the entrance to the alley.

In blind panic, Kip turned and ran.

Sophie's heart was pounding when she reached the low doorway of the draper's shop a little distance above the harbour. This was due partly to the steep climb up the narrow cobbled street.

But only partly.

The door was wide open to let in the sunshine and the customers. Master Hollar's shop was a favourite meeting place. Bolts of cloth were stacked on shelves against the walls: wool in sombre shades, worsted and kerseys, Irish straights and fustian; linens in white and cream and brown. And then, brilliant as a stained-glass window, all the silks and satins and velvets: watered tabby, sarsenet and paragon in crimson, apricot, indigo and jade.

A couple of neighbours were propped against the cutting table and gossiping with John Taylor, the aged assistant who managed the business during his master's frequent absences. The proprietor, Luke Hollar, was folding a piece of baize for a mason's apron, but he stopped when Sophie walked in. His long eyes surveyed her carefully before he said, 'Good day, Mistress Sutton. What can I do for you?' If he was surprised by Sophie's unexpected appearance in his shop, he did not show it.

'Good day. I was looking for some tabby silk. A couple of yards should be enough. It's for an underskirt for my mother.'

'Certainly.' He moved towards the shining column of materials. 'Was there any particular colour you had in mind?'

'I thought blue, maybe. Or perhaps green. It depends what you have.' Sophie could not imagine why her voice was coming out so wavery. She must be still out of breath from the climb up from the harbour.

In the leisurely manner of someone whose working life is spent waiting for customers to reach a decision, Luke lifted several bolts down from the shelf and laid them in a shimmering row on the cutting table. John Taylor and the two neighbours obligingly moved a little distance away, but they watched attentively, all pretence at conversation having ceased.

Sophie let her fingers trail across the nearest one, its watered surface rippling from smoky grey to deepest harebell blue. 'This one is very beautiful,' she said.

Luke was watching her, his face impassive. 'You like it?'

'I think so. I think my mother will like it. Two and a half yards should be plenty.'

John Taylor was trying to catch Luke's eye: he glanced meaningfully towards the ledger. Luke gave an almost imperceptible nod. 'Mistress Sutton,' he said evenly, 'before you make your decision, I have a piece newly arrived which I believe might suit your purposes better. Would you like to see it?'

'Yes.'

'It is at the back. This way, if you please.'

He pushed open the heavy oak door at the rear of the shop and held it while Sophie went through. She was expecting some kind of store, but found herself instead in the living quarters – a neat, airy room with an open fire, which had not been lit, a small table and three or four chairs. The few items of brazenware on the shelves had been polished, the hearth was swept. It had almost the air of a house waiting for its owner's return. He closed the door quietly. 'May I offer you some wine?'

'Please don't trouble. But I'd like to see the cloth.'

Luke smiled and raised his hands, palms flat. 'It was a pretext, so we might talk privately. To spare you unnecessary embarrassment.'

'Why?'

'Did you intend to pay for the silk in cash?'

Sophie found herself colouring. She should have expected this, but for some reason had forgotten about it. 'Surely my mother has an account with you.'

'Indeed she has, but unfortunately nothing has been paid against it in over twelve years. At my father's death the figure was over fifteen pounds. It must be more than double that now.'

'So large? I never knew. I am sorry to hear it. But the silk is not important anyway. It was merely an excuse to come and see how you did.'

'I am grateful for your concern.'

Sophie was moving slowly round the room as she spoke. She appeared both curious and uneasy. 'When you left Rossmere I was anxious about your injuries. You were too hasty. If you had followed my advice you would have let us nurse you for a few days more.'

'I did not want to put you to further trouble.'

'It was no trouble.'

After Treveryan's beating, Luke had been too badly hurt to be moved. Sophie had told Sir Richard he was being lodged in the grooms' chamber beside the stable, but in fact she had put a pallet bed in one of the storerooms next to the kitchen, where it was warmer. On the second morning Luke had insisted he was well enough to be helped on to his horse and had returned to Porthew. Since then, although she had seen him a few times at church, they had not had an opportunity to speak.

He said, 'You were an excellent nurse.'

'Your injuries were severe.'

'I have made a full recovery.'

'That is good.'

Luke stood quite still, leaning his back against the heavy door that led through to the shop and watching her while she moved around the room. He was wondering what was the real purpose of her visit, since clearly it was neither to purchase silk nor to enquire after his health.

She had not looked at him directly. She paused and ran her fingers along the shaft of a toasting fork that hung near the fire. She said again, 'I am sorry our account has grown so large.'

'Your mother's account, not yours.' He waited for a while before saying, 'Mistress Sutton, I would like you to have that silk. I'd prefer it if you used it yourself, but you must do as you wish, of course. It can be my way of thanking you.'

'For what?'

'For your care in the spring.'

'Oh, that. That was nothing.'

'It meant a lot to me. I should have thanked you sooner. Please take the silk – take it for yourself.'

'But I don't need anything.' All unconscious of what she was doing, Sophie touched the frayed cuff of her sleeve and Luke was reminded of the day when his father had sold that green fabric to be made into a jacket for her mother. It must have been twelve years ago. Mistress Alice Sutton had worn it for a few years then passed it on to her daughter. The realisation was oddly painful.

'You must allow me to repay you somehow,' he said. 'That's only right.'

'You have repaid me already,' she said, pacing to the window and peering out at the narrow strip of garden, 'by sparing me the embarrassment of a refusal in front of your neighbours. So, you see, we are even.'

'Hardly a very fair bargain. Won't you at least let me give you a glass of wine?'

'Oh, yes.'

He took down two goblets of Venetian glass from a shelf and set them on a table, then pulled the stopper from a bottle of wine. He was about to pour when he frowned, fetched a linen cloth and wiped the glasses carefully, inside and out.

'My best glasses,' he said ruefully. 'They are not often used.'

'Thank you.' She took the glass, raised it to her lips, but set it down without tasting it. 'Master Hollar, do you live here alone?'

'Since my father died, yes.'

'You were away during the summer. Was that business or . . . ?'

'Or?'

Sophie touched a geranium growing in a small pot on the sill and a couple of scarlet petals fell on to her hand. 'Perdita told me you travel from time to time with some actors.'

'That's right. But this time it was business.'

She moved away from the window.

Luke asked, 'Did my sister tell you *all* about our meeting?'

'She told me how she lost her mother's earrings.'

'They belonged to Treveryan's wife. Not her mother.'

'Yes, I see. But it was wrong to trick her, all the same.'

'The trick was harmless enough. And it gave me a chance to tell her about her mother. Our mother. You saw for yourself how shocked she was when she learned I was her brother.'

'Yes.' Sophie's voice was subdued as she remembered that last evening of Perdita's visit. When she had recovered from her initial shock, Perdita had insisted Sophie stay up half the night with her. She had talked almost feverishly, knowing that once she left Rossmere she would have no one to confide in.

After a while Sophie said, 'Your sister means to visit us at Rossmere with her father later this month.'

'Good.'

Something in the way he said the single word made Sophie glance at him quickly. The expression in his grey eyes was hardly reassuring. 'Why do you say that?'

'I am looking forward to my next meeting with Treveryan.'

'Perhaps it is better that you do not meet.'

He shrugged. 'It does not seem that way to me.'

Still restless, Sophie moved back to the fireplace. 'I ought to be getting back to the others. I said I'd only be a few minutes.'

'Master Edmund Menheire,' said Luke, with the merest trace of distaste.

'And my sister.'

'You have not drunk your wine.'

'Oh, yes.' She raised the glass and swallowed two mouthfuls. 'It is excellent.' And then, realising how her surprise must sound, she flushed slightly.

Luke had noticed the implied criticism, but he noticed also the way her eyebrows were of a slightly darker brown than her hair and the faint lines around her eyes and mouth. For the first time he felt that time was limited and so doubly precious. Fearing that she might leave before he had discovered the real reason for her visit, he said, 'Whenever I see you, I am reminded of the smell of honey.'

'Why?' That had startled her, and no mistake.

'That storeroom where you nursed me.'

'Oh, yes, the honey store.' She laughed. 'I wish we had provided a more elegant sickroom for you.'

'But I like the smell of honey. And, since those two days at Rossmere, I find I like it even more than before.'

'Than I shall bring you a comb when we empty the hives.' She moved back to the window. 'Perdita told me you play the fiddle.'

'Yes.'

'Do you have it here?'

'Of course.' He went to a low chest, lifted the lid and drew out the violin with a flourish.

'Will you play me a tune before I go?'

'What would you like?'

'What sort of music do you play?'

'Oh, I can do you all sorts. A doleful psalm, if you like . . .' He tucked the instrument against his shoulder and drew the bow over the strings in a slow, melancholy dirge. 'Or a sprightly march.' Adjusting the angle of the bow he struck up a cheerful tune. 'Or, if you prefer, I can play you a courtly dance . . .' And he demonstrated this with a few bars of a fashionable sarabande.

'I did not know you were so versatile.'

'I'm not finished yet.'

'There is more?'

'I can do you an Irish lament.'

'Too sad.'

'Or a love song.' He raised the bow and waited for her response, but there was none. He said, 'Love songs often have the best melodies.'

Sophie was looking down at her hands. 'Do they?' she asked.

'Maybe this is familiar.' He played a few bars, then stopped abruptly. 'Do you know it?'

She turned to look out of the window. 'Everyone knows that song.'

'Why don't you sing it while I play?' He had begun the tune again, but this time very softly, the bow light as a feather's touch against the strings.

'I am a poor singer.'

'Say the words, then.'

'Very well.' She smiled, then, and for the first time she raised her eyes to look directly into his. She held his gaze and spoke quietly, but without any trace of uncertainty,

> *'Drink to me only with thine eyes,*
>   *And I will pledge with mine;*
> *Or leave a kiss but in the cup,*
>   *And I'll not look for wine . . .'*

As the last notes faded away the room filled with silence. Sophie set down her glass. It was empty. She was still smiling, like someone who holds the key to a secret.

'Thank you, Master Hollar,' she said. 'You have been most helpful.'

Luke inclined his head, acknowledging her thanks. Their meeting was at an end. He pushed open the door that led back through the shop and into the dazzling sunlight in the street beyond. Outside again, Sophie turned, as though there were some last thing she wanted to say, but then she merely smiled at him once more, that secret, dazzling smile, and walked away briskly over the cobbles. Luke would have given a lot to know what she had accomplished to cause such a smile.

He stood in the doorway of the shop and watched her as she strode away down the hill towards the harbour. Seeing her again had revived, with agonising intensity, all the tumult of emotion he had felt during the two days he spent at Rossmere in the spring: his rage at Treveryan's barbarous treatment of him, his fierce shame at the way he had made a sport of Perdita's feelings, and then, more than all the rest, a deep and growing wonder at Sophie Sutton's tenderness and warmth. The bruises Treveryan inflicted were long since healed, but he doubted if there was any simple cure for the other legacy of those spring days at Rossmere.

John Taylor was lifting the watered blue silk to put it away, but Luke stopped him. 'Measure off three yards,' he told him. 'I will deliver it to Rossmere myself.'

Chapter Eighteen

Perdita had been looking forward to seeing Piers Menheire again. She found him and his brother, together with Louisa and Honor, among the crowd watching the Life of St Ewan behind the alehouse. They were laughing and exchanging rude remarks about the players, but when Piers caught sight of her, the laughter died on his face. He looked first shocked, then angry. As soon as he could speak to her without being overheard by the others he demanded, 'What, in God's name, are you doing here?'

She was baffled by the change in him. At first she attempted to deflect his rage with a pert smile. 'You have only yourself to blame, Master Menheire,' she told him.

'How so?'

'Why, it was you who told me St Ewan's Day was a treat not to be missed. So, you see, I have taken your advice.'

His expression remained grim. 'Is that what you call it? And I suppose your father is with you?'

'Of course. We would have been here two days ago, but the first ship we took had to turn back when a sailor was injured.'

'How very unfortunate.' The way he spoke implied that the real misfortune was that she had not drowned *en route*. He said, 'I hope the entertainment here has justified the sacrifices you have made.'

Perdita had intended telling Piers about their adventures since leaving Plymouth and, more importantly, to warn Kip, but faced with his hostility she said only, 'The fair is moderately entertaining. Of course, it hardly compares with St Bartholomew's in

London. If one has known nothing better, then I dare say it is amusing enough.'

He regarded her with contempt. 'All your efforts, and now you are disappointed.'

'It's the company of dull rustics that spoils the day,' said Perdita.

'Perhaps if you considered—' Piers began heatedly, but he broke off as Sophie approached them. Perdita turned to her with relief. At least, she thought, here was one person who was genuine in their greeting.

'Perdita! What a wonderful surprise!' Sophie embraced her. 'We did not expect you till the end of the month.'

Piers said harshly, 'Mistress Treveryan has stopped at nothing to be here. Please excuse me, Mistress Sutton, I have urgent business to attend to.' He made Sophie a brief bow and quitted them hurriedly.

Perdita watched him go. All the pleasurable anticipation at the thought of seeing him again – and now this. Let it be a lesson, she thought, never to be distracted by a handsome face and a charming manner. Sophie raised a questioning eyebrow, but Perdita said lightly, 'What a turncoat! Never mind him. Tell me all your news.'

Before Sophie had a chance to answer, Edmund bore down on them. He had barely said good day to Perdita when he turned to Sophie and fussed, 'You have been gone such a long time. I was growing concerned for your safety.'

Sophie laughed. 'In Porthew on St Ewan's Day? Really, Master Menheire, you must not worry on my account.' But Perdita noticed that she coloured slightly as she spoke. Almost as if she were hiding something.

'Then your business must have detained you longer than you anticipated,' said Edmund. 'I trust it was concluded to your satisfaction.'

'Yes. Thank you. It was.'

Edmund's face darkened. He had been expecting Sophie to explain the reason for her long absence. It was obvious that Sophie realised this, and had no intention of obliging.

Instead, Sophie slipped her hand through Perdita's arm and said, 'You're in time for the end of the play, at least. St Ewan has just killed the last giant in Cornwall – I'm sorry you missed that part – but you can see him being received into heaven with all of God's angels.'

Edmund fell into step beside them. Perdita noticed Louisa's dismayed expression as she caught sight of her. She lowered her voice so none but Sophie could hear and asked, 'Do you know where Kip is?'

'Somewhere hereabouts. You'll see him soon, I'm sure.'

'We ought to warn him.'

'Why?'

'My father has come with me. He is furious with Kip for running away from the ship.'

Sophie stopped in her tracks and turned to Perdita. 'Kip ran away?'

Edmund moved closer. He was frowning as he asked, 'Is anything the matter, Mistress Sutton?'

'Yes. No. I must have a moment to catch up with Perdita in private.'

Edmund fell back, annoyed, and Perdita whispered hurriedly, 'Didn't he tell you?'

'He said he hated the sea, but he told us Master Boulter agreed with him that it was sensible to leave. I assumed your father knew too. He said nothing about running away.'

'The part about hating the sea was true, at least.'

'Are you sure he ran away?'

'Jumped ship at the last minute. The master was furious. And so is my father.'

'Poor Kip,' said Sophie, searching the crowd for sight of her brother. 'Whatever will he do now?'

Kip did not return to Rossmere until the afternoon of the following day. Precisely where he had been was not clear, but it was obvious how the time had been spent. He was in that state where intoxication and hangover collide: sore-headed, dishevelled and ranting, he tumbled from his horse and staggered into the house.

'Kip, my poor darling!' Alice hurried to tend the miscreant. 'Where have you been? I was so worried about you!'

'Ah, Mother.' Briefly Kip slumped against her, then he straightened himself as best he could and said, 'Ale! Dear God, where's the ale?'

Alerted by the commotion, the various members of the household came running into the great hall from all directions. Honor, who had been resting in her room, came down the stairs, supporting herself against the banister. Francis came from his account books, Sophie from the dairy, Perdita from a stroll in the garden and Louisa from her sewing. All now gazed with mixed emotions at the prodigal and his mother.

Kip looked around at the assembled faces. He placed a hand against his mother's shoulder, as if for support, and roared out, 'Where is he, then?'

'Where is who, my dearest?' Alice enquired tenderly, and then, 'Oh, look, you poor child. You've hurt your head. Let me fetch you a bandage.'

'Treveryan!' Kip shouted. 'Where is he?'

'I don't know, dear heart,' fluttered Alice, 'but never mind him now. Let me—'

'Where is he?' Kip was bellowing like a young bull.

The answer came, deep and strong, 'Here!' as Richard stepped through the open door.

Kip quailed at the sight of him and stepped behind the long oak table. Shielded by its solid bulk he rallied and declared, 'And about time too!'

Disgust and rage made Richard's face terrifying. He stood four square across the table from Kip, but when he spoke, his voice was almost hushed. 'Well? And what have you got to say for yourself, eh?'

'I don't have to answer to you any more!' blurted Kip. 'Where the devil is that ale?'

'No more liquor. Explain yourself.'

'I'll not go back to sea! No one can make me.'

'That's not for you to decide.'

'I'll—' Kip's legs buckled under him and he collapsed on to a chair.

'Stand up when I talk to you,' said Richard, but Alice rushed to her son's side and put an arm around his shoulder.

'Don't be so unkind, Richard. Can't you see the boy's not well?'

Richard gave a snort of contempt. 'He can't hold his drink, that's all. Stand up, boy, and stop sheltering behind your mother's skirts. Twice you've run away, and you deserve a thrashing for both.'

'Hasn't he been thrashed enough already?' Alice turned on him in a fury.

'What?'

Sophie place a restraining hand on Alice's arm. 'Mother—' she began warningly, but Alice shook her off.

'Yes.' Alice was gaining confidence. 'The poor child has endured beatings and hardship and heaven knows what else on that terrible ship of yours. You should be ashamed of yourself, Richard, for putting my son at the mercy of such a fiend as your Master Boulter.'

Richard leaned across the table. 'Are you responsible for feeding your mother these lies, Kip?' he asked softly.

For answer, Kip merely groaned and laid his head on the table. It was a bad move. Richard reached over easily and caught him by the hair. 'Look at me when I speak to you! What other stories have you been making up?'

Kip's eyes rolled. An incoherent sound emerged from him. No words. He gagged.

'Stop it!' wailed Alice. 'You're hurting him!'

'Well, lad, are you going to answer me?' asked Richard grimly.

Kip continued to make strange noises, but his answer, when it came, was liquid. Richard released him and stepped back just in time as Kip was horribly sick.

'There!' Alice was triumphant. 'Look what you've done to the poor darling!'

'Dear God, woman. Just smell him. Your precious darling is a coward, a liar and a drunkard. I've a good mind to wash my hands of him entirely.'

And with that Richard turned and strode furiously out of the house while Kip's mother and sisters hastened to his aid. Perdita observed with interest as the youth her father had hoped she would marry one day groaned and retched and sobbed.

Most probably her father had abandoned his earlier plan; she was not in the least bit sorry. She had grown quite found of Kip, but only as one might be fond of a puppy or some amiable buffoon. More important, though, it must now be easier to persuade him to let her shift her attentions to Edmund Menheire.

And she need never play another game of merels, slam or shuffleboard as long as she lived.

Sir Richard Treveryan was not so easily defeated. The following morning he summoned Alice, Stephen and Francis to a meeting in the latter's office.

'What is this about, Richard?' asked Alice nervously, as she bustled into the room and he closed the door behind her.

'You know full well we are here to discuss your youngest son.'

'If we are to talk about Kip,' said Stephen, reasonably enough, 'don't you think he should be allowed to join us?'

'Not yet. It does the boy no good to know himself the subject of debate. I need the support of all present or I am wasting my time.'

'Support in what?' It was Francis who asked. He was pale after yet another sleepless night of worry and fearing the worst.

Richard placed his hands on the back of a chair and surveyed them all steadily. 'I do not intend to waste time listing Kip's faults. Even you, Alice, can be blind to them no longer. However, he is not yet twenty-one and in his defence I should say that he has been wickedly indulged. After yesterday's fiasco I was tempted to leave him to his own devices, but having considered the matter fully I am prepared to give him one more chance. Nicolas would have wished it, I'm sure. And Kip is not a bad youth, though he has been deceitful and a coward.'

Alice half rose from her chair and protested, 'Oh, Richard, that's not fair!' before fluttering down again, like some plump little bird momentarily disturbed on her nest.

'Believe me, Alice, I am trying as hard as I can to be fair. Your son has not made that easy at all.'

'But—'

'What exactly are you proposing to do?' Stephen intervened, before Richard and Alice became mired in a futile argument over Kip's character.

'Quite simply, I want to be allowed to treat the boy as one of my own sons. I want to give him the encouragement and the discipline that he needs, just as if he were my own. Without interference. If – and when – he proves himself worthy of it, I will see that he is well enough provided for to live as an independent gentleman, an asset to his family and not a burden.'

Francis looked startled. Stephen said quietly, 'That's generous of you, Richard.'

Only Alice appeared unimpressed. There was an oddly defiant little smile on her face as she asked, 'Does your plan include sending Kip to sea again?'

'To begin with, yes. If only for a single voyage.'

'Then it is out of the question.'

Richard restrained his impatience with some difficulty. 'Whatever lies you've been told, Alice, I can assure you he's suffered nothing worse these past six months than a bad bout of sea-sickness.'

'Just as I thought.' She bristled. 'You'd believe some strange captain rather than my own son.'

'All the same –' once again it was Stephen who intervened before a pointless argument flared up – 'is it really necessary to make him endure a situation for which he is so clearly unsuited?'

'Many excellent mariners have suffered worse than Kip to begin with,' said Richard. 'Most get over it soon enough. Kip must learn that he cannot solve problems by running away from them. If he is allowed to quit the sea because of his own cowardice in jumping ship, the task of educating him will be well nigh impossible. However, once he has made a successful voyage, even a short one, then he and I may consider what is best to do next.'

Francis was frowning. 'And you say that if he acquits himself well . . .' Here, he broke off and slid his forefinger inside his collar as though it had grown suddenly too tight. 'If he does well, then you will treat him . . . ah, he will benefit . . . ah, as a son . . . and independent.'

'You wish to know, perhaps, how much money is at stake?'

Francis looked more uncomfortable than ever, but did not answer.

Richard said, 'Your mother knows, Francis, that when I offered my help in the spring I told her my hope that Kip and my daughter might eventually make an alliance.'

'Your daughter – ah – yes.'

'All I need say at this stage is that her dowry will take into account what some people might consider to be the disadvantages of her birth. Of course, I know that no one here present would be so mean-spirited as to concern themselves with these matters. The long friendship between our two families would outweigh such considerations.'

Stephen smiled. 'Of course.'

'Ah.' For the time being this seemed to be the full extent of Francis's contribution.

Richard continued, 'Only a madman would settle a penny on Kip now. Anything he lays his hands on he drinks or gambles away. That is why his education is so important. I am willing to pledge my intentions in writing, if necessary, but I must be given absolute control over the boy.'

'Such a generous offer would be difficult to refuse,' said Stephen.

'Ah.' Francis was nodding vigorously. 'Yes.'

But Alice, who had remained silent longer than was usual with her, rose from her chair and said, 'It is out of the question.'

'What?'

She faced the three men. She was sure of herself, in spite of a slight tremor of the voice. 'I told you, the whole scheme is impossible. Kip is not going back to sea and there's an end to it.'

'But, Mother.' Francis struggled with his collar. 'Ah.'

Stephen said, 'Alice, do not be over-hasty.'

Richard gripped the back of the chair tightly, but said nothing.

Alice went on, 'I know what you're all about to say, that we must do what Richard tells us because of the money and the debts and the interest that is due at the end of the month, but I have Kip to think of and I'll not be threatened.'

'Richard is trying to help,' said Stephen, 'not to threaten you.'

'Oh, well, call it what you will, it amounts to the same thing.'

'I told you in the spring,' said Richard, 'that I'd pay the interest at Michaelmas, and so I will.'

'Whether you do or not, it is no concern of mine.'

Francis was appalled. 'Mother, what are you saying?'

'We don't need his money.'

'What? But the harvest's not in, the money is due in three weeks. How else can we manage?'

Alice was growing flustered, but she stood her ground. 'Others will help us if Richard backs out.'

'Others?'

'Who?'

'What kind of help?'

But she refused to tell them. She was adamant, however, that Richard's money, which in April had been all that stood between them and disaster, was now a matter of small consequence. The Suttons, it seemed, had other benefactors.

She said, 'It is all thanks to my efforts that we still have our home, Richard. Francis and Stephen will do well to remember that. And Kip remains here with me.'

'In that case,' said Richard, 'I am wasting my time. I will return to Plymouth as soon as possible, but I'll come back at Michaelmas as I promised. Maybe then, Alice, you will be more reasonable. Francis, tell your men to find me a couple of horses. Perdita and I will leave today.'

'Ah,' said Francis, more uncomfortable than ever. 'That might not be possible, Sir Richard.'

'Why on earth not?'

'I believe she has gone out riding with Sophie and Kip. They said it was something to do with a horse race.'

Chapter Nineteen

The group from Rossmere had met up with the party from
Trecarne near the gibbet on the edge of the Downs. Mercifully
the gibbet was bare for once, with only a few hungry choughs
strutting around to frighten the horses. They rode in a cheerful
group towards the open space that Kip and Piers had selected as
suitable for the race: six riders with a few grooms to attend them.
No dogs, not today.

Charger, the Menheires' horse, was a dark bay, almost ebony
and taller than Falcon by a hand, strongly muscled and powerful.
Excited by the presence of a strange stallion he plunged and
fretted at the bit and it took all of Piers's skill to keep him under
control. Falcon was more mannerly, but alert and interested in
everything going on around him, aware that this was to be no
ordinary gallop on the Downs. Sophie was enjoying his excitement, which fuelled her own: during the summer months that
she and the dappled stallion had passed together a profound trust
and respect had developed between them.

Edmund Menheire, imposing on his heavy cob, had trotted
up to ride alongside her, and Sophie acknowledged his presence
with a brief nod of greeting. As they rode upwards in the gentle
September sunshine he conversed with her gravely on a number
of topics that interested him. He was untroubled by her lack of
opinions and quite unaware that the smile on her lips, the
happiness that radiated from her like warmth from a flame, had
nothing to do with him.

Perdita and Louisa followed behind, both lost in their private
thoughts. Louisa had been delighted by the coolness with which

Piers and Perdita had greeted each other. Perdita was puzzled by his animosity, but did not waste any time over it: the future master of Trecarne, whose broad back she was following, was the sole object of her schemes. She was wondering what the key to Edmund Menheire's affection might be. In her experience everyone could be reached if only the right strategy was employed. Even her father – as she had discovered on the morning when he threatened to throw her in the horse pond and sheer fright had shocked her into standing up to him. The same trick had not, more's the pity, worked with Colonel Menheire, but she thought she had detected the first stirrings of interest in Edmund on that occasion. It irked her now that Piers had turned against her. Not that the opinion of an impecunious cousin was in itself of any importance, but she had been hoping to make use of his friendship in her campaign to win over the heir. More bothersome still was that she did not know why he had defected: Perdita liked to know the reasons for people's opinions.

Grooms and riders bunched up in an untidy gaggle as they reached the spot that had been selected for the race. Charger was frothing with excitement, unable to contain his energy any longer, and Piers rode him in a series of wide circles to calm him.

'Edmund,' said Kip, who was bubbling with eagerness, 'you stay here and start them off. I'll go down to the far end with your man in case it's a close finish.' He grinned. 'Five shillings says Falcon will win by three lengths or more.'

'I'll not stoop to gambling,' said Edmund coldly, 'but I'll start the race for you. Raise your hat when you are ready for me to begin them.'

'Right you are. Good luck both of you – especially Falcon!' And with a cheerful wave Kip cantered away down the track alongside the Menheires' groom. Perdita saw him turn in the saddle and shout out to his fellow rider and the two horses stretched to a gallop. She smiled. No doubt it was another impromptu wager.

Edmund dismounted carefully and walked across to Sophie. He attempted to take hold of Falcon's bridle. The stallion rolled his eyes and stepped neatly sideways. Sophie leaned forward to soothe him.

'There, there,' she said, running her strong fingers along the grey crest of his mane, 'not long now, Falcon.' She was watching Kip and the Menheires' groom who had nearly travelled the half-mile to the place where the race was to finish.

Edmund said, 'Mistress Sutton, may I assist you to dismount?'

'Why?' Sophie looked down in surprise at his upturned face.

'Your man will wish to change his saddle.'

'My man?'

'In preparation for the race.' Edmund was prepared to be tolerant of Sophie's absent-minded questions.

Her eyes lit up with a teasing smile. 'Surely, sir, you do not expect me to ride astride in front of so many people.'

Edmund curved his lips in a manner intended to show that he was not without a sense of humour, though clearly he thought her joke in poor taste. He lowered his voice as he replied, 'No more than you would wish your groom to endure a lady's saddle.'

'My groom? Whatever has he to do with it?'

'My dear Mistress Sutton, if he is to ride Falcon—'

'But he will not ride Falcon.'

'I see. Not the groom. Then why has your brother gone to the end of the field? Do you wish me to ride Falcon for you?'

Sophie burst out laughing. 'Not you, not Kip, not the groom. No one is allowed to ride Falcon but me.'

'That's right,' Louisa chipped in brightly. 'Sir Richard made Sophie swear an oath when he gave her Falcon. No one else is permitted to ride him.'

'Then how will he race?'

'Sophie will ride him, of course.'

Perdita observed with relief that Edmund had finally grasped the details of the situation. He was flabbergasted. 'But – but that's impossible!'

'I assure you, sir,' said Sophie, growing impatient with the joke, 'it is not impossible at all.'

'This is outrageous. You cannot possibly take part in a race. It is madness, complete madness. I cannot allow it. It is out of the question.'

'Please be calm, sir, you are upsetting poor Falcon.'

'There, you see, the horse is too strong for you. You cannot manage him even now.'

'He does not like it when people wave their arms and shout at him, that is all!'

'I will hold him for you.' And this time Edmund succeeded in catching Falcon's bridle just behind the bit. 'There, I have him now. There's no need to be frightened any longer, Mistress Sutton. I'll hold him steady while you dismount.'

'Really, I am not the least bit frightened.' Sophie had gone pink with exasperation. 'Please release him before there is an accident.'

'No, no, I insist. It would be entirely irresponsible of me to let this folly continue. If the boys choose to risk their necks in a reckless escapade then I'll not stand in their way, but for a young lady—'

'Is anything the matter?' Piers had been so occupied with restraining his own mount that he had not heard his cousin's argument. The ebony stallion's neck and flanks were already drenched with sweat. 'Kip is signalling us to begin. If I hold Charger back much longer he'll work himself into a fever.'

Edmund said sternly, 'There will be no race, Piers. There has been a misunderstanding. I cannot permit Mistress Sutton to endanger herself in this manner. Your young friend Kip has put his sister up to this. It is irresponsible madness and—'

'Is this true?' As Charger pranced sideways, Piers threw the question over his shoulder towards Sophie.

She was frowning. She said, 'Your cousin is under some misapprehension.'

'Not I, Mistress Sutton.' Edmund smiled up at her serenely. 'You have been led into error by the enthusiasm of others, but now that I have been able to explain things clearly, I know you will wish to be guided by me alone.'

'What?'

'Just get down from your horse and I will catch you if you fall. I can arrange everything.'

Precisely what happened next, it was difficult to say: Charger was pawing the ground in a lather of impatience. He plunged forward suddenly and kicked up his heels, almost unseating Piers. At the same moment Falcon, the whites of his eyes gleaming beneath pale lashes, jerked up his head and cracked the bony edge of his nose against Edmund's jaw. Edmund let out a cry of pain and staggered backwards, releasing his hold on the bridle. Sophie leaned over in the saddle and shouted, 'Now!' Falcon reared. When his front hoofs touched the ground again she gave him his head and he leaped forward, Charger beside him, and the two horses thundered away down the grassy track. In the distance, half a mile away, two tiny figures could be observed. One was waving his hat frantically.

As the hoofbeats faded, Perdita slipped from her horse and ran to Edmund's side. He had sunk on to his knees and was clutching his head with both hands.

'Dear heavens!' exclaimed Perdita. 'Are you badly hurt?'

'Stop them!' he groaned. 'Stop them before there is a terrible accident.'

'I fear it is too late,' said Perdita.

Instinctively Edmund reached out and she grasped him firmly by the hand and helped him to his feet. He watched the two riders, but from this distance it was impossible to see who was in the lead.

His hand still firmly held in hers, Perdita said softly, 'I was so relieved when you tried to stop their madness. I never thought Sophie was intending to ride Falcon herself.' And then she added, in a voice meant only for his ears, 'Women who have grown up in the country have no idea of what is proper.' She did not want Louisa to overhear her words and repeat them to Sophie. She was, after all, extremely fond of Sophie.

Edmund glanced down at her coldly and withdrew his hand. He said, 'I could not prevent them.'

'But you tried.' Perdita folded her hands demurely in front of her and said, 'Pray God Sophie comes to no harm. Already she is like a sister to me.'

She heard Louisa's scornful voice. 'Of course Sophie won't come to any harm. She's a better rider than anyone.'

'This is madness,' said Edmund.

'You did everything you could,' Perdita told him.

'It's all wrong,' Louisa said crossly. 'We should have told them to start the race at the far end and finish it by us.'

'Good heavens,' said Perdita, feigning alarm, 'and risk being trampled to death by those two brutes?'

At the tremor of fear in her voice, Edmund turned to look at her and she thought she detected a softening in his glance. She wondered if perhaps this, after all, was the way to reach him.

Louisa said stoutly, 'At least we'd have been able to see who the winner was. Oh, look, they must have finished! Was it Falcon? I'm sure it must have been Falcon!'

'So long as Sophie is safe,' said Perdita weakly. 'I can hardly bear to watch.'

Another glance from Edmund. Almost approving, this time.

Perdita felt a small spurt of triumph. She debated whether it might be in her interest to faint. A brief moment of reflection convinced her to keep that for another occasion. It might well prove to be a trump card.

'Of course Sophie is safe,' said Louisa. 'Oh, look, they are coming back.'

'Thank heavens for that,' said Perdita, 'I feel quite giddy with the suspense.'

'Here, Mistress Treveryan,' said Edmund manfully, 'why don't you take my arm?'

'Oh, thank you. That is such a comfort.'

She allowed herself to waver slightly as she rested her hand on his broad forearm. He led her to a small rise in the ground where she sank down, uttering faint words of gratitude. They were seated there, side by side, when the riders returned. Kip, Piers and Sophie were all laughing and excited.

'Who won?' shouted Louisa, as soon as they came within earshot.

Leaving Perdita behind, Edmund hurried towards them. 'Thank the Lord there's no harm done!' He was addressing Sophie, but this time, in spite of his concern, he was careful to remain at a safe distance from Falcon's tossing head.

'Falcon won by a length!' exclaimed Piers.

'I knew it!' Louisa was delighted.

'It was a draw,' laughed Sophie. 'They were neck and neck to the end.'

'Yes, and then Falcon pulled ahead.'

'It was Falcon all the way!' Kip was beside himself with pleasure.

'All thanks to your sister's excellent riding,' said Piers. Charger was blowing and puffing, his flanks creamed with sweat. 'You should have seen her, Edmund. I've never seen anything like it.'

Sophie beamed down at Edmund, proud of her achievement and proud of Falcon. 'There was nothing for you to worry about, you see. Falcon took good care of me. He always does.'

Edmund remained unsmiling. He said, 'The animal bolted. I do not consider a horse that runs away in that manner to be at all suitable.'

'Bolted?' Piers queried.

'I saw how Falcon galloped. Mistress Sutton was quite unable to restrain him.'

Piers laughed. 'Why would she want to do that?'

'The brute was altogether out of control. He was going much too fast.'

'For pity's sake, Edmund, it was a race,' said Piers. And then, grinning broadly, 'Horses are supposed to go fast in a race.'

Perdita was finding it hard to suppress her laughter and Sophie, she noticed, had turned aside on the pretext of adjusting her skirts. Edmund, however, was growing angry.

'This is no joking matter, Piers. Mistress Sutton could have been badly hurt, killed even. And I would have felt myself responsible. Had I known she was planning to ride the beast herself, I would never have consented to this whole scheme. Mistress Treveryan was seriously alarmed.'

'She was?' Piers looked intently at Perdita. She dropped her eyes.

Sophie exclaimed, 'Oh, Perdita, you shouldn't have worried about me. You knew I'd be all right.'

'You were going so terribly fast,' said Perdita, in a tremulous voice. 'It was quite terrifying to observe.'

Piers was continuing to look at her. The laughter had died on his face.

Edmund said, 'Mistress Treveryan, let me help you to mount.'

'Thank you so much. I must confess I feel quite weak.'

'I can't think what all this fuss is about,' exclaimed Kip, thoroughly bewildered. 'It was an altogether brilliant race. The ground was hard, that favoured Charger. Falcon would have won by three lengths easily if there had been rain. Why don't we try them again in a month? I know, best of three! And if Falcon wins all three then—'

'Mistress Sutton will not be racing again,' said Edmund firmly. Having helped Perdita to remount, he summoned his groom to bring his own horse to him.

His words, uttered with such absolute certainty, cast a mood of gloom over the group that affected even Kip. Sophie, leaning forward slightly in the saddle and ruffling Falcon's mane, had been watching him carefully. There was a curious expression in her brown eyes, but she did not contradict his statement.

'We will return home,' said Edmund, 'and hear no more of this foolishness.'

It was a more subdued group of riders who set off this time. Just as Perdita was about to leave with the rest, Piers said to his groom, 'Check the forefeet on Mistress Treveryan's mount. I think he may be about to cast a shoe.'

The man dutifully checked each of her horse's hoofs, but found no problem.

'Very well,' said Piers to the man, 'you may catch up with the others.'

The groom jumped on his small pony and rode off after the rest. Perdita was urging her own horse to follow, but Piers rode Charger across the path, cutting her off. 'What, in God's name, do you think you're doing?' He no longer made any attempt to hide his fury.

Perdita coloured. 'What do you mean?'

'All that nonsense about being frightened. And weak. Exactly what are you trying to do?'

Perdita said icily, 'I don't know what business it is of yours, but as it happens I found the whole enterprise extremely distressing.'

Piers snorted with contempt. 'Do you really expect me to believe that?'

'It's the truth!'

'My cousin might be taken in but don't try to fool me too.'

'I was terrified.'

'Mistress Treveryan, it is abundantly clear that a woman who visits a back-street cockfight alone in the roughest area of Plymouth Old Town is hardly going to get a fit of the vapours at the sight of two horses galloping in the opposite direction.'

'I was concerned for Sophie's safety. She is my dearest friend.'

'I would hate to be one of your friends, then, if that is how you treat them.'

'What are you suggesting?'

'Please don't insult my intelligence.'

'You have a vivid imagination, sir, that's not the same as intelligence at all.' Perdita tried to drive her horse on, but Piers was determined to stop her and Charger, still heated from the race, buffeted against her. Her horse skittered sideways and she had to grip his mane to prevent herself from falling off. Piers watched, but did not intervene to help her.

'I must say, I am surprised at you,' he said, when she had righted herself. 'Bad enough that you betrayed Kip, but to betray Sophie as well.'

'Kip?' exclaimed Perdita, still breathless from her near escape. 'What has Kip to do with it?'

'I suppose you are innocent of that one too?'

'What one?' Now she was genuinely bewildered.

'You're a fine actress, madam. I grant you that much.'

'For heaven's sake, tell me how you think I have harmed Kip!'

Piers only stared at her. Perdita did not at all like to be stared at quite so relentlessly.

'If you don't tell me, then how—' She broke off, remembering the sequence of events. She stared at him in horror. 'You think I told my father he had run away from the *Fearless*. You think that is how he knew!'

'Oh, bravo, Mistress Treveryan. Now we see the innocent surprise. Excellent entertainment.' But he did not look entertained.

'It's the truth!'

'Undoubtedly. If you say so.'

'Very well, think what you like. It is no concern of mine. But so far as Kip is concerned you could not be more wrong. I never told my father about Kip.'

'Then how did he know?'

'As it happens, it was the pilot who told him, the one who had escorted the *Fearless* out of Plymouth Sound. Master Boulter discovered Kip's absence almost at once and sent a message back to my father with the pilot, a certain Tom Cribbin. I was there when he arrived and you may ask him yourself, if you like. It was nothing at all to do with me.' She saw that he was tempted to believe her. She said, 'Besides, what reason would I have to tell my father about Kip?'

'So that you could return to Rossmere the sooner. Precisely as it has turned out.'

'And why would I want to do that?'

'I was wondering that myself. Today's little performance has given me the answer.'

Perdita was so angry she could hardly speak. 'This is outrageous. I'll not stay here to be insulted by you. Get out of my way and let me join the others or I'll – I'll—'

'Yes?'

For answer, Perdita raised her riding stick and would have brought it down on his head, or Charger's – it made no difference – had they not both skipped out of her way, leaving the track ahead clear. Her horse glimpsed the tip of her whip just as Perdita urged him on. In a panic he shot forward, almost unseating her, and careered off in pursuit of the others. Perdita had been too busy arguing with Piers to get a firm purchase on the saddle, the ground was uneven and at the first bend in the path she felt herself parting company with her mount. At the second bend she slithered, undignified and furious, to the ground. The horse cantered off after the rest.

Clatter of hoofbeats, and Charger's dark legs came to a halt in front of her.

'Are you all right?' It was Piers's voice.

'That was your fault!' She stood up and shook out her skirts.

'Yes, I suppose it was. Let us hope it teaches you to be more careful with your whip in future.'

Perdita saw that he was laughing.

He sprang down from the saddle. His blue eyes were sparkling. 'Are you quite sure you're not hurt?'

'Of course I'm not.'

'Such bravery. Can this be the same young lady who was so alarmed by the sight of two horses galloping?'

She said angrily, 'Mine has run away.'

'So I see.'

'You must let me have yours.'

'No, I don't think that is advisable. We may walk a while. One of the men is sure to bring your horse back soon, and the quiet walking will do Charger good. It will probably do us all good.'

'What do you mean?'

Piers had looped Charger's reins over his arm and started down the stony path. He said, 'I believe I was wrong to accuse you of betraying Kip. I owe you an apology.'

'At the very least.'

'So I apologise. Wholeheartedly.' He waited, but Perdita was in no mood for a gracious acceptance. He sighed and continued, 'That still leaves the problem of my cousin.'

'Edmund?'

'Yes. It is common knowledge that Edmund intends to ask Mistress Sutton to marry him.'

'Sophie will never accept.'

Piers stopped and turned to look at her. 'What makes you say that?'

'She told me so herself.'

'In the last few days?'

'No. In the spring.'

'I see.' He began to walk again, but more slowly. 'I think we may assume that her opinions have altered during the summer. At all events, she has given my cousin every encouragement.'

'That is because she is Sophie.'

'Meaning?'

'She is kind and generous to everyone. It is her way. It doesn't signify anything.'

'For her sake, I hope she has changed her mind since the spring. Or else that you misunderstood her meaning. If you have any real affection for her—'

'But I do. I care for her as much as anyone.'

His amused smile at this declaration might have indicated his opinion that this was a statement of little value, but he went on, 'She would make Edmund an excellent wife. More to the point, it would be a good match for her too.'

'That, surely, is for her to decide.'

255

'So long as there is no meddling by others.'

Perdita was about to protest, but then she thought better of it.

'I am sure,' Piers went on, 'that I need not mention that her family are in a poor way financially. An alliance with the Menheires would benefit them all.'

'I have no interest in financial considerations.'

Piers sighed. 'Just why do I find it so hard to believe that?' he asked.

'Are you always so intolerably rude?'

'Only when I am with you. Then it seems to come naturally. I believe usually I am thought to be a model of courtesy. You must bring out the worst in me.'

'You flatter yourself.'

'So be it. We must set ourselves to consider what is to be done about Mistress Sutton and my doting cousin.'

'They don't need any interference from us.'

'Precisely. And if you were safely returned to your home in Plymouth, then I would agree with you entirely. But you are not. You are most evidently here. And, for reasons I'd not dream of attempting to unravel, you would appear to have an interest in my dear cousin. No, no, don't waste time in denials, Mistress Treveryan. Besides, I have no objection to your ambitions and I can understand them easily. Edmund is my cousin – who knows his merits better than I do?'

Perdita did not answer. She was curious to know what was coming next.

'However,' Piers continued, 'I am also concerned about Mistress Sutton and her family. Perhaps we should strike a bargain, you and I. What do you think?'

'I must hear what the bargain is first.'

'Quite simply, that you leave Edmund and Mistress Sutton to their own devices until he has made his proposal. If you are correct and she turns him down – without any meddling by you – then I give you my word I will help you all I can.'

'You would help me?'

'Yes. If you wish to court my cousin I will give you every assistance. But only if I am convinced Mistress Sutton has been sincere in her rejection of him. I must warn you, however, that I believe she will accept.'

Perdita was silent for a little while, pondering. She said, 'This is most irregular.'

'Yes.'

'Why are you offering to do this?'

'It's simple. Sophie Sutton is everything I could wish for in a relative. If, as you say, she is not interested in him, then I am sure you would be an excellent substitute. More entertaining, certainly.'

Perdita decided to ignore this last remark. 'Are you to be trusted, Master Menheire?'

'Are you? However, I am prepared to take the risk if you will too.'

'And may I rely on your absolute discretion?'

'Have I not proved that already? Ah, good, your horse is being returned.'

The groom was full of apologies and concern as he ran towards them leading Perdita's mount.

'Don't worry, Jeffreys,' said Piers. 'We have enjoyed the walk.'

Perdita turned to him with a sudden smile. 'Indeed we have. It has been most rewarding.'

'Does that mean we have a bargain, Mistress Treveryan?'

'Yes. I think we do.'

'Excellent.' Piers turned away and gripped Charger's saddle, ready to mount before saying as an afterthought to the groom, 'Be careful how you assist Mistress Treveryan, Jeffreys. She has been much frightened by her fall. I believe she has a nervous disposition and is easily alarmed. We must be sure to take every care.'

By the time Perdita and the others returned to Rossmere, even Sir Richard Treveryan had to admit it was too late to set off for Plymouth that day.

'Have your bags packed at once,' he told his daughter. 'We leave at dawn tomorrow.'

'What about Kip?' she asked. 'What are you going to do about him?'

'For the time being, nothing at all. I shall have to see how the situation has changed by the end of the month.'

'Father, may I stay here until you come back at Michaelmas? It is only three weeks away and it seems as if we have only just arrived.'

'No, you will come with me.'

Perdita pleaded with him to be allowed to stay but, having been thwarted in his plans for Kip, he was in no mood to compromise. 'We leave at dawn and there's an end of it.'

'Yes, Father.' Perdita put her hand to her forehead. 'I only hope I'll be well enough to travel.'

'You will be,' he said grimly, as he left the room.

Furious, Perdita threw a slipper at the door as it closed, then stood lost in thought.

Suddenly decisive, she put on her outdoor shoes and hurried down the stairs and into the garden.

That night the whole household was aware of how violently Perdita had been taken ill. Honor was too afraid of infection to come near, but Sophie and Cary took turns to sit by her bedside. Even Louisa forgot her dislike of Perdita long enough to be seriously concerned.

By the time Richard went to see her in the morning, the dawn light revealed the deathly pallor of her skin, the greenish circles around her eyes, her all-too obvious weakness. 'Oh, Father,' she breathed, 'I'm so sorry . . .'

'There, there, Perdita,' said Sophie. 'You must not tire yourself with talking.'

Richard stared at her long and hard. He placed his hand on her forehead. It was damp with perspiration. He said to Sophie, 'Please see that I am kept informed.'

'You are leaving anyway?'

'Yes. If I was a betting man like your young brother, I'd lay odds she makes a speedy recovery.'

'Let us hope you are right,' said Sophie doubtfully.

He bade them both a brisk farewell. A few minutes later, two horses could be heard setting off from the front of the house.

Perdita would have liked to go to the window, but she was too weakened to do more than raise her head from the pillow.

'Has he gone?' she asked.

'Yes,' said Sophie, leaning out so she could see the beginning of the lime avenue, 'he's gone.'

'Thank heavens,' murmured Perdita. 'I think I'll sleep now.'

By the evening of that day Perdita was already on the mend and during the night, when no one was about, she was strong enough to take the few remaining berries, which she had hidden beneath her sheet, and throw them out of the window.

After only two days more, her recovery was complete.

Chapter Twenty

'You're looking mighty pleased with yourself, Edmund. Anyone would think she had accepted you already.'

'The outcome of our meeting can scarcely be in doubt.'

'I'm glad you think so. But too much confidence may be a mistake.'

Edmund merely smiled, and continued to ride in contented silence along the leafy lanes between Trecarne and Rossmere. He was convinced that Piers was wrong to advise caution. It was unthinkable that Mistress Sophie Sutton might refuse the offer of marriage he intended to make that morning. Assessing the proposed match as if it were a balance sheet – and Edmund knew of no other way to assess any situation – the advantages were all on his side. His family was wealthy and hers was on the verge of destitution and that was the beginning and end of the matter.

Though he was far from being the kind of mean-spirited fellow who gloats over the misfortunes of his fellow man, it would have been flying in the face of Providence for Edmund not to take advantage of opportunities when they arose, especially if those opportunities had been created by the errors or laziness of others.

His father's rapid rise to wealth and position in the county had been founded on this simple principle and Edmund had never questioned it. Father and son lent money at reasonable rates to people who were experiencing a period of temporary difficulty. When these difficulties increased, it was only normal business practice for the debtor to forfeit his boat, house or business to the lender. That was how things were done.

Edmund had occasionally heard wicked accusations levelled against his father: people had claimed he deliberately sabotaged the enterprises of those who owed him money, but since no one had ever come up with a single shred of evidence, it was clear that these were the vicious slanders of people who wished to lay the blame for their misfortunes at someone else's feet. He had no patience with such whiners.

After a while he said calmly, 'Mistress Sutton would never turn down a match so obviously to her advantage.'

'You make it sound as if money is the only consideration,' said Piers cheerfully. 'But, in that case, you'd hardly be about to propose marriage to a woman without any at all.'

'I have observed that Mistress Sutton is a woman of good sense, hard-working and agreeable. She comes from an ancient family. And, what is more surprising, my father indicated a few months ago that he was in favour of an alliance between our family and the Suttons.'

Piers regarded his cousin with amusement. He said, 'So Mistress Sutton's great charm and beauty have played no part in your decision?'

'There is no virtue in charm, Piers. She has a pleasant nature and will, I am sure, make a dutiful wife.'

'Dutiful?'

'Certainly.' Edmund had no doubts on this score. He had seen how Sophie toiled for her family, how she laboured in kitchen and dairy from morning till night and had even, so he heard, done farm work when necessary. If so, it could only be because she was obeying orders. He could imagine no other reason why a gentleman's daughter would stoop to such degrading activities.

Piers, however, remembered how Sophie had raced Falcon on the Downs, and thought his cousin might be in for some surprises after his marriage. Edmund had also been troubled by the events of that day. Of course, in his view, the horse had bolted and the race had been an accident, but even so, there had been alarming hints of wilfulness that must be checked before they grew worse. The sooner this matter was settled between them, the better for all.

During his many visits to Rossmere this summer Edmund had noticed the laxity of the Suttons' ways, an ease of conversation and behaviour, and a complete disregard for the proper distance between masters and servants. Clearly, the moment had come to bring such unruly activity to an end. His future bride had been too much in the company of her disreputable brothers and he must bring his influence to bear to calm her high spirits.

Even now, just thinking of the way she had ridden that stallion, there was a tight clutch of fury round his heart. The horse must be got rid of. A small carriage with a pair of matched bays and an elderly coachman to guide them – that was the way for the wife of Edmund Menheire to travel. He would have a coach made and bestow it on her as soon as they were married. From now on, she must accept gifts from no one else. He imagined her pleasure on first seeing the coach. His spirits rose.

Piers said, 'Your father approves and you believe she will be dutiful. Is that all that recommends Mistress Sutton to you?'

'Her family have a good name,' said Edmund, after some deliberation, 'though in recent times they have failed to do it credit.'

'And what her great beauty? Is that of no consideration at all?'

'I confess, I am hardly aware of it. Unlike you, Piers, I am not swayed by such frivolous concerns.'

At this last remark Piers raised a sceptical eyebrow, but judged it a waste of time to contradict it. Looking at the sober, confident face of the heir to Trecarne, there could be no doubt that he himself believed absolutely in the truth of what he was saying.

Piers had seen enough of the household in which Edmund had been reared to know that he had been educated to see the appearance of things as a snare and a temptation only. They had chosen to live at Trecarne because it was the largest house available in Cornwall: never once had they noticed the elegance of its proportions, the fine aspect sheltered by the oak woods and overlooking the bay. He knew that when Edmund looked at an orchard full of April blossom he saw only the value of the fruit that would be produced in the autumn and nothing else.

Even so, Piers knew that Edmund was only human, though he himself sometimes gave an impression of thinking otherwise. Edmund might believe he was guided only by notions of duty and advancement, but he was a man of strong passions for all that, passions that had been dammed up for far too long. Fear of his father had kept him within bounds until now: Piers wondered what might occur when his cousin finally slipped the paternal leash.

In the meantime, Piers had watched Edmund when he was in the company of Sophie Sutton and knew he was deeply affected by her beauty. He thought it a great shame Edmund could not allow himself to enjoy this aspect of his courtship but, then, Piers frequently thought it a pity that both father and son had created for themselves a life altogether bleak and narrow when they might have enjoyed so much more.

Maybe Sophie Sutton, once she was installed as mistress at Trecarne, would begin the process of their enlightenment. He himself had tried, but it had proved a thankless task. Now he confined himself to being grateful that he had passed the first fifteen years of his life with his improvident and mostly contented parents. Their capacity for gaiety and devotion had been beyond the imagination of the Menheires.

'Well, Edmund,' said Piers, as they arrived at Rossmere, 'I wish you luck in your enterprise.'

Edmund looked at him with some disdain. 'Luck, Piers? I thank heavens that I have a more solid reason for my confidence than a mere reliance on luck. Where the devil are those confounded grooms?'

'Mistress Treveryan, what a pleasant surprise. I assumed you went back to Plymouth with your father.'

'Unfortunately I was unwell and so unable to accompany him.'

'Unwell? I am sorry to hear of it.'

'Yes, it was most unpleasant.'

'Do you plan to stay at Rossmere long?'

'Until the beginning of October at least. My father will return before Michaelmas. I'm afraid that if I attempt to follow him to Plymouth, as he wishes, it may bring on a relapse.'

'To be avoided at all costs. Shall we walk in the garden? My cousin and Mistress Sutton are likely to be some time together.'

★　　★　　★

Sophie was in the middle of skinning a brace of hares when Louisa burst into the kitchen and told her excitedly that Edmund Menheire and his cousin had come visiting. That Edmund was wearing his grandest coat, the one with the silver trim, and had asked to speak with Sophie on a matter of great importance. It could only mean a proposal of marriage.

Sophie's first reaction was to lament the interruption. It was Louisa and Cary who chivvied her into removing her blood-spotted apron, fussed with the brown hair she had pushed under her cap first thing that morning and had forgotten about ever since, and who had fetched flower-water and towels to clean her hands and face. They begged her to change out of her everyday gown of brown wool into the green worsted with the taffeta skirts that she kept for best, but Sophie drew the line at that.

Stephen, who had dropped into the kitchen to pick up a hunk of bread and cheese before setting off for the fields where the barley was being cut, came to her aid.

'Even a fool could see Sophie's as lovely as any woman in Cornwall,' he said, putting his hands on her shoulders and surveying her with affection. 'No need for any other clothes. I only hope Master Menheire knows his good fortune.'

'Oh, Uncle, don't say that.'

'It's the truth.'

'Can I talk with you a moment, Uncle Stephen? In private. You see, I don't want—'

Louisa interrupted, catching her by the arm. 'Come *on*, Sophie. Don't keep him waiting all day. He may change his mind.'

Stephen smiled. 'We'll talk later,' he said.

He wondered why she looked so wretched as she was hustled from the kitchen by her sister. Perhaps it was only natural for her to feel some qualms of maidenly reluctance. He was sure that Edmund Menheire would think none the worse of her for that.

Because Edmund believed that the appearances of things were of no importance and that his carnal urges were a distracting nuisance, he was all unprepared for the fierce emotions by which he was often buffeted on the most inconvenient occasions.

Such as now.

Here he was, endeavouring to explain to Mistress Sophie Sutton the various practical benefits to be derived from a union between them, while all the time his efforts were being undermined by his own rebellious body. His heart was pumping like a horse after a fierce gallop, while his hands and chest were covered in a film of sweat. Worst of all, he had to keep altering his position for fear that other, less subtle signs of his agitation would become embarrassingly visible pressing against the cloth of his breeches.

He had expected, in so far as he had imagined this scene at all, that Mistress Sutton would be the one to be ruffled, not he. Yet she stood before him, silent and composed, while he blustered and stammered his proposal like a schoolboy with an ill-prepared lesson. He could not think what the matter was. Just as he was attempting to outline his remarkable generosity in not requiring her family to provide any dowry, he noticed a strand of brown hair that had escaped from her cap and was drifting idly and wantonly over the creamy skin of her neck. This conjured up vague images of rumpled sheets and softness and disarray, which led swiftly and disturbingly to the thought that the true purpose of marriage was the getting of children. His mouth was so dry at the prospect of fixing strong sons on her that he stumbled over his words and had to begin the sentence again.

At last the preamble was done. Having set out the reasons for the marriage, Edmund was just moving on to questions of timing and other details, when Sophie interrupted him. 'One moment, Master Menheire, I have not yet agreed to your proposal.'

Edmund blinked. He felt a shiver of annoyance at the interruption. He hated to be thwarted. Then he became aware of the scent that drifted from her, a kitchen scent of woodsmoke and herbs and something else besides, something warm and womanly. He said breathlessly, 'We can be married by All Hallows.'

'*If* we are to be wed. You are proceeding at too fast a pace.'

'Of course, of course. We must take our time.' Edmund

collected himself. Although her acceptance of him was obviously a formality, given their relative circumstances, he knew that in similar situations people in business frequently liked to maintain the pretence of being free to negotiate. Usually he had no patience with such shenanigans, but in this instance he decided it was as well to humour her. He said, 'My apologies. In my eagerness I have perhaps been over-hasty. One should never omit the proper forms.' He paused and stretched his lips into a smile before saying, 'Mistress Sutton, will you do me the honour of becoming my wife?'

'I do not know.'

'What?' The smile faded from his face. He was baffled, and more than a little annoyed. Then he told himself that this must be all part of some elaborate ritual that gentlewomen insisted on: it was, after all, the first and last time in her life that she would have even the semblance of power. He forced himself to say calmly, 'Perhaps if you explained to me the reasons for your uncertainties, I might set your fears at rest.'

Sophie frowned, then said, 'It is very simple. I do not know whether you and I are suited to be man and wife. I do not know if we would bring each other happiness, and I fear we might bring each other only grief.'

'Ah, is that all? Have no worries on that score. I have every confidence that you will make me an admirable wife.'

She smiled at that, for some reason. 'Maybe so, Master Menheire, but that was only the half of my concern.' But she saw he did not follow the thread of her meaning, so she said, 'I think, perhaps, I need time to consider this more fully.'

'Then I am prepared to wait. You will find me a patient man, Mistress Sutton.' He folded his hands in front of him in a pose intended to demonstrate his capacity for patience. It had the added advantage of hiding that part of his anatomy that gave the lie to his words. Sophie frowned slightly and looked down at her shoes. They were pliant and battered, misshapen from long use.

As he stood and watched her, Edmund was reminded of the first time he had singled her out for particular attention, just over two years before. He and Piers had been riding near the cliffs one hot afternoon towards midsummer. By chance they had come across Sophie and Kip together with a group of their friends, resting in the shade of a solitary oak. Having enjoyed food and drink they were diverting themselves with childish games. Piers had joined in at once. Edmund, disapproving but curious all the same, hung back and watched. There had been running races and jumping. Sophie and her brother had argued about some complicated handicapping system. She struck him lightly on the shoulder. He retaliated and, within moments, they were fighting together like young animals. She pinned him to the ground and tickled him until he begged for mercy.

Edmund had never forgotten the sight of those strong, pale arms holding her brother against the heath, the glimpse of white ankles beneath her skirts. The hint of so much more. Unable to hold back any longer, he took a step forward and said, 'Well, then, and have you made your mind up now?'

Startled, she raised her eyes, caught sight of his expression and then she actually laughed. 'Is this an example of your famous patience, Master Menheire? When I said I needed time in which to reach my decision, I was thinking of a little longer than this. Maybe if you come back in two days, I will be able to give you your answer then.'

'Two days! But that is ridiculous!'

'On the contrary, it seems to be hardly any time at all in which to make a decision of such importance to us both.'

Edmund knew that, in business dealings, there is a time to be lenient and a time to crack the whip. He decided the latter moment had arrived. He said firmly, 'Enough of this tomfoolery, Mistress Sutton. There is no reason to prolong these negotiations merely on a whim. You know full well that I have made my intentions clear over these last weeks, so my proposal can hardly have come as a surprise. I will not submit to the indignity of having to wait a further two days for an answer, which we both know full well must be in the affirmative.'

'It must?'

'Of course. After all, you are hardly in a position to refuse me.'

A dangerous edge entered Sophie's voice as she asked, 'Is that the case, Master Menheire?' but he did not notice.

He said, 'As your husband, I will, of course, treat you with all respect and honour due. The generosity of the marriage settlement I am proposing shows that quite plain. However, I refuse to put up with a delay. Such lovers' games might be gratifying to your pride, but—'

Sophie flushed as she interrupted him, 'I have no more interest in lovers' games, as you call them, than you do, but I insist on having two days in which to make up my mind. It is quite impossible for me to say yes to your proposal straight away – but, then, I do not know if I can refuse you either.'

'I should think not.'

'I need to discuss this with my mother. And also with Uncle Stephen.'

'As to your mother, she knows of my wishes and is entirely in agreement with them. In fact, she has indicated to me on several occasions that you welcome my attention, which has been my observation also. I fail to see that it has anything at all to do with your uncle.'

'It is just that I have always talked over any decision with him.'

Edmund felt himself to be back on firm ground again. 'Of course you have, Mistress Sutton, but only because you had no one else to lean on. Your uncle means no harm, I dare say, but he is hardly a man of any significance. Since your father's tragic death, your family has lacked firm leadership. During my visits here this summer it has been clear to me that your household suffers from the absence of a strong head. You will find matters very different at Trecarne. When we are man and wife, I can assure you that I will take care of everything!'

'Maybe that is precisely what I am afraid of.'

She smiled slightly as she said this. Edmund saw her smile as a signal that she was on the verge of capitulating. He took a step towards her. 'Afraid? You need be afraid no longer. From now on you will be guided by me alone.'

'If you are hoping to win my acceptance by such remarks, I should warn you that you are going about it in the wrong way.'

He took both her hands in his and gripped them close to his chest. His hands were surprisingly strong. 'It will be a fine thing when we are man and wife.'

'Please let go my hands.'

'Only when you have said yes.'

'I told you, you will have your answer in two days.'

'I cannot wait so long.'

'For a decision that must last a lifetime? It is not long at all. Now, let go of me and—'

'You will say yes. You must.'

'I must?'

'It would be madness for you to do otherwise.'

'Permit me to be the judge of that.'

'You are teasing me deliberately. I will not stand for it.'

'On the contrary—' Sophie made a final attempt to free her hands but Edmund only gripped them more tightly that ever and, leaning forward, he crushed his mouth down on hers.

In the narrow world in which he lived, he took orders from his father and everyone else took orders from him. Never had he been refused by a woman before. Never had he even had to wait or play the gallant. This was because he had always paid in coin for his pleasures, or singled out a woman who was not in a position to refuse. So far as he was concerned, Sophie Sutton was no different from the rest, for all that she had the airs of a fine lady; one glance at her battered shoes and threadbare gown had told him all that he needed to know. It could not damage his cause to show the real state of inequality between them. Besides, this was what his body had been urging him to do ever since he walked into the room. When Sophie twisted away from his lips, he seized her head between his palms and kissed her violently once again. Her hands were trapped against his chest and she had no way of freeing herself until he chose to release her.

As soon as he did she stepped swiftly away and positioned herself near the door. He saw, with some satisfaction, that she was flushed and trembling. 'You had no right to do that,' she burst out angrily.

Edmund smiled. 'Mistress Sutton, pray forgive me. I forgot myself. But, in the circumstances, I think I may be forgiven some slight excess of enthusiasm.'

'Believe me, sir, you do nothing to improve your chances when you act in such an ungentlemanly way. It does not seem to have occurred to you yet that I still have not consented to be your wife.'

Edmund folded his arms and regarded her. She was extending this little drama in a way that was growing tedious. It was time for him to play her at her own game and pretend to be withdrawing from the negotiation. By rights he ought now to tell her that if his offer did not meet with immediate acceptance then there was nothing more to be said between them. But he did not. He stood before her, his arms folded, and his expression was one she had not seen before.

'Mistress Sutton,' he said, as calmly as his ragged breathing allowed, 'I suggest we give up these childish games. You must be aware that you are in no position at all to turn me down.'

'What?'

'I have no wish to spell it out, but if you insist, then so be it. Your family's poverty is a matter of common knowledge.'

'That does not mean—'

'Be quiet and listen to me, you foolish woman. I will tell you precisely what it means. It means this whole household and everyone in it stands on the brink of disaster. It means that your mother is in debt to us for an amount she cannot possibly afford to repay. It means that you and your whole ragamuffin family can be turned out of Rossmere any time I give the word.'

Sophie stared at him in horror. 'Are you threatening me, Master Menheire?'

'Threats are unnecessary, in this case. Mere facts will suffice. It is really very simple. If no alliance takes place between us, then your family will lose Rossmere. It is only my father's great generosity that has made even this solution possible. By rights you should have forfeited Rossmere long since and I would have married a woman whose material assets would have helped our rise to prominence. You are not simple-minded, Mistress Sutton. I am sure you can see the situation plain.'

'Oh, yes, I begin to see much more clearly, thank you. But what of my wishes? Does it not trouble you at all that if I do agree to this marriage I might be acting only to save my family and not because I have any regard for you?'

'Why should it?' Edmund was genuinely puzzled. 'I am confident that once you are living with me at Trecarne as my wife you will learn to be perfectly agreeable.' He smiled. 'In fact, I look forward to it.'

Sophie shivered. Her hand was on the latch of the door. She said quietly, 'In that case, there is nothing more to be said between us.'

'Do you still mean to make me wait two days for my answer?'

'No, you can have it now. I will not marry you, Master Menheire.'

She lifted the latch, but he reached the door before she could open it and leaned the full weight of his shoulder against it as he said, 'I will try to forget that I ever heard you say this. Maybe I am not very good at expressing myself in words, maybe you expected a different kind of courtship, but when you have had time to reflect and talk this over with your mother, I have no doubt you will reach a different decision. I look forward to receiving word of your acceptance.'

'I hate to disappoint you, Master Menheire, but—'

'On the contrary, I am not in the least disappointed.'

He stood back with a smile of satisfaction, raised the latch and opened the door. Sophie felt more alarmed by his smiling confidence than she had been by his anger. She told herself he had been bluffing.

She was wrong. As he rode away from Rossmere, Edmund was almost contented with the morning's interview. Since her refusal of him made no logical sense, he decided that her words had been inspired simply by shock. Only give her a day or two to grasp the many advantages of the proposal he was making and she was sure to change her mind.

After all, her family's situation meant that she really had no choice.

Chapter Twenty-One

Towards late afternoon that day, a single horseman rode down the avenue that led to Rossmere. He wore a distinctive wide-brimmed hat and there was a small pack of cloth attached to his saddle. He paused on the gravel forecourt to observe the progress of the new roof, which was almost completed, then urged his horse under the arch that led to the stableyard at the rear. Although there was some inevitable loss of status by entering a house from the tradesman's area at the back, Luke had always found that this was more than outweighed by the useful information to be gleaned from a few minutes' casual conversation with the servants. Today was no exception.

Cary was sitting on a stool between the kitchen door and a low-silled window. An earthenware basin was clamped between her strong knees and a pile of pea-pods was growing beside her. She glanced up at his approach, but did not pause in her work. 'What brings you here, Master Hollar?' she asked.

'Is Mistress Sutton at home?'

'That depends which one you want.'

'Mistress Sophie Sutton. I have brought some cloth she ordered.'

'Leave it here, then. I'll see she gets it.'

'I must give it to her myself.'

Cary frowned. Not long after the dust had settled behind Edmund Menheire's retreating horse, the whole household had gained a rough idea of what he had said and done to Sophie. Sophie herself was angry, but not unduly upset. She took the view that she had had a narrow escape.

Her mother was less sanguine. Alice reacted with horror and insisted on talking to her elder daughter at once. Their raised voices could be heard in the winter parlour, but the exact substance of their conversation remained a mystery. What was apparent to all, when the two women emerged grim-faced, was that Sophie was deeply shaken by their meeting.

Cary had sat her down in the kitchen and mixed her a soothing drink, pouring in liberal quantities of their precious store of brandy. She was in no hurry to risk another upset, so she eyed Luke Hollar suspiciously and said, 'She may not be in the mood for visitors.'

Het had sidled over to stand next to her mother. Her mouth and hands were stained with blackberry juice. Seeing that Cary was distracted by the visitor, she dipped her hand into the basin of peas, took half a dozen and said, 'She sent him away with a flea in his ear.'

'Who?' asked Luke.

'Never you mind,' said Cary.

'Master Menheire,' said Het.

Cary jabbed her elbow against her daughter's side. 'Hold your tongue, young lady.'

'She did, though,' continued Het, undaunted. She remembered the Porthew draper from previous visits. Although often cool with adults, Luke enjoyed the company of children, and they responded with their trust. 'He tried to have his wicked way with her but she soon put him straight. I think perhaps she bashed him too, just to show him. Biff, right in the face. He fell down flat. We thought he was dead but—'

Sophie's voice could be heard from inside the house. 'Lord above, Cary, that child is worse than you with a tall story. By tomorrow the wretched man will have been decapitated at the very least – oh!'

Sophie was startled, as she laid her arms on the sill and leaned out of the window, to see that Het's story was being embellished not for Cary's benefit alone but for Luke Hollar. Her cheeks were already flushed from the brandy in Cary's hot posset, but her colour deepened as she said, 'Master Hollar, I did not know you were here.' Cary noted that Sophie did not look in the least

274

bit dismayed at the sight of him. On the contrary, she was most definitely pleased.

He bowed slightly. 'I brought the cloth.'

'Pay no attention to Het. She takes after her mother. What cloth?'

'We discussed it on St Ewan's Day.'

'But . . . wait a moment, please.' She tucked her head back in through the window and reappeared at the back door. Framed against the cool dark of the kitchen, she looked radiant, a vibrant contrast to the sorry creature Cary had been dosing only an hour or two earlier. Cary glanced from her to Master Hollar, and the first seeds of suspicion formed in her mind. Sophie said, 'You should not have gone to the trouble of bringing it yourself.'

'It was no trouble. As you know.' A smile on Luke's face.

'Yes, but I'm not sure if I can . . . We had better talk of this privately.' She reached down and ruffled Het's brown hair. 'Somewhere big ears won't be listening to every word we say and twisting them into goodness knows what. Come inside, Master Hollar.'

Cary stood up. 'I was just coming inside myself,' she said meaningfully.

'Why?' asked Sophie. 'You've not finished the peas yet.' Cary glowered at her. Sophie said, 'Oh, I see. Don't bother about me, Cary.'

'You've had enough upsets for one day, Mistress Sophie.'

'But I promise . . . oh, very well then. I'll take Bella her food and Master Hollar can come with me. Then you can watch us from here. If Master Hollar says anything to upset me I shall wave and you can come to my rescue. Will that do?' She retreated to the kitchen once more and emerged with a pailful of kitchen slops.

'Bella?' asked Luke as they walked away from the still-watchful Cary.

'Our oldest sow. She's due to be slaughtered next month so we're feeding her up. You should not have brought the cloth, Master Hollar. You know I cannot pay you for it, and I hate to think we owe you money.'

'You owe me nothing. Here, let me.'

They had reached a low-walled sty. A massive spotted sow

lurched to her feet as Luke took the bucket from Sophie. He emptied the contents into a stone trough and Bella fell on the food with glee. A couple of white doves settled on the roof of the sty and peered down, waiting their turn.

'Thank you,' said Sophie. 'That's very kind. About the cloth, I mean.'

'It's nothing.'

'I'll send you a side of bacon when it's hung.'

'Please, the money is of no importance.'

'Don't say that!' Sophie burst out with vehemence. 'It's everything, everything!' Her eyes had filled with tears.

Luke had turned and was watching her closely. He said, 'I take it there was some truth in the child's story.'

'Poor Bella. Bacon Bella. It's so sad.'

'Mistress Sutton, the Menheires can be dangerous enemies.'

'So I am learning.'

'Did he threaten you?'

Shocked, Sophie spun round to face him. 'Why do you ask that?'

'I know the kind of man he is. Edmund Menheire likes to play the gentleman, but only so long as he gets his own way. Neither he nor his father will accept anything less.'

'He is vile.'

'But very powerful.'

'You seem to know a great deal about him.'

'I have done commissions in the past for his father.'

Sophie's eyes widened. 'You work for the Menheires?'

'No. I never work for anyone but myself. From time to time, however, it suits me to accept commissions from others. I like to know what such men are doing.'

'But what business can you have in common with the Menheires?'

'I am a merchant. I travel a good deal. I can be useful to men like him in a great many ways. And no – I know what you are thinking. My visit here this afternoon has nothing at all to do with whatever passed between you and Edmund Menheire today. It is a coincidence, believe me.'

Sophie let out a sigh of relief. 'He does not have a black eye,' she said, 'whatever Het says.'

'More's the pity.'

'Yes.' She smiled.

Luke said, 'Mistress Sutton, I do not want to alarm you unnecessarily, but I advise you and your family to be careful in your dealings with the Menheires.'

'It is a little late for that.'

'This will not be the end of it. As well as lending money to your mother, I know that their man, Barnes, has been enquiring about your family's other debts.'

'What for?'

'He has been offering to take them over, at a small discount, of course.'

'But why would they do that?'

'Colonel Menheire still wants Rossmere.'

'They have the house and land at Trecarne, why do they want our home as well?'

'The why is not important. Colonel Menheire has already acquired several properties by lending large sums to the owners then claiming the land when the debts cannot be met. He will do so again, if he can.'

'Is there no way to stop him?'

'I don't know. Men like him are usually vulnerable in some way or other. I shall find out what I can and let you know. Maybe after church on Sunday we can talk together without attracting the suspicions of your cook, or anyone else. In the meantime, if there is any way I can help you, let me know.'

'Thank you, Master Hollar. I will.' She leaned forward and rubbed the bristly skin between Bella's ears. 'Sometimes I wish I was a pig, don't you? Life must be so much simpler.'

'Ask the sow about that come Michaelmas, when she's facing the knife.'

'I suppose so. But this year Michaelmas may well be difficult for us, too.'

Luke cursed himself for his lack of tact, since the loan repayments had to be made at Michaelmas, as he should have known. Having insisted that she accept the parcel of cloth, he made his farewells and left.

*   *   *

'What was my brother doing here?'

Perdita had seen Luke riding down the lime avenue towards the house, and she had taken care to remain out of sight until he was safely departed again. The memory of how she had responded to him in the spring still aroused her to anger and shame. It was simpler to avoid him. But now that he was gone, she was curious to know what had brought him to Rossmere.

She found Sophie hoeing cabbages in the vegetable patch beside the stables. Or, at least, Sophie had evidently intended hoeing the cabbages, but for once in her life she was too wretched and anxious to concentrate on the task in hand. She was leaning forward slightly, the handle of the hoe clasped between her breasts and with her battered hat tipped back from her face. She was gazing towards the near field where Amos and Sithney were leading the cows to drink from the stream, but from the look in her eyes it was not this tranquil, early-evening scene that she was contemplating.

Only when Perdita had repeated her question did Sophie turn and say, 'Oh, Perdita, it's you. Master Hollar brought some cloth that caught my eye on St Ewan's Day. He said it was to thank me for tending him in the spring.'

'Did Edmund Menheire really force himself on you?'

'Ugh, he is a loathsome man. I don't want to talk about it.'

'Poor Sophie, I've never seen you look so miserable.'

'I've never been so miserable in my life before, that's why,' said Sophie grimly.

Perdita felt restless. Perhaps it was seeing Sophie so unhappy, perhaps it was because the disturbing aura of Luke Hollar still lingered in the air about the house. Suddenly she said, 'Let's go for a ride. The men can have Falcon saddled in no time and one of the farm ponies will do for me. You always see things clearer when you're riding, you told me so yourself. Come on, Sophie. It won't do the cabbages any good to have you standing here looking like the face of doom.'

Sophie protested feebly, then allowed herself to be gently bullied by Perdita, and within a little while they were setting off along the track that led away from the demesne farm. Clouds of midges were dancing in the shafts of sunlight between the tall hedges and the ghostly shapes of evening moths fluttered against their faces. The air was heavy with the scent of late honeysuckle and meadowsweet. As Perdita had suspected, Sophie's spirits soon began to lift.

'You sent him packing anyway,' said Perdita. 'And good riddance too.'

'He threatened me, that was what was intolerable.'

'Well, and now you've done with him.'

'If only it was so simple.'

'What do you mean?'

Sophie leaned forward in the saddle to avoid an overhanging branch which Perdita, on her smaller mount, passed under without difficulty. 'When I said just now that he threatened me, I was not speaking of violence. Master Menheire said he could hurt my family badly.'

'That's just bully's tactics. Pay no attention.'

'That was what I thought. But when I spoke to my mother afterwards she said I must make up my quarrel with him, no matter what. I told her that was impossible, but then she cried and said in that case we were all as good as ruined.'

'How can that be?'

'She did not say, exactly. It's all to do with money she borrowed, and somehow that is tied up with arrangements for my marriage.'

'What arrangements? There has never even been a betrothal.'

'She did talk about it once or twice, but truth to tell, Perdita, I never paid her any heed. Now she swears I as good as agreed to it.'

'You probably smiled and looked helpful the way you always do and your mother came to all the wrong conclusions. Even so . . .'

'I was angry with my mother for exaggerating to get her way – at least, that's what I thought she was doing. But when I spoke to your brother just now he seemed to think that the Menheires do have the power to hurt us, and hurt us badly. It's all such a wretched tangle. And by now the whole county must know of our problems.'

'I don't suppose Edmund Menheire will be boasting about his triumphs today.'

'Ugh, don't. I cannot bear to think of him.'

Perdita did not respond and they rode on in thoughtful silence. They were passing through some airy woodland and the ground was soft beneath their horses' hoofs. The peacefulness of the leafy dusk, however, did nothing to calm their troubled thoughts.

Almost uniquely among the inhabitants of Rossmere, Perdita had been neither surprised nor unduly perturbed to learn of Edmund Menheire's bullying. She was sorry that Sophie had been upset by it, but secretly she was delighted at the refusal. Now there was nothing to prevent her from holding Piers to his promise and beginning her campaign to win his older cousin for herself.

Not for a moment had this fresh insight into Edmund's character tempted her to falter in her ambitions. A young woman who was guided by her head and not her heart – as she intended to be – was going to be attracted by a man with money and power. If Edmund was a bully, then that was a shame but not an impossible barrier. Everyone was likely to have faults of one kind or another. It was better by far to know from the outset the kind of man she was dealing with. Sophie had not been able to deal with him because she was always so direct. Perdita was confident of being able to manage him well enough. The heir to Trecarne was so convinced of his own superiority that an appearance of weakness was likely to fool him easily.

But now she found herself facing a far more difficult dilemma. Sophie had rejected Edmund and, by the terms of her bargain with Piers, Perdita was now free to pursue her own ambitions. But supposing the Menheires really did have the power to ruin Sophie's family? Ought she not try to persuade Sophie to reconsider? She had a suspicion that Piers would think so. He had made it perfectly plain that he considered Perdita to be devious and scheming – and maybe she was, though not without cause – but she liked to imagine his surprise and approval when she told him how she had pleaded Edmund's suit.

As they emerged from the wood she kicked her horse into a trot to catch up with Falcon and said, 'Maybe Edmund is not as bad as you think.'

Sophie turned and looked at her in surprise, then shrugged her shoulders and said simply, 'I detest him.'

'Why? Because he gets angry when you oppose him? No man likes to be contradicted.'

'Then I shall remain happily single till the end of my days and thank God for it. An old maid, as you said.'

'But what about your family? What of their debts?'

'I cannot help that. It is not my fault if my mother has borrowed money she cannot repay. I'd not marry Master Menheire if I was starving in the street.'

Perdita burst out laughing. 'I hope you didn't reject him quite so bluntly! No wonder he was angry.'

Sophie was startled by the laughter, but then the glimmer of a smile began to light her eyes. 'I wish I had, but the man is so thick-skinned he'd probably have taken it as a compliment.'

'Exactly. In many ways he is a complete fool, and you could have taken advantage of that. You'd have done much better to flatter him and make him believe he knows best about everything. I'm sure he'd be perfectly amiable then.'

'It's easy for you to speak, Perdita. No one is asking you to marry the terrible man.'

Perdita stared straight between her horse's ears and did not reply. Sophie looked at her with growing amazement. 'Surely you'd never consent to marry a man you despised, Perdita?'

'Of course I would,' declared Perdita. 'If it meant becoming mistress of a house like Trecarne.'

'Oh, Perdita, I simply don't believe you're as cynical as you pretend. I think you're still hurt because of what happened with your brother in the spring.'

'The reason doesn't matter,' said Perdita firmly. 'I don't care a fig for love or any of that nonsense. Just show me a man with a large house and a generous income. A man like Edmund Menheire.'

'If you mean that, then you can have him and welcome.'

'Thank you, Sophie, but unfortunately for both of us it is you he wishes to marry.'

'Not any more. Not after what happened this morning.'

'Oh, that. All you have to do is play your part right and he'll be eating out of your hand in no time at all.'

'Just what my mother said.'

'Really?'

'Yes, she plans to send Francis over to Trecarne tomorrow to tell him I have changed my mind and will be as sweet as pie from now on. I told her it was a waste of time, but she refused even to discuss it. I've never seen her so determined, never.'

'Oh, Sophie, what will you do?'

'I wish I knew.'

They had reached the height of land that overlooked Rossmere. From here the old house, its farm buildings, gardens, orchard, ponds and meadows were clearly visible spread out beneath them. Corn stood in stooks in the small fields nearest the farm. From here they could make out the figures moving silently through the dusk: Stephen driving a team of work horses back from the fields; Cary bringing washing in; ducks and geese waddling up from the pond; the doves ringing the barn roof like a necklace of pearls. Suddenly it seemed an impossible burden that to save all this for the family she loved she must not only leave her home, but give herself to a man she loathed.

Sophie leaned forward and ruffled Falcon's pale mane. 'Oh, Falcon,' she murmured, a catch in her throat, 'whatever can I do?'

The stallion flicked his ears and turned slightly. Then he tossed his head and whinnied to the horses and ponies down below. Their answering calls floated upwards on the evening air.

And then, suddenly, Sophie saw her answer clear.

Chapter Twenty-Two

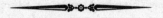

A buffeting wind, a foretaste of autumnal gales, was whipping a few early leaves from the trees as Francis and Kip cantered out of Rossmere the next morning. Francis was filled with foreboding at the task ahead of him, while Kip was wondering if they might take this opportunity to suggest a second race between Falcon and Charger. Perhaps this time he could ride Charger instead of Piers. The brothers were surprised, as they passed through the gates, to see Perdita waiting for them in the lane. She was mounted on a small dun pony and Amos was attending her.

'Perdita!' Francis exclaimed. Already he was imagining the worst. 'What is the matter?'

She lowered her eyes slightly then gazed up at him through her lashes in the manner that Francis had already come to find irresistible. 'I am coming with you to Trecarne,' she said, the gentle inflections of her voice making the statement sound like a request. 'I believe that, if I can speak with Master Menheire's cousin, I will be able to help Sophie's cause.'

'By all means. Certainly. But . . .' Francis looked flustered as all sorts of difficulties occurred to him.

Perdita smiled sweetly and said, 'I thought it best not to mention it to your mother or sisters but I knew that you would understand.' And she kicked her pony forward to join them.

They rode in a leisurely fashion towards Trecarne. By the time they reached the formal part of the Menheires' land, Kip had persuaded her to a half-crown bet that Sophie and Edmund Menheire would be married by Christmas.

Perdita reined her pony to a halt. 'You two go on,' she told them. 'I will wait here. Please tell Piers Menheire that I wish to speak to him.'

'In private?' Francis fretted. 'Is that not irregular?'

'Oh, Francis –' Perdita threw him a teasing smile – 'whatever do you think will happen? Don't worry. Amos will remain here as my duenna.'

Amos did not know what a duenna was, but the way Mistress Treveryan said the word it sounded an altogether improper thing. He grinned happily. Despite his advancing years, the company of Mistress Treveryan often made him feel surprisingly youthful.

Francis looked at her longingly, then rode on with Kip towards the house. Perdita felt her heart go with them. The long, elegant façade of Trecarne with its high windows and the towers at either end seemed to be beckoning to her, as if with outstretched arms. She felt such a tug of longing to be mistress of that house that she regretted ever having thought of trying to persuade Sophie to accept Edmund Menheire. She imagined bowling up to the front steps in her own carriage, her own servants opening the doors to welcome her home. In her mind, she possessed it already.

She had not waited long before Piers came over the wide lawns to join her, the two hounds who had so frightened Cullen on her first visit leashed and following at his heels. He looked as if he had just returned from a morning ride: a jacket was slung over his shoulders, his hair was ruffled and his cheeks glowed with fresh air and vigour. His blue eyes creased into a smile as he drew near. She slipped from her pony, told Amos to stay where he was and watch the horses, and went to meet him.

'Well, Mistress Treveryan –' he was conceding defeat with good-humour – 'I suppose you are here to hold me to my bargain.'

'Would that not be somewhat hasty?'

'Why? Although my cousin regards her refusal as a temporary setback, it sounded to me as though she meant it.'

'Indeed she did, but only because he handled their meeting so badly. If he had only been more generous in his approach . . .'

'Well, whatever the reason, the damage has been done.'

'But it may be possible to set matters aright. It all depends how we represent the situation to Sophie and your cousin. Since there is so much at stake, I believe we ought to do all we can to persuade them both to reconsider the matter. I have already spoken to Sophie about it.'

Piers slid her a suspicious glance. 'Why? Surely your own interests were well served by yesterday morning's events.'

'Certainly, but I have been trying not to think only of myself. It may interest you to know that I do care about Sophie and all her family. If anything happens to them, I would want to think I had done all in my power to help them.'

'Mistress Treveryan, you do surprise me.' Piers was looking at her intently and she felt a skip of pleasure: she had convinced him of her sincerity, and suddenly she found that she was sincere. She wanted Sophie's happiness very much indeed, and could not bear the thought of the Suttons' ruin.

Piers crouched to fondle one of his dogs. His face was turned away from her as he asked, with a show of nonchalance, 'Does that mean your own ambitions have altered too?'

'My ambitions?'

He glanced back towards the house. 'For Trecarne. And my cousin.'

'Not at all.' Perdita had only hesitated for the briefest moment. 'My ambitions – as you call them – are just as they always were. But I am prepared to wait and take my chance.'

'I see.' A shadow had fallen across his face.

'If your cousin refuses to try again, or if Sophie really will not have him, then I'll still keep you to our promise.'

Piers cupped the smaller hound's head in his hands and smoothed back her ears. Then, 'Of course you will,' he said, straightening up and smiling at her cheerfully. 'But first we must decide what can be done about our star-crossed lovers.'

'You must convince your cousin to be more gentle in his tactics. Sophie is the most generous-natured person in the world. I believe she would do anything for someone if she cared for them, and for that reason she will want to see the best in him, for her family's sake. But he must leave off threats.'

'Threats?' Piers's blue eyes had darkened.

Of course, thought Perdita, Edmund was hardly likely to have given an accurate report of the previous morning's encounter.

She said briskly, 'There's nothing to be gained by dwelling on what's past. All that matters is what happens next. I have been able to observe the Suttons at some length, and they are not like any family I have come across before. Sophie works from morning till night, harder than any servant, but she does so of her own free will. She is under no one's command. She has developed an unusual habit of independence. She will give it up, I am sure she will, but only through persuasion. Never through force. If your cousin can make a sincere apology, she may begin to think well of him again. I'll do all I can to make his roughness towards her seem like an excess of enthusiasm.'

'Have you always been such a dedicated matchmaker?'

'No, but I think I might have a real talent for it.'

'We shall see.'

They talked together for a while longer. Perdita turned down Piers's offer of refreshments. She did not want to risk a second humiliation by entering Trecarne until she saw how Edmund was disposed towards the party from Rossmere.

When Kip and Francis left the house, Edmund came on to the steps to see them off, which she took to be a good sign. They told Perdita they had informed him of Sophie's profound regret concerning all that had happened the previous morning – which was true, up to a point – and that he was invited to dine with the family at Rossmere the following day. Or any day after that.

Edmund had made no promises, but beneath his mask of injured pride he was secretly delighted. During the previous twenty-four hours he had drawn up a balance sheet in his mind, which weighed up his behaviour and that of Mistress Sutton. Although she had clearly acted foolishly and been wilful and irrational, he was not altogether pleased with his own behaviour either. He realised that it had been a tactical error to emphasise the relative strength of his position quite so forcefully. While it would be false to pretend that he was just another suitor who might be turned down, he should have given her some illusion of having a free hand in the decision.

He had also weighed up the relative merits of continuing with the courtship or going after some easier quarry. Sophie Sutton did not deserve a man of his wealth and calibre if she was foolish enough to be blind to his merits. A woman like Perdita

Treveryan, younger, more pliable and admiring, would perhaps suit him better. Until now his single condition had caused him few problems, but having once had the prospect of a wife in view, he found he was reluctant to give up the idea altogether. He was nearly thirty-five. He wanted children and the sense of being fully a man that a wife would bring. Suddenly, he was impatient to be wed. If not Mistress Sutton, then another candidate must be found.

It was his father who set him straight. Though Edmund might play the tyrant with others, with his father he was still a quaking boy, and when he returned with news of Sophie Sutton's refusal the Colonel had erupted in a rage. He called him an oaf who'd be incapable of landing any fish unless it swam straight into his boat first. He told him he must marry Sophie Sutton, that an alliance between them was essential to his plans. He told him he was an idiot, who did not deserve the fine future his father had mapped out for him. And much more besides.

So the news of Sophie's change of heart was welcome indeed.

He stopped trying to find reasons to dislike her, and remembered instead the delicious strength he had felt when he held her in his arms. How reassuring it was to learn that she regretted her impetuous refusal. How gratifying to imagine her repentance and submission. How pleasing to think of Sophie Sutton yielding to his generous forgiveness.

Even before Kip and Francis had ridden away, Edmund's mind was made up. He would go to Rossmere, not the next day – that would indicate too much eagerness – but the one after that. He would be gracious in his acceptance of her apologies. He might even admit to a small amount of error on his part – not error, exactly, but a certain over-hastiness. His eventual triumph would make such a small concession worthwhile.

Piers and Perdita parted on excellent terms. They had agreed to do what they could to help Sophie accept an alliance with Edmund Menheire, but if that failed, Piers would advance Perdita's cause. She had every reason to be pleased with her morning's work.

*   *   *

Not so Stephen.

That same morning, he had found Sophie in the pantry where she was weighing out greengages for preserving.

'Sophie, can I talk to you in private?'

'Of course. Close the door behind you. No one will hear us then. Here, have one of these. They're delicious.'

Stephen took one of the little yellow fruits, hardly aware of what he was doing, and closed the door quietly. Then he stood in front of it and gazed at her, the greengage untasted in his hand. He said bleakly, 'You know your brothers have gone over to Trecarne this morning to talk to Edmund Menheire?'

'Yes. I told Mother it was a waste of time, but she would not listen to me.'

'Then maybe you will listen to me.'

'Gladly.' She looked up and flashed him her easy smile. 'In fact, I was planning to ask your advice today anyway.'

'What about?'

'I had been wondering . . .' She paused and looked across at him once again, but this time something in the fixed expression of his face made her hesitate. 'Why don't you tell me what you wish to say first?'

'Yes.' Stephen cleared his throat to speak but looked more depressed than ever. 'It is very simple. If your brothers are successful in their mission today, I think you ought to agree to give Edmund Menheire a second chance.'

Sophie was appalled. 'What?'

'I am asking you not to reject him utterly until he has had a chance to explain himself.'

'But I loathe the man. No amount of explaining can ever change that.'

'Maybe you do not yet care much for him, but—'

'No, Uncle Stephen, I detest him. Heavens above, surely you of all people don't want me to marry a man I cannot abide.'

'Of course not. But . . . there are other considerations, apart from your wishes – wait, Sophie, hear me out first. Your mother has told me that Colonel Menheire's man lent her a large sum of money earlier this year on the understanding it would be absorbed in the marriage settlement between you and his son.'

'But she had no right to involve me!'

'She says you agreed to the idea of marriage.'

'I never did. Oh, Uncle Stephen, that's not true!'

'Maybe not, but now the damage is done and I do not see how the debt can ever be repaid otherwise.'

Sophie clenched her fists and pressed her knuckles against her forehead. 'Debts, debts, it's all we ever think of.'

Stephen said nothing. He had not the heart to comfort her when no comfort was available. He said, 'I'm not asking you to agree to marry him, Sophie. Not yet. Only that you will give him a second chance.'

'Do you really believe,' she asked bitterly, 'that I'll be allowed to turn him down a second time?'

Stephen did not answer, only stared at her. His face was haggard.

'Oh, Uncle Stephen,' she said wretchedly, 'I expected this from my mother, not from you. Never from you.' When still he said nothing, she turned to him and asked, 'Can you honestly look me in the eye and say you want to see me married to Edmund Menheire?'

He returned her gaze steadily. 'If that is the only way to prevent catastrophe for all your family, then yes, it is certainly what I want.'

'And what of your own comfort?' She flung the question at him harshly. 'After all, it would be inconvenient for you to have to find a new home for yourself when we are all turned out. Let's not forget that.'

All the colour drained from Stephen's face. His grey eyes for once were flinty and cold. 'You should not have said that.'

'But—'

'I am thinking of your family, Sophie. I have not thought of myself in years.'

He turned and strode from the room, brushed past Cary who was coming to see what had happened to the greengages and almost ran across the kitchen, through the stableyard and down to the farm. He roared at the men to get a couple of horses harnessed and spent the rest of the day struggling to pull a fallen tree up a steep and bracken-covered hillside. The work was energetic and exhausting, a welcome distraction from his present anger and self-loathing.

When he first heard of Edmund Menheire's rude wooing of his niece, he was glad she had turned him down. But that morning, for the first time in seventeen years, Alice had appealed to him directly for help. It was a measure of her desperation that she had smothered her pride and begged him, with anguished tears, to do whatever he could to persuade Sophie to change her mind.

'She'll listen to you,' Alice had sobbed. 'She trusts you, Stephen, she always has. She never pays any attention to me, she just thinks I'm a foolish old woman, everybody does. I dare say I am. And she's furious with me for accepting the money in the first place, but I was so certain she must want to marry him! I thought she only stayed here because we needed her and that this was her chance to make a good marriage. Oh, Stephen, I know we've had our differences in the past, but please, oh, please, talk to Sophie for me now. Make her see reason, for her sake, not just for everyone else's. Don't let Nicolas's children lose Rossmere just because of this, I beg you . . .'

And more of the same. Much more. Impossible to resist.

Besides, Stephen knew that in her muddle-headed way, Alice was right. Nicolas, doting father though he had been, would certainly have insisted Sophie marry Edmund Menheire if it meant saving their home. For seventeen years Stephen had accepted the responsibility for his brother's children − for all his brother's children, not just for Sophie − and this was not the moment for him to start changing course.

He knew that if he let Alice down now, the first time in her life that she had appealed to him for help, she would never confide in him again. In the difficult times that were sure to lie ahead, it was essential that Alice keep faith with him.

Over the matter of putting pressure on Sophie, there had been no choice.

But that did not stop it feeling like a gross betrayal.

Sophie thought this must be what drowning was like: as though the air all around her had been transformed into some thick substance like cloudy water. Familiar scenes and faces assumed a strange and faraway texture. Voices were booming, but indistinct.

Outside the winter parlour, a north wind was blowing. It rattled the windows and moaned in the chimneys, its chilly lament echoing the ache in her heart, as she looked at the people ranged around the dining table. Another meal, like a thousand others that had gone before, yet this time everyone had been changed for ever in Sophie's eyes.

There was her mother, cheeks pink with eagerness as she told Edmund Menheire how grand life had been at Rossmere in the old days before the wars. Before the wars. When I was a young bride . . . In the time when my late husband was still alive. The social calls and the entertaining. No anxiety about expense. All the servants in livery and every day a holiday. Not like today. Not like now.

Sophie could hardly bear to hear it. Could hardly bear the way her mother kept darting anxious glances in her direction. Smile, Sophie. Make yourself agreeable. We are all relying on you. Look how I have struggled and suffered and all for my children. Just be pleasant, Sophie, the way you always are.

Most agonising of all were her mother's frequent references to the quarrels she had had with her late husband – never, so far as Sophie could remember, mentioned before since Nicolas's death. 'Oh, of course we had our ups and downs. Doesn't everyone? All quite natural. In fact, I'm sure I would think there was something not quite right if a man and wife never argued at all. Only to be expected. Nothing to make a fuss about. And then there is all the pleasure of making up. Don't you agree, Francis?'

Francis? There he was, looking uncomfortable at every reference to his own marriage, as well he might, with Honor as pale and miserable as could be and Francis devouring Perdita with his eyes.

Perdita. In the echoing surf-sound of voices inside Sophie's head, she could not make out Perdita's actual words, but there was no difficulty understanding the message behind her gestures. Like this, Sophie. See, there's nothing to it. Only copy me and all will be well. Smile, pretend to be a ninny, he'll be butter in your hands in no time at all. Look, like this, it's perfectly easy once you know how.

And there was Kip, quieter than usual, watching her every

move. Michaelmas was approaching, soon Sir Richard Trever-yan would return. It had dawned on him that morning that, if their fortunes did not improve soon, even Alice would not be able to save him from having to return to sea. His brown eyes, silently pleading, not really understanding how this situation had come about, were fixed on her face.

Louisa's too. Her future was bleak enough even if they remained at Rossmere. No money for a dowry, hardly any chance of a decent marriage. But if they lost their home, what then? A life as maid-companion to her brother's wife in Camborne, if she was lucky. The maltster's bossy widow had never liked Charles's relatives and would work Louisa harder than a servant. A status lower than Cary's. All hope gone.

And there was Uncle Stephen, eating his meal in near silence and forcing himself to nod from time to time at some empty memory of Alice's and all the while he never smiled, or looked in her direction once. Since that dreadful meeting in the pantry two days before, he had avoided her. For the first time in her life Sophie felt utterly alone. In some ways it was worse than when the groom had brought her father's lifeless body back from the battlefield in far-off Somerset. A sharper pain of loneliness.

And there was Edmund Menheire . . . But no, she could not bring herself to contemplate him. He was skewering his meat with strong hands, as if even the simple task of eating a meal had to be a demonstration of his mastery. She loathed seeing the way his mouth worked to chew the food, the smear of grease on his lips.

She had only agreed to be present at this meal on the promise she'd not be left alone with him. Not yet. Bad enough that soon after his arrival that morning he had drawn her to one side and given her his opinion that they had both acted somewhat hastily before and ought to try to forget it. Sophie said simply that she was prepared to put the past behind her. Whatever that might mean. Secretly she was relieved that he seemed to regard himself as the injured party. Her greatest fear was that he might appear genuine in his apologies as that would have made it harder for her to remain resolute against him.

God knows, it was hard enough already. That morning she had heard Francis, gentle, tender-hearted Francis, telling Honor he wished he'd never married her. Some time later Honor had come into the kitchen to beg a soothing drink. Not surprisingly, she thought she had a bad headache coming on.

'What's the matter?' Sophie had asked her anxiously. 'Why are you and Francis always so out of sorts?'

Honor burst into tears. 'Poor Francis did not sleep a wink last night,' she sobbed. 'He is so worried about these terrible debts. He can think of nothing except how you will act with Edmund Menheire today.'

'But that's no reason to take it out on you.'

Honor blinked up at her through her tears. 'I'm sure he'll be himself again when you and Master Menheire are betrothed.'

'Nothing is settled,' Sophie told her sharply. 'A betrothal is most unlikely.'

But now, as she sat in the watery gloom of the winter parlour and listened to the wind beyond the windows and watched her family's desperate efforts to woo her suitor on her behalf, she wondered how much longer she would be able to stand firm against the massed hopes and fears of all those she loved most.

Chapter Twenty-Three

Sir Francis Sutton lowered his weight on to his ample knees and bowed his head. Around him, the voices of the congregation recited the prayers for the day in ragged unison, but Francis, though more sincere this Sunday morning than at almost any period in his life before, was addressing the Almighty on a quite different topic.

Oh, Lord, help me to reach a right decision. Guide me to choose what is best for my family and my father's heirs. Do not suffer me to be blinded by the snares of false affections . . .

Here, his voice trailed off into indecision. It was all very well to seek strength to withstand the snares of false affections, but how was he to know which ones they were? Was it the old protective care for his sickly Honor that was wrong, or was it this new passion beside which the whole of the rest his life seemed to have been merely a kind of sleep-walking?

If his marriage had been consummated, if Honor had even once offered herself to him, soul and body as his wife, there could have been only one solution to his dilemma. But she had not. Nearly four years married and she had never permitted him the satisfactions of a husband. All that time he had fretted and hoped and suffered, but now he saw there had been a purpose to the whole sorry business. Perhaps an unconsummated marriage was considered no marriage at all, perhaps it could be annulled. In time he might be free of the shackles that bound him to Honor.

Free to marry Perdita.

Boots scraping on the stone floor of the church, rustle of

petticoats and skirts. The congregation was rising to sing the psalm. A handful of raindrops rattled against the window of the church. Dazed by the conflict raging inside him, Francis placed his broad hands on the back of the pew in front of him for support.

The left side of his body felt as if it was on fire. He could sense Perdita beside him, warm and straight as a flame. As she stood up her arm had brushed against his, surely accidentally. She had murmured an apology, darting him a smile of such brilliance that he felt his heart turn over in his chest. Guiltily, he allowed his gaze to slide round to her: a single pearl was suspended from a thin chain around her throat. He became mesmerised by the way it rose and fell with her breathing, then trembled as she began to sing the psalm. Her voice was confident, though not especially tuneful. Her presence was strong and sure at his side. Perdita Treveryan was a woman he could take in his arms and make love to without fear of doing her injury.

Not like Honor, his wife who was no wife at all. She stood now on his right, chilling him. He had lingered too long a victim of her frailty. He had been so afraid of hurting her, so ashamed of his own gross desires. Even now, though the thought of her sickly body left him unmoved, it was hard to imagine causing her the kind of pain that must surely follow separation.

Where could she go? Not to her cousin, who was a notorious drunkard and had an inn near Bodmin. Nor to her younger brother, who kept house with a woman twice his age and was recklessly squandering the little money he had inherited. Francis was under no illusions; if he repudiated Honor, the shock and shame were sure to destroy her.

But if his family lost Rossmere, what future was there for her anyway? And if he sacrificed his wife, the rest might be saved. Sir Richard had talked of making a generous settlement if Perdita were betrothed to Kip. It seemed likely now that nothing would come of that scheme: Sir Richard was not likely to throw away either his money or his daughter on such an unreliable youth. But that did not mean the alliance between the two families was doomed. Surely Sir Richard would be even more generous if his only daughter was to become the wife of the elder son, the baronet? Enough, perhaps, to pay off the most pressing of their debts and get their affairs on a firm footing once again. Perdita, Lady Sutton: Francis savoured the name on his tongue. There was a rightness to it that delighted him.

More even than the thought of her wealth or her physical charms, Francis was attracted to Perdita by some quality he could not name precisely and of which he was only half aware. Beneath her superficial girlishness and her dainty manners, he sensed the determination at Perdita's core. Her strength was irresistible.

Francis was aware of his own failings – too much so. In fact, he blamed himself for all manner of calamities that were not his fault at all. He craved Perdita's toughness. With a wife like her beside him, he'd find a way through the quagmire of indecision that had brought them all to the brink of calamity. He'd be able to stand up to his mother, take the reins in his own hands. With Perdita at his side, he'd be a man at last.

The doxology: Glory be to the Father, and to the Son, and to the Holy Ghost. As it was in the beginning, is now and ever shall be, World without end . . . Amen.

The congregation sat. Francis placed his broad buttocks carefully on the smooth seat, then adjusted his position so that his hip was pressed against Perdita's. She made no sign that she had noticed; he interpreted this as acquiescence. His hopes soared. Dear God, it was surely sinful to have such lustful thoughts in a Sunday church, yet the wrongness of his desires only heightened his joy. He had been dutiful and good all his life and look what it had brought him: a wife who denied him the comforts of marriage and a household on the verge of bankruptcy.

Time now to throw caution away. If it was madness to desire Perdita so ardently, then let him be mad. It was, of course, all nonsense to imagine he might be free to marry her so long as Honor lived. Even if a separation was arranged, remarriage was out of the question. Yet surely a woman so frequently ill was not destined for a long life.

Meanwhile, there were other solutions. King Charles was setting a fashion for mistresses: Barbara Palmer was treated with the respect usually given to a queen. No one thought he would give her up when he married, a state of affairs that would have been unthinkable in the old King's time, when Sir Richard himself had shown his contempt for the married state by keeping house with Perdita's mother.

Francis almost laughed out loud to remember how shocked he had been when he knew Sir Richard's bastard daughter was coming to Rossmere. He had even worried about the insult to his wife! How much he had learned since then. Sir Richard Treveryan was a man he admired more than any other. He was a man who acted without regard for the opinion of others, a man who seized what he wanted and crushed anyone who stood in his way. Francis must learn to be like that. Sir Richard would guide him. Honor must be sent away. Perdita would become his wife in all but name. There would be children, whom Francis would treat as if they were legitimate as Sir Richard had with Perdita. Once Honor was dead, they might be married with all solemnity due . . .

They were kneeling for the final prayers. Francis felt like a man who has been stumbling through dark mist but who now sees his way clearly. He allowed himself another sideways glance at Perdita. Her hands were clasped in prayer beneath her exquisite chin and her eyes were closed. She shifted slightly, perhaps to move away from the pressure of his arm against her own. She let one hand drop to ease her skirts from under her knees. To Francis it was a signal, clear as a trumpet blast. His hand stretched down and seized hold of hers, his pale fingers closing over her fist, the secret contact of flesh on flesh a hammer blow in his breast.

Perdita's eyes flew open. Francis smiled . . . Surely she must know how passionately he loved her. She must respond as he did. But no, he had startled her, he had acted with too great haste. The colour flooded her face and she withdrew her hand. He tried to smile his reassurance. She frowned. Francis moved away, and Honor, as his arm brushed against hers, gave a small sigh.

Francis hardly noticed. He had been clumsy, that was a mistake he regretted, but the indecision that had inspired his prayers earlier was done with. He had made his choice.

The congregation began to file out of the church, into the blustery September morning.

To Francis, it was like emerging reborn.

*   *   *

From his vantage point on a rise of ground near the Suttons' graves, Luke Hollar observed the intricate dance taking place outside the church. It was obvious, to him at least, that Mistress Sophie Sutton was trying to escape from her family and come over to talk to him but without success. Her mother had hold of her arm and was tugging her into conversation with the odious Edmund Menheire. Honor, Lady Sutton, was clinging to her husband's side, however much he tried to shake her off. He, too, was talking with Edmund and Sophie, though his gaze kept straying towards Perdita.

His sister's attitude puzzled Luke. Usually so eager to be the centre of attention, she gave an impression of wanting for once to keep her distance from the others, even from Piers Menheire who had come over to talk to her. Her hands were folded demurely in front of her and her head was bowed. She appeared to be closed off from all that was taking place around her. Louisa moved across to talk to Piers. Kip followed her. Louisa drifted away. The figures in the dance continued back and forth: apparently random, but Luke knew each movement had a purpose. He could not unravel them all, but he was beginning to.

The fluid groupings were meandering towards the lych-gate. On the roadway outside the churchyard the usual cluster of boys lingered to admire Falcon and his dark rival, Charger. Luke sighed. He had positioned himself close to Nicolas Sutton's tombstone so that Sophie might have an excuse to seek him out, but he had reckoned without the limpet-like attention of Edmund Menheire.

He was disappointed, but there was no hurry. He had promised to tell her what he had discovered concerning the Menheires' intentions, but so far he had merely gained confirmation of what he already suspected: they were gathering as many of the Suttons' debts into their own hands as possible. The implications were obvious.

The last of the Rossmere party vanished beneath the lych-gate.

Luke was just about to move away, when he saw Sophie, alone this time, hurrying back through the stragglers towards the church door. Never once looking in his direction, she turned off and walked rapidly between the graves to the place where her father was buried.

Luke turned away, though he was keenly aware of her closeness. She stooped, as though placing something on her father's grave, and then he heard her say, 'Master Hollar, be so kind as to look beneath the flowers when I have gone.'

He did not look at her, but waited until her footsteps had hurried away once more. He walked slowly towards the far end of the graveyard, where his mother's resting place was. He glanced with loathing at the elaborate stone that had been put there in the spring by the man who, in Luke's opinion at least, had ruined his mother's life, then turned and strolled back towards where Sophie had been. The churchyard was now deserted, only the wind soughing through the yews and a few ruffled birds.

A handful of late roses had been placed on Nicolas's grave. Luke crouched and lifted them carefully. A sheet of paper, folded and sealed, lay underneath. He slipped it inside his coat and walked away.

Amazed at the risk Mistress Sutton had run, and wondering at the desperation that must have caused it, Luke hurried back to his home behind the draper's shop. The moment the street door closed, he tore open the letter. The words were misspelt, and so poorly written that Luke could barely read it, but the message was clear enough.

Dere Mastr Holar,
   I ned to ask yr advis on a matr of grayt ugensy. Ples be
at St Buran Well bifor sunset this evning.
   Yours, Sophie Sutn.

Even her name had been misspelt: Sutn. Clearly her schooling had been all of the kitchen kind.

Luke found he was very eager to know what had prompted this rare and barely literate letter.

Honor was so worn out by her visit to Porthew church that she retired to her room as soon as they were back at Rossmere and stretched out on the bed. Sleep was impossible. Her body felt soaked in pain. Her shoulders, spine and every joint from ankles to neck were agonisingly swollen. Her breathing was shallow and difficult.

Time was when Francis would have sat with her on the bed and offered doleful sympathy. Now she dared not even tell him she was ailing. She was too afraid of seeing that look on his once-kindly face, the look which said, as plain as words, Why do you not die, and be done with it?

She rolled on to her side and drew her knees up close to her chest, for comfort. But soon the pressure on her side was so unbearably painful she was forced to stretch at full length again. She ought to go down to the kitchen and get Cary to mix her something to ease the pain, but she kept putting it off.

It was not just ill-health that had driven Honor to seek the privacy of her bedchamber. She wanted to avoid the Suttons and their guests.

She remembered what it had been like when she first came to Rossmere. She had hardly dared to believe such a harmonious family existed anywhere: her beloved Francis, so gentle and concerned for her happiness; Sophie, all energy and warmth; young Kip without a care in the world. Stephen – Uncle Stephen, as she soon learned to call him – had seemed the most honourable of men. Even Louisa and Alice had made her welcome. Now Alice snapped at the least provocation, Louisa was angry all the time, Sophie tense and preoccupied, Kip moody and sullen and, most unbearable of all, Francis could no longer stand the sight of her. Almost as though the whole family had been infected with some malicious poison.

There was an atmosphere of disaster looming, as if they were trapped in a small boat rushing helplessly towards catastrophe. It was the debts that were affecting them so, always the debts. The slow days were ticking past till Michaelmas, when the interest must be paid, Sir Richard was due to return, Sophie must make up her mind.

And that was not all. There had been another change in the household recently. Honor thought that perhaps it had begun on the day of Edmund's hasty wooing of Sophie, as if the knowledge that she must be coerced into marriage with a man she loathed had laid bare that which is better left covered up. Honor had seen the naked desire in Edmund's gaze when he looked at Sophie, however hard he tried to disguise it as indifference. She had recognised it in Francis too, but not when he looked at her. Outside the church that morning, she had observed him undressing Perdita with greedy eyes. Even Kip, who used to think of nothing but sport and gambling, was beginning – Honor could tell – to regard the stranger in their midst with the lust of a grown man.

Honor was slow to blame Perdita. She, too, had fallen for her charm when she first came to Rossmere. Perdita had always listened to her woes. Now, however, she was adding to them.

Honor wanted Francis to look at her, his wife, the way he had looked at Perdita. She wanted him to love her. She wanted him to fold her in his arms and caress her. She wanted him to bruise her lips with kisses and touch her in those places where she had never been touched before. She wanted him to fill her with his loving, to fill her with his child.

Her hands touched her breasts, cautiously, tenderly. She imagined them full of milk. She imagined a child's small mouth tugging at the nipple. She heard her mother's voice, screaming in pain, but it had faded, as if it was coming from a great distance away. She imagined the very worst that could happen and saw Francis, standing beside her bed, weeping for the loss of the wife he had loved. She felt a timid happiness: better that than to die alone and unmourned. Better by far . . .

There was a brisk tapping at the door.

'Come in!'

Hope flickered and died. It was only Perdita who pushed open the door. She was carrying a tray with a jug and some other items on it.

'Perdita, what brings you here?'

'You did not come to table so I thought you must be feeling unwell.'

Sympathy always brought the tears to Honor's eyes. 'I ache all over,' she whispered.

'You poor thing. I've brought you some spiced wine and cakes. But first let me wipe your face and hands with this.' She produced a hot towel that was impregnated with pungent oils. 'There's nothing more soothing. See, like this . . .'

Perdita's touch was delicate, but firm. Honor had already forgotten that she had just been blaming Perdita for at least some of her woes. 'Thank you. I thought everyone had forgotten me.'

'Now why would they do that?'

Honor turned her face away. 'I am a burden to them all.'

'Nonsense.'

'Even to my husband. I am always unwell. He is growing tired of me, I know he is.' Her voice broke on a sob.

Perdita smothered a sigh of impatience. 'You cannot help being unwell, Honor. Francis is much too kind to blame you for that. Maybe it is just that sometimes you do not consider him as once you did.'

Honor glanced round at Perdita sharply, wondering what she might have guessed about relations between man and wife. 'What do you mean?'

'Here, have some wine, it will cheer you up. Would you like me to arrange your hair for you? It's really very pretty when you take care of it.'

'The combs hurt my head. If only I had a maid who knew how to care for me. But I cannot do it myself.'

'I'll help you. Not today, you're worn out, I can tell. But tomorrow. I can lend you some of my Imperial water, if you like. It's the most refreshing thing in the world. And when did you last have some new lace?'

'There's no money for lace, not any more.'

'I could find you something. I'll go and look later.'

'Did Francis notice I was not at dinner?'

Perdita was busying herself putting things back on the tray. 'Oh, everyone is so intent on trying to guess if Sophie will consent to smile prettily at Edmund Menheire they'd not notice if we all dropped dead of the plague. Now, have you had enough cake? It won't do you any good to go starving yourself. The wine will probably make you sleepy. I told Cary to put some drops in it. Would you like me to read to you for a while before you go to sleep?'

Soothed as much by Perdita's voice as by the medicine,

Honor fell into an exhausted sleep before Perdita had completed more than a dozen pages of her book.

Perdita observed her for a few moments: her mousy hair was tangled and dull, her skin pitted and pale, yet there was something touching in her dependence. Perdita could see why Francis had overlooked her lack of wealth and desired her for his wife. As he must be made to desire her again.

Ponderous footsteps on the landing, which she recognised at Francis's. Quickly she stood up, smoothed the bedclothes and hurried from the room.

When she collided with Francis, he raised his arms clumsily, as if wanting to steady them both, but somehow the gesture was transformed into a fumbling embrace. She pushed him away at once. 'Be careful, sir,' she spoke sharply, though keeping her voice low, 'or you will wake your wife.'

Then she almost ran down the stairs, appalled by the hunger visible in his eyes. She had hoped his ridiculous attempt to hold her hand in church that morning had been a momentary, never-to-be-repeated act of folly. This time, however, his intentions had been all too clear.

Luke reached St Buran's some time well before dusk, hoping to be the first there, but Sophie was already waiting for him. It was a lonely spot, about half-way between Rossmere and Porthew but set at a little distance from the road. It also happened to be a favourite trysting place for illicit lovers from the town. Briefly Luke allowed himself to indulge in the illusion that Mistress Sutton had romantic reasons for arranging this meeting, but then he checked himself. Her interest in him was sure to be practical.

She slipped down from her horse – the famous Falcon – and came forward on foot to greet him.

'You came,' she said simply. 'I'm glad.'

'You asked me to.'

'Yes.'

'I will help you if I can, but so far I have discovered nothing that can be used against the Menheires.'

'It is too late for that anyway.'

'Too late?'

She hesitated, nudged a stone with the toe of her shoe, then raised her eyes to search his face. 'Master Hollar, please do not be offended, but before I go on I need your assurance that you will not speak of this to anyone.'

Luke was offended, very offended indeed – would she have asked such an insulting question had he been a gentleman born? – but he said merely, 'You have my word.'

'Thank you.' Yet still she hesitated.

Luke said, 'I dare say my sister Perdita has told you that my word does not count for much. On this occasion, at least, I want you to know that I am sincere.'

'No matter,' said Sophie decisively, 'I will trust you because I have no choice. There is no one else I can turn to.'

He waited.

'You are a merchant,' she said.

'That's right.'

'So you understand how things are purchased.'

'Yes.'

'And sold.'

'Yes.'

'I suppose most of your trade is in cloth, that sort of thing.'

'For the most part. But I also deal from time to time in salt fish. Or tin. Sometimes I may oversee a shipment of spices. Or wine.'

'I see.'

But he could tell she was only half listening to him. Her expression was abstracted, as if she was thinking only of what she wanted to say. In an involuntary gesture she reached her arm over the stallion's mane and laid her cheek against his dappled neck. Luke told himself to be careful. He did not think he had ever seen a woman more beautiful, or less conscious of her beauty.

'Spices and wine . . .' She was echoing his words almost dreamily. Then she turned and looked him full in the eyes. 'And horses?'

'What?'

'I intend to sell Falcon.'

In his surprise, Luke said unthinkingly, 'Are you sure?'

'Of course I am. I have thought of nothing else for days. Master Hollar, I came here this evening to seek your advice about how best it might be done. Not to discuss the decision itself.'

She spoke sharply, as a gentlewoman addresses a tradesman who has overstepped the mark. Luke noted the rebuke. He did not like it. He said evenly, 'And this must be done in secret?'

'That is my whole purpose in asking you.'

He thought, then said, 'You had best send him to one of the larger horse fairs. This is a good time of year for it – another month and the dealers will be all back east for the winter. There are still some around who have come down from London and the north.'

'When is the next one to be held?'

'Truro, ten days from now.'

'That is too near to home. Besides, I cannot wait so long.'

'Wadebridge, then. In three days' time.'

'Perfect.'

'Do you want me to take him there and arrange the sale for you?'

'If that is not too much to ask. Of course, I'll pay whatever fee is customary on these occasions.'

He almost laughed. 'On what occasions? Mistress Sutton, what you're asking me to do is hardly a usual commission for a merchant like myself.'

'No . . . but I must pay you all the same.'

'More important, you must arrange for a groom to accompany me, someone who is familiar with the animal and knows his needs. Also, I will need a letter, signed by you, which authorises me to make the sale on your behalf. I do not want to be hauled before the courts on a charge of horse theft. Such a valuable animal is sure to attract a good deal of attention.'

'He is valuable, isn't he?' There was no disguising the eagerness in her voice.

'I'm no expert, but I'd say a hundred pounds at least at local prices. He'd probably fetch more up country, but then there'd be the risk of injury along the way. Since you require the money . . . urgently, then Wadebridge will have to do. I assume Falcon is registered under your own name, not Treveryan's.'

'Yes. Sir Richard gave me all the documents. I have them safe. When do you want to start?'

'If I'd had more warning, I'd have said this evening. I assume you want him to leave at night?'

'Yes. Then it will be some hours before anyone notices he's missing.'

'Have your groom meet me here with Falcon tomorrow at midnight. We can be well away before the alarm is raised. After that, the explaining will all be up to you.'

'Oh, that will be easy.'

Suddenly she was smiling, as though a weight had been lifted from her shoulders.

And so it had, thought Luke, as he journeyed through the darkening countryside towards Porthew. A hundred pounds or a hundred guineas – maybe even more.

Not nearly enough to solve all the Suttons' money worries, but more than enough to save at least one member of their family from a hateful marriage.

The wind had been rising all day. Perdita's cloak was filled like a sail and she had to hold it tightly to stop it blowing away. Her dark hair streamed across her face.

In front of her, Sir Francis Sutton hung his head.

'Sir, you have done me a gross wrong.' Her voice was raised to be heard above the wind. 'I am here as a guest in your house and now you have insulted me. Never did I expect such an outrage from you, and I assure you, if my father ever hears of it, he would be furious. Pray God I never have cause to mention this to him. His purpose in bringing me to Cornwall, as well you know, was to see if he might arrange an honest marriage for me to the son of his oldest friend. He was not to know your brother is still too immature to be an acceptable husband. But never, not for a single moment, did he or I entertain the notion that I might become the doxy of a married man!'

'But . . . I thought . . . the way you looked at me . . .'

'How dare you? If you have chosen to delude yourself, then you must cease at once. I can no longer remain under your roof unless you give me your solemn word that you will never again dare to address me in such vile terms . . .'

She did not let up until her anger was exhausted. He gave his word, of course. Sir Francis Sutton did not stand a chance against Perdita in a temper. But although she knew there'd be no more trouble from her host, still Perdita was worried as she hurried back to the shelter of the house.

She'd never admit it to anyone, but she was aware that there was some truth in his stumbled excuses that she had led him on. The habit of setting out to charm all those who might be useful to her had been so deeply ingrained since childhood that she had been slow to recognise it was a weapon of a different kind now that she was a woman. She felt like someone who has been in the habit of lighting a fire to warm their hands only to find themselves engulfed in flames. The coquettish ways of a delightful child had more serious consequences now.

But even so, she did not think Francis would have let his imagination run away with him had she not been tainted with the stigma of bastardy. His bumbling efforts to make love to her made her more keenly aware than ever of how vulnerable she was. Herself the product of illicit love, it seemed as though she must always plant such thoughts in the minds of others. The safeguard of propriety, which people like Sophie and Louisa took for granted, was something she lacked, leaving her with a kind of nakedness.

She had been caught out once. She did not intend to make the same mistake again.

'Listen to the wind,' said Honor. 'It's the first of the autumn gales.'

'Yes.' Francis had not spoken to her all evening. He had not spoken to anyone. He had sat alone in his workroom while the wind lashed against the windows. He pretended to be working, but in fact he merely sat and brooded.

Perdita had scolded him as if he were a child. He did not blame her. How could he have forgotten himself so and imagined she was encouraging his advances? Shame and remorse were overwhelming. He had botched the whole business, just as he made a mess of everything else.

He came to bed late, hoping to find Honor already asleep, but instead she was propped against the pillows, reading by candlelight. She laid her book aside as he came in. He sat down heavily on the edge of the bed and pulled off his boots, then stood up and loosened his breeches before removing those too. Outside, the wind was howling round the chimneys, while in their chamber the bed-curtains stirred and the corner of a Turkey rug lifted in the draught.

Sick at heart, Francis leaned over to blow out the last of the candles, but Honor placed her hand on his wrist. 'Leave it for a while,' she said gently.

'I'm sorry.' He drew back automatically. 'You are still reading.'

'Not reading, no.' Honor paused, but Francis was lost in thought and did not look at her. At length she asked, 'Do you love me?'

'Of course I do. You are my wife.' But his answer was wooden, no real answer at all.

'Then if you like . . . I know I have been afraid in the past, but that is finished . . . so if you still want me to . . .'

Francis had been staring at the movement of the curtains, now he turned slowly to look at her. He noticed that she was wearing a shift of some fine embroidered fabric he had never seen before. Her mousy-brown hair had been brushed to a dull shine and was spread out on the pillow behind her. Her skin gave off a delicate scent of flowers, which reminded him, painfully, of Perdita.

'Are you sure, Honor?'

'Quite sure.'

'But you were unwell only yesterday.'

'It is over now.'

'Ah.'

Still he stared at her, more puzzled than pleased. Honor had never imagined this would prove so difficult. She sat up and moved forward until her lips were pressing against his. He did not respond. She sank back against the pillows again.

'Do you still want me, Francis?'

'Of course I do,' he told her swiftly. Too swiftly. He needed to speak before she saw his doubt and despair. How many times had he waited for this moment? And now, when she was offering herself to him, his only emotion was a kind of helpless pity. He no longer desired the gift of her body.

But, still, he was her husband, and certain obligations were expected of husbands. He made himself smile, then placed his hands on her thin shoulders, leaned forward and kissed her. She responded eagerly. Then she took his hand in hers and placed it over her small breast. He touched it, but cautiously, and she wriggled slightly, pulling him down on top of her.

It was then that he knew, with the certainty of despair, that he was unable to give her what she was so unexpectedly asking for. However much he had wished to in the past, it had become impossible. His body had been restrained too long, and now, just when their difficulties might have been solved, it had chosen to let him down.

He pulled away from her, removed her frail arms from round his neck. 'This is too sudden, Honor,' he told her. 'Perhaps if we wait a day or two. After all, we've waited long enough already.'

He was aware that she nodded, though he could not bring himself to look at her directly. He was too afraid of the disappointment that must be written on her face. Once again, as so often before in his life, he had failed to come up to expectations. Just as he had failed to take his father's place, now he was failing to be a proper husband. He was doomed always to disappoint those closest to him.

Quickly, he blew out the candle and pulled the bedcovers over him. He heard Honor move down in the bed beside him.

'Good night, Honor.'

'Good night.' Her voice was small, like a child's. Soon she would be asleep. The wind was screaming now, a real autumnal gale. There might well be a tree or two down by morning. His hearing was playing tricks with him. He imagined he heard footsteps on the stairs, a door banging shut.

And then he heard another sound, closer, much closer, and this time there was no mistaking what it was. Beside him in the bed, Honor was weeping, but in a muffled way, trying not to be heard.

'Oh, Honor,' he groaned, 'don't cry.'

'I'm sorry . . .' The words were thick and indistinct. 'It's my fault. I didn't want to disturb you . . .'

He heard her fumbling for a kerchief. She blew her nose.

'Don't cry,' he said again. 'Please . . .'

'I didn't mean . . . It's all my fault . . . I'm so sorry . . .'

Francis sighed. 'You mustn't say that. Here.' He rolled over and put his arm around her shoulders. She nestled in close to him and soon his nightshirt was damp from her tears.

'You don't want me any more,' she sobbed, 'I know you don't. You did, you used to, but now it's gone and it's all my fault.'

'Please, Honor, don't upset yourself. You mustn't—'

But still she sobbed, broken-hearted as a child. 'I have always loved you so much, Francis, ever since the first time I saw you. I though when we were married everything would be all right, that I wouldn't be afraid any more. But then it just got worse. I wanted so much to be a proper wife to you, more than anything in the world, but each time I heard the screaming. I was so afraid I'd die, and then I couldn't—'

'I know, Honor. I know. You must not blame yourself.' He was patting her shoulder.

'But now I'm not afraid any more. At least I am afraid, but not of dying. Only that you might stop loving me. If you don't love me then there's nothing to live for, I might as well be dead. Oh, Francis, it's all my fault and I'm so sorry.'

'Please stop crying, Honor. I do love you, really I do. It's only that I can't show it, not the way you want me to . . .' He kissed her lips in a vain effort to reassure her, kissed the hollow at the base of her throat and the swelling of her breasts. And then, suddenly, he realised that what had been impossible only a short time ago was now not only possible but an urgent need.

He drew back. 'Honor?'

'Yes?'

'Are you still ready for me?'

'Yes.'

Moving rapidly, afraid that further delay might lead only to fresh disaster, he fumbled under her shift, pushed her thighs apart and tried to enter her. Twice he bumped against her, causing her to gasp aloud, but the third time he pressed himself home. Her whole body clenched against the shock of it, but he carried on and gradually she relaxed and her movements developed a clumsy harmony with his.

They whispered to each other as they made love, hardly

daring to believe that this closeness was such a simple thing after all.

Outside, in the storm-filled night, a horse whinnied in the darkness and a dog barked in warning, but Francis and his wife heard only each other.

At St Buran's well the wind was ploughing through the trees. The moon, when it rose, was nearing the full and the ragged landscape was awash with its pale light. Luke, who had been waiting for some time, was chilled to the bone.

Where was the groom with Mistress Sutton's stallion? Some mishap must have occurred: she had changed her mind, perhaps, or the groom had been intercepted before getting away or, more likely still, he had turned traitor and reported her plan to Sir Francis. Luke was debating how much longer he should remain in this forlorn place, before returning to Porthew and his own bed, when he saw a pale shape moving through the darkness towards him. Falcon. Seldom had Luke seen a horse with such grace and courage. He wondered what it must have cost Mistress Sutton to give up such a prize.

Luke urged his own horse forward from under the shelter of the hedge and shouted a greeting. The rider raised his arm in silent reply.

'I was beginning to think you were not coming.'

'I was delayed.'

Luke felt a chill of recognition as he heard the voice. Then the horseman let slip the hood that had been obscuring his face and the moon shone out from behind a cloud.

'Mistress Sutton!'

'Good evening, Master Hollar,' said Sophie calmly. 'I am sorry I kept you waiting.'

'What are you doing here? Where is your groom?'

'I have none. I have come alone. There is no one I can trust with this mission. I must do it myself.'

'That is impossible!' He was shouting to be heard above the wind.

'Why?'

'You cannot seriously intend to travel to Wadebridge alone.'

'But you agreed to come with me.'

'No, I did not. I said I would accompany your groom to the horse fair and get the best price possible for your stallion. I never offered to go there with you.'

'The journey is the same. And the commission. There is no difference.'

'There is all the difference in the world!'

'How so?'

'Don't play the innocent with me, Mistress Sutton.' As Luke's surprise passed he was angry, very angry indeed. 'You know full well that if you come with me to Wadebridge you'll be ruined. You must return at once to Rossmere and we will find another way of selling your horse.'

'No, Master Hollar. I have decided to go to Wadebridge to sell Falcon and that is exactly what I intend to do. If you refuse to come with me, then I must go alone.'

'Out of the question! You deliberately led me to believe you would be sending your groom.'

'Maybe I did.'

'You have tricked me.'

'There was no choice.'

'Well, now I have no choice either. I am going to Rossmere to tell your brother what you are doing.'

Sophie gasped. Then she leaned forward in the saddle and said, 'You must do as your conscience tells you. But remember, Falcon is the swiftest horse in all Cornwall and I shall ride him as hard as ever I can. No one will be able to catch us. Certainly not my brother, nor you either. I dare say I should thank you for your concern, but believe me, it is misplaced. If you had any care for me at all, you would do as we agreed before and not attempt to meddle in what you do not understand.'

'Oh, I understand you perfectly, Mistress Sutton. That's the whole problem. That is why you must turn back now, before you do something you are sure to regret for the rest of your life.'

'My only regret is that I was ever fool enough to seek your help. Good night, sir, I cannot afford to wait here and argue with you any longer.'

She reined the stallion around, touched his pale flank with her whip and cantered off along the Helston road.

Fast, much too fast. Despite the moonlight, the rocky track was treacherous enough for one of the sure-footed local ponies during the day. For a Barbary horse like Falcon, and in darkness, it was sure to be disastrous.

Luke cursed loudly as he watched them go. His anger was lost on the fierce wind. The pale horse was growing fainter: soon it would be hidden altogether by a bend in the road.

Suddenly decisive, he kicked his own horse forward and hurried after them.

Chapter Twenty-Four

As she walked in the garden after dinner, Perdita was surprised to see Piers Menheire riding down the avenue towards the house. As soon as he caught sight of her he jumped down from his horse and left it in the care of his groom. 'Mistress Treveryan,' he exclaimed, striding over the grass towards her, 'just the person I wanted to see.'

Perdita felt a small gust of pleasure at seeing him again, but she smothered it at once and did not permit herself even a smile. She was still shaken by Francis's clumsy overtures and did not want to make any further mistakes. She had been wondering, as she walked in the garden and brooded, if she had not allowed too much familiarity to creep into her dealings with Piers Menheire already. It was Edmund she wished to snare; good company Piers might be, but she could have no interest in a poor relation.

'Good day, Master Menheire.'

'Is anything the matter?'

'I don't think so. Why?'

'I've seen more cheerful faces heading for Tyburn in the back of a cart.'

'I was thinking,' she said crossly.

'Obviously an activity best avoided.'

Perdita turned away to hide her smile. 'Did you wish to speak to me about anything in particular?'

'Yes. I came over to say I think we should stop encouraging a union between Edmund and Mistress Sutton.'

Perdita was startled. She had never expected this. 'Why? Has he said he is no longer interested?'

'Not at all. He intends to ask her again soon. This time I think he means to involve her mother and Sir Francis first, which will make it harder for her to refuse.'

'But you think she ought to refuse him?'

'I am certain of it.'

'What has made you change your mind?' asked Perdita.

They were walking along the grassy path side by side. Perdita had forgotten she was supposed to be keeping him at a distance and was enjoying herself. He said, 'I'm not at liberty to say. But I overheard something that made me concerned . . . It hardly matters.'

'You heard your cousin talking about his intentions towards Sophie?'

Piers was frowning. 'Why the sudden curiosity, Mistress Treveryan? I am releasing you from any obligation to encourage the match. Isn't that what you wanted?'

'So whatever you heard it does not affect my own position in any way?'

'That depends entirely on you.'

'How can that be, when I do not have the faintest idea what has made you change your mind?'

He stopped and turned to face her. She was clearly as baffled by this impasse as he was. He laughed, but Perdita interrupted him. 'Your concern for Sophie may be unnecessary,' she said. 'She is not here.'

'What?'

'It is most probably nothing. Amos noticed at first light that Falcon had been taken. No one is permitted to ride him except Sophie, so everyone assumed she had just gone out for an early ride.'

'Was that likely?'

'Not really. She does go out riding sometimes in the morning, but she always tells someone what she is doing.'

'And this time?'

'No word.'

'She has not returned?'

Perdita shook her head. 'The men are out now looking for her. They are worried that she may have had an accident, but—'

'You don't think so.'

'No.'

'It seems the most likely explanation.'

'Maybe. But even so – she has been different this past few days. As if she was planning something.'

'Such as?'

When Perdita did not answer, Piers said, 'Do you think she might have run away?' Still no reply. 'Where would she go?'

'I wish I knew. Most probably I am imagining it and there is some perfectly simple explanation. I hope so. It's terrible to imagine that she might have fallen or—'

Her fear was left unspoken. She was relieved that Piers did not try to allay her worries with false consolation. There was a shared awareness that they had both tried to intervene in Sophie's affairs. In thoughtful silence they began to walk back in the direction they had just come.

As they neared the avenue, Piers looked up and said, 'There are her brothers now. Maybe they have found her.'

Francis and Kip were riding side by side. Even before their expressions were visible, it was obvious from the dejected slump of their shoulders that whatever news they had had it was not good.

'Well?' asked Perdita and Piers together, as they drew alongside.

'No sign of her,' said Francis wretchedly.

'But we've heard—' began Kip.

Francis stopped him with a warning, 'Kip!' and a meaningful glance towards Piers.

Kip said, 'There's no point trying to keep it secret, Francis. The news will be all over the district by nightfall.'

'The rumour,' said Francis. 'It is most probably a false alarm.'

'What rumour?' asked Perdita.

'We met the Porthew carter coming back from Helston,' said Kip. 'He said he'd heard a couple of people say they'd seen Sophie.'

'Or someone who looked like her,' interjected Francis.

'A woman riding a grey stallion, which must have been Falcon,' said Kip.

'Where?'

'Just the other side of Helston. And going north, as if she was heading towards Truro.'

317

'What on earth would she do there?' asked Piers. 'Do you have any family in that direction? Or particular friends?'

'She does have friends there. It may be she has decided to pay them a visit,' said Francis, as if giving due weight to this possibility.

Kip swung down from his horse and said firmly, 'With Master Hollar?'

'My brother?' asked Perdita. All at once an image flashed into her mind: Sophie kneeling on the ground by the old mews, Luke's head cradled in her arms. Piers caught her eye. She looked away at once.

'That's right,' said Kip. 'Sophie was not travelling alone. And at least two people said the man with her was your brother.'

'But that's impossible!'

'Not really,' said Kip. 'His assistant said Hollar told him he'd be away for a few days but would not say where he was going.'

Francis said hastily, 'There may be some perfectly simple explanation that we just haven't thought of and—'

But Kip interrupted him harshly, 'Of course she has, Francis. Quite clearly my sister is insane and has run away with the Porthew draper. You might as well tell your brother, Piers. He'll hear about it soon enough. Does anyone have any idea how we are going to break this to my mother?'

By the time Alice Sutton had recovered from her hysterics, her daughter was already well beyond Truro. They would have gone further still, only Luke insisted they stop for a couple of hours before noon to rest the horses. He found a patch of rough ground, which was hidden from the road by a clump of willows and scrub, and there, despite the continuing wind, he wrapped himself around in his heavy travelling cloak, lay down and fell at once into a deep sleep.

Sophie was far too agitated to follow his example. She kept an anxious watch and tried to soothe Falcon, who was as unsettled by this departure from routine as she was.

When Luke awoke he said they must now travel only on the side roads, which he knew well, since if her family had set off in pursuit at first light they might now be close to catching up.

Sophie was impatient at the delay, but the country beyond Helston was strange to her. In this maze of narrow roads and hillsides pockmarked with tin-works, she had no option but to follow his advice.

Towards late afternoon they halted at a smithy on the edge of a poor village and bought fodder for the horses, bread and cheese for themselves. The blacksmith took the horses to the rear of his cottage, where the water trough was. His large family gathered around Falcon to touch and admire him. Luke sat down on a bench in front of the forge to eat his bread and cheese. After observing him thoughtfully for a few moments, Sophie went to sit beside him. 'Master Hollar,' she said, 'how much longer do you mean to go on being angry with me? You've barely spoken a civil word all day.'

'You asked me to help you sell your stallion at Wadebridge and I will,' he replied coolly. 'I was not aware I was expected to entertain you as well.'

Sophie bit her lip. She crumbled a piece of bread between her fingers and watched as the wind gusted the crumbs away. She said, 'I did not mean to trick you, as you call it. Only . . .' Her voice trailed off.

'You realise, don't you, what everyone is now thinking in Porthew?'

'Well . . . yes. I am sorry, Master Hollar. I should have known that your reputation would be forfeit as well as mine.'

'I care not a straw for my reputation,' he told her angrily. 'What little I had was lost long ago. A man who consorts with travelling players is hardly dainty about his reputation. But you were well aware of that when you chose me for this task.'

Sophie was startled, more by the bitterness that lay behind his words than what he said. 'Believe me, Master Hollar, I never—'

'Ssssh!'

Alert to danger, Luke was gazing down the road. A party of horsemen was coming into view. He stood up, wrapped his travelling cape across Sophie's shoulders and drew her into the shelter of the smithy.

'Don't move!' he told her in a fierce whisper, as he pulled the edge of his cape across her face. He stood without moving for some minutes, Sophie quite still and pressed close against him.

Clatter of horsemen riding by and the roar of the smithy fire.

When he released her, Sophie's face was burning. 'Was that necessary?' she asked.

Luke stepped away and gestured towards the retreating group of riders. 'Young Godolphin and his cronies. They would have recognised you for sure.'

'I could have made up some story to put them off.'

Luke glanced at her. His long eyes were dark with anger, and something else besides. 'Oh, yes, of course. It's simple, is it not? You tell them you are visiting relatives . . .'

'Something like that.'

'With your loyal manservant to attend you.'

Sophie felt a tightening of her upper chest. 'I would never say that,' she told him.

'What, then?'

'I could tell them the truth.'

'The truth? Please tell me, Mistress Sutton, what exactly is the truth here?'

'Well, that I am on my way to sell my horse. And that you have agreed to help me and—'

'You see. It will not do, will it? No one will believe you. But that does not matter to you because it suits your purpose to have everyone assume the worst. You see it as a way to escape a marriage you never wanted.'

'And if I do? Where is the harm in that?'

'The harm, Mistress Sutton, is because you have used me. You knew I would not turn you down. My evil reputation suits your purposes exactly, but you had no right to trick me into this false elopement.'

'I did not mean—'

'We are wasting time. Let us get the horses. We still have Falcon to sell, whatever else happens. Or maybe you do not intend to sell him. Maybe that was merely the pretext.'

'Of course I mean to sell him.'

'In that case we have a good distance to travel yet today.'

Sophie stood aside to let him pass, then followed him into the gusty afternoon. She put her hand on his arm. 'Master Hollar, you are rightly proud and I have offended you, though it was never my intention—'

He shook her off. 'Spare me your sympathy.'

'But—'

'Hush. We are observed.'

The smith was leading the horses round from the back of his cottage. He looked curiously at the two travellers. Luke asked him how much was owed for the food. Sophie raised her arms in a brief gesture of exasperation, then followed him without another word.

As they rode along the riverbank towards evening and the spire of St Mary's church in Truro came into sight, Sophie felt weary. She had not slept at all in two days and had been too keyed up to eat much either. She had been wet and cold and worn down by the constant battering of the wind. More exhausting still, this journey had followed long days and nights of worry. She had fretted lest one of the horses might fall lame, one of her family might come after them or some accident she had never even imagined might occur. Now that she was in sight of Truro, her thoughts turned with relief to feather beds, blazing fires, warm food and drink.

Speaking for the first time since their argument in the smithy she said, 'Thank heavens, we're nearly there. Which inn do you recommend?'

'None of them.'

'Why not?'

'We are not stopping in Truro. We will not even go through it. Either you or Falcon is sure to be recognised.'

'Then where?'

'I know a place.'

His voice was cold, repulsing further questions, and Sophie had not the heart to insist. For the first time that day, bleak despair enveloped her. Dusk was spreading out from the shadows of the wood and a damp chill was rising from the river.

The warm kitchen at Rossmere seemed a hundred miles away from this darkening scene. She wondered what her family were doing now, what they were thinking. She had imagined their anger, which she was sure she could allay when she returned with the money. Now she imagined their worry. She hoped they were not anxious about her.

When she had planned this journey she had thought only of

the moment of return, her bag full of coins to pay off the debt to the Menheires, to free her for a future in which Edmund had no part. She had known, of course, that her disappearance must cause some alarm, but she had been confident they would understand in time . . . Now she was not so sure. In fact, she was no longer sure about anything.

'This is the place.'

Luke's voice jolted her from her reverie. Sophie realised she must have been nodding in the saddle. Reviving instantly, she saw they were nearing a small stone house, neither humble nor grand, which was set all alone in a deeply wooded valley. 'Where are we?'

'Jack Keagle's. He and his mother are respectable people. I've had dealings with him in the past and he owes me a favour. More importantly, no one would ever think of looking for you or the horse here.'

A man holding a lantern aloft came to the front door. He was wiry, with dark hair, a cautious face and something twisted about the shoulders. Luke slipped down from his horse and bade him good evening. 'We need shelter for tonight, Jack,' he said. 'Somewhere for the horses. Food and drink for my companion and me. We'll pay you, of course.'

Jack let his gaze rest on the silent woman riding a stallion the like of which he'd never seen in his life before. He said, 'You don't want a proper inn?'

'We prefer to be private.'

Jack examined Falcon more closely, then lowered his voice and asked, 'The stallion, Master Hollar, is he stolen?'

Luke clapped him on the shoulder and said easily, 'Certainly not. I wouldn't risk a hanging for the sake of a horse. He belongs to my companion and she has the documents to prove it.'

'In that case –' Jack's manner changed at once – 'come into the house and welcome. My mother will make you comfortable. I'll see to the horses.'

Luke showed Sophie into a low-ceilinged room and introduced her to Goody Keagle, a woman round and comfortable-looking as a plumped-up bolster, before going out to help Jack and make sure that Falcon was properly stabled.

Sophie took off her outer clothing and sat down gratefully on a settle by the fire. Goody Keagle stoked it to a blaze and seized the unexpected chance of company. Visitors were a rarity in her lonely home, especially visitors who were prepared to smile and be interested in the tale of her life: all those stories of small triumphs over adversity and huge griefs. Her husband had been killed at the beginning of the late wars, two of her sons had died at the siege of Bristol. Only last year her daughter-in-law had been carried off by diphtheria, and her two grandsons as well. And then there was the time her remaining son, Jack, had fallen from his horse and been left for dead and needed nursing for a whole year . . .

After a while, her remaining grandchildren, three girls ranged in age from four to thirteen, forgot their shyness and emerged from the kitchen to watch the strange lady as she chatted with their grandmother and sipped spiced ale from a pewter mug.

Goody Keagle retreated to the back room to rustle up a meal – luckily she had been baking only the previous day and the ale was freshly brewed – but after a while the oldest child appeared and asked, 'Why is the stranger lady sleeping?'

It was true. Sophie had fallen asleep where she sat, her head angled awkwardly against the back of the settle. Her face, beneath the grime of a long day's journey, was very pale, and her eyes were deeply shadowed.

'She's worn out, poor thing,' said Goody Keagle to the two men, who were just coming in through the front door. 'It seems a shame to wake her.'

Luke observed the sleeping woman, his expression almost tender. Then he stepped over and shook her roughly by the shoulder. 'Wake up, Mistress Sutton. First you must eat, then you can rest. Tomorrow will be just as hard.'

'Yes, yes. Of course.' Sophie roused herself with difficulty.

Goody Keagle hurried more than ever to set food on the table before her guest nodded off again, and Sophie, in spite of a growing dizziness, tried hard to eat as Luke advised, but it was no good. She was far too tired.

When her eyes had closed involuntarily for the fourth time, Luke gave up. He said, 'Goody Keagle, may Mistress Sutton share your bed tonight? Jack and I will shift for ourselves down here.'

Goody Keagle agreed at once. She had been wondering about the sleeping arrangements, but this was one solution that had not occurred to her.

'Please don't worry about me,' mumbled Sophie, forcing her eyes open once again. 'I could sleep anywhere.'

Goody Keagle fussed around her and guided her up the narrow stairs, the three little girls following curiously behind.

Jack reached for his pipe and turned to Luke. 'I thought you'd be wanting the bed with her,' he said.

'No.' Luke leaned back in his chair and sighed. 'And I need you and your mother to be our witnesses. It's one reason I did not stop at the inn at Truro. At the moment Mistress Sutton is not concerned about the possibility of scandal, but she may change her mind in future, and if she does . . . Well, this is the least I can do for her.'

Jack nodded. Above them the floorboards were creaking busily as Goody Keagle and her three granddaughters hurried to prepare the bed before Sophie collapsed on it.

Luke said, 'She intends selling the stallion at Wadebridge. The sale is to remain a secret until it is completed. She asked for my help.'

His companion waited to see if Luke was about to offer any further explanations, but when none were forthcoming he lit his pipe and said thoughtfully, 'Poor maid. She must have been desperate to turn to you.'

'Yes,' said Luke. 'I rather think she was.'

When Sophie awoke the next morning bright sunlight was streaming in at the window. It was the first time in her life that she had awoken anywhere but Rossmere and for a moment she thought she must be still dreaming. She could remember almost nothing about the previous evening after they had arrived at the house. She was alone in the large bed. There was a hollow in the pillow next to hers: clearly she had not passed the night alone. Suddenly she was very wide awake indeed.

She found Luke examining Falcon's leg in a low shed next to the house. He glanced up at her approach. He was frowning.

'Why did you let me sleep so long?' she demanded. 'We should have been on the road again at daybreak.'

'You needed the rest,' he said. 'Besides, you're not going anywhere, not today.'

'What?'

'It's probably a three-hour ride from here to Wadebridge, maybe more by the back roads. My plan was to spend tonight at an agent's house in Padstow. Now I think we'd better stay here. I'll go to Wadebridge this morning and make some enquiries. I'll be back this evening. Tomorrow, all being well, we'll travel on together.'

'Your first plan was better. I'll ride with you to Padstow.'

'No.'

'I am perfectly rested. The journey will do me no harm.'

'Your comfort is not my concern, Mistress Sutton. I was thinking of Falcon. He must have strained a muscle in his leg yesterday. I'm no horse doctor but I suggest you apply a poultice and we'll hope the swelling has gone down by tomorrow. There's no point in trying to sell a lame animal.'

Sophie ran her hand down Falcon's hind leg. The area just above the knee was inflamed and hot beneath the hair.

'This has happened to him once before,' she said. 'It's my fault for not checking him last night. How could I have been so thoughtless?'

'Don't blame yourself. I looked him over carefully myself and there was nothing showing then.'

'But still . . .' Sophie was smoothing Falcon's rump with her strong hand. 'I was so tired last night, I cannot remember any of it.'

Luke stooped to skim some chaff from the stallion's water bucket. 'By the way, he said casually, 'Goody Keagle tells me you talk in your sleep. She says you kept her awake half the night with your chatter.'

Sophie smiled. In her dreams it had been Luke's long body stretched beside her in the bed. 'Did she tell you what I said?' she asked.

'All nonsense, apparently.'

She sighed. 'Thank you, Master Hollar. When I asked you to help me sell Falcon, I never imagined it would be so compli-cated.'

'No?'

'No.'

'Don't thank me yet. There's good deal still to be done. Wait until after the fair.'

A little later he mounted Jack Keagle's horse, to give his own a much needed rest, and set off for Wadebridge. He tried to keep his mind fixed on the task ahead, but his thoughts kept sliding back and forming pictures of Sophie: the feel of her body pressed against his when he wrapped his cloak around her in the shelter of the wayside forge; her lashes so dark against the exhausted pallor of her cheek when she was losing the battle to fight off sleep the previous evening; her expression just now when she stood in the doorway of the stable, sunlight turning her brown hair to gold and she told him she had never imagined their journey would prove so complicated.

And she was not the only one, he thought grimly. Sophie Sutton was the kind of woman who could destroy a man's peace of mind while intending only gratitude and kindness.

Gratitude . . . The very idea of her thanks was lodged like a bone in his throat. God save him from her gratitude. Obviously she regarded him as little better than a stableboy or servant. Gratitude was worse than nothing at all.

In the days that lay ahead, Luke thought selling the stallion was going to be the least of the problems he was likely to face.

That day was one of the strangest of her life.

Despite the solemn purpose behind her journey, Sophie felt oddly light-headed, like a ship cast off from its moorings and drifting always further out to sea. The endless journey and the profound sleep that followed it seemed to have cut her off from her normal, everyday life at Rossmere. She told herself, as the hours passed, that now Cary must be setting out the food for dinner, now Uncle Stephen was coming in from the fields, now poor Honor was flitting about the house like a sad-eyed phantom asking for remedies . . . but she hardly believed it. Rossmere and all its inhabitants belonged in some other world, not this one. Not in this deep, secret valley with unfamiliar people and its strange rhythms and sounds, the echo of unknown voices through the house.

Goody Keagle found it difficult to place her guest in the scheme of things. She had the voice and manner of a gentle-woman, but her offer of help proved no empty gesture: she plucked and gutted a chicken for their supper in half the time it would have taken the old woman herself. Then again, her clothes were shabby and darned, yet she rode a horse any gentleman in Cornwall would have been proud to own. And, though anyone could see she had troubles enough of her own, she followed Goody Keagle's account of her own misfortunes with interest.

Sophie was discovering the delights of being among strangers, with its perilous illusions of privacy. She felt she could talk to this energetic old woman with a freedom impossible with her own family. During the afternoon she gave her a simplified account of the Suttons' difficulties and her reasons for selling Falcon. By early evening, when he still had not returned, their conversation turned to Luke.

'Master Hollar told me you owed him a favour,' said Sophie. 'Do you mind telling me what it was?'

'More than a favour. After Jack's accident he could not work for nearly a year. No work, and no money coming in. We used to sell our cloth to a Camborne man, but we fell behind. He was threatening us with all sorts of horrors, until Master Hollar lent us the money to get started again. No one else would have taken the risk. It was nearly five years before we could start to pay him back – it's all done now, thank the Lord, though he never pressured us, not once. Not like some. He's a kind man to his friends – but you know that better than I do.'

'I suppose so –' Sophie was sounding doubtful – 'though I never thought of it quite like that.'

Goody Keagle set down the pot she had been scouring and examined Sophie. 'Why else do you think he'd be going to all this trouble for you, then?'

'I don't know. I had not thought . . .'

The old woman leaned forward and patted her shoulder. She was beaming her gap-toothed grin. 'You'd know well enough if you'd seen the look on his face when you fell asleep at the table last night,' she said gleefully.

'He's angry. He thinks I've tricked him into helping me.'

Goody Keagle was still chuckling. 'You should've seen his face, dear. That wasn't the look of an angry man.'

When Luke returned, a little before sunset, Sophie was telling the Keagles the story of the Grey Lady of Tilsbury, and how the ghost had helped the Irish prisoners to escape death from slow starvation, and how Cary had blown up the Parliament munitions wagon and injured her face in the process. She had omitted the gorier details, so beloved by Cary, out of consideration for the smallest Keagle who had climbed on to her knee to hear the tale.

'You must be hungry,' she said, when Luke came into the parlour, brushing the dust of the journey from his wide-brimmed hat. 'The food is prepared. We can have the rest of the story after we've eaten.'

'No,' said Luke. 'There's no hurry. Finish the story.'

He sat down near the door and Goody Keagle fetched him a mug of ale. He was frowning and did not once look at Sophie as she gave a vivid account of Cary's escape from capture, and how she had come to live at Rossmere with her Irish husband. Sophie stole a glance towards him from time to time. She could not decide if he was even listening.

Over the evening meal, Luke told them that there were expected to be only two dealers at the fair who might have sufficient funds to buy a horse like Falcon. One was from the Midlands, the other from somewhere south of London. He had spoken to them both and they had expressed a cautious interest in seeing the stallion the following day.

'Of course, there might be local buyers who turn up. We'll have to wait and see. How is his leg?'

'Much better, but the swelling has not completely gone. I shall put a fresh poultice on tonight. He should be well enough to ride again tomorrow.'

'We cannot risk injuring him,' said Luke. 'Unless he is quite recovered, we'll have to forget about Wadebridge and wait for the next fair.'

To Luke's surprise, Sophie was not at all dismayed by the prospect of delay. In fact, she was thinking it would be a fine thing to remain with the Keagles and the three solemn little girls for a week more.

Or even a month.

Chapter Twenty-Five

'Look over there. Isn't that the Sutton girl from Rossmere?'

'You mean Sir Francis's sister? It can't be.'

'It is, you know. The older one. Can't remember her name.'

'What the devil is she doing here?'

A crowd had gathered to watch Sophie as she put Falcon through his paces. The stallion himself was novelty enough: his injury was healed and he was showing himself off to perfection, his dappled coat gleaming in the morning sunshine, iron-grey tail streaming behind him like a pennant.

Such a magnificent animal would have stood out anyway among the ponies and workhorses, but for once the rider attracted even more interest. It was rare enough for a woman to play an active part at a monthly horse fair among the usual assembly of traders and gypsies, local farmers and farriers, grooms and horse leeches, saddlers and scroungers, but it was unheard of for the sister of a baronet to do so. A murmur of disbelief rippled through the crowd, like a breeze over a field of summer corn.

Sophie was concentrating on showing Falcon at his best and thinking of the money to be made from the sale and so remained oblivious to the interest she herself excited. But Luke, who stood among the spectators, was only too keenly aware of it.

A woman's voice floated clear and shrill from somewhere at the back of the crowd. 'Whatever next? Does she want to be a laughing stock?'

'Look,' said one of the men standing by Luke, 'it handles well.'

'Which? The girl or the horse?' asked his companion.

'That's what I'd like to know.'

The two men nudged each other and snickered. It was all Luke could do to prevent himself from knocking their heads together. Tom Barber was a red-faced buffoon, a local farmer with pretensions to gentility, and his friend, Robert Yeo, was a squat little toad of a man with a gloating, lecherous grin, and nothing would have given Luke more pleasure than to smash their loathsome heads together. But Tom Barber had expressed an interest in buying Falcon, so for the time being he had to hold back.

Luke doubted if anything would come of the farmer's overtures: he seemed to be one of those types who enjoy spinning out the idea of a purchase for the satisfaction of haggling and the attention given by the seller. He was sure to find a reason to back out before the ritual of purchase was completed. But Luke thought he might be useful in forcing up the price eventually offered by one of the two dealers whose interest, though far less obvious, was still genuine. And since Luke's only purpose was to get the best possible price for the stallion, he did not intend to let Tom Barber and his companion goad him into retaliating. Not yet.

Besides, he was still angry with Mistress Sutton for exposing herself to the insults of scum like these. On the ride from Jack Keagle's home that morning, he had tried to persuade her to let him handle the sale.

'But what if they want to see how Falcon rides?' she had asked him. 'What then?'

'I can ride him myself. Or we'll find a lad to put him through his paces.'

Sophie had been perplexed. 'Where would be the sense in that? No one but me has ridden him since March. If he finds himself in a crowd of strangers and with an unknown rider on his back, the Lord only knows how he'd respond. With me riding him, everyone will see him at his best. Surely that will mean a higher price.'

'But you will make yourself a public spectacle.'

'That cannot be helped. And if it helps get more money for Falcon, then it doesn't matter about me at all.'

'A horse fair can be a rough place. I wouldn't like—'

'Please stop trying to alarm me, Master Hollar. My only purpose is to sell Falcon for the best possible price, and that is what I mean to do,' Sophie said crisply, putting an end to further debate.

Luke hated it when she spoke that way. As if he were a servant who needed to be snubbed from time to time to keep him in his place. Which was how she regarded him, of course. She was so single-minded in her determination to get a high price for Falcon that she had shut her eyes to everything else. Or maybe the simple truth was that the Tom Barbers and Robert Yeos of this world, like the Luke Hollars, were so far beneath her notice that quite simply their opinions were irrelevant. He told himself that she had only herself to blame if her blinkered pride made her a laughing stock . . . but when she rode over to where he was standing, he saw only her loveliness and her courage, no sign of arrogance.

'Do you think they've seen enough?' she asked Luke.

He turned to the four men standing by him. 'What do you think?' His question was addressed primarily to the two dealers. 'Do you want to see him at full stretch?'

Neither replied to this. One, a small, dark-haired fellow called Wilkes, was assessing Falcon through half-closed eyes. The second was a burly man from the Midlands, who demonstrated his lack of interest in the proceedings by scraping a piece of mud off the sole of his boot.

Tom Barber, however, smoothed Falcon's neck with his red hand – a hand that seemed to Luke to be straying unnecessarily close to Mistress Sutton's ankle – and said, 'A gallop, eh? That would be something to see.' He lifted his gaze to look boldly at Sophie. 'If that doesn't inconvenience you in any way, ma'am,' he added, with false civility.

'Not at all,' she said, accepting his civility as genuine and flashing him a smile. 'With Falcon it is always a pleasure. I shall go between those two trees over there. The crowds are too busy here – it might be dangerous.'

'How thoughtful you are, ma'am,' said Tom Barber, touching the brim of his hat.

Luke's fists were clenched so hard that his arms and shoulders ached. It maddened him that Mistress Sutton remained blithely unaware of the contempt of these so-called gentlemen farmers.

As she rode away, Barber said, in a voice deliberately loud enough to be heard by all about them, though not by Sophie herself, 'I'd like to put that young lady through her paces, that would be a sight to see.'

Yeo made appreciative smacking noises with his toad-like lips and both men sniggered.

'Hold your tongue, sir,' said Luke quietly, 'before I ram it down your throat.'

'Oh, ho! And what gives you the right to champion her ladyship, eh?' asked Barber, delighted to have goaded Luke into some response.

'He wants to keep her galloping all to himself,' said Yeo.

'It's a bit late for that, isn't it? They do say she went the distance with a certain wealthy gentleman and that stallion was her reward.'

He glanced sidelong at Luke, to see how he would take it. Luke was so angry that his vision clouded, and Sophie and her horse were no more than a pale speck of light in the distance, flying between the two trees she had designated. He knew, however, that Barber was only goading him because he had given up all hope of buying the horse, and that the two dealers were amused by the diversion and were watching him to see his reaction. A fight now, and he might as well say farewell to all chance of selling Falcon today. He forced himself to say, without any apparent emotion, 'Look at that stallion, gentleman. Did you ever see such a horse for speed?'

'A real goer,' agreed Yeo.

'Which?' asked Barber. 'The horse or the woman?'

Luke was not sure how much more of this he could take. Sophie reined Falcon back to a trot and was coming over to where they stood. He said, more to the dealers than to the farmers, 'I think, gentlemen, you've seen enough to know there's not a better horse to be had in all Cornwall. If anyone is interested in making a serious offer, they can find me at the Boar. I'll be in the side parlour.'

He walked briskly over to where Falcon was settling down after his gallop.

'What do you think?' asked Sophie, as she dismounted. 'Will they buy?'

334

'Maybe, if the price is right.'

'You're angry, Master Hollar. What is the matter?'

'Nothing, only that I wish to get this sale completed so we may quit this place as soon as possible.'

'We must not be over-hasty. I'll not let Falcon go cheap.'

'Leave it to me, Mistress Sutton. I promise you I'll get the best possible price for him.'

'I don't doubt it. Where shall we meet them to discuss terms?'

'At the Boar. But you do not need to be involved any longer.'

'It will be interesting.'

'It's better if you stay away.'

'Why? I promise not to interfere.'

'It's not that.'

'What, then?'

'Only . . . dear God, Mistress Sutton!' Luke broke out in exasperation. 'Why must there always be reasons? I'm a merchant. You asked me to help you because I understand about buying and selling and how it is done. If I tell you I do not want you to be present, then surely that is reason enough. Go and look at the stalls or the side-shows and leave me to do my job.'

A shadow fell across Sophie's face. The afterglow of ease and contentment from riding Falcon had faded. She said guardedly, 'I have not come all this way on a whim, sir. Selling Falcon may well be the most important act of my life. Do you seriously expect me to look at some pedlar's trinkets while the business is done? I insist on being present.'

'You know what they are thinking, don't you?'

'Their thoughts are of no interest to me.'

'Then don't blame me if—'

'If what, Master Hollar?'

'If those rogues do not treat you with the courtesy you are accustomed to.'

'Is that all? You really must not be so dainty on my account. So long as Falcon is sold for a good price.'

Luke gave up. 'The side parlour, then. I'll find someone to take the horse . . .'

Sophie went ahead of him into the inn.

*   *   *

The Boar in Wadebridge derived a good proportion of its income from the monthly horse fairs, and it had been full of drinkers since before daybreak. By early afternoon, when Sophie made her way into the dense press of people, enough ale had been consumed to float a small fleet. At the far end of the bar a fight had broken out between two men well on in drink. They swung punches wildly at each other, aimless as windmills, until one of them surprised himself by making contact with the other's nose. His victim slumped to the ground, bleeding copiously, but no one paid any attention.

Not even Sophie, who was thinking only of Falcon's sale. 'Which is the side parlour?' she asked a lad, who was struggling through the crowd carrying a pitcher of ale nearly as big as himself.

He gestured towards an open doorway. 'Through there.'

Tom Barber was obliged to stoop as he entered the inn. 'Mistress Sutton!' he exclaimed, his oafish red face lighting up with false familiarity. 'I must congratulate you on your horsemanship. Never seen anything like it!'

'Nor I,' croaked Yeo. 'Never seen a woman gallop so.'

'It is Falcon who deserves the praise, not I.'

'You are too modest!' declared Barber.

'A galloper and modest too!'

Sophie looked puzzled. Both men had obviously been drinking and she supposed this must be what Master Hollar had been warning her about. However, one of them might be interested in buying Falcon so she decided to ignore the unpleasant undertone to their remarks. There was no danger – except perhaps to her pride – in a crowded inn.

She continued into the side parlour to wait for Luke. Barber snatched a pitcher of ale from the potboy, then he and Yeo followed her, closing the door firmly behind them.

Luke arrived just in time to see the expression on Yeo's face as he pushed the door shut. He swore under his breath. He was still angry with Mistress Sutton for overruling him. He vowed in future to avoid all poverty-stricken gentlewomen with horses to sell . . . but now he had no option but to see this through.

Just then Wilkes, the dealer from south of London, appeared at his elbow. 'If that horse is still for sale,' he said, 'I might just consider making an offer.'

'By all means, come on through.'

'I'd rather have a quiet word with you here, Master Hollar, if it's all the same to you. No point everybody knowing our business, is there?'

Luke had been half expecting this. He knew neither Wilkes nor the other dealer were likely to make an offer with that buffoon Barber blabbing on all the time. In fact, his suggestion that they meet in the side parlour had been strategy to shake off the time-wasters. He had not anticipated – though God knows, he saw now he should have done – that Sophie would insist on following the false trail as well.

He threw an anguished glance towards the closed door of the parlour, then turned to Wilkes and said, 'Very well, then, how do you like the stallion?'

'I've seen worse. Shall we discuss this over a drop of ale?'

The deal was done with the minimum of fuss – though not nearly fast enough for Luke, who was seething with impatience. After a couple of false starts Wilkes offered a fair price for the horse, Luke talked it up as much as was reasonable, then the two men shook hands.

'Mistress Sutton must have the final say,' Luke told him. 'I'll go and tell her your offer.'

Wilkes nodded. 'I'll be hereabouts,' he said.

Luke elbowed his way through the scrum of people and pushed open the door into the side parlour, which was relatively empty. A couple of farm workers were slumped against the wall beside the empty fireplace. Both were dead to the world and snoring loudly. Sophie was seated at a small table under the window; Barber was beside her on the bench, Yeo on a stool nearby. Both men were leaning forward, crowding her. She threw Luke a look of undisguised relief as he came in. 'There you are, Master Hollar,' she exclaimed. 'I was beginning to wonder what had happened to you.'

Barber and Yeo moved fractionally away from her. Their expressions showed them to be less pleased at the intrusion.

'I was detained. Can I talk with you in private?'

'Of course.' She stood up. Neither of her companions shifted to let her pass. After a moment's hesitation she squeezed past the gloating Barber and came over to Luke.

He said in a low voice, 'Master Wilkes has offered a hundred and twelve guineas for Falcon and I have accepted, subject to your agreement. It is a good price and—'

'I thought the discussion was to take place in here?'

'Wilkes preferred to talk privately.'

'What about Master Barber? He may offer more.'

'It is extremely unlikely.'

'But you cannot be sure.'

Tom Barber pounded his red fist on the table. 'What's all this damned whispering in corners?' he wanted to know. 'I thought we were here to discuss the sale of your horse!'

'The stallion has been sold,' said Luke.

'What price do you have in mind?' asked Sophie.

'That all depends,' said Barber. 'Why don't we all sit down and talk it over?'

Sophie returned at once to the table under the window, pulled up a chair and sat down. Luke had no choice but to join her.

'How much have you agreed to sell for?' asked Barber.

'What are you offering?' asked Luke.

At the same instant Sophie said, 'A hundred and twelve guineas.'

'Mistress Sutton,' Luke spoke with barely controlled fury, 'I thought we had agreed—'

'Of course, I had forgotten. It's only—'

When Luke glanced at her, all his anger drained away. He saw once again how desperate she was to get the best possible price. She was thinking: if one man has offered a hundred and twelve then maybe one of these will offer even more. Maybe a hundred and twenty. Maybe even . . .

He turned to confront Barber. 'Well?'

Barber sucked in his shining cheeks. 'We-ell,' he breathed, 'that's a fair old sum of money for something with four legs and a tail.'

'You know he'd go for more than that up country.'

'Maybe so, maybe so. A hundred and twelve guineas is a powerful lot, you know. But then again, it is a fine animal, very fine indeed. No one can deny. A man would be proud to own such a horse.'

'So?' demanded Luke. 'Are you going to make an offer, or not?'

'I'll make Mistress Sutton an offer any day,' said Barber. Yeo snickered.

Luke's hand curled into a fist, but then he felt the grazing touch of Sophie's fingers, in a silent plea that he choose the least scurrilous interpretation of the fellow's words. She said coolly, 'It is my horse, Master Barber, but this gentleman is acting on my behalf. Please make any offers direct to him.'

'We are wasting our time,' said Luke.

'What's all the hurry?' asked Barber. 'Such delicate matters must never be rushed.'

Yeo said slyly, 'Maybe Master Hollar is impatient for a gallop on his own account.'

'What exactly do you mean by that?' asked Luke.

Barber raised his tankard with a laugh, but before he drank he said, 'I'll not buy the horse, Master Hollar, but it seems obvious to me that Mistress Sutton is mighty eager for some money. Since she's chosen you as her apple-seller, tell her she can have a gallop on my fine prick any time she wants and I'll gladly pay—'

He never finished his sentence. Luke was on his feet in an instant. He brought his hands down on the back of Barber's head, ramming his face against the brim of his tankard with such vehemence that his mouth was slashed to high up on the cheek.

Yeo was reaching for the knife he carried at his waist but Luke picked up a three-legged stool and brought it down on his head, shattering the stool and knocking him unconscious.

Barber staggered to his feet. Blood was pouring from the sickle-shaped wound to his face. He lunged at Luke, catching him around the waist, but Luke ducked his head and butted his opponent's chin, opening the wound still wider. Barber fell backwards with a roar of pain and stumbled over one of the snoring labourers. Luke reached for his own dagger, but Sophie, who had been watching everything in horrified silence, caught him by the wrist.

'No!' she said. 'Stop now. That's enough!'

Luke stared at her. His eyes were hard and unseeing, like grey-green stones set in his face. There was a blankness in his look, which frightened her.

'That's enough, Master Hollar.'

He shook off her restraining hand. 'They ought to be killed!'

Barber, struggling to rise to his feet, tried to curse Luke, but only managed to spit out blood.

'Please,' said Sophie, 'let's get away from here.'

Luke drew in a deep breath, then nodded, like someone awaking from a strange sleep. He set his dagger back in his belt and took her by the arm. 'We'll find Master Wilkes,' he said, 'and then a saddle horse for you. We'll not stay here tonight.'

'No,' said Sophie.

The Padstow agent at whose house they arrived an hour after nightfall was already in his nightshirt and on his way to bed when Luke rapped on his front door. It soon became apparent that the man had suffered a mild stroke since Luke had seen him last; he was shuffling and confused and utterly dependent on his housekeeper, who was already warming his bed for him. Both she and her 'brother' – a ruffianly looking fellow with a pock-marked face – made no pretence at being civil.

'There's food in the kitchen,' said the woman. 'Help your-selves if you must, but tidy away afterwards. We've enough mice already.'

'Thank you,' said Sophie.

'There's a bed in the chamber over the hall. It's not made up but there's a couple of blankets in the chest by the door. They may be damp, but I can't help that.'

'Mistress Sutton will have that room,' said Luke. 'I'll sleep down here by the fire.'

'Suit yourself,' said the slovenly woman, with a contemptuous glance at both Luke and Sophie, 'but don't go wasting wood. That pile has to last all winter. I suppose you'll be wanting a candle?'

'We need at least two,' said Luke.

The woman took a candle and broke it in half, giving one portion to Luke and one to Sophie. 'Make sure the back door is locked and bolted,' she said, as she turned to go back to her bed with the agent. 'We don't want thieves.'

'The worst thieves are always on the inside,' said Luke.

She pretended not to have heard.

When Luke returned from stabling the horses, Sophie was kneeling in front of the hearth, trying to coax the fire back to life. Her sleeves were rolled up and her forearms gleamed pale in the candlelight. Luke stood in the doorway, watching her.

She said, without turning round, 'Your friend keeps a wretched house. There's hardly any food and the ale is sour.'

'He's ill.' Luke crossed the room to stand beside her. 'Shall I try the fire?'

'It's going now.' She laid two pieces of furze on the glowing ashes and sat back on her heels as they crackled in the flames. 'I was afraid you were going to kill those two men today.'

'It was only what they deserved.'

'For being drunk and insolent?'

'They had no right to speak to you like that.'

'Only words – they meant no real harm.'

Luke stared down at her. 'You don't understand, do you? You've been so sheltered in your fine house at Rossmere, you've no idea what it's like in the world outside. How are you ever going to manage when your family lose their home?'

'*If* we lose our home, not when.'

'People are vicious and ugly. You talk as if words don't matter, but lives are destroyed by that kind of talk. *Your* life will be destroyed. Buffoons like Barber and Yeo have the power to drag you down—'

'But why are you so angry with me again?'

'Because you are deliberately throwing your life away. It is the waste of it.'

'How can that be?' Sophie put a few sticks on the fire, then stood up and turned to face him directly. 'I sold Falcon to save myself, not to throw my life away. Now I have the money to prevent a marriage that would have been a kind of death.'

'That's just foolishness. It would not have been so bad. You should have married Menheire. You would have been mistress of a fine house. Money and respect, these things are important.'

'Not to me.'

'That's because you've never known the lack of either.'

Sophie laughed aloud. 'Lord above, Master Hollar, you think we don't know about being poor at Rossmere?'

'Not in the way ordinary folk do. You think it means cutting back on servants, not paying your bills on time. But you can always retreat safe behind your high walls. You've always been protected from the worst. You say it's only words, but evil words can maim and destroy. You've never had to face the slander and the lies, day after day, no way of escape from it.'

'And you have?'

'Yes! When my mother—' Luke broke off, furious with himself. He flung himself away from her and sat down at the long table. It was covered in dust and grease. He said angrily, 'Where's that ale?'

'Here.' Sophie took a jug from a shelf and poured some for him. 'But I warn you, it's sour.'

'Give it to me anyway. Is there no food?'

'I found a few eggs. When the fire is stronger, I'll cook them.'

'I'll not wait. Haven't you found anything else?'

'Some rabbit pie, but it's old.'

'That'll have to do. Hurry, for God's sake.'

Sophie did not hurry. She moved around the kitchen with her usual calm efficiency, blowing the dust from a wooden trencher, cutting the green edge off the pie, setting all on the table in front of Luke. But she dropped a knife on the floor, and when she sat down at the table opposite him, she had to clasp her hands under her chin to control her trembling.

Luke tore at the pie with his hands, as though he was famished. Sophie gazed at him thoughtfully, then asked, 'How old were you when your mother took up with Sir Richard?'

'When she became his whore, you mean? I can't remember. It's not important.'

'You must have been just a child. I remember the rumours.'

Luke grunted, but he did not look at her, or speak.

'It must have been impossible for you in Porthew.'

'Not at all. I learned to use my fists.'

'But even so—'

He interrupted her. 'If you're not going to eat, why don't you go to your room and leave me in peace? We have a long ride tomorrow.'

'I'm not tired.'

'Well, I am. Leave me be.'

Sophie stood up and went to the fireplace. The fire was dwindling again, but she did not bother to add fuel. She said, 'All this time I've only thought about selling Falcon. Now that is done and the money is safe and . . . and I don't know what to do next.'

'It's simple. You go home. Hand over the money. Safe at Rossmere again.'

'And you?'

'What about me?'

'What will you do now?'

He shrugged. 'It doesn't matter.'

'It matters to me.'

'Why?'

'I don't know. Because you've helped me. Because we've done this together. Will you spend time with the travelling players again this winter?'

'I might do. But I'm getting too old for that, too fond of my comforts.' He took a swig of the ale and almost choked. 'Ugh! Mare's piss!'

'I warned you.'

'Is there nothing else?'

'Not that I could find. There's a cupboard over there, but it's locked.'

Luke stood up and went to the cupboard, examined the padlock that secured it, then took his dagger from his belt and eased the door off at the hinges. He removed the first of the two bottles, unstoppered it and sniffed the contents.

'Brandy, that's better. The lock must be to keep my poor friend away from his own liquor. He was always fond of a good brandy. I might as well enjoy it for him.' Luke raised the bottle to his lips and drank deeply.

'I'd like some too.'

He handed Sophie the bottle without wiping the rim or bothering to glance in her direction.

She leaned back against the edge of the table and drank.

When she did not return the bottle to him, Luke removed the second one and started on that.

After a while she said thoughtfully, 'You've only yourself to blame.'

'For what?'

'That I won't marry Edmund Menheire.'

Luke almost choked for a second time. 'It's nothing to do with me! I never asked you to come to Wadebridge, I never even wanted you to!'

'Not that. I meant that other time. When I came to your shop and you played the violin.'

'What of it?'

'I thought you knew.'

'I've forgotten. It was nothing.'

'No?' Sophie faltered. She took a long drink from the bottle of brandy, then said, 'It meant a lot to me.'

In spite of himself Luke was curious. He glanced across at her and asked, 'Why?'

'Because I thought maybe you cared for me.'

'Yes,' he laughed bitterly, 'and you saw how you might take advantage of that to make me a part of your sordid little schemes and—'

'That's not true, that's not what I meant.' Sophie's composure was rapidly crumbling. 'I knew then, after that time alone with you, that I couldn't marry another man if I felt the way I did . . . about you.'

Luke held her gaze for a long moment. He was breathing heavily.

Then he went back to the table and slumped down on a chair. 'It makes no difference,' he said thickly.

'No?'

'Leave me be, Mistress Sutton.'

'But—'

'Your horse is sold. You have the money. Tomorrow, or the next day, you will be back with your family. That's all there is to it.'

'But if—' She moved across to stand beside him, then touched his shoulder lightly.

He shook her off. 'No,' he said, standing up once more.

She placed herself in front of him.

He said, 'Why are you doing this?'

'Because—'

But he answered for her, 'You think you've thrown your life away so you might as well enjoy an adventure while you can, don't you?'

She frowned. 'What do you mean?'

He gripped her fiercely by the shoulders. 'Tell me, Mistress Sutton, why did Treveryan give you the stallion?'

'Because . . . I don't know why. He just did, that's all.'

'I don't believe you,' said Luke.

And then he kissed her.

It was an ugly kiss, full of all the anger and hurt and pain that had been building up for days. His lips bruised down against hers, his fingers were digging into her shoulder-blades.

At length he released her and she stepped backwards, shocked and bewildered.

'Is that what you wanted?' he demanded. 'Now, get away from here.'

She was hugging herself. She looked away from him and said, 'I never was Treveryan's whore. I've never been with any man. Until now. You know that, don't you.'

'Yes. But it's not important.'

'I love you,' said Sophie.

He laughed. 'That's the brandy talking.'

'Don't you love me?'

'You know I do. You've always known it.'

'So why must you make it so complicated? When two people care for each other, surely they have a God-given chance to be happy . . .'

'What, for a night? Two nights maybe?'

'For as long as they want. For ever.'

'That's not the way things happen.'

She moved slowly towards him. His face was wet with tears. She said, 'I love you, Luke.'

'No. You only think you do because you're away from everything familiar in your life and you don't know what to do next, you said so yourself.'

'Say you love me too.'

'I have always loved you.'

'Then it is simple.'

'Nothing is ever simple. Surely you've learned that much at least.'

'Have faith, Luke.'

'How can I when you're asking me to help in your ruin?'

She touched his cheek with her fingers. 'Why can we not be happy together?'

'I don't know how to be happy.'

'Like this.' She brushed his lips lightly with her own. 'And this . . .' She kissed him, briefly.

He said, 'I will only bring you misery. I'll not be your lover.'

'I want to be your wife.'

'You say that now but you don't know.'

'I know what I want.'

'It's impossible.'

'No, Luke, it's easy.'

He let out a groan that was almost a sob and rested his cheek against her face. 'Oh, Sophie,' he murmured, 'don't make me do this. We will destroy each other.'

'Ssssh.'

She took his face between her hands and kissed him. He returned her kisses, but gently this time, tenderly exploring her mouth, her cheeks, the hollow of her throat.

She said, 'Let's go upstairs.'

He nodded and picked up the candle, which had now burned down to a stump, placed his arm around her waist and climbed the stairs.

Three doors led off the landing; two were closed. From behind the first came a ragged duet of snores, from behind the second a grisly cough and the creak of bed-springs.

Sophie pushed back the third door, which was ajar. 'In here,' she said.

Luke held the candle aloft as they went in. It was a small room with an uncurtained bed and a couple of linen presses. The walls were black with mould and the atmosphere was heavy with the stench of rot and damp.

Sophie pulled a face, then smiled at Luke and began to undo

the buttons of her jacket. Next door the cougher had begun to hack and spit. Luke looked around him in dismay, then placed his hands over hers. 'Not here,' he said. 'This place is poison.'

'Then where?'

'I don't know. We'll find somewhere.'

'You're not just saying this to put me off, because you've changed your mind?'

'No, I promise.' He put his arms around her shoulders and kissed her once again. Then he released her. 'Come along.'

They crept down the stairs, whispering furtively like two children escaping from home on a midnight adventure. They left a couple of coins on the kitchen table to cover the cost of the brandy, then hurried out to fetch the horses. The moon was high and had been full the previous night so there was no difficulty finding their way.

By the time the morning stars were fading into the light of a fine dawn, they were following a track that led beside some open, moorland country.

'Here,' said Luke, reining his horse to a halt. 'This will do.'

Sophie looked about her. There was not a house to be seen anywhere, not even a shack. Seeing her disbelief, Luke grinned. He dismounted and came over to hold her as she slid down from her horse.

'This way, Mistress Sutton,' he said.

He took the pack from his own horse and tethered both animals to a stump of blackthorn. Then he grasped Sophie by the hand and led her along a path through the heather to an outcrop of boulders. There, in the shelter of some rocks, he spread out his thick travelling cape and said, 'Will this do?'

Sophie sank down on the cloak. 'A bed of heather,' she said, 'like in the songs.'

'You're shivering.'

'It's cold. But I brought the brandy. Do you want some?'

They each had a drink, then pulled Sophie's cape over them. On the rock above them, a solitary bird began to sing.

A little later, as the sun rose over the moorland, they made love. Gently, fiercely, lovingly, tenderly.

And afterwards, as the sun blazed across the empty moorland and the larks rose up to sing in the air above them and Sophie slept contentedly in his arms, Luke wondered if perhaps God had at last forgiven him, and granted him a chance at happiness, or whether, unredeemed sinner that he was, he had just been dealt the greatest punishment of them all.

Chapter Twenty-Six

As he rode west from Plymouth, Sir Richard Treveryan was not entirely sorry that such a mass of problems were waiting for him at Rossmere. The Suttons' debts, Perdita's disobedience, Kip's future prospects – or lack of them – these several annoyances provided a welcome distraction from melancholy.

Autumn was always the hardest time; the season when, during his long exile, he had found himself missing Cornwall most acutely. He had missed the damp winds and the fading light, the bracken-brown hillsides and the oak woods softening from summer green to tawny. He had missed . . . But, no, it had never been the landscape of Cornwall that he missed. Only Margaret. Always Margaret. Margaret Hollar, wife of the Porthew cloth merchant, mother of Perdita, the child she had lost. His own Meg.

And now, as he rode across the open moorland on the last stage of his journey west, he missed her with a hollow ache that would be with him until the day he died. How many times, in those months they had spent together at Trecarne, had he followed this same road, his spirits rising with each step of the way and all because of the woman who was waiting for him at journey's end?

He had been aware of his sense of loss when he travelled this way in the spring with Perdita, but not so acutely as now. This time, a few days before Michaelmas, the past and his memories were gathering round him like a shroud.

Enough of melancholy. He set himself to concentrate on the tasks ahead. Alice: he must devise some means of disentangling her from her family's affairs. Not an easy prospect. She possessed courage and a stubborn refusal to admit the possibility of defeat, qualities that had equipped her to keep Rossmere during the difficult years of Parliamentary rule but which now threatened to undermine her entire family. Sir Francis was never going to learn how to steer a straight course while his mother continued to insist he spend money the family did not have. Richard had observed how Francis looked up to his uncle Stephen: left to himself he would surely have been happy to be advised by the older man. Together they stood some chance of sorting out the family's tangles. Stephen must be brought in; Alice eased out. And Richard thought he saw a way to do it.

It all depended on Kip. Richard had long since abandoned all thoughts of an alliance between Kip and Perdita as much too risky. If they married, it was just possible that Perdita, with her hard-headed intelligence and determination, might be the making of Kip, but it was far more likely that the boy would prove to be her undoing. He had all the instincts of a born gambler: he lived only for the present, had no ambition, was convivial and eternally optimistic, happiest when doing least. A wholly unsatisfactory son-in-law.

So there was no reason, apart from a lingering loyalty to the boy's father, to insist he return to Master Boulter and the life of a sailor, as Alice was no doubt expecting. However, Richard did not intend to set her mind at rest straight away. Much better to let her believe that Kip's return to the *Fearless* was the price she had to pay for his continued help over their debts. Alice had such a horror of losing her precious child to the dreaded sea-captain she would probably agree to almost any concession to keep him at home. Not that Richard intended to let Kip off completely: some useful employment must be found for him, preferably at some distance from Rossmere. Perhaps a local tradesman might be persuaded to take him on – but not until he had served his purpose as a bargaining tool.

One stroke of luck in this whole hopeless tangle was that Kip and Perdita had never shown much interest in each other. Apart from her resistance to Kip's doubtful charms, Richard found no reason to be pleased with his daughter. He considered her violent illness at the beginning of the month to have been remarkably timely and Sophie's misspelt letter informing him of her recovery a few days later had not mollified him in the least.

His anger had increased when she had ignored all his orders to follow him to Plymouth. Richard had never expected disobedience from Perdita. She had been so eager to please him on his return to England a year before that he had quickly come to take her compliance for granted.

Some subtle alteration had come over her since their first visit to Cornwall in the spring. Six months ago he had found her determination to ingratiate herself with everyone she met distasteful in the extreme, but it had at least meant that she was easy to control. The more he saw of what lay beneath all that insincerity and charm, the less he liked it. In his opinion she was scheming, ruthless, selfish and calculating . . . very like himself, in fact. People rarely like to see their own faults replicated in their children, and Richard was no exception.

Still, he wanted to see her settled. He had spent some time with his two sons in the past couple of weeks and, so far as such things can be certain, their futures were clearly mapped out. When they had finished their studies at university they were to spend a year or so at the Inns of Court. From there he planned to send them abroad, to work with one of his agents, since a working knowledge of French and Spanish was invaluable to a merchant, especially one based in the south-west. Slowly they were being groomed to take their places in his business; he saw how eventually it might be divided to provide a decent living for each.

But Perdita? Since marriage to Kip was out of the question he must find some other security for her. One or two ideas were forming in his mind, and he planned to look into them more thoroughly on this visit west.

It puzzled him, and grieved him too, that Perdita had so little of her mother's essence in her. Even her features, narrow and dark, resembled his. What would it have been like, he wondered, if she had been more like his own Meg? He remembered how she used to stand on the bank near the bend in the road above Trecarne, how he had looked out for her each time he returned, how . . .

He brought himself back to the present. He must learn to curb this old man's habit of drifting back into the past. There was work to be done. They had reached the point where the road divided: left to follow the valley track, which brought them to Rossmere, right for Trecarne and the sea. Slipping back into old habits he had been about to take the latter road. He was angry with himself for such foolishness and drove his horse faster for the last few miles – to which Viney, stiff and uncomfortable from the long ride and struggling to keep up, took great exception.

White doves, like a handful of snowflakes, drifted over the roofs and chimneys of Rossmere. The autumnal beauty of the place undermined his determination and he half wondered if he might put off dealing with any of the problems that awaited him until the following day.

He reined Apollo to a halt in front of the house. Six months ago Sophie had run from the front door to make him welcome and he realised, as he sat there waiting for the Suttons' notoriously slow servants to appear, that a good part of his pleasure at returning to Rossmere was the prospect of seeing her again. Perhaps tomorrow he might persuade her to take some time away from her work and ride with him on the moors: a pleasant antidote to the grim tasks ahead.

The front door opened slowly. There appeared to be some confused movement just inside the house, with several people jostling as if to avoid being the first to emerge. Richard frowned.

Francis came through the door, pushed by unseen hands. His face was a study in dread, but he made an effort to look pleased to see their visitor as he walked across the gravel. Richard was uneasy. Such reluctance suggested bad news: had Perdita perhaps met with an accident? No, there she was, coming through the front door, but hanging back. Alice . . .

'Sir Richard, good day. We've been expecting you. Come in . . . yes. Ah, how was your journey?'

'Muddy, uncomfortable, long. Is anything the matter, Francis?'

'Not at all. Where *has* Amos got to? We had to get rid of Sithney a couple of weeks ago and we haven't yet found a replacement. Come in, you must be thirsty. We were just about to eat.'

It was only when the whole family had assembled in the great hall for the main meal of the day that it dawned on Richard who was missing. Honor, usually the one absent from meals, hurried into the room just in time to take her seat next to her husband: they bent their heads towards each other for a few whispered words and a furtive glance at the new arrival. Perdita had greeted her father with a warmth obviously intended to deflect any possibility of anger but, still, he detected an uncharacteristic reticence in her manner. Alice was flustered and hostile by turns, but that was only to be expected, since the hour of reckoning for her finances and Kip's future was fast approaching. Stephen . . . no change there that Richard could see, but he was a man who had been schooled by his years as a soldier into giving nothing away. Kip had met him with a cautious good-humour: not a youth to bear a grudge, he was still wary of what might be in store. Louisa was graceless and gloomy as ever. Even Cary, who brought in a platter of meats was much as before, but what about . . . ?

He looked around the table slowly. There was no place waiting to be filled. No one returned his gaze, not even Perdita.

'Where is Sophie?' he asked.

Silence.

Then, 'Yes,' said Francis. 'Sophie. Ah.'

Perdita laid down her knife and waited.

Alice said, half-way between anger and tears, 'This never would have happened in my husband's time, never!'

'What has happened?'

'She is not here,' said Kip.

Falcon, thought Richard, with mounting dread. 'Has there been an accident?'

'We don't know,' said Stephen. 'We think not but—'

'But what?'

Kip was tossing a couple of dice from one hand to the other. Their dry rattling noise was too much. Louisa, her nerves at breaking point, shouted at him to stop but Stephen said calmly, 'Sophie left here six days ago, Richard. We have no idea where she has gone. We've heard nothing since.'

'Sophie gone? Why would she want to leave Rossmere?'

'We-ell, it's hard to say, precisely,' said Francis. He beamed in a vain attempt to minimise the impact of his sister's absence.

'Was anything troubling her?' asked Richard.

'Yes,' said Stephen.

'We don't really know, to be sure,' said Francis. 'That is to say—'

Exasperated, Perdita said, 'She had turned down an offer of marriage from Edmund Menheire. Everyone thought she should have accepted and—'

'Is he involved in this?'

'Not directly,' said Perdita. 'She did not like him. She did not want to marry him.'

'I don't know why everyone is looking at me,' Alice burst out inconsequentially, since no one had been paying her the least attention. 'I'm not to blame, not in the slightest. It's all the fault of those terrible debts.'

'What do the debts have to do with Sophie?'

'Alice had . . .' Stephen began, but then his frown deepened and he began again, 'Colonel Menheire lent the family a substantial sum of money earlier this year. It came through an intermediary, but he was behind it. That is what made the repair of the roof possible. It now emerges that he was under the impression that the loan was to be part of the marriage settlement between Sophie and his eldest son. We therefore had no choice but to put pressure on her to reconsider young Menheire's offer.'

'Not pressure,' protested Alice, 'hardly pressure. I'm the one who has had to bear the pressure of the worry and the deciding. We merely asked Sophie that she cease thinking of herself and consider her family for once.'

'It wasn't such a hardship anyway,' said Louisa. 'Mother was only telling her to accept marriage to the most eligible man in all Cornwall and now she's gone and left us with nothing. Everyone always says how wonderful she is – well, now look what she's done.' Louisa had never forgiven Richard for singling Sophie out for special attention in the spring and giving her nothing.

'Be quiet, Louisa,' said Richard, his quiet voice masking a growing fury. 'Am I to understand that it is the general opinion that Sophie has run away from Rossmere in order to avoid being forced into a marriage she had told you quite plainly she did not want?'

'We-ell . . .' said Francis.

'Exactly,' said Stephen.

Alice was sobbing quietly. 'After all I did for her, and now this!'

'Lord only knows where she is now,' said Kip.

Richard looked around the room slowly. Never had his hooded gaze seemed more predatory and hawklike. 'Not only have you driven the girl into running away from her home, a home she had worked for harder than anyone else, but not one of you –' and here his wrath was concentrated on Kip – 'has had the wit and energy to go and look for her.'

'We did,' said Kip. 'We spent a whole day looking and asking questions. We thought she must have gone out riding and had an accident. We went all over the place looking.'

'A whole day? Is that all your sister is worth to you? One single day of your life?'

'It's not as simple as that, Richard,' said Stephen.

'No,' agreed Francis anxiously. Honor leaned over and clung to his arm.

Alice said, 'There's nothing anyone can do for her now. She has only herself to blame.'

'But—'

'There's more,' said Stephen. 'We haven't told you everything. Several people saw her on that first day. She took the road north out of Helston. And she was not alone.'

'Good. I hope she had a servant to attend her.'

'Not a servant, no,' said Francis.

'Then who?'

'That draper fellow from Porthew,' said Kip, throwing an uneasy glance towards Perdita.

'What?'

'Master Hollar,' said Stephen. 'It's true, Richard.'

And then, in case his identity was still in doubt, Perdita added coolly, 'My half-brother. Luke.'

★   ★   ★

Perdita was astonished by her father's reaction. He stood up, flinging back his chair with an oath and vowed that this time Luke Hollar had gone too far. This time he'd see him killed.

Suddenly all the pent-up tensions of the past few days erupted. Everyone stood up and began shouting at once.

'You're right, Sir Richard! He ought to be horse-whipped,' said Kip. 'But don't worry, he'll pay for it soon enough. You're not the first to talk of killing him. Edmund Menheire has—'

'Oh, how can you talk of the Menheires?' shrieked Alice. 'All they want is to ruin us and turn us from our home, and that wretched girl might have stopped them, but no, she thinks only of herself—'

'It's all my fault,' lamented Francis. 'If I'd heard her leaving, well, I think maybe I did hear her, but I did not think . . . I mean, I did not stop her because . . .'

'Stop torturing yourself, Francis,' said Stephen. 'We're all to blame for driving her into a terrible mistake.'

'Mistake?' screamed Louisa. 'Is that what you call it? Your precious Sophie brings us all to ruin and you call it a *mistake*?'

'Silence!' Richard pounded his fist on the table, making the untouched platters leap in the air, but everyone fell quiet. 'You're all mighty swift to accuse Sophie, but the girl must have been desperate. Perhaps, Alice, if you had remembered the Menheires' wickedness a little earlier, you'd not have plunged your family into this catastrophe!'

'Oh! Oh! How dare you blame me! After all I've done! After all I've suffered for my family's sake!' Alice was so frantic with rage that Perdita thought she might fall down in a fit, but she recovered enough to launch an attack of her own. 'You've no right to sit in judgement on me, Richard Treveryan, no right at all. You'd do better to consider your own part in all this. Yes, yours! Sophie was no trouble at all until you came along and turned her head. She was everything a mother could wish for. Then you had to give her a Barbary stallion, never a thought for the rest of us and how we'd have the worry of it and the expense. A Barbary stallion when we've not even a decent plough horse for the farm or a saddle horse for me and Louisa, but you never thought of that, did you? You never thought how it might affect her. That was when she started to change, that

356

was when she began going out riding when she should have been at home with her work. Of course, now we know that was probably just an excuse to meet up with that hateful man Hollar, but she'd never have gone astray if it hadn't been for the horse. It's your fault, Richard. I told you at the time that horse would be nothing but trouble, but no one listened to me, no one ever listens to me, they just blame me for everything and now she has gone and we are to be ruined and – and—' She was weeping great shuddering sobs of vexation and despair.

'Dear Lord, this is getting us nowhere,' said Richard. 'Stephen, Francis, we must work out how to find the girl and bring her home again.'

'What's the point?' asked Louisa. 'Edmund Menheire will never marry her now.'

'You surely do not want to abandon her, just when she needs her family most?'

'Of course not,' said Stephen. 'Richard is right.'

Perdita kept silence. In the days since they had learned that Sophie had left in the company of Luke Hollar, she had been bombarded by conflicting emotions. In some ways she felt it as a personal betrayal; sometimes, when she thought of Luke and Sophie together, two people who in their different ways had affected her profoundly, she felt a tormenting jealousy; sometimes she felt hurt that Sophie had not trusted her enough to tell her what she was planning to do; more than almost anything, Perdita grieved for Sophie – for the torment that must have led to her decision and for the heartache that must surely lie ahead of her.

Perdita's opinion of Sophie had changed radically since that first glimpse of her when she had run to greet them on their arrival at Rossmere. She remembered how surprised she had been by her open, easy manner and her even greater surprise when Richard Treveryan responded to her with teasing gallantry. At that time Perdita still viewed people through the lens Kitty had taught her to use: she had seen only the darned clothes, the strong, workmanlike hands, the way Sophie had hitched up her skirts and run.

Slowly, she had modified her views. She had been shocked when Sophie sat astride Apollo and galloped across the moorland

357

track, but there had been another emotion mingled with the shock, a tentative yearning for some quality she could not yet name but which she had recognised in Sophie, some quality that was a part of her fine freedom, her energy and contentment, but that was more than any of these. When Richard gave Falcon to her, Perdita had not been envious, only glad for her. It was as though Sophie's generosity of spirit had somehow spilled over and affected her too.

And then, on that terrible last night in March, when her father had beaten Luke Hollar and she had learned that he was her brother, it was to Sophie Perdita had poured out her heart. Or, at least, to Sophie that she had begun to pour out her heart, since for someone as practiced in concealment as she was, honest conversation was a new language, to be learned slowly and painfully. But she had trusted Sophie, and had been flattered when Sophie confided her own fears about Edmund Menheire. She had thought Sophie was speaking openly and honestly and she had admired her for it – and now she knew Sophie was a consummate deceiver and, worse still, a fool.

Only a fool would choose to run away with a common fraudster like Luke Hollar. Perdita had not untangled her own complex feelings towards her newly discovered half-brother, so it was simpler by far to hate and despise him. More than ever, now that he had destroyed Sophie. Sophie, the fallen idol. Only a fool would be taken in by him. Perdita had been a fool when he cheated her out of her mother's earrings: she had thrown away a precious trinket and learned a hard lesson, but Sophie had thrown away her entire life. To Perdita, this was the unforgivable crime.

No one knew better than Perdita how long the after-shock of scandal was bound to endure. She herself, even if she devoted her entire life to blameless respectability, would suffer the stigma of her mother's misdemeanours until her dying day. However well she married, she would always remain a bastard born.

How she had envied Sophie her place at the heart of a family of ancient lineage admired by all the country, no matter how poor they were. Sophie might do the work of a serving-woman, but she was a gentleman's daughter conceived in honest wedlock and welcome in any society. Everything Perdita must scheme and struggle to achieve, Sophie had been granted by birth. And now she had thrown it all away. The woman to whom she had looked up more than anyone else in the world had chosen to destroy herself.

No wonder Perdita felt it as a personal betrayal, and all the more bitter for that.

Towards mid-afternoon there was a clatter of horse's hoofs on the gravel beyond the window. Perdita saw her father react as they all had a score of times during the past long days of waiting. He strode to the window, hope lighting his face: perhaps Sophie had returned.

But the scene outside held no comfort. Dark stormclouds were massing above the lime avenue and a few leaves skittered across the gravel. The new arrival was not visible, but it was a man's voice that called out to Amos and a single horse that was led round to the stable block. Not Sophie, then. Hiding his disappointment, Richard turned back to face the others. 'Enough of argument,' he said briskly. 'We must consider what to do. Francis, I believe the interest on your debts is to be paid the day after tomorrow and—'

He broke off, looking with some surprise at the young man who now strode into the room. Everybody else regarded the newcomer with a combination of relief and expectation.

'Do you have any news?' asked Kip.

'A little,' answered Piers. His hat and shoulders were beaded with rain. 'I got here just in time. There's a storm breaking. Good day, Sir Richard. When did you arrive?'

'A couple of hours ago. What news?'

'I have reliable information that Hollar was sighted yesterday visiting a scrivener in Penryn.'

'Penryn?' exclaimed Francis. 'Then we must go there at once.' He stood up decisively and everyone turned to him in surprise. Honor reached up and laid a hand on his arm. He looked around him, his nerve failing, then sat down slowly saying, 'Penryn, eh?'

'Was anyone with him?' asked Stephen.

'My informant thought not. But someone else reported seeing him in the company of a woman.'

'Sophie?'

'Maybe.'

Alice was sobbing again. 'Oh, my poor girl,' she wept.

'Francis is right,' said Kip. 'Now we know where he is we can go after the fellow.'

'All in good time,' said Richard. 'It will be dark in less than an hour. We'll get nowhere this evening.'

'But—'

'This must be carefully planned,' insisted Richard. He paused. Stephen said, 'What are you suggesting, Richard?'

Richard was looking at Piers, who was picking pieces off a chicken carcass and sharing them with Kip's dog Tom. Richard said, 'Master Menheire, we are grateful to you for bringing news of Hollar, but the rest of the discussion must remain private.'

'Piers is our friend!' protested Kip.

And Louisa added stoutly, 'We've no secrets from Piers.'

'Then you ought to have,' said Richard. 'Have you forgotten that this man's family are the cause of half your problems? You must be mad if you think I am going to discuss your finances in front of any of the Menheires.'

'I thought we were talking about Sophie,' said Kip.

'So we are,' said Richard, 'but as the money on the loans is due to be repaid the day after tomorrow, you'd best decide what you are going to do about that before you start galloping all over the county looking for Sophie.'

'But he's in Penryn,' said Francis. 'We need only go to Penryn.'

'Yesterday. That's all you know for sure. By tomorrow afternoon he could be a hundred miles from there. Or even back in Porthew.'

'Sir Richard's right,' said Piers. 'I've been finding out as much as I can about Hollar and I reckon he'll be a slippery fellow to catch up with until he's ready. He knows Cornwall better than anyone. He makes a habit of disappearing and then turning up again when least expected, has done for years. Several people I spoke to reckon he was a spy during the late wars.'

'For Parliament?' asked Richard.

'Possibly. But the general opinion is that he worked for the

King. With his background, no one would ever have suspected him, and he was hardly more than a boy.' Catching sight of Perdita's baffled expression, Piers explained, 'His father was well known locally as a fierce man for Parliament. Everyone always assumed Hollar shared his father's beliefs.'

'That man has no beliefs,' said Alice, in a fury. 'He's just a common tradesman and a cheat.'

'Quite,' said Piers. He glanced across at Richard. 'It's all right, Sir Richard. I understand you want to talk it over privately. I'll go and cadge some food off Cary. Maybe she'll even tell me one of her stories.'

'Nonsense, Piers,' said Alice. 'We can't have you eating with the servants. Richard, I simply don't know how we'd have managed without Piers's help this past few days, he's been here every day and been like a son to me and—'

'Indeed, Alice? Did it never occur to you that your newfound son might be doing a little spying of his own? He is a Menheire, after all.'

'That's not right, Father,' exclaimed Perdita. 'You can't accuse him of plotting with his family. He's been on Sophie's side right from the beginning, not his family's. He's not like the rest of them. He only thought she ought to marry his cousin because he thought it would be a good match for her and would help her family too. Then when he heard something that made him change his mind and think she'd be better off without them, he came straight over here to tell me so that I wouldn't try to persuade her any more, only by then Sophie had already left and it was too late.'

Richard said, 'I fail to follow your logic. All the same—'

'Don't worry,' said Piers. 'I'd feel the same in your shoes, Sir Richard. I'll be in the kitchen if anyone wants me.' And he threw Perdita a smile as he headed for the door.

'Thank the Lord,' said Richard. 'At least someone round here has some sense.'

'I'll come with you,' said Louisa, rising from her chair and moving towards the door.

'And me,' said Kip, following swiftly.

'No, Kip,' Richard told him firmly. 'This particularly concerns you. Stay here. There's still the small problem of your future employment to consider. Or were you perhaps hoping I had forgotten about that?'

Kip threw himself gloomily into a chair and pulled the dice from his pocket. This time, when he began rolling them across the surface of the table, no one had the heart to stop him.

'We'll talk later, Kip,' said Piers. 'I'm not going anywhere in a hurry, not in this rain.'

It was true. The rain was falling steadily now, drumming on the new roof and on the gravel; a blocked gutter had already begun to overflow beyond the window. Night was falling early.

'Fetch the candles, Louisa,' said Alice, 'and take some of these dishes to the kitchen.'

Louisa threw a furious look in Perdita's direction. 'Why am I always the one who has to do all the work? Since Sophie left I've had to work like a skivvy!'

'Just as Sophie always did,' murmured Stephen.

When Louisa had stumped out of the room behind Piers, Richard said, 'Before we concentrate on finding Sophie and that scoundrel Hollar, there are two other matters we need to consider. First, how does Kip intend to redeem himself after the fiasco with Captain Boulter? Second, what is to be done about the debts? Exactly how much is owed to Colonel Menheire, Francis?'

'Ah, well. Exactly, yes. That is hard to say.'

'But not impossible, I trust,' said Richard drily.

'No, certainly not.' Francis glanced at Honor, who smiled at him with encouragement. 'The problem is, you see, Sir Richard, that there are two varieties of debt to Colonel Menheire.'

'Speak plainly.'

'Well, my mother . . . I mean, we borrowed a sum from him at the beginning of the summer to carry out some essential repairs to the roof and—'

'Where was the harm in that, I'd like to know?' insisted Alice. 'It was leaking like a sieve and all the ceilings rotting away. Am I supposed to stand by and let my children's home crumble around my ears? Is that what you think I should have done?'

'It's all right, Alice,' soothed Stephen. 'No one is blaming you.'

'And the second type of debt?' asked Richard.

'That is rather more complicated,' said Francis. 'It appears that, unknown to us, the Colonel has been taking over the debts that were outstanding with other lenders. At a discount, of course, but still . . .'

'When did you learn of this?' asked Richard, but before Francis could answer, Richard held up his hand, signalling silence.

The door opened. 'It's only me,' said Louisa ungraciously. She moved around the room, lighting the candles. No one spoke. When she had finished, she went to the door, then turned and asked sulkily, 'What's the matter? Are you all afraid I'm going to report back to the Menheire spy?' And with that she slammed the door shut.

All the candles bent sideways in the draught.

Richard said, 'I presume the most urgent debt is now the first one to Colonel Menheire. The interest on the others, whether or not he now holds them, can still be covered by my payment, as we agreed in the spring.'

'That's right,' said Francis. 'The terms on those ones are unchanged.'

'So what is the amount of the new loan?'

Francis looked at his hands and said, 'Two hundred pounds. Half is due the day after tomorrow, the other half by next Lady Day. And if we default . . . well, in theory . . . I mean, there is a charge on the house . . .'

'Dear God, Alice!' exclaimed Richard. 'Whatever were you thinking of?'

'But what was I to do?' wailed Alice, and broke into loud sobbing.

Richard turned away in disgust. 'Well,' he said, 'at least it is some comfort to know the Menheires will be taking possession of a house that does not leak. Now what?' For the door had opened again. 'Louisa,' he exclaimed, 'I thought I had made it clear we were not to be disturbed!'

Then he broke off. It was not Louisa who came in though the open doorway but Sophie. She looked around at the faces turned towards her in the candlelight. They were all blank with astonishment. She removed her hat and cape, shook the moisture from her hair. Her face was glowing. She said calmly, 'I was on my way to Porthew, but I was afraid you might be worrying about me so I stopped off to let you know that I am safe. And very, very well.'

'Safe?' shrieked Alice, leaping to her feet and hurling herself on her daughter. 'Have you any idea how much I have worried about you? And to think of you with that man! And now you say you are safe, but we will be ruined and all because of you!'

Alice struck her daughter about the shoulders, but then collapsed against her in tears. Sophie put her arms around her and said, 'Oh, Mother, I'm so sorry, but you left me no choice.' Alice was still sobbing loudly as Sophie guided her back to her chair. 'Please don't cry, Mother. I know it was wrong, but you won't be ruined, I promise. Not on my account, at any rate.'

And with that, she took the leather pouch that hung from her waist and loosened the string at its neck. She asked Francis, 'How much must we pay to Colonel Menheire?'

'A hundred pounds in two days' time and the same again—'

'Here is a hundred and ten guineas,' said Sophie, tipping the bag so the coins cascaded across the table in front of her brother. 'I had to spend two guineas on a saddle horse to get home again.'

The last coin rolled to a halt next to one of Kip's dice, and then there was silence, but for the steady thrum of rain beyond the window.

Stephen stood up. 'You sold Falcon,' he said.

'Yes.' She glanced quickly towards Richard. 'I had to.'

Richard said nothing.

Francis's mouth had dropped open in wordless astonishment. 'And Luke Hollar helped you to do it?' asked Stephen.

'I could not have done it without him.' She sank down in the chair closest to her brother and took both his hands in hers. She said fervently, 'Francis, I am sure this must be a shock to you, but I want you to tell Master Hollar of your gratitude. If we have the money to repay the Menheires, it is all thanks to him.'

'Master Hollar?'

'He is just outside,' said Sophie. 'I will ask him to come in.'

Richard was very still, watching the door and waiting.

Perdita had been holding her breath. Hoping against hope that her fears for Sophie had been groundless after all, she said,

'We thought you had run away with him! And all the time he was just helping you to sell Falcon.'

'Not all the time,' said Sophie, smiling as she went back to the door. She drew Luke into the room beside her. He was still wearing his wide-brimmed hat and his travelling cloak and the water ran from both on to the flagged floor. His eyes were watchful, anticipating opposition.

Sophie's happiness could be restrained no longer. She looked around the room and her face broke into a huge smile as she said, 'I'm sure you've been imagining all sorts of scandals in the past few days, but now I can set your minds at rest. Luke and I were married by special licence at Penryn on Wednesday. Please make my husband welcome at Rossmere.'

Chapter Twenty-Seven

It was Kip who broke the silence. He reached across the table, swept up his dice and said, 'Good Lord, Sophie! What on earth have you done now?'

She did not answer. No one spoke. Francis cleared his throat, and began to smile broadly, but then he checked himself and looked anxiously at Richard and Stephen.

Richard was immobile, every muscle taut. There was a frown on Stephen's face, as though he were trying to solve some puzzle. Alice had been so stunned by Sophie's announcement and Luke's arrival in her winter parlour that she ceased weeping abruptly, dabbed her eyes and croaked, 'Why?'

Sophie moved a little closer to Luke. She said, 'I wish I could show you everything that is in my heart. Then you would understand.'

Stephen nodded, as if in agreement, but his frown remained.

Richard said, 'And you, Hollar, do you have anything to say for yourself or are you going to let the woman speak for you?'

Luke turned towards his questioner. He did not bother to hide the contempt in his long eyes. 'What is it you wish to know, Sir Richard?' he asked softly.

Sophie looked from one to the other, and for the first time she betrayed signs of nervousness. She said, 'We plan to reach Porthew tonight. We only stopped off here because I wanted to reassure you, but now we really ought to be on our way and—'

'Slow down, Sophie,' said Stephen. 'I'm sure Master Hollar understands our surprise and knows we need some time to adjust. Won't you have a bite to eat before you finish your journey?'

'Well . . .' Sophie hesitated, but when Luke gave an almost imperceptible nod, she said, 'Very well, then.'

Luke removed his hat and travelling cloak and placed them carefully over the back of a chair. He was wearing the same jacket and breeches of simple grey that he had worn when he waited for Sophie at St Buran's well. Like hers, his clothes were rumpled and journey-soiled.

Richard watched them both closely, then said. 'To answer your question, Master Hollar, I'd like to know what you expect to gain from this marriage. You know, I suppose, that Sophie's family can provide no portion for her?'

Luke smiled. 'One glance at my ledger would have told me that, Sir Richard, but I am grateful for your concern.'

'You think that you can marry your way into the gentry, is that it?'

'Stop this!' Sophie insisted, hot colour flushing her face. 'Oh, Sir Richard, why must you be so cynical?'

'It is all right, Sophie,' said Luke. 'Treveryan assumes that everyone else is as unscrupulous as he is. His own marriage was an entirely mercenary business, though the unfortunate lady whose wealth attracted him was taken in for a while – and suffers for it to this day, so I hear.'

Richard's voice was harsh. 'If I have a low opinion of your motives then the fault is entirely yours. You tricked my daughter out of a valuable pair of earrings and told her God knows what nonsense about ghosts and unquiet spirits and then you had the audacity to try your luck with her again. Thank God I was able to stop you the second time.'

Luke moved swiftly to place himself in front of Richard, as if squaring up for a fight.

'Luke . . .' Sophie placed her hand on his.

He touched her arm in a gesture of reassurance. 'Don't be anxious. I've not forgotten my promise. Besides, there is no one in this world whose low opinion I'd rather have than Treveryan's. I'm not answerable to you, sir. I'm not answerable to anyone except my wife here, and what exists between us is our own concern and no one else's. As for seeking to use my marriage to better myself in the world, that is a wholly contemptible idea and only worthy of a man like you, who ruined the lives of all those who were ever foolish enough to care for him.'

'Quiet, you rogue, or—'

'Or what? Will you get your servants to hold me down again so I am unable even to defend myself? But I do not see them here, not this time. You're safe, anyway, Sir Richard. I promised Sophie I'd not quarrel with you.'

'So what do you call this?'

'Oh, stop, both of you, for mercy's sake, stop!' said Sophie.

Luke turned away at once and returned to her side.

'Luke,' she said. 'Oh, Luke.'

He laid his hands on her shoulders and smiled. For a few moments it was as though they were alone in the room.

Perdita could not tear her eyes away. She wanted to be angry and appalled – it was much safer to be angry and appalled – but there was such a web of tenderness spun between the pair that she hoped passionately their fragile happiness might last for ever.

Stephen had been watching everything intently. Now he stood up and came round the table. He clapped Luke on the shoulder, and said, 'Maybe this has not been the best of welcomes, but I hope you and Sophie will prosper and be happy together.'

Luke hesitated, then, 'Thank you, Captain Sutton.'

Stephen turned to Sophie. His expression was still solemn. He said, 'I have gone over our last conversation many times this past few days, trying to work out if I might have said it differently but—'

'Uncle Stephen, please—'

'It grieved me to think I had helped drive you from your home. At the time I felt it had to be said, but all the same I am sorry for it.'

'What conversation?' asked Alice. 'What are you talking about, Stephen?'

Sophie flung her arms around her uncle's neck. 'Please do not be sorry. If you only knew how happy I am now!'

'Then I am glad.' He smiled as he embraced her.

'Are you losing your wits, Stephen?' asked Richard. 'The girl has let herself be seduced by a rogue and you say you're glad? What is the matter with you?'

Stephen laughed. 'Stop growling like an old bear, Richard. You and I both had our chances of happiness and we threw them away. Maybe these two have more sense than us. I certainly hope so.'

Now it was Francis who heaved himself to his feet and went over to his sister. He was relieved that the storm appeared to be passing, relieved that Sophie had returned safely, relieved that now he need not traipse all the way to Penryn on a fool's errand, relieved most of all at the sight of the heaped-up coins still scattered in all their glory across the table.

'Sophie,' he began ponderously, but he never finished because the door flew open and Louisa burst in.

'So! You're back! Amos came into the kitchen and told us. Oh, why am I always the last to know anything? Piers, Cary, it's true, Sophie is home!'

Cary roared into the room like a fierce red-faced heifer and caught Sophie round the waist with her strong arms. 'My dear life, girl, but you gave us a terrible fright. Fancy running off like that with never a world to anyone, not even me! What got into you?' She scolded and hugged her and patted her cheek.

'Cary,' said Sophie, when Cary paused for breath, 'I have married Master Hollar.'

More pandemonium. Louisa declared they would all be ruined now for sure while Cary berated Luke and told him that Sophie was the best of girls and to see he never forgot. Luke was startled at first, but then he smiled and said that if ever he was in danger of doubting his good fortune he'd come to Rossmere and Cary could remind him. He was then rewarded with a grudging pat on the cheek and Cary supposed he might not be such a villain after all.

Piers had congratulated Sophie, then, catching sight of Perdita sitting silently at the far end of the table, he came over and took his place beside her.

'Why so quiet?' he asked. 'Are you not pleased to see Sophie again?'

'How can I be?'

'She looks happy enough.'

'Yes, but . . . I do not understand. An hour ago everyone was so angry with her and calling Luke Hollar the greatest rogue in the world, and now look at them all. How can they be so fickle?'

Sophie had at last succeeded in prying herself away from Cary's furious demonstrations of affection and had gone to sit beside her mother. From her face, it was obvious that Sophie was trying to explain to Alice the reasons for her hasty marriage and asking her forgiveness. Alice was eyeing her balefully, too fond of her elder daughter to resist for long, but still resentful that the fine prospect of marriage to Edmund Menheire had been jettisoned. It was plain, however, that Sophie's persistence and her overriding happiness were going to win the day.

Piers leaned back in his chair and crossed his legs at the ankle. He said, 'It is a perfect demonstration of the strength of fact over theory.'

'What do you mean?'

'Maybe she should not have done what she did,' he said, 'but now that she has there is no going back. They just have to get on and make the best of things. And quite right too.'

As Piers was speaking, Alice had finally bowed to the inevitable: she and Sophie were embracing each other warmly. Only Richard remained unmoved.

'I do not agree,' said Perdita miserably. 'What she did was not only wrong but it was senseless and stupid as well. She may look happy now, but how long will that continue when she is condemned to live out her life in that poky little hovel in Porthew?'

'Isn't that the house where your own mother lived?'

'Yes, and look what happened to her. She was wretched in her small house so she took a wealthy lover and then was more miserable than ever when he abandoned her.'

'Is that right? I always heard that it was your mother who abandoned him.'

'How could that be?'

'I don't know. Maybe you should ask Sophie's husband.'

'Master Hollar?' Perdita glanced across at her half-brother. He had not looked at her once since he had come into the room; he had eyes only for Sophie. She felt horribly muddled, as if she was part of a tangle she did not begin to understand. She said angrily,

'I'd never stoop to ask him anything. He was wrong to lead Sophie on so.'

'Perhaps she was just following the instincts of her heart,' suggested Piers.

'Oh, I dare say,' said Perdita bitterly. 'And if everyone did that, where would it lead us?'

Suddenly Piers was serious, and looking at her intently. 'Where indeed?' he asked.

Perdita drew back. He must be teasing her. He had twisted her words and used them against her. She began to protest, but he interrupted her, saying, 'I think perhaps you are angry with Sophie on your own account, not hers.'

'I don't know what you mean,' said Perdita.

'Do you not?'

'I know I would never be so foolish as to throw myself away on someone who had nothing to recommend them except a handsome face and a pleasant way of talking.'

Piers fell silent, considering this. At the other end of the table, Alice was stacking the coins in neat little piles. At length he said, cheerfully enough, 'How refreshing to find such an old head on young shoulders. Your father will surely be proud of you.' Perdita glanced at him to see if he was still mocking her, but he went on smoothly, 'Now that Sophie is so definitely out of the race, the position of mistress of Trecarne is once again open to all comers.' An idea occurred to him and he said, 'Maybe Edmund's thoughts will turn to the younger sister. I don't suppose Louisa would turn him down if she gets the chance.'

'Then I hope you will help me make sure she never does get the chance.'

'Certainly. I am still bound by my promise. Besides, I know that you regard my dear cousin with the most sincere affection and, were he the most low-born man in the kingdom with only a hovel to call home, your feelings for him would be undimmed and—'

'Stop it, you have no right to make mock of me.'

'I'm sorry. Never mind, Mistress Treveryan, I shall help you all I can. Already I sing your praises daily to my cousin. It can only be a matter of time before we have won him over.'

Kip came over and said to Piers, 'That's that, then. What a day, eh? How about a game of merels, Piers? Or we can play a three-handed game, if Perdita wants to join us.'

The chaotic gathering was at last breaking up. Sophie had automatically begun to help Cary clear away the table, but Stephen stopped her and said Louisa would do that, she must prepare a room for herself and her husband. Perdita offered to help Louisa and Cary: at least the work distracted her from painful thoughts of Sophie and Luke. She was hurt that neither of them even seemed aware that she was in the room, but when Sophie came over to bid her good night, she did not know how to act with her and retreated quickly. Kip and Piers had vanished to the kitchen to warm up some ale and play cards on Cary's chopping table.

Alice had been counting the neat stacks of money. When she stood up to retire for the night she said, 'Thank the Lord, we are safe for another six months anyway.' But all the colour had leached from her face and she looked frail, like a much older woman.

Sophie was about to quit the winter parlour with Luke when she noticed Richard, still standing near the window and apart from all the rest.

She went over and stood before him. 'Sir Richard, I owe you an apology.'

He stared down at her, his face unflinching, but he did not speak.

'Falcon was your gift to me and I sold him without consulting you. I can understand how angry you must be, but believe me—'

'If selling the horse were all,' he cut in, 'you would have my blessing. I might even have helped you. Falcon was the price of your freedom, that I can understand easily. What I will never understand, or forgive, is the way you have thrown away that dearly bought freedom by marrying the greatest scoundrel in all of Cornwall.'

'Don't say that, Sir Richard. Not even if you think it. Time will prove us right. Only wait and you will see.'

'Your future is no longer of any interest to me,' he said coldly.

373

Luke's eyes had been following Sophie all this while. Now he came over to her side and drew her away. She did not see the look that passed between the two men.

When Sophie and Luke had left the room, Stephen asked, 'Why so harsh, Richard?'

Richard sighed and went to stand in front of the dying log fire. He and Stephen were alone in the room. Outside, the rain continued. At length he said, 'I expected more from her. It is obvious she married him in a fit of temper.'

Stephen was surprised. 'Why do you say that?'

'She was angry with her family for trying to force her into a marriage she had made it clear she did not want. So she has married someone of her own choosing. Her anger shows in that she has chosen the most unsuitable man in the whole of the county.'

'Hollar may have made mistakes, but so have we all. There's sure to be some good in him. Anyway, you're wrong if you think she married him just to be revenged on her family.'

'Why else would she marry such a rogue?'

'That was what I was trying to decide. I couldn't work it out at first.'

'But you think you have now?'

'Yes.'

'And?'

Stephen was smiling as he began to move towards the door. Then he paused. 'I remember how Sophie was when I came back from the wars. Trying to care for the little ones, trying to support Francis, trying to protect her mother. She is brave and courageous, but above all she is loyal. For years I was afraid that would be her undoing, that she'd never allow herself to leave Rossmere. And I have to admit that underneath I was probably glad, I did not want her to leave. This business with Edmund Menheire showed her that her family were more than happy to face the future without her, in fact they were driving her away. Luke Hollar has arrived on the scene at precisely the right moment. At last she has found someone who truly wants her.'

'Only because he is scheming and ambitious.'

'No, Richard, you are wrong. I was watching him this

evening. He's a complicated character, I grant you, but I am sure that he loves her completely. And he has won Sophie's love because he needs her more absolutely than her family has ever done.'

Chapter Twenty-Eight

September 29: Michaelmas. A cool, grey morning with scudding clouds and a fresh wind from the south-east.

Francis had been dreading this day for so long that he had to keep reminding himself of his present good fortune. For here he was, riding with Kip to Trecarne, not, as he had so often anticipated, to throw himself on the mercy of their old enemy and implore Colonel Menheire for an extension to their loan, but with a fat leather bag containing all the money necessary to discharge one half of the debt now due.

Good fortune indeed. Never a man to indulge in rash hopes, Francis was beginning none the less to permit himself a little cautious optimism. It did indeed appear that the bad luck which had dogged him since childhood was changing to good.

First, and perhaps most selfishly, there was the great comfort he now enjoyed with his wife. The years of abstinence and waiting made their present joy the sweeter. Sometimes he worried that their pleasure was too great, for it was generally agreed that a man and wife must restrain their passion in marriage, which was for the begetting of children, not to fan the flames of carnal lust.

But Honor pointed out that if their coupling had been spread over the entire period of their marriage, and not crammed into a couple of weeks, as had been the case, they might yet be reckoned abstinent. Francis was ready to be convinced. Besides, he hardly knew if he could stop himself, and as for Honor . . . He chuckled to think he had ever imagined she might be too delicate to withstand his embraces. His fragile bride, though still prone to mysterious aches and pains and wheezes, was growing sturdier by the day; her own appetites were at least equal to his. She did not even wish to halt their activity when her monthly bleeding began: her disregard for the generally accepted taboo fired his passion to new heats.

The only anxieties that had overshadowed his pleasure – Sophie's disappearance and the need to raise the money for the debts – were banished when she returned and spilled the bag of coins on the table.

He thought it strange that both brother and sister had discovered the secrets of the marriage bed within a few days of each other but, of course, this was not something he could ever discuss with Sophie, since he had never confided his problem to her before and did not see how he might mention it now.

But, ah, the money. One hundred and ten precious guineas, which he had counted and recounted many times in the past two days. One hundred and thirty pounds now rested safe in his leather bag; half the repayment on the Menheire debt and the remainder – some of which Sir Richard had given them as promised – to cover the loans on the debts which Menheire had bought off the money-lenders. Somehow another hundred pounds must be found by next Lady Day, the end of March, but . . . sufficient unto the day is the evil thereof.

Reflecting on his life as he rode through the cool morning with Kip chattering on about some greyhound he had put his money on the previous week, Francis realised that, as far back as he could remember, his days had been measured from Michaelmas to Lady Day and on to the next Michaelmas. Panic and dread.

God willing, all that was now over. Yesterday, while he had been still recovering from the shock of Sophie's marriage and the money, Sir Richard had spoken with him at some length. Francis was flattered by the way the older man talked to him as if he really were the master at Rossmere.

Sir Richard explained that he had spoken with Alice. She had agreed that, in return for Kip staying close to home, she would hand over complete control of the household and the finances to her son. Sir Richard intended to have his own lawyer draw up the necessary papers, but in fact Alice appeared more than willing to put down her burden now that Francis was ready to shoulder his responsibilities. Of course, Stephen was always in the background if Francis needed someone of talk matters over with but, as Sir Richard said, the only way Francis was going to learn about business was by doing it.

Francis's confidence soared. So much, indeed, that he brushed aside Stephen's offer to accompany him to Trecarne and witness the settling of the debt. 'Menheire's a wily old devil,' Stephen warned. 'He'll still make trouble for us if he can.'

'Don't worry about me,' said Francis heartily. 'I can hand over a bag of coins without help, and I know how busy you are with the harvest. I might even give you a hand when I get back.'

'Watch out for Menheire, all the same. He still wants to get his hands on Rossmere.'

'Not while I'm around to take charge of matters. I'm sure I can deal with a fellow the apothecary gave up for dead six months ago. Besides, Kip is with me in case he laces my ale with poison, or if the local thieves have got word of our new wealth and decide to attack us on the road.' Francis had laughed easily at both these far-fetched possibilities. Stephen smiled at his nephew's unusual high spirits, and wished him God speed.

There were no thieves on the road that morning, only a couple of tenant farmers who were moving from one holding to another a few miles distant. And then a wretched family, known by name to Francis and Kip, who had failed to find the money for their rent and had been evicted that morning from the few acres of land and the hovel that had been their home.

Francis was so struck by the contrast between his good fortune and their misery that he hallooed them to stop. Only then did he recall that all the money he had with him was for Colonel Menheire and he had none of his own to give them. Nor, it transpired, had Kip. Suddenly resolute, Francis loosened the fastenings on the leather bag, dipped in his hand and plucked out a single coin. It was of a greater value than he had intended, but he tossed it to them anyway.

'What will you tell the Colonel?' asked Kip, as they continued on their way.

'I can pretend I miscounted. There's no crime in that.'

Kip turned round in the saddle. The family of paupers remained in the same spot; they were staring with blank faces after the two young gentlemen.

'Let's hope you haven't encouraged them to begin a life of highway robbery,' Kip said cheerfully.

When they began to ride down the final approach and the full glory of the Menheires' home was displayed before them, Kip exclaimed, 'Poor Sophie must have taken leave of her senses! Fancy choosing to live above a draper's shop when she might have had all this.'

Francis had been thinking the same. But he said firmly, 'We'll do our business with the Colonel then leave at once. No reason to draw it out. We can be home again by noon.'

He was remembering that Honor sometimes retired to her chamber for a recuperative rest after the midday meal. Once or twice in the past few days he had followed her, telling the others that she found it soothing if he stroked her forehead, or read to her. He had not read to her in months, but he had stroked her forehead. And many other parts of her anatomy also, places that he burned, now, just to think about. He was in a lather to be home again.

Edmund Menheire came down the steps to greet them.

Here was a fresh embarrassment that Francis had not antici-pated. Was the spurned suitor going to hold him responsible for the insult of Sophie's elopement? But no. Edmund, thank heavens, was as friendly as such a man knew how to be.

Yes, he had heard of Sophie's unorthodox marriage and he was sure he wished her all happiness, though he feared that her prospects with such a man and tied to a humble village house were not promising. Edmund declared he could imagine the anguish Francis must have endured: for his part he was heartily glad he had no sisters to plague him . . . and no brothers either.

'Where is Piers?' asked Kip, bored already with all the fuss over Sophie.

'Gone to Camborne on business for my father. One of our old agents has been ill for several weeks and we heard yesterday he had taken a turn for the worse. The Colonel wanted to know if his widow – I mean, his wife, poor lady – needed any financial assistance in these hard times. My father wishes to assure her that their home is hers for the rest of her life, though strictly speaking it goes with the job of agent. My father is not one of those employers who consider only the financial aspect.'

'Very commendable of him,' said Francis, reflecting that this incident showed Colonel Menheire in an altogether more favourable light.

'Still, it's a shame Piers is not here.' Kip saw his morning going to waste.

Edmund said, 'When he was leaving, Piers left instructions that if you came over I was to have Charger saddled for you. Something to do with a bet between you, apparently.'

Kip grinned. 'I beat him at cards two nights ago. My prize was a chance to ride Charger.'

'There you are, then,' said Edmund. 'The men are preparing him now.'

'I'll go out to the stables as soon as Francis and I have settled our business with your father.'

'Why not go now?' asked Edmund. 'I'm sure Francis can manage without you.'

'Excellent,' Kip agreed eagerly.

'But, Kip,' Francis protested, 'I thought we had agreed . . .'

Kip grinned. 'My job was to protect you from villains on the ride over. No one is likely to rob you between here and the Colonel's chamber. Besides, if I ride now it will save time and we can still be home by noon.'

That clinched it for Francis. 'Don't be long,' was all he told his brother.

As Francis entered the cavern-dark library where the Colonel was waiting for him, he realised that the only other encounter between them had been the occasion when the old man had insulted Perdita and been convulsed with a fit of rage. In the spring Colonel Menheire had looked like a man not long for this world. Now he merely looked a little unwell.

He was seated in front of a large fire and Francis, invigorated by his brisk ride, found the atmosphere in the room oppressive and stuffy. The Colonel wore an embroidered cap and a velvet gown and his slippered feet rested on a footstool. As ever, his manservant Barnes stood a little behind his chair. Several papers were neatly placed on a table close by, together with a jug of wine and two glasses.

'Sir Francis, I was expecting you. Come in, sit down. Have a glass of wine. I hear that fool sister of yours has run off with a Porthew man – what's to be done with women, eh? How is your mother? We see young Richard from time to time. Can't call him Kip, a name for a dog, eh? What do you think? Well, sit down, sit down. Make yourself comfortable. Now, then.'

Francis was bewildered by the Colonel's rapid, darting speech; so many questions that were left behind just as Francis was pondering how best to answer them. Barnes poured him wine and handed it to him as he sat down on a low chair. After his morning ride, Francis was thirsty and would have preferred cool ale, but he felt awed by the Colonel and did not like to appear ungrateful.

He drank the wine. 'I have the money we owe you, Colonel. It is all here in this bag.'

'Is that it? Good. Excellent. Give it to Barnes. He can count it. Make sure it's all there. Delighted we were able to help out. And the new roof. How is the new roof?' Francis opened his mouth to answer, but the Colonel rattled on, 'Trouble with old houses, always this and that to do. Fortunate to have this place. Solidly built. Treveryan may be a scoundrel but he knew how to build. Excellent house, this. More wine.'

'Thank you, no.'

'Give him more wine, Barnes. The lad looks thirsty. Why are you taking so long with the money, Barnes?'

'I'm recounting it. A guinea short the first time but—'

'Short? Short? What's that?' Colonel Menheire twisted his neck round as if he might pin down the error with his sharp eyes.

'Ah,' said Francis, squirming and sweating and drinking the second glass of wine in a single panic-stricken gulp.

'What's that?'

Confronted by the old man's searching gaze, Francis forgot he had been intending to declare it had been an error. Barnes refilled his glass. He drank for courage and then, emboldened by what Edmund had said about Menheire's charitable inclinations, he explained about the pauper family they had passed on the way. To his relief and amazement, the Colonel was sympathetic.

'Quite right, quite right. I'd have done the same myself. I'd have given them more. Isn't that right, Barnes? Always play the Good Samaritan when you can. Stop fussing with the money, Barnes. A guinea or two short is no matter. What was the name of the family? I'll send them some myself. Did I tell you, Sir Francis, that I am going to build an alms-house in Porthew? In my name, of course. Don't hide your light under a bushel, eh? Old man now . . . sons are provided for. Time to think of others, eh? What do you think?'

'It is admirable, sir.'

'Quite right. Have some more wine. Now, these debts. Here are the papers. All drawn up correctly. Checked by my lawyer. Half to settle now. And the interest on the others. We both must sign. Barnes the witness. Cause for celebration, eh? Why don't you drink the wine? Don't you like it? Chose the best in your honour. Drink up. That's better. Now then.' He picked up one of the documents from the side table and held it close to his eyes, frowning to read it. Barnes dipped a pen in the ink horn and handed it to his master. Colonel Menheire raised it with a flourish and a conspiratorial glance at Francis, then set it down again and said, 'A hundred pounds. That's due now. You've brought that, I'm glad. Excellent. Admire your family, tenacious bunch. Another hundred in March. Will you be able to raise that too, do you think? Any more sisters with Barbary stallions to sell? Not so easy next time, eh? Eh?'

He chuckled, raised the pen once more, then laid it down for the second time and stared at Francis for so long that Francis, already hot from the fire and the wine and the airless room, began to feel that he was melting slowly.

'We'll find the money, sir,' he said.

'I won't deny,' the Colonel said, his tone dropping to a more intimate, conversational level, 'there's been bad feeling between your family and mine. War's a hard game, winnows out the chaff, eh? But I've come through it and so have you. Time to bury old feuds. Hoped my son and that sister of yours . . . but never mind that. Maybe there's another way. Maybe I can help you now.'

'Colonel Menheire, you've already been most kind. The loan for the roof was—'

'Business. That was business. Now I want to help. Tell you what, young man, I have an idea. See what you think of it. Maybe it won't work, but still . . . give it a thought, eh? I'm fitting out a ship for the North Africa trade. The *Plaindealing*. Take out tin, bring back gold. There are fortunes to be made there. Couple of others are coming in with me. Tucker and Wagstaff from Penzance. Solid men, both of them. Know a good business prospect when they see one. They know the *Plaindealing*'s a good ship. I have the documents near here somewhere. You can have a look if you like. Barnes, fetch them here, you know the ones.'

'But, Colonel—'

'I wouldn't offer this to anyone I didn't trust. But, as I said, I want to help. How d'you like the idea of investing, eh? I'm prepared to put the loan aside for another six months so you can come in with me and the others. A hundred pounds invested now will be worth twice that by Lady Day. All your problems at an end. Might even be treble the value. Just imagine that, Sir Francis. All the debts paid off and a hundred surplus to spend as you wish. Trade's the business, Sir Francis. How do you think Treveryan made his money, eh? No family ever solved their problems by sitting on their hands. Farming is finished. Trade is the thing . . .'

Francis was almost tempted. When Sophie had spilled the coins across the table he had wondered, briefly, how the money might have been used if it were not needed to repay the loan. And now Colonel Menheire was offering him the chance to double, maybe even to treble, his original stake. It was possible, he knew that. The mention of Sir Richard Treveryan's name had struck a chord too: only yesterday he had told Francis it was time for him to start acting decisively. To seize opportunities when they arose. But then he remembered the reputation of the old man facing him. And then again he remembered all that he had heard of Sir Richard in the past, and how wrong that had proved to be. Why, the fellow had turned out to be their guardian benefactor. Maybe it was true that even the most ruthless men mellow as the final reckoning of death approaches. And then again . . .

He recollected himself. He took out his kerchief and wiped it across his face and said firmly, 'I am grateful to you for your offer, sir, but the money has been entrusted to me for the repayment of the loan, and that is what I must do.'

'Well, then, as you wish. It's the safe road. Remember the parable of the talents? The fellow who buried his money in the ground to keep it safe? And why not? Perfectly sensible thing to do. Never get rich that way, but not everyone wants to be rich, do they, Sir Francis? Let's drink a toast to caution, and then we can sign to show the money has been paid. I'm sure you'll find a way to get the other hundred by March. How is that charming wife of yours? Her grandfather Chapman was on the way to making a fortune in trade but now it is all gone. None of his heirs had the muscle to take a chance when one was offered. But you've said your piece and I respect you for it. More wine? Not everyone has the courage to make money. Put the money in a good ship and then wait for her to return. The *Plaindealing*. Solid name for a solid ship. Waiting for your ship to come in. Sounds promising, eh? Why don't we drink to that?'

Francis gulped his wine. The Colonel's face, seen through the distorting ripple of the glass, glowed with a strange light. Like a beacon offering hope across dark waters. Francis's head began to swim.

All the way home Kip maintained a steady stream of chatter, praising Charger, his strength and courage. Francis barely uttered. He was absorbed in his own thoughts and, as his head cleared in the fresh air, those thoughts grew increasingly sombre.

Either he had just taken the first bold step that was going to lift the Suttons out of penury and start them back on the road to wealth, or else he had played into the hands of their old enemy and ensured their speedy ruin. He hoped against hope it was the former. The sinking dread in his bowels betrayed his terror of the latter.

'Well done, Francis,' said Stephen, when he was back at

Rossmere. 'Another six months and we'll have that old rogue off our backs for ever.'

'Ah,' said Francis. He had planned to confide in Stephen of the unexpected use to which he had put the money. If his uncle thought he had acted rashly, then it might still be possible to pull out of the agreement with the Colonel and repay the loan as intended. But now he found he was unable to confess to what he had done.

That afternoon, Honor returned to her chamber 'for a rest' with a meaningful glance towards Francis.

For once he was too downhearted and anxious to respond.

Colonel Menheire spent the afternoon in his library, issuing orders, sending messengers, setting the trap. For the first time in months he forgot the ailments that tormented him and recaptured the thrill and energy that had driven him in his youth.

This time, he would not fail. All his life he had been guided by two ambitions: to see his son and heir wealthy, powerful and respected, and to destroy the Suttons.

He had come close to achieving both when he sat on the County Committee and the Suttons were branded delinquents for their opposition to Protector Cromwell's rule. It had rankled ever since that the prize had eluded him. The Suttons still remained in complacent possession of Rossmere – and of the potential riches at Widow Firth's farm at Polcreath, which they were too lazy and incompetent even to recognise.

At first, when he realised that Edmund was interested in their elder daughter, he had been outraged, but he came quickly to see how this could be fitted into his plan.

His single-minded pursuit of the Suttons had made him loathed by the Cornish gentry. He did not mind this for himself, of course – he had no interest in social niceties and preferred a fight to any other interaction – but he knew that, for his heirs to be called gentlemen, some accommodation must be made. And if Edmund was married to one of the Suttons then the pusilla-nimous Cornish gentry would accept the husband – and his children – for the sake of the wife.

But Edmund had blundered. Once again the Colonel had to

do everything himself. Destroying the Suttons had become an obsession. It was not enough for him to rise through the social ranks, he must see others fall. He remembered Nicolas Sutton, the young man, handsome, charming and utterly contemptuous of the scrivener's son from Launceston.

Colonel Menheire's only regret was that the arrogant young man had died a hero at the battle of Lansdown and had not lived to see his wife and children destitute and turned from their home.

Sophie opened her eyes slowly. Already the window was a paler square in the darkness and shapes were emerging in the room: the low slope of the ceiling, the chest where their clothes were stored, the dark rectangle of the Turkey rug. On a rooftop nearby a gull tipped back his head and uttered the first raucous cry of his day. Footsteps in the street below: the clack of wooden-soled shoes on stone.

She shifted slightly, moving closer to the warmth of the body stretched out beside her. Luke was sleeping soundly. She rested her knee against his thigh, but was careful not to wake him for she relished this private, early-morning period of adjustment.

The tenth day of her new existence as a good wife of Porthew stretched ahead of her and she rehearsed the sequence in her mind. No Cary stumbling groggily round the kitchen when she went down. Here she must kindle the fire herself, set food on the table for their early meal, fetch water, tidy and sew. A girl came in to clean and wash.

Luke was troubled to see her doing the work of a tradesman's wife, but Sophie told him truthfully that her present life was one of idleness and luxury compared to the days at Rossmere. There she had been always trying to do the work of half a dozen servants; here she need only do the work of one. With such a small house, and just two people to feed, she had plenty of time to enjoy the novelty of town life.

Her neighbours were already losing their shyness of her; there was gossip at the well when she went for water, fresh baked bread to be bought from the baker, ale from the alehouse, butter and cheese and eggs from the weekly market, and always there was the drama of the sea and the fishermen and their boats when she went down the hill to the harbour.

And there was Luke. When they married she had loved him without knowing him. Each day she learned new details of his life and likes; each evening was rich in pleasures. They talked together while she sewed, or else she sang the old familiar songs while he accompanied her on the fiddle. They made love and explored each other's bodies and their dreams. Sophie had always thought of herself as a contented person, wanting nothing. Now it seemed that all her days until these few had been a shadow only; this was the substance.

If she was in any way dissatisfied, then she herself was the cause. On the second morning she went through to the shop at the front of the house and told Luke she wanted to help him. John Taylor, the assistant who looked after the business whenever Luke was away, was in the early stages of a wasting disease and she knew Luke was anxious about finding a replacement. Luke set her to work checking the newly arrived stock against the inventory, but it soon became evident that Sophie's penmanship was not up to the task. Her schooling had suffered from the twin misfortunes of her being the oldest girl in the family and the general tumult caused by the civil wars. Luke was embarrassed for her, but she determined to make good her deficiencies.

A very small blemish in the present perfection.

She propped herself on her elbow and contemplated Luke's peaceful face: the long lines of mouth and eyes, the jutting cheekbones and the tumble of dark hair. The first rays of sunshine were slanting through the window, touching each surface with light.

Luke was waking. He opened his eyes and gazed up at her. She smiled. 'Good morning, husband.'

He frowned slightly, and did not answer, only raised his hands to smooth her eyebrows with his fingertips. She kissed his knuckles, then bit them playfully, but still he did not respond.

'What is it, Luke?'

'You looked sad just now. Are you missing Rossmere?'

'No.'

'Are you happy?'

'You know I am. Aren't you?'

'Sometimes I think I might be, but then . . .'

'Then what?'

'Then I don't know. What happens when you grow tired of all this and want to be back in your own home?'

'This is my home now.'

Luke rolled on his back and gazed up at the ceiling; the low ceiling and the small window and the four walls crowding close to the bed. Beneath the introduced scents of lavender and woodruff and cedar there was the unmistakable odour of an old house, meanly built, of walls and timbers where mice and insects made their homes, a smell of damp and decay.

He said, 'I want you to have a better home than this. Pritchard has a patch of land further up the hill. I think he'll sell. It's sheltered and there is a stream runs along one side of it, but it's not boggy. We can build there in the spring. It won't be a house like Rossmere, of course, but it will be a decent home. Better than this.'

'I told you, Luke. I like this house. I'm happy here.'

He refused to believe her. 'You must not be anxious about the expense. I'm wealthier than people think. It has always suited me to live simply because I wished to pass unnoticed. But not any more. I want you to have the best of everything.'

He spoke so earnestly that Sophie smiled. 'Careful, Luke. We don't want people to think I married you for your money.'

Luke lay quite still, his expression hardening, then he threw back the covers and climbed out of bed. He said tightly, 'You find it amusing when I tell you I am wealthy.'

'Oh, Luke, don't be angry over nothing.'

'So now it's nothing, is it?'

He turned his back on her and pulled on his breeches.

Sophie eyed him with exasperation. 'Dear heavens, why must you make everything so complicated? I told you I was happy here and it's the truth and for the life of me I cannot imagine how that has turned into an argument so soon.'

Luke did not answer. He had tipped water from the jug into the basin and was splashing his face and neck. Sophie watched him for a short while, then clambered across the bed in her shift and stood behind him, wrapping her arms around his waist. He tried to pull her hands away, but she gripped him strongly and kissed the side of his neck, still damp from the washing.

'It's you I love,' she said, 'you I want. Nothing else is important. How long will it be before you believe me?'

He stood without moving, his head bowed, his wet hands still grasping hers. Then he said. 'Maybe I cannot believe you. Maybe it will take a long time. Maybe a whole life.'

She kissed the sharp edge of his shoulder-blade. 'A whole life. What greater luxury could there be?'

He twisted around, all his anger vanishing as quickly as it had come. He kissed her lips, her eyes, her cheek, the curve of her throat. 'Show me,' he told her urgently. 'Show me how much you love me.'

'With pleasure,' she said, and crossed her arms in front of her to remove her shift over her head, but he caught hold of the fabric at the neck, tore it to the hem and pushed her back against the bed, pinning her down by her upper arms as though he meant to force her. Instinctively she twisted her body in an effort to free herself. She was nearly as strong as he was, but she was kissing him even as she struggled.

And then she found that she was aroused more swiftly than ever before. He had been tender with her in the past, tender and slow, but this time a kind of rage in him seemed to be engulfing them both with a new fire and she lost herself to the fierce joy of it completely.

Afterwards, when they heard John Taylor opening up the shop and they began hurriedly to dress, she half expected remorse from him: he was so often anxious that he had offended or disappointed her. But on the contrary he smiled at her slyly, pleased to have awoken such passion in her and placed his hand on the gentle round of her stomach. 'Are we making a child together, do you think?' he asked. 'A fighting, strong child?'

That afternoon they went together to look at the piece of land he was hoping to buy. A grey wind was blowing in from the sea and it seemed to her a desolate, lonely spot at first. But as Luke described the house he wanted to build she caught his enthusiasm and pictured a square, solid house filled with laughter and children and the music of singing and his violin.

He turned to her and said, with one of those shafts of honesty that always took her by surprise, 'People think you have married badly, Sophie. I cannot bear to think of anyone pitying you because of me. It means a lot to me to prove them wrong.'

'Who would think such a thing?' she asked. But, even as she spoke, she knew the answer clearly.

'Treveryan,' he said, his face darkening.

Sophie shivered. Luke wrapped his arm across her shoulder. 'Are you cold?' he asked. 'We'll go home.'

'Forget about Treveryan, Luke. For my sake. It frightens me how much you both hate each other. I know he has done you wrong in the past, but put him out of your mind. Sometimes you look as if you want to kill him.'

Luke laughed at her fear and tucked her hand into the crook of his arm as they turned to walk down the hill towards their home. 'Set your mind at rest, sweet wife. I'll not waste another moment on the old rogue. And as for killing him – why, that's all nonsense. He can find his own way to hell but I'll never help him there.'

'Do you mean that, Luke?'

'You have my solemn promise. I'll not touch a hair of his evil head. Not ever. Now, do you think one window will be sufficient for the front chamber? Or will we need two?'

Chapter Twenty-Nine

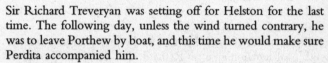

Sir Richard Treveryan was setting off for Helston for the last time. The following day, unless the wind turned contrary, he was to leave Porthew by boat, and this time he would make sure Perdita accompanied him.

His work in Cornwall was almost done; he thought he was unlikely ever to come this far west again. Francis was now handling his family's affairs: he was a grown man and must learn to sink or swim without Treveryan's help and, besides, Stephen was on hand to give wise counsel whenever necessary. Kip was going to work with a master saddler in Hayle. Richard did not expect this venture to last much longer than his days as a mariner, but the truth was, he no longer cared very much. Just one more visit to the lawyer in Helston on a matter of more interest to his heirs than to himself, then Richard was ready to quit Cornwall for good.

As he turned out of the Rossmere gates, Richard saw a young man riding down the hill towards him. His mind was still occupied with the business to be done in Helston and he was about to ride on with only a brief nod of greeting, when the other man stopped him. 'Sir Richard, just the person I wanted to see.'

'I am expected in Helston.'

'Then may I ride with you for a while?'

'The roads are open to all.'

Piers wheeled his horse around. They rode for a few minutes in silence, then Piers said abruptly, 'Sir Richard, I want you to give me a position on one of your ships.'

Startled by the suddenness of the request, Richard turned to look at him. Piers said, 'I have been meaning to ask you for some time, but since you are soon to leave—'

'Tomorrow, on the morning tide.'

'Exactly. Well, then, I wish to go to sea.'

'Can your uncle not arrange a place for you? He's a man of business. He must be familiar with most of the ships' captains in these parts.'

'My uncle would be content for me to spend my entire life chained to a desk in one of his gloomy offices. He's often talked about sending me abroad to work, but nothing ever comes of it. I'm tired of waiting.'

'I have no desire to encourage you to go against your uncle's wishes,' said Richard sternly.

Piers was undeterred. His face broke into a wide grin as he said, 'Stuff and nonsense, Sir Richard. You know you'd get great satisfaction from thwarting my uncle's plans.'

Had anyone else informed Richard he was talking nonsense he would have erupted in a fury, but not so with Piers. The young man was open and direct, not in the least awed by his companion, but there was no discourtesy in his statement.

Richard asked, 'How old are you?'

'Twenty-four.'

'Have you any experience of the sea?'

'None whatsoever, apart from a few local trips in small boats. In fact, I have no experience of anything very much.'

'So what makes you think one of my ship's captains should have the bother of you?'

'I cannot imagine. Still, I hope they will.'

Richard smiled. 'Why so eager? I'd have thought Kip's experiences would have put you off.'

'It is true that he was not especially enthusiastic. Yet, strangely, his account of shipboard life has only whetted my appetite. I am determined to go, Sir Richard.'

Richard reined his horse to a halt and examined his companion closely. Then he asked, 'What is your real motive in wanting to leave Cornwall so suddenly?'

Piers's gaze was unswerving. 'That must remain my own affair.'

'Your urgency indicates that you are running away.'

'If I am, then it is not for any shameful reason.'

'But you refuse to tell me why.'

'Are reasons important?' asked Piers.

'Maybe not. Leave me to think this over. I'll give you my answer before I sail in the morning. Meet me in Porthew tomorrow.'

'Thank you. Believe me, Sir Richard, you won't regret taking me on.'

'I haven't said I will yet.'

Piers grinned again and reined his horse round to go back along the way they had come. As he rode back towards Trecarne, Piers was well satisfied with his conversation with Sir Richard Treveryan.

Was he running away, he wondered. If so, it was because he could see no other way out of his present dilemmas. He knew, from the whispered conferences, and the activity of messengers and agents, that his uncle was engaged in some enterprise he intended to keep secret. His guess was that it concerned the Suttons and that, if he knew the details, he would be disgusted.

However, as things stood now, he was powerless to interfere, even if he had known what the Colonel was up to. And, for all their faults, the Menheires had taken him in at a time when he had nowhere else to go. For that, at least, he still owed them loyalty, however distasteful it was.

His instinctive reluctance to put himself any further in his uncle's debt had prompted him to ask Sir Richard for a place on one of his ships rather than approaching the Colonel for help.

Besides, if he was employed on a Plymouth-based ship he would be more likely to see Perdita again. This was an added attraction.

White doves rose up like spindrift on either side of his horse's hoofs as Piers trotted into the stableyard at Rossmere. Through a flurry of white wings, he saw Perdita coming out of the house. She was wearing a simple gown of brown worsted and a pair of battered leather riding boots, somewhat too large for her small feet. She crossed the yard to where Amos was holding the quietest of the Suttons' saddle horses by the bridle.

'You are going riding?' queried Piers superfluously.

She nodded. 'Will you come with me?'

'Delighted. I was coming over to say goodbye anyway.'

'We are leaving tomorrow.'

It occurred to Piers that Perdita was unusually distracted. He noted once again her shabby clothes: not quite the pauper's costume in which she had first made his acquaintance but, still, nothing like the elegant attire he had come to associate with her. He thought he had seen the skirt and boots on Louisa in the past and wondered why Perdita had borrowed them for this ride in particular. With Perdita, he knew, there was bound to be a purpose.

Stephen emerged from the stable, a pitchfork in his hand. He looked harassed. 'Piers,' he exclaimed, 'excellent. Now you can go with Perdita on this ride of hers. Amos has more important things to do than prance around the countryside acting the lady's maid.'

Perdita was dismayed. 'You cannot expect me to ride without an escort. It is not proper.'

'Proper be damned. This is Rossmere, not the Hoe at Plymouth. I'm sure I can persuade Piers to promise not to molest you. Isn't that right?'

'I shall make every effort to be honourable,' said Piers.

Stephen thrust the pitchfork into Amos's hand and told him to make a start on the cow byre.

'It is no laughing matter,' fretted Perdita, as they rode out of the stableyard side by side. 'We must hope no one sees us.'

'I shall try to make myself invisible. But tell me, what is the matter with Captain Sutton? I don't think I've seen him ill-humoured before.'

'The Lord only knows, and I am sure I do not care. The whole household is out of sorts these days. I cannot wait to be quit of this place tomorrow. Nothing has been right since Sophie went and married that man. Mistress Sutton hardly speaks to anyone, Uncle Stephen is gloomy as a tomb, Kip has to go and live in Hayle, and as for Francis, he is the worst of all. He sits by himself all evening and drinks himself into a stupor,

I cannot imagine why. He was never like this before. If this is how country folk prepare for the winter, then thank heavens for the city.'

'Is Sophie so badly missed?'

'I suppose it must be that, but Francis was perfectly cheerful when she first went away. In fact, I thought it was quite odd. He and his wife carried on like a couple of lovebirds and no one could make it out at all. And then when Sophie came back he was so pleased he was almost sprightly – Francis, of all people! But he's been in a foul mood ever since he went to see your uncle at Trecarne.'

'Has he?' Piers seized on Perdita's irritated remark. 'Do you know why?'

'I've no idea. All he did was hand over the money. We were expecting to celebrate in a fine style that evening, but you'd have thought it was a wake.'

'You're sure he paid back the loan?'

'Of course he did. He must have done. And Kip was with him anyway.'

Piers said nothing and for a little while they rode together in silence. He seemed to be deep in thought. Above them, the clouds were breaking up and a fitful sun shone through. At length he said cheerfully, 'You've not mentioned Honor or Louisa.'

'Oh, them. Honor just fusses over Francis as if he were made of glass, and as for Louisa, she is always so bad-tempered, I do not see how she could possibly get any worse.'

'It does not sound as if there is anyone in Cornwall you will miss.'

Perdita thought of Sophie, whom she missed already: she had not seen her at all since her return from Wadebridge with Luke. Although she tried to persuade herself that Sophie had been a fool and was no longer her friend, she cared about her too much to believe that for long. And as for her brother Luke . . . The muddle that she always felt at the thought of him was still painful. She told herself that it was illogical but, all the same, she could not prevent herself from feeling left out when she thought of the two of them, so contented together in their little house in Porthew.

But gradually, as they rode together in companionable silence, she realised there was one person she would be sorry to leave behind in Cornwall.

'I will miss you, though,' she said. And then, in case he might have misunderstood her remark, she added, 'I mean, it's good to have a friend, to know there'll never be anything else . . .' She stopped. She did not seem to be expressing herself very well.

Piers digested this as he watched a flock of starlings wheeling high above their heads. He slid her a sideways glance and said, 'I told your father I wanted a place on one of his ships. He promised he'd consider it.'

'That's wonderful!' exclaimed Perdita. 'You will be able to come and see us in Plymouth when your ship is in port, just like Kip did. I hope he agrees.'

'What about your own plans? Have your feelings about Trecarne altered at all?'

'I never give up on a thing once I've set my mind to it, but I think I'd have as good a chance of seeing your cousin in Plymouth as here. He never comes to Rossmere, and I never go anywhere else.'

'It does not sound very promising.'

'You must persuade him to come to Plymouth on business. I know, you can leave something for him at our house and then he will be obliged to come and collect it himself. That might be a start.'

'I'll see what I can manage,' said Piers.

Perdita was no longer paying him any attention. They were on the Downs, near to the place where Sophie had ridden Apollo. She said thoughtfully, 'This will do.'

'Do?'

'Can I borrow your saddle for a little while? Or, better still, your horse.'

'Why?'

'Never you mind. Oh, well, I suppose there's no harm if you know. I had meant to keep it a secret but you don't really count. I know I can trust you not to tell anyone. I want to try riding the way Sophie did, but you must promise not to watch . . .'

Once he had understood the nature of her request, Piers promised readily. He dismounted and led Perdita's horse away, leaving her the use of his, but it quickly became apparent that Perdita, who had only ever ridden pillion or side-saddle, was finding it difficult to mount without help. Piers's horse, an independent-minded gelding, took advantage of her inexperience to wander in search of a few choice mouthfuls of green stuff that were still to be found among the heather and gorse of the moors.

Perdita swore robustly. Then, 'Damnation take the wretched animal,' she exclaimed, hopping awkwardly in his wake, one of her too-large boots still firmly stuck in the stirrup.

Piers, who had been standing with his hands ostentatiously placed over his eyes, asked mildly, 'Do you need help?'

'No, don't look. Oh, the devil's in this horse, yes, of course I do! Sophie had help, though I suppose Kip is her brother and that makes a difference, but . . . why won't the fiend keep *still*?'

Laughing, Piers came over, tugged the gelding's head up and told him to stand. Looping the reins over his arm he removed Perdita's boot from the stirrup and told her she was fortunate not to have sprained her ankle. Then he knelt down and told her to put her foot in his cupped hands . . . But by now she was shaken by her previous failures and her first attempt was disastrous. Somehow she managed to get both knees on the saddle and, alarmed at the prospect of pitching head first over the other side, she slithered back down the way she had come. Piers was quick to break her fall.

'Are you all right?' he asked, steadying her.

She gasped, 'I think so.' She had a sudden sense of his closeness and of his eyes, very blue and piercing and so close to her own that she could have counted the dark lashes that fringed them. He was looking at her as if he had just seen something in her face that he had overlooked until now. She said breathlessly, 'Let's try again. I'll be more careful this time.'

'Very well.'

He seemed to be in no hurry to remove his arm from around her waist and Perdita suddenly remembered Stephen's joking instructions that he must promise not to molest her. The ridiculous thought swam into her mind that it might, after all, be a pleasure to be molested by Piers Menheire. His eyes were no longer smiling, but serious and still fixed on her face.

She found herself examining his mouth in minute detail. It was not far from hers.

Remembering the purpose of this expedition and the perils of following her erratic emotions, she said briskly, 'Will you do the stirrup business again, then?'

This time she ended up with one leg on each side of the horse.

'Lordy, however did Sophie make it look so simple? What am I supposed to do with all these skirts?' She was talking too much, she knew, but did not seem able to stop herself. 'There! How is that? It feels very odd. I suppose I must bunch them up and sit on them. Thank heavens there is no one here to see me.'

'Just as well Amos did not come with you, then.'

'I was planning to make him wait down by the crossroads but, still, I am glad it was you.' She looked away quickly, afraid Piers might misinterpret her words.

But he merely laughed as he said, 'I shall cover my eyes with my hands, like this. But just to make sure you come to no harm I shall separate my fingers and watch from time to time, so . . .'

Perdita was still smiling as she rode away down the grassy track that led across the moorland. She remembered the way Piers had looked at her when she had slipped from the saddle and once again she experienced that strange sensation, a tightening of the upper chest and an inner warmth that was quite new to her.

She thought it was lucky that Piers Menheire had become so much like a brother to her, not at all like the other young men she had come across, that there was no possibility of any awkwardness between them. After all, he had pledged his help in her plan to become mistress of Trecarne, so he must have only brotherly feelings towards her, which again was entirely fortunate.

The track curved slightly. She glanced behind her. Piers was watching her progress. She could not make out his expression, but she raised her hand to show that so far her experiment was going well and he waved back as though encouraging her to try a faster pace.

So she gathered up the reins and kicked the gelding to a canter. A startled woodcock lofted out of the path in front of her and winged away over the heather. The air felt fresh and clean against her cheeks and she felt a glow of health and excitement.

Then the track opened up ahead of her, she urged the gelding on and he broke into a gallop and at last she began to understand what Sophie had enjoyed that March day on the moors: a glimpse of freedom and adventure.

Kitty would be horrified, if ever she knew. In Kitty's world there was no room for the exhilaration that came from flirting with danger. She knew that it was in Kitty's narrow world that she must ultimately succeed, but just once, just for now, it was thrilling beyond words to sit astride the horse and hear his laboured breath and his hoofs pounding the turf as she flew along the mossy moorland track and around in a huge arc to the place where Piers was waiting.

Luke was returning from a visit to a family of weavers who were late in a delivery of cloth. They insisted he stay and drink with them to celebrate his recent marriage. It was pure bad luck that he left them later than he meant and so rejoined the Helston road just as Sir Richard Treveryan was returning that way to Rossmere.

Instinctively, both men reined their horses to a halt and paused, each regarding his foe. The air was gloomy in the autumnal dusk and a handful of leaves swirled across the road between them, then settled and were still.

Luke noted that Treveryan was for once alone, with no manservant to attend him. He remembered, with a quickening of excitement, that other evening in the spring and the gross indignity of being held down and beaten like a criminal. A longing to even the score surged through him.

He smothered it at once. He had promised Sophie, not once but several times. The old feuds were over. He'd not even give Treveryan the satisfaction of a quarrel. The fellow was not worth it. This chance encounter on a lonely road provided a heaven-sent chance to prove how greatly he was altered since his marriage, all his bachelor impulsiveness behind him. He smiled with secret pleasure at the image of Sophie's delight when she heard that he had passed Treveryan on the highway and that nothing more warlike than a salutation had been exchanged between them.

He urged his horse forward and touched his hat briefly as he drew level with Treveryan. Hatred flew between them like sparks from a blacksmith's anvil, but all Luke said was, 'Good evening to you, Sir Richard.'

Richard nudged his horse back, blocking Luke's path.

'Not so hasty, boy,' said Richard. 'And take that insolent smile off your face when you talk to me.'

'A man's face is his own business on a public road, Treveryan.' And then, when Richard continued to block his path he said, 'Out of my way, I've better things to do than parry words with you. My wife is expecting me.'

'You're a sly piece of work, aren't you, Hollar? God, how it sickens me to hear you call that woman wife. Couldn't go courting her like an honest man, but you had to take her away from her family to seduce her, and then subject her to the shame of a secret marriage.'

'Why so angry, old man?' Luke could not resist the temptation to taunt him. 'Did you want her for yourself? All those expensive presents, but still she turned you down. Now you're in a fine sweat because she chose a young man who wanted to marry her, not an old rake like you who would have made her his mistress for a while and then left her.'

'You're a foul-mouthed brat, aren't you? She'll discover her mistake soon enough, if she hasn't already. How will you endure that, eh? You think you've done well for yourself, but all you've done is ruin the life of an innocent girl.'

'Something you know all about!' blazed Luke, and then, fearing he'd soon forget his promise to Sophie, he said, 'Get out of my way and let me pass. I do not seek to quarrel with you.'

'Are you running away? Is cowardice to be added to your faults? Do you want it known that you turned tail and ran like a beaten dog?'

'Never! Damn yóu, Treveryan, but I will not fight with you!'

'No?' Richard raised his whip and would have brought it down on Luke's head or shoulders, but Luke raised his arm to protect himself and caught hold of the older man by the wrist. Richard roared out in fury and the horses, alarmed by the sudden commotion, leaped sideways, unseating both their riders. Still locked together the two men crashed awkwardly to the ground. Luke felt a stinging pain shoot up his leg, but it was nothing compared to the rage that billowed through him at the sight of his old tormentor, sprawled in the mud of the highway.

'Fight me, then! Go on, fight me!' yelled Luke, lifting Richard from the ground by his coat, but he appeared stunned by the fall and flapped his arms uselessly.

Luke dropped him back on the ground and knelt beside him, exulting in his fall. 'Go on, Treveryan, now's your chance. Fight me – here I am! Show me how you can fight!'

And then Richard did. Summoning all his strength he half rose from the mud and caught Luke a ringing blow with his gloved fist to the side of his head. Luke cried out, fell sideways. Another blow followed, more punishing than the first.

Luke scrambled to his feet, blind madness gusting through him. He brought his boot down against Richard's head, knocking him to the ground. He kicked him twice in the ribs, then fell on him and beat him around the face and head until the hated features were almost unrecognisable, a mass of broken skin and bruises and hot flesh swelling.

Luke sat back on his heels and surveyed the horror of his handiwork in the thickening dusk and laughed out loud. Laughter that rose from deep inside him and bubbled out like crazy sobs.

In front of him in the road, Richard groaned once or twice, moved slightly, and then lay still, a small stream of blood from cuts around his eyes and nose the only movement.

Staggering, hardly aware of what he was doing, Luke went to his horse and mounted. The pain in his leg was so intense he almost fell.

Then he wheeled his horse around and rode as fast as he could into the night. Appalled, furious, weeping, he took the road that led away from Porthew. Away from his home, and from Sophie, who even now was lighting the candles and awaiting his return.

Chapter Thirty

It was a room he recognised, a room he had inhabited long years before and visited many times since in his dreams. The tower bedchamber at Trecarne. On one side was the high window that looked out on to the trees behind the house, and facing it the view reaching down the valley to the sea. The two songs were mingling now, the west wind drifting through the oak woods and waves breaking on the distant shore: soothing sounds, lulling him back into sleep – tormenting sounds, reminders of vanished pleasures. Richard felt weak tears sliding down his cheeks and yet, despite the aching in every limb, he was filled with great happiness.

Somewhere out of his line of vision there was the click of glass vessels being tidied on a tray. Then a woman's light footsteps.

Margaret? In the muddled state from which he was surfacing, which must have been a kind of sleep, he had seen Margaret often. She remained as beautiful as ever he remembered, but her face was sad. *Why are you tormenting my boy?* she asked him. *Why injure my Luke?*

He tried to explain himself, to reach out and hold her there with words, but no words came.

But now the thought came to him with sudden eagerness: if she really was there in the room with him, he could at least tell her it was over. The fighting between him and the boy was done. There was no hatred left any more. The anger was all spent. He must tell her at once.

'Margaret?' His voice was a ragged croak.

'It's only me, Father.'

'Perdita.' Her narrow, dark face appeared at his bedside,

anxiety and relief mingled in her eyes. His mind slid forward nearly twenty years to accommodate the empty present.

'Heaven be praised, you are better,' she said. 'I shall fetch the physician at once.'

'Wait. I thought I was dreaming. What am I doing here? Why am I at Trecarne?'

'Hush, don't fret. You've been feverish. Piers Menheire found you by the roadside. You'd been left for dead. He fetched some of his uncle's men and they brought you here. You kept insisting on this room, so Piers ordered a bed made for you. I came over as soon as I heard. The Colonel has been very kind.'

'The Colonel?'

'Colonel Menheire. This is his house.'

'Of course. I had forgotten.'

He lay quite still, his eyes flickering over the contours of the room, so familiar and yet so different from the place of memory. 'This was your mother's room,' he breathed at length.

'I thought so,' said Perdita, with a shy smile.

He lapsed into silence once again, his eyes closed. Thinking that he slept, Perdita laid her hand lightly over his. His fingers gripped hers tightly, then his eyes opened and he was smiling, as if at some secret understanding.

'What happened?' he asked.

'You must have been attacked by footpads, though there was no money taken. No one can make it out. But now that you are recovered Colonel Menheire will send for Justice Brown and you can tell him. Your attackers cannot have got far. They were probably local men. Did you recognise them?'

'Who?'

'The footpads who beat you.'

'Not footpads, no. Not footpads.'

'What was that, Father?'

Treveryan smiled and closed his eyes once again. To think that in the spring he had chastised the boy for fabricating ghosts and unquiet spirits, and here he was, taking orders from them.

'Footpads, yes,' he said. 'Two of them. But it was dark. I could not see their faces. But I know they were not local men.'

★   ★   ★

Perdita had been horrified by the news of her father's accident. Despite her anxiety about encountering Colonel Menheire again, she hurried over to Trecarne the instant she heard what had happened, determined to nurse Richard back to health.

Once installed in the magnificent house, however, it would have been unforgivable to ignore such a precious opportunity to engage with Edmund. Luckily for her, the Colonel was confined to his room with a low fever; luckily for her father, the physician who had been summoned to treat the Colonel was already on hand to dress his wounds and give him the elixir that helped him to rest easy. All in all, Perdita was beginning to see the hand of Providence at every turn, and she fully intended to assist it with a small nudge of her own whenever possible.

She did not therefore confine herself to her father's sickroom, or to the chamber beneath it which had been assigned to her. When Richard was awake, she read to him and tended him as carefully as she knew how. When he was asleep, she left Viney to watch over him. The elderly manservant was feeling his advancing years in every aching joint and found sickroom duty far more congenial than his master's usual turbulent pace of activity.

With the two old warriors confined to chambers at opposite ends of the house, Perdita was free at last to roam the rooms her mother had once inhabited. Despite its grandeur, Trecarne was a house that revealed its full beauty slowly, and with each day that passed Perdita's love of the place deepened.

After a difficult night at her father's bedside, she had only to go to the main hall, where the servants were busy sweeping and polishing, and she was soothed by the elegance of the proportions, the smooth curve of the stair rail and the beautiful dome overhead. She discovered a small room beside the library, with a deep window-seat where she could settle in solitude for half an hour and watch the changing colours of the sea and sky, all the deepening blues and purples of autumn.

The best times were when Piers persuaded her to walk with him down to the shore. The afternoon when she had ridden his gelding across the moors seemed to have sealed the friendship between them. When she was with him she never had to watch what she said, or worry about the kind of impression she was making on him. She sensed that he liked her, as she did him, as a friend, and this was a new and altogether pleasurable feeling. He talked to her freely about his concerns that the Menheires were intent on ruining the Suttons and his frustration at being powerless to intervene. She realised that part of the attraction he felt at the prospect of going to sea was that he'd be removed from a household he was finding increasingly abhorrent. Perdita thought he was probably exaggerating the Menheires' vindictiveness, perhaps because of the treatment his parents had received from them years ago. Certainly, on the few occasions she had spoken to Edmund he had seemed concerned to hear about the Suttons. Besides, she could not imagine why anyone would want to leave a home as beautiful as Trecarne. The longer she spent in the house, the more appealing she found the idea of one day living there as its mistress. She made sure, therefore, that her ramblings occasionally took her to those places frequented by Edmund Menheire.

Thus it was that on an October afternoon of slanting sunshine, she was to be found in the long gallery, near to the mantelshelf carved with the Latin words that also appeared on her mother's tombstone. She had been pacing back and forth, pausing every now and then to gaze through one of the high windows at the gardeners who were tidying the box-edged flowerbeds at the front of the house in readiness for winter, when she heard a man's footsteps approaching the door at the far end of the gallery. Quickly she resumed her seat and took up a piece of embroidery she had brought with her from Rossmere. She detested sewing, embroidery in particular, and had been working on the present piece since the previous winter, but men were invariably impressed by the sight of a young woman employed in some useful activity – though the exact purpose of an overdecorated pipe-holder eluded her.

However, she knew she made an attractive picture seated beside the fire in her dress of deep blue, warm sunlight glinting on her dark hair as she bent her head earnestly over her work. The footsteps paused when the intruder caught sight of her, then rang out boldly as he crossed the polished wooden floor to join her.

'Mistress Treveryan,' said Edmund, 'I trust I am not disturbing you.'

'By no means.' She glanced up and flashed him a radiant smile. 'Your company is always a welcome distraction when I am working.'

He drew up a chair, sat down facing her, then said, 'How is your father today?'

'Much better, thank you. He was sufficiently recovered to be angry with Viney this morning, a sure sign of improvement. What is the news of the Colonel?'

'Not good, I fear.' Edmund adjusted his features into a proper expression of dismay. 'His fever is increasing. Dr Bartlett has said that in view of his general low level of health, we must prepare ourselves for the worst. Yet he has recovered from these bouts of fever many times in the past, and we can only pray that he does so again.'

Perdita was amused. It was obvious Edmund was bursting with impatience to see his father safely buried so that he might take control of the house and business, and quite sensible too. No one in their right mind would regret the death of Colonel Menheire. She thought no worse of Edmund for his ambition, or for his hypocrisy. She intended never to think anything but good of a man who was soon to be sole possessor of this house and the fortune that went with it.

She said solemnly, 'My prayers are joined with yours.'

'Thank you for your concern.'

They sat for a while in silence. Perdita was conscious of Edmund's gaze fixed on her as she worked. She was stitching a large and, in her opinion, especially repulsive blue flower that might well have been a rose but for the colour. Each petal seemed to take an age and she had only done two. After a time she said quietly, 'You seem preoccupied. Is something else troubling you?'

He sighed. 'My father's illness has come at a most awkward time. There are many decisions to be made in our work. I cannot consult him as he is too ill, yet I know he would think I was going behind his back if I went ahead anyway.'

'A dilemma indeed. What in particular needs deciding now?'

'I must not bore you with my business concerns.'

'Oh, you could never be dull, Master Menheire.'

There was a small silence. Perdita could sense him puffing up like a bullfrog with pleasure at the compliment. She worked on diligently.

At length he said, 'We have the chance to buy a holding near Helston where deposits of tin have been found. We cannot tell how much, and the price is high, but we need to make a move before Godolphin gets it. He has far and away the lion's share of the tin trade already.'

'Tin,' said Perdita, without thinking, 'how fascinating that sounds.'

'That's where the money in Cornwall is to be made these days. The price is rising all the time. There's not much to be found in this part of the county, more's the pity, but—' He broke off abruptly, then ended up, 'Well, there's fortunes to be made in tin if one knows how to seize the chance.'

Perdita heard the passion in his voice, the determination to rise above all rivals. She laid down her work and raised her eyes to look at him. She had never seen him so animated: he looked almost handsome. She bit her lower lip in a gesture indicating breathless excitement and which, she had learned from previous experience, showed her to especial advantage. 'Oh, Master Menheire, what a lot you must know about it. Please, do tell me all about tin.'

He hesitated only seconds before proceeding to do exactly that, omitting no detail. Perdita had long since mastered the art of the intelligent-sounding question and Edmund remained talking to her for much longer than he had intended – a whole bright blue rose petal of time, in fact.

Later, after he had visited his father's sickroom and received the galling news that the Colonel was much improved and all danger of his imminent demise had passed, Edmund consoled himself by reflecting on the enchanting female who was lodged beneath their roof.

Perdita Treveryan was not beautiful like Sophie Sutton, but she had a quick sympathy and a liveliness that were most beguiling. Besides, his experiences with Sophie had put him off well-born young ladies for the time being. He had come to the conclusion that he'd had a merciful escape where she was concerned and he looked forward to seeing her grow thoroughly miserable in her rash marriage. Perdita Treveryan was altogether more his sort of woman.

It was therefore a great shame, in his opinion, that the idea of marriage to her was quite impossible. An alliance with a bastard, however alluring, was not for him. Edmund Menheire knew his family's origins were not equal to his ambitions. If he was to consolidate their position among the gentry, a careful marriage was going to be essential. Breeding was far more important than wealth in his future bride, as his father had known when favouring the match with Sophie. Perdita had to be ruled out.

As a wife, at any rate. Edmund thought it a great shame Treveryan had not been killed outright by the elusive footpads. Once her fierce father was out of the way, Perdita's step-mother was sure to push the cuckoo child from her nest and the girl would be alone in the world. In which case, she was going to need a protector. A man of wealth and substance, a man she already regarded as a friend and to whom she might well be persuaded to turn in her hour of need.

A man very like Edmund Menheire.

'Carefully, Mistress Perdita. He's sleeping now.'

'That's good.'

Perdita padded on slippered feet into the tower chamber, closing the door quietly behind her. A single candle was burning on the table beside her father's bed and Viney was slumped in a chair near the fire. To his surprise, Perdita sat down close to him. To his further surprise and great delight she produced a flask of French brandy from the folds of her gown and poured him a glass.

She smiled as she handed it to him. 'You've been working so hard looking after my father,' she said. 'I thought it was time you had a reward.'

She was looking at him intently, but he did not notice. He downed the glass in a single gulp and she poured him another, which swiftly followed the first. After the third glass had vanished in the same manner, she asked, 'Would you care for some more?'

'Indeed I would.'

'Very well, then.' She lifted the flask as if to pour more, then said, 'You knew my natural mother well, I believe.'

'I was her servant for many years.'

'I want you to tell me about her.'

Viney's eyes were fixed on the brandy flask, poised in mid-air above his glass. He ran the tip of his tongue over dry lips and said, 'What exactly do you want to know?'

'Everything. What manner of woman was she?'

'That's hard to say. She was an ordinary sort of woman, but then again,' he added hastily, as he struggled to think of some nugget of information that would result in more brandy ending up in his glass, 'she was not like other women at all. She liked her books, poetry and Latin, that sort of thing I believe it was, though of course I can only sign my name myself. But for all her learning she was a good woman.'

'Don't just say what you think I want to hear,' said Perdita briskly. 'Tell me the truth. She was never a good woman, surely.'

'Well, no. Not from the outside. Some folk were quick to judge her, because of your father and other things too, I believe. But if you knew her, well, it's hard to say exactly, and I was only her servant so . . . but things never looked so black when you were standing close to her, if you know what I mean.'

Perdita did not. She said, 'She was wrong to leave her husband.'

'I suppose so, but then again, after he sent the boy away—'

'Luke Hollar? He was sent away?'

'Yes, well . . .' Viney glanced anxiously towards the bed, as though he had already said too much. Hastily Perdita poured him another glass, which he drank at once before continuing with renewed enthusiasm, 'It was after she took up with Sir Richard. Master Hollar, her husband, sent the boy away. Said she wasn't a fit mother, which anyone could have seen was a pack of lies. Fair broke her heart, it did, and he was only a slip of a lad. So maybe she thought she had nothing to lose when she came here.'

'If that was the case, why did she not stay?'

'Well, you see, I believe she was always pining for the boy. Hoping he'd return. Then the wars came, we got rumours that

Luke was marching with the Parliament men, though he was still hardly more than a child. She was frantic with worrying. And I believe the parson persuaded her to quit this house. Said the Lord was more likely to send her boy back safe and well if she did.'

Perdita poured him another drink.

'Praise the Lord,' said Viney, 'and he did. But that was much later. After I'd brought you here. She wanted to know you were safe.'

'Sweet Jesus,' came a harsh voice from the bed, 'I do believe the girl is making you drunk. What gibberish you're talking.'

Viney downed his final glass and said, 'Begging your pardon, sir, I was just remembering the day we brought Mistress Perdita here to you. Me and Dorcas.'

'Well, you can stop remembering and help me sit up, damn you.'

'Yes, sir.'

Perdita went with Viney and together they eased Richard into a sitting position. His face was still a mass of bruises, but most of the cuts were healing. It was his chest and stomach that pained him most now.

'She was a good woman, Sir Richard,' said Viney, his usual silence undermined by the brandy.

'I know that, you fool,' said Richard. 'I don't need you to tell me. Good God, man, what's the matter with you? It's this house, it's making you maudlin. And me, too, if the truth be known. Time to quit this place. Viney, go and tell Menheire's men to get hold of a litter. I'm going back to Rossmere.'

'But, Father, you cannot possibly travel. The doctor said this morning—'

'If I listened to doctors I'd have been dead years ago. Viney, do as you're told this instant. We'll leave at first light. And, Viney, go to Diggory Fitch in Helston. Tell him to come and see me at once. I'll be at Rossmere. And tell Piers to come here right away. Hurry, man.'

Viney knew better than to argue with his master and he disappeared at once. Exhausted by his brief efforts, Richard laid his head back on the pillows and his eyelids drooped.

Perdita settled herself more comfortably in the chair beside the bed and prepared to wait. She listened to the wind soughing through the oak trees, and the logs wheezing in the grate, content to try to imagine what it must have been like for that other, unknown woman who had once found love in this tower chamber and then thrown that love away. A cold draught of air passed through the bedchamber, bending the candles sideways and for a moment Perdita felt as if an unknown presence was filling the room and she herself was wrapped in tenderness. Then she remembered how she had been tricked in the back room of the Mitre and she told herself not to be so foolish a second time. Yet something of the passing serenity remained with her.

Automatically she smoothed the coverlet that lay across Richard's chest.

'Stop fussing, girl.' His bruised hands flapped her away.

'I thought you were asleep. Besides, I like to fuss.' After a little while she asked, 'Is that why you hate Luke Hollar, Father?' She waited, watching him. His mouth seemed set in a stubborn line, but when he did not answer she asked again, 'Viney said she left you because of Luke. Is that why you still hate him?'

'Not hate,' said Richard, half opening his eyes. He sighed. 'Not any more. Your mother was always afraid that her boy would come back to Porthew and not find her, so she never came away with me . . . changed her mind eventually, but by then it was too late . . . always too late . . .'

'Why? I don't understand.'

'That's because you're like me. You try too hard. Always chasing after what you can't have and miss what's in front of you. Maybe you'll learn in time. Not like me. Don't be a fool and leave it too late . . .'

His voice drifted into silence. Don't be a fool, he had said, and leave it too late. A picture of Piers came into her mind, Piers, waiting for her on the moors while she rode his gelding back and slipped, excited and breathless, down into his waiting arms. In the stillness, Perdita heard a small movement. Looking up, she saw Piers standing on the opposite side of the bed.

'Am I interrupting?' he asked.

She shook her head, indicating with a brief gesture that her father was sleeping once again.

He drew up a chair and sat down. 'I'll wait,' he said.

Perdita had no wish to talk to anyone just then, but she was glad of his silent presence in the room.

For the first time it occurred to her that her father was mortal, this huge and difficult man who had dominated her whole life, either by his absence when he was in exile or now by his enigmatic presence. She realised, too, that no matter how much people told her about the woman Margaret Hollar whose natural child she was, she had no hope of ever coming close to knowing her.

She wondered what her life would have been like if she had remained to be brought up by the woman who had inspired such love in Richard that he had carved those words on the oak mantel and then, nearly twenty years later, had them inscribed on her headstone.

No other love . . . What would it be like to feel so strongly about another person? To throw away all caution and common sense for a few months or weeks or even days of fleeting passion?

She checked herself. She, of all people, could not afford even to imagine such a luxury. In her longing to find out more about her mother she had been desperately hoping to grasp hold of some insight that might indicate how she should live her own life, but there was none. If anything, all that she had learned about her natural mother merely reinforced the lessons she had learned from Kitty: wealth, position and a strict adherence to the conventions were the solid bedrock on which a successful life must be built. Those who were influenced by sentiment and emotion always found their own road to misery. She might wish it were otherwise, but those were the facts.

She blinked back the threatening tears and glanced across at Piers. His eyes were fixed on her face, almost as if he expected to find the answer to some problem there. *No other love* . . . As her eyes locked with his, she felt a tremor of danger. It would be so easy, so perilously easy . . .

She said, 'There's no need for you to stay here. He'll probably sleep till morning now. With any luck he will have forgotten all about this hare-brained scheme to go back to Rossmere.'

'The devil I will,' Richard's voice broke in angrily. 'We leave as soon as the litter is ready. Perdita, I want you to write a letter to my wife. Inform her that I fell from my horse but will be fully recovered by the time she receives the letter and will be on my way to Plymouth. The last thing I want is for her to come fussing around me.'

'Don't you think Lady Treveryan will want to know the truth about your injuries?' asked Piers.

'No sense worrying her over nothing. Now then, Piers, you're going to deliver the letter to her for me. And you'll take another for Master Boulter. You can write it out for me. He's the captain of the *Fearless*. Tell him I am recommending you for whatever position he thinks fit. Let's hope you make a better job of it than that fool Kip did.'

'Thank you, Sir Richard.' In his enthusiasm, Piers leaped to his feet and looked as if he meant to seize his benefactor by the hand. Just in time he remembered the extent of Richard's bruising and restricted himself to a broad grin.

'Now, go away, the pair of you. I want both those letters drafted by the morning so I can sign them. Tell Viney to come back here at once. He may as well sleep off his drunkenness where I can keep an eye on him. Once he gets started he's the devil to stop, as you well know, Perdita. Leave me in peace, I want to sleep.'

'Very well, Father.'

Once Viney had been located and informed of his orders, they went through the dark house to the library, where writing materials were stored. Perdita was anxious about her father's determination to return to Rossmere when he was still pitifully weak, but Piers was so delighted at the prospect of being employed on board the *Fearless* that he was unable to remain sombre for long.

He fetched a bottle of sack and insisted that Perdita join him in drinking to his great good fortune. Infected by his excitement, Perdita felt her own mood shift at once. They toasted Richard then Master Boulter, and the *Fearless* herself several times. After the fourth toast Perdita forgot her worries altogether and allowed herself to be swept away by his enthusiasm.

'You must go to Barbados and find Cary's husband!' she exclaimed.

'That's the first place I'll visit. Then I'll go to the Andes and find the lost gold of Montezuma.'

'Take care! You may be captured by Barbary pirates and turned into a galley slave.'

'They'd not stand a chance against me. I'd capture their ship and set the slaves free.'

'Just think of all the places you'll visit.'

'Genoa and Rome.'

'Venice and Barcelona.'

'Oporto and Bordeaux.'

Soon the lists of faraway names became more intoxicating than the wine itself, and it was some time before they remembered they were supposed to be writing serious letters.

Perdita wanted to write to Kitty that her husband had been set upon by a band of twenty footpads, all known murderers and wanted by the justices in at least six counties, but he had slaughtered every last one of them and suffered only minor scratches to his hand, now healed.

Piers then suggested that he write the letter to Master Boulter and described himself as the most seaworthy man who ever set foot on a ship, half merman, half monkey, as useful in a wreck as up a mast, with the strength of an ox and the courage of a lion, proficient in ten languages at least and able to exist for a month on a cup of water and a single ship's biscuit.

Perdita watched him as he strode around the library. With his dark hair and eyes the colour of a summer sea, he was looking quite remarkably handsome in the candlelight. It was lucky he was leaving soon, she thought. If he had shown any inclination to stay in Trecarne for much longer, she might have been in serious danger of forgetting her purpose in making a good marriage to his highly eligible cousin.

After the anxiety of the previous few days, it was a blessed relief to laugh, and they might have continued that way through the night, if Edmund had not come into the library.

'What is all this commotion?' he asked stiffly. 'I could hear you on the stairs.'

Perdita glanced at Piers. He was standing by the open window, his head thrown back. He had been in the midst of striking a theatrical pose as he described his plans for thwarting attacks from privateers. For a moment she wanted him to pick a fight with Edmund. She felt reckless, as though she wanted to burn all the boats she had been so carefully assembling since she arrived at Trecarne.

But, of course, Piers had promised to help her in her quest to win Edmund. He would do nothing that might harm her cause.

'We were writing letters,' Perdita explained.

'Very important letters,' added Piers.

Edmund said coldly, 'May I remind you both that there are two sick men in this house. Your frivolity does you no credit.'

He withdrew.

Piers sighed. 'Damn my cousin,' he said, in exasperation. 'He's always had a grotesque sense of timing.'

'We ought to get the letters written all the same.'

'Yes.'

For a little while nothing could be heard but the scratch of pen on paper. As she reached the end of hers, Perdita realised that Piers's pen had fallen silent. She looked up. He was staring at her thoughtfully. 'What about you, Perdita?' he asked. 'When I come back from all my travels, what will have become of you?'

It was the first time he had used her name. Perdita flushed, but luckily her earlier recklessness had faded and she was able to reply calmly, 'If I get my way then I will be able to welcome you back to Trecarne as mistress of this place. I shall be your cousin. Will that be to your liking, sir?'

'Of course it will, why not?' he replied.

She bent her head once more to finish the letter. After that neither of them felt like laughing any more.

Chapter Thirty-One

It was the dark evenings Sophie found hardest. For the first time in her life she was quite alone. Alone in the room, alone in the house, alone in Porthew. Until now she had been surrounded by people, family and servants, the noise and busyness of a large household. Often in the past at Rossmere she had longed for a little time to herself. Now she had all the peace and quiet she could wish for — and she hated it.

At first she assumed Luke must have been delayed by the family of weavers he had been visiting. After her first night alone and sleepless, she was afraid he had met with an accident. She alerted her neighbours; the constable was informed. She borrowed a pony and searched along the route Luke would have taken then returned a different way. They asked the weavers, all those who lived near the road. No sign of Luke anywhere.

By noon came the news that Piers Menheire had discovered Sir Richard lying beaten and barely conscious by the roadside and had taken him back to Trecarne. Sophie's neighbours were alarmed by the news: if a band of footpads was terrorising travellers then most likely Luke had also been their victim. They redoubled their efforts to find him, but when they returned that evening, still with no sighting to report, Sophie began to place her own interpretation on events.

Sir Richard's injuries and Luke's disappearance, the time and the place, all pointed to a single conclusion. Her first reaction was one of outrage: how dare Luke exact revenge on the man when he had promised her so many times he would forget the past? Worse still, how could he run off without telling her what was happening?

As the days passed and still there was no word or sign from him, she began to despair. Rumours reached Porthew that Sir Richard had recovered consciousness enough to say that he had not recognised his attackers and was sure they were not local men. By now Sophie thought he must be suffering a loss of memory or, for some reason, that he was lying.

She took in a grey kitten she found cowering under a mound of nets near the harbour. It was in many ways an unsatisfactory companion, but better than none. During the days she kept herself busy around the house and practised her handwriting by copying passages from the Bible or from the ledger in the shop. But as darkness closed in and the footsteps and voices from the street fell silent, she gave up all pretence of activity and simply waited.

There was nothing else to do. With the grey kitten curled in a contented ball on her lap, she sat by the dying fire and waited. Always waiting.

She missed Luke wretchedly. Her anger flared up only occasionally; most of the time, all she wanted was to have him back again. She missed the feel of his presence in a room, the rise and fall of his voice as he spoke with customers in the shop, missed the way his whole expression was transformed each time he caught sight of her, missed the way his lean body fitted so snugly against hers when he pulled her close to him, clothed or naked, missed the touch of his hands passing over her skin.

She had been so sure he loved her, but now in the darkness she began to doubt. Maybe there was another woman who had a prior claim to his affection, maybe he had intended all along to leave her and never return. But how could he go with never a word to say why, or to tell her when he might return? And if he had planned to stay away, then surely he would have taken his fiddle with him?

She took Luke's violin down from the high shelf near the back door and, taking care not to disturb the kitten, she leaned the instrument against her shoulder. Luke always played it held against his upper arm. There was comfort in the silky gloss of the wood, polished smooth over the years by the touch of his fingers. She plucked one of the strings gently and the note, awkward and out of tune, jarred through the silence.

She was praying silently for Luke's return. She believed he had been Sir Richard's attacker, but supposing Sir Richard had inflicted damage of his own? She was haunted by the possibility that Luke was lying somewhere, injured, maybe dying. Needing her. Every day she had walked the roads he might have taken. Tomorrow she must do the same again. Until then, she could only wait.

Waiting. Hoping. Despairing.

She remained sitting quite still, the kitten sleeping in her lap, until she heard the church clock strike the hour.

Then she rose from her seat. No one travelled the roads at this time of night, he'd not return, not now. In the morning she'd set off before dawn and hunt for him again.

She set down the kitten on a cushion near the fire and locked the door that led into the shop. Then she went to bolt the back door.

It opened as she approached and Luke stepped over the threshold.

Wrapped in a dark cloak, he looked pale, thinner than she remembered, and his deep-set eyes were guarded.

Sophie let out a cry. He raised a finger to his lips in warning. She moved forward, anticipating his embrace, but he remained quite still, hands dangling by his sides.

She stopped where she was and lifted the candle to see him more clearly. There was no sign of injury, but his face was altered all the same. 'Luke, where have you been?' she asked, her voice frayed with the long strain of waiting. 'What happened?'

He came into the room, bolting the door carefully behind him, and shrugged off his cloak. 'Is there anything to eat?' he demanded. 'I haven't had a proper meal in days and I'm famished.'

'Tell me what happened. Where have you been?'

'Oh, here and there. Nowhere in particular.' He noticed the kitten, which had awoken and was stretching out tiny claws as it eyed him sleepily. 'Who is this?'

'Damn you, Luke, answer me! You've been gone for nearly a week with never a word, while I've been here alone imagining the Lord knows what horrors. Now you walk in here as calm as you please expecting food as if nothing had happened. Don't you know how worried I've been?'

'You'll get used to it,' he said coolly. 'I warned you from the beginning it would be hard.'

She examined him silently as he stooped to stroke the kitten's tiny head. 'It was you, wasn't it?' she said. 'You attacked Sir Richard and left him by the roadside.'

Luke shuddered. He went to the fireplace and nudged a pile of ashes with the toe of his boot. They glowed briefly, then faded back to grey. 'Well, then, what of it? Is the villain dead?'

'He was gravely ill for three days, but now the word is he will recover.'

'More's the pity,' said Luke. 'It would have been better for us both if he died.'

'How can you say that?'

'Consider for a moment. If he had died right away, no one would ever know who injured him. As it is, he will have alerted the justices. I must go into hiding. You'll have to get used to being on your own from now on.'

'No one else suspects you. Sir Richard is telling people he was attacked by footpads.'

'What?'

'It's the truth, Luke. He said he did not recognise them. It was dark, there were two at least, but he does not think they were local men.'

'The fellow must have lost his wits.'

'I think not. He is at Trecarne.'

'What, in God's name, is he doing there?'

'Piers Menheire found him after . . . after he was injured. He took him to Trecarne. Perdita went over the next morning. Cary told me she is there still.'

'You are *sure* he has said nothing about me?'

'Quite sure. No one has even mentioned your name.'

'Then it must be a trick. He wants to lure me back to Porthew so he can trap me.'

'I don't think so,' said Sophie. 'There's been no one looking for you. If you were under suspicion, then the justices would have been here by now.'

'We'll see.' He looked up and met her eye. 'But you, dear wife,' he said bitterly, '*you* suspected me from the beginning.'

'What else was I to think? When you did not return that first evening, I assumed you'd met with an accident, but when the news came about Sir Richard and still you did not come home – why, then, I knew it must be you. I've always known how much you hated each other. That was why I asked you to promise you'd never fight with him.'

'It's your own fault,' said Luke contemptuously. 'You should never have trusted me. I always break my promises. Didn't anyone tell you that? Come now, surely they did. I dare say I told you myself. Well, at least now you know the kind of man you have married. How do you like it? Don't you wish you were snug back at Rossmere instead of shackled to a worthless fellow who cannot keep his word even for a month?'

'Oh, Luke, stop tormenting yourself! If only you had come back here and told me straight away. Of course I was angry, but that doesn't stop me caring about you just the same. It doesn't make me wish I was back at Rossmere. I want to be with you, no matter what.'

He looked away. 'You're talking gibberish. Is there nothing in this house a man can eat?'

'How can you stand there demanding food when you will not listen to one word I'm saying? Couldn't you have trusted me enough to come back here instead of leaving me to worry all this time? How can you be such a blind fool? Why won't you tell me what happened?'

Luke flung himself into a chair. He did not look at her. 'I did not want to hurt him. I thought when I saw him on the road that I could ride past and bid him good evening. I was going to tell you that. But then he tried to stop me, and we fell . . .'

'You did not want to hurt him?' Sophie stared at him incredulously. 'It does not sound as though Sir Richard got his injuries just by falling from his horse.'

'He provoked me,' he said simply. Sophie waited, but he stood up briskly and went to the pantry where the ale was stored. 'I see I shall have to fend for myself. And, of course, you are right. It was my doing entirely. I did not mean to hurt him, but all the same I beat him within an inch of his life. And him your friend and a fellow nearly twice my age. What kind of man does a thing like that?' He took a pitcher of ale and poured himself a glass. He sounded almost light-hearted. 'And now it looks as if I will get away with my crime since Treveryan is obviously suffering a lapse of memory. These things happen after a blow to the head. Or, in his case, several blows. Footpads, eh? I suppose now they will arrest some luckless pair of vagabonds and they will be punished in my place. All of which goes to prove my belief that there is no justice in this world. Shall we drink to that? Why are you staring at me so goggle-eyed, woman? If you love me one half as much as you pretend, you must be delighted at my escape. Or are you perhaps thinking it is your duty as a citizen to tell the justices who the real villain is? If Sir Richard dies then I might yet swing for murder and your troubles will be at an end.'

'Stop it! Stop it!' Sophie hurled herself at him, and struck his shoulder with her fists. 'What is the matter with you? Why do you have to twist everything around? Why do you hate me so much?'

He caught hold of her wrists. His face was white with shock. 'I do not hate you, Sophie.'

'Then why do you always have to make it so hard? Why do you never believe me when I say I want to be with you? Damn it, Luke, I'm your wife. I care about you.'

'How can you say that after what I've done?'

'You had no right to leave me, it was not fair.' She twined her arms around his neck. 'I could not bear it here without you.'

He buried his face in her hair. 'Why?' he asked.

'You and all your questions, will they never end? Why can you never just let a thing be? Stay still and do not talk, only let me kiss you. I have missed you so much.'

He groaned. 'I was sure I had lost you.'

'Never.'

They held each other tightly, their bodies fitting together like two halves of a perfect whole. Then Luke murmured, 'Not here. Upstairs.'

'But you're hungry.'

'That can wait.'

Sophie lifted the candle and slipped her hand into his. 'Don't ever go away without telling me again. No matter what.'

He looked at her steadily. 'I promise. I—'

He broke off. Fists pounded on the back door so loudly that Sophie dropped the candle, which blew out, leaving them in darkness.

'Who can that be?' asked Sophie, crouching down to retrieve the candle.

'At this time of night? It's the justices. I knew it was a trick. Treveryan was only waiting till I came back. They've been watching the house.'

'You must hide. I'll not let them in.' Sophie's hand was trembling so much that even when she had found the candle it took her an age to light it from the last embers of the fire. The banging on the back door was louder.

'What's the point? They know I'm here. This whole thing has been planned. What part did you play, Sophie?'

'How can you ask me that?'

'I didn't mean it. I—'

And then they both stopped; they were listening. A woman's voice was calling through the door.

'It's Perdita!' said Sophie. 'She sounds as if she is in trouble.' She ran to the door.

'Sophie, stop! It's sure to be a trick!' shouted Luke, but she pulled back the bolt and the door flew open.

Perdita swept in. Ignoring Luke, who had retreated to the foot of the stairs in preparation for flight, she seized Sophie by the hand and her words tumbled out in a rush. 'My father is outside on a litter. He insisted on leaving Trecarne, though we all said it was madness, but then we feared it would be worse for him to be thwarted. They tried a horse, but the pain was too great for him so the men started to carry him. And that was nearly as bad – they had to keep stopping to allow him to rest. We begged him to go back to Trecarne but he wouldn't hear of it, and the way was endless, I've never known it so bad. Then it started to get dark, I thought we'd have to spend the night on the road and the cold would kill him. I told my father we'd stop at Porthew and he said here, not the inn. And now he is in too much pain even to speak and I'm afraid it is killing him. Oh, Sophie, you must help us!'

'Of course,' said Sophie at once, not looking at Luke, who was watching them, horrified, from the foot of the stairs. 'Tell the men to bring him in.'

Perdita awoke in the darkness. She had no idea of the time, but she feared she must have overslept. She had meant to rest only for a couple of hours, but she was so exhausted that her body was slower to wake than her mind. For some time she lay as if paralysed in the strange room, remembering the events that had brought her to the draper's house.

For her the nightmare that day had begun when Piers Menheire left for Porthew to find a boat to take him to Plymouth. He was in excellent spirits and Perdita could tell that in his eagerness to begin a new life on one of her father's ships he had already turned his back on everything he was leaving behind in Cornwall – herself included. She was pleased, for his sake, but the house seemed empty once he had gone and she felt briefly depressed.

But as soon as she realised her father meant to stick to his plan to quit Trecarne, there was no time for anything but the practical arrangements for the journey.

Edmund Menheire insisted on taking control of the preparations. 'Leave it to me,' he kept saying. 'I will arrange everything for you.' But since he paid no attention at all to her father's wishes, his help caused nearly as many problems as it solved. He was adamant her father must travel by coach, as a gentleman ought, ignoring the fact that the deeply rutted roads and the constant jolting made this agony for Sir Richard. They abandoned the coach less than a mile from Trecarne.

By late afternoon it became obvious that they had no hope of reaching Rossmere in daylight and her father insisted they go to the draper's house, not the inn. Perdita was dismayed. She had seen neither Sophie nor Luke since the stormy evening when their marriage had been announced, and she had convinced herself it was better that way. But when she saw Sophie in the little room behind the shop, all her misgivings vanished: Sophie was practical and warm-hearted; Sophie would know what to do. Perdita forgot she had ever felt betrayed by Sophie's rash marriage and remembered only that she had liked and admired her more than almost anyone she had ever known.

Her brother was more enigmatic.

Luke had acted strangely from the moment she entered the house. He had watched with an odd expression on his face as the men brought her father into the house. Sophie held a candle aloft and directed them to take the litter into the parlour next to the kitchen. Luke remained always at a slight distance, hanging back as though he wished to keep out of sight, reaching forward as though he wanted to help. And all the time he never once ceased to stare at the face of the injured man.

It was true that in such a short time the change in her father had been shocking, even to Perdita who had watched the alteration day by day. His face was still disfigured by the beating; he had not been shaved in more than a week and his bruised jaw was covered by a brindled stubble. He had eaten little and the flesh had fallen away, leaving his cheekbones and his fierce eyes more prominent than ever. His breathing was rapid and painfully irregular, and at first he was struggling so much against the pain that he was unable to speak.

Sophie ordered a mattress brought down from one of the bedchambers. She herself fetched sheets, pillows and blankets and then, as gently as they could, they eased him from his litter. Richard's face was grey and shining with sweat but he never cried out, not once.

Perdita was awed by his endurance. All day his strength and obstinacy had dominated those around him. Sick and helpless he might be, but even so no one dared go against his commands.

When he was laid on the makeshift bed in the parlour, Viney touched his master's lips with a sponge soaked in some painkilling potion, but Richard jerked his head away impatiently. 'Awake,' he muttered. 'Stay awake here.'

Viney stood back. Sophie drew up a stool on one side of the bed, Perdita on the other. Richard's eyes closed and it seemed from his breathing that he slept.

'He is so ill,' whispered Sophie. 'Why ever did he want to travel?'

'I do not know,' said Perdita.

Viney had retreated to the shadows at the side of the room.

He leaned his back against the wall and slid down into a crouching position. His eyes closed.

Luke took a couple of silent steps forward. He could not drag his eyes away from Richard's face as he asked Perdita, 'Why did he want to come here? Did he mention me by name?'

'He's been delirious,' whispered Perdita. 'It's hard to follow what he says.'

There was a movement from the bed and Richard was fully alert. He turned towards Perdita and said, 'Your mother . . . in this house . . . nearly died in Porthew before . . . saved me then . . . never knew . . .'

'Yes, Father. Hush, now, do not tire yourself,' said Perdita. She was afraid that the effort of talking after all he had endured that day might prove too much for him.

Luke had moved to stand at the foot of the bed. Richard caught sight of him. His lips drew back slowly in what might have been a smile, or maybe a grimace of pain. 'Luke . . .' Richard gasped, his words barely audible, 'always get it wrong . . . but your mother . . .' He was silent for a long time. He seemed to be struggling to find the words, or maybe it was simply breathing that was hard. At length he said, 'Beware of footpads, Luke . . . take care . . .'

Luke was shaking from head to foot. He backed out of the room. Sophie watched him, then rose and followed him into the kitchen. Perdita could hear the murmur of their voices; she heard Luke say, very distinctly, 'It's a trick, don't you see? He still means to trap me . . .' And then Sophie's voice, soothing and indistinct.

A little later, Luke showed Perdita into the back bedchamber where she was to sleep. He had smiled, that odd, tentative smile of his, half devious, half shy, and told her it was the room she had been born in. Her own room. Her mother's room. She was shocked and wanted to ask him more, but he slipped away before she had the chance and she returned to the room where her father was resting.

Perdita remained by his side through most of the night. The men from Trecarne were all lodging at the alehouse, Sophie and Luke had retired to their room, only Viney remained. At some stage he had snored himself awake, staggered to his feet and told her to get some rest, he'd watch for a while. Thinking of all that lay ahead the following day, Perdita at last agreed.

Now the stars were beginning to dim in the east. It was going to be a clear day. Perdita hauled herself from the bed and wrapped her cloak around her shoulders against the morning chill. She had slept in her clothes, had not even removed her shoes.

She went down the stairs. The kitchen was deserted, except for the small grey kitten who mewed plaintively at her approach, then darted forward, demanding to be fed. Perdita scooped it up in her hand and set it down on a chair where it was less likely to inflict damage on the hem of her skirt. There was no sound from the parlour next door where Viney must still be watching by her father's side. No doubt both men were sleeping.

Perdita decided to use the privy at the rear of the house before going in to her father. The back door was unbolted and the morning air felt cool as spring water against her cheek. In a hen coop in a the next-door garden a cock was crowing lustily. Suddenly Perdita remembered that she had barely eaten anything the previous day and now she was ravenously hungry. Through a chink in the roof of the privy she could see the morning star fading in an emerald sky.

She returned to the house just as daylight was filling the rooms. The kitten made a second assault on her skirts and this time Perdita set him down on the table before going into the parlour.

Her horrified cry echoed through the house.

The parlour was deserted.

The litter was there, propped against the wall, the makeshift bed, the chairs, her father's travelling bag, even his cloak. But the bed was empty, the covers thrown back, and both Viney and her father had vanished.

She shrieked again and spun round. Hurried footsteps pounded above her head as Sophie and Luke were roused by her cry. They clattered down the stairs, Sophie dressed only in her shift, Luke still tying his breeches.

'What's the matter?' asked Sophie. 'Is he dead?'

'He's gone.'

'Gone?' Luke looked into the empty parlour.

Sophie put her arm around Perdita's shoulders. 'Don't fret, he cannot have got far. We'll find him.'

Perdita shook off her sympathy. She ran back into the parlour and picked up the linen towel she had been using the previous evening to soothe her father's forehead. It smelt of Hungary water and sweat. She pressed it against her cheek, and then she had an idea.

'I think I know.'

Sophie and Luke stood side by side, watching her. 'Wait,' said Sophie. 'We'll come with you.'

Perdita was too impatient to linger while they fussed with shoes and clothes. Leaving by the back door she ran through the strip of garden, then along the narrow lane that led behind the houses down to the harbour. The little town was waking, men setting off for the boats or the fields, women going for water, emptying slops, exchanging the first greetings of the day. They paused in their work, surprised by the sight of a young lady, whom most of them recognised, racing through the streets, her eyes wild and her hair disordered.

She crossed the piece of open ground behind the alehouse. A dog ran out and barked at her, but she hardly noticed. She hurried up the steps that led into the churchyard and under the slate roof of the lych-gate. As she ran between the gravestones and the yew trees the sun appeared on the horizon. Sunlight flowed down the stone tower of the church and glittered across the wide expanse of sea.

Her instinct had been right. She saw him. Sobbing with relief, Perdita flew down the soft grass to the grave at the far corner by the wall that overlooked the sea. His feet were visible, protruding slightly across the path.

'Oh, Father! I thought you had gone without me!'

He was sitting with his back propped against the new headstone he'd had inscribed with those Latin lines from Catullus. Viney was nowhere to be seen.

Perdita dropped to her knees and grasped his hands. The sleeve of his shirt was soaked with dew. 'Oh, Father, whatever were you thinking of? You'll catch your death of cold.'

He did not answer with the annoyance she had come to expect from him when she fussed. She looked at him more carefully. He was staring out beyond the low wall towards the golden shimmering sea-path of the sun.

Staring, but not seeing.

'Father?' Perdita stared at him, not yet understanding his unusual silence. Then, gaining courage, she touched his cool face with her hand. Only then did she wrap her arms around his neck. She held him tightly, hugging him and rocking back and forth as the first harsh tears rose in her throat. For once, his chilly, stiffening body offered her no resistance.

Close to him in death as she never had been in life.

Chapter Thirty-Two

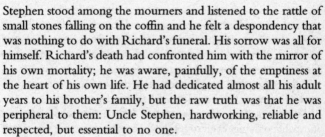

Stephen stood among the mourners and listened to the rattle of small stones falling on the coffin and he felt a despondency that was nothing to do with Richard's funeral. His sorrow was all for himself. Richard's death had confronted him with the mirror of his own mortality; he was aware, painfully, of the emptiness at the heart of his own life. He had dedicated almost all his adult years to his brother's family, but the raw truth was that he was peripheral to them: Uncle Stephen, hardworking, reliable and respected, but essential to no one.

He looked across at Perdita, draped in cloudy black from head to toe. Like everyone else he had heard how Luke and Sophie had discovered her in the graveyard, clinging to her father's dew-soaked corpse only a couple of feet from where she stood now.

Later, when Viney was found in a drunken sprawl beside the alehouse, they learned that Richard had insisted that he help him – carry him, more like – to the graveyard. Viney had stayed with him for some time; when he realised his master was dying he set off to get help, but his nerve had failed him and he opted for drunken oblivion instead. It was Perdita who had found her father, guided by God knew what instinct to her mother's grave, Perdita who had been sobbing as if her heart must break.

Hard to imagine that now. She looked so resolute and strong – no, that description was too charitable. She looked stony and unbending, like someone who no longer has a heart that can be broken. Pale, with dark shadows under her eyes, she some-how repelled all pity. It was as though some of the grim determination of the father had been transmitted to her at the moment of death.

Stephen was dismayed by his own lack of sympathy for her, but he could not help it. He lamented briefly the loss of the bright-eyed, eager girl who had first appeared at Rossmere. Still, however unfeeling she appeared at his graveside, she had been distraught at the time of her father's death. There was no one who would lament Stephen's death with such a fierce passion.

His gaze shifted sideways to settle on Sophie. She and Luke stood side by side, their heads bowed. Luke appeared as deeply affected by Richard's death as his wife was. Just why Luke should mourn a man who had always treated him so harshly Stephen did not know. Perhaps because hatred sometimes forges bonds closer than love. It was obvious, however, from every look and gesture that passed between them, that husband and wife were far from happy, but their anguish seemed to be drawing them still closer together. Stephen felt more distant from his niece than he had even in the first days of her marriage.

Stephen sighed. He was cursed by a remorseless honesty; incapable of lying, even to himself. The shaming truth was that it was the change in Sophie, more than Richard's death, that was causing his present discontent. Ever since his return from the wars he had persuaded himself that he was happy to devote his time to caring for his brother's family, but in reality it had always been Sophie for whom he had laboured. She had been the daughter he would never have, she had grown into the young woman he could never marry, and now she had abandoned them all and left her family to make a separate life for herself, as was only right and proper. As he himself ought to have done, years ago.

The service was over. Alice, her hat draped in black ribbons, was inviting the mourners back to Rossmere. Most of them had started out from there that morning anyway, apart from Sophie and Luke. Richard had had few friends in the neighbourhood and his old enemies had stayed away.

There had been whispered surprise among the congregation when Edmund Menheire appeared in the church. Stephen thought he might have been sent by the Colonel as a mark of respect since Richard had spent the final week of his life at Trecarne, a guest of sorts, but seeing the way Edmund watched Perdita and seemed always to position himself as close to her as possible, he thought there might be another reason for his attendance.

People were moving away from the graveside. Only Perdita remained motionless. Suddenly Stephen sensed how brittle her seeming strength really was. He was about to go and offer her some words of comfort, but then he saw Edmund glide up to her and speak. Stephen could not hear the words, but he saw Perdita's reaction. She flinched, as though startled from a dream, then turned to Edmund and bestowed on him a smile as radiant as it was insincere.

Stephen turned away. He was sickened by a gesture of such calculating hypocrisy at the very moment when the earth was being heaped on her father's coffin.

He strode out of the churchyard, barely remembering to acknowledge those he passed. He gave a coin to the lad who had been waiting with his horse and mounted straight away. He was intending to go straight back to Rossmere and continue the work of patching up the roof of the cow byre, which he had begun that morning, but on an impulse he turned off the road and took the narrow track that led to Polcreath.

At this autumnal season of the year, it seemed as though Biddy Firth's little farm was being clawed back into the damp earth from which it had been formed. The thatch was blackening and covered in moss; ferns and grasses grew in every crack of stone and cob, and the farmyard ooze was rank with nettles and dock. The interior of the tiny farmhouse was losing its struggle against the wild: trails of ivy twined in through the window frames and chickens pecked at the mosses covering the damp floor.

Biddy Firth showed neither surprise nor pleasure at the sight of him, but as always she made him welcome with ale and cheese and an apparently endless list of the calamities that had befallen her since his last visit: all her autumn chicks taken by badgers, the corn attacked by mould before it was winnowed, a cow with an infected udder and the well-water brackish and not even fit for washing in.

Stephen should have been used to it by now. He knew it gave

her some strange satisfaction to lay her woes before him, that she valued his patient listening almost as much as his practical help and their bedchamber pleasures. Yet for some reason, perhaps because it too closely reflected his own feelings of waste, this afternoon he found her litany of disaster well nigh intolerable.

She did not notice. At length she sent her son Tod off on some errand in their far field and said cheerfully, 'We can go upstairs now, Captain Sutton. The boy won't be back for a while yet.'

Stephen nodded. He stood up. He started to follow her to the narrow stairs, but then he placed his hand on her arm. 'Wait a moment, Biddy.'

She turned her weather-wrinkled face to look at him. 'Is something the matter, Captain Sutton?'

'Not the matter, but . . . I have decided not to visit you like this any more. Of course, I shall continue to call in to see how you and your son are doing, and I shall help out in any way I can but . . .' Stephen knew there was no easy way to say what he wanted. He took the coward's way out and let Biddy fill in for him.

'There's to be no more sport upstairs, is that what you're saying, Captain Sutton?'

'That's right. I shall miss it, but—'

'You will not, or you'd never have decided to call a stop,' she said, but quite without bitterness. 'Well, that's a shame. I have enjoyed our times together, but you must go your own way. Not thinking of getting married, are you, Captain Sutton?'

Stephen laughed. 'Who would want to marry a penniless old bachelor like me?' he asked.

Before he left, Stephen promised to send down some ointment for her sick cow and he placed twice the usual amount of money in the jar above the fireplace.

But as he rode away from Polcreath, Stephen wondered only that he had not ended this strange liaison with the widow long since. He was amazed that he had ever been satisfied with such a tawdry exchange. Biddy's refusal to engage in any of those small acts of intimacy which, in Stephen's opinion, set men's appetites apart from those of mere beasts had never troubled him before. Now he despised himself for having settled for so little for so long.

He realised, with a certain weary irony, that her question had been more accurate than she knew: what he wanted now was a wife. But his question to Biddy still stood: who would want to marry a penniless fellow like him? Although he was only forty-five, he knew that an old bachelor was invariably a figure of fun. He did not want to make a fool of himself with a young wife, nor yet put up with an old one. If he had looked around fifteen years ago, he might have married some apple-cheeked yeoman's daughter and had a parcel of children, but it was too late for that now.

He was condemned to live and die alone, and no doubt it was better that way. He had loved only one woman in his life and now, when he remembered those brief months of happiness and grief in the summer when the old King's cause was lost at Naseby, he wondered if his memory was playing tricks on him. Had he ever known what it meant to be the centre of another's universe? Had he ever known those moments of complete joy when past and future fade to nothing and only the endless present exists? Or had he dreamed it? Imagined it, and wasted all hope of happiness since because nothing in this real world was ever going to match up to the perfection of the dream?

By the time he reached Rossmere he had uncovered no answers to his questions, but he had developed a powerful thirst. There was no sign of Amos, and he decided to leave the cow-byre roof until the next day. Entering the house through the kitchen, he found Cary filling a pitcher with hot wine from a cauldron set near the fire. 'Captain Sutton!' she roared, her cheeks flushed from the heat of the fire and probably a fair quantity of the wine as well. 'Take this through to the hall and be quick about it!'

'Can Viney not help you?'

'That old tosspot could not help himself to find his own pecker in his breeches.'

'Mind your manners, Cary,' he told her.

'I'll do that when I get paid for once. Three years it's been owing, Captain, as well you know. If I'm expected to do the work of ten, and all for nothing, then I need help from time to time. And you can tell that idle brat Louisa to get off her backside and give me a hand with the trays of food.'

'Cary, you're drunk.' Stephen took the pitcher and decided to have a word with her – when she was next sober. Besides, it was easy to understand her present arrogance towards the family. The household could not possibly function without her, and she'd have no difficulty finding another position elsewhere if she chose. Since she was correct about her lack of wages, the family were dependent on her goodwill, but this imbalance of power had never been apparent until Sophie's departure. Since then Cary had grown ever more domineering. Right now, Stephen did not see that much could be done to prevent it.

Following Stephen across the inner courtyard to the winter parlour, Cary quickly settled herself among the family with Honor and Alice. She ladled out wine in generous measures, especially to herself. Looking at the assembled gathering, Stephen saw that this was to be a wake in the old style.

Francis was already well on in drink, though recently this had become his usual condition of an evening. Speaking through frequent tears, Alice was telling Honor that Richard had been her first suitor when she was a young girl and much admired, and he had even fought a duel with her future husband for her. It was Edmund's first visit to Rossmere since Sophie's marriage, and the first time he had been in a room together with her and her new husband. Perhaps to cover the potential awkwardness of the situation he had agreed to a game of cards with Kip. He had also drunk a fair amount of wine, so that Kip was doing rather well out of him.

From time to time Edmund stole a glance at Sophie and Luke. He must be deriving a good deal of satisfaction from the sight of their discomfort, thought Stephen. Once again he was aware that they were bound together in some strange web of intimacy quite different from the happiness or even shyness Stephen had often noticed in newly-wed couples. They did not appear the least bit comfortable with each other, nor yet as if they had quarrelled. More like fellow conspirators, plotting some dark crime, thought Stephen – and the image startled him.

Suddenly he was weary of the problems and conflicts at Rossmere, weary of this family that was not truly his, yet was all the family he'd ever know. He ladled himself a generous measure of wine, drank it at a single draught and helped himself to more.

He looked around at the assembled company again. There was something – or someone – missing. Of course. The chief mourner: Perdita. Maybe he had judged her harshly earlier. Maybe she was one of those people such as himself who prefer to keep their emotions to themselves. Maybe even now she was giving way to her grief in the privacy of her bedchamber.

Wrong. When she entered the winter parlour a few moments later, Stephen could detect no trace of sadness in her features: on the contrary, she appeared strangely elated.

Diggory Fitch, the Helston lawyer who had been handling Sir Richard's affairs in recent months, followed close behind. A dishevelled, birdlike man, he hovered for a while on the fringe of the family gathering. Dusk was falling and it was obvious he was hoping to be invited to remain at Rossmere. However, Francis and Alice were both too sunk in their own wine-sodden miseries to notice him, so eventually Stephen said, 'Diggory, have a glass of wine. It's too late for you to go home tonight. We can find a bed for you somewhere.'

'That's very kind of you, Captain Sutton. Very kind of you indeed. I'm happy to accept your offer. Most happy. A glass of wine would be most welcome. Yes, yes, I'd appreciate a glass of wine.' Stephen remembered wearily that the fellow made a habit of saying everything twice. 'A glass of wine, good. Excellent. Much appreciated.' Sometimes three times.

Cary, who was sprawled in a large chair, her cap drooping over her face, lurched towards Perdita and demanded, 'Well, then, Mistress Perdita, what's in the will? You can tell us now!'

'Shame on you, Cary,' said Sophie. 'It's none of your business.'

Cary was unabashed. 'Don't be such a hypocrite. Everyone is in an itch to know how Sir Richard left his wealth, so where's the harm in asking?'

A roar from the games table gave news of another victory for Kip.

Perdita had gone to stand near the fire. Perhaps it was purely by chance that it was a position from which she could be viewed to advantage by at least one of the players at quits, but Stephen doubted it.

'Go on, Mistress Perdita,' insisted Cary. 'Has your father made you rich, then? Will all the men be forming a line to get their hands on your purse – and your person?'

'Cary!' from Alice.

'Cary!' from Louisa, but giggling all the same.

'Purse and person, that's good!' Cary was whooping with pleasure at her own verbal dexterity. 'Purse and person! How d'you like that, eh, Captain Sutton?'

Stephen ignored her and helped himself to more wine.

Perdita said, 'I do not like to have secrets from my dearest friends, but still, it is hardly right for me to tell you before my mother knows.'

'Quite right,' hiccuped Francis.

Both Kip and Edmund looked up from the card table.

'Therefore,' she said, 'I must remain silent.'

All the same, she looked like a cat that had found the cream as she slid a glance towards the gamesters. Stephen thought he detected something predatory in the way Edmund met her gaze, but Perdita, the little minx, did not seem in the least perturbed by it.

'Never mind about the details, then!' roared Cary, with such vigour that her cap slid off altogether. 'Give us the bare essentials of it. What's a bastard daughter worth, these days? Has he left you a wealthy bastard or no?'

There was a shocked silence. Perdita flinched, all the colour draining from her face. Just then she looked every inch the orphan child.

Even Stephen, who knew Cary better than anyone, had not realised quite how much she had drunk already. She must have been hard at it since early morning.

He stood up and went across to her. 'That's enough, now, Cary. No more drink for you tonight. I'm taking you back to the kitchen.'

'Won't you take me to bed, Captain Sutton?'

Kip let out a roar of laughter. 'There you are, Uncle Stephen, there's an offer you can't refuse!'

Suddenly furious, Stephen caught Cary by the arm and hauled her to her feet. By the time he had manoeuvred her across the courtyard to the kitchen she was bellowing.

Later, she began to cry. 'It's funerals that does it, Captain Sutton. You don't know how it hurts me to see the coffins put in the earth. I keep thinking of my poor Michael and where he is and who was there to care for him at the end. You don't know what it's like, the not knowing, it's eating away at me all the time. I can feel it like a pain in my belly.' She crossed her broad arms over her stomach and rocked and sobbed. 'I wake up with the pain and I fall asleep with it at night. It's killing me for sure, Captain Sutton. What can I do for him? I cannot bear the thought that he's lying all alone under some heathen sun for the birds to peck at, or rotting at the bottom of the sea. I'm sure he must be dead – he'd have come back to me otherwise. If I could only give him a proper Christian burial, like Sir Richard had today, then I'd rest happy. There's no peace for either of us until then. Oh, Captain Sutton, it's so hard not to know!'

Stephen offered her what comfort he could, though it was little enough and they were each repeating words they'd said often in the past, ever since O'Rourke had been reported captured. She continued her lament for some time, frightening her daughter Het, who had been sleeping in their chamber beside the kitchen. Stephen stayed with them, quieted Het's fears and resisted Cary's demands for more liquor. Eventually Cary keeled over on the settle and snored. Stephen covered her with a large baize apron and moved a chair alongside so she did not fall off.

Then he fetched himself a generous supply of wine.

He noticed Luke, standing in the shadows near the door.

'Who was Michael?' Luke asked, coming closer.

Stephen sighed. 'Cary's husband, O'Rourke. An Irishman who fought with me in the late wars. He was a good man, though he had a wild look to him. He got caught up with Penruddock and the rest when they rose against Cromwell. We tried to help him but it was too late. He'd been sent on a ship to Barbados. There's been no word of him since.'

'Have any returned?'

'A few. Most died.'

'So O'Rourke is dead?'

'Probably, but no one can be sure.'

'That was quite a performance Cary put on just now. Her

man's been gone for more than seven years. According to the law she's now a widow.'

Stephen glanced at Luke and said, with distaste, 'I do not think Cary's heart is guided by the law.'

'Whose is?'

Luke sat down across the table from Stephen and helped himself to some wine. Stephen, who had been looking forward to numbing his misery in solitary drinking, saw with dismay that Luke was determined to sit out the evening with him. By now Sophie and the others were probably retiring for the night. No doubt it was the wish to avoid his wife that had guided Luke to the kitchen, as much as any desire for Stephen's company. Stephen hoped he might for once be spared the confessor role: if husband and wife had reasons for wanting to avoid each other, then he for one did not want to know about them.

For a while, both men drank steadily and neither spoke. On the settle, Cary snored, loud, irregular snores. Stephen thought how harshly time had dealt with them both: that summer of '45 she had been a serving-girl, not beautiful, but with all the freshness and charm of youth. Her large brown eyes and bold, cheerful manner had attracted the admiration first of his lieutenant, Jack, and then of the Irishman, O'Rourke. It had been a summer of fighting and death and love. This evening he wanted to remember only the love.

Luke had been staring into the depths of his glass. Now he asked, 'Have you ever done a thing, Captain Sutton, that you regretted with all your heart?'

'Yes.'

Luke was startled by the unhesitating nature of the reply. He said, 'I do not mean those petty failings and peccadilloes that folk usually like to berate themselves for. I mean an action a man could truly regret his whole life through. An action so contemptible—'

'Yes,' Stephen cut in. 'That was what I meant too.' His clear grey eyes were fixed on Luke's face.

'Like betraying the person you care for most in the world?'

'Exactly.'

In spite of himself, Luke was curious. He knew Captain

Sutton only as a man of upright character, hardworking and reliable. Sophie's uncle was renowned for his unswerving honesty. Yet here he was admitting to dark betrayals.

He asked, 'Will you tell me?'

'No.'

But it was an amicable no.

The drink passed between them, back and forth. Stephen no longer minded the younger man's company.

Luke said, 'If you had your life to live through again, would you do anything in it differently?'

Stephen considered this carefully, then answered, 'How can one answer yes to such a question? If it was not possible to act in any other manner the first time, how would it be different a second time?'

'But it is a terrible thing to live with regret.'

'True.'

'A man might go crazy with the burden of it.'

Stephen sighed. He was well on the way to being satisfyingly drunk and he did not want to know the details of his niece's marriage, but the habit of caring for her happiness was too hard to be broken. At length he said, 'What is it you have done, Luke?'

'That is my business.' Luke was pale and his hands were shaking. Like Stephen, he had drunk far more than was his habit. He said belligerently, 'It concerns none but me.'

'And your wife.'

'And my wife.'

The drink was finished. Walking with the stiff attention of the inebriate, Stephen fetched more from the pantry. He sat down once more, refilled their glasses and said firmly, 'You must make amends.'

'Not possible,' slurred Luke. 'Too late for that.' Suddenly it was vitally important to him that Stephen understand the complexities of his position. He said, 'My father told me I was special, one of God's elect. I used to think that, really I did. But he was wrong. I learned that in the fighting. Sheep and goats, like it says in the Bible. I've done bad things. All my life, y'see, been a bad person. Evil, wicked, through and through. Didn't matter, though, because only me. But now there is

Sophie. Thought I had changed. Because of her. Then did the worst of all. A terrible thing.' He said the last words speaking into his glass, which he then emptied down his throat, frowning all the while.

Stephen, blearily, imagined a sexual lapse. He said, 'You must tell her you won't do it again.'

For some reason Luke appeared to find this hilariously funny. 'Not possible to do it *again*, even if I wanted to. Which, of course, I don't.'

'Never mind,' said Stephen. 'Sophie will get over it. She'll forgive you.'

'Oh, *yes*. No problem there. Forgiven already. Everyone forgives me.' Luke raised his hand to his eyes. 'It's the damned forgiveness that's worst of all.'

Stephen was baffled by this, so he said nothing. He poured himself more wine and watched Luke's eyes as they separated out and became four, then slid back through three into two again.

Luke announced, in the manner of someone making a discovery of huge importance, 'Must change! Show Sophie! Can be different! Not bad any more. Do something *good*!'

'Quite right.'

'One thing. Only one. Wipe out the bad. Make amends that way.'

'Excellent.'

'What can I do?'

'Can't imagine.'

Luke looked annoyed. 'Must be something I can do.'

There was a sudden commotion as Cary rolled over, crashed into the chair Stephen had placed against the settle and slithered on to the floor. Stephen and Luke watched the sequence, then, when all was quiet once again, they went over slowly to help her up.

'Like a crusade,' said Luke.

'Better put her to bed,' said Stephen.

Cary, her eyes still swimming with drink, squinted up at Stephen and said something quite remarkably obscene. Luke giggled. Together they stumbled with her to her bedchamber beside the kitchen.

'Poor Cary,' said Stephen, as he fumbled his way back to the kitchen.

'Don't worry about *her*,' said Luke earnestly. 'I'll find her husband – what's his name?'

'O'Rourke.'

'I'll bring him back.'

'Or his body,' said Stephen.

'Or his body.'

'Proper burial's important.'

They debated this truth over more wine. Then Stephen gripped both Luke's hands in his. 'Make Sophie happy,' he said. 'Don't throw it away, Luke. Got a good wife. Don't lose it. Don't know how lucky you are.'

'So lucky.' Luke began to weep. 'You should have a wife too, Captain Sutton.'

'Too late for me.' Stephen leaned back in his chair, releasing Luke's hands. His expression was bleak. 'Not possible anyway. Only one woman I ever wanted.'

'Doesn't she love you?'

'Yes. At least, I suppose she must do.' Stephen's words were slurred. 'Would have sent the necklace back otherwise.'

'Necklace?'

'It was a sign.'

'She loved you. You loved her.' Luke was putting the pieces together slowly. 'Then why didn't you—? Ah!' Illumination dawned. 'I understand you now. Married, eh?'

Stephen bowed his head in gloomy confirmation.

'Time to find another woman,' said Luke firmly. 'Can't spend your whole life waiting.'

'Maybe you're right. It's terrible to spend it alone.'

'I'll find you another wife.'

'Good. I'd like that.'

'Let's drink to that, then.'

And they did.

For months afterwards, the day of Sir Richard Treveryan's funeral was famous locally for the evening when Captain Stephen Sutton, the calm, sober, hardworking and upright Stephen Sutton, became quite heroically drunk.

Most people assumed he had been drowning his sorrows at Sir

Richard's death, but Biddy Firth, who heard the news from the boy who brought the medicine for her sick cow, decided his grief had been caused by the end of their liaison.

It was the best compliment she could ever remember.

Chapter Thirty-Three

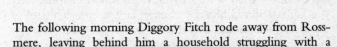

The following morning Diggory Fitch rode away from Ross-mere, leaving behind him a household struggling with a collective hangover of massive proportions.

When she awoke, Honor was alarmed by raised voices and the sound of scuffling. She peered round her bedchamber door only to see Louisa and Kip coming to blows at the top of the stairs because she had accused him of treading on her skirts. Francis, pale and puffy-eyed, could barely pull on his breeches without groaning. Most startling of all, Stephen appeared to have spent the night slumped at the kitchen table beside Luke; he was observed tipping a pail of ice-cold water over his head and shoulders in an effort to clear his brain. Alice did not make an appearance until late morning and Cary was too ill to stir from her bed.

Though Luke had drunk a fair amount, he was much less affected than Stephen by their carousing. If anything, it seemed to have acted on him like a thunderstorm after a period of hot weather; he was brisk and energetic, even cheerful. When he and Sophie departed for Porthew, the tension between them appeared to have eased.

Perdita also was unaffected. She had drunk only a small cup of wine. As always she was neatly turned out and composed; she had a final meeting with Diggory Fitch then set about the preparations for her own departure for Plymouth.

Edmund, who was suffering nothing worse than a headache and dry mouth, noted with approval her bright appearance when he came across her in the great hall. She was instructing

Amos to find Viney and bring him back to Rossmere at once. He had last been seen heading in the general direction of the alehouse, but Perdita intended him to switch his allegiance immediately to her and escort her back to Plymouth.

When she was finished, Edmund suggested that, as she was soon to quit Cornwall, they might take a turn together in the garden. Perdita agreed at once, pausing only to send for the black cloak Alice had lent her while her own mourning was being made up. As she came out of the house to join him, Edmund thought how very young she looked in the hideous black, like a child forced to dress in widow's weeds. Her youthfulness stirred him. By contrast he felt himself a man of the world, mature and powerful. It was an agreeable sensation and he was smiling as she approached.

They talked of matters autumnal until they had walked some distance from the house. Edmund knew that he did not always appear to advantage in the company of women – the image of Sophie's abhorrence was a recent reminder of this – and one of the things he liked about Perdita was that conversation always flowed smoothly between them. Her smiles and interested questions implied she found him a stimulating companion. He decided it was time to come to the point.

He said solemnly, 'Your father's death must be a grievous loss for you.'

'Indeed it is.'

'You have lost not only a father's love but also his protection.'

'He was everything a daughter could wish for,' said Perdita, with genuine emotion. She had already begun to overlay the imperfect reality of Richard's memory with the image of the father she had dreamed of during the years of his exile. She was mourning them both.

'It is a tragedy for you,' insisted Edmund.

'Yes.' Perdita was blinking back tears.

Edmund took her hand and tucked it in the crook of his arm. Through the layers of doublet, shirt, glove and cloak, he had the impression that her fingers were clinging tightly to his flesh. He said, 'You must never feel that you are completely alone.'

'Thank you, Master Menheire. I am fortunate to have so many good friends.'

'You will soon need someone who is more than a friend.'

The pressure of her hand against his arm increased slightly. Tension flowed through the thick layers of clothing between them. Swathed in her layers of funereal black, every inch of flesh and shape except for her watchful, narrow face shrouded and invisible, Perdita was still somehow vibrant. Edmund had a disturbing image of the movement of her legs and hips against the rustling of her petticoats.

They were walking along the gravel path that led down to the area devoted to ninepins and bowls, a place invisible from the house. Edmund looked down at her. Perdita continued to walk with her neat, short steps, her gaze fixed on the ground a few feet ahead of them, but two spots of colour had appeared on her cheeks and her eyes were very bright.

'More than a friend?' she asked.

'Much more.'

She was silent for a while, before saying quietly, 'My father has been in his grave less than twenty-four hours. It is too soon for me to consider anything more than friendship. But –' and here she softened her words with a smile in case they had sounded like a rebuke – 'I am grateful to you for your concern.'

'I understand. It is advisable to wait. But not for too long. Meanwhile, I hope you will think of me if you ever need help.'

'You are most generous.'

'In time,' said Edmund, who was by now congratulating himself on handling this whole conversation with rare finesse, 'I hope to be able to show you just how generous I can be.'

Perdita came to a halt. Edmund stopped also. She turned to face him. She was composed and, despite her reference to her father's death, she seemed almost to be enjoying herself. She said, 'Master Menheire, are you suggesting that there should be some kind of understanding between us?'

'Precisely.' He wondered if he should now seal their discussion with an embrace, but he was wary of repeating the errors committed with Sophie. 'Since you are so recently bereaved, it is improper to make any arrangements immediately, but I hope that in a few weeks—'

Smiling, she interrupted him. 'I confess I share your

impatience, but we could not possibly announce a betrothal until six months at least have passed.'

'Betrothal?' Edmund started backwards as if he'd just been stung by a bee.

'I thought that was what—'

'Certainly not!'

'Then I do not understand . . .' Her smile faded. She frowned and said, 'I was under the impression, sir, that you were saying you wished eventually to marry me, even though my present circumstances mean the need for delay.'

'My dear Mistress Treveryan, you surely cannot have thought I was talking of marriage. Your circumstances, as you call them, make the whole idea of marriage quite impossible.'

'What?'

'I was offering you my protection.'

Now it was Perdita's turn to step back. 'Your *protection*!'

Edmund was puzzled by her reaction. 'There is no reason to be affronted. I am suggesting just such an arrangement as that which existed between Sir Richard and your mother. You, of all people, cannot object to that. Only consider. While your father was alive, you enjoyed privileges uncommon for a young woman of your dubious status. You will find his death has changed all that. People made an exception for you, but only because of him. A case in point: your step-mother is hardly going to continue the pretence of treating you like her own daughter now. If you refuse my offer, who else will you have to turn to?'

'Do you seriously expect me even to contemplate the possibility of becoming your mistress? Of becoming an object of scandal?'

'There is no need to regard it as scandal. You have been enough in town to know that mistresses are all the fashion now. There is no shame in it for you – and much to be gained. You have been fortunate up till now, but without a powerful father to shield you, you will find the world a dangerous and cruel place.'

'Sweet heavens, Master Menheire, you have a strange way of wooing. I suggest you learn some manners before you dare to speak to me again.'

'I need no lessons in civility,' he said stiffly, 'especially not from the likes of you.'

Perdita was shaking with rage but she restrained herself and said, 'I do not wish to quarrel with you, sir. We have both been labouring under a misapprehension. I thought that you admired me—'

'Of course I do, dear girl. That is why—'

'And that you wished to make me your wife.'

'Impossible!'

'Then our conversation is at an end.'

She turned and began to walk swiftly towards the house, but Edmund strode after her and caught her by the arm. 'Mistress Treveryan, Perdita, wait. You are angry now, but that simply proves how sheltered you have been by your father's protection. Do not make a decision you are sure to regret later. The world is full of men who are less scrupulous than I am, who take what they want without asking. They will be quick to take advantage of your orphan state.'

'Do not dare to threaten me!' She shook him off. 'My father may be dead, but thank God, I am not altogether without friends in this world.'

'Who? That fellow who calls himself your brother? A tradesman? How do you imagine he can help you?'

'I do not count him. I have two other brothers, but I was not thinking of them either. Sir Francis and his family have come to regard me as one of them.'

This time Edmund laughed. 'The Suttons? Please, Mistress Treveryan, do not place your faith in a family who are sure to be ruined and turned from their home before another year is over.'

'How can that be?' Perdita was so startled that she forgot her own rage in a genuine desire to learn the truth.

Edmund blustered, a man who knew he had let slip too much. 'They are so improvident. Sure to bring about their own ruin.' He returned to the attack. 'Besides, they did not even stop their own cook from insulting you last night. What kind of protection do you think you can expect from them?'

Perdita made a superhuman effort to control herself as she said, 'I am grateful to you for your concern for my safety, but I assure you, it is very much misplaced. Maybe it seems laughable for me to expect an honest marriage but, believe me, I will settle for nothing less. You might be less quick to mock me if you knew the terms of my father's will.'

'He has left you wealthy? I am glad of that, for your sake, but it makes no difference to me.'

'Not just wealthy.' There was a gleam of malice in Perdita's eyes as she continued, 'I am sure you are aware, Master Menheire, that the legality of your father's claim to Trecarne has long been open to doubt. While Parliament ruled, the claims of Royalists did not stand a chance. Now that England has a Stuart king once more all that is changed. You may be interested to know, sir, that my father left his claim on Trecarne to me, and me alone.'

Edmund smiled his contempt. 'A meaningless bequest, I'm afraid, which is probably why he left it to you and not to his wife or legitimate heirs. You delude yourself if you think otherwise. Our claim is good enough for the Cornish courts. No one here would dare to turn us from our home for the sake of a dead man's bastard.'

'What a very eloquent turn of phrase you have, to be sure. And maybe if it was only a matter for the law you might be right. But His Majesty, as you yourself pointed out just now, is more broad-minded in his opinions. One of the last actions of my dear father's life was to draw up a petition requesting King Charles to restore Trecarne to him – or to his designated heir. I think His Majesty might well favour the family of a man who made such sacrifices for the royal cause, don't you agree?'

Edmund stared at her in stunned silence. Then, 'This – this is preposterous!' he sputtered.

'Is it?'

She was smiling up at him. Hands folded in front of her. Very composed.

He stared.

She said mildly, 'A long court case would surely be ruinous to all concerned. However, if the petition is successful then only your family will face ruin. What a pity it is that you were so contemptuous of the amicable solution to our difficulties which I thought you were suggesting. Now, if you will excuse me, I must prepare for my journey to Plymouth. Where my dear mother, contrary to your cynical view of matters, will be awaiting my arrival with all impatience. In her hour of bereavement, she will especially value the comforts of her only daughter. Good day, Master Menheire. You will have to complete your walk without me.'

This time, when she started back towards the house, Edmund made no attempt to stop her.

Her composure lasted all the way back to the house, through the hall and up the stairs. Only when she was safely in the privacy of her chamber, with the door closed firmly behind her, did she give way to the rage she had been struggling so hard to rein back.

How dare he? *How dare he!*

She tore off her cloak, her gloves and flung them across the room. Was this the kind of insult she must expect the very day after her father was laid to rest? Was it really true that he had been all that stood between her and the contempt of every man whose attention she might attract? How dare Edmund stand before her and cold-bloodedly tell her that the best she could ever hope for was to be a wealthy man's mistress, without the respect of society or the security of marriage?

Her only comfort was the memory of his stupefaction when she told him of her father's petition.

She only wished it was true.

In the final draft of his will, her father had indeed stipulated that if ever King Charles saw fit to restore Trecarne to his heirs, then Perdita was to have it, but Diggory Fitch had made it clear that both men had thought this unlikely.

The lawyer had mentioned that morning that just before he died Sir Richard had considered petitioning the King, but had not yet begun the process. In the heat of the moment, faced with Edmund's blind certainty and her own panic as all her worst fears were realised, Perdita had converted the thought into a fact. Whatever the risks, it had been worth it, she was sure, to see the satisfaction wiped off his face.

As she journeyed towards Plymouth, Perdita had plenty of time to reflect on her conversation with Edmund. It was several days before she could remember her own naïve hopefulness without her cheeks flaming with embarrassment. For a while she was certain that she never wanted to see the hateful man as long as she lived. But there was a core of rage inside her that refused to be so easily defeated.

By the time she was once more in Kitty's house and her mother was absorbed in choosing the finest black silks and velvets for their mourning clothes, Perdita's courage reasserted itself. There was only one way to wipe out the memory of her humiliation.

Edmund Menheire was not going to be allowed to escape so easily. He had said that he admired her; half the battle was already won. The more she thought about it, the more determined she became.

The man who had insulted her by coolly suggesting she should put herself under his protection and become his whore, must be made one day to go down on bended knee and beg her to be his lawful, honoured wife.

'Why were you asking Cary all those questions?'

Sophie had come through to the shop just as Luke was measuring out some lengths of cloth to be delivered the next day to the draper at Penryn. He leaned the yardstick against the cutting table and said, without looking up, 'Questions?'

His evasion only increased Sophie's suspicions. She had waited until she heard John Taylor leave for the evening before seeking Luke out. In this darkening season of the year, there were few customers once the sun had set and little reason to keep the old man from his own fireside.

She said, 'All about Tilsbury and O'Rourke and the wars and Cary's life. Why are you interested in all of that?'

'I know you're fond of the woman. No particular reason.'

Sophie folded her arms and prepared to wait. She knew Luke well enough to know he was lying, but she did not know why. Mercurial as ever, he had changed yet again since the evening of Sir Richard Treveryan's wake.

She had thought at the time that anything would be preferable to the anguished guilt that had tortured him since his fight with Sir Richard, but now she was not so sure. He was courteous towards her and even-tempered; they made music together and they made love; he still talked about the house they would build in the spring. Yet all the time she could feel him slipping away from her, growing more distant with each day that passed.

'You were asking Uncle Stephen questions as well.'

'Yes. He is a fine man. I can see now why you have always been so devoted to him.' He laid down the scissors and began to fold a length of cloth.

It was Luke's present calm that was so difficult to bear. It was a calm that excluded her completely. Resisting the impulse to tackle him, Sophie cast around for some more neutral topic. She said, 'Perdita must have reached Plymouth by now.'

'Probably.'

'Do you think she'll come back?'

'Doesn't that depend on Master Menheire?'

He looked up and smiled at her as their eyes met.

'Cary says there's a rumour Sir Richard left her his claim to Trecarne,' she said. 'Do you think that's true?'

'Maybe, but it won't do her much good. A lifetime of litigation would not shift the Menheires. Treveryan must have known that.'

They discussed the fluctuating fortunes of their neighbours for a while and Sophie began to feel more easy with him than she had since Sir Richard's death. When Luke had finished wrapping the cloth that was to be sent to Penryn, he came over and put his hands on her waist. She felt, as always, the quickening of excitement at his nearness. He kissed her gently on the bridge of her nose, then her mouth. He said, 'It may be that I have to go away for a while.'

'Why?' She had been expecting something like this.

'I have some business to do in Plymouth. The stocks are falling low and—'

'No, Luke. Tell me the real reason.'

'I told you—'

'Is it to do with Treveryan?'

His expression hardened. His eyes searched her face, then he turned and crossed the room to the cutting table and began briskly to put things away.

Sophie followed him. 'How long will you be gone?'

'A couple of months.'

'So long!'

'I'll be back by Easter.'

'But that is *six* months away!'

'So . . .'

'Why must you go now? Why not wait until the spring when travelling is easier?'

'I cannot.'

Sophie felt chilled to the bone. She said slowly, 'You do not plan to come back at all, not ever. You are leaving, and all because of me.'

'No!' He spun round and gripped her shoulders. 'No, Sophie, you could not be more wrong. I will come back, I promise, but only when—'

'Yes?'

'When I have done something that will make you proud of me.'

'I don't understand. I'm proud of you now.'

'That's just words, it does not make it true. You must despise me for all the harm I've done to people. I must do something to make amends. You have given me your love, but it does not seem that I have any right to it, I've never earned it. Can you understand that?'

'No. You make it sound like a ledger, like one of your sets of accounts.'

'You're a tradesman's wife,' he said, with a rueful smile. 'That's how I understand things.'

She smothered her shock and asked, 'What do you plan to do?'

'First of all, I want to find out what happened to Cary's husband. He may still be alive somewhere but without the money to return. Only try to imagine if I could fetch him back to Rossmere for her!'

Sophie laughed, in spite of herself. 'You're surely not going to Barbados, are you?'

'Not if I can help it. There's plenty to be done nearer home. The Menheires have business dealings in the east of the county. I intend to find out all I can about that. They still have designs on

456

Rossmere, I'm sure of it, but I cannot understand why they want it so badly. Besides, every family has secrets to hide. If I can uncover some of theirs, it may help Sir Francis in his battles with them. Your brother thinks you've married a nobody, and maybe he is right, but he'll have to change his mind if I find a way to save his family from ruin.'

'Do you really think you can do that?'

'I can try.'

'I'd rather you stay here with me.'

'I'll be doing everything for you.'

'But that doesn't make sense. I hate it here when you're gone.'

'Then go back to Rossmere. I'll be easier in my mind knowing you're with your family.'

'How soon are you planning to leave?'

'In two days. It is all arranged.'

Now Sophie understood the secrecy and the evasions. She was confused, sick at heart at the thought of the long separation, but also glimpsing how much this journey meant to him. Less than a month married, and already he had found a reason to leave her.

Yet she believed him when he said he loved her.

On the evening before his departure, as they lay together in the darkness, Luke said, 'My mother loved the old stories – all those gods and goddesses who carried on no better than a pack of travelling rogues. There was one I liked, a fellow by the name of Hercules. He went mad, as I remember, and killed his wife and children. Then the gods gave him all these tasks to do to make amends. One of his jobs was to clean out the biggest stable full of horse shit there ever was since the world began.'

'That's simple, then, Luke. No need to go off on your wanderings at all. Uncle Stephen can give you a pitchfork, there's always plenty of that kind of work at Rossmere.'

'I'm serious, Sophie.'

'I know. Did the gods bring his wife back to him when he was done?'

'No, they couldn't do that. They made him immortal, I think.'

'Is that what you want, then?' she asked. 'To be immortal?'

'I'll settle for this life.'

'They say that having children is a kind of immortality.'

'The very best kind. I hope we have a score.'

He rolled on his side and propped his head on one hand. With the other he touched the weight and fall of her breasts, the warm mound of her belly. Then he dipped his head and closed his lips around the swelling fullness of her nipple, caressing it with his tongue until she felt such a surge of pleasure that she said, 'Oh, Luke, don't go!'

'I must, you know I must.' He kissed her gently on the mouth, then said, 'I feel such a lame, shabby creature for all the bad I've done. You know I'll miss you. I'll miss you every day, but our real life together will begin when I come back.'

'I thought it began when we went to the horse fair. I thought it began when we married. Isn't this real, here and now?'

He did not answer. He was moving to come on top of her. She could see the outline of his shoulders in the pale light from the moon beyond the window, the dark hair falling across his forehead.

She said, 'Is there nothing might make you change your mind?'

'Nothing.'

She reached up and kissed him fiercely, knowing how long it might be before she held his lean body in her arms again. She made love to him with a slow and deliberate passion, as though she could seal the press and thrust of his flesh on hers, as though she might store up such a harvest of loving that it would help her to endure the barren winter months ahead. Almost as if it might be for the last time.

The following day Luke left Porthew soon after sunrise. By early afternoon, Sophie was riding on a borrowed pony down the lime avenue to Rossmere.

As she entered the house, Francis appeared at the top of the stairs. 'Sophie! What brings you here?'

'Luke has gone away for a while.'

She had been dreading the moment of explanation, but Francis was so distracted that he did not notice the strangeness of their separation, only its convenience.

'Thank the Lord,' he said. 'I was going to send for you anyway.'

'Why? What is the matter?'

'It is Honor. She is so distressed that I can do nothing with her. I cannot make it out at all, but if I so much as mention sending for a doctor she becomes hysterical.'

'Is she ill? Oh, never mind, Francis. I'll go and see for myself.'

Suddenly it felt to Sophie as if she had never been away, as if Luke and the horse fair and Porthew and the new home they planned to build together had never even existed. Rossmere was folding her in its dramas and rhythms, the beat and flap of doves' wings rising in a cloud beyond the window, the smell of faded tapestries and the touch of wooden floors polished to a ripple by generations of feet.

Honor was in her bedchamber. Standing sideways to a small looking-glass she had propped against a chest, she was smoothing her skirts down over her hips.

Barely glancing at Sophie she said, 'Do you think I have narrow hips, Sophie? Cary says she has never seen hips so small as mine but only once. She says that time the woman was so long in labour that both she and the baby were like to die . . . She says the doctors tried to break her bones to let the baby out but they could not so they took a saw and began to—'

'Honor, that's enough now,' said Sophie firmly, catching hold of her sister-in-law before she fainted away with the sheer terror of it. 'You should know better than to listen to Cary's stories – you know what she is like. Why, I remember once I had a splinter under the skin of my thumb and before she picked it out Cary had told me of a woman whose whole hand had turned green, and then her arm . . . Dear heavens, never listen to Cary.'

'But she seems to know so much. And my hips *are* narrow. Look, just place your hands on mine. See? There is hardly any width there at all.' Honor had seized hold of Sophie's hands and laid them against her hips, but she was gripping her so tightly that her own chilly fingers were white with the strain.

'Honor,' said Sophie, very slowly and carefully, 'are you with child?'

Honor gave a scream and her eyes, wide with shock, rolled backwards under her lids. 'No!' she shrieked. 'No, I cannot bear it! I'm not strong enough! I shall die, I know it, I know it! Help me – help me to get rid of it! I cannot do it, oh, Sophie, I can't, I can't! You must help me!'

Sophie hardly knew whether to laugh or be angry. No wonder poor Honor had been so affected by Cary's usual tales of dismemberment and agonising death. She soothed her as best she could, but Honor was in the grip of an all-consuming terror. Alerted by the sound of his wife's screams, Francis had come to stand in the doorway.

'What ails her?' he asked, looking in anguish at his bedraggled, shivering wife.

Sophie smiled. 'Come and comfort her, Francis. This is your doing.'

'Mine?'

'God willing, you are going to be a father.'

'Is that why . . .'

Sophie nodded. Perplexed and anxious, Francis came and put an arm around his wife's shoulders. She tried to push him away, then clung to him, sobbing hysterically.

Sophie moved away, took off her hat and cloak and laid them on the edge of the bed. She said, 'By my reckoning, your child must be due some time around midsummer. Do not be so downhearted, Honor. At least you are going to have company in your ordeal. And maybe it will not be so bad after all. Not for either of us.'

Francis raised his eyes over the top of his wife's trembling head and looked at his sister questioningly.

'That's right,' said Sophie. 'If all goes well, there'll be two lusty babies in the family by midsummer next.'

PART THREE

Luke
May 1662

Chapter Thirty-Four

The woman he had travelled so far to see stood near the fireplace in the main chamber of a well-appointed house in the Gloucestershire town of Tilsbury.

Luke had no need of the family portrait dominating the room to know that Mistress Taverner had once been a remarkably good-looking woman. The evidence was before him now. Her black hair was streaked with grey, but her figure was still good and her fine-boned face strikingly handsome. Above all, it was the eyes that attracted: strange eyes that skewed the face away from classic beauty. Dark eyes a man might spend a lifetime trying to forget.

Luke was astonished and intrigued. When, on the night of Sir Richard Treveryan's wake more than six months before, he had persuaded Stephen to recount some of the details of his time as a garrison commander – far more, Luke was certain, than had ever been divulged to anyone else – he had formed a mental image of the woman being described with such reverence. He thought she might have been attractive once, in a pallid, girlish way, but undoubtedly by now she would have sunk into a plump and dowdy middle age. Nothing was further from the truth. Mistress Taverner must be over forty, but she held his gaze more proudly than many a much younger woman.

She had not invited him to sit, nor offered him any refreshment. She was looking at him very intently.

'You say you come from Rossmere?' Her voice was deep, attractively husky, and still carried traces of her foreign origins.

'Yes, it is in Cornwall.'

'I know where it is,' she told him. She remained silent for a while. Her eyes had dropped to look at a patch of sunlight, but he had the impression that she was looking with her inner eye at something visible to her alone. He glanced once more at the portrait: the painter, though not especially gifted, had been trying to pin down that very expression, inward-looking, remote and austere.

He said, 'I have recently married Mistress Sophie Sutton.'

'Sutton?'

'Stephen Sutton's niece.'

'Ah, yes. He spoke once of his brother's family.'

'He has been like a father to them, so they say.'

She tilted her chin with just a hint of defiance as she said, 'So Captain Sutton has been talking about me?'

'We were drunk when he spoke to me. And I am sure he has never talked of you to anyone before. You may be assured that he said nothing that was not to your credit.'

'And he said?'

'That you were beautiful. I thought he was exaggerating but—'

'What else?'

'That you were not English, had come from some foreign country to be married here when you were barely out of childhood. I thought he said Germany, but maybe I was mistaken.'

'I was born in Spain. My father joined the Spanish army in Germany. That was where I met my husband.'

'Stephen also said that he had loved you.'

She drew in a sharp breath, then turned away and walked towards the window. Luke was unable to see her face when she asked, 'Why did he tell you to come here?'

'He did not send me. He does not even know I am here.'

'Then why did you come?'

'I want to help him.'

She turned. 'Help him? How?'

Luke hesitated. Mistress Taverner had not tried to conceal that there had been some kind of liaison between them when Captain Sutton was commander of the garrison in Tilsbury, but even so he was aware that he was treading on dangerous ground.

464

He said carefully, 'From what Captain Sutton told me, I gather that there once existed some kind of – some kind of understanding between you. He was not at all specific, but he did say that was the reason he has never married.'

'He is not married?'

Her question was just a fraction too eager, but Luke pretended not to have noticed as he continued smoothly, 'No. As I say, I gained the impression that he felt he was still under some obligation to you, which stops him from making any arrangements of his own. His thoughts have recently turned towards marriage.'

She drew in a quick breath. 'Who is the woman?'

'There is no one in particular, not yet.'

'But there must be someone who has attracted his attention?'

'Not that I know of. We were very drunk, but I am sure marriage was only mentioned in the abstract, as something he might aspire to. I believe he said merely that he was tired of being a bachelor.'

She was thoughtful. 'I see. And now he wishes to find a wife.'

'Exactly. But he is prevented by the idea that he remains bound by some obligation to yourself.'

'How can that be? You must have misunderstood, Master Hollar. Perhaps you were more drunk even than you remember. Whatever happened once, I was a married woman, he can feel no obligation to me.'

'He mentioned a necklace . . .'

Her hand flew up to touch her throat. It was covered by a plain white falling band. An item of jewellery might easily be obscured beneath it. Mistress Taverner's costume was in the old style and could not have been simpler. Despite her evident wealth, she wore no ornaments, not even a ring. Yet the young woman in the portrait was as richly adorned as a young infanta.

'You have it still?'

Her hand fell to her side. 'Maybe. I do not know. I will have to search for it.'

'Thank you,' said Luke. He wondered why she was troubling to lie about the whereabouts of the necklace when she had made no attempt to deny its significance. 'If I take it with me back to

Cornwall, I am sure Captain Sutton will feel he can begin to look for a wife.'

'Of course. He should have married years ago, I dare say. He must have the necklace again.'

'I am lodging tonight at the Lion. I'll return in the morning.'

'I am sure I will be able to find it by then.'

There was a clamour in the hallway, a man's voice calling for ale and food. Luke had had enough difficulty with jealous husbands in the past to have an instinctive urge to avoid Master Taverner.

'I have taken up enough of your time.'

'There is no hurry. The cook can see to his needs.'

'But I am sure that your husband . . .'

'My husband?' She turned to him with a smile, the first he had seen, an extraordinary smile, sad and bitter, yet with a trace of mischief in it too. 'That Master Taverner is my son. My husband died five years ago.'

After Luke had gone, Dolores Taverner retreated, as she always did when troubled, to her stillroom. She inhaled the rich, sweet smell of flower waters and charcoal, spices and bruised leaves, all familiar and calming.

She ran her fingers along the rows of jars and gallipots. There were potions and remedies for every affliction: medicine to ward off the plague, ointments for burns and cuts, infusions for green sickness and fevers, for colic and constipation, gout and head-aches. There were even some drops – she had used them once to good effect – that induced a sleep so profound that for several hours nothing could wake the sleeper. But among all her famous battery of medication, there was no panacea to make a soul forget.

Was that really what she wanted? No, not forgetfulness. She had hoarded her memories as jealously as her husband hoarded his jewels and gold coins. Resignation, then, maybe that was what she sought, a calm acceptance that the past is a place which has vanished for ever and can only be revisited in dreams.

She had been unprepared for Luke Hollar's arrival. He had turned up in her home quite out of the blue just when she was putting cowslips to steep in a crock of warm water. As soon as he began to speak, she had guessed he must be from Stephen: that same Cornish resonance to his voice that she had not heard in years, that gentle sing-song, questioning accent that swept her back in an instant to the summer of 1645 when the Royalist soldiers had garrisoned the town and one of them had captured her heart.

Her first thought was that Stephen had died, that he had sent this emissary with some final deathbed message. She had nerved herself to hear the worst. But, no, he must be in good health for he was thinking of marriage. It was something, anyway, to know that he thought of her sometimes and even remembered her with affection. She had always assumed he must have forgotten her long since.

All unconscious of what she was doing she raised her hand and touched the ridge of metal that lay across her throat. Stephen had given it to her as a pledge of his love, and she had promised never to return it so long as she still loved him.

At the time he had said that he would always love her; at the time, she had believed him. All the foolish talk and promises that lovers make – but she was sorry now that it had prevented him from finding happiness in his far-off Cornish home. Seventeen years. Too long, much too long. How typical of Stephen, with his dogged honesty and loyalty, to feel bound by it till now.

It struck her as strange that Master Hollar had come such a long way on his eccentric errand. There was something unusual, secretive about him and she had only half believed him when he said he had business in the neighbourhood and thought that he might as well pay her a visit and do his new wife's uncle a favour at the same time . . .

She would ask him in the morning. Suddenly she realised what a great deal there was she wanted to know. She must be careful not to waste this chance, there was certain never to be another. Luke Hollar could tell her about Stephen, about his present life and all that had happened to him since they parted. That would be something for her to treasure. And was there any message that she wanted him to take to Stephen? Only that she was well and contented and hoped that he found happiness too.

She must find a way to convey to him that she had been more

fortunate than anyone could have expected, given the circumstances of her early life. At his death, her husband had left her well provided for. Though she was always going to be treated with the wariness due to an outsider, she was respected locally and had no enemies. Her four children had all survived into adulthood. Of course, it was a shame that Beth's home was now so far away – she had married a Somerset man – but it was good to know that she was settled and, so far as Dolores knew, reasonably happy. The two younger boys were both away from home too: Pip had joined the army. He had never shaken off the excitement of those months when all their lives had been turned upside down by the garrison. Robert, who had been a baby then, was now a young man of seventeen, studying at the Inner Temple. A lawyer to his fingertips already.

For a while, it was true, she had mourned their going. But Harry had remained at home to continue his father's business and his young wife was expecting their first child in the autumn. She was sure that once the house echoed to the laughter and cries of children again, the melancholy she so often endured was likely to ease.

And if Harry was grown rather too much like his father for her comfort, and if his bride often seemed to her like an empty-headed, quarrelsome girl – well, these were minor vexations.

Her life had turned out much smoother than she had ever dared to hope and she was sorry that loyalty to the love they once shared had prevented Stephen from having children of his own. She remembered his gentleness and care with hers: Beth, in particular, had adored him and on one occasion at least he had saved Pip's life.

Yes, she had much to be grateful for. Once again, she touched the bump of the necklace around her throat. Tomorrow, then, she must give it to Master Hollar so he might return it to Stephen. That would be a proper conclusion to the secret passion there had once been between the Cornish captain far from home and another man's Spanish-born wife.

The tap room at the Lion was spacious and comfortable. Like all the main buildings in Tilsbury, like the Priory House where

Luke had just left Mistress Taverner, it reflected the wealth of the area, wealth derived from the wool trade. Sheep and fleeces and cloth, the riches at the heart of England.

Luke ordered a pot of the best ale and a shilling dinner, then went through to the garden at the back of the inn and settled on a bench in the sun. A songthrush was serenading him from a may tree. He was well pleased with his morning's work. Now that the last of the tasks he had set himself was almost accomplished, he began to look forward to returning to Cornwall. Already he had been away longer than he had planned and he was impatient to be united with Sophie again.

The delay was partly because it had taken much longer than he had expected to find reliable information about O'Rourke. During the autumn he had combed all the ports and harbours from Penryn to Dawlish, asking for news of the Irishman in every place where sailors gather. One or two remembered O'Rourke from when he was captured and awaiting transportation to Barbados, but no one knew what had happened to him after that. Luke began to fear he must have perished almost at once and that no one had survived to tell his tale.

In December, in a rain-lashed tavern near Exmouth, he at last encountered a young mariner in the final stages of a consumptive illness. Yes, he had known O'Rourke, had known him well. The Irishman had befriended him on the hellish voyage to Barbados and had helped him to survive those first terrible months on the plantations. But by the time conditions improved, O'Rourke's health was broken. A year ago they had set out together on the voyage home, but O'Rourke had died in mid-Atlantic and his weighted body was cast into the sea.

This was not the news Luke had been planning to send back as his first gift to the household at Rossmere. A novice in the ways of helping people, he decided to improve on the truth. He stayed with the young consumptive until his death, then oversaw his burial and had a simple stone placed on the grave. He wrote to Sophie to inform Cary that O'Rourke had indeed died, but peacefully, with Luke beside him and that his last words were of his wife and daughter. In case the widow ever happened to make a pilgrimage to her husband's last resting place, Luke paid for O'Rourke's name to be inscribed on the new gravestone.

It was the best he could do, but it was not enough. If Luke had been able to convey O'Rourke back to Rossmere in person, he might have been content to return then. But news of a death, however cleverly the dismal reality was disguised, was hardly the kind of triumph he'd had in mind when he made his drunken promise to Stephen.

His enquiries about the Menheires, which he had been conducting at the same time, had yielded some interesting results. In order to find out more, he travelled to London in the New Year and befriended a couple of merchants who dealt in Cornish tin. This exercise was equally fruitful and Luke was on the point of returning to Cornwall when he fell ill with a fever that left him so weakened it was over a month before he could contemplate travelling again.

Since he was already in London it needed only a small detour to visit Tilsbury on his way back to the West Country. It was useful professionally too. He made contact with a Gloucester cloth merchant with whom he would have direct dealings in future. From there it was less than a day's easy journey through the spring countryside to visit the mysterious Mistress Taverner of whom Stephen had spoken so warmly that night. Perhaps it would prove possible to release him from whatever promises had prevented him until now from finding a wife of his own.

Luke was not entirely motivated by his desire to see Stephen happy, nor even by an urge to impress Sophie and her family. He was aware of the deep bonds of affection that existed between uncle and niece and he could not help being jealous. He wanted Sophie for himself alone, and to that end he wished Captain Sutton to be occupied with a wife and family of his own.

And in Tilsbury he thought he might gather useful information. Wherever there were secrets, Luke knew there were opportunities: all his life he had collected secrets as other men gathered money or land. He had hardly ever had cause to threaten anyone directly with disclosure; usually it was enough to let a man know that his secrets had been uncovered.

Not that he ever expected to want to use that kind of information against Stephen Sutton – he liked and respected the man and would have been happy to call him a friend – but, still, the old habits were not easy to break. Stephen could well be a useful ally at Rossmere one day, so it was only going to be to his advantage to know more about his past than anyone else.

By late afternoon Luke had spoken with a number of people in the town who were glad to share their memories of the summer months of 1645. All spoke of the young Cornish captain with affection and respect. There was no hint of any impropriety between him and any woman of the town: clearly he had covered his tracks well.

That evening he also paid a visit to the farm where Cary's brothers still lived and worked the land. He looked forward to telling Cary all her family's news. Her goodwill might well come in useful one day.

He went to bed after an excellent supper, well satisfied with his day's work. That night, however, he was troubled by several bad dreams. In the last one he and Sophie were walking together on the cliffs above Porthew. She turned to say something to him, but he did not catch her words and he asked her to repeat them. This time when she answered she was moving away from him. She reached out her arms; he tried to grasp hold of her, but he was not quick enough. He tried again, but she was sliding towards the cliff edge. As she realised the increasing danger she called to him to help her. He ran to her, caught hold of her hands. They slithered from his fingers. She fell, endlessly falling, and there was nothing he could do to stop her.

When he awoke he was sobbing and his body was soaked in sweat. For once there was no relief in the knowledge that it had been only a dream. Fearing that it had been a portent of disaster, he was gripped by a passionate desire to return with all haste to Cornwall.

'Master Hollar, it is fortunate I am an early riser or you'd have been obliged to wait.'

'I leave for Cornwall this morning. If I make good time I can reach Bristol tonight.'

'Then you must be all impatience. I promise not to keep you long.'

This time Mistress Taverner was prepared for his visit. Food and drink had been set on a side table. More importantly, a simple chain necklace was visible over the linen collar she wore across her throat and shoulders.

'Yes, as you see I found it,' she said, following the direction of his gaze. 'It was lying forgotten at the bottom of a box of trinkets. It is a thing of no value at all. I cannot imagine why I have kept it for so long.'

Luke was amused. Like all inexperienced liars, Mistress Taverner made the mistake of being too elaborate in her deceits. He did not hold it against her. If anything she struck him as more beautiful today even than on first sight. There was a poise and animation about her, a vitality that was almost feverish. It is remarkable, he thought, how the memory of a past intrigue can rejuvenate a woman.

He said politely, 'I am sure Captain Sutton will be pleased to know that you kept his memento for so long.'

She was looking at him very directly. She said, 'Captain Sutton was a man of remarkable qualities.'

'So he is now.'

'Yes, you must tell me all about him. Will you take some ale?'

'Thank you, but I have breakfasted already, since I was hoping—'

'Yes, of course, to be in Bristol this evening. You are impatient. But you must stay just a little longer. There is so much I want to ask you. Tell me about Captain Sutton. Is he bald now? Does he have a beard? How do you like him?'

'He is not bald and he is clean-shaven and I like him well enough. I do not suppose he has an enemy anywhere.' Luke saw that she would be happy to while away the entire day in reminiscences. An image of Sophie came into his mind, Sophie as she had been in the dream. Sophie slipping for ever from his grasp. He said quickly, 'If you would be so good as to give me the necklace, Mistress Taverner, I have a long day's ride ahead of me.'

'Certainly. I have no right to detain you. I shall give you this at once and then you can go.' She put her fingers on the chain, as though to remove it, then swung quickly away from him, saying, 'Is it true that our old servant Cary is in Cornwall too?'

'Cary? The woman with the scarred face? Yes indeed. I don't know how the Suttons would manage without her.'

'She is a good worker?'

'She does the work of ten. Or so you'd think if you listened to her.'

She laughed. 'And does she still tell tales fit to make your hair stand on end?'

'Frequently. Sophie told me some terrible story about a ghost who helped to free a pack of soldiers. I didn't believe a word of it. At Rossmere any impossibly tall tale is called a "Cary story".'

'I can imagine. She was only a girl fresh off the farm when she worked here. I put her in a room with two of my children because I thought they needed company while the house was full of soldiers — mercy be, what a mistake. Poor Beth had nightmares for months because of Cary's bedtime stories. Mind you, I was too blind to notice what was happening under my own roof. It was your Captain Sutton who suggested the possible cause.' She looked at him with sudden wistfulness as she added, 'He must be much loved by his brother's children.'

'I believe he is.'

'Please tell him that mine are all well. Harry remains at home, as you know. Beth is married and has gone to live in Somerset. Robert — I don't suppose he even remembers Robert, who was just a baby — he is studying law in London. And Pip, you must tell him that Pip likes to be called Philip now that he's a man. He has gone away to be a soldier. I had a letter from him last year. He was in France. Stephen will like to hear about Pip.'

'I will tell him about them all. And now—'

She interrupted him, 'What about Cary? Does she have children?'

'A daughter. I think her name is Het. Cary's husband was an Irishman but he was captured after Penruddock's rebellion and he died a year ago.' Luke paused before adding thoughtfully, 'He is buried near Exmouth.'

Mistress Taverner bowed her head. 'O'Rourke, I remember him. Poor Cary. I am so sorry. Maybe I can give you something for her. I might find an old shawl of Beth's. I know Beth would like Cary to have it.'

'I am afraid there is no time. Cary is well cared for by the Suttons.'

'Well, then. And that is something.' She lapsed into silence. She seemed lost in thought.

Luke saw there was to be no rushing this meeting, but he thought he might be able to jog matters along, so he said, 'I noticed that you have rosemary growing by the side of the path. If you wanted to put some in with the necklace . . .'

'The herb of remembrance, an excellent idea. I shall do that at once.' She was brisk once more and Luke saw his chances of reaching Bristol that evening increase. 'There now, help yourself to food and drink, it will fortify you for the journey. I shall be only a short while, and then I promise I'll detain you no more. I must find a bag or purse to put the chain in, together with the rosemary. I should have thought of it myself. Thank you, Master Hollar. Rosemary for remembrance . . .'

Before Luke could protest, she had hurried from the room. However, she was as good as her word and returned a few minutes later, a spray of grey-green rosemary and an embroidered purse in her hand.

'Here you are, some rosemary, just as you suggested,' she said.

'And do you have a message for him?'

'There is no need. The necklace says it all.' She put her hand on the chain and smiled at him. 'What a simple, worthless trinket to carry such a weight of memories!'

'I am sure. May I take it now?'

'Certainly. Let me just . . .' She dipped her head forward in the gesture women make when they are about to remove a necklace and Luke observed that she had a fine neck, elegant and pale. She raised her arms and took hold of the chain. Then she paused. Her breathing was suddenly grown very rapid and shallow.

Luke asked, 'Is something wrong?'

'No, nothing. Nothing at all. It is just . . .' But her hands were trembling.

'Can I help you?'

'Yes, if you would. I'd be grateful . . .'

But as Luke lifted his hands, she moved swiftly away. 'No, wait. I think maybe there is a fault with the catch.'

He waited.

She sank down on a chair and turned her face away from him. Then she took hold of the chain and pulled it taut, running it back and forth between her long fingers. 'I never knew parting with it would be so difficult,' she said, and Luke saw that her eyes were swimming with tears.

He gave up all hope of Bristol. He drew up a low chair and sat down in front of her before asking quietly, 'Why? What exactly does it mean?'

'Oh, nothing. Only . . .' She smiled at him through her tears. 'Did Stephen not tell you? Well, Master Hollar, I'm sure you know the kind of foolish promises lovers make. For we were lovers. Did he tell you that? I expect you guessed. I don't think anyone knew. Apart from my husband, of course. I never talked of this to anyone. It feels so strange to be talking like this to you, when I do not know you at all. But you have come from Stephen, and you will see him again . . .'

'I promise I'll never breathe a word of this to anyone.'

'I do not fear a scandal. Once upon a time I did, for my children's sake, not mine. But they are grown and gone. Besides, who would ever believe you? Sometimes I almost wish that everyone had known about it. You've no idea how difficult it has been never to be able to talk about him. Tell me, is he well, my Stephen?'

'Yes. He is in good health.'

'I am glad. I am so glad. And you must tell him that I am too. I would not want him to think . . .' She turned away.

'I will tell him you are still beautiful.'

She laughed. 'You must not forget to tell him about my grey hair. That will amuse him! And then he will find himself a young wife. Yes, the chain. I will send it back to him. How strange to think he still remembers it after so long. I thought he must have forgotten it. Nearly seventeen years – can you imagine how long that is? You must have been still a child when . . .'

'Yes?'

She sighed deeply. 'He gave this to me before he left. He said – well, it does not matter what he said. But I promised to return it when I no longer loved him. Such foolishness – as if one could still love a person after so many years!'

'At least you know he has not forgotten you. Only now he needs the chance to find a wife of his own. Maybe even children.'

'Yes, he'd like that. He deserves that. I never imagined this little chain was preventing him. It was never meant to be any kind of obligation – how could there be such ties between us? It was only a token . . . But, yes, of course, you're right. I must release him from it now. I expect he has someone in mind, if he has talked to you of marrying. He was a handsome man when he was here. There were others in the town who thought so, not only me. Is he handsome now?'

'I don't suppose he is much changed.'

'That's good.'

She was silent. Still running the chain back and forth between her fingers and gazing with her magnificent eyes at some distant scene invisible to Luke. A single tear rolled down her cheek but she did not notice.

Luke waited.

At length she rose from her chair and walked slowly across the room to the window that overlooked the street. A couple of drovers were passing the front of the house with a small flock of ewes and lambs. The anxious cries of the animals mingled with the men's shouts and a neighbouring dog barked.

All unaware of the commotion outside she said slowly, 'I cannot let you have the chain, Master Hollar. Go on your way. I have detained you long enough. Go back to Stephen Sutton and tell him he is free from any obligation to me. Tell him he is free to live his life however he chooses and I wish him every happiness and joy. But I will not give up this necklace. I must keep it. There is nothing else.'

Silence.

Then Luke asked, 'Are you sure?'

'Yes.'

'Why don't you tell him yourself?'

'And how do you suppose I can do that?'

'Come back to Cornwall with me. See him again.'

She spun round, horrified. 'Are you mad, sir?'

'Most probably.'

'That is the most ridiculous suggestion I have ever heard!'

'Why? There is nothing to stop you now. Your husband is dead, your children are gone. We could be at Rossmere within the week. I am serious, Mistress Taverner. Come with me to

Cornwall and talk to Stephen face to face. He still thinks of you with affection. Who knows what might—'

'Stop it. Stop it at once! It is quite impossible. Look at me, I am too old to go rushing about the countryside on a fool's errand.' She was pacing the room. 'My hair is white. In a few months I shall be a grandmother. What an extraordinary man you are! You must think I am a simpleton even to suggest such a thing. But it's my own fault, I should never have spoken to you so freely. Go. Now. At once. You should never have come here. I have cowslips that need attention. Soon it will be elderflowers, then the roses. I cannot leave this place, this is my home, my family are here.'

'And Stephen?'

She sank down on to a chair and put her hand over her eyes. 'You must tell him I have lost the chain and that is why I cannot return it. Tell him I never think of him at all, I did not even remember his name. Tell him I am dead. Tell him it was all a kind of madness, it was impossible. I never loved him. Tell him he is free.'

'Tell him yourself. Face to face.'

'You make it sound so simple. But how can I do that? What would I say to my son?'

'You can pretend you are going to visit your daughter in Somerset. No one else will ever know. You can be back here within the month.'

'You want me to lie?'

'Why not? You lied to me yesterday about the necklace.'

She smiled. 'You're right. I wondered if you had noticed. I wear it all the time. Foolish, isn't it, when I have always hated to wear jewellery?' She glanced up at the portrait with distaste. 'My husband brought back so much from the wars – all stolen and looted. He liked me to wear it for him. I always hated it. But this – this worthless, foolish, feeble little chain! I must have had it mended a hundred times, there's no strength in the metal at all. Yet it reminds me that once I was happy.'

'And so was he.'

'A long time ago. It is over.'

'Perhaps it can begin again.'

'That's dreamers' talk. Leave me, please, Master Hollar. You are wasting your time here and I know you're in a hurry to be in Bristol.'

'I have changed my mind. I'll stay another night at the Lion and leave for Cornwall tomorrow. You can come with me.'

She laughed bitterly. 'Just listen to the boy, how easy he makes it sound! Did you say you were recently married? Then hurry back to your wife and leave me in peace.'

'You're frightened, that's all. But why not take the risk? What do you have to lose?'

Anger fired through her once again. She stood up and faced him, her dark eyes flashing with pride. 'Everything, that's all! Everything that I have! You stand there and smile and tell me to take a risk, but you do not know how cruel it is, what you are suggesting. You think it is an easy thing, a kind of game, but you could not be more wrong. Don't you understand anything at all? How can I go with you to Cornwall? I am different now. I am not the woman Stephen loved. That was seventeen years ago and we have both changed since then. Maybe he still thinks he loves me, but he loves a memory, not the person I am now. If it was anyone else but Stephen, maybe it would be all right: we'd see each other again and the dream there once was would shatter at once. He'd realise the past can never be recaptured, that it was gone. Then he'd be free to find a young woman who can love him and give him children and I could come back to my home and . . . and . . . But you know what Stephen is like. He has remained faithful to those foolish promises through seventeen years of silence. How could he turn from me if he saw me again? He is a kind man. I could not bear to see him pity me.'

'Why, in God's name, would he do that? You're still beautiful—'

'Stop. It is over. The dream is over.'

'Maybe you are afraid that Stephen will be changed. Maybe you are just afraid that you could not love him now he is changed and older.'

She threw him a look of utter contempt as she said, 'I will never love anyone else. Nothing can change that.'

'Don't you think his love might be as strong as yours?'

She faltered. 'Maybe, but even so . . . it is too painful. I have my life here. It is enough.'

'Are you really such a coward?' asked Luke. She turned away, shaking her head, but he caught her hands and held them tightly as he said, 'I came here because I wanted to help Captain Sutton. He has been good to me. When I married Sophie, all her family were against me, all but him. He wanted us to have the chance to be happy that he had never had. He knows it is worth risking everything for the chance to make a life with the person you love. I know he was thinking of you when he told me not to throw that chance away.'

She held his gaze for a long moment, then withdrew her hands slowly. 'You are very eloquent, but it is too late for us. It was always too late. Please go, you are wasting your time. Say to Stephen whatever you must to set him free, but leave me alone. I cannot come with you to Cornwall.'

Luke picked up his hat. 'My offer still stands,' he said. 'I shall stay at the Lion tonight and call again in the morning. If you wish to travel with me to Rossmere, I would consider it an honour to escort you.'

She was standing very straight and still by the window.

She made no reply.

The following morning, Luke returned to the Priory House. Determined to do everything in his power to persuade Mistress Taverner to go with him, he had purchased a quiet saddle mare and was leading her, as well as a packhorse laden with cloth. If Mistress Taverner declined, which seemed likely, he could easily sell one of the horses when he reached Bristol.

The door was opened by an elderly serving-woman who said that her mistress had left soon after dawn to gather dandelions for the stillroom. She had said she'd not be back until the afternoon. No, she did not know where she had gone, there were several places hereabouts where the flowers grew thickly, but if the young gentleman's business was urgent, she'd send a couple of the men to look for her.

Luke told the woman not to bother. Mistress Taverner had made her wishes known in the most effective manner possible and there was no reason to waste any more time in futile argument. He consoled himself by rehearsing how to tell

Captain Sutton the gist of the previous day's conversation. It would probably not be long before Stephen travelled to Tilsbury to plead his suit in person. His visit had not been wasted.

As he rode out of the town he began to think of his return to Cornwall and being reunited with Sophie.

He could forget about the bewitching Mistress Taverner.

And then, just at the point where the Bristol road began to climb steeply through a patch of woodland, he saw her.

Mounted on a sturdy cob, she was waiting just out of sight of the last houses in the town. A light travelling cloak lay across her shoulders and two panniers were fastened to her saddle. Luke's horse ambled to a halt.

She urged her horse forward to join him.

'Good day, Master Hollar. You look surprised. Do you know, this is the very place where I saw Stephen first?' She was frowning.

'In a few days you will see him again.'

'Am I mad, do you think?'

'Maybe.'

She smiled for the first time. 'We must hurry. Isn't it ridiculous? After all these years, and now suddenly I am terrified I'll be too late.'

'We'll travel as fast as we can.'

They rode on in silence up the hill and Dolores never once looked back at the little town she was leaving so abruptly.

Chapter Thirty-Five

This time Perdita came by sea. The ship, the *Speedwell*, dropped anchor off Porthew in the early afternoon and she and her servants were rowed ashore by four muscled sailors. Perdita was almost tempted to travel on with the *Speedwell*. It was going to Penzance and from there round the point of Land's End to the north coast of Cornwall, then across to the southern ports of Ireland.

They had journeyed from Plymouth on a fresh southerly wind, and there had been a heavy swell. Perdita found that the roll and pitch of the boat did not make her feel the least bit unwell; on the contrary, the salt air gave her a fine appetite and she slept even more soundly than usual.

It was the dry land that felt strange when she stepped ashore.

She walked slowly over the flat rocks at the head of the beach, then turned to look back at the *Speedwell*. There was still time, while she waited for the horses that would take her to Rossmere, to change her mind and return to that fine ship.

Her own ship.

She had not thought it necessary, when she was telling Edmund Menheire of her father's fictitious petition to King Charles, to mention that Richard had in fact left her a more substantial proof of his affection: ownership and control of one of his ships. Such a bequest had raised a few eyebrows in Plymouth, but it was by no means unheard of for a woman to own a ship: Kitty had possessed three at the time of her marriage.

Perdita was only sorry it was not the *Fearless* he had given her

– it would have been amusing to have been in control of Piers Menheire's fate. But she soon discovered the reason for her father's choice. The *Speedwell* was a solid, capacious and reliable merchant ship, and its greatest advantage was its master. Captain Matthews had nearly half a century's experience of the sea to recommend him. As a youth he had been one of the few survivors of Sir Walter Raleigh's doomed voyage to Guiana and since then he had roamed all over the world. As well as being a skilled mariner, he was a capable trader. He was able to give Perdita sound advice about shipments and prices, and Perdita was shrewd enough to let herself be guided by him. She knew she had a great deal to learn before she was able to make the best use of her new possession and she was impatient to begin.

It was only a grave emergency that had persuaded her to go on to Rossmere instead of continuing with the *Speedwell* to Ireland.

She turned away with a sigh and went on into the village. On a warm summer's afternoon Porthew was a singularly tranquil place: fishermen were sitting cross-legged on the ground, mending nets and smoking their long-stemmed pipes. A couple of old women sat knitting in their doorways, barefoot children played in the dust. A grey cat stretched her limbs in the sun.

Perdita remembered her first arrival at Porthew by sea the previous September, less than a year past, though in many ways it seemed much longer. Then she had arrived with her father in the midst of the colour and noise of St Ewan's Day; now she was alone and the little town was drowsing in the summer heat. Then she had been looking forward to seeing Piers again and telling him of her adventures at sea. Now she knew that Piers was himself enjoying the excitement of life on board ship: the *Fearless* was due to return to Plymouth from the Mediterranean in a few days' time. She was sorry she was going to miss him yet again. He had visited Plymouth twice during the winter and early spring, but on both occasions she had been absent in London.

This had been a busy winter for her. She had devoted herself to ensuring that her position in society was as secure as possible. Edmund Menheire's warning, the last time they met, had cut deep into her fears.

She had been relieved to find Kitty as fond of her as ever. Widowhood had increased her dependence on her only daughter. No mention was made of Perdita's irregular status in the family. Kitty appeared incapable of denying her anything.

Or almost anything.

In March, Perdita remembered that the interest would soon fall due on the Suttons' debts. Since her father had agreed to maintain the payments to stop them falling into even worse difficulties, Perdita suggested that Kitty should keep up this generous course. Kitty categorically refused. The one subject that was sure always to provoke an angry outburst was any mention of the Suttons, Trecarne, Porthew, or even Cornwall in general.

In the end, Perdita had decided she would have to find the money from her own funds, something she was fairly loath to do. She wrote to Francis, asking him to let her know details of how much money was due in interest, and to whom it must be paid. For some weeks she heard nothing. Then, to her astonishment, she received a brief and fairly illegible letter from Sophie telling her she must not trouble about them any more: their affairs were now in a hopeless state and they would have to leave Rossmere by the end of the year.

Perdita was horrified. However, there was little she could do straight away as she was about to set off to London again, this time in the company of Lord and Lady Harper who had promised to introduce her to a number of families influential at court. Perdita's first instinct had been to cancel her visit and go immediately to Rossmere to see what had happened, but this would have caused gross offence to the Harpers, and the opportunity to be the protégée of such a respectably grand couple would not come again. A brief struggle took place between her ambition and her loyalty to old friends – and ambition won.

The decision appeared to be paying off when she was attending an evening party given in honour of the Countess of Castlemaine, the King's mistress and Queen of England in all but name. Suddenly she caught sight of Edmund Menheire: he was hovering on the outskirts of the fashionable group of which she now formed a much-admired part. She had graced him with a smile of haughty condescension then moved on, leaving him quite delightfully dumbfounded.

Later that same evening she had heard rumours that he was in London to distance himself from some scandal that had surrounded his father in Cornwall that winter. She tried to find out more details, but the accounts were conflicting. She had no doubt she'd find out soon enough.

She had not entirely given up hope of gaining possession of Trecarne, however that might come about. She managed to persuade Kitty, after many stormy scenes, to send a petition to King Charles asking for the restoration of her late husband's Cornish home. It joined the mountain of such petitions mouldering in a back room of his palace, their wax seals nibbled by undisturbed mice.

Perdita had also instructed Diggory Fitch to let it be known locally that she was continuing with her father's efforts to have his house restored to him. Although, as Edmund Menheire had said, it was hard to believe that any Cornish court would find in favour of her claim, she thought it no harm to indulge in some noisy sabre-rattling.

And, having once seen Edmund Menheire in London, she looked out for him at future gatherings. Given the nature of their last encounter at Rossmere, she thought it highly unlikely she'd ever become mistress of Trecarne through marriage to him, but she had not abandoned the idea entirely. In the meantime, she intended to use that as a benchmark for future offers. Any man she married must be at least as agreeable as Edmund, at least as wealthy and with a house the equal of Trecarne. The first part was not a problem, since most men were more agreeable than he, the second presented more difficulties and the third seemed well nigh impossible. She had already turned down one suitor because, even though he was affable enough and possessed a reasonable fortune, his home was in Lincolnshire. She had no intentions of severing her West Country links. Not yet, at any rate.

In some ways Perdita would have been content to remain single indefinitely. She was learning to enjoy her independence and freedom. There were, however, risks involved. She had been appalled by Edmund's remark that now her father was no longer there to protect her plenty of men would not hesitate to take by force what she refused to give voluntarily. It was true that her irregular background, combined with her considerable wealth, made her an object of some fascination. And she had noticed, this last winter in London, the second of King Charles's reign, a new licence in men's behaviour towards women, which did not bode well for the future.

There were several horror stories in circulation about heiresses being abducted and forced to marry against their will. Whatever the punishment meted out to their violators, the fate of these unfortunate women was almost always the same: they were effectively ruined and their chances of a decent marriage much reduced. For Perdita, already struggling with the stigma of illegitimacy, it would have been a disaster.

She made sure she never left her home without a formidable retinue of servants – not just Cullen and Adam, but also Rudd, an amiable giant of a fellow. His low forehead, fierce expression and bulging arms were enough to deter anyone, though he was gentle and mild-tempered.

He was sitting with the others on a bench outside the alehouse. When the horses arrived, half a dozen of the small Cornish ponies most suited to the narrow, stony paths of the area, Rudd looked at them with some surprise. He made a pretence of trying to ride the smallest one, but his feet touched the ground on either side like a Colossus and the pony walked on, leaving him straddling air. He then made as if to pick up the pony and carry it, instead of the other way around.

The net-menders, knitters and playing children all paused in their activities and watched the pantomime with growing merriment, and when Perdita set off, several of them called out to her in friendly greeting.

Clearly there were unexpected benefits to be gained from the presence of this humorous giant in her retinue.

As Perdita rode down the lime avenue towards the house Rossmere and all the countryside around were looking lovelier than she had ever seen them. The hay meadows were starred with bright flowers, and foxgloves grew thickly in the shade at the edge of the woods. And the mellow buildings of Rossmere rested like a slumbering stone beast in the hollow of the hills. Perdita felt a sudden gust of anger towards all the Sutton clan: what endless catalogue of incompetence had brought them to the point where all this, their family home for generations, must now be forfeit?

Her anger was replaced by altogether different emotions as the afternoon wore on.

'Why did you not tell me in your letter?' she exclaimed as she jumped down from her mount and ran over to greet Sophie. It was hard to embrace over the barrier of her most pregnant belly.

Sophie laughed. 'I'm not much of a one for letters,' she said truthfully.

Evidently pregnancy suited her. She was glowing with health and energy, straighter, prouder and more beautiful than ever before.

'What has happened?' asked Perdita. She linked her arm through Sophie's and they walked slowly into the cool gloom of the house. Ale and food had been set out in readiness on the table in the great hall. 'Why have you come back to Rossmere? Has anything happened to Luke?'

'So many questions! He went away last autumn. He should be back by now. He has been delayed in Somerset. I had a letter from him a few days ago. He said he'd had a fall from his horse, nothing serious, but he was unable to ride for a few days. Lord knows when he will be home. Soon, I hope – but, then, I've been hoping that all winter.'

'Doesn't he know you're with child?'

Sophie shook her head. 'I did not tell him before he went because . . . Well, I do not know exactly but I didn't. Since then I've heard from him often but he never sent an address where I could get in touch with him so I could not have told him even if I'd wanted to. He likes to be secretive, I think. Even this last letter gives me no address. He did say, however, that he has a surprise for Uncle Stephen that will amaze us all.'

She turned as she said this and smiled at Stephen, who had just come in from his work in the fields. He looked older, more careworn than Perdita remembered him, but he welcomed her warmly and said, 'Sophie's husband is full of secrets and surprises.'

'What kind of surprise could he be planning for you?' asked Perdita.

'A measure of decent tobacco would not go amiss,' said Stephen, helping himself from a jug of ale and settling down to enjoy a pipe. 'Still, Luke is in for a surprise of his own when he does return.'

Sophie placed a hand on the mound of her stomach. 'I hope he comes soon,' was all she said.

It was Francis himself who told Perdita how Rossmere had been lost. She was appalled to hear of Colonel Menheire's deceit in persuading him to invest in a high-risk trading voyage when he knew the family needed to hoard every penny they had to pay off their loans. The ship that had carried all his hopes with it had not yet returned. The second payment on the debt had been due at the end of March, together with the first, which had been delayed. Since there was no hope of either sum being found, Colonel Menheire was legally entitled to claim Rossmere.

It was the last thing he did.

He had died, peacefully and well satisfied with his life's accomplishments, at the beginning of April.

'So Edmund Menheire is now the owner of Rossmere and there is nothing that can be done to prevent him,' said Perdita.

'Yes – may he rot in hell for all he has done to us!' Perdita had never seen Francis so vindictive before, but she was hardly surprised. Francis took a long drink of wine and said bitterly, 'He has graciously permitted us to remain in *his* house until the end of the year. To give us time to wind up our affairs and make other arrangements.'

'So what will you do?'

Francis sighed heavily. 'I expect Louisa will go to live with Sophie and the baby at Porthew. Kip will remain with the saddler he is working for in Camborne. As for my mother, I do not know what will happen to her. Sophie has offered to give her a home.'

'In that tiny house?'

'It is better than nothing, though my mother does not see it that way. The great problem is that she blames Sophie for all our misfortunes and will not hear of going to live with her. We may have to make other arrangements, but I cannot think what.'

He drained his mug of wine and looked about him bleakly. Francis had never been a fighter, but Perdita could see that the looming catastrophe of the past months had knocked out of him what little stuffing he had had. His ponderous, once handsome face was developing the puffy contours of the heavy drinker. The gentleness that Perdita remembered with affection had been overlaid with bitterness and impotent fury.

'What about Uncle Stephen?' she asked.

Francis shrugged. 'I'm sure he is making his own plans,' he said, but obviously his uncle's future no longer interested him. Perdita suspected that nothing interested him very much any more.

But there she was wrong.

'What about you and Honor?' she asked. 'Where will you go?'

He looked at her bleakly. 'That all depends on . . . I hardly dare to look so far ahead.'

'Why? Is she ill?'

'Not . . . exactly. She is due to have a child in a week or so. But she is not strong.' He spoke rapidly and with agitation. 'This pregnancy has been a terrible ordeal for her. We thought we were losing her many times. You cannot imagine how she has suffered. It has been an agony for her. I do not know how she has borne it. And knowing all the time that the worst is still to come! Dear God, if there was any way I might spare her, or suffer and die in her place! But all I can do is watch and wait and—' He buried his face in his hands.

Perdita thought he must be weeping. She stood up and went to put her hand on his shoulder, but when he looked up he was dry-eyed.

'If anything happens to her,' he said, with greater firmness than Perdita had ever seen in him before, 'then I do believe I will die here with her at Rossmere.'

Perdita was dismayed. 'Dear heavens above, Francis, what a time to talk of dying. Just listen to yourself. All this talk of doom and hatred, no wonder the poor woman's sufferings have increased if that is all the comfort she's had from you.'

'I know, I know, it is all my fault,' said Francis recklessly. 'But don't worry, I mean to make sure that Menheire suffers for all he has done.' He took another long drink of wine and Perdita, seeing that further conversation with him would only provide more of the same, went in search of his wife.

Honor had spent most of the day resting on her bed, and had now gathered sufficient strength to rest beside the kitchen fire. Although the day was warm and the fire was hot, she had a heavy shawl over her shoulders and was shivering.

Perdita had assumed Francis was exaggerating when he described her sufferings – in his fevered state of guilt and foreboding his troubles were much magnified – but one glance at Honor showed that indeed she had been wretchedly ill. Her stomach was huge, but the rest of her was pitifully thin, her face haggard and her arms no more than sticks. There were purple shadows, like bruises, round her eyes. Worst of all, she had a haunted look. Perdita had heard of people seeing in someone's face when they were not long for this world, and now she knew what they meant.

She hid her misgivings as best she could, but her bright greeting was lost on Honor.

'Perdita –' Honor's small hand gripped hers tightly – 'I never thought I'd see you again.'

'Why on earth not? Do you think I'm so easily got rid of?'

'No, but . . . I wanted Sophie to send for you, but she said we must not add to your troubles with ours.'

Perdita was touched. 'Well, Honor, and now I am come anyway. I intend to look after you all in the next few weeks. This whole place is about as cheerful as a pest-house. Only think of your baby being born into such a home of long faces.'

Honor smiled sadly. 'Yes, I think about my baby all the time.' Her eyes filled with tears. 'I think of my baby, and my dear kind husband. Oh, Perdita, I've been frightened for such an age, you've no idea what it's been like. But now that the time is almost here, I am hardly frightened at all. Well, not so much. It is worst at night when Francis is sleeping and everything is dark and I feel so alone and . . .' She struggled to collect herself before continuing carefully, 'No, I must try to be brave. I know how much it distresses him to see me like this. He blames himself, you see. Not just for the child, but because his family are to lose Rossmere. I cannot bear to add my own sufferings to his burdens, he has so many already.'

The tears spilled over and rolled down her cheeks. For once Perdita was at a loss. It occurred to her that both husband and wife squandered so much energy on being miserable because of the other's distress that she could see no end to it.

Honor's next words startled her even more. 'That's the reason I wanted you to come here, Perdita. You are so strong and brave, not like me. They told me how you stood up to Colonel Menheire. I could never have done that. Francis needs a wife like you, not a foolish, feeble creature like me. I want you to promise me, Perdita, that after . . . after . . . after I am gone . . . you will take care of him for me. I know how much he admires you, I know he thinks well of you and all I want is for him to be happy when I am—'

'Oh, for mercy's sake,' exclaimed Perdita, thoroughly exasperated, since Honor was working herself into a fit of hysteria. 'Women have babies all the time and most of them are fine. There's no point getting into a state over it now.'

'But I can't help it!' wailed Honor. 'Look at me, it's hopeless. My hips are so narrow and the baby is already huge, look how big I am *here* and how narrow *here*!'

'Stop this,' said Perdita sharply. 'Stop it at once!'

Honor gripped her hand more tightly than ever, gulped back her tears and said, 'You see, Perdita, you are so much stronger than me. It is probably better this way.'

Cary, who had stumped into the kitchen with a wicker basket full of washing, regarded Honor with contempt and said, 'She's been like this for months. Frightened of her own shadow, that one is. There's a lot of nonsense talked about child-bearing. I had my Het with no trouble at all, just popped out like an egg out of a chicken. But she'll get herself into all sorts of trouble working herself up the way she does. I wouldn't be surprised if she doesn't die of fright, pure and simple. Lots of folk think that's impossible, but I saw a man once with my own eyes who had died of fright and it was the most terrible sight you ever did see.

His tongue was swollen and blue and lolling out of his mouth like an old fish and his—'

Honor was moaning in terror and Perdita said firmly, 'Cary, don't be so unkind. You know you're only making her worse.'

Cary grinned and set down the washing. 'Well, maybe I am, but we've tried making her better a thousand times and it came to nothing.'

'At least you're just the same as ever.'

'Not entirely. I've had word of my Michael since you were here last. I'm a widow now, good and proper.'

'I'm sorry, Cary. Do you know what happened?'

'It was that brother of yours found him. It was a terrible shock when I heard, but it's better to know the worst. When the family are away from here and have found somewhere to go, I'm taking Het with me to see the place where he is buried. Master Hollar paid for a proper headstone and all. I'd pay him back only I've not had any wages in so long I've forgotten what real money looks like. Still, it will set me at peace to see the place where he lies.'

'Master Hollar found him?'

'Strange, isn't it? But he's not all bad, that brother of yours. Have you seen Mistress Sutton yet?'

'No, I ought to go and find her now and pay my respects. Is she well?'

'As well as can be expected,' said Cary, which Perdita had always considered to be no kind of answer at all.

She soon discovered that in this case it meant that the person under discussion was far from well. In fact, when she found Alice sitting alone in the winter parlour, Perdita was more shocked at the change in her than in anyone else at Rossmere, even Honor. Alice seemed to have aged ten years in the few months since Perdita had seen her last. Her hair was white, her face drawn and deeply lined. All the animation had leached away. 'Ah, Perdita,' she spoke listlessly, 'they told me you were coming.'

Perdita pulled up a chair and said brightly, 'So, Mistress Sutton, you are soon to be a grandmother twice over. Cause for congratulation, I should think. Do you suppose Sophie or Honor will be the first to have their baby?'

'Babies?' Alice gazed at her emptily, then said, 'You must not talk to me of Sophie, she is a bad girl and I do not want to see her. Francis tells me we must cut back on our expenses in future and that is all because of Sophie. She was going to marry Edmund Menheire, you know, she'd told me many times about it. And then she changed her mind. It is all her fault. I won't have her name mentioned again. Thank heavens she is living in Porthew so I do not have to see her every day.'

'But—'

Alice leaned forward and said, as if afraid they might be overheard, 'Tell me, Perdita, how is your father? Did I ever tell you that he wanted to marry me once? I turned him down, I had to. Nicolas was so much more suitable. Much more suitable in every way.'

'But surely you have not forgotten,' said Perdita, in some confusion, 'that my father died last year. He is buried at Porthew.'

Alice looked startled and retreated slightly. Then she said, with a little smile, 'That's right, I remember now. How silly of me. I must be getting old. I forget things sometimes, but Richard, yes, I knew he was dead. So sad.' She fussed with the silk tassel that hung from her girdle. Then she beamed at Perdita and said, 'It was so kind of you to tell me about Richard, my dear. I was always so fond of him.'

She fidgeted for a few moments more. Perdita could not think of anything more to say. After a while Alice glanced across at her, her head to one side like a little bird. She smiled and said, 'Your face looks familiar, somehow, but I do not believe we've ever been introduced. Please tell me what you are called.'

Perdita stared.

By the time Perdita retreated to the privacy of her bed-chamber that evening, her earlier annoyance with the Suttons had been replaced with a slow-burning rage against Edmund Menheire.

Yes, indeed, the Suttons had made errors. Alice should never have borrowed the money for a new roof when their debts had already been so great, and as for Francis, she could not imagine how he had been so foolish as to sink the money Sophie had made from Falcon's sale into such a treacherous enterprise.

But theirs had been errors and misjudgements only. The Menheires had been guilty of cold-blooded deceit and destruction.

For whatever malicious reason – and Perdita guessed there must be some ancient grudge between them that had caused the malice of the upstart family – Colonel Menheire and his son had set out quite deliberately to bring an old and much respected family to its knees.

And how successful they had been! Their cruel triumph was etched deep in the face of every single member of the household. Even Louisa, never one to arouse warm feelings in Perdita, had become an object of pity now that her future prospects were so grim.

Perdita lay awake half the night plotting how she might thwart Edmund Menheire and help her friends, but she could see no solution to the present tangle. All the comfort she had was from the thought of what she would say to Edmund when she saw him next.

She did not have long to wait.

Chapter Thirty-Six

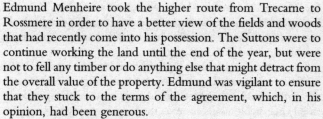

Edmund Menheire took the higher route from Trecarne to Rossmere in order to have a better view of the fields and woods that had recently come into his possession. The Suttons were to continue working the land until the end of the year, but were not to fell any timber or do anything else that might detract from the overall value of the property. Edmund was vigilant to ensure that they stuck to the terms of the agreement, which, in his opinion, had been generous.

Now, as he rode past the green fields of corn and barley and the cut hay meadows, he calculated the likely profit from each and decided he had been too generous in his provisions. It looked like being a good growing season and the Suttons had been in no position to negotiate: he could probably have got away with insisting on half shares.

His father would have been displeased.

Edmund had not yet adjusted to the fact that he no longer had to face the daily ordeal of his father's wrath. Though the Colonel had been laid to rest, his voice still sounded in Edmund's head. A voice sharp-edged as the teeth of a saw, rasping, nagging, never letting go.

Edmund had expected to feel liberated by his father's death, not to mourn him. The present situation was thoroughly unsatisfactory. It was not that he missed the old man exactly, rather that he was weighed down by an awareness of his solitary state. The Colonel had filled his universe for so long and now there was nothing and no one to take his place.

While he had remained alive, plotting each step with

meticulous care, the trajectory of the Menheire family's advance had made complete sense. Now Edmund was left holding the pieces of his father's vision, but they no longer seemed to fit together quite so snugly. Or if they did, he had forgotten how it should be done.

He knew the plan was for the Menheires to gain possession of Rossmere; he knew the reasons why that was so important and he knew the Suttons must be ousted . . . but some element of the grand design was missing. He had been going through all the possibilities in logical order, as his father had taught him, and he had recently reached the conclusion that he needed an heir. The Colonel's efforts had not been for himself alone, they had been for Edmund and future Menheires yet unborn. Once Edmund had found himself a wife who would give him sons that he could mould and direct as his father had moulded and directed him, he'd find his bearings once again.

Continuing in this same logical progression he reasoned that his father had wanted him to marry Sophie Sutton. Marriage to the Suttons' elder daughter would have been satisfying enough simply because it would have set the seal of equality between the two families. For the son and grandson of the Launceston scrivener, who had suffered from a hundred petty snobberies in the past, this was a rich prize. But it had the added advantage of masking the harsh reality of the Suttons' destruction. If a Sutton bride remained as mistress of her family's ancient home, if Sutton blood was mingled with the Menheires', then the catastrophe for the rest of the Sutton clan would have been easier to overlook. As it was, Edmund had considered it best to absent himself for a month or two during the winter so that he would not be associated with his father's final ruthless master stroke, but even so a good deal of the hatred his father had inspired had now attached itself to him.

Edmund knew it would be sensible, therefore, to transfer his interest to the younger sister, Louisa. Having been twice rebuffed at Rossmere he thought it would be better to make the arrangements through her older brother. It did not occur to him that even Louisa might think twice about agreeing to marry the man responsible for her family's ruin. He thought only that, despite the obvious advantages, the prospect of marrying Louisa did not appeal to him much. He assumed this was because she had no wealth. Apart from that there was nothing wrong with the girl, so far as he could see. She simply did not much interest him.

Not like Perdita Treveryan. Edmund had not forgotten that tantalising glimpse of her at the evening party for the Countess of Castlemaine in April. Of course, marriage to her was not a possibility, for a whole host of reasons, but if a woman *like* Perdita were to present herself . . .

Just as this thought was progressing through his mind, Edmund rode down the last stretch of lime avenue and saw Perdita. Since it was more than six months since her father's death she had set aside full mourning, except for formal occasions. Today she was wearing a dress of watered green with only an edging of black and she was throwing corn from a little basket for the doves. She made a decorative picture, her dark hair against the pale green, the white birds forming a ring around her skirts, the lavish gesture of her arm as she scattered the corn.

Edmund's mind saw none of this. His mind registered that a guest ought not to perform tasks properly done by servants and that anyway the corn being so wastefully squandered was now his corn, and since the doves were unproductive, they should not have it. He decided to have them slaughtered before they made further inroads on his profits.

His body, however, especially that neglected and shrunken part of him generally described as the heart, responded to the sight of Perdita in an altogether more immediate way. It was as though he had just downed a glass of the finest French brandy at a single draught.

'Good day to you, Mistress Treveryan,' he said, as he dismounted. His grooms led the horses away. 'I did not expect to see you here.'

Perdita levelled at him a gaze of the utmost contempt. 'Nor I you. I wonder only that you dare to show your face at Rossmere.'

He stiffened. 'This is my house,' he said coldly. 'It is customary for a man to visit his own properties, especially when there is so much work to be done on them.'

'Indeed? I would have thought you had done enough mischief at Rossmere to last anyone a lifetime.'

For once, Perdita had not thought before she spoke. She was still seething with impotent rage at the misery of the Suttons and when she saw Edmund, smugly satisfied as he rode like a conquering hero up to the house and ordered his horses fed and watered without so much as a by-your-leave, she felt such a gust of anger that it was all she could do not to strike him.

He said, 'And what is that supposed to mean?'

'Are you really so blind that you cannot see how you have destroyed the family here?'

'It is their own folly has proved their undoing.'

'There is no crime in being foolish, but you and your father have tricked them deliberately. The Colonel knew full well Francis must not risk his money on a shipping venture when all his money was needed to pay their debts.'

'That agreement was legally binding and Sir Francis entered into it of his own free will. Besides, it was settled between him and my father. I had no part in it.'

'I do not believe you. As you are the sole benefactor of the scheme, there is no need to pretend innocence to me. The Suttons may be taken in by your deceptions, but I am not so easily fooled.'

Edmund stared fiercely at her, then said in a tight voice, 'The opinions of a bastard are of no interest whatsoever. You must excuse me. I have business with Captain Sutton.'

'The pity of it is,' said Perdita, in a cool, clear voice, as he began to walk past her towards the house, 'that you damage your own cause even more than theirs.'

'On the contrary,' he said, with a smile, 'my own cause has never been in better shape.'

'I am amazed you can be so foolish as to think so. In your way, Master Menheire, you are every bit as innocent as the Suttons.'

That stopped him. 'Innocent? What do you mean?'

She smiled and tossed another handful of corn towards the strutting doves. 'There, you are surprised, which only goes to prove I am right. You believe that wealth is all that matters, which is as limited as the Suttons' belief that fine breeding is all important. What good will your great riches do you when you are ostracised by every decent family in Cornwall? Your grand-father was a scrivener, your father not much more than a money-lender, though he was dressed up in fine clothes, like you. You want to call yourself a gentleman, but you forfeited that chance when you set out to ruin the Suttons. I suppose you know that the scandal of your behaviour was all the gossip in Plymouth last month and that people even spoke of it in London? An ugly story it made, believe me. I wonder you dared to show your face in society.'

Several times Edmund opened his mouth to stem the tide of her anger. He told himself he did not have to listen, he ought just to walk away . . . but he stood quite still, like someone in a trance. No one had ever spoken to him like this before. Certainly no woman. And yet, in an odd way, it felt familiar, as if he was back in territory he knew well. His father had never lost a chance to scold him, and he had never known how to respond except to bow his head and promise to try harder in future. But with Perdita, he was sure he could gain the upper hand, if he could only think what best to say.

In the meantime, there was no stopping her. 'And what,' she was asking him scornfully, 'do you expect to gain from all this intrigue against the Suttons? All they have is this house, which is hardly any distance from one you own already. Do you really imagine you can live in them both at once?'

Edmund interrupted her quickly, glad that he was at last on firmer ground. He said, 'We are not so foolish as you think. Our reasons for wanting Rossmere are rock solid and it is nothing whatsoever to do with this house. It will probably be pulled down within a year or so to make way for—'

'For what? You cannot expect to derive any great riches from the few wretched farms still attached to the house. Do you mean to turn Biddy Firth out of her hovel and scrape a living from her few acres or—?'

She stopped. She had been in full flight, but something about Edmund's reaction to her last statement made her pause. He had coloured as if she had touched a nerve. Had it been the mention of Biddy Firth's tumbledown farm? For a moment she wondered dizzily if Edmund had hopes of replacing Captain Sutton in the widow's affections. She said, 'Is it something to do with Polcreath?'

Edmund said, 'My motives are none of your concern.'

Perdita was intrigued. She wanted very much to know what reasons he was hiding. She realised that by her present outburst she was throwing away any chance of persuading him to make her a more honourable offer than his last and she was furious with herself for allowing her anger to override her schemes.

Still, since there was nothing more to lose, she might as well make the most of this chance to hit out on the Suttons' behalf. She returned to the attack. 'My concern, sir, is for my friends, but that is something you will never understand. You have no friends, nor ever will have. You can gain only enemies. Last time we met here, you were chivalrous enough to remind me of my troubled origins. Your daintiness on that subject shows how sadly you lag behind the times in this Cornish backwater. You will never be able to make real progress since you have no understanding of London ways or how real business is conducted. Do you imagine the child the Countess of Castlemaine has just borne the King will be given anything less than the highest respect? Of course not! Whereas you will be an outcast and despised for the rest of your days.'

'I do not have to listen to this. Besides, by our actions we have only hastened the inevitable. The Suttons were sure to lose Rossmere sooner or later.'

'Oh, I don't doubt it. And you might have come to possess it in their place. You might have reached the same goal without alienating every decent person in Cornwall, if you had only had the wit to handle matters more carefully. Your family's tactics may have been suitable in a scrivener's shop in Launceston, but now that you aspire to higher rank you must learn how to court the good opinion of others, or face ruin.'

'Public opinion is of no interest to me,' said Edmund. It was something he had heard his father say many times. Perdita heard the way he spoke, as if he was reciting a lesson. She noticed also his troubled expression and she guessed that Edmund, contrary to his words, wanted others to think highly of him. She began to understand that Edmund was a man at odds with himself. The exterior was just as his father had made him, logical, ruthless and cold. What lay beneath was far more uncertain. She wondered how she might exploit this insight to the Suttons' advantage.

She said coolly, 'It is always wrong to underestimate the importance of public opinion. Just suppose, for instance, that when my family's claim to Trecarne comes before a court, the presiding judge turns out to be an old friend of Mistress Sutton's. Is it not likely that he will be inclined to find against the very family whose persecution of her has caused her to lose her wits?'

'You exaggerate the lady's indisposition.'

'Indeed I do not. The worry has quite destroyed her. She cannot remember anything for two minutes together. This morning she has already asked me several times if we have been introduced.'

Edmund frowned. 'Such a decline is common in the elderly. Her afflictions cannot be laid at my door.'

'You do not even believe that yourself, Master Menheire, so you can hardly expect others to be so deceived.'

'I really do not see—' Edmund began heatedly, but Perdita interrupted him.

'No, and that is the whole trouble. You are blind to almost everything around you. It would be almost pitiable if others had not suffered so much more because of your follies.'

Edmund was amazed by the boldness of Perdita's speech, and even more amazed that he was still engaged in conversation with her. There was no earthly reason why he should endure her scolding. He should be talking to Sir Francis about the work that still needed to be done clearing ditches in the lower meadows . . . but some fascination held him there still. Though he was furious with her for spouting such empty nonsense, Edmund felt more alive than he could remember in years. He said, 'You are very free in your criticisms.'

'Only because I see much to criticise. What you want, Master Menheire, is someone of good sense who can advise you on business matters. You are like a man who has cut down a stout tree with his axe and now wishes to make a delicate piece of furniture from the timber, but has only the axe with which to do it. You need someone who can show you how to negotiate what lies ahead with subtlety and skill.'

Edmund sneered, 'And are you offering yourself for the

position of adviser?' But even as he spoke, he thought what an excellent solution this might be, and he saw that the same idea had just occurred to her as well.

All she said was, 'I'd not dirty my hands meddling in your affairs even if you asked me on bended knee. But the time will come when I have more knowledge of business matters than most men, yourself included. It may surprise you to know that my father showed his faith in my abilities by leaving me one of his ships. I intend eventually to use the profits from trading to take out shares in another, though I shall make sure it is a more reliable investment than the luckless voyage your father sold to poor Francis. I shall rely on the advice and support of my friends. At least I am not so narrow as to imagine that good practice is a matter only of profit and—'

She broke off.

She and Edmund had been so engrossed in their argument that neither had noticed the sounds of commotion coming from the house.

Now a young lad mounted on a dun pony came hurtling under the stable arch and clattered off down the lime avenue as fast as he could go.

'What is going on?' Perdita asked no one in particular.

From the open windows of the house she could hear raised voices, running footsteps and then, faint but chilling, a woman's scream.

Forgetting Edmund, she ran into the house and almost collided with Cary, who was rushing towards the stairs, her arms heaped up with linen clouts.

'What is happening?' Perdita asked.

'It's Mistress Honor,' said Cary, starting up the stairs two at a time. 'Her labour has begun but—'

The rest of Cary's sentence was cut short by the piercing wail that ripped through the whole house. Perdita was suddenly sick with anxiety. Honor had vexed them all for so long with her worries and ailments that they had long since stopped listening to her, but maybe her terror had only been a premonition of the horrors ahead. Maybe this was indeed one of those grim occasions when the chamber of birth was destined to be a chamber of death as well.

Upstairs a door opened, a dreadful moaning could be heard, then the door was closed once again. Sophie had hurried in from the kitchen courtyard. She was carrying a heavy pail of water.

'Here,' said Perdita, 'let me take that. It's too heavy for you.'

Sophie smiled as she handed over the bucket and straightened up, her hand in the small of her back. She was stately and serene, proud and contented in her pregnancy. Then they heard another scream, more agonising than the first, and Sophie grimaced. 'Poor Honor, what a noise already, and it is only just beginning. Her strength will all be used up by nightfall. Don't look so worried, Perdita. You and I have work to do. I think my brother is going to need almost as much attention as his wife. Shall we take turns? I'll go up to Honor now and you can find Francis and stop him getting in everyone's way. The midwife will be here shortly.'

'What can I do for him?'

'Distract him as best you can. Persuade him to go somewhere he can't hear poor Honor screaming all the time. There she goes again. Something tells me this is going to take a long time.'

Chapter Thirty-Seven

'You have missed my daughter by more than a week,' Kitty told her unexpected visitor. 'She sailed for Porthew on the *Speedwell*. It is her own ship now, you know. Her father left it to her in his will. Some people have been surprised at him for doing such a thing, but he knew she would have me to advise her. I had three ships left me by my first husband and I managed them very well. And then I had the running of my husband's affairs when he was obliged to be out of the country after the late wars.'

Kitty had been bored that morning, a day of languid summer heat, and the arrival of such a vigorous-looking young man was an unexpected tonic. He had eyes like chips of blue sea-glass and though his clothes were not fashionable, he was handsome enough for her to overlook this shortcoming. She remembered now that he had visited her in Plymouth once before, the previous October. It had been he who had brought the letter from Richard, which said he had had a fall from his horse and was delayed but would be joining her in Plymouth soon. Her husband must have been already dead by the time she had read it.

Piers said, 'I was sorry to hear of Sir Richard's death. When I left him at Trecarne there was no indication that his injuries were mortal.'

'It all happened so suddenly,' fretted Kitty. 'There was no time to get in proper mourning clothes. I simply had to make do with what I had for nearly a week.'

Piers reflected that she had made up for that delay since. He had never seen such elaborate mourning. Even in this fine summer weather, she sat like one entombed in layer upon layer of black silk, black ribbons, black-trimmed lace, an enormous mourning ring weighing down her finger. He hated to think of Perdita similarly shrouded.

His anxiety to see her again increased. He said, 'Is your daughter likely to remain in Cornwall long? I need to see her urgently, but I do not want to travel to Rossmere if she is already returning to Plymouth. Do you know her plans?'

Kitty's features crinkled into a scowl. 'She said she'd not stay long, and she only took enough clothes for a few days. I urged her to take more, but she was very stubborn. She insisted on going. My late husband's friends the Suttons are in some kind of difficulty, everyone is talking about it. But I cannot be bothering with other people's worries when I have so many of my own to contend with.'

'Yes,' said Piers grimly, 'I have heard of their misfortunes.'

'And now this morning she sends me another letter to say she will not return until the babies are born. I am trying to decide whether to send her more gowns and linen. It is hard to know what she will need.'

'Babies?'

'Mistress Sutton's daughter is expecting, and her son's wife. It is really most inconvenient and I do not see what it has to do with Perdita. I'd have thought my own needs were greater than theirs. She was a great comfort to me in London last winter, Master Menheire. Even though she was in mourning, her costumes were much admired everywhere she went. It was generally agreed that she did me great credit.'

Piers grinned. 'I am sure your daughter will attract attention wherever she goes.'

'Yes, she takes after me in that.' Kitty smoothed the fabric of her skirts with quiet satisfaction.

Piers uttered some meaningless words of agreement. This was neither the time nor the place to tell Lady Treveryan his own observation: that Perdita might outwardly conform to her mother's standards but there was something wilder about her also, something that had nothing to do with Kitty's narrow world.

Eight months as a sailor had been a challenge and adventure

Piers would not have missed for the world. He had seen and experienced much, just as he had hoped. Moreover, the time away had altered his perspective on his home, family and friends. During the long winter nights on board ship he'd had time to reflect, and many topics to reflect on. On calm starlit nights, with no sound but the creak of the wooden hull and the rush of water alongside her bows, and on days becalmed in a clinging grey mist, he had thought long and hard about Rossmere and the Suttons, his friend Kip, Edmund and Trecarne. And about Perdita herself.

Although he had grown fond of her the previous year, he had always known that she had no interest in a man who was going to have to rely on his wits to make his way in the world. He was attracted to her, and believed she felt the same about him – at least in those rare moments when she let her guard drop. It was obvious, however, that nothing would ever come of it and he saw no sense in exposing himself to unnecessary disappointment. He had assumed that, once he was away from Cornwall and facing the challenges of shipboard life, he would forget about her soon enough.

He had been wrong.

Not that he considered himself in love with her: given their circumstances, that would have been a pointless waste of time. It felt more as though he was unable to shake her off, as though somehow she had become lodged in his mind and remained there to surprise him when he was least expecting it. When the other men on the *Fearless* were talking about women – wives and girlfriends and mistresses, whores past and whores anticipated – in an endless round of sexual banter, Piers found himself remembering Perdita. On the few occasions when he was with other women, whether well-born young ladies or the less genteel women who thronged the harbour side when the *Fearless* came into port, he always found them strangely insubstantial compared to Perdita. As a good-looking young man he had more than his share of opportunities, and he took advantage of several, but the woman was always forgotten as soon as he stepped back on board ship.

He thought it might be because the course of his relations with Perdita had followed such an unusual route. From that first sight of her standing her ground at Trecarne as the dogs streaked towards her in the mist and her 'sister' cowered behind her, when her haughty manner was so much at odds with her ragged clothes, he had been struck by the contrast between her outward appearance and all the fire and longing that she tried to keep hidden from the world. On that first occasion, she had put him in mind of one of those princesses in fairy-tales who were brought up in the forest by a woodcutter and his family. Even now he sometimes found himself aroused by the memory of her pale feet and ankles, smeared with mud and bleeding, as she stood and glared at him in silent fury.

That first mystery had been quickly solved, but there were others that were harder to unravel. She was clever and brave and appeared to be ambitious. Someone who did not know her well would say she must have a good opinion of herself, since she was aspiring to be mistress of Trecarne. But Piers was convinced she was selling herself short. Perhaps because of her irregular origins, perhaps because her position in her father's household had always been open to question, she did not, after all, believe in herself enough to think she deserved what a woman like Sophie Sutton took for granted: to be loved and cherished for herself alone.

Piers recognised the fear and self-doubt that lay beneath the surface, perhaps because his experience with the Menheires had in some ways mirrored her own: both had known they were peripheral, and could be discarded if they slipped from favour. Whatever the reason, he was certain that Perdita deserved better than marriage to Edmund. Just what she deserved was not altogether clear to him. But not Edmund.

His views about his adoptive family had changed dramatically since he'd gone away in the autumn. When Piers had first come to live with his uncle's family, soon after his parents' death, it had been enough to have a place to live; he was not inclined to be critical of his successful uncle and cousin. Still, he disliked many aspects of their life and behaviour. He had felt himself an outsider, part of the household and yet separate from it, and this distance enabled him to endure his uncongenial relatives. He devoted himself to enjoying what he could and ignoring the rest, since he was powerless to change anything. During this time,

Kip had been the ideal companion, with no interests beyond horses and dogs, sport, cards and ale.

Like everyone else, he had heard as soon as he came ashore that the Suttons had lost Rossmere. The news shocked him profoundly, shocked him more even than other people because he knew at once that he should have seen it coming. All the apparatus for their downfall had been in place for months. Edmund and his father had never included him in their discussions, but the signals had been clear enough.

Even without the evidence that had stunned him when the *Fearless* dropped anchor in Genoa two months before.

He thought Perdita would be nearly as interested in what he had to say as the Suttons themselves.

Now he said to Kitty, 'Do you have a letter you'd like me to take to your daughter? I will leave for Rossmere this afternoon. I only hope I am not too late.'

Luke had had a variation on the same dream every night for over a week, and the frustration of it, and the horror, had become blurred with the reality of these sunny June days in the minister's house just outside Wells.

The exact location of the dreams changed night by night, but the texture and atmosphere were always the same. He had agreed to a rendezvous with some unspecified person; he set out in plenty of time; the journey took longer than he expected; the places along the way were further apart than he remembered them; he thought he had arrived at his destination only to find it had shifted and he was hardly half a mile from where he had started; he travelled by sea and the winds blew him back; he travelled by land and his horse fell lame; he travelled on foot and the ground stretched out under his feet.

Time slipped away.

After five days, he could bear it no longer.

'We will leave here tomorrow,' he told Dolores. 'We have wasted too much time already.'

'As you wish,' she said calmly. 'I can give you medicine for the pain, but it will not alleviate it entirely. If you would rather wait a few more days, I am happy to remain here with my daughter.'

In any other circumstances, Luke would have agreed. Three days after setting out from Tilsbury, they had stopped for the night at the house of Mistress Taverner's daughter, on the outskirts of Wells. The following morning, soon after they began their day's journey, Luke's horse was alarmed by an adder. The horse bolted on a long hill. Just as Luke was reining him back, his mount stumbled in a pot-hole and fell heavily, crushing Luke's leg. Luke was badly bruised, his shoulder sprained and the base of his spine was agony. It was all they could do to get him back to the house they had just left.

Once again, Mistress Taverner's daughter and her husband made them both welcome. Beth was not at all like her mother in looks: no trace of the Spanish beauty, she had a homely, blunt-featured face and a mass of cinnamon-coloured hair. But she was warm-hearted and an excellent nurse. Luke spent several days so drugged against the pain that he had hardly any idea where he was, or why. It was only later that the dreams began.

'Your daughter has been most kind,' he said now, 'but, as you know, I am impatient to get back to my wife.'

'A day or two more will make no difference.'

Luke winced. Dolores assumed it was the pain in his spine that troubled him, but her words had ignited a flame of panic. 'A day or two,' he muttered, 'just a day or two. I cannot explain it to you, but I have an instinct to make haste.'

'Then we will follow your instinct. I will go and tell Beth we leave tomorrow.'

She found her daughter in the nursery. Beth had married a man as plain, chubby and good-natured as herself and already they had two plain, chubby, good-natured children and another on the way.

Beth had made it no secret that she thought her mother's present enterprise showed she was losing her wits. When Dolores had first arrived at her home and told her the purpose of her journey, Beth had been stunned.

She clearly remembered the summer Captain Sutton had spent in their home in Tilsbury. She herself had adored the Royalist officer who had become such a vital part of all their lives during those months, but never, either then or since, had she imagined any kind of intrigue between him and her mother.

Beth was shocked to think her mother had ever been unfaithful to her father, but more than that, and much more uncomfortable, she was jealous. Captain Sutton had been her special soldier, though she had been only eight years old. She had always treasured the memory of his affection towards her. It was painful now, as well as shameful, to learn that she had always come second in his heart.

Now she said crossly, 'I cannot believe you mean to continue in this scheme to travel half-way across England on such a fool's errand. Whatever do you expect to gain from it except saddle sores and battered pride?'

Beth had never spoken to her mother quite so frankly before and the novelty of the experience left her breathless. Dolores was not angry, however, but neither was she deterred. In fact, the criticism only strengthened her resolve.

She said, 'Do not worry about me, Beth,' for she knew that anxiety lay behind her gentle daughter's scolding. 'I'm sure you will see me again in a week or so. I'll be safely on my way home again with my curiosity satisfied and no one but you and I will know what has happened.'

'So why do it? And with Master Hollar, of all people. I do not think I trust the fellow, though sometimes I think I like him well enough. I never met such a muddling sort of man in all my life.'

'I could not make him out to begin with either. Nor did I like him. But I've come to think he is not so bad after all. He merely believes he is wicked, which is not the same thing.'

'Now you are talking nonsense. If you were so keen to get away from Harry and his wife, you could have come here. We have plenty of room and the children love to see you.'

'Thank you, Beth, but that's not the same.' Dolores was seated on a high-backed chair, her hands folded in her lap and a secret smile lighting her face. She said gently, 'And here's another thing you will find it hard to understand, though maybe when you are older you will remember this and think, yes, I know now why she did it. When I set out from Tilsbury with Master Hollar, it was like no other action in my life. Everything I've done until now has been caused by outside events, things that I had no control over – the wars that destroyed my family when I was a child, marrying your father because there was no one else to turn to, living in

Tilsbury and doing what I did. I am not complaining, in many ways I know I have been fortunate, but there has never been a choice. Even those months with Stephen, it was the war that brought him to our house, other people who forced us to part. I had no say in any of it, not really. Then, when Luke suggested that I go with him to Cornwall and see Stephen again, I saw that for the very first time I had the chance to act freely, without regard for anyone but myself. I knew if I turned that chance down I would be throwing away something that would never come a second time. So you see, Beth, it hardly matters what happens when I get to Rossmere, this journey will have been worthwhile. Can you understand that?'

'No, I cannot.'

Dolores was still smiling. 'When I set out from Tilsbury, I felt like a ship weighing anchor and leaving its safe harbour. Can you imagine how it feels to be a fine ship, with the wind blowing against the sails, skimming over the sea and no knowing what lies ahead?'

'No, I'm pleased to say I can't. Just imagine if it had been you falling from that horse instead of Master Hollar, what then? All this talk of being a ship, what will it be like when you run aground? Or, worse still, you may be wrecked and sink altogether. What then?'

'Ask me in a month.'

'I can see that nothing is going to make you change your mind.' Beth stood up and wrapped her arms around her mother's neck. 'Since you are going anyway, you may as well give Captain Sutton my love too. Tell him I have not forgotten him either.'

The brief midsummer night faded to a misty dawn, larks singing in the cornfields, birdsong cascading over the mossy walls and a smart new roof at Rossmere.

It was over.

The pain and the blood and the mess, the hurrying midwives and the anxious consultations, the screams of agony and exhausted groans, the long, weary hours of waiting and watching, the suspense and drama and the sleepless nights, all over.

Once again, the early-morning stillness inside the house was disturbed only by the contented sounds of two healthy babies suckling at their mothers' breasts.

Honor had amazed everyone, herself most of all, by being only eight hours in labour.

'There you are,' said Cary, bringing her a jug of hot spiced wine to build up her strength again and pausing to admire the tightly swaddled infant sleeping in his wooden crib. 'What did I tell you? Just like a hen laying an egg.'

Honor was still so shocked and disbelieving at her own good fortune that she only smiled wearily and murmured, 'Oh, Cary, the things you say . . .'

Sophie had had a harder time of it. Her labour began when Honor's baby had just been born, but she herself was so busy she did not notice right away. The midwife resigned herself to having only a hastily prepared meal and no rest at all between the two. Her baby needed turning and she was in labour two days and three nights before the child slithered out. Another fine infant, a girl this time, strong-limbed and bonny as her mother. They put the baby in Sophie's arms and she held her daughter close, but she was too exhausted to speak much. Later, she slept.

Perdita sat in Sophie's bedchamber and watched the room fill with midsummer sunlight as the dawn broke over Rossmere. Never in her life had she felt so weary: she had carried water, changed bedding, coaxed and soothed and bullied; she had distracted Francis and comforted Sophie, she had praised Honor and encouraged Louisa and been ordered around by Cary for more days and nights than she cared to remember. She had not known it was possible for a body to feel so worn out.

'Go on to bed now,' Cary told her. 'Get yourself a few hours' sleep. That's what I'm going to do.'

'Yes,' said Perdita automatically. Like everyone else in the household, this past few days, she had fallen into the habit of obeying Cary without thinking. Then she yawned and said, 'Thank heavens it is all over.'

A familiar frown creased Cary's scarred forehead. 'Don't go speaking too soon,' she said ominously. 'The danger's not over for a fortnight at least, not until they're both churched and the babies given a Christian baptism. Haven't you ever heard of childbed fever? I remember a woman in Tilsbury who gave birth to twins and was up and doing within three days, no one healthier than her. Then six days after that her belly began to swell again, and then the poison spread into her arms and legs and—'

Tears of exhaustion prickled the backs of Perdita's lids as she began to giggle helplessly. 'Oh, Cary, please, not now. Not another of your terrible stories, I can't bear it.'

'This is no joking matter,' said Cary sternly. Then she grinned, gave Perdita an unexpected pat on the head and trudged off to bed.

Perdita knew she should do the same, but for once her limbs refused to move. She ached all over and her head was throbbing. She wondered if perhaps she was falling ill, and she thought it would be a strange turn of events if the two new mothers came through their ordeal unscathed while one of their nurses fell sick.

Cary had left the bedchamber door open and after a little while Perdita became aware that there was someone standing in the doorway: Francis.

She shifted slightly in her chair. 'Come on in, Francis,' she told him. 'Come and say good morning to your little niece.'

Francis tiptoed across the floorboards with exaggerated care, making them creak even more than usual. Sophie opened her eyes as he loomed over the bed. She smiled up at him.

'How are you?' he asked.

'Sore,' she said, shifting herself into a more comfortable position. 'But apart from that I'm fine. Have you seen my baby?' She indicated the crib with a slight turn of her head.

'Not yet.' He peered cautiously at the sleeping child, as if fearing that even his glance might be enough to wake her. He whispered, 'She looks so small.'

'I know,' said Sophie. 'Like a little mouse.'

'What will you call her?'

'That is for Luke to decide.'

'But . . .' Francis frowned.

'He will be here soon,' said Sophie firmly. 'Don't ask me how I know, but this time I am sure of it.'

Francis had given up all hope of his brother-in-law, but he did not want to upset Sophie so he remained silent. He lowered his weight cautiously on to the chair beside the bed and gazed at Sophie with a fond and vaguely hopeful expression. Perdita wondered if she should leave them alone together but she was still too exhausted to move. There was something dreamlike about the scene, brother and sister together in the dawn light, no need to talk out loud. She sensed how even now Francis was drawing strength from Sophie. Despite all the dramas and anxieties of the past few days, he did not look as if he had been drinking. Perdita wondered if fatherhood was going to provide the necessary goad to make a man of him at last.

After a while, Sophie said, 'How is Honor?'

'She grows stronger by the hour.' Francis appeared baffled by this. 'She has already walked around her bedchamber and she talks of going downstairs in a day or two. It is a miracle, after all her fears, I can hardly believe it. We have so much to be thankful for, and the boy is thriving.'

'What name do you have for him?'

'We have not yet decided,' said Francis. 'Honor says she would like to call him Nicolas, after my father, but I am not sure it is a good idea.'

'That would be beautiful,' said Sophie, 'and will give our mother much pleasure. How can you possibly object?'

'Well, clearly it is for Honor to have the final decision. After all she has been through I do not want to contradict her but, still, I do not think . . . I mean, I am so happy for her, so very happy . . . so . . . so happy . . .'

His voice broke on a sob. His face was streaked with tears and he made no attempt to hide them. He said, 'She has given me a son, praise God they are both well and yet . . .'

'What is it?' asked Sophie.

'Oh, Sophie, the child is heir to nothing – nothing at all! I always thought my son would grow up here, the way we did. That he'd learn to ride in the first meadow and fish in the stream and get into trouble for climbing on the stable roof and all the rest of it. Just the same as us. But he won't. He'll only know this as the home his family was forced to give up. Why should we burden him with my father's name when he will have nothing else? I never thought Honor was going to survive. I even persuaded myself it was all for the best: no wife, no child to endure the pain and the humiliation. And now there is no escape from it. Each time I look at the child and Honor, I am so happy they are both well, and the next instant I think of what lies ahead of them and I feel nothing but shame and despair.'

'Oh, Francis,' said Sophie sadly.

Perdita said nothing. She thought what a fine thing it would be if Francis's son could grow up to have all the courage and strength his father lacked, if he could rebuild the Suttons' fortunes and win back their home and lands from the Menheires. But when she looked at his weeping father and remembered the frailty and timid nature of his mother, she had to admit that such a happy outcome was not likely at all.

Chapter Thirty-Eight

The fine midsummer weather continued. The hay was cut and gathered in, corn was growing strongly and the animals were thriving. Kip rode over from Camborne to admire his little niece and nephew and see them baptised. Sophie was briefly distressed that the choice of name for their child could not be delayed until Luke's return, but her uncharacteristic tearfulness was attributed to the weakness that always follows delivery. She chose the name Lucy for her daughter, since it was the closest to Luke that she knew. Honor's son was called Nicolas after his grandfather and Francis raised no further objections. Since neither of their mothers was well enough to make the journey to Porthew church, Perdita found herself standing in for both of them at the christening.

All the Suttons' friends and neighbours for miles around rode over to celebrate the safe delivery of the two babies. Cary and Louisa brought in extra help and worked like carthorses to prepare lavish food for their guests. The great hall and the gardens were filled with talk and laughter and good cheer. Alice talked so much about the old days that she began to think the good times had returned to Rossmere and all their troubles were over. Kip was in his element, with as much bowls and skittles as he wanted and a full moon to guide their guests home at the end of the day.

But beneath all the celebration and thanksgiving lay the dread certainty that this must be the last time the Suttons presided over a large gathering at Rossmere. Hosts and guests all avoided mentioning the doom hanging over the house, but the

Menheires' name was whispered in corners. Vague threats were muttered, but there was a general acceptance that Edmund's progress was inevitable and, before long, must be accepted.

Perdita began to see that Edmund's belief in the all-conquering power of wealth was mostly correct: soon the Suttons would become an embarrassment to their former neighbours, while the owner of Trecarne was made welcome in their place. Luckily Edmund himself did not attend the christening, or the festivities that followed.

He did not visit Rossmere until two days later, when Perdita and the two new mothers were sitting with Kip in the garden, enjoying the warm sun.

It was the first time Honor had been persuaded to leave the house and risk the fresh air – not because she was anxious for her own health: all her worries now were for the brown-haired, blue-eyed, crinkle-faced infant who was sleeping inside in his crib. She and Francis fussed around their son every minute of the day and night: he was too hot, he was too cold; he was feeding too much or not enough. Perdita thought it would be a miracle if baby Nicolas did not grow up to be the most fussy, demanding youth in the whole of creation.

Honor, however, was utterly transformed. She was still painfully thin, and the shadows around her eyes had not yet gone away, but her cheeks were gaining a healthy colour and she was eating three times more than she ever had in the past. Her breasts were swollen with milk. Like Sophie, she had insisted on feeding her infant herself, which shocked Perdita more than anything. Honor was far too protective of her child to entrust him to a wet-nurse's care, while Sophie found nursing her daughter a pleasure she saw no reason to miss.

Little Lucy was more fretful than her placid cousin, but she fed lustily and was much doted on. Her father's absence, not spoken of directly by anyone but never quite forgotten either, made everyone especially tender towards her. Stephen, on coming in from the fields, always went at once to her crib and treated the simple act of opening her eyes or sneezing as evidence of great cleverness and nobility of character. Then he remembered himself and praised Nicolas equally.

This morning, Honor had brought out a piece of mending,

Kip lounged at their feet and played knucklebones in the dust and Perdita raised her face to the sun and enjoyed the feeling of warmth on her face. Kitty would have disapproved, but for now Perdita had forgotten about Kitty. Only Sophie seemed out of sorts, but since everyone assumed they understood the reason this was not commented on.

Eventually Sophie got to her feet and said, 'I am going inside. The sun hurts my eyes and I have a headache.'

Honor gazed up at her with sympathy. 'Do you want some of my drops? They have feverfew in them and are very good for headaches.'

'Don't bother,' said Sophie crossly. 'Cary can get me some cool ale. Not everyone treats a little twinge like a mortal illness.'

Honor blinked with surprise at the unexpected rebuke.

When Sophie had retreated into the cool gloom of the house, Kip said, 'You offering Sophie medicines, Honor. There's a turnaround no one ever expected to see.'

But soon he, too, grew bored and wandered down towards the stables.

'He's right,' said Perdita. 'You have changed. Do you remember that fortune-teller on St Ewan's Day who said you'd have a child within the twelvemonth? You were so worried at the time, and now look at you.'

Honor smiled, with quiet satisfaction. 'I feel different, that's why. Ever since I was a little girl I worried almost every day about having a child of my own. I was so convinced I'd never survive it. That was why . . . well, my husband and I . . . but that is not important now. I've done the one thing I thought I could never do and I feel as if nothing can ever frighten me again. Unless, of course, anything happened to little Nicolas – that would be impossible to endure.' Her lip trembled. Then she turned to Perdita with an anxious frown. 'Did you hear him cry just now? No? I was sure I heard something. I'll go and check, just to be on the safe side. You never can tell . . .'

She hurried off, leaving Perdita smiling and alone.

Crunch of feet on the gravel and Edmund Menheire stood before her.

Perdita looked up at him with disdain. 'If you wish to speak with Francis, I believe he is in his office.'

'No, it is you I have come to see.'

'Me? I do not think you and I have any more to say to each other. If you will excuse me . . .'

She rose from her seat but he gestured with his hands as if to push her down again and said, 'Be quiet for once and listen to me.'

'Master Menheire—' Perdita began angrily.

But he interrupted her and said, 'Last October, when you thought I was making you a proposal of marriage, you would have accepted, is that right?'

'I hardly think—'

'Damn it, woman, I'm not interested in what you think. Just tell me, would you have accepted or no?'

'An honourable proposal, yes, but what you were offering was—'

'Then will you accept one now?'

'*What?*'

'It's perfectly plain, just answer yes or no. Will you be my wife?'

Perdita was so shocked she almost laughed. She said, 'Is this another of your cruel jests?'

'Why would I jest about such a matter? Well, give me your answer. If it is no, I'll leave at once and we'll say no more about it.' Already he was turning, as if to go away again.

Perdita said quickly, 'Wait. You have taken me by surprise and I need a moment or two to consider. My mind has been full of nothing but babies for days and . . . Why don't we walk in the gardens and we can talk?'

She was thinking very fast. She believed his proposal was genuinely meant and she knew at once that she could not turn him down. To be mistress of Trecarne had been her chief hope and ambition for more than a year and she was not about to turn away from it now. But she had to handle this carefully: there were many factors to be considered.

No trace of her rapid calculations showed on her face as she rose from the seat and said, with an easy smile, 'This way, Master Menheire. This is our best chance of talking without interruption.'

He followed her and said, 'What is there to discuss? Just give me your answer and we can leave it at that.'

'In some ways, of course, you are entirely right, and I may as well tell you that I am inclined to accept your offer, but even so, there are many details to be considered.'

'We can leave those to the lawyers.'

'Quite. But I seem to remember you had strenuous objections to my irregular origins and I cannot help wondering what has made you change your mind.'

'I have weighed up the situation carefully and have come to the conclusion that the defects of your birth need not be such a barrier after all.'

Perdita slid a glance at him as they walked towards the skittles lawn. He did not look much like a man who had been weighing up matters carefully. He looked more like a man who had passed several sleepless nights and was at present in the grip of an all-consuming passion. She felt herself grow calmer as she understood the strength of his inner turmoil. She said, 'I am delighted to hear it. A man of fashion and influence can ill afford to be burdened by such petty and old-fashioned worries.'

'If that is all, then—'

'No, my next concern is the Suttons.'

'You must forget about them. They do not interest me in the least.'

'Nor I,' declared Perdita, drawing a murmur of surprise from her companion. 'But I confess I have no wish to be married to a man who is hated by everyone and welcome nowhere. It is therefore essential that we find some way for you to achieve your ends while giving the impression of acting more generously than has so far been the case.'

'I do not see how that is possible. But I can assure you that money has a way of winning people over in the end.'

'Maybe so. But still . . . it might assist me to think of a solution if I knew why you so particularly want to gain possession of Rossmere when the house itself is of no interest to you.'

To her disappointment, he did not take up the bait. He said merely, 'Rossmere is mine. The Suttons have only themselves to blame for their misfortune.'

'Oh, yes, I do so agree. But others do not always see things as clearly as you and I. That is why it is so important to present your actions in the best possible light. For instance, if you do not want the house itself, then maybe you could let the family remain here as your tenants. Or there might be some other property of yours which they could be allowed to inhabit. Such a solution would cost you little and be more than worth it in terms of public approval.'

'The opinion of others is of no interest to me,' said Edmund automatically, but she could see he was intrigued by the idea.

She said, 'We need to weigh up the different options with regard to the Suttons and see what is best. For you and your family, of course. Not for them.'

'Indeed, yes, yes. That is all very well,' Edmund burst out impatiently. 'What I want to know is, will you be my wife?' He turned to face her as he asked the question.

She saw his red face, handsome and perspiring in the warm sunshine. She saw his hunger and his eagerness, and behind him, in her mind's eye, she saw the long, elegant façade of Trecarne.

She smiled and said calmly, 'I have no wish to keep you in suspense, sir, and as I said, you have every reason to be optimistic but . . .' Edmund took a step towards her as though to take her in his arms, but she raised a hand in warning and said, 'I share your eagerness to see this matter to a swift conclusion, but – not here. At Rossmere there is always the risk of being overheard. Given the way things stand between you and the Suttons, I prefer to conclude our discussion without fear of interference from them or anyone else. This is what I suggest. If you do whatever business you have with Uncle Stephen and Francis and then leave, I will ride over to Trecarne this afternoon and we can discuss it further in private. After all, it is your house which has brought us together, is it not? I am sure my petition to His Majesty is in some part responsible for your present overtures. What could be more appropriate than to set the seal on our agreement there?'

'Then you do agree?'

Once more, Perdita neatly sidestepped his approach. 'This afternoon, Master Menheire. You will have your answer then. At Trecarne.'

*　　*　　*

Perdita had not seen the house at midsummer before. Now it was as though Trecarne had been waiting for this moment: it stood serene and beautiful in the afternoon sunshine, the wide façade and twin towers spread before her as if in welcome.

She had told no one at Rossmere where she was going, but she knew they'd find out soon enough. She intended telling anyone who was interested that she had visited Edmund Menheire to see if she might persuade him to treat the Suttons with greater leniency. This, at least, was partly the truth.

She had half thought to confide to Sophie the real reason for this visit, but Sophie was still complaining of a headache and Lucy was crying loudly, so Perdita decided to talk to her when she returned – but by then her own future was sure to have been decided, one way or the other.

'That's a fine house, Mistress Treveryan,' said Rudd, reining his horse to a halt behind her. She had brought along the big man as well as Adam just in case Edmund Menheire was tempted to resort to rough tactics. She remembered his warning last autumn about less scrupulous men seizing by force what they could not get by legitimate means: there was always a chance he might have been describing his own inclinations. She was fairly sure she could handle him herself and that his proposal was sincere, but she did not intend to take any chances.

She said now, 'My father built it before the wars.'

While thinking to herself, and soon, if I play my hand right, it will be mine. I will have won.

Edmund was waiting for her outside the house. While they were still some distance away, Perdita said to Adam and Rudd, 'I have private business to conclude with Master Menheire. One of you must remain within calling distance at all times. If I need you for any reason I will shout and you must come at once. Even if you have to break the door down to do so. Is that understood?'

'Yes, mistress,' said Adam and Rudd in unison. Adam looked excited, Rudd depressed at the prospect of having to do battle with the Menheires' doors and servants.

Perdita said tersely, 'Good. However, I do not expect it will be necessary.' Then she gave her attention to greeting her host in a manner that combined warmth and grandeur in exactly the right proportions.

Edmund was frowning, every muscle taut with expectation. He said, 'You are here. Excellent.'

They walked into the house in silence, Adam and Rudd at their heels.

Edmund said to them, 'Don't follow so close. Go round to the back and wait there.'

But Perdita said, 'They have instructions to attend me here.'

Edmund showed no further emotion as he ushered her into a large, well-proportioned chamber. Perdita recognised it as the one they had first entered when they visited Trecarne in March, more than a year before. This time the windows were un-encumbered and the air was filled with afternoon sunlight. It was even more beautiful than she remembered and she caught her breath at the thought that soon she would be walking through these rooms as their rightful owner.

'Well?' he said, as soon as the door was closed. 'What is your decision?'

Their business was quickly concluded. Perdita insisted that their betrothal must be kept a secret until her mother had been informed and the legal niceties dealt with by Diggory Fitch and Edmund's lawyer. Some proper provision must be made for the Suttons, which was more generous than that presently proposed: she thought, though she did not choose to tell Edmund this, that she'd talk it over with Sophie and Francis and see what would best suit them. Edmund raised no objection to her plans for the Suttons, even when she said that any arrangements must be drawn up by a lawyer and signed by all the interested parties.

She wanted his verbal undertaking that she might keep some control over her ship, the *Speedwell*, though she knew that in this matter she was dependent on his goodwill and her own cleverness, since legally all her property would become his on their marriage. She also requested a contract that would ensure the *Speedwell* reverted to her in the tragic event of his death, just as he would be able to keep the ship should she predecease him. Similarly Trecarne must be made over to her and any heirs he might leave behind him.

Edmund merely nodded as she went through all the topics she had listed in her mind on the way over. It did not seem to surprise him that his future bride should be so concerned with financial and legal details at a time like this; if anything, she saw, it excited him. Contracts and balance sheets were the only world he knew, and to hear them discussed in Perdita's clear, firm voice was a potent mingling of the familiar and the unknown, which made him desire her more than ever.

At length she could think of nothing more to say. Edmund unfolded his arms and moved towards her. 'Is that everything?' he asked.

'It must remain secret until I hear from Lady Treveryan.'

'I have already agreed to that.'

'Well, then—'

'You accept?'

'I accept.'

She remembered, as she spoke the two words of agreement, that last October she had vowed he would one day make her an honourable proposal on bended knee and she wondered briefly if there was any way of insisting on this added refinement, but the moment passed more rapidly than she could have expected. He had caught her in his arms and crushed her to him

'Then you will be my wife,' he breathed urgently, somewhere in the region of her ear.

'Yes, of course. I—'

The rest of her sentence was silenced by the pressure of his lips against hers.

The kiss was like the man: impatient, grasping and quite without subtlety or finesse. Perdita had already calculated how much it was prudent to allow, but she was startled by the unexpected strength in his forearms and was relieved to think that Adam and Rudd were stationed outside the door. She did not in the least enjoy his kiss, but then, to her satisfaction, she found she was not repelled by him either. And it occurred to her that a man of such urgent and unschooled desires might prove a good deal easier to manage than a man of either greater experience or less passion. While his palms pawed the small of her back and his mouth was crushing her lips against her teeth, she reflected that once she had learned how to exploit this aspect of her husband's nature to the full, they might learn to get along together very well.

When he was forced to pause and gasp for breath, Perdita

escaped with a laugh, as she exclaimed, 'Heavens above, you leave me quite breathless. We shall have to fix a date as soon as possible or the Lord only knows what will happen.'

'Perdita . . .' He was staring at her with smoky eyes, but she had no great desire to endure another of his bone-crushing embraces just yet so she patted her hair, straightened her collar and said, 'All in good time. We will not have long to wait. I confess, I am almost as impatient as you.'

A little later, when she was preparing to depart, he looked at her with great intensity and said, 'You and I have much in common. A year ago I thought I wanted Mistress Sutton, but now I see that you will suit me better. We want the same things. We understand each other.'

'An excellent basis for a marriage, I do so agree,' said Perdita brightly.

But when she was riding back to Rossmere in the fading afternoon sunlight, she kept remembering his words, and instead of the elation she had been expecting, she felt depressed.

She told herself firmly that this was no time to indulge in pointless regrets. She had set out to become the lawful mistress of Trecarne, the house where her mother had once been happy and where she herself had been conceived, the grandest house in all this part of Cornwall which had been wrongfully taken from her father. By every form of natural justice Trecarne should have been her home and now her determination was making that happen. She had every reason to be happy and none at all for gloom. She tried to divert herself by imagining her future life as the wife of Edmund Menheire.

The alterations to be made to the house kept her amused for over a mile. Then there was the accommodation in London to consider, since Edmund was properly ambitious and the Cornish stage would soon prove too small for them. She would visit Kitty frequently in Plymouth. She might even see Piers from time to time, though for some reason this prospect was not as cheering as she had expected. She turned her attention to the paintings and furnishings she would purchase for Trecarne, the carriage and fine horses. Her hospitality would be famous throughout Cornwall. Sophie and Honor and their babies would be frequent visitors to Trecarne. Even Louisa.

Still, the hollow ache remained. She wondered if achieving one's ambition was always such a bitter-sweet sensation. Maybe it was the struggle itself that was the pleasure, rather than the attainment. Maybe that was what a man like Colonel Menheire had understood all along. Maybe she needed to set new goals for herself: she might persuade Edmund to turn his back on Cornwall altogether and try his luck at court.

She remembered Edmund's final words. Yes, it was true, they did have much in common. She understood him as Sophie could never have done. He was ambitious and ruthless, and so was she. It gave her no pleasure to admit how similar they were, since in so many ways she disliked him. But there was no changing human nature, everyone was agreed on that.

By the time she was back at Rossmere she had thought of everything she could, but still her spirits weighed heavy. She decided to find Sophie and talk it over with her: it was a relief to think how pleased all the Suttons would be to discover that there was, after all, to be at least a partial solution to their problems.

The sound of raised voices, anguished and angry, drew her across the courtyard to the kitchen. Kip was there, Cary and Louisa too, but there was no sign of Sophie.

It was a few moments before Perdita's eyes grew accustomed to the shadowy interior of the kitchen so she did not see straight away what Louisa held in her hands. She did, however, see that Louisa's pretty and so often angry face was streaked with tears.

'How could he?' she wailed. 'How can he be so cruel? Just look at them, all dying or dead already! And for what? Oh, I hate him! May he die in everlasting torment and – oh, how could he do such a thing?'

'What? What has happened?'

Louisa turned to her in a fury. 'Look, this was out by the horse trough. Kip found two more in the barn. Look, oh, it is horrible!'

She thrust what she was holding into Perdita's hands. It was white and feathery, still warm. Perdita could feel the dove's heart still beating rapidly, but otherwise it did not move. Its beak was open and its round eyes filming over.

'What is wrong with it?' asked Perdita.

'We think Menheire's man must have laid poison for them this morning,' said Kip wretchedly.

'We *know* he did,' said Louisa. 'I saw him putting corn for them on the roof of the sty. I thought it odd but, dear heavens, I wish I'd had the wit to stop him then. It was all laced with poison.'

'The doves?' said Perdita stupidly. 'Why would Menheire's groom want to poison the doves?'

'Because he is a fiend!' shrieked Louisa.

'Because they eat his corn,' said Cary.

'Well, and what is wrong with that?' Louisa rounded on her. 'What's a little corn when there have always been doves at Rossmere? Oh, I wish I could put poison in his food. I'd like to see him suffer too!'

'Edmund Menheire thinks only of his profits,' said Kip.

Perdita gazed down at the white dove in her hands. She could no longer feel its heartbeat. Its head lolled brokenly. She felt something cold and hard, like a splinter of ice in her heart. She thought: this is the man I have chosen to marry, there is no turning back. I have chosen my path and I know what I am taking on. And then she thought: but the man is a fool, to cause such outrage and all for a few handfuls of corn. I will talk to him about it the next time I see him. There will be white doves at Rossmere again before we marry.

Little Het stumbled into the kitchen, her arms heaped up with white doves and deposited them in her mother's lap.

She said to Cary, 'Why do they all keep lying down? Are they sleeping?'

Perdita could bear it no longer. She pushed the dead bird back into Louisa's hands and hurried from the kitchen.

Just as she was crossing the courtyard, she saw Honor. 'Have you seen Sophie?' Perdita asked her.

'Yes, she's lying down.' Honor was pale and her forehead creased into a familiar frown. 'She says it is nothing but I think she may have a fever. Francis is sending for the midwife. I'm going to get Cary.'

'The midwife? What's it to do with her? Why not the apothecary or a doctor?'

Honor spoke in a low, anxious voice, as though afraid they might be overheard even though they were alone in the sunny courtyard. She said, 'It is only six days since Sophie's baby was born. She is not out of danger yet. There is still a chance of childbed fever.'

She hurried on. Perdita stood quite still. Out of the corner of her eye she could see something pitifully small and white lying like a dropped kerchief on the ground beneath a window-ledge. She remembered how she had laughed off Cary's dire warning on the morning following Lucy's birth.

Just another Cary story.

She did not feel like laughing now.

But when she saw Sophie, her fears were eased. She was lying fully clothed on top of her bedcovers. She brushed aside Perdita's fears. 'Just a headache,' she told her. 'And maybe a bit of a chill. The sun has been very strong today and I think perhaps I've been overdoing things. I hear you disappeared on a mysterious errand today. Was it to Master Fitch about that petition of yours? I hope the King does give you back Trecarne. Lucy and I will enjoy visiting you at Trecarne.'

Perdita smiled. 'I'm glad to hear it. I intend you to visit me often. Edmund Menheire proposed to me today.'

'Oh, I am sorry.' Sophie pulled a face. 'Was it horrible?'

'Only in parts. I have accepted him.'

'What? Oh, Perdita, you cannot mean it!'

'It's a secret, you must not tell anyone yet. And that is not all. He has agreed to change the terms of the agreement with Francis over Rossmere. It's not all fixed yet, but I've told him I'll not marry him until it is done properly by a lawyer. Either he has to find somewhere else for Francis and his mother to live, or else they must be allowed to remain here as tenants. What do you think they would prefer?'

Sophie was frowning. She gripped Perdita's hand tightly and said, 'You must not marry that man for the sake of my family. It is too much to ask. I know you want to help them, but . . . it is still not too late to change your mind.'

Perdita had been looking forward to getting some credit for her actions, but not as much as this. She said hastily, 'You mustn't think I'm marrying Edmund just to help your family. Surely you know I'm not so self-sacrificing. Mostly I am doing this for myself.'

'Why? Do you really think you can care for such a man?'

'Not especially. But I already care for his house very much indeed. You know I've had my heart set on living at Trecarne ever since the first time I saw it. And in order to get the house I must marry the owner. He's not so bad as all that.' Perdita hastily blotted out the image of little Het, her sorrowing face over the pile of white doves as she went on, 'I dare say it will be a struggle sometimes, but I think we'll get along well enough together.'

Sophie's frown had smoothed into a look of puzzled affection. 'I hope you know what you're doing,' she said. 'It all seems very odd to me.'

Perdita noticed that Sophie's hand, still clasping hers, was shaking. 'Are you cold?' she asked.

'A little.'

Perdita helped her under the covers. Sophie's tremors grew stronger. Beads of perspiration covered her face, but her skin was cool to the touch.

Stephen hurried in, still in his working clothes. 'Cary says you have a fever,' he said, his voice ragged with anxiety. 'How are you feeling?'

'It's nothing, Uncle Stephen. You must not worry about me. It is just a headache and bit of a chill. I'll be fine again by morning.'

'Thank God for that.'

A thin mewing noise from the crib. Perdita automatically went over to the tightly wrapped infant. Sophie was struggling to raise herself on the pillows. Stephen stepped forward eagerly to help her.

'Poor little Lucy,' said Sophie. 'She's hungry again. Nothing seems to satisfy her today. Will you bring her to me, Perdita?'

'Of course.' Perdita leaned over the crib and lifted the baby, all hungry mouth and bawling impatience. She turned to Sophie with a smile and said, 'Just look at your daughter. She's as greedy to be satisfied as a certain gentleman we've both had dealings with.'

Sophie smiled. Perdita was just crossing the room, the baby in her arms, when Cary burst in through the door and snatched her away. 'Dear heavens above, Mistress Perdita, what are you doing?'

'Don't frighten me so!' snapped Perdita. 'I was only taking Lucy to be fed.'

Sophie's eyes were locked on Cary's face. 'Let me have my baby,' she said.

'Not now,' said Cary. 'Not while you've got a fever.'

'But—'

'Do you want Lucy to catch it from you, then?'

'Oh!' Sophie turned her face away and put her hand to her mouth, biting the knuckles fiercely in her pain. Tears were spilling out of her eyes. She said, 'Go on, then, if you must. Take her away.'

But Cary already had.

There was a steady stream of visitors to Sophie's bedchamber after that – all the family trekking in and out, the midwife and the physician, even the minister from Porthew – so it was not until much later that Sophie and Perdita were once more alone again.

Sophie had been shivering helplessly with the fever, but now the attack seemed to be passing. She patted the edge of her bed, inviting Perdita to sit. She said, 'I keep thinking of you and Edmund Menheire. Do you really think you can be happy with a man like him?'

Perdita considered this for a while, then she said, 'I'll not look to him for happiness, but I believe I can be content to be his wife. As content with him as anyone.'

'I always thought his cousin was more to your taste.'

'Piers? If he had a house like Trecarne, then he might do very nicely, but I'd be a fool to let myself be wooed by a man with only a handsome face to recommend him.'

Sophie said teasingly, 'So young and yet so worldly wise.' They remained together in silence for a while, before Sophie said, 'Do you remember when you first came to Rossmere and you asked me if I was not afraid to die an old maid?'

'Did I?'

'Yes. And now look at me. Not very young, and certainly not a maid.'

'But you're not—'

'Of course not. I'll be fine again in the morning.' Then she burst out, in anguish, 'Oh, Perdita, I was so certain Luke would be here by now. What can have happened to him?'

'I wish I knew.'

A little later, when the sky was turning from the emerald of dusk to brief midsummer darkness, Sophie muttered. 'This afternoon, when I was sleeping, I dreamed of Falcon. I wonder who has him now. It was so good of your father to give him to me, the best gift in all the world. I don't think I ever thanked him properly.'

'What nonsense. You never stopped thanking him, as far as I can remember.'

'Good.'

And a little later Sophie said softly, 'Dear Perdita, I feel as if we've known each other for ever. And when you're at Trecarne we will be neighbours always. I do hope you will be happy.'

She smiled at that, and so did Perdita, but in her heart the words sounded like a valediction.

Chapter Thirty-Nine

Outside the gates to Rossmere, the two riders reined their horses to a halt.

Luke turned to his companion with an eager smile. 'This is where the Suttons' land begins. The end of our journey.'

He was urging his horse forward, but Dolores said, 'You must go on without me.'

'What?' Luke wheeled his horse round. 'You're surely not going to change your mind now.'

'I will wait here. Tell Stephen I have come and then . . .'

Luke did not want to waste time in argument. Both he and Dolores had been so impatient to complete their journey that they had left their Truro inn at sunrise and had ridden without stopping since. Luke had even been tempted to leave the packhorse there to be brought on later so that they might reach Rossmere more quickly.

His back was giving him a great deal of pain, in spite of the powerful medicines Dolores had brought with her from Wells. He was furious with himself for being the cause of their delay.

He looked at Dolores. Though she was outwardly calm, he could detect the tension beneath the surface. He had imagined taking her with him into the great hall at Rossmere and was looking forward to seeing her first meeting with Stephen, but he realised that after so long this meeting was going to be hard enough for both of them, even away from the curious gaze of Stephen's family.

So all he said was, 'I'll find Captain Sutton for you. Promise you'll stay in this same place. If he is working in one of the far fields he may be some time.'

She smiled. 'It's been seventeen years, Luke. An hour or two will make no difference to me now. Do not worry, of course I'll stay here. Where else would I go?'

'Don't forget to tell him I was the one persuaded you to come.'

'I'll make sure you get full credit for your actions.'

'Thank you.' Luke was smiling, slightly sheepish about his own insistence on being praised, but determined all the same. 'You are my gift for my wife's family,' he said. 'I want them to think well of me.'

'I know, but don't pin all your hopes on this. I will probably be on my way back to Tilsbury this evening.'

'At least you will both be free of the past.'

She nodded, then said, 'Besides, you have other gifts for the family.'

'Yes.' There was O'Rourke. Also, as Luke had told her on the journey to the south-west, he now knew why the Menheires were so desperate to get their hands on Rossmere.

'Go on, then, Luke. Go to your wife. I will wait for Stephen here. Good luck.'

'And good luck to you, Mistress Taverner.'

Suddenly both were aware that the strange partnership which had developed between them during their journey was about to be broken. The circumstances of the past three weeks would never be repeated and each was about to be caught up in the stream of their separate lives, Luke with his new wife and his business in Porthew, Dolores . . . But her future was uncertain.

Luke tied the packhorse to a branch in the shade and set off down the lime avenue. He kicked his own horse to a weary canter; suddenly he was filled with a fear that Sophie might have returned to Porthew and he'd not see her until evening.

Just before he reached the house, he saw Amos. He was making a half-hearted attempt to scythe the long grass and weeds at the edge of the drive.

Luke called out to him, 'Where is Captain Sutton?'

Amos glanced up and then indicated, with a brief movement of his head, the tall figure seated on a bench in the shade at the side of the house. Luke drove his horse on and came to a halt in front of him.

Stephen looked up slowly. His face was ashen and he looked as if he was recovering from a long illness. His body was limp and exhausted.

Luke smiled. In a short time Sophie's uncle would be singing a different song.

'Luke?' asked Stephen. 'Why have you come now?'

'Good day to you, Captain Sutton.' Luke had imagined this moment many times but still the words seemed awkward. 'Take my horse and go to the gates. Did Sophie tell you I have a surprise? Someone is waiting there to talk with you. Someone with a message for you from Tilsbury.'

'What?'

Captain Sutton was grown very slow, Luke thought. He said again, 'From Tilsbury. Hurry, man. Don't keep your messenger waiting.'

He jumped down from the horse and pulled Stephen to his feet, pressing the reins into his hands.

Stephen stared at him in amazement.

'But, Luke,' he said, 'have you not heard?'

It was Captain Sutton who was not hearing very well, thought Luke. He was standing like a man in the first stages of paralysis and Luke had practically to hoist him into the saddle.

'Just outside the gates,' he said, slapping the horse on its rump to drive it forward. 'And be prepared for a surprise. Do you know where Sophie is?' Stephen was frowning. Impatient now, Luke said, 'Never mind, I shall find her myself soon enough. I'll see you later, Captain Sutton. I only wish I could see your face when . . . but some things are better private.'

And, flourishing his hat in a salute of encouragement, Luke hurried on into the house.

Dolores had tethered her horse in the shade beside the pack-horse. She was pacing up and down, back and forth. Already she felt as if she knew each blade of grass that grew beside the track, each jagged stone and sunbaked ridge of mud.

A songthrush was serenading her from a bush and skylarks

sang in the misty blue of the sky over the cornfields. She noticed every smallest detail: her senses were more alert than they had ever been in her life. Her heart was pounding fiercely but at the same time she felt an icy calm.

She knew what she had to do.

When she had first turned down Luke's suggestion to accompany him to Rossmere it was because she could not bear the thought of Stephen pretending an emotion that had long since died, simply because he felt sorry for her. His pity would be the cruellest pain of all. She had only changed her mind because she remembered that Stephen had always been incapable of pretence. Unless he had altered out of all recognition, he'd not be able to keep his true response a secret from her. If he was dismayed to see her again, she would know at once.

She would leave Rossmere immediately and the past they had once shared would be laid to rest for ever.

Her pacing stopped. She listened.

Horse's hoofs moving with painful slowness over the hard ground towards her.

Her mind was racing as she considered the possibilities. It was Stephen: in that case, Luke must have told him she was here and he was in no hurry to see her again. However, it was possible Luke had not told him her identity. Or perhaps it was not Stephen at all but Luke himself with bad news. Stephen might have met with an accident. Stephen was dead. Stephen—

Horse and rider came into view. It was Stephen.

As soon as he saw her, his face, already pale and drawn, became blank with shock. Whatever he had been expecting, it was not this. She stood very still, waiting, prepared to turn round and ride back the way she had come.

The reins fell from his hands. Weary and no longer sure what was expected of it, the horse came to a halt beside the other two. Its head dropped and it snatched a few mouthfuls of grass.

Still staring, his face drained of all expression except disbelief, Stephen dismounted. He was moving heavily, like a man whose body had become detached from the messages sent by the brain. He came towards her, then stopped when still a few paces away.

She waited.

'Dolores,' he said at last, his voice barely audible. 'Is it you?'

She said, 'Have I changed so very much?'

'But I never thought . . . Is it really you?'

'Yes, Stephen.' She smiled. 'I am not a ghost. Not this time.'

His face was anguished. 'But why?' he asked her. 'Why have you come now?'

'I travelled with Luke Hollar. He came to see me in Tilsbury.'

'Luke. Dear God.'

There was silence. Neither moved.

The smile faded from Dolores's face and she felt some foolish flame of hope flicker and then die inside her. It was only what she should have expected. After seventeen years, had she really imagined they might attempt to rebuild what had once existed between them? And what had that been anyway? If all the women who once thought themselves loved by a soldier far from home set off to find their old sweetheart again, then the roads of England would be impassable to normal traffic and every woman a fool.

In one respect she had been right. Stephen was not able to mask his true feelings. Never had a man looked more appalled to see anyone than Stephen did now at the sight of her.

She cursed herself for her folly in believing what Luke had told her. Of course Stephen was not still faithful to the pledges they had made. Probably the confidences Luke had overheard that night of drunkenness at Rossmere had been about some other woman entirely.

The realisation, once absorbed, was not so very hard after all. She had not forfeited much, as she had said to Beth. Only a few weeks of her time and the end of a a futile dream.

She said calmly, 'Luke told me you were thinking of marrying. He said you were prevented from looking for a wife because of the promises you made to me when you gave me the necklace. He said that if I sent it back to you then you would be free to marry at last. I am sorry, Stephen, that you have waited for so long. I never meant it to be a burden to you.'

'Stop,' he said. 'I don't understand. Does Josiah know you have come?'

She hesitated, then, 'My husband is dead.'

'When?'

'Five years ago.'

'*Five years* – why did you not tell me sooner?'

'Would you have been interested? I assumed you must have forgotten me.'

'No.' Still Stephen looked dazed. 'No, I never forgot you.'

'But now you are sorry I have come. Do not be anxious, Stephen. There is no need to pretend. Just let us say I came here on an old woman's whim. I shall go away at once. I'll not come to the house, that would only be embarrassing for us both. Tell Luke that I—'

'No,' he broke in. 'Don't go, Dolores. Not yet.'

'But why . . . ?'

He stared at her helplessly. Then he raised his hands in a gesture of despair and sat down on a boulder beside the road. 'Don't go,' he said again. 'Not like this.'

'But it is better . . .' She stopped.

Tears were pouring down his cheeks. His shoulders rocked. He was weeping with the raw agony of a man who has not wept since boyhood and has long since forgotten how it's done.

'Stephen, what's the matter? I did not mean . . .' She went and stood beside him. She had never imagined this meeting would be so painful. She said, 'I am sorry. I should not have come.'

But he caught hold of her hand and said, 'Don't go, Dolores. I never thought I'd see you again. Don't go now. It's Sophie, my niece. She had a baby, little Lucy. She wanted Luke to be here so much. She had a fever. She said it was nothing, but then . . . She died two nights ago and now you are here, and Luke. Are you real? I cannot believe it is you.'

'Sophie? Luke's wife is dead?'

He nodded, wiped his face on his sleeve. Dolores crouched down in front of him. Instinctively she put her arm across his knees, the comfort of touch. He looked up at her, his face very close to her own.

She said, 'Poor Luke. Poor, poor Luke. He was so eager to be back and now . . . I cannot take it in. And now he is too late.'

Stephen did not answer. He raised his hand and touched her cheek wonderingly with his fingers. 'But you are here,' he whispered. 'I never thought I'd see you again.'

'It was Luke's idea. He said you were thinking of getting married.'

'Why would I want to do that? Is Josiah really dead?'

'Yes. I'm a respectable widow now.'

'Well, I'm sorry to hear it, of course.' His face brightened. 'Damn it, that's a lie. I've wanted him dead a thousand times. Sometimes I even wished I'd killed him when I had the chance.'

She nodded. The same thought had been with her also, but Stephen must know that.

Stephen was smiling. 'Do you still have the chain I gave you?'

'I am wearing it now. I always wear it.'

His fingers followed the ridge of metal that lay against her throat. He closed his eyes. 'Oh, Dolores, my God, but I've missed you so much.'

She tilted her head, brushing his knuckles with her cheek, then turned and kissed the sun-bleached hairs and the tendons on his brown hand. He let out a groan and grasped the back of her head, drawing her towards him. He kissed her, then drew back to examine every detail of her face. 'It's a miracle,' he said. 'I keep thinking you're not real.'

'Oh, I'm real.' She took his hand and placed it against her breast. 'This is real.' She was smiling at his pleasure, but then she frowned. 'Are we too late, Stephen? Like Luke and his Sophie? Have we left it too late?'

He stood up, taking her hands in his and raising her to join him. 'No,' he said, his voice deep and very sure, just as she remembered him. 'Time doesn't matter any more. Even if it's only an hour, a day, a month, we've found each other again. That's all that matters.'

Dolores was laughing. She had thought she remembered every detail of his face, his body, his voice, but there was so much she had forgotten after all: the way she knew, when she was with him, that he was utterly without deceit. What he showed her was what he was, through and through. And the way his brown hair curled over the top of his ears. And the way he looked at her, as though she was the only woman in the world.

He wrapped his arms around her and folded her against his chest. Their bodies moved together as naturally as if they had never been apart, as if it had been only hours not years since they were last together. A seventeen-year absence was swallowed up in their embrace.

For a long time they stayed together by the entrance to Rossmere as the afternoon shadows lengthened across the track. Sometimes talking, always touching, and wondering. Never ceasing to hold each other and be amazed.

Later they unhitched the horses and led them, walking side by side, down the lime avenue towards the house.

Chapter Forty

Piers heard the tolling of the mourning bell as he was being rowed ashore. The harbour was deserted. All the people of Porthew had gathered near the church to see the funeral party arrive and the coffin carried past. The pall-bearers, who had walked from Rossmere with their load, set it down on the open patch of ground between the alehouse and the church while a final jug of ale was passed between them.

The mourners were making their way to the church. Piers recognised Perdita, draped in black from head to toe, as she went up the steps and through the lych-gate into the churchyard.

'Who has died?' he asked an elderly man with few teeth, who was holding a battered hat clasped to his chest as a sign of respect.

The old man turned to him with tears in his eyes. 'Mistress Sutton,' he said. 'Terrible, terrible. Happened so quick.'

Piers remembered Alice as he had seen her last. He felt a kind of weary pity: no doubt the shock of losing Rossmere after all her struggles during the Parliament years had finally proved too much for her. It occurred to him that this was probably one of those bereavements that fall into the category of merciful release: at least she'd not have to witness her family being turned from their home. Her death was sad, but not a tragedy. Given the dangers of childbirth, he had been afraid it might be Honor or Sophie being buried, or one of their new babies.

He saw Stephen walking slowly towards the church. There was a woman at his side Piers had never seen before. Her dark hair was streaked with grey and her face still showed traces of a haunting beauty. They walked in silence, side by side. As they reached the steps, Stephen touched her elbow with his hand and she inclined her head slightly towards his. Gestures of profound intimacy without the need of words. Then they vanished from view, leaving Piers baffled.

The next moment he saw Francis and Kip with a black-draped figure, whom Piers assumed must be Sophie or Louisa, between them. They paused in front of the coffin and murmured their thanks to the pall-bearers before turning around and walking to the church.

Only then did Piers see the face of the woman who walked between them: neither Sophie nor Louisa, but Alice herself.

He shivered, as though he had seen a ghost.

Then the old man's wife standing next to him said, 'Not Mistress Sutton, you old fool. Mistress Hollar she was now. Been married nearly a year.'

And the old man shook his head and said, 'Still think of her as a Sutton, somehow.'

'Sophie?' asked Piers.

'That's right.'

'Sophie Sutton is dead?'

He looked again at the coffin heaped with midsummer flowers. The pall-bearers, their thirst quenched, were once more hoisting their burden on their shoulders and stepping out in weary unison towards the church.

'That's right,' the old man said again.

'No, it can't be true.'

But the stricken faces of the pall-bearers, the silence of the crowd as they passed by, the grief for a young life cut short, all showed that this was no ordinary death.

Piers turned back towards the sea. He had a wholly irrational urge to head back at once to the ship that had brought him here from Plymouth. I should never have come, he thought. As if, by removing himself from Porthew, he might somehow undo the tragedy that had been enacted during his absence.

He remembered the day Sophie and he had raced, Falcon against Charger, across the wide spaces of the Downs. He remembered her energy and joy. He wished with fierce anger that he had not come back to Porthew to face this.

Suddenly resolute, he left the crowd of onlookers and

followed the coffin into the church just as the mourning bell tolled for the last time and the funeral service began.

Perdita happened to turn her head just as Piers entered the church. She felt a brief moment of joy, then a fist of unease curled around her heart. Why had he come back now, of all times? How had he heard of Sophie's death?

All around her the sound of muffled sobbing mingled with the words of the service. The parson was speaking with unnecessary slowness, Perdita thought. He seemed to be determined to drag out the ceremony for as long as possible. Perdita was seething with impatience. She was too stunned by all that had happened in the last weeks to be able to grieve for Sophie yet; she knew only that her mourning clothes were hot and scratchy and made her look terrible. She envied Honor, who had the babies as an excuse and had not been obliged to attend, and Cary, who was busy preparing food for the mourners and had stated quite clearly that to attend another funeral would probably be the death of her too.

Only a fortnight ago there had been a christening party at Rossmere, and now it was to be a wake.

The service droned on. She gazed at the other mourners. Alice looked as though she was on the verge of fainting clean away; only her two sons, one on either side, were keeping her on her feet. Francis had a dumb, bruised expression, like an ox that had dragged a heavy burden for too long. Kip was standing very straight and blinking frequently to keep back his tears.

Luke was on the other side of the aisle. For some perverse reason, which Perdita could not understand, he had refused to sit in the Suttons' traditional pews and had taken his place among the townsfolk of Porthew.

She had felt desperately sorry for him when he first returned to Rossmere three days before. He had looked so light-hearted, boyish even, when he came into the house and demanded to know where he could find Sophie.

In her shock Perdita had replied, 'She's in her bedchamber,' and then she had run after him up the stairs saying, 'Luke, wait, you must not go in!'

But he had ignored her.

The rest was too painful. Even now, she could hear his cry of anguish ringing in her ears. Forgetting all the tensions that had come between them in the past, she had wanted only to ease his pain. He had flung himself across the bed where Sophie's corpse was lying and his body shook with sobs. Perdita had put her arms around him, tentatively at first. His grief had been angry, vengeful. He raged against the cruel God who had snatched away his wife just when he was bringing her the gifts of his love, just when their real life together should have begun. Perdita held him and offered no consolation – there was none that she could think of. He clung to her so fiercely that his fingers dug into her flesh and later, when she undressed, there were bruises on her upper arms and shoulders. Despite her anguish, she wondered if this day might mark the start of a new intimacy between them, the intimacy proper to a man and his half-sister.

Now she felt she had been foolish even to imagine such a thing. He had not stayed long at Rossmere once the first wild outpourings of grief had died down. Nor did he seem much interested in his baby daughter, and that was just as well, thought Perdita. Little Lucy was well cared for at Rossmere and doted on by all. No one wanted Luke to take the child back with him to the lonely draper's shop in Porthew.

She glanced across at him now. It was hard to believe that the tall man standing among the townsfolk was the same person who had sobbed like a child in her arms only three days before. He did not look much like a grieving husband now. His expression was cruel and twisted, almost as though he had been expecting disaster to engulf him all along.

Perdita began to think the service would never end. The summer heat and her stiff mourning seemed to have brought on some kind of rash. She tried to scratch her side, where the itching was worst, without anyone noticing, but the itch only moved round to the small of her back. Then the skin on her ankles and feet crawled, as though tiny insects were stealing across. It was intolerable.

She could not see Piers. She wondered if he was looking at her. His return now was somehow disturbing. She was glad to see him, and yet she wished he had not come back. She wondered if Edmund had told his cousin of the marriage plans. He had promised to keep it a secret until Kitty was informed and the betrothal formally settled, but maybe he did not consider Piers to be part of that promise. Or maybe he was not a man who was in the habit of keeping promises.

Perdita was surprised to find that she did not relish the prospect of Piers knowing she was to marry his cousin. Not that it was any of his business, nor did she care what he thought, but all the same she would have preferred him to stay away until she was safely installed as mistress of Trecarne.

She told herself she must try to stop brooding on all the hurt and miseries of the past days. Mistress of Trecarne. Kitty would have told her that passion always leads to misery. Look at Sophie, look at Luke. Kitty's faith in bricks and mortar and the security of money and position had been entirely vindicated.

Mistress of Trecarne. Perdita told herself fiercely that it was all she had wanted for more than a year, and soon her ambition would be realised. She had every reason to be satisfied with that.

After the funeral service, Luke did not return to Rossmere, but Piers did. He borrowed a horse from one of the townsfolk and he and Kip soon detached themselves from the main party and took a detour that followed some high, open ground. Here they let the horses have their heads in a long gallop.

After the horror and grief of the service, both found a kind of release in the speed and exhilaration of the ride, but as they reined their horses to a walk, each was thinking the same thing.

'Sophie would have enjoyed that,' said Kip.

Piers nodded. He wondered how long it would be before either of them could indulge in a race across open country without the agony of remembering Sophie, and the pleasure she'd had in Falcon.

As they rode quietly down towards Rossmere, Kip brought Piers up to date on all that had happened in the time he'd been away. He himself had only a sketchy understanding of how and why Dolores Taverner had come to be in his home, but he had no doubt at all about the effect on his uncle.

'You should see him,' said Kip. 'He follows her around like a moonstruck youth. Amos thinks he is bewitched.'

'I can think of worse ways of being bewitched,' said Piers, with a grin.

He asked Kip about his work with the Camborne saddler, which Kip found surprisingly congenial since it gave him ample opportunity to discuss the finer details of horseflesh with their customers. He then asked Piers about life on board the *Fearless* and Piers gave him a brief account of what he'd done in the past few months.

Each was baffled by the other's pleasure in their occupation: their differing experiences caused a barrier between them. Kip felt obscurely betrayed that Piers was now enjoying the life that had caused him such anguish; Piers could not see how Kip could be content with a life so narrow and dull. The old easy friendship between them was waning.

As soon as he reached Rossmere, Piers went in search of Perdita. She was helping Cary and Louisa with the food and drink, and her manner implied that she could not be expected to break off such an important task just to greet an old friend. Piers persevered, but when it became obvious that she would use any excuse to avoid talking to him, he withdrew and watched her from across the room.

She had changed, no doubt about it. The first time he had seen her, she had been disguised by the clothes of a pauper woman; now it was a cold, arrogant manner with which she hoped to protect herself. His two meetings with Kitty had given Piers some idea of the values with which Perdita had been raised. He was angry with her for reverting to the chilly mask of her step-mother's world.

But even so, he thought he knew her well enough to detect the hurt and fear that lay beneath her outward show: she must have suffered much since last he saw her – Treveryan's death, now Sophie's. And there had been no mention of any attachment to Edmund, so her hopes had come to nothing.

A wake was not the time to talk of such serious topics, but Piers thought that when he was able to tell her what he knew about Edmund's dealings with her friends the Suttons she would be relieved to know that she was not, after all, to be married to such a man.

There were other changes to surprise Piers at Rossmere. He was shocked to find that Alice did not know who he was. The only pleasant surprise was provided by Honor. He hardly recognised her. The wet-nurse who had been brought in for Sophie's baby had proved unreliable and slovenly and for the past two days Honor had fed both infants. It was a task that clearly agreed with her. Her breasts had swelled, her face had filled out and she was developing an apple-cheeked roundness that made her look almost pretty. She had quickly discovered that Mistress Taverner's father had been an apothecary and that she herself had acquired many of his skills. She was already the grateful recipient of a whole armoury of potions and ointments for everything from sore nipples to a suspected rash on little Lucy's arm.

She was enjoying her new importance as mother and foster-mother. Ever since she arrived at Rossmere, Honor had been in awe of Sophie. Her sister-in-law was so remarkable in every way that there seemed no area in which Honor was not pitiful by comparison. Like everyone else she was still stunned by Sophie's death, numb with shock and amazed to find that life carried on somehow without her: the babies cried and slept and fed, mealtimes came and went, people went to bed at night and woke in the morning.

No one was ever going to take Sophie's place; no one would ever even try. Honor would continue to be timid and anxious and Louisa would always be discontented and short-tempered. But each of them was beginning, in a tentative way, to discover in themselves qualities they had never known they had. Honor had amazed herself by surviving the expected horrors of childbirth and even flourishing. Two babies now looked to her for nourishment and comfort, and she was able to provide both with what they needed. Louisa worked in the kitchen with Cary, as Sophie used to do. They shouted at each other and argued constantly, but with no older sister to show up her faults at every turn, Louisa's confidence began to grow.

And then there was Dolores.

Somehow, following the cataclysm of Sophie's death when the world at Rossmere was turned upside down, she had slipped almost unnoticed into their lives. She had a self-contained dignity, which the more easy-going and explosive Suttons might have found intimidating except that she was always prepared to help out in nursery or kitchen and possessed an instinctive tact. They were not to know that, for Dolores, her new position in the household was much easier than the one she had left, with an opinionated and unskilled daughter-in-law competing with her at every minute of the day.

The only person who had mixed feelings about Dolores was Cary. She had been enjoying her importance as household tyrant and was looking forward to wielding fresh power over Honor and the babies. Dolores, who had been her first employer, had put a stop to that at once.

Cary's displeasure was partially mitigated by the fact that, a few days after Dolores first arrived, Stephen had come into the kitchen and had given her all the back wages that were owed. She was planning a trip to visit the site of O'Rourke's grave.

That midsummer of such sadness and such change, with the two new babies and Stephen's great happiness and the huge grief of loss, while all the time the certainty of leaving Rossmere hung over them all, had a dreamlike quality.

No one could remember such a long spell of dry weather. Nights of thunder that rolled across the sky, summer lightning and occasional fierce downpours that were over almost as soon as they began, long days of sunshine with warm breezes carrying dust.

An air of unreality.

Waiting.

Chapter Forty-One

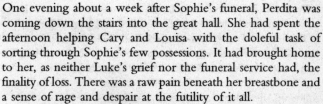

One evening about a week after Sophie's funeral, Perdita was coming down the stairs into the great hall. She had spent the afternoon helping Cary and Louisa with the doleful task of sorting through Sophie's few possessions. It had brought home to her, as neither Luke's grief nor the funeral service had, the finality of loss. There was a raw pain beneath her breastbone and a sense of rage and despair at the futility of it all.

And then she caught sight of Stephen and Dolores. They were coming in from the kitchen courtyard; he had his arm around her waist. They were laughing, perhaps at something they had been saying, perhaps simply for the pleasure of being together.

Perdita caught her breath. She had never imagined that such grief and happiness could exist side by side.

Dolores noticed her first. She looked up and said, 'Perdita, what is the matter?'

Her hand on the stair rail, Perdita did not know how to answer. She was afraid that if she spoke she'd be unable to hold back her sadness.

A shadow fell across the open doorway and she turned. It was Piers. Perdita felt a stabbing pain in her throat at the sight of him, tall and full of energy.

'Captain Sutton,' he said at once, not noticing the figure watching him from the stairs, 'I need to talk with you and Sir Francis on a matter of great importance.'

Stephen looked puzzled but he said, 'Of course, Piers. Francis is probably in his office, we can talk to him there.'

Only then did Piers turn so that Perdita could see his face

properly. His expression was grim. For some reason she felt sick at heart. It had been easy enough to avoid him when he came back to Rossmere after the funeral and she had not seen him since. Now her emotions felt too close to the surface for her to be able to deal with Piers on top of everything else.

Instinctively she turned to retreat back up the stairs, but Piers's voice called her back. 'Don't go, Mistress Treveryan. I especially want you to hear what I have to say.'

She hesitated. More than anything, she wanted to be alone to nurse her grief and find the strength to deal with the days ahead. Kitty was expected to arrive from Plymouth shortly, the final negotiations would soon be complete and her betrothal to Edmund publicly celebrated. All this required a cool head, and just now she felt hot and muddled and miserable.

Piers was waiting, and watching her. He looked purposeful and strangely elated. He said, in a voice that did not allow for contradiction, 'You will find it most interesting, I promise.'

Her curiosity was aroused. She went down the stairs and followed the others to Francis's chamber.

'Well, Piers,' asked Stephen, 'what is all this about?'

Piers stood in front of the empty fireplace and surveyed his audience calmly. 'I meant to speak to you as soon as I returned. But then, because of Sophie's death, I decided to wait until now.'

There was a brief silence. Francis was seated at his desk, his habitual anxious frown deeper than ever at this unexpected invasion of his privacy.

Stephen and Dolores stood near the window. Dolores had automatically come to hear what Piers had to say, not because anyone supposed that it concerned her in particular, but because it had already become accepted at Rossmere that Stephen was never easy if she was separated from him for long. It was as though he was afraid she might vanish, like some desert mirage, if he did not keep her by him at all times. Even now, as they stood side by side and waited to hear what Piers had to say, they were touching, shoulder to shoulder, hip to hip.

Perdita settled herself on a stool. She was wondering if Piers already knew that she was to be betrothed to Edmund as soon as Kitty arrived. If so, he should be pleased for her, since it was what they had schemed together the previous year. All the same, she felt apprehensive but could not understand why. Piers himself had changed: his easy-going patience had vanished. She found herself remembering that last evening in the library at Trecarne when they had composed their extravagant letters and drunk toasts to all the faraway ports he'd visit in his travels.

A great deal must have happened to him since then. Certainly a great deal had happened to her: Treveryan's death; Edmund's two so different proposals; Sophie . . . . Small wonder if their former friendship had been squeezed out by such huge changes.

If she'd had any space in her heart for more sorrow, she might have regretted the passing of their former genial alliance. As it was, she was almost able to convince herself that she felt nothing.

Piers was speaking. He said, 'Sir Francis, I understand that at Michaelmas last year my late uncle persuaded you to invest in a shipping venture of his.'

Francis's frown deepened. 'Ah, yes,' he said. He picked up a loose heap of papers and riffled through them helplessly. Then he sighed, and said, 'I agreed to it, yes. God knows, it was the worst mistake of my life.'

Piers continued, 'The *Plaindealing* was due to call at Cadiz and Gibraltar and should have returned to these shores early this year, by the beginning of March at the latest. The returns would have been more than enough to repay the whole sum that was owing, both the amount from the previous year and the balance that was due on Lady Day.'

'Yes,' said Francis. 'It seemed a sound investment at the time, but I should never have taken such a risk. When the *Plaindealing* went down, I lost everything.'

'No,' said Piers, 'you were duped.'

'How?' asked Stephen, listening to Piers's words with close attention.

'Contrary to reports, the *Plaindealing* was not lost at sea. I saw her with my own eyes when I sailed into Genoa on the *Fearless* two months ago. Her crew had been paid off and her name changed. She was in the process of being refitted by her new owner.'

'But I don't understand,' said Francis. 'Why the confusion?'

'Colonel Menheire deliberately tricked you, Sir Francis,' said Piers. 'He persuaded you to put money in a ship, and then he gave orders to the *Plaindealing*'s captain that the ship was to vanish. Lost, presumed sunk at sea. But, in fact, it was sold on at a low price to an Italian merchant who wasn't too particular about the reason for the bargain.'

Francis stared at him. 'The *Plaindealing* did not sink?'

'No.'

'Why would Colonel Menheire deliberately sell his ship at a low price?' asked Stephen.

'To get his hands on Rossmere,' said Piers.

'Just as Edmund has now done,' said Francis.

Stephen said, 'Did Menheire know what his father was up to?'

'I'm sure of it,' said Piers, with a glance at Perdita. 'After all, he is the only person who stands to gain from it now.'

Perdita felt herself begin to colour. All around her was a clamour of voices exclaiming at the wickedness of the Menheires and calling Edmund every kind of scoundrel.

Although she was as startled by Piers's revelations as anyone else, she could see that it would be awkward for her when her betrothal was announced if she kept silent now.

She said firmly, 'You have no reason to assume that Master Menheire was a party to his father's deceptions. Besides, I have it on excellent authority that he will not, after all, turn you and your family from Rossmere, Francis. He has promised he will allow you to remain here as tenants at a low rent. And, moreover—'

Piers was raking her face with his eyes as he cut in, 'How do you come to be so well informed about my cousin's intentions?'

She rose and shook out her skirts before replying, with a calmness she was far from feeling, 'It was intended to remain a secret until my mother arrives from Plymouth, but as she is expected at any moment I might as well tell you now. Your cousin has asked me to become his wife and I have accepted. The final details will be settled as soon as Lady Treveryan reaches Trecarne.'

There was a stunned silence. She tried to avoid looking at Piers, but she could see that he had reacted with horror to her announcement. She knew she had to ignore him. She must not allow herself to be distracted from the goal she had set for herself, not now, just when she was so close to gaining everything she had ever wanted.

Remembering Sophie's generous interpretation of her motives, Perdita continued, 'I made it clear to Master Menheire that proper provision must be made for you and your family, Francis, as corollary to the marriage contract, and he raised no objections. So you see, though the Colonel was undoubtedly a rogue it is not fair to condemn his son equally.'

To Perdita's dismay, no one seemed in a hurry to congratulate her on her success with Edmund, nor to praise her for negotiating on behalf of the Suttons.

Piers had taken a step towards her. He was searching her face, as though looking for the answer to some problem.

He asked, with quiet fury, 'When did you agree to marry Edmund?'

She faltered. Then, 'It was the day Sophie was taken ill.' And she thought: was that really less than two weeks ago?

'It still does not fit together,' said Stephen. Piers remained staring at Perdita, but Stephen continued, 'I cannot understand why the Menheires have gone to such trouble to get their hands on Rossmere land then let us live here as their tenants. What possible value does the place have, apart from the house?'

Piers said, 'Maybe Mistress Treveryan can enlighten us on that as well. She seems to be better acquainted with Edmund's motives than anyone.'

Perdita felt horribly vulnerable and alone. It was not fair that she should be blamed for Edmund's crimes when she had tried only to protect the Suttons. 'I know he has no interest in the house itself,' she said, 'only the land. But I do not know why.'

'And even if you did know,' said Piers, 'why would you want to betray the secrets of your future husband?'

Perdita gasped, then darted him a furious glance before saying, 'It is something to do with Biddy Firth's farm at Polcreath and that is all I know. Believe me or not, it makes no difference to me what you think.'

She turned away quickly, so that no one would see the tears that had sprung into her eyes.

Dolores spoke for the first time. She said, 'There is one person who does know his reason for wanting the land.'

All eyes turned towards her. 'Who?'

'Luke Hollar.' She spoke deliberately, her words still fractured by the lingering traces of her Spanish accent. 'He told me so as we were travelling here. He said there were three things he had done for Sophie and her family. Not as many as Hercules, but he hoped it would be enough. One was to find O'Rourke and see that he had a Christian burial. The second was to come to Tilsbury. And the third was to discover why the Menheires were so determined to get Rossmere. He said he thought he had found out enough to save her family from ruin.'

'Then why did he not tell us?' asked Francis.

'For the same reason I have not mentioned it until now either,' said Dolores. 'The horror that was waiting for him on his return must have made him forget everything else. Even the debts.'

'Then we must ask him immediately,' said Stephen.

'Quite right,' agreed Francis, setting his papers in an orderly pile. 'We'll go to Porthew first thing in the morning and ask him ourselves.'

'No,' said Piers firmly. 'We'll go at once. This whole affair has dragged on long enough. Why don't you come too, Mistress Treveryan? Or perhaps you are afraid that if you find out too much about your future husband you might run the risk of discovering you have made a terrible error in your choice.'

'There is no chance of that,' asserted Perdita. His words hurt her more than she would ever let him see and she had to draw on all her reserves of pride and anger to be able to answer without betraying her real feelings. She said haughtily, 'I am more than content with my decisions.'

'Excellent,' said Piers. 'Then you will come with us. If we leave right away, we can be there and back by nightfall.'

Sometimes Luke lost whole hours at a time. He might be standing at his cutting table measuring out lengths of cloth, he might pick up his pen to make an entry in the ledger, or else take up his violin to tuck it against his shoulder and play . . . and then he would become aware that an hour had passed, the shadows had travelled across the floor and the time had vanished. He had accomplished nothing. Lost in thought.

If you could call it thinking.

Over and over he remembered those last few days with Sophie before he left just after Michaelmas. He remembered her questions: are not children a kind of immortality? Is there nothing that would make you change your mind?

She had known then that she was expecting his child. There had been hints aplenty, but he had been too blinded by his own feelings of guilt and remorse to hear what she was trying to tell him.

This was one of the certainties that galled him most. He, Luke Hollar, who had learned the currency of secrets at an early age, who had always prided himself on knowing what no one else knew and putting that knowledge to good use, who had once fancied himself a spy, in the end had not even known that simplest of all truths: that his own wife, whom he loved more than life itself, was expecting their child and needed him to stay with her.

Some of the townsfolk, seeing his sorrow, tried to comfort him with the assurance that his presence would have made no difference. Childbed fever was a scourge that was feared almost as much as plague or leprosy, and countless women survived the rigours of childbirth only to fall ill and die within a few days of their delivery. They told him he could have done nothing. He must not blame himself.

But, of course, he did.

Besides, if he had stayed he would at least have had the comfort of knowing he had not squandered those pitifully short months of their marriage.

Instead he had insisted, against all her hints and pleading, on going off on a fool's errand, chasing after a long-dead Irishman and another man's mistress and all for the sake of his own pitiful pride.

Vanity had been the only motive driving him, he saw that quite plain. He had told Sophie he had to achieve these goals so that she would be proud of him. She had told him it was not necessary, she was proud of him already, but he had not listened.

He understood so clearly now. It had been important for him, not for her. Still less for her family. Even when he thought he was acting for the good of others for the first time in his life, he was still only gratifying his own selfish needs.

He'd have done better to stay in Cornwall and get busy with a pitchfork in the muck-filled stables at Rossmere, as Sophie had laughingly suggested. And he had reacted with hurt pride and gone anyway.

And had returned in time only to find her corpse and see her buried.

All his dreams of happiness gone.

He was so wrapped up in misery and bitterness and an incessant, grinding remorse that he never heard the fists beating at the door of the shop.

He still did not hear when footsteps came up the path in the back garden and a face peered in though the window of the kitchen where he had been standing for over an hour, fiddle in hand, while the room filled slowly with the midsummer dusk.

He did not notice until the back door was pushed open and Piers Menheire came in. Behind him was Sir Francis. Luke had been expecting a visit from Francis, but he was surprised to see Piers. And even more surprised when Perdita slipped into the room after them.

'Master Hollar,' began Francis awkwardly.

But Luke said, 'I know why you are come. You want to know the reason why Colonel Menheire set out to gain Rossmere.'

Chapter Forty-Two

Late that afternoon Kitty, Lady Treveryan, made her triumphal entry into Trecarne. Having long ago discovered that sea travel was torment, and since the roads in this south-western part of Cornwall were impassable for carriage traffic, she had no choice but to journey on horseback. She had made up for this indignity by bringing almost her entire wardrobe with her, as well as the majority of her household and outdoor servants.

This impressive cortège came to a halt on the gravel sweep in front of Trecarne, and Edmund met his future mother-in-law for the first time. A messenger was sent to Rossmere to inform Perdita of Kitty's arrival and to escort her back to Trecarne so that the final arrangements for the betrothal could be set in place.

A couple of hours later, as dusk was falling, the messenger returned to report that Mistress Treveryan had left for Porthew with Sir Francis but was expected to return at any moment. The messenger assured them he had left word with Lady Sutton, who had promised that Perdita would join her mother at Trecarne the following morning.

Edmund was in a fever of impatience to have Perdita safely under his roof and all the negotiations completed. He had hardly seen her since the day she had agreed to become his wife: the Sutton family's bereavement combined with his own plans for Rossmere had convinced him it was best to keep his distance for a while.

But he had never been a man who liked to have to wait for anything. To be obliged to wait for his union with Perdita was turning out to be hardest of all, and did nothing to improve his ill-humour.

Nor, it soon became obvious, did the company of Lady Treveryan. Edmund's experience of female relatives had been limited and his own mother had been a subdued, shadowy figure. Kitty Treveryan's ceaseless shrill torrent of words was something quite new for him.

He had never expected to be grateful for his future bride's bastard state, but after an hour he had seen and heard enough to be thankful that Perdita was not going to inherit either Kitty's looks or her character. He announced he had urgent business to attend to and bade her a brisk good night. A servant showed Kitty to the lower tower bedroom which she, like her wounded husband before her, had requested specially, while Edmund retired to the library to draw up a list of tasks that must be done the following day.

He was wondering whether to ride over to Rossmere in the morning so that he could escort Perdita to Trecarne himself when the door opened and Perdita stepped in.

He sprang to his feet and hurried towards her, but then he stopped in amazement. She was not alone. Piers entered the room after her, then Sir Francis. Luke Hollar was the last to come in. He closed the door firmly and leaned his back against it, then looked at Edmund with an expression that was not quite a smile, something wilder altogether. Edmund was annoyed. He was not accustomed to visitors arriving unannounced. And what was Perdita doing with his cousin? Or Luke Hollar with either of them?

'My God, what do you mean—' he began, but Perdita came across the room to join him. Her eyes were glittering and her cheeks were flushed.

He wanted to get rid of the intruders so that he could crush her in his arms but she raised her finger to her lips, and said, 'These men have some questions for you. I am sure you will know how to answer them.'

'Questions?' Edmund was confused and angry. 'Perdita, your mother has arrived and is waiting to see you now. How dare these people burst in here like this and—'

'Silence, you fool,' said Luke, with casual brutality. 'Listen to what your cousin has to say.'

'How dare you? I'll not be ordered around in my own home by a common—'

But then, as Piers began to speak, Edmund fell silent.

He remained, standing motionless, while Piers described how he had happened to come across the *Plaindealing* being fitted out under another name and with a new owner in Genoa. Perdita stood close by. She kept her eyes fixed on his face, partly to avoid the necessity of watching Piers, but partly because she was curious to know how her future husband would respond to these accusations.

When Piers had finished Edmund said coldly, 'Is that all? You dare to burst in here unannounced and all because you think you *might* have seen a ship of mine in a foreign port when it was thought to have been lost at sea? Don't waste my time, Piers.'

Piers was resolute. 'Are you denying that you and your father set out deliberately to defraud the Suttons of their investment and thus of their home?'

'I'm not answerable for my father,' said Edmund, moving calmly to stand in front of a high-backed chair so that a large table was between him and his accusers, 'but I can assure you that so far as I know the *Plaindealing* sank, as we have been told.'

'In that case,' said Piers, 'why did the captain of the vessel have a draught against a Flemish merchant and bearing your signature as of March this year?'

'Do you have this remarkable document with you?' asked Edmund, with a sneer.

'I saw it, that was enough. The fate of your father's ship seemed unusual, but at that time I did not know it had been reported sunk at sea. Nor did I know until recently that the Suttons had been persuaded to put their money into the voyage. So there was no reason for me to bring back proof of your far from plain dealing.'

'Not a shred of evidence and you think people will believe you?' said Edmund contemptuously. '*I* don't, and nor will anyone else. Except, perhaps, poor Sir Francis here who is so desperate he'll clutch at any straw he can find, and a local tradesman of no account who, as everyone knows, looks out only for himself. Just what you think you'll gain by involving my future wife in this, I cannot think. Get out of here, Piers, before I have you thrashed and thrown out as you deserve. Is this how you repay all my father's great kindness to you? By attempting to blacken his name when he is no longer alive and able to defend himself?'

'My loyalty to your father,' said Piers, 'for his grudging and belated kindness, has kept me silent far too long. Last autumn I went away to sea rather than stand by and have to witness his efforts to undermine the Suttons. I never thought he would defraud them deliberately of their money. I realise now that I should have stayed and helped them fight you in any way I could. My only excuse is that I had no idea you would stoop to such gross deception as this.'

'Nor have I been guilty of any deception,' said Edmund calmly. 'You are mistaken, Piers. It was not the *Plaindealing* you saw. There must be a thousand ships in the Mediterranean of similar size and build.'

'The *Plaindealing* is a Penryn boat,' said Piers. 'I helped draw up the bill of lading for her myself before she sailed. I know it was her.'

'But you can never prove it,' said Edmund, adding hastily, 'for the simple reason it is not true. No one will ever believe you.'

Francis looked from one man to the other, his expression a study in misery. 'He is right, Piers. You have no proof. We should have thought of that before.'

'Nonsense,' said Luke. He was leaning with his back against the door, one knee bent, in the pose that reminded Perdita of the first time she had seen him in the graveyard at Porthew. Alone of all the people in the room he seemed to be enjoying himself. At all events, he was still smiling that mysterious smile of his. 'All the proof we need is right here in this room.'

'How can that be?' asked Perdita.

'It is written on Menheire's face,' said Luke. 'If Piers was mistaken about the identity of the *Plaindealing*, if Menheire had lost his own investment as well as Sir Francis's, even if his father had carried out the deception without telling him about it, then he'd be outraged by the very suggestion. As it is, he is not outraged in the least. He merely denies that it is true, calmly and reasonably, but without any hint of shock or disgust.'

'That's a lie!' exclaimed Edmund, suddenly angry. 'I think it is altogether despicable to try to—'

'Too late.' Luke raised a hand to interrupt his protests. Without a doubt, he was enjoying himself.

Piers looked across at him with approval, then said to his cousin, 'Besides, there is another detail we've not yet mentioned. Master Hollar knows your reason for wanting Rossmere.'

Edmund turned to Luke with an expression of undisguised contempt. 'I cannot see that my ambitions have anything to do with your draper friend, Piers.'

'Maybe not,' said Luke, moving away from the door and coming to face Edmund across the broad table. Now he was no longer smiling, but spoke with passionate intensity. 'But it had a great deal to do with my late wife, and anything that affected her touches me also.'

'What was it?' asked Perdita, her eagerness to know stronger now than her feelings either for her future husband or for the Suttons.

Luke glanced at her briefly. 'Still as curious as ever, Perdita?' Then his face hardened again as he turned back to Edmund. 'When I was in London during the winter I came to an excellent understanding with two gentlemen by the names of Fernor and Beech.'

'What of it? They are nothing to do with me,' insisted Edmund.

'Who are they?' asked Perdita.

Luke said, 'Two London merchants specialising in the purchase and shipment of tin. Unfortunately Master Menheire has not had much cause to do business with them until now, tin being a metal not much found in this part of Cornwall. Or so it has always been thought. However, Master Menheire recently told them to expect large and increasing shipments from the middle of next year when a certain scheme that his father set in motion last year comes at last to fruition.'

'But I don't understand,' said Francis.

'Polcreath Farm,' said Perdita, earning a furious glance from Edmund.

'Is that where it is?' asked Luke. 'I had been wondering, but I couldn't be sure.'

'But . . .' Francis was more bewildered than ever.

Piers explained, 'The reason the Menheires have wanted Rossmere for so long is that they have found evidence of large amounts of tin below the ground at Polcreath Farm, and very likely at other points nearby as well.'

'Ah yes. I see,' said Francis, labouring to piece the information together. 'Biddy Firth at Polcreath. She told Uncle Stephen last year that there'd been strangers on the farm at night. She said there'd been digging. We thought they were smugglers. But now, Master Hollar, you think they might have been seeing if there was tin on the place. I see that now. Uncle Stephen will be interested to hear that. Yes.'

In spite of everything, Perdita felt a skip of satisfaction at a problem solved. She smothered her smile and turned to look at Edmund. He did not appear in the least bit put out by recent revelations.

He said coldly, 'Is that all? You force your way into my home with nothing but a string of lies and insults and guesses, not a scrap of evidence or legal proof. What do you expect to gain by this? Get out of my house before I set the dogs on you. Perdita, you will go to your mother at once and we shall talk again in the morning. I regret that you have been subjected to this.'

'It's true,' said Francis, subsiding instantly into despair again. 'Without proof we can do nothing.'

'Quite right, Sir Francis,' said Edmund. His lips drew back in a cold smile as he continued, 'I am glad you are beginning to see sense at last. I may decide to believe that you have been persuaded to take part in this ridiculous confrontation against your better judgement. It is well known that you are weak and easily led. Out of consideration to Perdita here I may even continue with my plan to let you remain at Rossmere as my tenant. In return I shall expect your full support in refuting these wicked slanders that have been aired here this evening. I hope you understand.'

'Well,' muttered Francis, 'that does seem generous.'

'What?' exclaimed Piers. 'How can you let this man trick you out of your family's home and property and still call him generous?'

'But what else can I do?' said Francis.

'Nothing at all,' said Edmund briskly, sitting down at the table as though he meant to continue with his work. 'I see you are a man of better judgement than I thought, Sir Francis. It is all perfectly straightforward. Your mother signed the papers authorising the final loan and offering Rossmere and its land as surety. You yourself signed the documents transferring those monies to be invested in the *Plaindealing*. A ship which, as everyone knows, has tragically failed to return to port. Therefore Rossmere is forfeit. All the rest is mere supposition. So far as the law is concerned—'

'The law be damned!' said Luke.

Before anyone else knew what was happening, Luke had moved around the table. Usually his gestures were slow and deliberate, so his burst of speed caught everyone by surprise. Lithe and quick as an animal, he went behind Edmund's chair and, just as Edmund twisted to see what he was doing, Luke reached out and imprisoned his head in the angle of his arm. His fist was clenched against Edmund's cheek as he yanked his opponent's head back viciously against the polished carving of the chair.

Edmund let out a strangled cry of rage and shock. Instinctively he raised his hands and began to drag at the V of Luke's elbow pinned against his throat.

Perdita gasped. There was a flash of bright metal as Luke raised his free hand and brought a dagger, a short blade of silver with a lethally sharp edge, against the flesh of Edmund's jaw. Luke pressed the flat tip against his skin and said, with unmistakable relish, 'Try to escape and I'll cut your throat.'

Either Edmund did not believe him, or else the instinct to free himself was too strong. He continued to struggle. The muscles on Luke's forearm stood out and he was panting with the effort of holding the big man's head pressed against the chair back. All at once, his patience seemed to snap. He said, 'I'm warning you, Menheire,' and then, as though to reinforce his point, he adjusted the angle of the dagger so it was poised on its tip, then twisted quickly, nicking the gleaming point into the flesh of Menheire's jaw. Edmund cried out in pain. A small berry of blood sprang up, to mingle with the sweat and stubble on his cheek. Luke hissed, 'Don't press your luck, Menheire. I mean what I say.'

Edmund's arms fell to his side and he gasped, 'Perdita!'

At that moment, Luke looked as though he meant to murder Edmund, and Perdita was confused and frightened. Whatever she had thought the outcome of this meeting would be, Edmund's death had never been part of the plan. Instinctively she moved towards the door, but before she had taken more than a couple of steps, Piers moved to cut her off. 'No,' he said angrily, 'we're going to see this through.'

'But—'

'No buts,' said Piers, and then, to reinforce his point, he caught hold of her arm and drew her close to him.

At once her fear vanished. She trusted Piers. This encounter was not going to end in madness after all. She relaxed and, without thinking what she was doing, she allowed her body to rest against his.

Luke was watching her. He still held his dagger close to Edmund's face, though his victim had ceased to struggle. Luke said, quietly, but with absolute conviction, 'If you call out or make any attempt to help him, dear sister, you'll find yourself courting a corpse.'

Edmund sat rigid with strain, his eyes flickering back and forth as he tried to think of a way out of his trap.

Francis stood between the two pairs of antagonists, Piers and Perdita close to the door, Luke and Menheire locked in a vicious embrace behind the table. He let out a moan of indecision.

Luke said with icy calm, 'You don't give a damn about the law, Menheire, and nor do I. But other people are more dainty than we, so we'll set about this legally. Where are those documents you spoke of just now?'

At first Edmund refused to say, but Luke dipped the tip of his dagger in the smear of blood and held it in front of his eyes, then laid the blade against the artery on his neck. Edmund was soon persuaded to change his mind.

Luke ordered Francis to go to the small coffer at the side of the room and remove several documents. 'Burn them,' he said.

Francis grunted as he squatted down in front of the empty grate. After much fumbling with dry tinder, he was successful and the documents flamed.

Edmund was gasping, still imprisoned by Luke's arm circled

round his throat, the dagger tip still denting the skin of his neck, but he said, in angry triumph, 'Much good will that do you, Sir Francis. There are copies of them all lodged with my lawyers.'

'Exactly,' said Luke. 'And that is why we are now going to draw up a fresh document in your name, acknowledging how you have tried to defraud the Sutton family of their rightful home, which you now see was a gross and wicked error, and renouncing all claim to that property. We might as well put in a clause wiping out all the monies they owe you too. That seems a small enough compensation for the grief and anxiety your crimes have caused them.'

'You must be insane,' said Edmund, 'if you think I'd ever sign such a document.'

'I very much hope you do,' said Luke, 'because otherwise I'll cut your throat.'

'I don't believe you,' said Edmund. He twisted in an effort to escape Luke's restraining arm. 'Only a madman would risk a hanging just to save another man from debt!'

'*Only* a madman? Do you think I'm not mad, Menheire? Don't you know me at all, even now?' And then, as easily as if he was drawing a pen across parchment, he drew the tip of the dagger the length of Edmund's cheek. Only instead of ink, it left a line of bright blood. 'Fear for your life, Menheire,' said Luke, 'because I don't give a tinker's damn about mine. Don't you know I'd gladly face execution if I thought it would help my Sophie's family? Do you imagine I fear a hanging? Don't you know how much I'd love to die?'

'Luke, not yet,' warned Piers.

But there was no need. Edmund was already convinced of Luke's intentions. His face was grey and shining with sweat. His whole body was limp, all opposition gone. He looked as if he was on the verge of fainting away altogether.

Francis was almost as terrified as Edmund when he sat down at the end of the broad table, picked up a pen and paper and wrote hurriedly to Luke's dictation.

Perdita watched with growing disbelief. Although the sky outside was still the deep blue of twilight, inside the room it was almost dark. Piers had released his hold on her some time before, but she had not noticed, and had not moved away from him.

When Luke drew his dagger across Edmund's face and the blood spurted out, she had gripped Piers's arm and held it tightly. She hardly noticed when Piers put his arm around her waist, but for reassurance this time, not restraint.

Edmund appeared to be shrinking in front of her eyes. Some inner certainty in him had been shattered by his fear. It would take a long time for that confidence to return. Perhaps it never would.

Luke watched intently. He looked almost disappointed that Menheire had put up so little opposition, that he'd had no excuse to do him greater injury. It was easy to believe him mad. Francis scratched pen across paper so fast one might have thought he was the man being threatened, not his old enemy.

At length, and in silence, the document was complete. Luke released Edmund, lit a candle and read it through slowly. Then he handed it to Edmund for signature. When Edmund had put his name to it, Luke witnessed the signature with a flourish and a smile, then sprinkled sand on both their names.

The job was done. No one seemed quite sure what to do next. Somehow they had to cross the bridge that would reconnect them with their everyday lives.

Perdita became aware that she had been circled by Piers's arms all this time. She could feel the beat of his heart against her back, the pressure of his hand against her waist. Her hands had been gripping his arm, but now, as she released the pressure, he caught her fingers and entwined them with his own. A sudden giddiness threatened to overwhelm her. With a huge effort she pulled herself together, extracted her hands, moved away from Piers and stood once more alone, watching.

Francis pushed back his chair and stood up. He had raised his arm, as though he meant to reach across and shake Edmund by the hand in the manner that business dealings were normally concluded. Then it occurred to him that the present circumstances made this inappropriate. His arm dropped to his side and he said, 'Ah, yes,' and frowned.

Only Luke remained in full command of the situation. He shook the sand off the new document, rolled it up neatly and tucked it inside his jacket.

'I'll keep this safe for you, Sir Francis. I doubt if we'll ever have cause to make it public, but just in case I'll have a second copy drawn up and Menheire can sign that too. I'm sure he'll raise no objections.'

Edmund looked up at him, appalled, still terrified. He touched the crimson seam that ran the whole length of his cheek and his fingertips were smeared with blood.

Luke smiled down at him. 'That may leave you with a scar. Let us hope so. It will be a reminder to you never to try to undo what has been achieved here this evening. If there is tin at Polcreath, as you believe, then the Suttons will get rich from it, not you. Remember, they have a madman to assist them now. They have me, and I am that worst of enemies, Menheire, a man who has nothing to lose.'

Edmund opened his mouth to speak, but no words came out.

Francis said, 'Yes, well, I suppose I had better get back to Rossmere.'

He followed Luke from the room. Perdita went quickly after them, leaving Piers alone with his cousin. She knew instinctively that Edmund was mortified above all that she had been a witness to his humiliation. She wondered how that would change the way things stood between them. She was not sure if she cared any more.

She went down the steps after Luke and Francis into the warm summer twilight. The air smelt of new mown hay.

'Are you riding back to Rossmere with Sir Francis?' asked Luke.

'No,' said Perdita. 'My mother is here. I will stay with her.'

'Well, then,' said Francis, 'that's good.' He looked more mystified than pleased. It would be a long time before he understood that the events of the last hour had made his home safe for him and his heirs once and for all. The old habits of worry and uncertainty were not so easily broken.

Luke was observing Perdita in the dusky light. He said, 'Have I shocked you again?'

'Yes,' she said truthfully, 'very much.'

'Menheire could never have got Rossmere, not once the truth about the *Plaindealing* was public knowledge. He knows Piers and I can get all the proof necessary, but it would have taken too long. My way was quicker, and just as effective.'

'Yes,' she said again.

Luke hesitated, as though waiting for her to say something, but when she remained silent he raised his shoulders and smiled briefly, that odd smile of his, half calculating, half shy. Then he turned away from her and went over to where his horse was waiting with one of the Trecarne grooms. Perdita followed him and touched him lightly on the sleeve.

'Luke,' she said. He turned round at once. His eyes were almost eager. She said, 'Sophie would have been proud of you.'

He did not answer. But his face softened with a look of such gratitude and hope and grief, a glimpse of the kindly, affectionate brother she might have known if their lives had followed different tracks, that all at once she understood why Sophie had cared for him, and been happy, for however brief a time.

Chapter Forty-Three

Sleep was impossible that night.

Perdita had gone to the tower bedroom and watched from the open window as Francis and Luke rode off into the moonlit night.

Behind her, in the darkness, Kitty was snoring in the large four-poster bed where Perdita had nursed her father. She was thankful she did not have to deal with her step-mother's questions and chatter until the morning.

Her mind was whirling with all the scenes and images from the evening, but coherent thought was impossible. When she considered all that had happened it was hardly surprising that she was muddled and uncertain. The only fact she felt sure of was that tomorrow the final details of her marriage contract would be settled and her betrothal to Edmund made public. And if the prospect made unwelcome tears spring to her eyes, then she told herself it was only because that scene in the library had left her overwrought. Tomorrow cool reason would have reasserted itself. Marriage to Edmund Menheire had been her ambition for too long: she could not afford to lose her nerve now.

Because of Sophie's death, it would be necessary to have a quiet wedding, and in her present mood Perdita was glad of that. But though Sophie's death had touched her more deeply than any relative's would have, she had been a friend only, so there would be no reason to delay the marriage for more than a month or so.

It was midsummer. By Michaelmas she would have achieved all she had wanted: a lawful, honoured wife, all the stain of bastardy obliterated so far as that would ever be possible, wealth and position. Above all, mistress of Trecarne.

She wondered how the events of that evening would affect her relations with Edmund. Not only had he been outmanoeuvred and reduced to a state of helpless terror, but he had suffered the additional indignity of having his future bride witness his defeat. She was going to need all her skill in the morning to persuade him that he had been heroic, noble in his suffering and that his bravery had increased her admiration for him.

She did not relish the prospect, but she knew she was equal to the task.

It occurred to her that she might be tainted, in Edmund's eyes, since his most deadly attacker, the one who had reduced him to a state of witless terror, had been her own brother. Probably the damage was not so great. Edmund's great consciousness of rank was her chief ally here. In his eyes, Luke was a draper and Perdita a wealthy gentleman's daughter: close kinship was impossible between two people with such contrasting positions in society. She should have been glad, but this certainty only increased her depression.

Her feelings of restlessness and unease increased.

By now her eyes were accustomed to the darkness and she found a shawl of Kitty's neatly folded on a wooden chest. She decided it would help calm her mind and prepare her for the day ahead if she took a walk outside and saw her future home in all the secret beauty of moonlight. She put the shawl over her shoulders and slipped quietly down the spiral staircase from the tower bedroom.

She was thwarted. All the outside doors had been secured for the night by Edmund's servants. In spite of her agitation she smiled. This was surely an example of locking the stable door after the horse had bolted – or in this case, not just a horse but an entire estate and a fortune in tin besides.

Without thinking of what she was doing, she made her way to the long gallery. Its beauty in the moonlight brought a lump to her throat. High windows cast lozenges of chequered silver light across the floor, shadows rippled when the breeze stirred the leaves of the creeper that grew against the front of the house.

From the rocky bay came the sigh and murmur of small waves breaking on the shore. Somewhere in the oak woods, a nightingale was singing.

This was the reassurance she had been seeking. A woman was right to stake everything on gaining possession of such a prize.

She breathed a sigh of relief, as if a question had been answered. Then she stiffened. Footsteps echoed on the main stairs, the door at the far end of the long gallery opened and a fan of candlelight spread across the ceiling.

A man was approaching. Her heart sank. She was not ready, not yet, to deal with Edmund's wounded pride.

Not Edmund.

Piers.

A different kind of tension knotted the pit of her stomach.

'Mistress Treveryan?' he said in surprise, as she was revealed by the light. 'What are you doing here? I thought you were with your mother.'

'I could not sleep.'

'Nor I.'

He hesitated, then set the candle down on a low table. He smiled ruefully. 'After everything that has happened this evening, it's not really surprising.'

'And your cousin?'

'Barnes gave him some kind of sleeping draught. I think he was afraid Edmund might be taken by one of the choleric fits my uncle used to suffer. I've never seen anyone so angry. He's sleeping now.'

'Will he try to go back on the document Luke made him sign?'

'He cannot, and he knows it. That is why he is so angry. He knows he's lost Rossmere. I told him I intend to get the proof that he falsified the disappearance of the *Plaindealing*. He knows Hollar will not hesitate to use it against him if he ever causes trouble for the Suttons again.'

'*You* told him that?'

'Yes.' Piers smiled. 'From his response I gather that I am no longer welcome in this house. But that suits me admirably.'

'What will you do?'

'Return to the *Fearless*. Master Boulter told me he'd always have a place for me. There's a ship dropped anchor in Porthew this afternoon, which is bound for Plymouth. I shall join it in the morning.'

It was only what she should have expected, but all the same this news of his imminent departure made her utterly wretched. She knew it was inevitable: Edmund would never forgive Piers for his part in the day's events. Most probably it would be years before she saw Piers again. She told herself that was just as well: their friendship had been a fine thing but they had both moved on. Both were about to achieve their ambitions and had no need of each other any more.

It was no use. She had a horror of this parting. She forced herself to say evenly, 'So you are going at once.'

'Yes,' he said, 'and you?' His eyes were searching her face. 'Do you still intend to go through with this marriage to Edmund?'

'Of course.' She tried to make her voice sound light-hearted and flippant, but it did not work. 'Why should I change my mind now?'

'I would have thought,' he said bitterly, 'the discovery that your future husband was a liar who had set out deliberately to ruin your friends and deprive them of their home and lands might have altered your feelings towards him.'

He was looking at her as if he hated her. She could not bear to be so unfairly accused. He had no right to stand in judgement over her.

'Why?' she demanded angrily. 'You know full well I had no illusions about the kind of man he was when I agreed to be his wife. What you and Luke revealed this evening only confirmed what I already knew.' Still he did not look convinced. She carried on, 'In my experience all men are either fools or scoundrels. It seems to me I am fortunate in knowing the worst about my future husband right from the beginning. Surely that's better than starting married life in foolish ignorance and finding out the truth when it is too late to do anything about it.'

Piers was silent. He was frowning, no longer angry. He asked quietly, 'Why do you always pretend to be so cynical?'

'I am simply realistic, that's all.'

'No. That is not all.'

'What do you mean?'

'You are turning your back on everything you really care about.'

She laughed. 'Look around you – everything I care about is here.'

'Is it? What about respect and honour and regard?'

'My position as mistress of Trecarne will give me those.'

'What about love?'

Perdita gasped and took a step away from him. Her heart was beating rapidly. She had known that Piers was going to try to persuade her not to marry his cousin and she was determined to stand her ground. A year ago he had been happy enough to help her in her ambitions, so why was he now so eager to thwart her? Nothing had changed.

She said firmly, 'I have no patience with that. It is an illusion that leads only to grief and misery.' She had retreated to stand near the fireplace and, almost without being aware of what she was doing, she raised her fingers to trace the words that had been carved there before her birth. *Nullus amor.* She said, 'Look what happened to my natural mother. Look at Sophie. Don't dare to talk to me of love. You know nothing about it.'

'Don't I?'

'No. It means being poor and miserable and despised by everyone. It means putting yourself in the power of someone who can hurt you and abandon you any time they choose. It means losing every chance of happiness you ever had.'

'Is that honestly what you believe?'

'Why would I say it otherwise?'

'That's what I can't decide.' Piers turned away. For a few moments he did not move. Then, suddenly decisive, he came to stand in front of her before the fireplace. 'Damn it,' he said, suddenly angry, 'but I will tell you what is in my mind.'

'I don't want to hear it.'

But Piers put his hands on her arms, holding her in front of him as he said fiercely, 'I don't care what you want or what you think you want – God only knows which it is. I'm leaving here in the morning and I won't be coming back. Even if I wanted to, Edmund would probably have me killed if I showed my face here again, so there's nothing more to lose. Don't go through with this marriage, Perdita. If you do, you'll regret it for the rest of your life.'

'No!'

'You think you can marry a man like Edmund and not be changed by him, but you're wrong. It will change you, just as I was changed by all those years living here with him and my uncle. I thought I could distance myself from what they were doing. I thought I could stay Kip's friend and ignore their scheming because it was nothing to do with me. Then when it got worse I went away to sea rather than face up to what was going on.'

'So? I don't care why you went away. It doesn't affect me.'

'But it already has.'

'How?'

'This evening, in the library, when Edmund called out to you, you were going to help him. The Suttons are your friends just as much as they're mine, but you were going to summon help so Edmund could defeat them.'

'That's not fair! I thought Luke was going to kill him. Anyone would have tried to prevent their future husband from being murdered, especially as Luke would have gone to the gallows too. I've always wanted Francis to keep Rossmere. This is the only house I have ever wanted. I'm nothing to do with Edmund's schemes and lies.'

'Not yet, maybe. But you will be.'

'And if I am, what does that have to do with you?'

'It's everything to do with me, you fool. I care about what happens to you.' He paused. His hands were still gripping her shoulders, and though the pressure of his fingers was biting into her skin, she made no attempt to free herself. She was terrified of what he was about to say, yet she could not have dragged herself away if the house had been burning down around her. He released his hold on her, then said, 'It's obvious, isn't it? I love you, Perdita.'

There was a glow of pleasure at the sound of his words, deep in the heart of her. How long had she been waiting to hear him say that? But it was no use. She whispered, 'You must not say that!'

'Are you afraid to hear the truth?'

'But it's not. It's just words and empty promises and it doesn't mean anything at all.' Even as she spoke she wondered: is that really what I think? But her question frightened her. She had to cling to the only certainty she had ever known.

He must have noticed her hesitation because he asked, 'Is that honestly what you believe?'

'Yes. It is.' She knew this was what she had to say. 'People who follow their hearts always live to regret it.'

He turned away. She hated to see his disappointment: his face looked haggard now and much older. She said, 'I do care about you, Piers, you know I do. You've been a friend to me and helped me and I'll always be grateful for that. Maybe if our circumstances had been different then I could have said I loved you too. But we have to make the most of what we find in life. Edmund is offering me everything I have always wanted. You have nothing.'

'Nothing? Is that what my love means to you?'

'I don't mean it like that. But love never lasts. We might be happy together for a while, but we'd be sure to regret it sooner or later. And I couldn't bear that. I don't want to live my whole life knowing I'd thrown away the best chance I ever had. And Edmund is giving me that chance.'

'Edmund has a house and money, that's all.'

'Those things matter to me.'

'So I'm beginning to realise.' He waited for a moment, then said thoughtfully, 'But what about Captain Sutton and Mistress Taverner? You say love never lasts, but theirs has lasted seventeen years of separation. You only have to look at them to see how happy they are together. Don't you think we could be like that too?'

She said swiftly, 'It's different for them.'

'Why?'

'Because . . .' She had been going to say, 'Because he is a good person and I'm not,' but she knew that wouldn't make sense to Piers, so she shrugged and said, 'I don't know why, but it is.' When he remained silent, she said softly, 'I'm sorry, Piers. I wish it was different, I really do. But we can't change the world.'

For a little while, neither of them spoke. Outside the

nightingale had ceased its song. There was only the soft boom of the waves and the whisper of leaves against the window.

'So be it.' Piers stood up wearily. 'We'll say goodbye, then, Perdita.' He smiled. 'Now I am glad I cannot return to this house ever again. I could not bear to see you another man's wife. Especially not Edmund's. I'm glad I'll not have to come back here and watch you get more scheming and narrow and tyrannical with every year that passes. All your worst faults magnified by your life with him.'

Perdita had never imagined words could hurt so much. She tried to laugh and said, 'Are you flattering me again, Piers?'

'I don't need to flatter you. There's never been any need for pretence between us. I love all of you, Perdita. You're generous and brave. You never cease to surprise me and—'

'Stop,' she cut in. His praise hurt even more than his disapproval. 'That's enough.'

'Almost. Not quite.' He took a step towards her and, very gently, brushed a strand of hair from her cheek. Then he leaned forward and touched her lips with his own.

A shiver ran down her spine. She closed her eyes. The touch of his lips moved her as his words had not. She could fight words with words, but she had no defence against the physical longing that was coursing through her body. His lips were dry and warm. She wanted him to circle his arms around her and refuse to let her go. She wanted him to kiss her long and hard and caress her body and make her love him. Her lips parted under his. She wanted more.

He drew back.

She opened her eyes. His expression was questioning. 'Do you really want me to go?' he asked.

She groaned and turned away. There could be only one answer.

'Yes,' she said.

And still he hesitated. Still his eyes scanned her face. She felt giddy with misery and longing, as though her whole future was swinging in the balance. If he only raised his hand and touched her now, she would forget everything she had ever wanted and follow him blindly.

But he did not. He nodded, as though finally accepting her

decision. His face was set and hard. 'Then there's no more to be said. Farewell, Perdita. I can't wish you well with Edmund, but I hope you find what you're looking for. I'll not forget you.'

He turned at once, before she had a chance to speak, and walked quickly away. She heard his footsteps ringing out in the moonlit emptiness of the long gallery, then the door closed and his footsteps faded into silence.

She was alone.

Alone in the beautiful shell of the house she loved. The long, empty years stretching ahead.

She felt engulfed by a huge tide of desolation. It was not fair! Everything she had worked so hard to achieve was hers, and yet she had never felt so wretched in her life.

Piers had no right to try to make love to her on the eve of her betrothal to his cousin. He had always been her friend. They had worked together. This had never been part of the bargain between them.

She tried to compose her mind to be ready for the day to come. She had to deal with Kitty's questions and Edmund's wounded vanity and the legal details of their contract. She needed to be calculating and level-headed and . . . and all the time her thoughts kept coming back to Piers.

Their friendship had been different, right from the beginning. She had never even bothered to flirt with him, but beneath his teasing and his banter there had always been another quality, a depth of sympathy and understanding that she had never known with anyone else, not even Sophie.

She had called it friendship. Now he was calling it love.

Tears were pouring down her face. He was right, of course. She should have known. She did love him. She remembered the time when she rode his horse on the moors. He had caught her in his arms when she fell. Maybe she had known then, but had tried to pretend it was not happening.

And that last evening, when her father lay injured at Trecarne and they were together in the library, she had loved him then. But he was so eager to leave and begin a new life away from her, she had thought he had no feelings for her beyond friendship. And he thought she wanted to marry his cousin so he must have assumed she felt nothing for him.

It had been a muddle all along. Now the muddle was cleared up, but had that changed anything?

If she loved Piers, that did not stop Edmund from being the master of Trecarne, the house she had vowed to make her own. If she loved Piers it did not make him rich, or able to provide the honour and position she so desperately needed to wipe out the stain of her bastard birth. If she loved Piers . . .

She had always held firm to the belief that love was a fleeting distraction, and that those who followed their hearts found only disappointment and grief. Nothing Piers had said this night changed that.

She had been pacing up and down the long gallery, pausing every now and then to glance out through one of the tall windows. The moon had sunk lower in the sky. A long trail of silver stretched across the sea.

In her mind she heard her father's voice: your mother always longed to go to sea.

Suddenly she felt utterly bereft and alone. There was no one she could turn to. She crossed the long gallery and stood before the fireplace.

Nullus amor . . . She had learned from one of the oldest servants that her mother had had those words carved there just before she left. Why? Why write such a testament to love then leave, never to return?

She had no way of knowing. She learned her forehead against the carved oak and her tears spilled on the floor.

If her mother had still been alive, perhaps she would have been able to offer some solution to her dilemma.

'Oh, Mother,' she whispered, 'what am I supposed to do now?'

But the long gallery was filled with silence. Besides, she had no faith in ghosts, not since her humiliation in the back room of the Mitre.

She thought of Edmund, the life of security and wealth that he was offering, and then she thought of Piers, setting off to join an unknown ship with all his worldly goods in a small canvas bag.

Outside, the brief summer night was drawing to an end and the first light of morning was appearing in the eastern sky.

★   ★   ★

Piers rode away from Trecarne just as dawn was breaking over the sea.

He had been planning to go to Rossmere to take his leave of Sir Francis and the others, then to bid farewell to Luke Hollar, but now he wanted only to quit this whole area as fast as he could.

He felt too wounded and angry at Perdita's rejection, though he knew he should have expected no different. He, who knew her as well as anyone did, understood what a vital place security and rank held in her world. He knew the significance of the fine house at Trecarne, home of the mother she had never known. He knew the shame and hurt that lay beneath the ruthless façade.

He should not be angry, he should not even be surprised. But, still, he was disappointed. Disappointed because he also knew the other side of her, the side he loved, her courage and her sense of adventure, her cleverness and fun. He had staked their future on the chance that this other, daring side of her would ultimately win through, but he had been wrong.

He had lost.

It hurt, but he knew that in time the pain of it would ease. A man who has lost both his parents in the space of a month when hardly out of boyhood knows that all wounds become bearable in the end. What made this particularly hard to bear was that it had been caused not by a random accident of fate but by deliberate choice. And a wrong choice, he was sure of that.

He handed his horse to the Trecarne groom who had ridden with him, slung his canvas bag over his shoulder and set off to find someone who would row him out to the ship that had dropped anchor offshore the previous afternoon.

It was the *Speedwell*, a sturdy vessel on its way back to Plymouth from the southern Irish ports.

He set his mind to think of the days and weeks ahead, and to forget about Perdita.

As he sat in the small rowing boat and listened to the dip and creak of the oars, and the laboured breath of the old fisherman who was rowing him out to the *Speedwell* he could see the small figures moving around the ship, preparing to raise the anchor and journey on under the spell of the gentle southern wind.

The old fellow seemed to be rambling on, but Piers's mind

was full of all that had happened and all that must be done in the days ahead, and he paid him no attention.

And then he caught sight of one figure on the deck of the *Speedwell*, who was somehow different from all the other hurrying, roughly dressed sailors.

Someone with a broad hat, dark hair and a narrow, eager face. Someone with eyes that were smiling with excitement at his approach.

'Perdita,' he breathed. And then, as the old fisherman looked at him in surprise, he shouted, 'Perdita!'

She leaned her forearms on the rails of the ship as the rowboat pulled alongside. Her eyes were shining.

'Welcome aboard the *Speedwell*,' she said.

A little later, as Edmund was soothing his injured pride by threatening his servants with dire punishments if they did not find Perdita Treveryan at once and bring her back to him, and Kitty was choosing what to wear for her daughter's betrothal and which dress to keep for the wedding, a small ship appeared in the bay beyond Trecarne, a small ship that both of them were too busy to notice.

On board the *Speedwell*, Perdita and Piers separated themselves from the long embrace that had caused such a barrage of good-humoured banter from the sailors as the little ship got under way. They walked over to watch in silence as the magnificent façade of Trecarne came into view: more beautiful than ever in the early-morning sunshine, with its two towers at either end, the long high-windowed façade, and the soft green of the oak woods behind. Cormorants were standing with wings outstretched on the rocks at the side of the bay.

Gradually Perdita became aware that Piers was looking not at the house but at her face. She knew the unspoken question that was in his heart. 'No, Piers,' she said. 'I'll never regret this morning.'

They remained, standing side by side in silence, as the house was revealed in all its glory for the last time, then vanished from view for ever.

Epilogue
Rossmere, Midsummer 1671

Honor laid the sleeping baby in his crib and straightened the front of her dress, then went across to the writing table and picked up a sheet of paper to read through what she had written earlier that day:

> *My dear Perdita,*
>
> *Your letter from Oporto reached us by carrier a month ago. I would have written to you sooner, but I was brought to bed of a fine boy three days after. He is with me now as I write. I fear he is of a delicate disposition like his brother and sisters, but Francis and Kip tell me I must not fuss, and indeed, if you could see them all now playing in the hayfield together with their cousin*

There she had been obliged to halt to tend to the needs of the bonny boy being written about with such pride and affection. She picked up her pen, dipped it in the ink and continued;

> *You would not think think there was a healthier family of children in all of Cornwall. We are so lucky to have Dolores with us. She has a remedy for every ailment, and I tremble to think how little Nicolas would have managed with his weak chest last winter were it not for her.*
>
> *Your niece Lucy takes after her mother in that she is never poorly for a moment. She has much of Sophie's*

*character, but is far more mischievous than ever Sophie was
and leads the others into all kinds of trouble. Last week I
heard Kip has been teaching her to ride her pony legs astride,
like a boy, which he says her mother used to do, though I
cannot believe that and where such goings on will end I
dread to think. Still, her father is the worst one for
encouraging her waywardness. Sometimes I think he does it
on purpose to worry me.*

*But I must not allow myself to complain about your
brother since my dear Francis says the tin works would never
have flourished as they do if Luke had not taken over the
running of it. Certainly Luke has a good head for figures
and keeps a cool head on his shoulders when things go wrong
as they do from time to time even in the best-run operations,
or so they tell me.*

*He is teaching Lucy to play the pipes and they make very
pretty music together when he plays the fiddle with her.
Sometimes we sing together and even dance. He says that
when she is older he will take her with him to join a band
of travelling players and they will tramp the roads of
England together as he did as a young man, but I am sure
he only says that to vex me because he knows the very
notion is abhorrent to me. Besides, Luke likes his comforts as
well as anyone and there is no place so comfortable in all the
world as Rossmere.*

*Moreover, it is common gossip now that Edmund
Menheire owes Luke a deal of money. Francis explained to
me that the Menheires were never so rich as they made out
and they stretched themselves to the utmost when they took
Trecarne, and then again with all that trickery over the
Plaindealing and buying up our debts. I do not understand
it all, but there is some satisfaction in the knowledge that the
wicked do not always have to wait until the next world to
meet with their just desserts. Cary says there are rumours in
Porthew that Luke will soon be able to make him sell him
Trecarne, and that Luke means to live there one day with
Lucy, though as you know your brother is such a secretive
man we would always be the last to know such a thing.
Still, it is strange, when you consider that his mother once*

*lived there and your own father built it and dear Sophie
might have lived there had she not married him and*

Here Honor found that she had written herself into such a knot
that she did not know how to untangle it. After a few moments'
anxious reflection she crossed out the last word and wrote,

*But there are many strange events in this world, as we are
reminded almost daily. Lousia and her husband visited us
again last week, but I cannot say their visit was an altogether
happy occasion. They do not appear yet to have found the
harmony together that my dear Francis and I are blessed
with, but I know full well the early years can be difficult and
they may be more comfortable together when the child is
born. Everyone sends you their love, and wishes to know
when you and Piers will visit us, but I tell them they must
be patient. I am sure you will come to visit us one day.*

She paused. A noisy rabble of children were racing past the
window, led by a tall, brown-haired girl who was waving a stick
wildly above her head and urging the others on. Lucy was like
Sophie in so many ways, Honor thought, but then again, she
could be a terror too, and so unpredictable, just like her father.
Honor was in no hurry for Perdita to visit. She enjoyed having
someone to exchange letters with. She wrote,

*My husband does not have to concern himself much with
the tin works these days, since Luke says he can manage it
better himself if he does it alone. I think my dear Francis is
too much a gentleman to understand the workings of
commerce. Uncle Stephen still supervises the work on the
farm so Francis is more at leisure, which I must say suits us
both very well. He has a clever plan to enlarge the horse
pond so that we will be supplied with fresh fish at all times,
which will be an added blessing.*

So many blessings, she thought. Even a dedicated worrier like
Honor had occasional moments of tranquillity, and this midsummer afternoon was one of them.

The white doves, which had been disturbed by the rush of children's feet, fluttered down to peck and strut across the gravel again. Lucy's strident voice was growing fainter. Honor felt a great sense of well being. She picked up her pen once again.

> Well, and that is all my news for now. I hope this reaches you in Oporto before you sail again with your husband. Do your sons never feel they lack a settled home or does your gypsy life suit them as well as you and Piers? Do write to me when you have time. I keep all your letters and read them out in the evenings when Cary does not feel like telling stories any more. The tale of your journeys is as good as any story, everyone is agreed on that. We all love to hear of your adventures.
>
> Ever your loving, Honor

And with a little sigh of satisfaction that she was only hearing about adventures, and not obliged to live them out herself, Honor set down her pen.

JOANNA HINES

THE CORNISH GIRL

Margaret has always been slightly set apart from the others in her village. When she falls pregnant at sixteen, her refusal to name the father of her unborn child leads her into trouble and she is driven to marry William Holler, a stranger with his own secrets. Longing for love, Margaret turns to wealthy landowner Richard Treveryan, a bitter cynic loathed by her family and friends. With him she finds a passion she never dreamt possible.

Then the Civil War threatens all she holds dear, forcing her to choose between her beloved son and the only happiness she has even known.

Utterly compelling and heart-wrenching, *The Cornish Girl* brings to life seventeenth-century Cornwall and an unforgettable woman.

'A fine novel of Cornwall, beautifully written'

A L Rowse

'A long, escapist wallow in the seventeenth century'

Daily Mail

'A fantastic tale of trust, honour, courage and fate'

Company

HODDER AND STOUGHTON PAPERBACKS

JOANNA HINES

THE PURITANS' WIFE

Few of Mistress Doll Taverner's acquaintances would be able to tell that beneath the façade of prosperous merchant's wife and mother of four lies a scared Spanish child who was brought to England by her husband as the spoils of war. Even Doll herself doesn't quite realise it, until the King's soldiers, led by the Cornishman Captain Stephen Sutton, arrive to garrison the village and she is forced to confront the horrors of her past and the demands of her present.

The Puritan's Wife is an evocative, engrossing love story set in the Cotswolds against the vivid and dramatic backdrop of the Civil War.

'An enjoyable historical novel . . . the love story is engaging, with a pair of very credible protagonists, and the background of the period well felt besides being well researched . . . but perhaps the greatest merit of this very readable novel is its underlying sense of the horrors of civil and religious war'

The Tablet

HODDER AND STOUGHTON PAPERBACKS